VAMPIR̶ ̶ ̶ ̶ ̶ ̶ ̶ ̶ ̶
VAMPIRE IN DEFIANCE
VAMPIRE IN CONFLICT

BOOK #4–6 OF FAMILY BLOOD TIES

DALE MAYER

Book in this series:

FAMILY BLOOD TIES BOOKS 4–6
Dale Mayer
Valley Publishing

Copyright © 2014 Dale Mayer

All rights reserved. Except for use in any review, the reproduction or utilization of this work in whole or in part by any electronic, mechanical or other means, now known or hereafter invented, including xerography, photocopying and recording, or in any information storage or retrieval system, is forbidden without the written permission of the publisher.

This is a work of fiction. Names, characters, places, brands, media, and incidents are either the product of the author's imagination or are used fictitiously. Any resemblance to actual events, locales, or persons, living or dead, is entirely coincidental.

ISBN-13: 978-1-988315-33-1

Vampire in Deceit

Hurt and hurting, Tessa wages war against her own as she tries to protect those she loves and save those that can't save themselves.

Exhausted by the constant attacks, afraid for her friends and family, Tessa is driven to the end of her reserves as she strives to beat back the never ending wave of vamps. Thankfully, she's never alone...inside or out.

Kidnapped and injured, Cody struggles to escape and find the girl whose connection to his heart, mind, and soul is growing by the moment. The chances of all of them surviving this chaos are slim...but he just knows he can't live without her.

Jared is determined to help his father and friends. He can't leave them alone to their fate, even when his own life becomes endangered...again. Only this time, he has allies on his side... or does he?

The war unites human s and vamps as the conflict escalates to survival of the fittest...but the people most deeply involved can't take much more. And then they find out the worst...

Vampire in Defiance

This was it. For Tessa. For Cody. For Jared. Her family. Her Friends.

Moltere's Mountain is collapsing. With Tessa, her friends and family still inside. Tessa won't go out without a fight...and she won't leave the others behind. But as she races to save everyone, time runs out.

Grounded with an injured wing, Cody wants Tessa to leave while they still can. But most of their friends and family are missing. He wants to do the right thing and save them all...but it's too late...

Jared had led the army into the mountain. Only to find they were looking to annihilate all vamps, not just the bad ones. He can't leave his friends vulnerable to yet another attack. But the mine is a death trap. And he could be the one that ends up dead.

The pressure is on – to save friends, family, each other – only the enemy is just as determined that no one survives.

Vampire in Conflict

The blood farm is gone. Those behind it have either died, been caught, or are on the run. Time to return to the real world.

Only normal life isn't quite what Tessa expected. Good thing, because there is no 'normal' anymore. She's different. Her family is different. Her friends are different. The world around her is different. Trying to find her place is not easy. She wants nothing more than to be a normal teenager and join Cody and his friends on a Friday night out.

Cody wants the trouble to be over so he can get back to living the life he used to with one major addition – Tessa.

Only Ian and Jewel aren't healing well, Rhia is acting out of character, and Jared keeps tripping over dead bodies. Then there's David, who'll do anything to help Jewel…even something he knows he shouldn't do.

Something is wrong, and once again it's up to Tessa to figure out what is happening under the surface of this 'normal' life.

Sign up to be notified of all Dale's releases here!

http://dalemayer.com/category/blog/

COMPLIMENTARY DOWNLOAD

DOWNLOAD a *__complimentary__* copy of TUESDAY'S
CHILD? Just tell me where to send it!

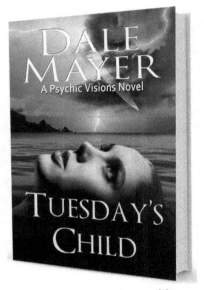

http://dalemayer.com/starterlibrarytc/

Vampire in Deceit

Book #4 of Family Blood

Dale Mayer

PROLOGUE

*This is the last chapter of book 3, **Vampire in Design**. We left Tessa after this point...*

TESSA STEPPED INTO line behind her father as he searched the area for vamps. She hadn't seen anyone yet. Not that she'd been allowed to enter any of the rooms they'd come upon. Like usual, she'd been relegated to being a...girl.

It both pissed her off and made her feel loved.

Cody walked up behind her. "Tired of being in the background again?"

She smiled. "It's a bit unnerving to have my role switched depending on the people I'm with."

"True enough." He slung an arm around her shoulders. "Feels good to know you can handle yourself when the need arises though, doesn't it?"

"Yeah," she murmured, "it does."

Just then, the elders walked back out. "This place appears empty," her father said.

"Does that mean that we can release the captives?" Tessa looked around. "Then maybe go home and fight the rest of the war from there?"

"We have the captives' location saved on the GPS," David said, holding up the phone.

"As this place is empty, let's do what we can for them and

get the hell out of here." Cody wanted away from this place.

Goran added, "We came here to find you, so if we're all here, let's check on the others. I'd like to see this room full of drugged vamps so we can help our own people and determine who's on whose side here."

Plan in place, Ian used the GPS on the phone to guide them back to the room full of drugged humans. Checking out the energy trails, Tessa realized no one else had come by since she'd last been here. So far, so good. Maybe the other team had finally run out of bad guys.

After a quick check on the still-drugged humans, Ian led the way back through the other rooms to where the vamps had been drugged. It was still empty. Or almost empty. They found Motre standing there, staring at the empty beds.

"Where the hell have you been?" Cody asked. He didn't know how Motre fit in here, but it was good to see him alive.

Motre grinned at them. "There you are. I've got the vamps in another place. Glad to see you're all doing okay."

He nodded to Serus and Goran. "Good to see you two."

"How is Councilman Bushman?" Goran asked.

"Awake and pissed." Motre's grin widened. "After we got separated, not by my choice, by the way," he rubbed his head and winced, "I decided to use the tracker and return to guard our people. Come on, I'll take you to the councilman. There are many of us up ahead."

They fell in behind him and entered the vast room to see that they were surrounded by vamps. Motre strode ahead toward a door on the far end.

Tessa stopped to study the faces of those around her. They didn't look familiar.

As the color of everyone's energy swirled around her, she realized that she recognized several from her treks to meet up with her friends and family. But none of them looked like allies. She whispered, "Shit."

She felt rather than saw Cody glance her way.

What's the matter?

They aren't on our side.

Are you sure?

No. But almost. And we're surrounded. So now what?

We kick butt.

❧ ❦

RHIA SLIPPED AROUND the back of the huge mansion. Sian crept up behind her. Rhia's head still pounded and her limbs had a weakness she didn't like. She was getting stronger by the hour, but the hours had become too short and moved too fast. She had to get this information to people they could trust. And fast.

Damn it all. She wanted this mess over with. And her family home safe and sound.

"Is anyone there?" Sian whispered. "And why are we skulking around again?"

"Because we don't know who else might be here. We need to speak with Councilman Adamson only. Preferably in private."

"Right. He has no spouse, does he?"

"No. Or kids, as far as I know," Rhia murmured, struck by how different a life that meant. She had three children and Serus to fill her day. How lonely would her life be without them all? She couldn't imagine.

She returned her focus to the door at the back of the house. The house appeared empty. She hoped not.

Taking a deep breath, she rapped on the back door.

The door opened under her hand, the creak loud enough to make her jump. Sian's gasp had her looking behind. "Is there someone there?"

"I don't know." Rhia stepped into the dark interior, her senses on high alert. This could be a trap, but no one, and she meant no one, knew they were here.

She walked straight through to the main room, Sian right behind her. "Is the place empty?"

"It might be. Or," Rhia hesitated, "he might be hiding."

Sian looked at her curiously. "And why would he do that?"

"Because of the times we are in. If he had any idea of the other councilmen's involvement, he might feel like he's in danger."

A heavy brush of wings filled the air.

Rhia stiffened. There was more than one vamp landing. Were they good or....

"You dare enter my home without an invitation?" Councilman Adamson questioned, his voice lethally sharp. A second vamp landed at his side. Rhia studied her. She thought it was Gloria, the dragon lady who kept the council in line.

That could be a very good thing.

"We called out," Rhia said. "But as we couldn't be sure if you were home or not, we decided to come in and check."

"And what is so important that you felt you were justified in doing such a thing?"

Rhia exchanged a quick glance with Sian. She took a deep breath, pulled out the laptop, turned it on, and brought up the saved material. Giving him a hard look, she spun the laptop around and held the information up to him.

"This."

❧ ❧

JARED WATCHED AS a man in a white lab coat came around the corner of a row. A human doctor. "What are you doing here?"

Jared tried to smile. "I'm sorry. I'm Jared." At his name, the other man's face relaxed.

"You're the one that got away. I'm Taz. Tessa is a friend of the family. I was brought in to help these people out."

Jared relaxed. "Thank you. There was no one here when I arrived, and I was afraid something was wrong."

"Oh, we're here – just a few less than we started with. We were attacked and taken prisoner. Tessa's father and Goran came to rescue us."

"Oh, wow! I'd so hoped the bad guys were out of the picture now."

"I don't think so." Taz smiled. "How did you get here?"

"I came up with Seth, Tessa's brother, and three of his friends. They were already planning to come, I just hitched a ride."

"Really? There's no reason for any of them to be here." He frowned as he studied the area around them. "I'll need to find them and see what they want. They shouldn't roam around here freely."

"I haven't seen them since I separated from them at the exit over there." Jared pointed toward the way he'd come in.

"And why did you come back?" Taz asked, his voice low, solemn.

"I have reason to believe that my father is one of the humans hanging here." He took a deep breath, adding, "And has been since I was little." He hated the pity and compassion that came over the doctor's face. Taz was a good man. And he'd know all the implications of what Jared had just said.

"I'm sorry."

Jared nodded. He swallowed hard. "My uncle did it. He also sold me to the farm. I'm going to make sure he pays. I'd love to see him hanging up here." He motioned upward to the man hanging beside him. "Like this guy."

"No, you don't." Taz grabbed his arm and tugged him down the row. "Let's go down to the office we're using. There are computers there. And some food and drinks. Your father might be in the database. I don't know that they have any names there, though."

"That's why I'm walking the rows." Jared looked up and came to a dead stop.

Taz studied his face "What's the matter?"

Jared wasn't listening; his attention had locked on the face before him. Could it be? There was enough resemblance to his own face and a younger uncle's to make him recognize the family line. But it was that inner conviction that made him sure. He could sense a connection. Sense a link between them.

It was his father. He knew it at a DNA level.

And it broke his heart to see this. To see the proof before his eyes. He dropped his gaze to the computer hanging in front of this man's body. Number 97239.

"It's my father."

TESSA'S HEAD SNAPPED back as a blow came out of nowhere. "What the..." Only she was knocked forward into yet another blow. She went down...hard. Damn it, she was too tired for this.

Don't say that. Get up. Hurry. I can't keep them off for too long.

Crap. Tessa bolted to her feet, desperate to shake the fog from her rattled brain. A flash of silver had her instinctively shifting to the side and grabbing the hand behind it. She pivoted and stabbed the chest in front of her with her own spike.

Ash floated down around her. She groaned as another vamp stepped up and took his place, a ferocious grin on his face. They were all starting to look the same. Mean, ugly, and way too happy to be here for comfort. She backed up a step and hit someone. She pivoted, spike between her fingers, her nails long and dripping.

And found Cody staring down at her. She grinned up at him, loving the surge of warm power she felt between them. Then his eyes lit up in horror. He snatched her up and pushed her behind his back as the vamp she'd taken her eyes off charged.

And went down. She peered around Cody's shoulder to see it vaporize in front of them.

"I'm never going to enjoy a warm fire again."

Cody nodded silently. "I hear you."

There. She gasped. *David and Ian are in trouble.*

Let's go.

And go they did, meeting vamp after vamp, delivering blows and kicks, and taking too many for comfort. Finally they were in the center, where David and Ian had backed up against each other, chests heaving as they faced the enemy encircling them.

An enemy whose numbers never seemed to dwindle.

Tessa and Cody immediately took up positions next to them. Their last stand. She hated having that negative thought. Especially at this moment, with the four of them exhausted.

And surrounded.

"Where's Jewel?" David rasped, his voice low and hoarse and full of pain.

Cody answered, "She's with my father and yours."

Tessa couldn't see his face, but his relief was so strong she felt the physical wave that washed over her brother. His whispered "Thank you" hit a spot in her own heart. It also brought to life how very real and deadly this war had become.

They were all going to lose someone before long. They had to. The war was too big and too harsh for all of them to survive. She didn't want to lose anyone. She didn't want her way of life to die. And she didn't have a clue how to get through this.

Ready? Cody's voice filtered through her mind. His warm tone bolstered her flagging energy. "Everyone stay focused. We aren't alone."

She glanced over at him.

"This looks like the last group. Motre and the others just finished theirs and so have the elders. They'll attack from the outside. We just have to stay alive a little longer."

Ian's voice, exhausted but still game, said, "A little longer I can do. These bastards are tough, though. With them having spikes, it's all about speed. Get them before they get you."

David added, "We need a better way to attack."

Just as he said that, a wave of black filled the room. Cody swore, "Shit. There are more."

"Ours or theirs?" muttered David.

Tessa turned to Cody. "Can you fly low and scrape the spikes along their backs? I can jump and get one or two, but if we split up and attack on all sides..."

"Two in the air. Two on the ground. A scratch might not

kill them, but it will slow them down a lot."

"Good. Let's do it."

Ready?

Absolutely. She'd rather go out in style, fighting to the end. And she'd rather die than face life without her family and know she'd caused their deaths. The guilt would be far worse.

One...two...

And they both took to the air. Tessa couldn't jump high from a standstill, but she gave it her best shot. She jumped up smoothly then glided low. The silver spikes stuck out from between her fingers as she slashed and punched at the backs and heads of the group surrounding her brother. David and Ian came in low and dispatched the stumbling vamps.

Woot! Tessa pumped her spike-laden fist in the air.

That bunch is done. I'm going over to help my father. Cody took off to the fighting going on at the right, where the damn doors seemed to let in even more vamps.

Tessa landed and spun around to make sure she wasn't under attack, checking to make sure David and Ian were fine. Ian was breathing hard but appeared unhurt. David raced over to Jewel, who struggled with one last vamp. David stabbed him in the back and stepped over the still-fiery ashes to tug Jewel into his arms.

On the opposite side of the room, Motre and his men were dispatching the last of the vamps. Quickly, efficiently, and ruthlessly.

She closed her eyes and groaned as the last vamp fell. Then again, she was doing a slow slide to the floor herself. She wanted to giggle as her butt hit the floor but she just had no energy left. And from the looks of it, her friends weren't in much better shape.

David had his arms wrapped around Jewel, who was barely able to keep standing. But she wasn't ash on the ground, so all was good. At least, as good as any of them could be. She searched behind Jewel to find her father in conversation with Goran. They'd both been through so much and for so long. She was amazed they looked as strong as they did.

Ian was on the other side, bent over, chest heaving with exhaustion. He looked wasted.

It was over.

It had to be. Surely they'd finally purged this farm of bad guys.

Surely?

She ran a shaky hand over her forehead, wondering if they'd actually managed to get through this battle unscathed.

It would be unbelievably lucky if they had. There were many piles of ashes, but she couldn't bear to think of anyone she knew as being one of them.

She started counting heads. Motre was there. Good thing. He'd been a godsend in this war. And his cronies didn't do too bad either. Although he appeared to be surrounded by a smaller group now than before. Yet...there were still a dozen or so.

She could see both elders. David and Jewel. Ian. Cody? Where was he?

Ice formed in her stomach. She bolted to her feet and searched left and right.

Her panicked gaze searched the clusters of people for his familiar face. Bile raced up her throat and her heart constricted in fear. There was no sign of Cody.

Cody? Cody!

CHAPTER 1

"**C**ODY?" TESSA SCREAMED as loud as she could. "Where are you?"

In her mind, she whispered, *Damn it, Cody, please answer me.*

Silence. Inside and out. There wasn't a sound in the room – except for the raspy breathing of the survivors as they stared around the smoky room with dawning horror.

Tremors started from her toes and slowly worked their way up her spine He had to be fine. *He had to.*

She couldn't lose him now that she'd finally found him.

"Cody? Stop fooling around. Where the hell are you, boy?" Goran bellowed, fear beginning to show on his face. He pivoted and searched the men in the room.

"He was over by the door the last time I saw him," David said, already striding to the door. "Maybe he went out to carry on the fight."

En masse, everyone raced to the door. Tessa was slightly behind, her muscles slow to react as the shock of impending disaster warred with hope. She couldn't help take a last glance at all the still smoldering piles on the floor.

So many dead. So many gone and no one would be able to identify the remains. Did they all have families who would now wait endlessly for someone who would no longer come home?

She might be able to deal with that...as long as they weren't *her* family and friends. Selfish? Yes, and she didn't care. Trying to ignore the smoldering piles, she ran behind the others.

In the large outer room, they separated and spread out to search for Cody.

Except Goran. He'd halted several yards in, and hands on his hips, roared, "Cody? Where are you?"

Only there was no answer.

Tessa, after the initial panic had drained what little energy she had left from the fight, could barely think with the fear still snaking through her. Cody had to be alright. Anything else didn't bear thinking about.

But there was no sign of him. Tessa stood in the middle of the cavernous room when the shakes started. She didn't know when she tumbled to the ground. Next thing she knew, she was on the floor with her knees up to her chin.

David came running over to her. "Tessa, are you okay?"

She looked up at him, her voice heavy with pain. "Where's Cody?"

The worry lines on David's face deepened. "He'll be here. He has to be." He crouched down and gave her a hug. They stayed like that for a long moment as the others continued to call out Cody's name.

Goran came back, his steps heavy, his face aged and full of agony. "He can't be dead. I'd know if he were."

David started. He pulled back slightly to look at Tessa. "Tessa?"

Confused, she stared up at him. "What?"

With a glance around to make sure that the others couldn't hear him, he said, "Have you tried to talk to Cody using mindspeak?"

She blinked up at him. "I'm not even sure that's what we're doing." She took a shaky breath. "And I've been trying, but I'm not hearing him."

He leaned closer. "Can you sense him? Anything at all that indicates he's alive?"

"Tessa?" A deeply pained voice sounded behind her.

She twisted slightly to see Goran standing there, a ravaged look on his face.

"Can you try again? Please?"

Damn. Still, she had to get past her own fear to be able to talk to Cody. "I don't know if it will work," she warned. "It doesn't always."

"Try," said David.

With a last worried glance at the room full of smoldering ashes, she nodded and closed her eyes.

Cody, where are you? Can you hear me? Are you alive? She waited several long minutes but heard no response.

A shudder slid down her spine. She looked at David. "I can't hear anything."

"Try again. Please. He could be unconscious. What if *he's* been kidnapped this time?"

"Oh no," she cried out softly. And yet why not Cody? She'd been in trouble several times. So had Jewel and Ian. Then there was her mother, who had been injected with some kind of mind-altering drug. So it was quite possible for Cody to have been overpowered, or injected with something to make him lose consciousness.

Unfortunately, even Cody could be overtaken. It had already happened once. David and Cody had been drugged and taken to the platform up high. Instinctively, her head tilted back and she stared at the cavernous ceiling high above. Why hadn't she looked for his energy? God, she was a fool. She turned on both sets of vision as she bolted to her feet.

"Sis? What's up? Can you hear him?"

Goran took a hopeful step toward her.

"Not at the moment. If he's unconscious, then I don't think I could anyway." She held up her hand as both Goran and David started to speak. "*But* I should have looked for his energy trail."

She spun around, but the energy was a crazy mess. "Goran," she snapped, "Get everyone to stand still. I need to sort out the different signatures."

With Goran bellowing at the top of his lungs, she crouched down to see better. She realized that she was standing in the middle of a large ball of energy. Straightening, she backed up and stopped at the doorway. From here, she could see most of the large room laid out in front of her, the vamps frozen in position. There, she squatted again to search the smoky mess of energy.

It twisted and mixed on the ground in front of her. Slowly, she was managing to read the story. A fight had spilled out into this huge room.

There. Cody's energy.

"His energy is here," she shouted excitedly. She backed up slightly in order to see more.

Goran came running – and man, could he move! "David said he was here before the battle. Could that be what you're seeing?"

She shook her head. "No. It's too vibrant. He was in a fight here, on this side of the room and then…" her voice trailed off as she moved slowly to the left in Motre's direction. "The fight brought him over here."

The energy blended into one confused mass. She stopped and turned around slowly, looking to pick up the trail. "But I can't see where he went next," she cried out in frustration,

"That's okay. Take your time. If you saw that he'd been over here, then he wasn't incinerated in the same room where we were. That's what matters. Take another look. He might have been thrown over someone's shoulder. Would that change the energy pattern? Would you need to look higher?"

"Higher?" Her gaze shot upward. She turned in a slow circle. Cody was a flier. "If he'd managed to get airborne, he could have gone anywhere."

"But he'd have come back here if he could have." Goran was absolute in that statement. Cody wouldn't have left them to fight alone.

"Yes," she said slowly as she continued to study the air. "Several fliers came in from that direction." She lifted her arm and pointed. "There was a skirmish of some kind and all the energy mixed..." She gasped. "Cody, with at least two fliers, went that way." This time, she pointed back toward the area under construction. The way they'd come.

Goran ran to her side and stared up into the air. "Do you recognize the fliers?"

She frowned. "The energy is murky. For all I know, there could be more than two as I can barely separate them at this point. But I can see Cody launching upwards, not very strongly, injured maybe." She ignored Jewel's horrified gasp as she tried to decipher the meaning of the energy. "Maybe as an attempt to get away from whatever fight was going on below, but he ended up cornered by fliers." And he struggled hard. But she didn't say that out loud. "His energy doesn't look good. I can see it, but it's pale."

"Pale? What does that mean?" Goran's voice rose to a roar at the end.

Tessa winced at the sudden ringing in her ears. "Sorry.

The energy looks slack and lifeless, almost as if he's hurt. Or maybe he's been drugged. It's possible he's not flying at all, but that someone else is flying him away."

"Then I'm going up there and finding those assholes. They'll be damn sorry they ever decided to touch my boy."

"Whoa. Hold on." Serus said, his quiet authority evident as everyone turned to look at him. "You're tired and injured and although we grabbed some sustenance at the hospital, you've burned through the bulk of that already. You can't go alone. Not if there are more than a couple of these fliers around."

"There aren't enough fliers here to stop me." Goran snapped. "And if you think you're going to stop me from going and saving my son, you're not the man I thought you were."

"I'm not going to stop you. I'm trying to find a way to get a team to go *with* you." Serus growled. "Any more cracks like that and I'll slug you."

The two ancients glared at each other, the air fairly crackling with testosterone.

"Hey, you two. Knock it off. Let's try to help Cody instead of wasting time." Tessa didn't realize she'd yelled until David walked over to her and wrapped an arm around her shoulders.

"Easy, Tessa. We'll find him," he said.

She closed her eyes and buried her face against his shoulder. Damn. She hated reverting to that helpless Tessa. That Tessa who couldn't do anything. But she needed a moment. Just one. Okay, that was enough. With a headshake, she threw off the weakness and took a deep breath. Then she stepped away from her brother's protective arms.

"I'll be fine." She threw him a confident smile before

turning to face the others. And she would be now that she knew Cody hadn't died…yet. "If you two are done…?"

Serus gave a snort. "That's my girl." He reached out and smacked Goran on the shoulder. "Let's go."

While the others stood and watched, Goran took to the air, with Serus not far behind.

"We have to give them ground support," Motre called to the rest of them. "Let's go."

"Already gone," Tessa called back as she picked up speed and went past him. Behind her, she heard Jewel laugh and call back to her brother. "Come on David, or you'll miss the party."

"Like hell."

Tessa grinned. She quickly lost it as Motre and Ian steamed past her. She barely had the energy to do what she was doing. How the hell were they beating her? And they hadn't had a meal in how long? Damn. They'd fought hard too.

"Shit." She was such an idiot. They were drawing energy from their vampire heritage. Although how long that would hold out, she didn't know.

Why the hell couldn't hers just kick in automatically? She mentally ordered her body to draw on that side of her DNA to power up. Before long, she was coasting along smoothly. She grinned. Now if only they could find Cody alive and well…

Damn it, Cody. Where are you?

Then she heard it. A moan, deep and dragging inside her mind. "It's Cody," she yelled. "I can hear him. He's alive!"

CODY GROANED. AT least he thought he did, but no sound

came out. And maybe that was a good thing. His brain was too scrambled to figure out why. Besides, everything hurt too much to care. Especially his arm. Damn it. Had he broken something? Surely a break couldn't hurt this much. He should have already healed. Unless he'd just broken it. And that brought him back to nothing making any sense again.

He tried to shift his shoulders and moaned.

Silently.

Cody? Can you hear me?

Tessa's worried voice screamed through his thoughts. He winced as the power of her voice bounced around his brain. Still, just knowing she was there made his heart beat louder. He struggled to get his thoughts coherent enough to answer her. *Tessa?*

Yes! Are you okay? You don't sound so good.

I don't know. Just coming back to consciousness, I think.

Be careful. You might have been drugged.

Drugged? Oh shit. I can't remember.

Yes. The battle is over. Only we couldn't find you. I think other fliers must have captured you.

At her words, images and sounds filled his mind. Emotions thrummed through his veins. Panic, screaming. The sound of vamps dying. Sounds of friends crying. The fight had been intense. He'd gone to help his father and Serus by the door. That had led to more fighting outside. He'd been surrounded. Had fought hard, then bolted up as high as he could to catch his breath. And then…and then nothing. He didn't remember anything after that point.

Damn. She was right. He'd had to have been taken by other fliers.

That's what I figured when I saw the energy trails.

He cracked his eyelids open a sliver and tried to see where

he was. He tried to lift a hand to rub his burning eyes, but it was locked down at his side. Lying on his back, the truth slowly sank in. He was strapped to a bed or table of some kind. His left arm burned. His aching wings were folded under him. Slowly, trying to make the motion natural as if he were asleep, he let his head roll to the side and froze. Yards of tubing crisscrossed his view. *Christ.* He strained to hear anything.

Was he alone?

His heart pounded. If he was, he was getting the hell out of here. But what if he wasn't? The last thing he needed was a heavier dose of drugs. And this was his second time. Shit. Double Shit. He had to get out of here. And hope his wings weren't paralyzed like Ian and Jewel's were. That would so not be good.

Do you know where you are? Your dad is flying, trying to follow your trail. The rest of us are on the ground looking for you.

He started to smile, but held it back at the last moment. He didn't want to give himself away. But damn, it was good to know the cavalry was coming. He'd hoped they'd all survived.

We did. We're here. We're coming for you.

Good. I'm going to get out of here – somehow.

Do that. But be careful. Those drugs are deadly.

Yeah. I hear you.

Pissed now, Cody opened his eyes and stared up at the ceiling. A white tiled ceiling, like so many he'd seen before. He fisted his hands and tested his bonds. Both wrists were bound and his wings were killing him. It was not comfortable, with him lying on top of them. And with that thought, they started to throb. Shit.

He shifted his legs and almost sighed with relief when

they moved. They ached something awful, though. What the hell had the assholes done to him? He lifted his head slightly and took in the room with a glance. Empty. Good. Now to free himself.

Tessa. I'm in a room, strapped to a bed. So far I'm alone.

Damn. Get out if you can.

Working on it.

And he was. But he wasn't getting anywhere. In fact, a strange lassitude was filling his veins. He wasn't tired, but foggy. Confused. He shook his head to clear it. His eyes really hurt too. It had to be the drugs. Or the lack of food. Damn, he didn't dare go down that pathway. He didn't want any of the blood from this farm. But it wasn't like there were any synthetics available.

He sat up and pulled at the straps. They were tight. But... he closed his eyes, gritted his teeth, and pulled. And pulled.

Nothing. Tessa's retractable claws would come in handy right now. What the hell? He was a vamp, he had more muscle strength than ten humans. But these beds...they had to have been prepared for vamps.

Shit.

He collapsed back on the bed. He was so tired. Even though their vamp lineage could keep them awake for long periods as long as they stayed out of the sunlight, it couldn't sustain them indefinitely. They all needed rest and blood. Some things that they weren't likely to get anytime soon.

Still, there was no way he was going to stay here and wait to be rescued. He'd never live that down. Even Tessa had managed to escape. Plus she'd shown him up enough these last few days. He closed his eyes and urged his vamp heritage to match the slow building fury inside. He'd had enough of being beaten down, drugged up, and confined in rooms. To add insult to injury, he was tied up again *after* being beaten.

Enough was enough. He could feel the energy surging through his veins. Opening his eyes, he stared at the white tiled ceiling he hated. Gritting his teeth, he slowly clenched his fists and tightened his muscles. With a burst of anger fueling his body, he lunged off the bed. There was a momentary strain before the straps snapped, sending him hurtling forward. He cried out as needles were ripped out from his arm. His wings unfurled, barely stopping his collapse to the floor.

Gasping with euphoric relief, he stood in the center of the small room and stretched out his wings and arms. He cried out. His left wing throbbed. It wasn't broken, but the feathers were bent back on one side. He stretched around but couldn't reach the spot. He shook them freely several times, but the left one was damaged just enough that he wasn't sure flying was something he should be trying anytime soon. And that just pissed him off even more.

He'd heal. But would he heal fast enough?

He straightened, folded his wings into place, and muttered out loud, "To hell with it. It has to be good enough." He took several steps forward, testing his muscles. Damned drugs. He hated the weakness coursing through his muscles, not to mention the fear that they might have used mind-altering drugs on him, like what they'd pumped into Rhia.

And that scared him more than anything else they could do to him. He'd seen the results of their drugs. Not just with Rhia, but also with Ian and Jewel. He shuddered.

That so wasn't going to happen to him.

Then he heard a noise outside his door. Time was up. Someone was coming.

Shit.

☙ ❧

Number 97239.

THE REALITY STARING at Jared was too much. He dropped to his knees and bowed his head.

"Are you sure?" Taz spoke, his fingers already checking the data on the computer unit attached to the hanging male. "This is one of the older units. He's been here for a long time. I'll have to check the information in the computer system to see just how long."

Jared's voice cracked when he said, "At least 13-14 years. I'm 17 and he's been gone most of my life. I have the barest of memories of him."

Taz's sucked in breath was audible in the eerily silent living morgue of the blood farm.

"Damn. I'm sorry, son. That's a tough one."

"My uncle sold him." Jared stared at the ravaged body of his father, a hatred he'd never imagined possible forming inside him. "I overheard him and my aunt talking about having gotten rid of him for good. I was supposed to be hanging up here beside him. And I would be, except for Tessa."

"I'm sorry Jared. Even knowing what you've found, I wish you weren't here. This is no place for you. And we have no answers yet. Especially not for anyone who could possibly have been hanging here for as long as your father might have been."

Jared struggled to his feet, hating the moisture collecting at the corner of his eyes. "I had to come," he said simply. "Once I knew, I just had to."

Taz sighed. "I understand. Come with me and let's see

what information we can find in the computer system. Maybe we can download this man's history and either confirm or refute his identity."

Jared stared up at the plasticized version of so many of his own features and felt like ripping his father down from the ceiling hooks. "I want him down from there."

Taz stopped and turned around. "If you do something, you are likely to kill him."

Jared closed his eyes. He knew that. But to see his father hanging, helpless, victimized into this living dead state…he shuddered.

A heavy hand landed on his shoulder. "Come on. Let's do what we can on the computer end first."

Jared let himself be led away. With a final look at the hanging man, he said, his voice cracking, "He can't be helped, can he?"

There was a heavy silence, then Taz said, "I don't know. I hope so, but if he's been hanging as long as you believe he has been, then it's probable that his system, muscles, and bones are too damaged to have a chance of recovery." He turned to glance at Jared. "But we don't know that for sure. While he's there, he's alive. And every day gives us a chance to find the answers we need to help him and the others."

There was some truth to that. If his father could stay alive, then maybe they could find something to help him. He'd been hanging for so long now…as much as it was hard to leave him there, it might be the best answer. At least for today.

Still, he had no plans to leave his father alone here. Not now that he finally found him.

"Thank you."

Taz looked over at him in surprise. "You're welcome." He grinned sheepishly. "I'm about to become a father, so you're definitely hitting my buttons with your find."

"Yeah, and I wouldn't have known about it except for what I overheard today."

"You can tell me all about that now. We'll write up a report and make sure no one slips through the cracks. We want to make sure everyone pays for this nightmare they've created."

"I'm all for that. I'd like to see my aunt and uncle hanging up here themselves."

"Well, that won't happen." Taz shook his head. "But that doesn't mean they will get away with this."

"Good. Then let's go find the proof."

Jared smiled, a feral smile of vengeance. "And then they can spend the rest of their lives in a different kind of prison."

CHAPTER 2

"**W**HAT? YOU CAN hear him?" David raced toward her. Goran and her father were too far ahead to hear her, same as the others.

"Yes." She shouted gleefully, almost dancing in place. "He's strapped down on a bed in a room, alone. He's trying to get loose and has no idea where he is."

David held up his hand for a high five. "It doesn't matter. We'll find him." He turned and started running after the ancients in front of the group, calling behind, "It would be good if he could get free, though. He could give us directions on how to find him."

"I know."

She fell into last place, with all the other vamps running ahead of her. She hated to be last, but her energy wasn't the same as theirs and now that she knew Cody was alive…she wanted to talk to him. But… *Hey Cody. Any luck getting loose?*

Yeah. I'm loose but it looks like I'm about to have company.

Shit.

Actually double shit. Gotta go. Things are about to get…busy.

Tessa picked up the pace, now flat out running behind the others. Cody needed help and fast.

Up ahead, she caught sight of Goran circling in place. Energy filled the air around him. There was a lot of colorful

27

swirling energy that hadn't been there very long. They were either catching up to the assholes who took Cody or the other vamps had caught sight of Goran and booked it. Of course there could be many other scenarios, but she liked the sound of that last one. Anything that had the other guys running away worked for her.

She came to a staggering stop as the rest of the vamps gathered below Goran.

"What's he doing?" Motre asked.

Tessa had no idea. And where was her father? Usually where there was one ancient, you could be sure to find the other. She found him on the far wall resting on some kind of ledge. "Look, there's Dad."

The others stared in the direction she pointed. As they watched, Serus dropped to the floor below. And onto something...or someone.

Goran flew down in a fast plummet to join the fray.

Motre roared and the next thing Tessa knew, she and Jewel were the only ones left standing in the same place.

Jewel, her eyes huge and exhausted, looked over at her. "Will this ever end?"

"Yes, it will. And soon." Tessa answered with a firmness she didn't feel, then whispered to herself. "It has to."

She didn't think she could keep doing this.

Then all selfish thoughts disappeared as Cody screamed through her mind. *A little help would be good.*

Cody! Shit. *We're on the way.*

RHIA AND SIAN stared at Councilman Adamson and Gloria as they scrolled through the names and numbers. There was no break in their hard blank glares. At least the glares were now directed on the screen and not at them. Thank heavens for something.

"Where did you get this?" snapped Councilman Adamson, his gaze narrow and cold as he glared at Rhia. Rhia glared back. She'd taken a big chance showing him this material. Gloria too. But Gloria had lost her husband and son in the last war, and Rhia was betting that she'd be more than helpful. Vamps were many things, and pissed off vamps were especially known for getting their revenge.

Without warning, Rhia snapped the lid closed. "We picked it up from the blood farm."

"The blood farm?" Gloria took a step closer to the laptop.

Rhia held the laptop to her chest and watched the dragon lady approach. "Yes. The one my daughter just found."

Both sets of eyes locked on her face. She could feel their intense scrutiny. She stood firm. Sian sucked her breath in at her side. "There is more than one blood farm. It's a huge operation and in this laptop we have the who, when, and how."

Councilman Adamson stared at her, his gaze hard and unreadable. His tone of voice was not. He was pissed, but curious as he asked, "And? Why are you here?"

Rhia took a deep breath and said, "Because your name is NOT on this list of board members."

He reared back in shock, a frown rippling over his face.

Gloria gasped. "Surely, you're not saying everyone else is on that list?"

Sian shook her head. "No. Not everyone. But it's enough that we can see those who are and those who aren't. And of course we have to consider the group that each side is very close to."

Rhia understood what she meant even if Councilman Adamson gave no indication to his thoughts. Last time, the council was firmly divided. So many of the council were on the side of humans and against blood farms, while just as many had come down on the other side. By looking at their friends and associates, it was easy to guess where each member stood. Some, like Gloria, remained in the grey area. And that's why she kept her gaze on the older woman.

"Rhia? Is this true?" Councilman Adamson asked.

"Mostly. Not everyone's name is here, but enough for us to realize how dangerous it is for us to be the only ones with this knowledge." She curled her lip at the surprised look passing between the two of them. "Of course, we have passed on this information to a few others. Just in case…" and her smile dropped several degrees in temperature. "…we're wrong."

Gloria turned back to her and snapped, "Well, I certainly don't have anything to do with this mess." She tossed her hair, the haughty look on her face cold and superior.

"I know," Rhia said gently. "You're still alive, aren't you?"

Gloria narrowed her gaze then spluttered as she understood what Rhia was implying. "You'd have come into my home to kill me?"

"Your home?" asked Sian gently. "We came here to see Councilman Adamson. Not you."

The three women stared at each other with distrust, the temperature of the room dropping steadily.

"Easy, ladies." murmured Adamson. "We're all on the same team here." He motioned to Rhia and Sian to come further into his house. "This has been a shock, but let's deal with this calmly. We don't want to go making accusations that aren't warranted."

Gloria snorted. "Goran already contacted me about this blood farm. He wanted me to find the enforcers."

"And did you believe him?" Sian asked. "Or did you delete the message?"

Gloria raised an eyebrow. "You can't know Goran very well if you think he panics over nothing. Or that he would waste my time."

Rhia smiled. Maybe they'd made the right decision after all. "So you're on our side?"

"Not having heard all the details yet, I'm not willing to go that far," said Councilman Adamson. "But I do see names on there that don't surprise me. In fact, I've wondered about some of them for a long time."

Sian nodded. "I know. There are a few names in here that will surprise you. But it's big. Bigger than you can imagine."

Councilman Adamson's face went dark. Then he sighed, almost seeming to age in front of them. "Good enough. Let's take a closer look."

∂> ⤵

SERUS TOOK A fist to the jaw and kept on moving. He'd landed on the back of one vamp and crushed him to the ground, but a second had jumped him while he was trying to get back up. Now that he was moving forward, two piles of ash at his feet, nothing was going to stop him. Enough of this bullshit. He was tired, hungry, fed up, and wanted to go home to Rhia. But first they had to find Cody. That boy was like a son to him. He couldn't imagine how Goran would handle it if anything happened to Cody.

It was too horrible to contemplate. But if Tessa said the kid was alive, then he was good with that. They all needed hope.

Especially Goran.

They were both too old for this shit, but it didn't matter. They hadn't taken care of business the first time around so there was no ducking it this time. The last thing he wanted to do was leave this mess for his kids to sort out.

Another blow came out of nowhere and Serus realized he'd been standing in a daze while the fighting went on around him. Shit.

"Come on boy, wake up. It's not that I can't handle this pack of dogs without you, but no whining afterwards that I didn't share," shouted Goran.

Serus laughed, a booming sound that made the guy in front of him suddenly turn and look for an exit. And he got it. Goran lifted and tossed him in one fell swoop. The guy hit the wall and fell, bouncing a few times before he hit the ground and stayed there.

"Look out!" shouted Goran.

Serus pivoted and ducked, a silver spike raking along his shoulder and catching on the leather of his coat. "Hey," he roared. "I love this coat." He grabbed the arm holding the spike and twisted it around, forcing it into the guy's back. Instantly, the vamp turned to ash in front of him.

"Asshole," muttered Serus. He spotted a vamp several feet to one side fighting with Goran. It was almost too easy, but he figured they needed to conserve their energy. He took a spike from his pocket and stabbed the first vamp, then withdrew it and stabbed the second vamp who was about to step into the dead guy's place.

"Where did they find so many bad guys?" Goran asked. "And are they imports or created?"

"Created in a lab most likely," Serus said. "These are not normal vamps."

Another male snorted and waded through the ash piles toward him. "Hell no, we aren't. We're much better." And he threw a punch, silver glinting in his fist. Serus managed to duck just enough that it skimmed safely over his head. He pivoted and stabbed his spike upward, impaling the vamp in the side.

The man fell to the ground gasping, but it wasn't the normal turning into ash scenario. Instead, there was a slow hissing sound and weird 'off' smell as the large vamp appeared to cook from the inside out.

Backing away, Goran held his nose. "Jesus. What the hell are they doing to these guys?"

"Nothing good." Serus coughed several times to clear his throat, backing away several steps behind Goran. "Is that all of them?"

"All that are here right now." Goran looked around. He nodded toward the group of young males making their way over to them. "There you are. Leave all the work to us ancients, huh? Talk about lazy."

But his voice was cocky and pleased. Serus figured he'd been delighted to show off and crack a few heads. Dealing with younger vamps was always a bit of a struggle. Supposedly the ancients were stronger, bigger, and according to the ancients, smarter. But sometimes that wasn't even close. However, the younger generation was often cockier, more arrogant, and thought they knew more. In truth, they had no experience to back anything up.

Serus searched the crowd, happy to see David and Jewel there with Ian. But where the hell was Tessa? That girl could get into more trouble than the three of them combined. Ah, there she was, running to catch up. The look on her face…

He called out, "Tessa, what's going on?"

Her grin widened, making her look even more like her

mother.

"Cody is awake. He's loose from his straps, but said he could use some help because company is on the way."

With a spring to his step, Goran walked over the ash piles toward her. "Does he know where he is?"

Tessa shook her head. "No. Apparently, he's being held in a room similar to all the rest except it's only got one bed. He thought he heard someone coming, but that was a few minutes ago and I haven't heard anything since."

"I'm still trying to figure out how you're hearing him," Motre muttered. "Mindspeak is not for younguns."

Serus watched Tessa stiffen and glare at Motre. "It doesn't matter who it's supposed to be for. It's happening to me whether you like it or not, regardless of how old I am. Deal with it."

He had to hide a smile as Tessa jutted out her chin and glared at the largest male vamp in the area. And one of the largest Serus had ever seen. Tessa sure had changed. He was glad for it, but he knew it wasn't going to be an easy road ahead. She'd changed and her world had changed. How the two were going to fit together now still remained to be seen.

"Let's keep moving. They have to run out of bad guys soon. And we need to find Cody."

On that note, Goran took to the air again. Serus, hating that sense of wanting to just go home, picked up the pace and jumped behind his best friend.

CODY FLATTENED AGAINST the wall behind the door. His heart slammed against his chest. He wanted someone to enter so he could bash his head in. But whoever stood on the other side, hand on the knob, appeared to be talking to someone else. Only Cody couldn't hear their conversation.

But the knob on his side of the door kept twisting and then releasing. He closed his eyes, straining to make out the words.

"More traffic…"

"Greater numbers…"

"Need to solve this problem first."

This problem? Were they talking about him? Hell. He opened his eyes and glared at the stark white room, wishing they'd get on with it.

They were right. He was a problem. And he'd make sure they remembered that. But damn, he didn't have time for this crap. He had things to do and vamps to punch. And Tessa to get back to. Like what the heck, every time they got everyone back together again, someone went missing. With chagrin, he realized it was his turn. And boy, were Ian and David going to tease him over that.

The door opened, and he realized that anyone would see the empty bed without having to actually enter the room. So not good.

But the person was still talking as he entered. "Will do. Let me finish this up, then I'll—"

The door widened. Cody grabbed him, snapped his neck, and dropped him in place just inside the room.

Cody immediately grabbed the door and opened it wide enough for him to exit. And found two startled vamps on the other side. He stepped forward in a smooth motion, as if he was supposed to leave the room all along.

"Hey fellas. Were you looking for something?" He kicked out with his right boot and connected with the first guy's chin. His head snapped backward, but Cody was still moving, bringing his right fist forward and giving an award winning upper cut to the second vamp's chin. Both men howled and stumbled back. Cody brought out his silver stake and gave them a couple of quick jabs, dispatching both vamps efficiently.

Not wanting anyone left alive to rat about his escape, Cody went back to the first vamp in his holding room and stabbed him.

As he stood over the smoldering ashes, he felt worried for a moment. Were all assholes in this facility guilty? Or were some of them innocent – and therefore shouldn't be killed? As he glared down at the remains, he realized they had to know about the blood farm if they worked here. That made them guilty. As least as far as he was concerned.

With a grimace, he realized it was a little too late now to worry. They were all dead and he planned to take out every other one he met on his way back to the others as well.

Glancing in both directions, he realized the ashes were likely to arouse suspicion, but he could hardly sweep them away. Better to escape and hope he could get a head start before anyone found out.

To that end, he chose to go left.

Too bad his wing was still injured. Otherwise he'd try flying. If he could get into open air, he'd try regardless of his wing. He tested that by giving his wing a shake and gasped.

Shit.

Are you hurt? Tessa's warm voice popped into his mind. How odd to know she could hear him…know him that intensely. That intimately.

Shaking off the musings, he answered her, *No. I'm fine.*

And he would be. Soon.

CHAPTER 3

T ESSA TRAILED IN last place again. But she didn't feel last. Not with Cody in her head. And what kind of miracle was that? One that made her toes wiggle with joy.

She didn't know how the system worked or why it happened, but she wasn't going to say no. It was too special. And so was he.

She gave a happy sigh and started to run. Somehow, the others had gotten ahead. It was not a safe distance. Not after all they'd been through. She so didn't want to get isolated again. The long hours had caught up with her though. And the lack of food. She hurt in places she didn't know existed. And that was just stupid.

Urging her vampire genes to give her flagging energy a boost, she was able to keep the others in sight. In a way, she was surprised she'd been allowed to fall behind. After having been kidnapped a couple of times, she thought her father and brother would keep a closer eye on her. Or else they'd figured she could look after herself.

Honestly, right now she doubted she could do much to defend herself.

"Hey sis, you look like you're ready to drop. You okay?"

David's voice pulled her out of her reverie. He'd stopped up ahead to wait for her. She gave him a bright smile. "I am. Although a couple of days in bed sounds good right about now."

He laughed. "To you and me both."

He waited until she stood in front of him before asking, "Any more word from Cody?"

"Not really." She added, "He's injured but I don't know how badly. Oh, and he's free."

David's eyebrows shot straight up. "You *really* can talk to him using mindspeak, can't you?"

She shrugged, a difficult move while jogging. "It seems like it."

"That's really unusual."

"Yeah, I got that. But right now, it's damn useful."

"Yeah." David sounded like he wanted to say something else but couldn't quite figure out what to say.

"Just spit it out." She fell into step beside him as they followed the others. "It's obvious something is bugging you."

"You know Cody isn't exactly prime boyfriend material, right? I mean I love the guy, but he's got girls all over the place."

"Meaning I can't compete?" Tessa didn't mean to sound bitter about a lifetime of not being good enough, but she couldn't help it.

"No," he rushed to say, "that's not what I meant. In fact, after this mess, you're likely to be overrun by interested males."

"That is so not what I want." She shuddered. "Ugh."

"Want it or not, it's still going to happen," he said seriously. "And Cody is definitely interested."

She cast a sidelong glance at her brother. And just what did that mean? "So are you warning me away or putting him up as a suggestion?"

He laughed, his features so young looking now he barely

looked tired at all. How could that be without rest or food? She felt like a wreck beside him. She hated that. Or maybe not. But damn, she'd like to not be so tired right now.

"Like Cody would stand for either," David said, still chuckling. "I'm just warning you to take things slow. You're not used to men hanging around you like they will be soon enough."

Really? He was concerned for her? That was kinda cool actually. "I think you're exaggerating. I doubt any of the males will give a damn."

"And what about Jared." David added, a doubtful tone in his voice, "If you and Cody have this thing…"

"I didn't say I had a thing with Cody," she said. And if she did, she so didn't want her brother to know the extent of it. At least not yet. And she had no idea what to think about Jared. He'd been her first crush. And she still really liked him. But Cody sent her reeling sideways.

"And yet the two of you can mindspeak?"

She shrugged and moved faster. She didn't want to delve too deeply into her connection with Cody. The relationship was too new. Too private. And she was too uncertain of just what it was yet. "Obviously not for the same reason that mom and dad can though."

"You don't know that. We have no idea when they started doing this or why. They don't talk about it."

And that she could now understand.

She didn't want to share either.

JARED STARED DOWN at the computer monitor in front of him. He had a bottle of water in one hand from Taz and a candy bar from his pocket in the other. He took another bite of chocolate. Taz was munching on a granola bar. He had brought up his father's number. Figures scrolled down, bright green on black, a confusing and never ending stream. Dates. Times. Quantities.

"What does all of this mean?" he asked, not understanding why there was so much.

"It means your father has been here for a long time. A *long* time." Taz shook his head but never took his gaze off the monitor. "How could no one have known?"

"They did know. But no one cared." Jared wanted to both cry and hit something. "How could they do this to their own brother?" he snapped. "It's despicable."

Taz nodded. "It is that. And it's criminal. Some big money had to go into keeping this quiet." He turned to study Jared's face. "Surely there were other people in your father's life? People that would have looked for him when he went missing. Friends? Coworkers? Bosses?"

"How would I know? As far as I knew, he died when I was little. That's all my aunt and uncle said."

"What about your grandparents? Other relatives." Taz hesitated. "Your mother?"

Jared shrugged. "My mother died when I was little and I never met any other family. As far as I knew, it was just my aunt and uncle. Neither of them are married anymore and neither have kids." He frowned. "I don't suppose they got rid of the spouses here too, did they?"

Taz's left eyebrow shot up. "Wow. That's a hell of a way to get out of a divorce." His lips twisted as he considered the matter. "We'd have to ask the police to follow up on their whereabouts today."

Jared could only snort at that. "I don't trust the police.

One of the cops that questioned me is probably in on it. He wasn't helpful, friendly, or supportive. He basically accused me of making it all up!"

"Really? Do you remember his name?" Taz asked, a frown forming on his forehead. "There's got to be some police involvement in this operation for the vampires to have kept this many missing people a secret for so long. We're going to need to ferret out who we can trust. And who we can't."

"I say trust no one. Just think, both my aunt and uncle are involved along with that cop and I've only been free for what, a day – or is it two now?" How sad, he had no idea what day it was.

Taz nodded. "The problem is finding out who we can trust to help us."

"I think one of my friend's father is a cop."

"Do you *know* him though? Because he could be either good or bad. Somewhere along the line, we need to find an honest one and have him on our side."

"Sure, ask for a miracle, why don't you," Jared scoffed. "I'm starting to wonder if there is such a thing."

Then Taz narrowed his gaze and tapped the screen. "Look. There are cross-references here."

Jared leaned closer. "To files? Another system? Another person? What?"

"No idea. But we need to find out."

Just as the green numbers stopped scrolling, the lights in the room went out.

Taz whispered, "Shit."

COUNCILMAN ADAMSON HELD out his hand. "Let me see."

Rhia hesitated. She'd come here for help, but until now, this laptop had remained in her keeping. She was loath to let it out of her hands. She stared into the Councilman's black gaze, wishing she could see into his soul.

·"We came this far," Sian murmured at her side, "But it's your decision. We can leave if you want to."

Gloria shook her head. "Don't be stupid. You came to us because you believed in us. Let's get past this foolishness and figure out what we can do to stop this war before it gets any worse."

Rhia hesitated a moment longer. With a sigh, she handed over the laptop. "So long as you know this isn't the only copy of the information."

The councilman gave her a hard but real smile. "Good. I suggest we make sure there are several copies so that the information can't be buried again."

Sian nodded. "True. Half the council is listed here."

Gloria's gaze sharpened. "Half?"

"At least," Rhia added. "There are a lot of names here. If I were to guess, I'd have to say that at least a tenth of the vamp population is involved."

"That is not good news."

"No." Councilman Adamson turned to his main seating area. "Come. Let's sort through the list and find the information we need, then come up with a way to clean out the clans. This time, let's make sure it sticks."

∂◊

CODY MADE HIS way down the hallway, urging his genes to speed up the healing. He hated feeling at a disadvantage with his injured wing. These guys were giving no quarter, and he hated going to war in less than perfect shape.

I knew you were injured.

Damn it Tessa, it's nothing. Just a few bruises.

Even he could hear her snort in his head. How did that work again? How could she sound so clear and hear his every thought? He didn't think her parents could do that. Although they did finish each other's sentences and appeared to mind-speak easily. Maybe it was the exact same thing. How odd.

Odd? Is that what you call it?

He grinned at her aggrieved tone. *Yes, odd.*

I guess.

Then his mind went empty and he could only assume she was gone.

Are you there? He asked, testing the emptiness in his mind.

No. But there was laughter in her voice. And then a real emptiness filled him. And he knew she had left for real this time. So weird.

He grinned. "Okay. Now to get the hell out of here."

"You should have done that before, boyo. Now you left it a little too late."

Cody froze and closed his eyes. Damn. He turned around very slowly and came face to face with three vamps. Three overgrown vamps. Too big, too ugly, and too damn bad – for them.

Without warning, he spun forward and did a quick mid air twist and let his boot lash out, carried by the momentum, to connect with the biggest of the three vamp's jaw. He landed lightly on his feet on the other side. He crouched, spun, and slammed his right fist into the second vamp.

Crack!

Cody straightened, a sense of satisfaction surging through him. A sense of control. A sense of power. He'd be damned if these assholes would take him down.

Not Cody. No siree!

The third vamp stared at the biggest vamp crumpled on the floor then at the second one lying unconscious on the ground. He backed up a step. Then another.

Cody smirked. "What's the matter? Not so tough now that you're all alone, are you?"

Meaning to scare the guy even more, Cody put his hand into his pocket and pulled out a spike. He held it up and shook it in front of the other guy. A bead of sweat formed on the other vamp's forehead. Cody laughed and took a step forward.

The other vamp's gaze widened in horror.

Cody had the asshole right where he wanted him. "See, I took this off a friend of yours. I've put it to good use since I confiscated it."

The big vamp swallowed. Cody shook his head. "So if you have something to say that might sway the case to *not* killing you, maybe you should speak now."

The other man's gaze went from the spike to Cody's face and back again. He appeared to be completely terrorized by the spike. Interesting. "Haven't you been issued any of these?"

The other vamp gave a frantic head shake.

"But you know what it is? Right? And what it does?"

Now the vamp nodded rapidly.

"So you know I can annihilate you and your friends very quickly?"

Cody felt like he was speaking to a mute child. He studied the vamp's face. He was seriously scared. Cody risked a quick glance behind him. The hallway was empty.

And now Cody understood a little of what Tessa had tried to explain but hadn't wanted to hear. Apparently not all the vamps *were* willingly on the wrong side. Some had been forced. Some had no choice. And he didn't know for sure, but he was starting to realize that the vamp in front of him didn't even want to fight.

He stood contemplating the man, trying to figure out what to do at this point. What was the right thing to do?

And then he heard Tessa's compassionate voice. *Talk to him. Find out what you can. And give him a chance to choose his own future.*

He groaned, startling the other vamp, who hurriedly took another step back.

Damn it Tessa, I can't convert this guy. He's on their side.

By choice?

How the hell am I supposed to know?

Silence.

And he groaned again. "Okay. Why the hell are you here? Are you working for these guys? By choice?"

The vamp shook his head.

It was starting to piss Cody off. "Do you talk?"

The vamp nodded.

"Then say something."

The vamp wiped the back of his hand across his mouth. "I don't know what to say."

"How about – please don't kill me?" Cody glared at him. "Jesus, was this guy dense or what?"

"Please don't kill me?"

Cody studied him, wondering what the hell had just happened. It seemed like he'd stepped off a cliff into another world. He didn't have a clue what to do. He couldn't just kill the vamp in cold blood. Killing in a fight was one thing. Killing in self-defense another. But killing a man that just stood there staring at him in terror – yeah, that was something else entirely.

And he realized he couldn't do it.

He dropped his arm. "What the hell."

The vamp's gaze followed the spike in his hand. Really? Cody decided to test his theory. He moved the hand holding the spike to the right. The vamp's gaze followed. He moved his arm to the left. And again the vamp's gaze followed. Cody slipped his hand back into his pocket and let the spike go.

The vamp's gaze locked on Cody's pocket. Slowly, Cody withdrew his hand and held up his open palm.

"See? I put it away."

The vamp stared. Looked at Cody's face and then grinned.

He jumped Cody and knocked him to the ground, landing on top of him.

The asshole brought his legs together and squeezed tight. "So glad you did that. See, I don't have a problem with you or this place. But now those spikes...."

Cody gasped for breath but he couldn't get any air. His injured wing screamed at him. Damn, he was a fool.

Then the asshole punched Cody in the face – hard.

Damn. Cody realized the big-assed vamp had been waiting for just this moment. And he'd taken the opening Cody had so foolishly given him. What an idiot.

Another fist hit his chin, knocking his head to the side. "Shit."

"Yeah. Like what are you going to do now?" The vamp gave him a huge toothy grin.

Cody glared back. He could hardly breathe with this guy on his chest but he'd be damned if he'd give in so easily. He had to get free. Somehow.

"Don't like a fair fight, do you?" he gasped.

The toothy bastard's grin widened. "It was fair. You just let down your guard. You were worried about me." He imitated Cody's voice in a mocking tone. "And look where it got you."

And because he could, he punched Cody in the face again.

Under the guise of groaning in pain, Cody worked his left hand into his pocket and smiled as his gloved fingers closed around the spike in his pocket. He clutched it tight, then stabbed upward – through the material of his pocket, through the jeans the vamp wore – right into the inside of the vamp's thigh.

Cody barely had time to take a breath and turn his face away as the vamp screamed and his body combusted. Cody rolled to one side as the ashes floated down on him. He scrambled to his feet, shudders wracking his frame.

So gross. So horrifying. And so wrong.

If this big guy could die so easily, what kind of chance did any of them have? On a bad day – none.

And he so wanted to live.

Then he heard a sound that sent shards of ice down his back. A scream. Tessa's scream.

Cody! Help!

CHAPTER 4

TESSA HADN'T SENSED the attack until the vamps were on top of them. There seemed to be dozens. She and David were surrounded, but up ahead she saw another cluster surrounding her friends. Damn it. They'd been split into two groups. She felt like an idiot. A mad idiot. A really pissed off idiot.

She stood with her back to her brother and glared at the three vamps in front of her. "David?"

"Easy, sis. There are a lot of them."

"I don't care. I'm not being taken."

"We can't fight them all."

"Goran and Dad wouldn't have been taken," she snapped. "They'll come to the rescue."

"Maybe, but possibly not in time." His calm voice helped steady her own nerves. She was jumpy, but that was from trying to hold back killing these assholes. "We need the element of surprise here." She studied the circle of vamps. "Something to break their concentration."

"We could use Dad's help right about now."

"Or Ian. Or Jewel. Or hey, Cody would work too."

"They've probably got him locked up tight."

"Nah, he's on his way toward us."

She turned, catching David's surprised look. "Yes, I'm talking to him. Okay?"

"Tell me he's just around the corner. Then it will be fine." David motioned to the leader of the group in front of them. "He wants us to move toward the others."

"At least then we'll all be together." She took a quick glance around to see who could hear her, then whispered, "And Cody is coming, but he's not that close yet."

"Like that's a help." Still, he grasped her arm and tugged her toward the others. She stumbled behind him, loath to take his pacifist way. She wanted to kill more vamps. In fact, a surge of bloodlust ran through her with such force that it shocked her. Scared her.

She didn't consider herself a vamp in the traditional sense. Angry, cold, and aggressive – she wasn't any of that. But she was learning that in some ways – she was all vamp.

Someone shoved her forward to stand beside Jewel and Ian. Too bad they were still suffering from the effects of the drugs and couldn't fly out of here. Motre was there with another half dozen vamps. What the hell? There were enough on her side to fight. Why were they giving in so easily?

It didn't make any sense.

"Finally we have you all." A formidable looking vamp spoke to the right of Tessa. She studied his features. She should know him but couldn't remember who he was. Except she thought he might be yet another councilman. Taking a chance, she gave him a cold smile. "What a surprise seeing you here, Councilman."

His cold gaze drifted over her, stopping to study her face before moving to David beside her. His gaze narrowed as if recognizing her brother. His gaze zipped back to her face. "Do I know you?"

"Yeah, I'm Councilman Serus's freak daughter," she answered, her voice equally cold. In the distance, not taking her attention off the dangerous man in front of her, she heard gasps coming from both sides. But she was so done with respect where it wasn't due. And these assholes were not vamps deserving respect.

His thin lips moved in a parody of a smile. "Ah. The lab rat."

She snorted. "In your dreams, asshole."

The smile dropped away. "No one speaks to me like that."

"Easy, sis." David was standing still beside her, but his muscles were knotted with tension, desperate to fight but not knowing when or what move to make first.

"I just did." She shrugged. "I reserve respect for those that deserve it."

"Oh, a do-gooder." He laughed. "Feel sorry for animals, do you? Feel a kinship to your ancestors by any chance?" he mocked.

"Only to the good vamps. You're the animals here. Not us. Not the humans you have hanging in the blood farm. No, *you're* the animals."

That same thin cruel smile showed up. If she had any sense, she'd be backtracking right now. Even the vamps on either side of him were shuffling their feet uneasily. "You got part of it right. We're the predators and you, the humans, and the weaker vampires are the prey."

"I wonder what the rest of the council will think of that?" she asked, deliberately keeping her tone of voice thoughtful. Inside, her mind was racing, seeking answers. They needed a distraction.

Shit. Come on, Cody. Where the hell are you?

"Grab her. The rest of the group will be so much easier to deal with without her influence." He motioned to a group of six vamps standing to one side. "Take her to the lab and keep her secured. Don't return. And if you lose her, you'd better keep running because your punishment will be death."

The six vamps approached.

And Tessa did the only thing she could think of. She screamed in her head again. *Cody! Help.*

⚜ ⚜

SERUS WATCHED FROM the shadows high above the group as his daughter was surrounded and corralled away from the others. Damn. There had to be forty plus assholes down there. At any time, he'd take it as a compliment, but in this instance they needed to narrow the odds in order to have a chance of success. His group was tiring and they weren't taking enhanced drugs like these guys were.

That they were separating Tessa from the rest of the group made him sick to his stomach. She had proven that she could handle everything that had been thrown at her these last few days, but this could be too much.

"What do you want to do?" Goran asked from behind him.

"Kill some vamps," Serus growled. "They are separating Tessa again. Going to take her to the damn labs."

"That we can't have. We need a distraction. Something to scatter the bad guys and give us an opening."

"If they're planning to drug the rest of our friends and family, we might have time. But they might just as likely decide that our group is too much trouble and kill them off immediately."

The air thickened as Goran and Serus watched the vampires tighten the circle around the remaining group. Serus hated to see David and Tessa split up. He needed to help them both. Torn, he did nothing but watch helplessly as the second group was herded in the opposite direction from Tessa.

"Damn," whispered Goran. "We need reinforcements."

"I don't think there are any more we can call."

"Not that we have a way to call them either. I sure hope Rhia and Sian are getting somewhere."

"Yeah. They can send reinforcements any time."

Goran nudged him in the direction where they'd taken Tessa. "She can't take on six herself, can she?"

"I suggest we split up and find out," Serus said, twisting around to see Goran's features. He smiled and was rewarded by an equally cold smile on Goran's face.

RHIA STILL HAD misgivings but settled on the couch beside Councilman Adamson. Gloria chose the other side. Sian, not to be left out, walked around behind the three of them and watched as they searched through the information on the laptop. Gloria had a tablet in front of her where she made notes as they worked slowly, page by page.

It wasn't long before Rhia and Sian switched places so Sian could get off her feet. Her pregnancy wasn't showing yet, but Rhia knew she needed to rest. Tessa wasn't so old that Rhia had forgotten the fatigue that came with pregnancy.

Gloria rose and retrieved several sheets of paper they had printed. "This is the list of warehouses that they are using for distribution." She held up several pages clipped together. "These are the supplies they are using to make the warehouses operate smoothly." She held up other clipped pages and tapped a long bloodred nail on the top sheet. "These are the main players behind the warehouse."

"Not quite." Council Adamson studied the laptop. "I only see up to the top echelons, but not the main players. I see the councilmen, several high hitting businessmen, and even several ancients, scholars, and scientists, but I don't see a clear indication of who is running this place. This is like the who's who list of everyone down the line – but not showing who is sitting at the top."

Rhia understood. She paced the living room, wondering how to find the final names that could clinch this problem. She stopped and turned to Councilman Adamson. "Who owns the laptop? He's the boss. If I were making a list, I wouldn't put my name on the top. I'd put those below me. So whoever owns the laptop is the boss."

"Or one of them. But how do we sort out who owns the laptop?"

"Check the logs. I wish David or Ian were here. They're both computer nerds." Rhia was good, but she didn't know how to hack into a system. Those two did.

"Adamson, hand it over. Let me see what I can find."

Gloria resettled the machine on her knees and started clicking away. She opened up a black screen with a little text, but what was there seemed to make her happy. She clicked and clicked and clicked. Eventually, her joy turned to a frown, then into frustration and finally, she looked downright pissed off.

"There's nothing to identify the owner on this laptop. Damn."

"That makes sense." Sian said, "If I was involved in something like this, I wouldn't leave my name on anything."

Gloria nodded. "I know, but I had hoped." She glanced over at the paperwork she'd set aside. "We have a lot to go on, but we need to coordinate this carefully. We need to take down all the suppliers and the councilmen at the same time. Make sure they are all under house arrest and separated where there is no communication between them while we round up the others. The warehouses have to be shut down and..." she tapped the laptop screen, "we have to find the last of the blood farms and put them under heavy guard."

Rhia loved the sound of all of it. She just wasn't sure they had the manpower or the time to do all of it. "How?" she demanded. "We barely know who is involved. There have to be hundreds and we're going to accidentally contact some of them. There's no way to avoid it."

Councilman Adamson narrowed his gaze, deep in thought. "There must be a group of people we can call on to help us."

"Humans."

Sian's suggestion came out of the blue and shocked them all. Rhia stared at her oldest friend. It wasn't hard to understand where she was coming from. After all, she had married a human and knew the species better than all of them in the room. She had insider knowledge that could help them. "Do you think Taz would know who to contact?"

Sian nodded. "There have to be humans involved in this as well, but I doubt it's to the extent that the vamps are."

Gloria said, "That's true. Some of the cops will be involved. Accepting payoffs to look the other way, to bury missing persons' files, etc. But I doubt the Human Council is involved. The vamps wouldn't want to let anyone in power know. They'd have to split the profits. And the council has no purpose in letting their own people become victims like this. Even many of the cops might not know exactly what was happening to the people they chose to turn their backs on."

"And yet Jared had some suspicion that his uncle might

have had something to do with him being in the blood farm."

"Jared? Hmmm. He was the young man that started all this, wasn't he?" asked Councilman Adamson.

"He's the young man whose disappearance started this chain of events, yes," Rhia corrected him. She wasn't going to have any more misunderstandings. Jared was not to blame. And that just reminded her that she hadn't heard from Goran or her family in way too long. She thought she'd have heard back from Seth by now. She pulled her phone out and checked yet again. Still no messages.

Sian cleared her throat. Rhia looked up, caught her questioning look, and shook her head.

Rhia watched as Sian dropped her gaze, her shoulders slumping. She hadn't heard from Taz either then. They were both waiting for word knowing that the longer it took, the worse the news was likely to be.

"We could contact the Human Council for a meeting today. See what they have to suggest and go from there." Gloria turned to Sian. "Can you coordinate that? Maybe you'll get a better reception with them because of Taz."

Sian nodded. "I can't guarantee anything, but I'm willing to contact them. Most of them know Taz and me." She shrugged. "Like the vamps, that doesn't mean they like us."

Councilman Adamson stared at her. "You have an interesting relationship. I'm sure there have been many challenges along the way."

Sian's gaze lit up at his understanding. Rhia assumed this was the first he'd mentioned anything to her. Her best friend had gone through a lot with Taz but she knew how strong and loving their marriage was. She also knew the difficulty Sian would face when Taz aged and she didn't. To have loved one lifetime might make it worthwhile for Taz, but at the end of his life, he'd be leaving Sian alone for eternity.

She had to wonder if Sian had considered turning Taz and if Taz would be receptive to the idea. It was illegal, but Sian could petition the council with a request. The response would be interesting. Like her own daughter, both Sian and Taz had faced a backlash of prejudice.

And like Sian and Taz, Tessa had learned to live with it gracefully.

Now if only they could all live in peace again.

CHAPTER 5

TESSA'S MUSCLES WERE starting to cramp, she'd locked them down so tightly. How the hell had these assholes gotten the drop on her? On them? Somehow, these guys had come out of nowhere and surrounded them all. Their numbers were so vast, the thought of fighting never entered the picture. She didn't know where the ancients were or if they'd even been seen. She'd been quickly segregated and shoved into a tunnel away from the others.

She desperately wanted to make a move but knew it was too early. She had six guards. Six. Like what the heck was she going to do against all of them? She could handle one. Might be able to handle two. Would still try against three, but six? So not doable.

And that just pissed her off even more.

None of them were fliers though. And that could be her ace in the hole.

She needed one chance to jump and get clear of them. But she was in a tunnel with a low ceiling. She couldn't take advantage of her skills here. She'd have to make a run for it. Anything was better than being locked up and drugged. That whole lab rat thing was so not going to happen.

"Look at her. She's like a trapped mouse, looking desperately for a way to escape." One of the men behind her laughed coarsely. "Too bad she doesn't understand her days of running away are done. She's here as our guest for all eternity."

More laughter, this time from several assholes. Boy, were they delusional. "Must be the drugs they gave you," she said in a conversational tone.

Up ahead, the tunnel was coming to an end. If she was lucky, it would lead to that big cavern and the half finished medical rooms where she'd found Cody and the others a little while ago. The ceiling there was high enough for her to jump up and hopefully hide out in the nooks and crannies of the cave. At least long enough to formulate plan B.

"Hey now. What's she talking about?"

"Forget her. She don't know nothing."

That last speaker had to be the slouched oversized soft-looking vamp slightly behind her. She thought he might be stronger than he looked. She'd seen guys like him before. They looked out of shape and huge but somehow they had the power and strength of two smaller men. And she didn't doubt this lumbering oaf would be even more powerful. He'd be the one to put down first.

But she had to choose her moment carefully. And get a hold of the spikes in her pocket. She couldn't slip her hand inside because her arms were being manhandled.

"Come on, stop struggling."

She laughed. "What? I'm supposed to just walk to my slaughter. Like you guys? Do you really think I'm as stupid as you?"

"Shut up. You don't know nothing." The vamp holding her left arm jerked her forward. "You don't scare me."

"Good. You shouldn't be scared of me, you should be terrified of what you let them do to you." She smirked.

"What are you talking about?" The vamp holding her right arm scoffed. "You're just trying to save yourself."

"Really," she muttered, "why would I do that?" Idiots. They were so not strong in the IQ department. Like that was a surprise.

"Stop listening to her. She's just trying to rattle you."

"And I'm getting rattled," growled one of the vamps from behind Tessa.

She kept her grin hidden. A little more of this and she might actually set them against each other. Good.

"Just shut up. And keep her quiet too." That was the big sluggard one. He was the leader here. The boss. And the one she'd take down first.

A shout behind them had her being jerked to a stop. A whispered conference from the others behind her kept her guessing. She tried to hear enough words to make out what was going on, but their hushed voices blended with the background noise. She could only hear a few words here and there.

"Come…"

"Two of you…"

"Wait…"

She turned around, noticing her two guards were also more interested in what was going on. But they still held on to her arms tightly. Damn. She watched, muscles tense. They were only ten yards away from the end of the tunnel. She just needed a chance.

And maybe this was it. Two of the six guards took off back the way they'd come. Good. She was down to four now. Good enough. She'd take her chances.

Her arm was jerked forward.

She glared at him and jerked her arm free. "Don't be so rough. Geesh, what's your problem?" She slipped her free hand into her jacket pocket and palmed the silver spike.

"Shut your mouth and get moving." This time, her arm was grabbed and used to haul her forward. Her hand came free from her pocket. She almost smiled as the spike stayed hidden under the leather cuff of her coat. Instead, she snarled at the two henchmen.

"What's the matter? Didn't you get picked to go help the others? Are you pissed off that you got put on babysitting duty? Huh. Not good enough for the real fighting like the big boys, are you?"

The men glared at each other and dragged her forward. She let them. She wanted them off balance both mentally and physically.

That the biggest vamp of the lot was still behind her and trudging slowly along just meant he was closest for her to take out. They were only a yard or so from the end of the tunnel when she realized it was the cavern she'd been hoping for. If she spent much more time in this damn mine, she'd actually start to find her way around.

Perfect.

In a flash, she elongated her long nails and dug them into the arms of the two men.

"What the—"

The vamps howled as she drew blood. She pulled backwards, freeing herself, then spun around. With her spike out, she stabbed the big-assed vamp in the chest.

She continued her spin to face the next closest vamp and slashed outward, catching him across the face. Both vamps went up in ashes.

Now the odds were much better. She turned slowly to look at the two assholes who'd been dragging her down the tunnel. She held up the spike and flashed her long nails, still dripping with their blood. She stalked toward them, tired, frustrated and…pissed off.

The first asshole grinned and jumped her. His own spike was out and slashing like mad. She snorted. "Like that will do you any good." She leapt over his head and dragged the spike across his head.

He screamed in agony.

She landed and took out the fourth one before he even understood what the hell had happened.

Yeah, geniuses they weren't.

Alone again, she stood for a moment to catch her breath. Those screams should have brought reinforcements – if there were any close enough to have heard them.

She waited, but there were no sounds of running footsteps. That didn't mean they weren't there though. Besides, her plan had been to escape these guys into the cavern, but now that she'd taken care of them, she needed to go back and help the others.

Good idea.

A light burned brighter on the inside at the sound of his voice. She smiled. *Cody, where are you?*

Who knows? Are you okay now? I could hear you earlier but wasn't sure if I should interrupt. Your thoughts were full of plans.

Really? That's just bizarre. And it was. But it was also kinda cool. *I'm free again. I need to go back and help David and Ian, not to mention Motre and his group. They were surrounded by way too many vamps when I was led off in a different direction. And I have no idea where our fathers are.*

I should be close to you. I think I'm almost at the big cavern where they had the half-finished medical research area.

Really? Cause I'm right there too. I'm coming up to the tunnel entrance. You have to be very close to me.

I'm now at the cavern. Where are you?

She stepped into the cavern and stared.

∾ ∽

"WE HAVE TO do something. They are moving the whole lot of them somewhere. And we don't know where. It's going to be hard to track them in the tunnels."

Shit. Serus hated this. "I'll go after Tessa. You keep an eye on the others."

"You can't do that. We have to stop this lot from moving too far into the tunnels. I know you want to save Tessa, but they aren't going to kill her right off. You know that. She's a lab rat to them. But David is just a troublemaker. They are likely to kill him immediately."

The painful truth was enough to send a shock wave down Serus's spine. He couldn't take that chance. If Tessa did get injected with drugs, chances were good that the effects could be combated by other medicine in the same way they'd worked for Rhia.

He had to save his son David.

Easy, slugger, whispered Goran in his head. *I'm right behind you. Let's wait until they get everyone moving, then we can pick off the men in the back one by one.*

As if on cue, several of the vamps started straggling behind, deep in conversation with the two that had come back from escorting his daughter.

Perfect.

Now.

Serus dropped like a rock to the floor of the open space. Not a hallway and not a cavern like the big one they'd all passed through a while ago, but something in-between. He'd have called it an anteroom. Since this was an old mine completely hidden in a mountain, who knew what or where these tunnels led to. There was some kind of miniature railway that wove in and out of the mine as well. That he had yet to see. He landed silently just a few feet behind the last man.

The vamp turned. "Wha—"

And Serus stabbed him with a spike. He'd rather break the vamp's neck, but this way the vamp couldn't come back after them again. And before he'd even finished that thought, he had the second vamp floating in ash around them. And a third, with Goran finishing the last of them.

Instantly, Serus turned and raced to catch up with the group ahead.

If there was one thing vampires did well, it was stealth. But being stealthy against your own kind levelled the playing field. Or so Serus would have thought, but these vamps had none of the same finesse or superior vampire qualities he was used to. These had to be turned vamps or enhanced – designer vamps, as Tessa called them. With Goran at his side, he snuck up, grabbed the closest of the guards, stabbed him with the spike, and kept moving. Between them, they had five guards down before David noticed them. He reached out and smacked Ian and Jewel lightly. Both glared at him before twisting slightly to see what was going on.

An evil grin lit up Ian's face. He walked faster and caught up with Motre. Seconds later, Motre's big back stiffened. Serus swore he could read each vamps' body language as they got the news.

He didn't know how to time this for everyone to move at the same moment, but just as he was about to let out a war cry, everyone in front of him attacked the vamp closest to them.

The two ancients stopped in place and stared in astonishment as a mini war raged in front of them. Before they had time to join the fray, the designer vamps were vanquished and Motre was finishing off the leader of the group.

"Well, look at that. Maybe the odds are finally in our favor." Goran beamed happily. "They did good."

Serus snorted. "Damn well better have. These assholes seem to be getting dumber and dumber."

David approached with a big grin on his face. "I'm thinking the bosses don't have the time to make the enhancements or programming take like they used to. We're killing so many that they may have been forced to pull in reinforcements before they were ready."

"Now that actually makes sense." Goran said. "It's also good news. Means we're slowly winning this war."

"Slowly isn't good enough," growled Serus. "This has to stop."

"It will. We're getting there." Goran motioned around the room. "Look how well everyone did."

"Yeah Dad." David punched Serus gently on the shoulder. "Now shall we go and get Tessa?"

Serus brightened. "Absolutely." He turned and headed in the direction he'd seen Tessa disappear earlier. The others could be heard falling in behind him. He made it partway down the tunnel and came to a shuddering stop.

In front of him were four piles of smoldering ash.

❧ ❦

CODY STEPPED OUT carefully into the cavern. He'd been caught in this place once. He didn't plan on it happening again. But Tessa was somewhere close.

He searched the skies. Nothing moved. Absolutely nothing. Hoping his wing was up to it, he jumped lightly into the air and up onto the roof of one of the partially finished rooms. So far so good. His muscles ached with the movement, but the wing was functional. It would heal the rest of the way soon enough.

Staring into the massive room, he realized it was silent and empty. He frowned.

Tessa? Where are you?

Here.

She sounded like she was standing right beside him, and yet he couldn't see her.

Then she laughed.

He spun around to find her standing behind him, grinning wildly.

Cody opened his arms.

She launched herself into them.

He hugged her close then picked her up and spun her around. When he lowered her to her feet, she giggled and tried to step back, only he tugged her forward and squeezed hard. When she protested, he pulled back slightly.

Damn, she looked good.

Thank you.

Heat suffused his face. *Okay, this is embarrassing.*

Her smile faltered. *But is it okay?*

He grinned. *Yeah. Besides, it's not like we know how this started or what to do about it. For all we know, it will stop just as suddenly as it started.*

Tessa nodded. *True. I just wonder what it all means.*

I don't care. It's special. You're special, and I'm glad we can talk this way.

He watched her eyes widen then start to warm, a light glow shining from within. He felt happy and sappy and so not like himself.

And then he realized the two of them were alone. Like really alone. Tucked up high in the shadows above the main room. There was no one around see them.

He couldn't resist.

He lowered his head.

And kissed her.

$$\approx \ll$$

"WHAT WAS THAT?" Jared asked, hating the sense of panic clawing at his throat. The darkness was absolute. He spun back around to the computers, relieved to see the lights on the machine. "The computers didn't go offline."

"These ones haven't. But I don't know about the others. I'm assuming they have a decent backup system to keep the liquids flowing. If that were to stop…"

Jared stared out at the vast warehouse, but couldn't see anything in the dark. "There should be more than one backup system. All these people would die if the system went offline for a long time."

"Exactly."

Taz fiddled with several of the dials on the machine beside the computer. There was so much equipment here and Jared didn't understand half of what he was seeing. Didn't want to know more either. He was sure it had to do with nasty body functions and he so didn't want more details on those.

"What's the chance that some asshole turned off the lights to sneak up on us?"

Taz glanced over at him. "I'd probably take that as a given right about now. But there are more of us here so it's not going to be all that easy. Goran and Serus and many other vamps are fighting in the mine somewhere."

That sent a wave of relief though Jared. "How can we contact them? Cause I'm starting to think maybe we should."

"We can try cell phones, but it's sort of hit and miss here." Taz straightened then walked over to the door leading to the warehouse. "They should be back soon. They released me and the others from a locked room and took off, but that was hours ago."

"Or maybe it's Seth and his friends playing a joke on us." Jared both hated the idea and loved it. It would be typical of their age group and would mean that killer vamps weren't about to jump out of the dark at them.

"Forgot about them." Taz turned to stare at Jared. "Why did they come up here again?"

"I assumed it was to help the others." Jared glanced over at him. "Ask Rhia."

"I asked Sian and she said something about making an agreement to keep Rhia in the hospital." He shrugged. "She didn't stay there anyway."

"Shit."

Jared spun around, his nerves starting to get the better of him. "What's wrong?"

"The computer is going on the fritz. Whatever is happening out there is starting to affect the electronics in here."

"Uh-oh. That's not good."

"Especially not for people like your father." Taz looked out at the warehouse then back at Jared. Before Jared understood what he planned to do, Taz was already running out of the room, calling behind him, "Stay here. I'll be right back."

CHAPTER 6

T ESSA MELTED AS Cody took her lips in a warm caring kiss. She tried to stop her knees from buckling, but she couldn't stop from sagging against him. Thankfully, he didn't pull back. Instead, he shifted his arms, tucking her in closer and deepening the kiss. She sighed gently, their breath mingling, warming each other. Then he teased her lips open. She'd have gasped, but his tongue surged inside to stroke hers then retreated, teasing, tasting, tormenting.

She moaned softly.

He started to pull back.

She stretched up on her toes, her hands sliding up his chest to rest on his cheeks to hold him in place.

Tessa. We have to stop.

Noooo, she whispered softly in her head. This time, she took the initiative and tugged his head lower so she could slide her fingers though his thick dark curls as she deepened the kiss.

He shuddered then took her kiss and turned it into something so hot, so fierce, it left her wanting so much more.

Suddenly he stepped back, holding her at arm's length. *Someone could come at any time. They'd see us.*

She closed her eyes, swaying in place, hating the cold air between them. She just wanted to snuggle closer and stay that way. Bravely, she stepped closer and hugged him, letting her head rest against his chest. He wrapped his arms around her and held her closer. Just held her. Letting her know she wasn't all alone any more.

So nice. She stayed close, soaking it in for a moment longer. Then she stepped back and looked up at him. The concern in his eyes made her realize how worried he was about her. He was just that much older. That much more experienced.

It didn't bother her. But it might bother him.

So not.

She gasped as heat washed up her neck and warmed her cheeks. *You're right, that is definitely not easy to know you can read my every thought.*

"Not read them – hear them." He said out loud. Then he frowned as if thinking hard. "We must be able to turn it on and off sometimes, but I'm not sure how."

"There must be a way or this would be very invasive."

"I don't know about invasive, but it is definitely personal."

"Yah think?" she snorted. "You're already hearing things I'm uncomfortable with."

"And that goes both ways. It's not like we're used to guarding our thoughts," he added, consternation is his voice.

"No, and I don't think that would be easy to do."

"Then I guess we're stuck with it for now."

And what did that mean? She had to wonder. As his gaze narrowed, she realized he could hear that thought too. She groaned.

"I mean that this is the way it is," he clarified. "Not that I'm upset about it, or worried and will read the wrong thing into your thoughts – it means it's odd, different, and weird. But we can do this."

She sighed. "Thanks." She sighed. "I'm feeling fairly out of my depth."

He grinned boyishly. "So am I, Tessa, so am I. My age and experience is of no help these days. We're both out of our comfort zones."

"Maybe that's a good thing. Level playing field and all that." She had to admit it did feel good to know he wasn't miles ahead of her on this one.

Why don't we look at this as yet one more thing we can learn together?

She smiled up at him, then heard something off to the right.

She spun around.

Cody stepped up beside her, his arm wrapping around her shoulders possessively as he pointed to one of the tunnels.

David. And her father.

❧ ❧

GORAN SEARCHED THE area David was pointing at and saw Tessa and Cody.

"Oh thank God." Goran whispered.

"I'll second that." Serus ran a hand down his face, hating that sensation of having barely skimmed through safely once *again* by sheer dumb luck. But he was afraid that the next time, they wouldn't be so lucky. How many times could they walk through fire and not get burned? He didn't know what he'd do if he lost his kids. Any of them. He loved them all.

And Rhia would be devastated.

"They look awfully close," Goran said, his tone of voice confused yet curiously cautious.

Serus studied his daughter and the young man who he'd

73

looked upon as yet another son for so long. "They do, don't they."

David turned to study their faces. "And you might want to get used to it. Cody is confused enough about all of this as it is without you two going all possessive and becoming know-it-all fathers here."

"Harumph." Serus didn't know what to think. Surely mindspeak wasn't possible at their young age. The two had some link, but he doubted it was telepathic. Then again, Tessa had been showing all kinds of abilities. And that would make mindspeak a whole different thing with them. Maybe it wasn't as personal as it looked. As David seemed to think it was. He said slowly, trying to feel his way here, "She's awfully young."

David grinned. "Not as young as she used to be. And she's not as young as *you* see her. Most girls have been dating for awhile at her age."

Serus felt that old shudder of rejection as the thought went through him. She was his daughter and *that* made it somehow different than it was with his sons. And he knew both his wife and daughter would jump on him for that. He'd thought it great when the boys had entered into the dating scene. That had seemed natural. Normal. All men wanted their sons to have lots of fun. Only now, he was the father of one of those daughters the boys had fun with. And that couldn't happen. Not with his daughter. And he didn't care how unfair and sexist that made him. He was going to protect his little girl. In fact, he wanted to grab Tessa, race her home, and keep her locked up where the others couldn't see her.

"She's turned into a very desirable young woman when you weren't looking." Goran stood at his side, looking at the two in the distance.

Serus didn't know what he was thinking. At the moment,

the door between him and Goran was closed. Goran's son and Serus's daughter. Who would have thought?

"Oh, I was looking," Serus sighed. "I just didn't know what to do about it."

Goran laughed. "I have to admit that I'm glad I had sons. Raising girls...at this age...no thank you."

"Harumph." Serus said. "It's your boy standing with his arms around my daughter."

Goran leaned closer for a better look. "A friendly bit of support, maybe?"

David laughed. "I don't think so."

"Well, we're not going to be able to change whatever is happening so maybe you should look on the bright side, Serus," Goran said with a grin.

"Yeah, what bright side?" How could anyone see a bright side to this mess? His baby was growing up.

"You can bet that if Cody is standing by her side, none of the other eager young bucks who try to go after her will succeed. Cody doesn't take competition well. He'll knock out anyone who even gets close."

"Damn. I'd forgotten about the other young punks. Once word gets out about Tessa..."

"They are going to be calling day and night." David's grin split his face. "And I'm sure Cody won't appreciate that fact either."

"Staking his claim early," Goran crowed. "That's my boy."

Serus growled. "And just how much of a claim is he going to stake?" Serus snapped. "She's not a plaything. She's my daughter."

David rolled his eyes. "Before you two start fighting over who has the better kid or Cody's character, of which you'd be in perfect agreement if the woman in question wasn't Tessa, I suggest you remember your original statement about not being able to change whatever is happening."

Both of them looked down at him.

He just shrugged and walked away, calling behind, "I'm going to talk to them. Sit here and gossip like old women if you want to."

Serus reached out and grabbed his son by the shoulder. "No, you're not. I want to see what's in Cody's eyes for myself. You can join us in a few minutes."

Ignoring Goran's gasp behind him, he took off in a high strong glide to take him to his daughter and the young man who was holding her a little too close.

DAVID WATCHED HIS father take off, his glide strong and sure and showing no sign of his advanced years. He just hoped Cody was ready for this.

"He's not taking this development as well as I'd hoped."

With a quick spin, David looked up at Goran. "You knew?"

"I saw signs. I don't know how far it's gone but the mind-speak is a huge indicator that something special is happening. Serus knows this. But having his daughter hit this age and stage so fast...well, I guess that would be enough to startle any father."

"And Cody?" David asked, "Are you okay with him being with Tessa? Up until now, she was barely higher than a full-on freak in most vamp's eyes."

"Hmpph." Goran frowned as he watched Serus land beside his son and Tessa. "But she isn't. She's also saved my life several times. She's a good kid."

"And yet, I'm hearing a 'but'..."

"If this is serious, Cody has chosen a hard road very early. Serus won't allow for anything else. Hell, I'm not sure in this instance that I would either."

And Goran took to the air.

David stood and watched him. What had the man with so many relationships behind him meant?

He was right that Cody would have his work cut out for him. Tessa had taken a lot of crap from her peers, and vamps were nothing if not vindictive. If they wanted to, everyone could make Cody's life hell for choosing to date Tessa. On the other hand, Cody most likely wouldn't care. And that attitude alone would make the difference.

❧ ❦

CODY STIFFENED AS Serus landed in front of them, a hard look in his eyes. Cody lifted his chin and stared back at him.

"Glad you made it, sir."

Serus's gaze narrowed and he studied Cody's face. Damn, had Serus seen him kiss his daughter? Crap. He straightened his shoulders but refused to remove his arm around Tessa's shoulders.

Start the way he meant to go on. He was connected to Tessa one way or another. With Serus's approval or not.

He felt Tessa's slight start. And remembered that she could hear his thoughts, too.

"Hey Dad, about time you got here. Cody escaped and so did I." She beamed a smile up at him. Cody waited, tension running down his back. Would Serus soften or was he on a rampage at seeing a relationship developing between Cody and his daughter?

And why did Cody, who'd done so well overcoming all kinds of challenges these last few days, feel his knees quivering in the face of Tessa's father's potential displeasure?

Their families were close. Maybe too close. Maybe this relationship with Tessa was bound to happen eventually.

Tessa stepped forward, seemingly unaware of the tension crackling in the air. She reached out to Serus and stepped right up in front so that she could look directly in his face. "Dad? Is there a problem?"

He tore his gaze from Cody to stare down at Tessa, then with a heavy sigh, he eased back a bit. "No. Everything is fine."

Cody released a silent sigh of relief. War averted for the moment. Tessa's back stiffened and Cody whispered in his head, *Sorry. But he knows. Just not so sure he's happy about it.*

Her smiled eased and became so loving, so caring, Cody didn't think he'd seen anything like it. From her. From any girl.

And then she surprised him again. She brought the issue right out into the open. Cody could only listen in surprise.

"Thank you. Cody and I are struggling to sort out what's happening between us too. At the moment, just know that we care about each other. Where it goes or how deep it goes is something we can only wait and see."

Serus stared down at her. "You're too young."

"No." Again that gentle smile. "I am young. But not *too* young. Besides, Cody is only a few years older. I could have had this happen with someone your age. *That* would be difficult."

Cody struggled to hold back his laughter at the shock rippling over Serus's face. Then the laughter disappeared when

Serus lifted a hand and cupped her cheek.

"I've almost lost you several times these last few days," he started.

Tessa reached up and clasped her hand over her father's. "But I survived."

"Thankfully." He smiled so very gently. "And I've come to realize how much you've changed and matured these last few days. Just..." he glanced over at Cody, his gaze hardening as he pinned him in place. "Take it slow. Okay?"

Her smile lit up the darkness in the cavern. "I promise."

Cody let his breath out slowly, scared to break the moment, and nodded.

Serus gathered Tessa in a deeply loving hug.

Cody felt a band around his own heart loosen. Tessa looked so cherished. He could barely begin to understand what Serus must be going through right now.

Just then his own father arrived beside him. Goran dropped a warm heavy hand on Cody's shoulder. "Does the old heart good to see this." He nodded at Serus and Tessa. "Serus had to get to this point. He can't be worrying about what might be between Tessa and you while this war is going on. The distraction could get him killed."

Cody nodded. "Sorry for adding to the troubles we're all dealing with."

His father shook his head. "Don't be. Sometimes fate knocks us on our ass, but just as often it gives us a hand up." He squeezed Cody's shoulder. "Serus needed this."

At his words, Cody glanced over to see Tessa engulfed in Serus's arms. "So does Tessa," he admitted.

"Yes, those two have had their troubles these last few years and although Tessa has changed so much these last few days, she's always going to be his baby girl."

"Is that a warning, sir?"

Goran laughed. "Hell no. If you see something worth going after, then by all means go after it. You're awfully young to make a final decision though."

Cody wondered if everyone planned to warn him and Tessa about that same issue. He didn't know about Tessa, but he wanted to see where this went. But there'd be no trifling with Tessa like Cody might have done with other girlfriends. She wasn't in the same category as previous girlfriends.

Damn right, I'm not.

Cody was saved from having to answer by the arrival of David and the rest of the group. They gathered on the ground and looked up at the group.

"See, I get all this family stuff, I really do. But..." David paused for effect. "Do you think we could have this meeting at home instead of here where we're likely to get attacked at any moment?"

Tessa pulled back from Serus's hug and smiled. "You're right. It's time to finish this show and go home."

She walked over to Cody. She stood in front of him, a gamine grin on her face and said, "Right?"

He tugged her back to his side and wrapped an arm around her shoulder possessively. "Damn right."

CHAPTER 7

T ESSA LAUGHED AT her brother. She jumped down to his side. "Glad to see you managed to extricate yourselves this time."

David gathered her up in a big hug. "Same to you." Keeping an arm anchored around her shoulders, the two waited for the others to jump down and join them.

After the greetings were over and Cody had been slapped on his shoulders and back several times, the group stood around talking.

"Game plan?" Tessa asked when the noise calmed down. "We've taken out dozens of bad guys but that doesn't mean there aren't more around here."

"There are more. And more captives we have to save." Motre stood, his legs in a wide stance and his arms crossed across his chest. "We need to free as many as possible. The assholes need to have their supply of basic vamp models taken away from them. I don't know where they are getting their supply from, but let's not have our friends and coworkers be the next wave we're up against."

Several of the men behind him nodded. "I'm missing several good buddies. If they are here, I know they'd want to help us kick butt and rescue them if we can."

A rumble of assent moved through the group.

Tessa stepped back slightly and watched as the conversation went in one direction then the other. She closed her eyes and groaned silently.

Here they went again. The conversation got louder and louder. Voices rose as each struggled to be heard over the other. Another five minutes and fights would surely erupt.

Then she couldn't stay quiet any more. "Hey!" she shouted. And no one listened. She groaned louder. Vamps were always like this when they got together. And she hated it.

She put two fingers in her mouth and let loose a piercing whistle.

Silence.

As if on cue, they all turned to look at her. Of the faces she could see, only Cody and David were grinning. Goran and her father looked their long ancient noses down at her and frowned.

She rolled her eyes and shook her head. "Could we get back to the real issue on hand, please?"

Motre snorted. "Exactly what I've been trying to say. Look, I'll take a group and go searching for more of my people. See if we can find a councilman or two. If we can bolster our numbers, that will be a huge help right now."

"Right." Tessa realized she'd forgotten about so many other people she'd heard had been found and lost again. "This place is a maze. It's more likely that you'll get lost."

"No." Motre straightened his back, making him look even bigger. "I'm great at navigating. It's what I do. I'll be fine." He looked at his wrist as if to check the time. "I need to find the councilman and the rest of those captives." He glanced around. "There are human and vamp captives everywhere. We'll release the ones we can and save the GPS location of the others so we can come back for them."

"I'm going with him," piped up one of the vamps standing right beside Motre.

"So am I."

"Me too."

Very quickly, a small group of men moved off to the side. Goran slapped Motre on the shoulder. "We're going back to the cavern meeting rooms to see if we can round up any more bosses. Stay close and stay in touch."

"Will do."

And the group took off.

Tessa watched them leave. It seemed weird after all they'd been through to have them split up again. But this group was big enough to handle it. In fact, both groups were. They'd collected enough good vamps to be able to separate and cover twice as much ground. And that was good news.

"Speaking of humans, how long before we can get help for Catherine and Jill?"

David frowned. "Let's get back to Taz and give him the location of all those people. He can get a medical team to take them to the hospital."

"We don't know how long they've been here, but with the right treatment, your friends will be fine." Jewel smiled up at Tessa. "But we need to get them help as soon as possible, I think."

Tessa nodded. There was only so much they could do. She really needed to connect with Taz again.

"We'll get them the help they need." Her father stepped up in front of her. "How about you go home and stay with your mother?"

She smiled. He'd do just about anything to get her out of danger and into their home, where she'd be safe. "See that would be nice, but I'm here. You're here and every time we part, someone gets into trouble. I know David and Jewel would also like to go home. They also need some healing time and blood. Not sure about Cody, but the thing is, while we're here, I think we need to keep pushing their front line back."

David spoke up. "She's right. Every time something goes wrong on our end, we give them a chance to regroup with new reinforcements. We need to get more of the bad guys out of here, and get more of the good guys in."

Jewel's gentler voice spoke from behind. "As much as I don't want to stay, I really don't want to be separated from everyone to go home. Bad things happen when we do that."

Ian snorted at Jewel. "No kidding. We're forever getting into trouble. Just look at the two of us. We can't even fly out of here with all the drugs they injected into our systems." He tried to stretch his wings and growled when they still wouldn't move. "We stay here and then we go home together. And I'm totally okay with going home now – but that's got to mean everyone."

"So let's do a sweep of the offices then head back to the blood farm and make sure Taz and that group are still fine. Hopefully they've heard back from Gloria. There should be reinforcements coming sometime soon. For all we know, they might be here already."

That concept perked everyone up. Tessa marvelled at how much straighter everyone stood. How much more positive they all appeared. "Good. A quick sweep, back to Taz to check in and then home."

Everyone nodded.

Tessa wanted to laugh. Since when had anything been easy in this place?

RHIA WASN'T SURE how she'd ended up here at the Human Council offices, but Gloria and Councilman Adamson thought it would be better for them to approach the humans for help on their turf. Sian had agreed.

The four of them stood outside the darkened building.

"It doesn't look like anyone is here," Rhia commented.

"It's night time." Sian shrugged. "They won't be standing around in the dark waiting for us."

Gloria turned to Sian, a frown on her face. "But why not? It's almost morning for them, shouldn't they be up and ready?"

Sian patiently answered the seemingly endless stream of questions about humans, making Rhia realize how involved her friend had become in the human world. It was to be expected given that she lived with a human, but for Rhia, she hadn't realized how deeply that partnership had impacted Sian's life.

Who'd have known? Sian wasn't quite accepted into either world and neither was Taz. But they'd created their own world and at this point in time, they appeared to be wonderfully happy.

"We don't just stand around in the dark waiting for vampires to come and visit." A testy voice snapped from behind them. "Most of us are asleep at this hour." He strode past the small group and unlocked the large double doors. He flicked on a light switch that instantly cast a warm welcoming light in the dark interior.

"Come in, come in." He kept walking forward, as if uncaring as to whether they did or not.

Rhia hated the uncertainty that coiled inside her as she entered the building. She was more powerful, older, and wiser, but humans had been killing vamps for centuries and that wasn't the easiest of thoughts to put away. She couldn't help but consider that this meeting might be a trap. Adding to that uncertainty was the knowledge that some humans had partnered with the vamps from the blood farm.

The four of them stood uneasily in the front entranceway, the door still open behind them in case staying wasn't an option. The human returned, a big smile on his face. He reached out and shook Councilman Adamson's hand. "Good to see you again, sir. Come in and sit down. The others will be here soon."

Councilman Adamson strode forward. Rhia wished she felt even slightly as comfortable he looked. She'd been surprised when the councilman had decided to come with them. His official presence lent more weight to the seriousness of the problem.

That Gloria had come as well was also good. The more the merrier, as far as Rhia was concerned. She'd had no word from anyone in hours and hours. Even Seth hadn't checked in. That scared her even more. That damn blood farm was a giant sinkhole. It just kept eating up more of her family.

She wanted them all back.

As she stood there, sounds of other people arriving had her turning to face the front door. A good dozen men and women streamed inside. Signs of weariness, mussed hair, and hefty yawns attested to the early morning. Most had probably been pulled away from their warm beds.

As much as she hated disturbing them, this was a necessity.

"Good, everyone is here." The first human greeted the new arrivals then led the way to a large round table. "Everyone take a seat, please. And let us begin."

Rhia chose a spot beside Sian while Councilman Adamson sat on the far side beside Gloria, strategically placing themselves on both sides of the table and minimizing the sense of them against us. As she went to take her seat, her gaze was drawn to the still open front door.

She'd assumed it had been left open for other people that were due to arrive.

As she watched, the door slammed shut.

And the bolt on the inside of the door snicked shut.

Shit.

❧ ❧

CODY LED THE way back up to the main office area above the massive cavernous room still under construction. They hadn't seen anyone the last time they'd been in this area, but they'd been cornered soon after. He knew there still had to be well hidden areas, and that in theory they could spend months down here and never find all the nooks and crannies. And for that reason, he doubted they'd be able to flush everyone from here. They'd have to set up traps above ground and catch the others coming and going. It also meant that none of the medical staff working to help the victims would be safe either.

They'd need a full battalion of guards. All the time. Just in case.

"Cody."

He turned at the sound of his father's voice. "What?"

"I'm going to scout ahead. Why don't you come with me?"

Cody wasn't sure if his dad was trying to separate him from Tessa and Serus or because he wanted his son with him. Still, he decided it was better to go.

His father lifted up and flew off with a grace that always

amazed Cody. He could only hope he had the same strength and agility as his old man when he reached the multiple century mark. He'd asked his father how old he was years ago, but Goran had refused to answer.

Cody launched behind him. He caught up with his father, who was gently circling high above the crowd.

"Are we here for a reason?"

"A couple. The biggest being, I don't like seeing everyone in a single group. This way we can scout ahead. Make sure we aren't going to be under attack again."

Cody wondered what his father was getting around to. He understood the benefit of scouting ahead and didn't need a reminder. Not after having been taken captive last time. He had no wish for a repeat of that experience.

Nor I. Tessa's warm voice filtered through his consciousness.

"So how bad is it with Tessa?"

Ah, there it was. "What do you mean by how bad is it?" Cody didn't think anything about it was bad.

"How serious?"

Cody sighed. Here it was. His father's turn to ask about his relationship with Tessa while they were alone.

Tessa chuckled and whispered, *I'm gone.*

He wished he could disappear with her, but no such luck.

He could feel his father's gaze searching his face, and he really didn't want to look at his sire. But he needed to. He glanced up, caught his father's gaze and said, "Honestly? I have no idea."

Goran frowned. "You're not new to this relationship stuff. You must have some idea of how you're feeling."

"Some. But it came on hard and fast and I haven't exactly had time to analyze my emotions or even my thoughts."

"Speaking of thoughts…"

"Yeah, what the hell is with this mindspeak?" Even as he said it, he understood Tessa was there in his thoughts. In his mind.

No, I'm not. I so don't want to hear this. I'm gone. He spun around in the air, searching for her, but she was there standing beside David. And she was no longer inside his head. Damn. How did she do that?

"Now that's a good question," his father said. "I've never heard of anyone having that ability this young. I never had it with your mother. With Serus, we've been able to do this type of communication for centuries, but we'd been close buds for decades before we even started. And that's another thing, it started off slow and we can't do it all the time."

"Whereas we appear to have started suddenly and have extreme capabilities." Cody snorted. "As an example, she just left my mind to give us privacy to talk. Twenty minutes ago, we were discussing that we didn't know how to do that. All our thoughts were open for each to read."

Goran stared at him in shock. "Wow! That's harsh."

"It was a shock. We didn't notice it because we kept on getting separated in here, but the more time we spend together, the stronger and clearer we can communicate."

"And you're okay with that?" Goran studied his features closely. "I'm not sure I would be."

Cody snorted. "You forget – I haven't got a choice. Nor have I had time to figure out if I'm good with it or not. It just happened."

"That's crazy." Goran did a slow circle around him, searching the area. "I don't see anyone anywhere."

"Yeah, you should probably tell Serus it's all clear."

Goran laughed, that deep rolling laugh that Cody always

remembered. "I already have. There are definite advantages to mindspeaking."

"Yeah, but there are definite disadvantages too," Cody muttered, "Especially when you can't help but notice how hot someone looks."

Goran surged around to come up in front of him. His eyes were wide with shock. "She can hear those kinds of thoughts?"

At Cody's nod, Goran shook his head. "Oh wow. I had no idea."

"Yeah, there isn't much privacy this way."

"And what about that whole attraction level? This is Se-rus's daughter. David's kid sister, you know."

"I know," Cody said coolly. "I do understand that. I didn't expect this to happen. I certainly didn't plan on it. She's too young."

"She's young, yes, but the years will go by very quickly."

"She hasn't had a chance to experience life. As much as I like knowing I'd be her first relationship – I don't like thinking about how she hasn't had a chance to experience other relationships. Once she's mine, I'm not going to let her go."

"Strong words, boy. You're too young to be settling down."

"I never said I was ready to settle down."

Goran gave him a hard look. "You remember whose girl you're trifling with."

"I'm not trifling with anyone." And he wasn't. The problem was he didn't know exactly what he was doing. But trifling wasn't a word to apply to Tessa.

"You'd better not."

Thankfully, his father's gaze was diverted by movement in

the open window area overlooking the cavern. "Company up ahead."

"I see them." Cody flew higher, trying to catch a glimpse of who was in there. But he couldn't see clearly. "Let's go."

"The others will meet us there."

Great. At least this time they had backup. With his father in the lead, Cody swooped down to the open ledge high up in the middle of the room. They landed silently, but the open area was empty. Quietly, they did a sweep to the left and entered the first room. Nothing. They then checked the second room. Still nothing. Silently, Goran pointed out a doorway around the corner.

Cody slipped in behind his father.

Goran held up three fingers then silently counted down.

They both jumped into the room. And found two vamps waiting for them.

Goran took a hit to his jaw and fell backwards into Cody, who tried to move out of the way but got jumped instead. Cody ended up with his back on the ground again. His wing, still not fully healed, was so painful that he felt paralyzed for a few seconds. Before he could move, a big vamp straddled him.

"About time you assholes got here. What you think, we got nuttin better to do than wait for yer slow asses to make your way here?"

A second punch caught Cody on the nose. The vamp sitting on his chest laughed. But it was his still healing wing twisted beneath him that pissed him off. That poor wing would never heal at this rate. He grabbed the man's knee and in a sudden move he lunged up and over – nicely reversing their position. Only he didn't waste time mocking the asshole. Cody dug his spike out and incinerated the guy while he was still pinned down.

Then he shifted a few feet, stabbed the second vamp on the back of his shoulder, and watched while his ashes floated over his father.

"Dad, you okay?" he asked, staring down at his father.

Goran groaned. "I'm getting too old for this shit."

"Aren't we all?"

"You don't have anything to whine about. You're barely out of diapers," Goran growled.

"Ha, and you're almost back in the damn things," Cody said with a grin as he rose to his feet easily then held out a hand. "Come on, up and at it."

Goran glared at the hand, but reached out to grab it.

Surprised, Cody pulled him to his feet. His dad couldn't be feeling very good if he accepted a helping hand. Normally, his father held his pride as a shield. But then, he *had* been through a lot lately.

Once on their feet, they heard sounds of racing footsteps coming up the stairs. Goran straightened and his face bore a haughty look that Cody recognized as the facade he always showed the world. He felt honoured that he was able to get a glimpse of his real feelings for just a moment. And it made him feel closer to his father. More of an equal.

David came through first. He slid to a stop, relief apparent on his face. "Are you okay?"

Cody grinned. "Absolutely. Two more incinerated."

David smacked him on the shoulder. "Yes. We're actually starting to win the war. At least for the moment."

Serus stepped closer to Goran. "You okay old man?"

Goran's eyes blazed and his brows knit together in outrage. "Who are you calling an old man? Who got here first? And who took forever to make it up those stairs?"

Serus grinned. And turned as Jewel and Ian and the rest of

the group finally arrived. He pointed and said, "Them!"

"TAZ?" JARED CALLED out softly. The friendly doctor hadn't returned and by now Jared was well past worried and headed straight to panic.

He did not want to be lost alone here. Seth and the others were here – somewhere. But where? And in the dark like this, Jared was at an even bigger disadvantage. He couldn't see. Not like the vamps could. They'd know he was there long before he'd know he wasn't alone.

Unfortunately, it was the same for Taz. Although he had to admit Taz appeared comfortable, friendly even, with the vampires. He wasn't sure but from the bits of conversation he'd heard, Taz might have a relationship of some kind with a vamp. If so, that was way cool. And maybe dangerous. Jared didn't know which.

But given that Tessa was a vamp…

He peered around the corner to look into the vast warehouse. He thought he heard something on the far side. Dare he go look? Taz had told him to stay put. And that's what he wanted to do, but if Taz needed help…

Jared groaned softly and flattened himself against the warehouse wall. Why him? Why couldn't there be dozens of doctors and techs working away under bright lights with security guards posted at all entrances? But no, the guys he'd arrived with had taken off and the only person he'd found had just run into the pitch black warehouse leaving Jared, once again, all alone in this house of horrors. Like who else had such shitty luck but him?

The noise grew closer. Jared sucked in his breath, hoping

he wasn't visible. Was he safer in the office or here? Where would the new arrivals be heading? Jared would like to know who the newcomers were before he identified himself as a human. He'd had enough of being the vamps' lunch…and dinner.

And surely he'd be forgiven if he admitted that an itch on the back of his neck was warning him that he was about to become an early morning snack. He held off as long as he could, but his nerves screamed at him to run.

Three, two, one…and he bolted to the nearest hiding place he could think of.

Amongst the rows of bodies.

CHAPTER 8

TESSA STAYED AT the bottom of the stairs when the rest of
the group had charged into the fray. They'd all raced
forward after hearing the sounds of a fight going on. It had
seemed relatively minor by the time she hit the bottom of the
stairs.

And that's when the weariness hit her. Again.

She'd been at this forever. And damn, she wanted this to
be over. Back to the blood farm, then home. That sounded
pretty damn good right now.

Giving in, she parked her butt on the bottom step and
slumped against the wall. Just for a moment. She closed her
eyes.

She didn't need long, just a quick power nap so her vampire genes could fire up again.

A warm hand landed on her shoulder as Jewel sat down
beside her. "Are you as tired as I am?"

"Yeah." Tessa gave her a half smile but didn't even open
her eyes. "I just want this all to be over."

"Yeah, you and me both. I so badly want a shower and
some sleep." Jewel groaned and leaned against Tessa. "I want
my life back." In a half whisper she added, "And I want to be
able to fly again."

Tessa winced. That last part had to be tough. She knew
the drugs would slowly drain from Jewel's and Ian's systems,

but in the meantime, not being able to do something that had come so naturally since birth had to be tough. She was glad that the drugs didn't affect Cody's flying abilities the same way. She loved seeing him fly.

David jumped over their heads, spun, and crouched down in front of them. There was a big grin on his face. "It's all good now. Just think. Two more done and gone."

Tessa gave him a tired smile. "Good. Home time?"

"Almost. We'll just keep heading toward Taz and take out everyone we find in between. Oh, and rescue all the rest. Taz should have news from the councils. Maybe there's security on the premises by now." He tugged both girls up to their feet and wrapped his arms around their shoulders. "Once we're sure security has arrived to keep Taz and the others safe, we can leave."

"Sounds good to me." Jewel stood up and walked with a new bounce to her step.

Tessa wished she had that same energy. "Anyone heard from Mom?"

"Not yet. And it's almost impossible to communicate from in here. We'll need to go to the computer rooms and contact her that way."

"I still have Bart's phone, but the battery looks dead."

"The batteries die much faster underground."

Just then, the others made it down the stairs and walked toward Tessa and David.

"If you're ready," Serus said. "let's go."

He led the way forward, Goran at his side. Still walking with her brother's arm wrapped around her shoulders, Tessa trudged forward. She yawned. Then yawned again.

"Wow. Sounds like bedtime." David laughed. He removed his arm from her shoulders.

"I wish."

"Good. It's definitely time we got out of here. The fresh air will do you some good." Serus said. "Come on, let's get back to the blood farm."

Just go slow, Tessa. Cody said quietly as he walked up beside her. *You'll get through this.*

Yes. I will. But it pisses me off that I have to remind my vampire genes to actually kick in. If they'd done it automatically a while ago, then I wouldn't be in this pickle.

His warm laughter flitted through her head.

Trust you to find the humor in the situation.

Yeah. I know, she said glumly. *Like why me?*

Because you are special.

You know how much I hated being told that growing up. It only meant I wasn't like the rest of my family. By now, Cody was half supporting her. *I can walk on my own now, you know.*

Too bad. I'm not taking that chance. I want you home and away from this house of horrors.

She smiled. *You and me both.*

IT SEEMED LIKE forever before Goran realized that they reached the warehouse section of the mine. "Here's the blood farm."

"Thank heavens for that," Tessa whispered.

"You're doing good," said Cody. "We'll get Taz to check you over in a few minutes."

Goran added, "He's the one to look for. He should have the updates on this place."

They approached the blood farm warehouse warily, with Tessa and Cody and Serus in the back.

"The room is pitch black." Goran came rushing back to them. "There's no sign of anyone. We have to assume there's something wrong."

Oh, not again.

Goran was getting pretty damn fed up with fate pissing in his world. He'd done everything right and still these asshole vamps kept turning up. He glared at the open doorway of the blood farm, barely seeing discernable shadows ahead. There were flashing lights on the small computer boxes associated with each victim. So this wasn't a power failure. Or else the computer boxes wouldn't flash those bright colored lights.

Someone had somehow turned off the lights to the large warehouse area. But why? To conserve power? He couldn't see a place like this having a shortage of power. Besides, turning off the lights would have minimal impact on the energy saving process.

No, chances were good that turning off the lights was meant to confuse or scare someone. As vamps could see in the dark, the only ones adversely affected would be humans. The human doctors and techs working to save the humans. Taz. Damn it.

He turned back to Serus. "I think someone is after the humans again. There's no other reason for turning off the lights."

The look on Serus's face was impressively cold. He said, "I've had enough of this crap."

"Yeah. Me too." Goran strode up to the doorway. "I'll go left."

"I'll take the right," Serus said. "You others split up and follow behind us. Nobody gets left behind. And for God's sake – stay out of trouble."

❧ ❧

CODY SLIPPED HIS arm down Tessa's back to rest at her waist. At the doorway, they stopped for a moment and listened. The barest of sounds could be heard as the two groups made their way around the massive room.

Cody urged her to the left. She resisted, asking instead, "Are you hurt?"

"Me? No, I'm fine."

"You hurt your wing earlier. Are you sure it's okay?"

"Sure," he glanced at her curiously, "What's the matter?"

She sighed and motioned upward. "I was just remembering last time how the vamps grabbed you and David and took you to that little room up top. What if they're up there again?"

He cast a glance toward the high ceiling and twisted his lips in thought. "I suppose I could fly up there. But I'd have to take you with me. There's no way I'd leave you behind. Especially when you're still not at full strength."

"I'm fine. Just tired. And that's normal. At least the new normal for these last few days," she said. "And I wouldn't mind going up there. But I don't want to hurt you."

He glared at her, puffed out his chest, and snatched her up into his arms. "I'm fine." And he lunged upward, his huge wings unfurling behind him.

Tessa gave a small gasp and threw her arms around him.

Damn if that didn't make him feel even more powerful. He clasped her tightly against his chest, grateful when he only felt a slight tug from his wings. He healed fast for a vampire, but these constant injuries required more recovery time than normal.

He could really use a couple of days off. Go see a movie,

watch a game, catch up on all the meals he'd missed. Something laid back and normally taken for granted in his old life. This seemed to be the new world and although he loved the action, making a mistake here had fatal consequences.

He had centuries ahead of him. He had no intention of dying in this nasty place.

Good.

He glanced down at Tessa. She'd become a woman these last few days. A light chuckle rippled through his mind. Damn if he didn't feel some heat rising up his neck. He shook his head. This was so not easy.

No, it's not. Sorry. I'll stop listening.

Instantly his mind felt empty. Bereft. And he didn't like that much either.

"How did you do that?"

"I just thought it and it happened. Cool huh?"

"Absolutely. And a little weird."

"Weird maybe, but at least now we know it's possible. If we try to respect each other's privacy, then it should make it easier."

"Yeah, but how are we going to know when that is?"

He flew high up to the office space and hovered off on one side. If there was someone there, he didn't want to alert them of their presence. He could hardly fight off an attack with Tessa in his arms.

Thankfully it was empty.

"See? There is no one here." He landed lightly and let her stand on her own. He watched as she walked across the small space and looked over the side.

"Everything is amazingly clear from up here."

"Which is of course why it's here." He stood beside her and looked down on the blood farm. "It's hard to pick out the immobile humans from the mobile ones from down there."

"Yeah, but I can see loads of colourful energy from here. It's quite pretty."

"Pretty or helpful? Are there energies down there that shouldn't be there?"

She glanced over at him. "I'm not sure. There are a lot of energy signatures below, but it's not surprising. Over a dozen of us entered, plus there's Taz and whoever is helping him."

"I suggest you take a closer look and see if there are energies you recognize and ones you don't. The lights are off here for a reason. We don't want them off because someone is sneaking up on or has already taken Taz."

"I wonder if I can pick out Taz's energy here."

Cody walked to the far side. "Check over here. He should be in the computer lab room. The individual monitors were downloading information to that set of computers. He was trying to figure out what nutrients these people were being given to keep them alive. To see if they could duplicate the process and bring these people out slowly without killing them. Although I'm pretty sure anyone who's been hanging for longer than a few months is likely already dead."

"But we don't know that." Tessa cried out. "And we have to remember that these people are brothers and sisters, sons and daughters to someone. There has to be someone who cares about them. For them."

"There might have been at one time, but this many people? Makes me think no one cared about them at all."

She studied the layout below them then stiffened.

He glanced over at her curiously. "What do you see?"

"It's not what – it's who." She turned to stare at him. "I see Jared's energy."

Cody shrugged. "So? He was here for a long time. His

energy should be here."

"Yes. But this is fresh."

⌘ ⌘

RHIA STUDIED THE looks on the faces of those around her. No one appeared bothered by the locked door. But she sure as hell was.

So was Sian, for that matter. "Who locked the door?" Sian asked the leader of the humans.

"What? Oh, that door. It locks automatically once we start our meeting. Just a precautionary measure. It's fine, I assure you."

Sian glanced over at Rhia and nodded. Rhia frowned and sat down. They'd come to have this talk and regardless of how spooky things were, they needed to clear the air.

Councilman Adamson opened the talks while Rhia and Sian stayed quietly in the background. No one said a word while he spoke. When he was done and fell quiet, the humans looked at each other, then at him.

It's as if they didn't believe him or didn't know if they should believe him.

"It's true," Rhia said. Somehow they had to get through to these people. And fast. She couldn't get rid of that horrible feeling of impending disaster. She wanted to go up there herself.

Sian nodded.

"We've heard about the blood farm. How could we not these last few days? But I had no idea the corruption was that widespread in the vampire world."

Gloria reared back and raised her nose to a haughty angle. "It's not just the vampires. The humans are involved in a big way, too."

The Human Council stared at her. Not accepting, but not arguing either. As if to say they were too polite to discuss it.

Sian snorted. "Do you really think this many people could go missing and stay missing without the humans involved?" She swept her arm open wide in the direction where they'd found the blood farm. "There has to be a large vein of corruption to keep something of this scale quiet. Humans have been turning a blind eye on the problem. Or worse, have been selling off their own kin."

The human leader gasped in shock. He pulled his heavy sweater tighter around his chest. "Sian, that is a grave charge."

One of the other men at the table spoke up. "Obviously there has to be some humans involved. But it doesn't have to be a large percentage of the population."

The other members nodded their heads. One of them said, "There is always going to be a certain amount of corruption at all levels of the government. A few crooked law enforcement officers can easily make files disappear. That's bad, but it's not at the level you appear to be suggesting."

Rhia leaned forward, her gaze hard and angry.

"They were able to make a thousand files disappear. Or is that not serious enough for you either?"

CHAPTER 9

TESSA GASPED IN shock. *What the hell?*

Cody spun to look at her.

"My brother Seth is here, too." She stared down at the confusing energy below.

Cody stared down below. "Are you sure? I can't see him."

"He's not *here* here, but he's here. As in I can see his energy. It's older though. It's already starting to dissipate. It's a few hours old at least."

"Was he supposed to come?"

Distracted by the myriad of colors floating on the ground below, she took a moment before turning to face him. "There's no reason I know of, but if he and Mom got worried, he might have come up looking for us. Mom should be still be in the hospital and she might have sent him in her stead." She frowned and studied the energy. "He headed out the way we came in, so we should have met up with him here."

"And how did Jared get back here? Not to mention why?"

Distracted again, she looked at him. "I don't know. As long as he's not one of the hanging dead, then I'm fine with it. He said something about other young men hanging that he wanted to make sure they were brought down safely." She shrugged. "He's that kind of guy."

"What kind of guy?"

That caught her attention. His tone of voice wasn't one

she was used to hearing from him. Cool. Controlled. Distant.

Like what was his problem? She studied his face and wondered if she should open her doorway to his mind. Or was that one of those times when she'd be intruding? Then again, they needed to be open if they were going ahead. And something about Jared had set him off on this tangent. Now if she only knew why.

"He cares about others," she explained. "If he knew some of the other people hanging here, then I could see him wanting to make sure they were taken down and given the care they needed to pull through this."

"But enough to come back up here? I doubt most people would."

She automatically answered, "Jared isn't most people." She pursed her lips and thought about it. "If it was someone he really cared about, he would."

"Like your friends?"

Her eyes widened. "Exactly.

She turned to look over the edge again.

"There appears to be a lot going on here that we don't know about. For instance, Jared and Seth." He studied her face. "Maybe we should focus on those two problems while we can?"

She knew he was right. "Fine." She leaned over to judge the distance. She could jump that. She was feeling much better now. So much stronger. She didn't know how or why, but she'd take it.

"Forget it."

"Forget what?"

Then she let out a squeal as Cody gathered her up in his arms and jumped over the edge.

"A little warning would have been nice," she muttered

against his neck.

He grinned. "Sorry."

She laughed lightly. "So not."

Then she realized he wasn't landing. She twisted in his arms, loving the steely strength of him. He rarely showed off his strength and given that all vampires were strong, maybe he wasn't super elite but to her, he seemed it.

Thanks.

She laughed. "So where are we going?"

"I thought maybe we'd make a pass around the room and make sure it's safe to land."

She shrugged. "We haven't heard any sounds of fighting yet from either side, and we should have if things had gone wrong."

He snorted, his eyes peeled below. "Really. Are you actually thinking that all this 'dead' silence around us is natural? That there is nothing wrong because we haven't heard anything wrong yet?"

"I never thought of that." She tried to look around, but it was hard to do when she was crushed up against his chest.

"Quit wiggling. I might drop you."

She gasped, then caught his smirk. "You are so going to get it when I get down on the ground."

"Get what?" He leered at her, making her heart jump and her body so aware of the strong physical male holding her.

She giggled. And then laughed when she heard the sound coming out of her mouth. She sounded like the girls in school when they were with their boyfriends. A sound burned into her memory as always being the one on the outside. She'd often wondered if such a day would ever come for her. And now here she was in Cody's arms.

Yeah, and what's wrong with me? he growled under his

breath.

Oh no. He'd read her mind. Again.

But not on purpose. He flew around the suspended office to the other side. "And you didn't answer. What's wrong with me?"

"Nothing. It's more that you're Cody – dreamboat, hunky Cody."

The look he sent her way had her giggling again. "Are you blushing?"

"No." He said shortly. "And you should know better than to listen to crazy gossip."

"I didn't have to listen to anyone. I could see it with my own eyes. You were always surrounded by gorgeous women and you played with lots these last few years."

Now no amount of darkness could hide the flush on his skin. She smiled. "Of course, as a female, I could also hear the girls squeal about you at every gathering."

"They did not." But his voice was gruff. Was he embarrassed? Maybe?

She shouldn't tease him, but it was too much fun not to.

"And you, did you gossip with them?"

"No," she said gently. "I never did. And I never heard them be mean. Everyone adores you. They all wanted to be with you." Some of the stiffness in his shoulders relaxed and she reached up to cup his cheek. "You never crossed my radar because I never thought you'd even look at me. I was just David's kid sister."

He snorted at that. "That last part is so true. And as David's kid sister, you were out of bounds."

She reared back slightly to see his face better. "Really?"

"Of course. And then sometime in this last week you stopped being his kid sister." Cody sighed. "And now we're here."

She loved his humor. "And the worst is over."

He glanced down at her, as if considering her words before saying, "You could be right."

"My dad and brother both know. Your dad knows and your closest friends know. The rest will gossip regardless." She leaned against his shoulder. "And who cares what they think?"

She felt the rumble in his chest at his warm laughter. Still, he didn't know what it was like to be the butt of every joke.

"That is exactly how we should look at it."

"It will be harder for you."

"In what way?" His tone was amused, as if he was just humoring her.

"I'm used to being laughed at," she said honestly, realizing the pain of having fingers pointed at her all the time no longer affected her. She'd come so far that the Tessa of last week was hard to even imagine.

His arms tightened gently and he cuddled her closer. What a feeling. Held against his heart, flying through the air. For all the danger, there was magic in the moment. Too bad they weren't flying outside instead of inside this vast monstrosity.

"They won't laugh anymore," he said, his voice cool.

"No. They won't." She grinned. "And if they do, I won't care. Not now."

He looked down at her, one eyebrow raised.

She stretched up and dropped a kiss on his chin. "I'm not that Tessa anymore."

The heat in his gaze made her heart sigh, but his words warmed her soul.

"No, you sure aren't. And I for one am damned glad."

ॐ ॐ

DAVID SLAMMED INTO his father. Ooops. Serus turned and glared at him. David grinned and lifted his shoulders in a shrug. He kept quiet though. Who knew what was out there?

His father turned and strode forward, his steps soundless in the empty room. How did he do that? David tried to imitate it, but he couldn't pull off that same stealthy move. And then there was Ian clomping behind him. Jewel was much quieter, but fatigue was making her clumsy. Considering that their wings were still paralyzed, this trip had been more brutal for them – probably more so than anyone realized.

Goran had been drugged too, but he was bigger and too damn ornery to let the chemicals stop him from flying. Also, unlike Ian and Jewel, he was an ancient – the drugs seemed to have a different effect on him and Cody, allowing them to retain their ability to fly.

Or maybe they'd just been given different drugs.

The group had been through so much already that it was hard to believe they were finally back here safe and sound.

His father stopped up ahead. He held up a hand in warning.

David turned to nudge Ian and wrap an arm around Jewel. "There's something ahead. Be ready," he whispered into her ear.

She nodded and visibly tried to pull herself together. She might have been exhausted but she was a trooper, always ready to step up to the plate. He was damn proud of her.

Ian nudged them from behind. "If you two would stop mooning over each other, we'd have caught up to your father."

Startled, David realized his father had gone on ahead and David had missed his signal. "Shit," he said under his breath. Slightly louder he said, "Let's go."

And they raced ahead.

GORAN KEPT HIS back against the wall and methodically swept through his half of the warehouse. Something was off. His instincts were telling him to go up high and get out of a waiting trap, but with every step that he expected a trap to be sprung – there was nothing. He couldn't believe it. Something had to have happened for the lights to be off. He could see lights still flashing on the individual computer boxes on the victims. He stopped and stared at the rows of victims. Would turning the backup power off be one way of determining who could still survive? If they lived then they were viable, and if turning off the power killed them, so be it.

It sounded harsh, but many of these people had been hanging dead for decades. If they could find the newest arrivals and start with those, they would quickly understand how far back they could go to save these people. He didn't think anyone hanging for longer than six months could be saved. They were humans after all.

Then he remembered there were also vampires hanging. Moltere himself might be saved as their line could essentially last forever. The man shouldn't have survived the last war – to think he could survive this one was not acceptable.

But a couple of his kid's friends were here too, and they needed to be helped. Everyone had jumped to the assistance of the humans, but where were the vamps to help out the vamp victims?

He strode ahead. There were several of Motre's vamps with him. He didn't know any of them, but they'd fought bravely in the last skirmish. He'd seen his son fly overhead with Tessa and knew Serus had the other kids. Making him the only one without friend or family to guard his back.

He wanted to count on the men behind him, but it didn't feel right. Since entering the warehouse, the vibe of those behind him had changed. And this inactivity, this sense of waiting for something bad to happen was driving him nuts.

And his instincts were screaming at him to move. Giving in to his instincts, he jumped up, gave a strong pull of his wings, and cleared their heads.

As he went over them he caught the look on their faces – shock, and there it was, on the third vamp – anger.

☙ ❧

OKAY, THIS SO wasn't good. What the hell made him think that hiding amongst the quasi-dead was a good idea? Except that maybe they wouldn't expect Jared to be here.

In the dark, all sounds were amplified. He swore he heard wings. Like what the hell? His eyes were slowly adjusting to the deep black, but he sure wished he could see in the dark like the vamps could. Human and vamp. So different. Yet as Tessa had proved – also so much the same.

He wished he could see her. Had seen her before he left. Had been able to tell her what he was doing. And why.

Not having gotten cell numbers from the other kids who'd helped him, he felt disconnected from everyone. When he'd met Taz, there'd been a rapport because the doctor was human. He understood what Jared had gone through and could possibly help his father. Although he hadn't sounded too positive about that. And if Jared was honest with himself, he didn't see much chance there either. But there were many young males that couldn't have been here for long. Surely they should be focusing on getting them out of here? Then again, an older male who hadn't been here very long deserved the same chance as the younger ones.

Damn, this place was making him crazy.

A heavy rustling sounded overhead. He ducked and crouched to one side of the row. So he wasn't alone.

He thought he heard whispers from the left. Damn it. Or was the sound coming from a couple of rows over?

Shit. He ran a shaky hand over his forehead. He so didn't want to end up in the wrong side of this war again.

Then he thought, no, he swore he heard a female voice.

He straightened and spun around in that direction. And heard it again.

Tessa.

CHAPTER 10

TESSA LOVED THE sensation of flying. Of course, special moments in Cody's arms weren't bad either.

Snort.

She grinned. *You deserved that.*

Uh-huh. Let's land and check on Taz.

Good idea. He should know what's going on.

Can you see his energy?

She twisted in his arms and searched the rows of bodies. "It came from the office there," she pointed, "And darted across to the main computer room."

"Then let's go there first."

She studied the energies as they came closer. "Wait. Oh my God. That's Jared."

Cody pulled up to hover in place. "Where?" he demanded. "He shouldn't be here now."

"I know. It's got to be him." She pointed below and off to the left. "In between the rows."

"What the hell." Cody said in a resigned voice. "I thought I finally got rid of that guy."

Tessa smacked him lightly. "Never. Jared is a nice guy. You just haven't had a chance to get to know him."

"Right. So not going there," Cody muttered.

She let that pass as he was landing gently at the end of the row where she could see someone crouched down low. "I hope he's not hurt."

Cody stayed suspiciously quiet. She tried to take a step and found the ground wavy. It was as if she'd been on a boat for so long that the ground didn't stand still when she finally hit land. "That's so weird."

"You get used to it." He grabbed her hand. "Come on. Let's check this out."

She squeezed his hand and approached cautiously. There was no reason for Jared to be here, but she couldn't mistake that energy signature. And it shone strong and bright. If he was injured, it didn't appear to be bad.

About ten feet from him, she could see him pivoting in the crouch position, trying to see what was going on around him while staying hidden.

"Jared?"

The figure jerked. Stilled. Then bolted to his feet.

"Tessa?"

"Oh my God. It is you." Tessa tried to drop Cody's hand but he didn't let go. She shot him a startled look just in time to see a typical bored Cody look cross his face – the one he got whenever he didn't like what was happening.

She pulled him forward with her and stretched out her free hand to grab Jared. "It's so good to see you."

He stepped forward as if to hug her but stopped at the sight of her hand firmly held in Cody's. "Same here."

She smiled up at him. "What are you doing here? I thought you were still in the hospital."

"Yeah, I was. Then in a halfway home because…well, I'm not sick but I can't go home either."

"And you came here, why?" Cody asked, his voice cool and cold.

Easy Cody. Jared hasn't done anything wrong.

Nor has he done anything right. He's put himself right back in danger.

But you don't know why.

She turned to Jared, realizing that he was staring at them curiously. With effort, she shook off Cody's hand and linked her other arm with Jared. "Why are you here?"

His face twisted with pain. Quietly, leading her and Cody through the rows, he explained. He came to a stop and pointed to a man hanging. "This is my father."

She gasped, tears coming to her eyes. She turned to Cody, reaching out for him with her other hand. He grasped it tight and tugged her close. She leaned in, accepting the comfort he offered. "How could they do something like this?"

She stared at the vast warehouse of hanging victims. "Do you realize how many families are affected, destroyed by what's been done here?"

"Thousands of people," Jared said, his voice cracking. He turned away, his head slightly bent as he struggled to regain control.

Tessa reached out and stroked his back, offering what little comfort she could. "Do you know how long he's been here? If he has a chance to survive?"

Jared shook his head. "Probably not. He's been here since I was just a little kid. But I'm not sure. Taz looked up his records."

"Speaking of Taz? Where is he?" Cody studied the darkened room. "And what the hell happened to the lights?"

Jared shrugged. "Damn if I know on both counts. We were in with the medical computers when the room went black. He was concerned about the monitoring system and was checking something, then all of a sudden he bolted out of the room. I never did see where he went."

"And you haven't seen him since?" Tessa asked. "'Cause that's not good."

"I know. I came out because I was afraid to get pinned down in the computer room in case this power outage was another attack."

Even now he searched the room warily. "I wish I could see in the dark like you guys can."

"Yeah, but it's not that great a help right now as there's nothing to see," said Cody.

And he was right, but vamps could see what there was and she knew the humans would only be seeing shadows at this point. "What about the other people working here?"

"Honestly, I haven't seen anyone but Taz."

"And he seemed normal when he was with you?" Tessa asked curiously. "According to our fathers, they rescued a huge mixed mess of vamps and humans, including Taz, earlier when they first arrived. Took out a bunch of bad vamps in the process. Then they came searching for us."

Jared turned to study the two of them. "Were you two captured? Again?"

Cody bristled at the last word. "It's not like we did anything stupid to get caught."

Jared just looked at him.

"Easy Cody. Jared wasn't saying that."

But Cody wasn't having any of it. "Sure he was. And we did just as much as he did to get caught."

Jared turned on him, his shoulders squared and jaw jutting out.

"Oh shit," she muttered. "Come on, you two. This is the wrong time and place for a fight, okay? We've got other things to worry about."

The two glared at each other. Tessa stepped between them. "Enough already."

He shifted his gaze to her, his eyes warming with humor. "Yes, dear."

Jared made a strangled noise and Tessa realized he hadn't seen her since his rescue and lots of things had changed in the meantime. She shot Cody a disgusted look and turned to deal with Jared. "Hey, it's okay. Let's go find Taz."

He studied her face, looked as if he wanted to say something, and closed his mouth again. He hooked his arm through hers and walked her toward the end of the row.

"Smart boy," Cody muttered behind them.

Be nice, Tessa admonished him mentally.

Why? The guy's a prick.

And you're acting like a jealous teenager.

Jealous? There was a long pause in her head. *I know I said I wouldn't push you and I'd give you time to decide what you want but…is there a reason for me to be jealous?*

What? No! She stopped and turned to look back at him. The cold look on his face chilled her inside. *I'd never do anything to make you jealous. You know that, right?*

Jared jerked on her arm lightly, trying to get her to move forward again. She resumed walking by his side but waited anxiously for Cody's response.

I don't think I could stand it if you did, he growled. *That was Xana's favorite trick. She did everything she could to make me jealous.* He took a deep breath. *And I hated it. Hated that feeling and even more, I hated knowing she was doing it on purpose.*

Tessa didn't know what to say to that. After a long moment, she said, *Is it wrong to be happy that she's dead? I don't think she was a very nice person.*

His tired laughter rolled through her mind. *No, she so wasn't. And no, I don't think it's wrong to be happy that she's gone. It saves us from trying to fight her again.*

Yeah, there is that point. I'm tired of fighting these guys. Or girls, in Xana's case.

Jared spoke up. "Are you two talking to each other?"

She looked at him and sidestepped the issue. "Why on earth would you think that?"

"I don't know. There's a weird hum going on. And you've got a really preoccupied look on your face."

Preoccupied. She had to wonder just what the others saw when she and Cody were talking to each other. It had to look odd.

Then again, that was nothing new.

They reached the end of the row. Tessa peered around the corner. Energy floated gently on the ground but it was starting to disperse already. So no one had travelled down here in the last few minutes. In fact, she only saw Jared's energy as he made his way through the rows.

Twisting her head slightly, she said, "It's clear. Doesn't look like anyone has been through here since Jared."

They stepped into the wide hallway and walked toward the computer room where Jared had last seen Taz. At the darkened doorway, Tessa studied the energy. But she couldn't see much that was new. "I only see older energy here. There's nothing new since Jared left."

"So where is everyone then?" asked Cody.

"Good question." Tessa studied the surrounding area, searching for energy pathways. "They all have to be here somewhere."

"Why?" said Jared.

"Because we didn't arrive alone either. The two of us flew in, but we have groups that split up to sweep both sides of the warehouse. We were hoping to find the bad guys before they even knew we were here."

Jared looked around. "Then where are your groups?"

Cody groaned. "That's the thing. They should be here by now."

Tessa shook her head. "Maybe not. We flew, and that is so much faster."

"But you forget, we went to that suspended office first, then circled around. Something must be wrong." His worried tone had her stopping to study his face. He was serious.

"Damn. That means both groups met up with trouble."

"Or one went to go help the other."

"And how would they know the other group was in trouble?" Jared asked curiously.

Cody snorted. "Mindspeak. Both our fathers can communicate that way."

"And would have called on each other only as a last resort," Tessa reminded him.

"True. But that doesn't change the fact that one group has run into trouble. Or most likely both groups."

Jared shook his head. "I'd so hoped that everything would have been dealt with already. I asked your brother about it, but he really didn't say much." He frowned. "Come to think of it, maybe I didn't ask him. Seth sure doesn't talk much does he?"

"Seth? You came here with him?" Tessa asked in shock. "Why did he come?"

"He didn't say. In fact, none of them talked much."

"Them?" Cody asked quietly. "Who else came?"

"I have no idea. But we drove from Tessa's house, then we stopped somewhere along the way and these three young vamps were waiting for us on the side of the road. Really weird. They got in and we drove up here. We separated at the entrance. I focused on finding my father so I have no idea where they went. And Taz found me not long after. He wasn't happy to hear about Seth and the others though. He was quite worried. Said it wasn't safe here."

"And it's not," Cody added. "We're still trying to get away from these assholes. Adding new guys that don't know the score can get them killed. In fact, there's no way to know if they have been hurt or not."

Tessa shuddered. "I haven't seen Seth. I've seen his energy, but I couldn't make sense of it. Now I'm just scared that he's heading into a trap. He might have come at Mom's urging to make sure we're all fine but he's not going to know what side is doing what. And anyone who doesn't know him is going to take him out."

"Yeah, there have been so many attacks the feeling is more like if you're here and not one of us, then you're one of the bad guys." Cody added.

"At this point, no one is going to ask questions. They are just going to kill," she cried out. "We have to find them. Help them."

"Hey, they seemed to know where to go just fine. I certainly didn't get the impression that they'd never been here before. They came to the garage and down the hallway as if they knew exactly what to do."

His matter of fact delivery in no way eased the impact of his words. Tessa's mind raced for answers. Raced for an understanding that was reasonable and so not the instant one that came to mind.

Easy Tessa. Cody's warm comforting voice slipped into her mind. *We don't have the facts at this point, so let's not jump to any conclusions.*

Easy to say that, but my mind is already all over the place. How would he know about this mountain? Even if he'd been told about the garage, that doesn't it make easier. He'd have fumbled, looked around, maybe even asked Jared.

I know what it sounds like when you first hear it, but we can't jump to conclusions, he stressed. *This is too big and too important for that. You know Seth. It's not likely he'd be involved in this.*

No. She smiled, relief washing through her. *He wouldn't.*

Unless his friends had gotten him into it?

That sent shards of ice through her veins. *Damn.* She struggled to remember tidbits of conversation these last few months. But she couldn't lock onto anything. Nothing specific.

But there was a sick feeling in her stomach. Either way, Seth being here was bad news.

And that the others still hadn't met up was another bad sign.

In fact, this whole final segment of their journey was starting to look like seriously bad news.

"We need to find the others."

"I'll scout around." Cody unfurled his wings. Jared took a hurried step back.

"Jesus," he said just beneath his breath.

"It's okay, Jared." Tessa turned to Cody. "Be careful."

He nodded. *I will. And you keep your pretty face safe too.*

And he took off.

JARED STUDIED TESSA'S face, watching the emotions flit across it as Cody took to the air. He didn't particularly like that lost look. As if she was about to be separated from her best friend. And from what he'd seen, there was more than just friendship going on. And that couldn't be good. He didn't know how he felt about her but knew he wanted them to have a chance.

He could hardly compete with some guy that could pull out a set of wings and fly through the air. He didn't know how many vamps could fly, but he hadn't seen anyone other than Cody and his father. So they had to be rare.

Great. The oh so much older and protective Cody could fly. That would make him a god in women's eyes. And it was something most guys would kill for.

He was only human. How could he compete? And did he want to? Hell, he'd always thought of her as his girl, but they'd only gone to the movies as part of a group. A night that had ended in disaster.

Since then, she had been the light that kept the darkness at bay while he endured all the torment her people inflicted on him. No, not her people. No matter what the vamps had done to him and to these other poor victims, they could never be in the same category as Tessa. She'd been the only one that had come after him. The only one who'd cared enough.

So the question really was – did she care for him? Or did she care for everyone and he was nothing special in her eyes?

And wasn't that a depressing thought?

"Let's go back to the computer room. See if we can learn anything useful."

Jared started at her voice. She was all about business now. Had he imagined her melancholy over Cody leaving? God, listen to him. He was starting to sound like a girl, worrying over everything. Pathetic.

Resolutely, he turned and followed her into the room.

RHIA STARED MOODILY at all the members involved in heated arguments. Everyone agreed that something needed to be done, but so far no one had any idea what to do. Ideas were tossed into the ring and trashed immediately.

For the first time, she understood her daughter's constant complaints about vampire meetings. Lots of talk and no action. This time she was the one waiting to get out of here with a plan of action. But no one knew what to do.

"It was a mistake to come here."

Silence.

It was as if she'd shouted the words at them.

One by one, the humans drew back and glared at her.

"Really? And why is that?" said the leader, anger cutting through the suddenly thick atmosphere.

"Because you aren't doing anything. We need to act. Fast. The warehouse is full of people that could be saved or need to be given a decent death and burial or whatever it is you do with your dead. And there are vamps risking their lives to save other humans and vamps alike. Kids have gone missing. Adults have gone missing. Council members have gone missing. It's happened to both sides."

Sian reached over and covered her hand with hers. Rhia stared down, belatedly realizing she was clenching her fists so tight she'd drawn blood. She leaned back and folded her hands on top on her lap. "I'm going up there. If I die fighting your war, at least I'll have done what I can to save my family."

She stood up, edgy and pissed. Anger flowed through her, giving her the strength to walk to the door, intent on ripping the door off its hinges if necessary to get out. That urgency was so much worse now.

"Rhia, wait. We need their help." Sian rushed toward her.

With a shake of her head, Rhia rejected that idea. "They

have no help to give. They are victims with a victim mentality. They have no idea what to do or how to find out who amongst them are serving their own people up on a platter to these guys. And I'm not sure they care."

She reached for the handle on the door when Councilman Adamson lashed out. "We came to ask for their help. What was the point if we don't give them a chance?"

"They won't make a decision," she cried out, pivoting on her heels and striding a few steps back toward them. "We don't have time. Even as we speak, they are gathering their forces. Making plans. Capturing more people. *Killing* our people."

Sian stood in front of her. "Rhia. Listen. We're here. Let's give them a little longer and if it doesn't go anywhere – I'll come with you. I need to connect with Taz too."

Rhia felt some of the anger drain away. Sian had as much to lose as Rhia. She closed her eyes briefly and prayed for patience. "How long?" she asked, her voice hard and cold.

"Half an hour. That's it. Let's try to find a solution and then I'll go with you up to the blood farm."

She stared into Sian's beautiful eyes, so warm and caring. She'd been a wonderful friend through the years. They'd worked together, played together, laughed together, and cried together. Sian had been there for her. In this instance, Rhia figured she could give Sian half an hour more. But she wasn't going to let them waste the time. Something needed to happen here and now. Or else.

Hooking her arm with Sian's, the two walked back to the table. As she retook her seat, Rhia snapped, "Fine. But a solution happens or I'm going to start looking at this group as being part of the problem."

CHAPTER 11

C ODY SOARED TO the top of the warehouse and flew deep into the heavy machinery that criss-crossed the ceiling. The space allowed for his wings to expand fully, pull, and then glide.

He couldn't imagine the amount of science or mechanics required to keep the warehouse functioning at optimal levels. He doubted he'd find anything up here, but it occurred to him that since they had found one suspended office, it was possible that there could be more. There'd been no time for a thorough search. And this wasn't the ideal time now either, except....he was searching for their missing people.

Silently, he glided through the vast space, then pulled his wings closer to his body and zipped between and around several huge pipes. Could he trace this pipeline to the main machinery room? Would that help? It would if it led to the other warehouses. There were three other blood farms that they'd heard about but had yet to see. They hadn't had a chance to explore the railway tunnel either. That could lead to all of them. They'd thought to secure the place and then leave it for others to sort out. Now he realized he wasn't quite so complacent that they would do that again. And he wanted to be a part of this clean up. To make sure it really *did* get cleaned up.

He slowed down to hover in the air and search below.

Nothing moved. Where was his father? He'd have taken to the sky if he'd gotten into trouble. Presuming of course that he'd been able to get away.

And if he had to take to the air, would he be flying around attracting attention? No. He'd be holed up somewhere where he had the best view while he contacted Serus. Or he could already be on his way to helping Serus.

Damn. Again, too much speculation and not enough information. So it was up to him to do a slow and quiet circle of the area below and find the others. To that end, he pulled in his wings even tighter and began a silent glide to the far end of the room, following the direction his father had gone.

Nothing. He'd almost made it back to where Tessa and Jared were when he heard a rustling sound. He charged straight up, hoping his youth would give him the advantage over whoever was creeping up behind him. Then he suddenly reversed directions and came down behind the other flyer.

His father.

With a big grin on his face, Goran pulled up and hovered in place. "Learned a few tricks, have you?"

"Yeah. Out of necessity." Cody looked down at the warehouse below. He was still on the opposite side of the room from Tessa and there was no one else down there. "What happened to your group?"

"Good question. I got that nasty suspicion that I was heading into a trap, held it off for as long as I could, then bolted into the air." He shrugged. "I looked down to see what the hell was going on and the six guys in my group were gone." He snapped his fingers. "Just like that."

Cody stared at him. "All six? As in they found a bolthole to hide in? Or were they taken?"

"I really don't know." He studied the area under them.

"I've not seen anyone since."

"And Serus?"

"See, that's the other thing." Goran shifted several feet over. "I can't see or hear him talk."

Uh oh. "And normally you would be able to in this warehouse – correct?"

His father nodded. "Unless he's unconscious, locked inside one of these nasty thick walled rooms, or…dead."

"But you could talk to him before when you were locked up, so I think we have to assume that he's either unconscious or…" Loath to say it, Cody changed the last word in his mind to, "…worse."

Goran nodded. "I vote we find him first."

"Yeah. David, Ian, and Jewel are with him, too."

"And my group could have been the bad guys." Goran glared down at the vast space below them.

"Is that really possible?" Cody stared at him. "They were all fighting on our side before. I know several of them were really vicious. Weren't they part of Motre's group? Or did he take all of his people with him?"

"I don't know. Either way, that doesn't mean that one or all of them didn't change sides or were already spies in the first place. If it was the last guy in my group, he could have spiked everyone before they had a chance to fight back. And if there were two spies in that group, their job would have been much easier. Honestly, I saw the look on the third man's face. He looked pissed when I suddenly flew up." He shrugged, a motion that spoke of years of understanding the duplicity of his own kind. "You know we can't trust anyone."

Cody groaned. "I was hoping we could at least trust these vamps."

"Not going to happen. You can trust me and Tessa's family and likely Jewel and Ian. Beyond that…"

Shit.

Not wanting to waste time, Cody led the way back to where they entered the warehouse. When they reached the spot, he turned toward the left where Serus's group had gone.

"Where the hell are Taz and the techs? We released a dozen people earlier. Vamp and humans alike," Goran added as they zipped along.

"We found Jared, only he was alone." Cody quickly filled his father in on Jared's trip back with Seth and his friends.

"Damn fool," Goran growled. "We got more people running around here that don't know what's going on. How are we supposed to find and save them all now?"

Cody hated to say it, but they both needed the reminder. "Especially when they've been here long enough to have been captured and drugged. At this point, they could be on either team."

"This is beyond stupid," Goran growled. "We need an army to lock this place down until the drugs have time to get out of everyone's system and we can figure out who is who."

"Even then, the bad guys are just going to play along and pretend to have been victimized," Cody pointed out, his gaze never leaving the floor below. He flew at such an angle that he could see into the rooms slightly. But he saw no sign of anyone.

No one? Tessa's worried voice whispered through his head.

Just my father. Everyone else is missing.

Turning to his father, Cody said, "They've likely been locked in a room somewhere."

"I'm not sure about that. At this point, I think they are killing everyone right away. We're causing too much trouble. If they can take us all out – who will be left to cause trouble?

Rhia and Sian. That's an easy answer for everyone," Goran said, his voice harsh, cold.

"Not good." Cody was about to say something else when his father's face brightened.

His father said, "Serus just contacted me." His face darkened. "They've been surrounded by those that had been in my group. Serus overheard them talking about taking them to the mini railway."

"I know where that is." Damn, that's one of the places they'd meant to explore and never got around to. "Let's go."

"And fast. Serus doesn't sound good."

❧ ❦

DAVID STARED IN shock at the vamps he'd last seen following Goran. They all held silver spikes in their hand and every one of them were glaring at his group. How? And why? He didn't understand, and neither did his father. Tired, they hadn't expected an ambush from within their group.

"Damn."

Jewel leaned against him, her fear almost palpable. "Why?" she whispered. "I don't understand."

"And you don't need to understand nothing." said the asshole closest to her. "You're all such great sheep. Following the leader and never seeing the wolves in the pack."

Ian tried to take a step forward, but one of the vamps brandished a spike in his direction. "Stay back."

"You all fought on our side in the last skirmish." Ian held out his hands, palms upward. "Why are you doing this?"

David didn't know if Ian was playacting or as tired and confused as he sounded, but the vamp appeared to think he really was exhausted. That could play into their hands.

"So why not kill us outright?" David asked curiously. "Why surround us? What do you want?"

"Some people want to see you." The biggest of them, and for some reason David had counted on that one being on the good side until now, motioned them forward. "Be good and you get to live. For a little while." He showed the spikes he held in both hands. "Or give us an excuse to take you out now. The bosses will never know."

His father straightened at the word *bosses*.

David could almost see his mind turning over that idea. If they were being taken to see the bosses, in theory, they could find out who was behind this nightmare and kill them off. And for that to happen, they had to stay alive. He didn't dare ask about Cody and Tessa. That they weren't here was a good thing. It gave him hope. But he also knew there was a chance they'd been picked off first. He wanted to ask his father about Goran but didn't dare. That the vamps weren't crowing about killing an ancient gave him more hope. Goran was a cagey vampire. He wouldn't be easy to kill.

"We're moving." Gently, David urged Jewel to move in the direction they were pointed at. Down the stairs to the mini railway tunnel.

Yes! Excitement surged through him. That tunnel led to freedom as well. That's how Jared had managed to escape.

Which way did he want to go?

Fight and possibly escape? Or stay captive and possibly meet the bosses?

TESSA HATED THE waiting. Hated the dark. And really hated knowing that her father and brother were in trouble. Again.

Cody? Any news? Can you find out where they are being tak-en?

Dad can talk to your father now, but he says Serus doesn't sound good.

"Tessa?"

Startled, she turned to face Jared. And felt heat wash over her face. "Hey. Sorry about that."

"You were talking telepathically, weren't you?"

She nodded. "Yes. Some of us can do that. I didn't know I could until recently. I still can't communicate with many though."

He studied her quietly. "That would be so cool."

She grinned. "It is."

Tessa, the group is being herded down the stairs to the mini railway.

Tessa gasped. "Do you know where the mini railway is? The others are being taken there."

Jared walked past her and studied the doors closest to him. "That's how I escaped. I think I can find the right door again."

"Cody and Goran are heading there now."

They've left two vamps behind to keep watch for anyone who might follow. But they are only staying a short while before racing to catch up with the main group. Serus said something about them having big plans for the place. He got the impression that it wasn't nice plans.

Tessa stopped in shock. She asked cautiously, *Like what kind of plans?*

Like they wouldn't have to worry any more about anyone left behind because they wouldn't be alive for much longer.

"Oh shit."

She quickly relayed that information to Jared. "We have

to act. Taz is here somewhere. I don't know what these guys have planned, but I have to search for and hopefully save them."

"Surely they wouldn't do something to this place." Jared stared the people hanging. "There are too many people here. If they think we'd die, then so would all these people."

"Maybe, and maybe they don't need these people any longer. Maybe these ones are too old. Or maybe they are just trying to cut their losses and get away to start up somewhere else." She tossed the last bit behind her, racing from room to room in search of Taz. She should have done this right away. Every minute could make a difference. Cody's last words had nasty images coursing through in her mind. She didn't know if they'd blow this place up or try to seal it or fill it with gas, but she couldn't just stand by and watch.

Empty room upon empty room and still no sign of the others.

Jared ran ahead of her, checking the other rooms, helping them cover the distance twice as fast.

We're going after the two vamps left behind. Get out of there!

Not without helping Taz. He's here somewhere.

Damn it Tessa, we can't save everyone.

I know. Go. We'll follow as soon as we can.

No. Go to the surface. Get out. You should be safe there.

She didn't bother answering. *Too late, we've already made it to the far end.*

Damn it, Tessa. At least go to the right and check that end first. We didn't find any closed doors on the left.

She crossed the room and raced down the far side. "They have to be here – somewhere."

"Unless they were killed, or taken to the railway themselves." Jared called out, running at top speed ahead of her.

She raced after him. "I don't think they'd kill the humans. They need to replenish their stocks at the blood farm."

She watched him head into the next room and heard him shout. "This door is locked."

He pounded on the door and heard someone pound back from the inside.

"Move aside, Jared."

He backed up without an argument.

She leapt into the air at the last moment, using the momentum of her jump to deliver a powerful kick to the doorknob. The door popped open as she made a clumsy landing.

Taz rushed out of the room, pushing her out of the way as a half dozen techs stampeded out.

"Tessa?" Taz said, "you shouldn't be here."

She laughed, or would have if she had the chance. "So not a choice. You have to get out of here. Apparently my father and friends have been taken to the mini railway down below. They were warned that everyone up here is likely to die. I don't know if it's gas they have planned or something else, but we have to move."

The others cried out and raced to the far end, where the white tunnels led to the surface. She raced alongside them. "Taz, is everyone else all right?"

"Yes. There were vamps with us but they were separated. Only the humans were left behind.

Shit. Those vamps could have joined the others or been taken out permanently.

Cody, where are you?

She heard the grunting and fighting sounds in her mind and knew he was trying to overpower the two guards. Hopefully his father was helping. Damn.

"Jared, make sure they get up to the surface. And get off the mountain if you can. Get in whatever vehicles there are and drive like hell. I don't know what these assholes have done but it's bad. Go, go!" She yelled. Taz turned as if to protest and she shook her head. "Go, Taz. Save the others."

"What about you?" he protested.

"I'll check on Goran and Cody. Then we'll all follow you. We can fly faster than you can run. Go!"

She wasted another precious minute making sure they were able to make their way safely to the end of the warehouse.

Then she turned in the direction of the door that Jared had pointed out earlier. She leapt into the air and glided to where she landed almost in front of it.

She could hear the sounds of a horrific fight going on and that worried her more than anything. Two on two should have easily made Cody and Goran the winners. That there was even a fight was disconcerting. Who were these two that were causing such trouble?

She opened the door to find the small room empty. Shit, was this the wrong room? Surely not. Then someone slammed up against the wall in front of her. She raced inside the room to find a partially hidden door. As she reached for the knob, the room went deadly silent.

Shit. Hang on, Cody. I'm coming.

She opened the door.

CHAPTER 12

TESSA LUNGED THROUGH the door, her claws extended like the lethal weapons they were.

"There you are." Goran said with a grin. "About time."

She stared at him in shock, then glanced over at Cody who was grinning at her. She straightened and rolled her eyes at the two of them.

"You could have told me," she muttered. "Looking stupid *all* the time isn't exactly a goal you know."

Cody and Goran both laughed. Cody walked toward her, his lethal grin making her heart beat faster. "That wild warrior woman look will never make you look stupid. And thanks for coming to our rescue. But as you can see, we got it covered."

In fact, three piles of ash burned around them.

She tilted her head. "Three?"

"Yeah, another one joined them from somewhere."

"Probably one of the guys who locked up Taz and the others."

Goran turned to stare back in the direction of the warehouse. "Did you find them?"

It was Tessa's turn to grin. "Sure did. And they are all racing to the surface of this damn place with strict orders to get off the mountain until they hear from us." She glanced over at Cody. "I sent Jared out too. It's really dangerous for humans in here."

He snorted and pointed to the ashes. "And for vamps."

Goran moved down to the entrance of the tunnel. "Let's get moving. I'm having a hard time hearing Serus in my head."

"That could be the damn tunnel and the sheer amount of mountain between the two of you." Cody led the way through the door, with Tessa close behind. Goran took up the rear position.

Cody looked down as he stood at the top of the stairs. "These steps go on forever. It's faster if we fly, but there isn't enough room to open our wings."

"I'll race you," Tessa said. She reached out and smacked Cody on his shoulders. "Tag, you're it." And she took a leap off the top stair and landed on the landing below then took off again. Using the longest jumps she could, she barely kept ahead of Cody racing behind her, who was laughing and swearing as he just missed her at every landing.

The stairs went on forever. She just kept extending her jumps until finally she could see the last one ahead. She was about to take the final jump that would take her to ground level when Cody grabbed her arm. "Shhhh. We don't know if there are more guards."

Startled, she pulled back and caught her breath as they waited for Goran to join them. By the time he arrived, she was feeling more or less calm from the rush of jumping so far. With a warning glance at both of them, Cody dropped lightly down the last flight of stairs. He walked the few steps to the doorway and put his ear up against the door. Then he shook his head and motioned for them to join him.

With the three of them in position, he cracked the door open just a hair, listened, then pulled it wide enough for him to look out.

Tessa waited impatiently.

Cody turned and opened the door fully. "There's no sign of them anywhere."

Crap. Tessa stepped through and looked first in one direction then the other. He was right. There were no obvious signs that her family had even been here.

Cody pointed to the left. "That's where Jared disappeared and made it out of here last time. I'm pretty sure that means our group would have been taken to the right."

"Why?" Goran frowned. "Does that go deeper into the mountain?"

"To another blood farm possibly?" Tessa murmured, staring down the track to the left. If Jared had left that way, it would be an easy way out. But her family was in trouble. Resolutely, she turned to the right and studied the size of the tunnel. The energy trails confirmed that a large group had travelled in that direction.

The tunnel was just barely big enough to fly in. "Well, we have the advantage here."

Goran looked at her. "In what way?"

"The tunnel is big enough that we can fly or glide and catch up to them faster."

Both men eyed the tunnel. "It would be harder work here, but still doable." Goran nodded. "I'll fly ahead and scout the tracks. See if I can find something.

"No," Cody said, causing both Tessa and Goran to stare at him. "I'll go. Then I can tell Tessa if there is a problem up ahead without having to come back."

Now she understood. "Good thinking. Go. We're right behind you."

Cody took off smoothly and flew forward with ease.

Knowing she was the weakest link, Tessa started off with

her long ballet jumps. By the third or fourth one, she was covering twenty or more feet in a single jump. Goran hovered by her side.

Tessa, I can't see them.

Keep looking. They have to be there somewhere. Are there doors up ahead? Curves in the track? Any place they can go?

Not that I can see. I'm flying further ahead.

She shared Cody's findings with Goran.

He frowned and stared down the dark tunnel. "There has to be an end to this thing."

"But it could be ten miles or more." Of course that was likely to be an exaggeration but then again, maybe not. It was an old mine. How extensive were these things?

Tessa? I think I see something. The tunnel splits into two tracks up ahead.

She told Goran.

"Tell him to wait for us. We don't want him going off on his own."

She told Cody, listening as he laughed in her head.

That sounds like my father.

He's right. If you get into trouble, we're too far behind to help out.

She picked up the pace as much as she could without tiring herself out. There was no point in arriving at their destination exhausted. That wasn't going to help anyone.

Actually, I think you might be almost here.

In the darkness, she could see Cody racing toward them.

"Hey. How much further?" Goran asked.

"Not much." Cody pointed ahead. "It's right around that bend."

Three more glides and she was there.

"They've likely gone to the right. The tracks are much

shinier, as if they'd been used more often." Goran said. "The tracks on the left are darker."

Cody turned to Tessa. "Do you agree?"

She stopped to study the tracks. She turned on both sets of vision and studied the tunnels. "Definitely the right. They can't be more than a few minutes ahead."

"In that case, we stay together."

Cody nodded. "Tessa, you set the pace. We'll keep up with you."

She nodded and took a leap into the air. As soon as she landed, she immediately took off again.

Cody flew up beside her. "You can really cover some serious ground this way, can't you?"

"More and more all the time. I wasn't anywhere near as good at the beginning, but now…"

She warmed at the admiration in his voice. It wasn't flying, but it was what she could do and as her dad had kept up with Goran these last few centuries in the same way, she figured it would work just fine for her too.

It was Goran from behind her who sent out a gentle warning, "We need to keep quiet. I think I hear something."

And just then, so did she.

Voices.

She strained to make out the words.

She raced ahead, trying her best to land as soundlessly as possible. They had no place to hide. And no place to go if they were attacked. She shoved her fingers into her pockets and pulled out two spikes, one in each hand. She'd be damned if she'd leave any more asshole vamps alive.

Especially not ones that double-crossed them.

SERUS TRIED TO keep his shoulders down, his demeanor quiet and beaten. It wasn't that hard actually. The amount of silver they were all waving around might just be affecting him. They'd already come close to killing him once. A slash of silver had cut through his coat and grazed his skin. It was as if a poisonous arrow had scraped him raw. He wasn't dying. He knew his vamp genes would heal that eventually – but it was taking time. And time was one thing he didn't have.

They had to get out of here and he needed to be at full strength to achieve that. He'd managed to connect with Goran. The good news was that Goran, Cody, and Tessa were on their way. Tessa had also found the techs from the warehouse and had sent them to safety. Now why his daughter hadn't left with them was both agonizing and terrifying. He wanted her safe and away from here.

Still, she was riding to the rescue once again. She'd like that.

He almost smiled, then remembered that he was supposed to be cowering in fear. Yeah right.

"God. Look at the old man. He's a broken down relic. Just like most of the ancients. Why do we keep them around?"

"Cause the boss said so. And you know what happens to those that cross the boss."

The first man gulped and pulled at the neckline of his t-shirt. "What about the girl? Do you think he'd let us have her?"

Serus felt David's back go rigid even as he felt Jewel's withdrawal into herself. He took a step closer to Jewel. These assholes were going to pay for that comment with their lives. If he didn't take care of it, he knew David would. These assholes couldn't be allowed to live and terrify their own species.

Centuries ago, there'd been an attempt to cull the vampires and keep only the purebloods. It was not that they wanted good vamps back then. They wanted ones of like mind. To that end, hundreds of vamps had gone missing in the span of a month. No one ever claimed responsibility or dared raise their voices but he'd always wondered. He remembered telling Rhia to keep a low profile. Even then, he hadn't been able to contemplate life without her. She'd been everything for him. And now he was blessed with three kids. That Goran said Seth was lost in this nightmare as well was just too much.

He didn't dare lose any of them.

The vamps talked among themselves, seeming not to care if the captives heard them.

Serus listened and planned. "See, the young one has more fire in his blood than the old guy. I say we should just kill him off. It will make the young ones much easier to handle."

"No, it won't. It will piss them off and we'll end up having to kill them just defending ourselves. We have to bring them *all* in."

"Talk." A different vamp on the right side of him spit on the ground. "That's all they do. How about a little more action?"

"I don't know. I kinda like this."

"Well, I don't. I'd rather have a good fight any day."

He straightened and walked over to the first guy.

Serus watched his movements. Then he heard Goran in his head.

Serus. Get ready. We're almost there. Three. Two.

Serus turned to look.

And the vamp who'd asked about keeping Jewel incinerated in front of everyone.

❧ ❧

CODY SHOOK HIS head. Tessa had turned into an aggressive vamp. That her chosen victim was the asshole asking about Jewel wasn't lost on him, but he figured David might have wanted to have that honor. But then he was too busy taking down the two vamps bringing up the rear to argue with her choice.

With the vamps turning to ash and being blown away by the wind, he turned to confront the rest. And stopped.

There was no one left. David was standing over a smoldering pile with smoke still floating around his arms. Ian and Jewel were still recovering from their fight, the two weaker ones sticking together and watching each other's backs. Both the ancients were huddled together at the other end of the tunnel, talking.

Tessa sniffed the air and grimaced. "I'm never going to light a fire and roast marshmallows again."

Everyone stared at her.

"Marshmallows?" asked Jewel. "What are those?"

Tessa threw her head back and laughed. "A human treat that they roast over ashes."

On cue, the group stared at the fiery ashes all around and groaned.

"Oh gross." Jewel made a retching sound.

Tessa giggled. It was a wonderful sound of resilience that never failed to entrance Cody. Yeah, he had it bad.

"Not over vamp ashes, silly," Tessa added, "over a fire made of wood."

"But why?" Ian asked. "I don't get it."

"Yeah, you'd really have to be there to understand." She smiled warmly up at Ian.

Cody realized how much of her life had centered around human activities. Human school. Human field trips. Human friends. What would she do when this was all over? Would she switch to vamp school? He was in university himself. But he thought she had one or two more years to go before then. He wished she was going with him to university. He was taking legal counseling so he could work with the Vampire Council. He had no idea what her plans for the future were. If she had any.

She was so young. He regretted that part. Only because he felt that by locking her to his side, she was going to miss out on so much. And a part of him didn't care. Right or wrong, he didn't want to let her go and find someone else. Or give her time to get to know her own mind.

Damn. He was a fool.

NOW THIS WAS much better. Rhia strode out to the vehicle. The Human Council, once they'd realized she was serious, had gotten down to business. They'd pulled together some kind of secret service group and special army members. She didn't understand what their titles meant, just that they were loyal to humans and could be trusted not be corrupted over this process.

She had to trust someone. The teams were being assembled now. If need be, there were more of these groups around the world. But that would take time. And she didn't want to alert the vamp community of the widespread movement of humans. It was so much better to do this under their noses. If they learned of it, they might get the wrong idea and both sides would be facing a war for a totally different reason.

She waited by the vehicles, staring as the first rays of light peeked above the mountains. They had maybe an hour if they were heading to the blood farm. Although she wasn't sure that was the best place for them to be. More people rushing in without any warning could not be a good idea.

"Let's go." Councilman Adamson and Gloria got into the front seats of the SUV while Sian and Rhia hopped into the back. Behind the heavily tinted windows, they would be safe no matter which direction they travelled.

Sian's phone went off. She looked at the number and gasped in shock. "It's Taz."

"Finally," Rhia said, "Answer it."

Sian rushed to say hi to her love, then cried out at what she was hearing. The councilman waited for her to finish her conversation. But Sian was already dialing the Human Council leader.

Rhia listened in as Sian spoke on the phone.

"Jackson. I just heard from Taz. He says there were threats to do something to that whole warehouse. He didn't know if they were talking about gas or explosives, but make sure to warn your men."

"Explosives? Gas?" Rhia's stomach was ready to hurl. "That is not a good development."

Sian closed her phone and reached over to clutch Rhia's hand. "And it gets worse. Serus and his group, including David, Ian, and Jewel have been taken. Cody, Tessa, and Goran have gone after them."

"Deeper into the mountain?" Rhia asked, tears springing to her eyes.

At Sian's nod, she leaned her head back against the seat and tried to control her panic. "Did he mention Seth?"

The long slow sigh from Sian was painful to hear. "No.

He never saw him, but he heard from Jared that Seth drove him up to the blood farm."

"Jared is there too?" Rhia asked, horrified.

"He's outside with Taz and the other human techs. The vampire techs were taken somewhere else."

Another problem to think about. "They will need to be picked up."

"They actually have a vehicle and are on their way down the mountain." Sian said, not looking up from her phone's screen. "But Taz has not heard or seen anything of the others since Tessa released them."

Her lips pinned together to hold back the cries, Rhia swallowed hard and said, "What can we do to help?"

"Nothing. The human army is on the way," said Councilman Adamson.

"Doing nothing is not acceptable," Gloria snapped. "We are not useless and there is much we can do. I suggest we head to the first of those property listings. They are most likely storehouses or suppliers. If they fight, we kill them. If they want to talk, we imprison them and stop them from contacting anyone else."

Rhia brightened at that idea. "And we'd be cutting them off at both ends." She turned to Sian. "What about you?"

"I'm in." Sian put her phone away and opened the laptop. "The first of the properties is about ten minutes from here."

"Councilman Adamson spoke up. "I think we should bring in Councilmen Baker and Wilson. They will want to help."

"I'll call them", Gloria said. "I sent them an email earlier but we need backup *now*."

CHAPTER 13

TESSA STUDIED THE group. Her father was hurting, but she wasn't sure what the cause was. Jewel looked like she was done. But then she'd been exhausted and worn out a long time ago. All that girl wanted was to get the hell out of here and never come back. It was the same thing Tessa wanted.

Except the vamps needed blood. But she knew none of them would avail themselves of any they found here. They'd gone without for so long that she hadn't worried about it, but now realized how fast it was becoming an issue.

"Any idea where you were being taken?" She asked Ian, who stood quietly beside her.

He snorted. "The bosses apparently wanted to talk to us."

"And where is that meeting supposed to take place?"

He opened his arms. "No idea. But they stopped here. We don't know if the others were coming to join us or if there is a doorway somewhere. You attacked before we found out anything more."

"Good. We'll be fine without them. The world is better off without those traitors." She sniffed in disgust.

"Yeah. Except this wasn't all of them. Several stayed behind."

She cut him off with a wave of her hand. "Cody and Goran took care of them. And Jared and I found Taz and his group and they bolted out of that nightmare warehouse. They should be halfway down the mountain by now."

"You hope." David said, his arms wrapped securely around Jewel. "Jared's not very good at taking orders."

She frowned. "I'm hoping he did this time. If they are set to do something destructive with that blood farm, no one is safe." And that saddened her. "Jared came back because he found out his father is hanging there. He found him too."

Jewel spun around, horror on her face. "Please tell me you're kidding?"

With a shrug, Tessa said, "Sorry, but he found him in one of the rows. Been hanging there for a long time. Most likely since Jared was a little kid. I don't think Jared's father can be saved. Not sure any of them can be actually. That was the original warehouse and the bulk of those people might have been there for decades. I highly doubt there is anyone hanging that has been there for less than six months. They probably have those in a different warehouse.

"Except Darren." Jewel frowned. "Although he has been missing longer than six months."

"At least that long," David piped up. "If you think back, it's probably been longer than a year."

"But he can still be saved," Jewel cried. "The vampires here can't die from just this."

"Maybe, and maybe not." Cody spoke up for the first time. "Their muscles are still wasting away from lack of use. And you don't know what else has been done to them."

Jewel shuddered. "I sure hope they don't have any females here. Not after what that guy wanted."

"Yeah well, he won't be asking for that again." Tessa glared at the piles of ash. "We heard him while we were coming down the tunnel. Asshole."

"Okay, everyone listen up," Cody said, "We have a choice

to make."

Serus nodded. "Exactly. We can go back down the railway and get out. We know from Jared that there is a way out from there. Or we go after the bosses."

He waited for someone to say something.

Tessa just raised an eyebrow and stared at him. He glared at her. "You're tired, Tessa. Home makes the best sense for you."

"So are Jewel, David, and Ian. Besides, you're not looking all that ready to dance either," she retorted, her gaze narrowed and locked on his face. "Besides, none of you have eaten in how long? I'm starving but will last longer than any of you."

David chuckled. "Give it up, Dad. She's not going to leave until the rest of us do." He looked down at Jewel. "Except Jewel might want to go home."

"Not anymore," Jewel said. "Sure, I want to leave, but that vamp's suggestion made me afraid that there are female vamp captives here that might need rescuing." She shook her head. "I'm not leaving them behind to suffer any more because I'm tired."

"I got news for you. I don't think they'd care one bit if the women were vamp or human." Tessa snapped out at the group in general. "I sure didn't see any young attractive women hanging in that damn blood farm, that's for sure."

That made everyone stop and stare at her.

It was Ian who verbalized what they were all thinking. "I sure hope you're wrong about that. But if you aren't, then every last vamp in this place gets taken out permanently 'cause that is wrong in so many ways."

Goran walked over. "This is the end of the tracks. Now I'm not seeing a door, set of stairs, or any place to go but further along by foot." He swept his arms open toward the black hole of a tunnel. "Does anyone see anything different?"

"Tessa?" Cody asked. "What about you?"

She walked over to the front of the mini train and studied the energy ahead of her. "There's nothing going down the tunnel. Nothing recent anyway."

She turned and studied the wall on the left. "I can't see anything in this direction either." She turned to look at the right wall. Then shrugged her shoulders. She turned back to face the mini train and its bright ball of combined energies and wondered what she was supposed to do with that. She caught sight of something on the wall to the left. She walked over, her hand instinctively reaching out to trace a faint line in the tunnel wall. Painted a dark brown dirt color, the wall blended in with the darkness.

Cody's hand reached over and traced the same door. "A door from the looks of it."

"Yeah, but how do we open it?" Ian asked.

David laughed. "Most likely like this." He lashed out and kicked it dead center.

Silently, the door opened.

JARED STOOD OUTSIDE the garage and wondered what the hell he was doing. The others had tried to coax him into the vehicles and leave with them, but he hadn't been able to. He couldn't help but think that someone should stand watch. In case the asshole vamps came out or more arrived. Besides, Taz had given him a small camera. He planned to take a picture of anyone coming or going. It made him feel useful.

It was almost morning so maybe there'd be no one in or out, but he wasn't prepared to take the chance. If they had security cameras out here that would be a different story but they didn't, so he'd take on that job.

And he really had nowhere else to go.

Besides, Tessa and his father were still down there.

How could he just leave? He was surprised that Taz was leaving until he realized the doctor was planning to return with his own reinforcements. Medical staff that he could trust. People who would be able to make decisions on how to save the people below.

Jared knew in his heart it was unlikely they could still save his father. He'd wondered about the other kid he'd spoken to in the blood farm. He hadn't been moving all that much, but he'd been capable of talking and thinking and surely that was worth saving. But...Jared hadn't seen him hanging. In fact, it seemed like no one hanging was younger than forty, if not sixty. A scary thought.

Then he remembered what one doctor had said about there being different programs and that Jared wouldn't be given a choice which program he went into. He'd forgotten about that.

Was that information worth contacting Taz about? He had Taz's phone number saved in his new cell phone and now that he was outside again, he had reception.

He called Taz and quickly relayed that information.

"It's possible the younger healthier people are in another place altogether. But we can't go down until it's cleared and we know it's safe. I'll try to return in an hour with more medical staff. And there's going to be some special forces and a special military group arriving soon. Stay out of their way and answer any questions they might ask. Got it?"

"Got it," Jared said. "Glad I called. They'd have scared the crap out of me arriving out of the blue like that."

"In fact, you might be able to show them the way in through your escape tunnel. I'm sure they'd like to know about that bolthole. To plug it, if nothing else."

Jared stared at the still empty road. "I think I can find the way again." At least he thought he'd pointed out the right door to Tessa. In theory, he'd be able to show the army the same door.

"Good man. Hold tight. I'll be back soon."

Jared hung up the phone and looked for the best place to stand and watch the proceedings. He didn't want to be in the open and he didn't want to appear like he was hiding. There. In the shadow of the front steps up by the double doors. He could stand there and appear to be part of the house until he knew for sure it was safe.

As he ran up the steps, he had to wonder at the ashes on the ground in various places. There were still several parked vehicles and in a pinch, he'd drive out if necessary – if he could find the keys. He studied his spot and nodded. "This should work."

He leaned against the wall of the alcove and stood watch.

∽ ∾

CODY STEPPED FORWARD and studied the staircase in front of them. "I'll go first." He didn't bother waiting for the inevitable argument. He stopped at the first step, almost afraid of what might happen. Booby-trapped like almost all the others they'd tried? But the stair held. Silent and dark, with no way to go but up.

Taking a deep breath, he walked up the stairs as quietly as possible. If there were vamps waiting for him, he didn't want to give them any warning.

The others traipsed up behind him just as quietly.

The staircase appeared to go on forever. How did that work? They came down one part of the mountain only to climb back up another side of it? Why not go straight across? Was that even possible? His mind reeled with questions that had no answers.

See anything?

Tessa's curious voice made him smile. He answered. *Not yet. Just stairs and more stairs.*

It feels like a trap.

I'm half expecting someone to jump out of the walls. Or at least to be waiting for us at the top.

All of us came inside. I wish we'd left a couple of us behind in the tunnel. Maybe I should go back.

No! That's not good. No more splitting up. At least any vamps travelling down the tunnel will think that we were taken to meet the bosses.

Yeah, except for the piles of ashes we left behind.

True. Cody came to a stop at the top step. There was nothing there but a small landing. He stretched out a hand to find a wall in the small landing, but there was no apparent door. No handle or obvious way to open it. Again.

"Damn."

"What's wrong?" Ian asked from behind him. "Is there a door?"

"No idea. I can't find a way to open it."

"Kick it."

Right. Except there wasn't much room. He motioned for Ian to watch out, then moved his leg back and gave the wall an awkward kick. The door didn't move. He kicked it again at a different spot. This time, there was a loud scraping sound as the door opened.

So much for stealth.

Be careful, Tessa warned.

Yeah. And with that, he stepped into the unknown.

THIS WAS NOT how she'd imagined shutting down the blood farm business. Rhia thought it would be dealt with by the various enforcers and council members. Not with her being at the forefront of a raid on the first of the addresses found on the laptop. Daylight had hit full force. The vamp members were in full motorcycle gear to protect them. But she found the leather constricting. With the gauntlets on, she couldn't use her lethal claws. Wearing the heavy boots, she'd lost the ability to be quiet.

More protected than normal, yet she felt more vulnerable than ever. She hated it. But the options were limited.

Sian squeezed her arm. She turned to look at her best friend. At least she was smiling. Rhia had to grin. "You look ridiculous."

"Almost as silly as you do."

Rhia rolled her eyes at that, then turned to stare in the direction of the warehouse front door. The others should be in position at the back of the building. They had several guards on this side, but she couldn't imagine that anyone was in the warehouse at this hour of the day. At least not any vampires.

Still, better to be careful and all that. The guard opened the front door and slipped inside. Rhia waited for their signal.

There. The guard opened the door and motioned to them. Rhia and Sian strolled across the street, pretending to unbuckle the chin strap of their helmets. Rhia couldn't wait to remove it, but it was only coming off if the interior of the warehouse was safe.

Inside, they stood for a moment and reoriented themselves. It looked like a large warehouse full of shelves and boxes. Everything was labelled.

Then she realized that the warehouse was cool – cold even. As if the contents of the boxes need to be kept at that temperature.

The guard took off his helmet. "The place appears to be empty."

Councilman Adamson spoke up. "I'm going to the office to see what we can find."

"I'm coming with you," Rhia said, happy to have her head free of the helmet. She shook out her long hair. "Sian?"

"On it." The three raced upstairs. "If there's a computer, we need to grab it, too."

The guard said, "We'll stay down here and search the back."

Everyone, and there had to be a dozen vamps on this raid, spread out as Rhia reached the second floor.

The office was empty. But there was paper everywhere. Sian snagged the computer and took it to a side counter. She studied the contents while Rhia searched the desk and found an accounting book. "Names and dates on this ledger."

"Grab it. We'll use it to find more of the missing pieces."

Councilman Adamson called out from the far side. "Grab everything. Gloria just said that the raid on the second location went off without a hitch too. As if no one was expecting our presence."

"Good, but we don't have much time. Let's grab what we need and leave the rest for the team to secure. There's a clean up crew coming. They'll take care of this place. It's in our hands now. We need to move on to the next address on the list."

They were planning to hit as many as possible – they had to. And fast. There were several teams coordinating the hits.

Rhia nodded, gathered up the ledgers, checked the drawers for more, collected a large stack of paperwork, and checked the rest of the room. There was nothing more that she could find. She handed everything to a guard that had followed them upstairs. With Sian right behind her, she led the way down the stairs and headed to the front door.

Only it opened as she reached for the knob.

CHAPTER 14

BEING CAUGHT IN the middle of the line sucked. Tessa couldn't see much in front and even less behind her. Goran stood in front and her own father was coming up behind in last place. Both were big and protective. She wished she was in front with Cody. The line had stalled while he tried to open the door. The problem was, she couldn't help but think they were sitting ducks in here. Who would know or even find them if the doors at both ends suddenly sealed shut.

She couldn't stop the shudder that rippled through her at the thought.

Then Goran went up several more steps and she realized that Cody must have found a way through.

I did. But there's nothing up here. Seems to be a small landing and another big empty room, but I can't see anything inside.

Well, if I could join you, maybe I could see if anyone was up there recently or had been for a while. But getting there is taking a bit of time.

You'll be here in just a moment. Patience.

She let a snicker out at that. And drew a frown from Goran as he turned around at the unexpected noise. Damn. She gave him an apologetic smile and rushed up the last of the stairs.

By the time she'd entered the room at the top, her father had reached the top of the stairs as well. She walked into the room. Cody grabbed her arm.

Easy, he whispered. *We don't know if we're alone.*

She nodded. *I have to check for energy signatures, and that means I have to get away from the ball of energy from the group. It's too hard to see otherwise.*

He dropped his arm and she took several more cautious steps forward before turning to look back. The combined energies glowed bright in the dark. She shifted to stare at the rest of the space. There didn't appear to be anything in the room.

She frowned and squinted. There had to be something. There. A sound had her freezing. She spun around and searched the dark corners. Still nothing. Then that weird sense at the back of her neck urged her to look up.

There. She smiled. And pointed.

The sound of rustling wings whispered beside her as Goran and Cody took to the air as one. Serus wasn't far behind.

Tessa moved back to the group while trying to keep watch on what was going on above them. To have another flier here would be unusual. Cody's line only had a handful of relatives left, and there were few others that could fly. They'd already caught several fliers, so chances were they were all related.

The fliers reached the cloud of colored energy she'd seen up above.

But she couldn't tell what was happening.

"Tessa, can you tell how many are up there?"

She shook her head. "It was too far away. I doubt there is more than one or two, but I don't know. I also don't know if they were all fliers. There could be rooms full of vamps up there."

"Let's look for another way up." Ian and David ran around the room checking the walls for doors or stairs, anything that would let them join the fight. Jewel and Tessa just stared at each other. Tessa shrugged. "I'm happy to leave it to them. I didn't see any energy trails at this level, but that doesn't mean there aren't any."

A faint smile crossed Jewel's face. "You've been right every time so far."

"Yeah, and that's when I'm likely to be wrong." Tessa grinned as both Ian and David came back, frustration and anger on their faces as they tried to keep watch on the proceedings up above.

Tessa, we're good here. Bringing two assholes down.

Oh good. She laughed. "Cody said they caught the two up there."

David looked at her, then up at the high ceiling. "Good. I wonder who they caught."

She shrugged and continued to stare upwards, looking for Cody. "Doesn't matter to me. I don't know any of them."

"No, but I might."

As they watched, Goran and Serus came down with another winged vampire in their grasp. He didn't look so good. And he was old. Like seriously old.

She was surprised to see the lines on his face, the pain showing in his bent over stance. But she had no time to sort it out as Cody came down carrying the second vamp. An unwinged and much younger vamp.

"Interesting." David asked, "Who are they?"

Goran snorted and pointed to the old one. "He's an ancient. Haven't seen much of him in centuries. Didn't know he was still alive. And he doesn't look so good."

"Will he talk?"

Serus shrugged. "Who knows? He's been around too long to care at this point."

Ian circled the ill-looking vamp. "Other ancients don't look like he does."

"No, he appears to be dying," Serus said, "And I'm not sure from what."

Tessa remembered Bart and his comment so long ago. "Bad blood?"

David glanced over at her. "There was something about bad blood a long time ago. Surely that wouldn't still be affecting him, would it?"

"It could." Goran studied the old vampire crumpled on the floor. "Depends on how long he was drinking it and if he's had so much that the good stuff can't heal him anymore. Bad blood is a slow poison that can seep into his system and slowly eat away at him from the inside."

"But that would mean he's been doing this for a long time," Jewel protested.

Goran straightened. "You may not like this, but there are some ancients who have never had anything but fresh blood. For centuries, that's all most of us had. In his case, he might not have converted to the synthetic stuff."

God, what a horrible thought. Tessa studied the old man, wondering how many people he'd killed. Sure, it was their way. It might be their nature, but they had a choice. They could take what they needed and leave the humans alive. And clear their memories so that no one would remember. Now with synthetic blood available, they didn't even need to do that.

He really didn't look good. She asked, "So he's not looking that way because of his age?"

"Hell no. He's older than we are, but not by that much."

Ian piped up, "He looks like Moltere."

That name caught everyone's attention. "You have a good

eye for details, Ian," Goran said, "He's from the same family line. Their fathers were brothers. One winged and one not."

"There aren't going to be many left after this culling," said David. He glared down at the old vamp. "He looks dead now."

"Well, I'm not," snarled the old vamp. "And if it's my time, so be it. It will be yours soon enough."

There was just enough power in his voice to make Tessa wary. "Who is the second male?"

Cody kicked the younger vamp lying crumpled on the floor where he'd tossed him. "Another henchman, maybe. I don't know him. I've recognized so few here that I have to wonder where they've all come from."

The old one spoke again, "Many don't know anything other than this farm. They don't know the towns and cities around the world. They've spent their years living here and in other similar places. He's one of them."

Surprised, the group stared at each other.

"Never going to school? Council meetings? Friends? Family?"

"Their friends and family are all here. Those that you've left behind."

Tessa walked closer and bent to study the younger vamp's face. She gasped.

"Tessa?" She shook her head and lifted the vamp's chin to get a better angle. The vamp was young. Older than her by a couple of decades maybe. And he looked familiar. Why? She didn't recognize his energy. The color was normal, healthy if not vibrant. But there was something...off about it.

"I've seen his face or someone similar to him before." She straightened but continued to stare down at him, urging her brain to kick in fast. "But I can't place him."

"Not him. He lives in here."

She studied the old guy. "Maybe he does, but I recognize him or his family line from somewhere."

The old guy snorted. "You are nothing. Just a girl. An odd one at that."

"So true. And you are nothing but a diseased animal," she retorted. "The real question is what to do with you. We came here to meet with the bosses, but you two aren't them."

The old ancient struggled to rise as anger flashed on his face. But then he crumpled to the ground where he lay gasping. "Why can't we be the bosses?"

Jewel stepped forward. "Because you are too weak. The younger bosses would have risen up and taken your spot."

So true. Tessa studied his skin. He really didn't look good. She glanced over at her father. "What did you do to him?"

"Nothing. He was already injured or dying when we got up there." Serus shrugged defensively. "We didn't do any-thing."

"I wonder if Jewel isn't right. And did that takeover do this to him?" She bent over and opened the old ancient's coat.

"Whoa Tessa, what are you doing?" David asked.

"Looking for the damage." She found a long shallow slice in the ancient's shirt. Several of them. Meticulously sliced into the skin, but so very shallow that it was not that noticeable. His neck held the same marks. "Look. I bet they took a silver stake and swiped it across his skin. Or something silver at least. Not enough to incinerate him. Not enough to kill him even, just enough to poison him. A long, slow death."

"Ugh." Ian bent at her side. "That's just mean."

Jewel shook her head, her face twisting in revulsion. "Wow, someone hates you."

"Hated. He's dead." The old ancient glared at her. "I will be too, soon."

"And the young guy. Was he on your side?"

The ancient nodded but the effort seemed to be too much, and he collapsed back on the floor. "He's the one that killed my attacker. There were two of them. Thought I'd be easy. We showed them."

"Do you know who is trying to take your place? Who is the new boss now?"

A faint smile drifted across the ancient's face. "There will be two – until they fight to the death."

"A challenge?" Goran asked. "Haven't had one of those in a long time."

Serus spoke up, "And I doubt there will be one now. Chances are that one will kill the other before it comes to a proper fight."

The ancient laughed and laughed, but the sound was so broken and pained that it just felt off. Tessa wanted to calm him down, offer him some comfort, but at the same time she wanted to stab him with silver and finish him off.

"You think you know what's going on here, but you don't know anything. Many fingers are spreading out into the world. You can try, but you'll never stop this. It's too big. Too widespread."

"Maybe, but that doesn't mean we can't shut this mess down on our end."

The old ancient coughed several times, blood and something else sliding from the corner of his mouth as he collapsed yet again. "Maybe, but you don't know who you're really fighting with or against. I'm the last on my level. Moltere will not survive the experiments that I volunteered him for. We used to be partners. Now the young dogs will fight." A horrible rictus of a grin slipped out, making Tessa shudder.

"You hung Moltere up there? Why?"

"He carried our bloodline. Thought we could put it into other lines. Create bigger, better vamps."

"Well you did do that," Cody snapped. "But they are also more stupid."

"Yeah, but then they weren't all that bright in the first place. Look at what they signed up for."

"And Darren? What did that kid ever do to you? He's a young vamp. He could have had a wonderful life."

"That was young Jacob's idea. He hated Darren. Wanted him gone. So I put him in the experimental program. He can't survive the farm either. No vamp can. Or humans, for that matter."

"Are you sure about the humans? Some of them are young. They haven't been hanging for very long."

"Maybe the younger ones in the new farm. But not the others. Too late for them." He tried to shrug, but the movement obviously hurt too much. He opened his mouth and gasped, "No matter. It's too late for all of you as well."

A short silence swept over everyone.

Cody leaned down and grabbed the ancient by the shoulders. "Why? What have you done?"

"Me, nothing." He could hardly get the words out. "It's the new boss. It's what he's done. And you have no idea who that is. And you aren't going to like it when you find out."

Cody shook the dying man hard. "Who are you talking about?"

A weird rattling sound came loose and the ancient's eyes rolled into the back of his head.

Cody dropped him back down.

The frail ancient barely made a thud as he hit the floor.

Goran bent over and checked for a pulse, then looked up at the group. "He's dead."

JARED HID IN the shadows, cursing that he'd stayed behind all alone. Surely someone else could have stayed behind with him. He didn't use to hate being alone. But after almost being hung in that damn place, it was a little hard to not think about those that lurked in the dark.

Vampires. God, he hated them.

That thought pulled him up short. Because he didn't. Not really. He hated the asshole vamps. The ones who'd put in the farm, but he didn't hate Rhia or David and certainly not Tessa. Although Cody... No, he might be an asshole and after Tessa, but hate was too strong a word for how he viewed him. Besides, the guy had a hand in saving Jared's ass.

The sound of a truck coming up the road brought his head around from the garage entrance he'd been watching. Given the fact that Jared was more or less helpless against a vamp's strength, he'd been half hoping that the bad vamps wouldn't come up to the surface.

Typical.

The sound of a heavy engine grew louder. He considered his position, then decided to slip around the side of the house just in case these guys were looking to go inside. He'd have no place to go should that be the case. Alternatively, he could run across and hide near the garage entrance to the blood farm. As he quickly considered the pros and cons, he realized that his view would be much better from the other side.

He dashed across and slipped into the shadows just as a vehicle came into view.

❧ ❧

RHIA MANAGED TO step to the side at the last minute as the door opened, letting two vamps in. She jumped the first one and pulled him into a headlock as two of the guards that had followed her jumped the second. Neither intruder made a sound as they collapsed to the ground.

Breathing heavily, Rhia pulled the helmet off the first man.

She didn't know him at all. "Anyone know this guy?"

"Yeah, he works for Councilman Stenger."

Rhia looked up and pinned him in place. "Are you sure?"

The guard nodded. The second guard beside him spoke up. "He's a bodyguard."

Rhia looked over at Sian, a question in her eyes.

"I'd take him out. If he didn't come here with us, he came here because he knew of the place."

"Anyone got a problem with that?"

She didn't get a chance to get an answer. Councilman Adamson reached down and did something. The vamp jerked once, then a second time before becoming still.

Rhia stepped back and stared at him. "What did you do?"

He held up his hand to show her a weird metal ring that released a sharp object when he flipped a tiny switch. "It's a special alloy. A blend of silver and other metals. It kills vamps but doesn't burn them."

The closest guard walked over. "It would be better to burn them. This way, we have to deal with the body."

"And what about this second one," asked the guards standing over the second motionless vamp. "Same thing?"

"Take off his helmet," the councilman said.

When they did, Rhia gasped and said, "But that's Jacob's

brother."

Sian looked down at the vamp on the ground. "I don't know Jacob or this one. I've seen him around of course, but never had a name to put to him."

"He's also an apprentice at the council. Also to Councilman Toncher." Councilman Adamson frowned, pulled out his cell phone and texted someone.

Rhia waited for him to make a decision. She was all for culling the vampire society of the assholes, but they had to make sure that they were assholes. And how did one know?

Adamson's cell phone rang. "Gloria?" He appeared to listen for a bit, and then nodded. "Okay, we have Jordan and Paul, the apprentice on the council. Make a note somewhere so we can keep track of who is involved. Right." He closed his phone, nodded to the guards and said, "Kill him. From here on out, if the vamps are in the wrong place, we kill them."

The guard pulled out some kind of small gun and before Rhia could blink, Jacob's brother burned to ash. She stepped back, realizing how deep and destructive these next few days were really going to be.

"Let's go." Councilman Adamson said, "We're behind schedule."

CHAPTER 15

D AVID LOOKED DOWN at the vamp near Cody's feet. "Hard to get answers from a dead man."

"Good thing we brought along a spare." Goran grabbed the second man and tossed him in front of the group. The vamp groaned.

Tessa turned away. The whole killing while in the midst of a battle was one thing. Torturing them for answers, that was a whole other issue. She couldn't do it.

She felt more than saw someone come up beside her. Jewel. A sick looking Jewel.

"Not into torture?" Tessa asked lightly, already knowing the answer.

Jewel's skin took on a greener tinge. She shook her head, sending her hair flying everywhere. "So not," she whispered. "I can't stand what this whole place is about. I so want to leave."

"Let's hope he hands over the answers we need," Tessa answered quietly. "Personally, I've had enough death for a lifetime. And considering how old we can live, that is saying something."

"A couple of weeks ago, I'd never have believed everything we've gone through was even remotely possible."

"Nor would I." Tessa studied the dark blank walls of the strange room. "I went to the movies with a group of friends and started a war."

"It's not your fault," Jewel said softly. "You know that, right?"

Tessa quirked her lips in response. "Still…"

"No." Jewel shook her head again. "We needed to know. Needed to stop this. Needed to save those poor people."

"I don't think they can be saved." And that was a hard pill to swallow. "We did this to them. What kind of animals are we?"

"Not us. The others. The old ones."

"Not all of them or all of us. Goran and my parents had nothing to do with this. And we can't say none of the younger group had anything to do with this – look at Jacob."

There was a sad silence.

"We can only be responsible for our own actions." Jewel stared out into the darkness but from the unfocused look in her eyes, Tessa knew she wasn't really seeing anything.

"True enough. And be authentic to who we are every step of the way."

At that statement, Jewel turned to look at her. "I've learned more about myself these last few days than all the years I've been alive."

"You already knew who you were, you just became better acquainted," Tessa said fairly. "You're still the same girl. Just remembering, understanding, and recognizing who and what that is."

Jewel laughed lightly. "You're years younger than me and in some ways years older."

"Yeah, sometimes life dishes out things and what you thought you were getting turns out to be something completely different." Tessa smiled. "I've just learned to take it and say thanks anyways."

Jewel smiled, the first real smile Tessa had seen out of her in a long time.

She opened her mouth, hesitated and then said slowly, softly, "I want to apologize."

Tessa turned to face her more fully. She tilted her head and looked at Jewel. Her face looked so sad. What was this all about? "Really? For what?"

"For before." Jewel said painfully. "For the way I treated you. I didn't know you. But I *knew* you, or thought I did. And like all the others, I laughed and said some things that I'm not proud of now."

Tessa was silent, wondering what it cost the other girl to admit that. "I can't say it doesn't matter, because back then, it *did* matter," she said honestly. Sometimes it had hurt a lot. "People did a lot of stuff to hurt me. To make themselves feel better at my expense. And it was painful."

She sighed. "But like you said, you didn't know me. And like you also just said, you've learned a lot about who you really are. So what matters... is what you do from here on out."

Jewel stared at Tessa. Her face was blank, as if she hadn't expected that response. And true enough, Tessa hadn't expected it either. It sounded a little too philosophical to be her own words. The thing was, as she thought about all that she'd discussed with Jewel, they were true. And she meant every word she said.

Tears came to Jewel's eyes.

Tessa gasped. "Oh don't cry. Please don't cry."

Jewel laughed, yet tears still pooled in the corners of her eyes. "I never cry."

"I always figured it was just my throwback genes," Tessa joked, hoping it would stop the waterworks before they really got started.

"No." Jewel wiped the corner of her eyes. "I am tired, and feeling shitty, but that's not the only reason. You are a good person, Tessa, and I for one have learned to see beneath the surface to what is really on the inside."

"And that's a good thing," Tessa joked, "'Cause my brother is uuugly!"

Jewel gasped, then burst into howls of laughter.

David chose that moment to approach them, his face both wary and curious. "Okay, so what the hell is going on over here?"

Tessa grinned at him. "Oh nothing. Just a little girl talk."

David's step faltered. And now he looked worried. Jewel couldn't stop laughing. She took the last few steps and hurled herself into David's arms. He gave Tessa one last wary look before wrapping his arms around Jewel and holding her close.

I heard that. Cody's warm voice swept through her mind, melting her insides. *Nice job.*

Someone had to let her off the hook. She didn't do anything different from everyone else.

Not me. Besides, that's nasty girl type behavior.

It is. But then lots of guys like to get in touch with their feminine side.

The gasp of horror in her mind had Tessa laughing. She turned to find him in the crowd and saw him beside her father, staring at her.

Not a hobby of yours?

He glared at her. *So not.*

She giggled.

Serus glanced at Cody. "Did you say something?"

"Only to your irritating daughter," Cody snapped. Then realized what he'd said and to whom. He groaned and backed up quickly. "Sorry, sir."

Serus laughed. "Don't apologize to me. You're just starting on this journey. I've been living with her mother for centuries. You've got a lot to learn."

"And you're blessed to have Mom, aren't you, Dad?" Tessa walked close enough to stand between the two men. When he didn't answer, she repeated her last sentence with force, "Aren't you, Dad?"

He chuckled. "That I am. And you, for that matter."

She grinned and was reaching out to Cody when the vamp on the ground suddenly surged up in a smooth move. Something flashed in his hand.

"Look out," Goran shouted.

Cody and Serus stepped forward to grab him, but he spun and twisted and stabbed. Goran's hand flashed. But not fast enough.

Just before Goran's spike found his mark, the prisoner drove a silver spike through Tessa's hand.

❧ ❧

JARED WATCHED AS the vehicle pulled up and parked. It was an old car. Beaten up and rusted out. So not what Jared had been expecting. The driver got out. He looked human, but Jared wasn't exactly betting that he was a good human. A lot of bad humans had taken part in this blood farm.

He waited, camera ready for a chance to take a picture of the man's face. A second human exited from the passenger side. No uniforms. No bags. Nothing.

And that made him leery. He watched to see what they'd do. Was Taz coming in a separate vehicle? Or did these guys know of this place because they'd been here before? There were no other people exiting the vehicle so he assumed it was just the two of them.

But then they walked toward the garage – and him.

Shit. He ducked out of sight. Good thing he could still hear the conversation.

"No one is here."

"No one is topside, you mean. The others could be down below."

One guy coughed several times before continuing. "I doubt it. Most are too scared to go down there in case they never get out."

"Well, they did pull Peter out of the last meeting and made an example out of him. Remember that."

Jared shuddered. He didn't want to know what they meant by that. He kept an ear tuned in to the conversation.

"Hell, I'll never forget. This place is my worst nightmare."

"Just a couple more jobs and we can get the hell away from here for good."

"Says you." The man's voice rose to a high-pitched whine. "I'm afraid they won't ever let us go."

"Nah. You heard the boss." The first man coughed a second time, his voice hoarse as he answered, "They just need us to take care of the doctors they got locked up inside."

"Great, now we're killing our own doctors. And why us?" There went that high-pitched voice again. "They sent us up here just for that? They could have taken care of this on their own."

Jared had to ask the same question. Then he realized these guys had come to take care of the medical team that he'd helped rescue.

"Maybe it's a test. We're not exactly on their good side after the last couple of problems we had."

"It wasn't our fault. Jesus, those kids are a pain in the ass."

"That one wasn't supposed to leave the group home alive, remember?"

Jared closed his eyes, scared to breathe in case they heard him. This was his first confirmation that he had been targeted. And boy, was he glad he'd chosen to go to Tessa's house instead of returning to that home.

"Yeah, but that wasn't our fault. By the time we got there to haul him down to the station, he'd booked it. Hell, everyone there is in deep shit."

Back to the station? Oh crap. Jared finally realized that these two were cops. They weren't in uniform and they certainly didn't look official, so they were likely off duty. Also, he'd never seen them before.

"Yeah, but not like we're in trouble for that. We didn't do anything wrong. It's just things didn't go right."

"I think they are the same thing to the boss."

Their voices faded slightly as the garage floor lowered, the grinding noise drowning them out.

Jared peered through a hole in the wall and took a few pictures before they were too low to get a face shot. His mind was still reeling from what he'd heard. He had left to buy a new cell phone and while he'd been gone, they'd actually come for him. Jesus. The close call scared the crap out of him.

And then he thought about what he knew and what they didn't.

The vamps had done something to the mountain so that everyone in there wouldn't survive. And those guys were sent to go down there anyway.

He smiled.

Maybe there was justice after all.

RHIA STAYED IN the vehicle when they arrived at the next place. Sian sat beside her. They were talking to Gloria, who was coordinating the raids from the council headquarters. So far, the other buildings had been taken without a hitch. A good half dozen or more vamps had been taken captive and the rest had been killed. The captives were being transferred to the human jail. That was the safest place for the moment. And the cops had silver on them in case the vamps resisted.

The captured vamps had all been low-level operatives and appeared cooperative. Then again, they were vamps, and that made them liars and cheats and not trustworthy. For all anyone knew, they could be much higher up on the food chain.

They had just arrived at what Rhia hoped was the last warehouse. It was much larger than the others. Because of that, they had a second team here for back up. There were still suppliers to pick up. Apparently, several Special Forces teams were rounding them up. It was assumed that they were humans, but who knew?

The sweep had been going wonderfully well.

And that scared her.

It was going too well. That meant it was going seriously bad somewhere for someone. Given the news Taz had passed on, she just hoped to hell that it wasn't with her family.

"Taz is trying to organize a biohazard team to go up with him and the other doctors. And a military team. They'll check out the place first. Who knows what these assholes might have done?"

"Or are planning to do."

Sian reached across the seat. "We'll get your family out."

Rhia smiled and clasped Sian's hand. "I know. I just feel so helpless. It seems like they've been up there forever."

"Not that long really. Besides, with it being daylight, there is only so much they can do. They could be hiding out in the trees again."

Rhia knew Sian was trying to make her feel better, but if Serus was hiding out in the trees he'd have contacted her by now. Especially after not doing so the last time. She hadn't done it in front of the kids, but she'd reamed him out good in private. They could communicate, so therefore they *should* communicate. Especially now. Especially when her whole family was inside that torture chamber.

"Oh, there's something here from Gloria."

"What?" Rhia leaned over to see a large image open up on the laptop screen. "What is that?"

"I don't know." Sian rotated it. "But I'm thinking it might be a blueprint of the mountain. Or at least part of the mountain."

Rhia looked closer. "There's the garage that Tessa found. That's where we entered."

"And there is the blood farm below." Sian used a long nail to outline the path that led down below. "This is great. We should be able to have the entire thing searched this way. Look at all these rooms."

"I don't understand all the writing, but some of it appear to be under construction. Like there, it says Phase 3, medical labs. Look how big that area is."

"And what do they need medical labs there for?"

Sian and Rhia stared at each other.

"For experiments. Drug experiments?"

"We certainly know about those." Rhia studied the drawings carefully. "There is the mini railway. And look at the other end of it. There are all kinds of rooms in there. We'll have to make sure we check them all out."

"It could be another warehouse. Look at how the small room on the side seems to lead deeper into the mountain. And to that massive cavern or room ahead."

"I wonder what's in there." Sian wondered.

"Nothing good."

CHAPTER 16

P AIN LIKE SHE'D never experienced before shot through
Tessa's body and mind. She understood that the silver
stake had been removed from her hand and that blood
dripped steadily from the injury. But comprehending anything more than that was beyond her. Ice and fire melded in
her palm. The ice was winning. Was that a good thing?

She could hear the shouts and screams all around her, but
it was the voice in her mind that she latched on to.

Cody.

Hold on, Tessa. We're trying to help you.

There's nothing you can do. That's silver.

*But you're not fully vampire. Maybe we can save you. We
have to try.*

Shakes slithered through her tired body. *I'm so tired. Feel
so odd.*

*Don't sleep. You have to stay awake. The silver didn't incin-
erate you, so something is working.*

Old vampire. Poison.

*No. I won't accept that. Call on your human genes to fight.
Throw it off. Silver isn't poisonous to humans like it is to vamps.*

She understood what he was saying, but it was hard to do
anything. Her body shivered as if some internal battle waged
deep inside. Her head felt heavy. Too heavy to hold up. She
wanted to drop it, only to realize she was being held in Cody's

arms. He was trying to support her, trying to keep her alive.

It's too late, she whispered. *I might be a hybrid, but my vamp system is in shock.*

That's good. Your throwback genes can handle this. It can spit out the poison from your system with no problem. But you need to call on it like you do for your vampire genes. I've heard you. When you're tired or frustrated at not being able to do something. I've heard you call on your vampire heritage to pick up the slack. Now you need to call on the human side of your body. You are both.

Am I? My mother said her great-grandmother, a Leant, was like me. Maybe I'm just two different types of vampire.

And that's fine too. But whatever you are — you can do this. Look, you're still alive. Any of us would be ash by now. You didn't get scratched, you were stabbed. The spike went clean through your hand. You're not burning up; you're not even showing signs of starting to smoke. You're weak. You're cold. That's good. Use that to fight off the poison.

My hand...

Yes. I know. But the hand is still there. And yes, there is some kind of discoloration around the injury but you can still move your fingers. Right? Tessa, move your fingers, he urged. *Let me see.*

She tried to feel her hand, but that damn iciness made it almost impossible.

Come on, damn it.

She struggled past the numbness, struggled past the pain, and urged her fingers to move.

Tessa?

Trying to.

Try harder. Now.

And she did. Her fingers, coated in fiery burns, moved.

The effort it took to make that happen was too much to handle. She slipped into the deep dark abyss waiting for her. The last thing she heard as she went under was Cody's cry.

Tessa? Tessa!

☙ ❧

HORROR AND ANGER surged through Serus as he stared at his beloved daughter. This was one time that he really hoped her throwback genes carried human DNA.

"It's a good sign that she's still alive," Ian said with forced cheer.

Jewel said, "Not if she's going to die slowly, poisoned like the old vamp."

Cody shifted her in his arms. "She was talking to me until just a few minutes ago. I made her move her fingers to prove her hand was still functioning. That the poison wasn't working further though her system." He rested his cheek on the top of her head. "It was after making that effort that she became unconscious."

"Maybe that's a good thing," Goran said, "Maybe her humanity will save her."

"Only we don't know exactly what she is, do we?" Serus snapped. "We've all treated her like she was part human, but according to Rhia she might be part Leant. And although they were vamps, they were different in so many ways."

"But she's alive." Goran pointed out. "And she doesn't appear to be showing the same symptoms as that old asshole."

"Or it's too early to tell. Does anyone know what silver does to humans?"

Ian said, "Outside of metal poisoning, I don't think there's anything to worry about. They wear jewelry made of the stuff." He leaned closer. "Look at her hand. It's pulpy around the edges, but it's not even black. If that were any of us…"

"We wouldn't be here to talk about it. We know." David straightened from his crouched position. "I wish we could ask Taz."

"He's not going to be able to help us. No one is. Like so much in her life, Tessa is going to have to handle this battle on her own," Goran said, his voice sober but calm. "We have to trust that she can do that. Vamp. Human. Something else. As she's already done so much we didn't know about, who knows what else she's capable of doing?"

"Look." Jewel exclaimed. "Look at her hand."

Everyone crowded around Serus to the point that he had trouble seeing anything. "Back up," he ordered. Then he carefully lifted Tessa's injured hand for everyone to see.

"Wow," David said in a soft shocked voice. "How is that possible?"

"If she was vampire and it was anything other than silver – it's what we'd be doing."

"So she can survive silver and heal like a vamp?" Ian asked. "I think I'm jealous."

"She hasn't survived yet, and the effort to heal appears to take a lot more out of her than it would from us. We normally regain our health and strength much faster and without the same effort. She's unconscious, for heaven's sake. That would kill us in battle. Our enemies would finish the job while we struggled to heal."

Serus nodded. "True, but Tessa shouldn't be in this battle. I've been saying that since the beginning."

CODY LET THE conversations and suppositions go on around him. He didn't care what conclusion they reached – he just wanted to hear Tessa's voice again. To know that she was going to be fine. This connection with her was a part of him now. He couldn't have imagined such a thing happening before, but now he couldn't imagine life without it. The dead emptiness in his mind right now was horrible. Like a massive black pit. Cold and dark. Waiting for someone to return. Someone who was having trouble finding her way back.

Tessa? Are you there? Please be there. Talk to me.

Silence

He closed his eyes. He didn't know what to do for her. No one did. He understood his father's words to mean that this was new for Tessa too, and she'd have to handle this on her own. But that didn't make it any easier. Cody needed her in his life.

A sudden movement had him lifting his head to look at her. She shifted again, trying to move. But her eyes were closed along with her mind. He couldn't sense her at all.

She twisted as if in agony, but her face was pale and expressionless.

"What's she doing?"

Cody thought it was Ian who asked, but no one had an answer. They could only watch as Tessa's body struggled.

"Look at her hand now."

Serus raised her hand again so they could all see. The puckered edges of the fleshy palm was slowly becoming smooth again.

Jewel gasped. "Is that hole closing?"

It was hard to see as the flesh had closed in on itself after the spike was removed. It had left a bloody red circle but as Cody stared, it appeared that the circle in the palm of her hand was getting smaller.

"She is healing!" he exclaimed.

"Good. Now do we all stand guard here while it's happening, or should some of us head off and look for more assholes?" Ian asked.

"We stay here. Together." Serus said. "No more splitting off."

"Besides," Goran said. "We came here to meet the bosses. We met them and killed them. Sounds like it's time to go home. We could just as easily carry Tessa down to the tunnel and exit through the other side. Can't say I'd be sorry to get out of this place."

Jewels faint gasp of hope had Cody considering the issue. He could easily carry Tessa. But was that the right thing to do? How could getting the hell out of here be wrong?

"What about the other bosses," David asked. "The ones they wouldn't tell us about?"

"I don't think we will be able to find them now." Serus straightened but stayed close to Cody and Tessa. "I think given Tessa's condition, we need to get her out of here and home as fast as possible. We have to keep her safe until she's strong enough to fight off any attackers."

"To that end, I suggest we get back down those stairs and through the tunnel to the outside." Goran said, straightening up to look back at the way they'd come.

Ian nodded.

David stood up and wrapped an arm around Jewel's shoulders. "I guess we've done our part. Now it's time to get some help in here to take care of the rest. I think you mentioned Gloria would be able to contact people to help." He looked over at Goran. "It would be good to get out, reconnect with everyone, and create some kind of organized plan to finish this." He looked down at his sister. "Her safety comes first and I know Jewel is tired. She needs to go home and rest too."

"So am I." Ian snorted. "I like a good fight as well as the next guy, but this fight never seems to end. I really hate not being able to fly."

"Good." Goran placed a hand on Cody shoulder. "Are you carrying her or am I?"

"I am." Like hell he was letting anyone else take Tessa anywhere. She wasn't that heavy and he was an ancient like his father. He stood up in one smooth move, shifted Tessa's body in his arms, and looked at his father. "If I need to switch off, I'll let you know." But his voice was hard, as if to say it wouldn't happen.

Goran stared from Tessa's unconscious face to his son's and sighed. "Fine."

Serus wasn't so agreeable. "Are you sure?"

Cody glared at him. "I'm fine. And I've flown with her before." Surely the gentle reminder that it had been Cody who had saved her before wouldn't hurt right now.

Serus's gaze was hard as he stared into Cody's eyes. "If you need help, tell us. She's been through enough without you dropping her."

He turned away, leaving Cody gasping. "I wouldn't drop her," he muttered out loud.

David smacked him on the shoulder. "Nope, you wouldn't. And if he didn't believe that, he wouldn't be letting you carry her either."

"Now that's all settled, can we get out of here, please?" Jewel's voice trembled with exhaustion. "This place is getting on my nerves. I can't help but think something else is going to go wrong before we're all safe and sound."

"Yeah, they have bad guys hiding around more corners than I could imagine this place having." Ian turned to study the large open empty room. "This place is a nightmare."

"It's actually a maze, and given a chance to reconnect with a laptop, I'd love to track down some blueprints. I think we need to do a complete sweep and make sure that no one is left behind in one of the many hidden rooms here. And after all this time, we still haven't found any sign of the three other blood farms."

"I wish we had a way to contact Motre."

"There are going to be many captives here somewhere." David pointed out. "And we'll find them, but not right now. We'll come back with help."

Jewel turned to look at the closed door where they had originally entered. "Did we close that door?"

Cody got a horrible sinking feeling in his stomach as he turned to look. "No. I don't think so."

The ancients were staring at the door. Goran reached out and kicked it. Nothing. Serus did the same.

Still nothing.

Shit. Cody dropped his head. He was getting damn tired of this place.

❧ ❧

JARED WAS TIRED of waiting around. Talk about an anticlimatic ending. He'd been sitting here for an hour. The two humans hadn't returned to the surface and Taz hadn't returned with more staff.

Like what the hell?

Part of him wanted action while the rest just wanted answers. He couldn't help but feel it was too late for his father.

Taz hadn't been hopeful, and depending on what the assholes had done to the blood farm – if anything – then his father might be gone for good.

A father he'd only just realized he'd had. Grief and anger and yes...hatred burned inside him.

He stared at the garage entrance. His father was dead, or more or less dead. What did he do with that? He couldn't grieve properly because his father wasn't really dead. And until Taz came back with specialists that said he couldn't be saved...he wasn't ready to let go of the idea. He loved the thought of living out the rest of his life with his father at his side.

That he had no mother either made his insides hurt. Could she be in there too? He didn't think he ever knew what had happened to her. But if his uncle could have, he'd have gotten rid of her too. Bile rose up in the back of his throat. Surely not.

But how to know for sure? He looked at his cell phone and wondered. What could he find out from here?

RHIA WALKED INTO the council chambers. The building hummed with activity. Probably Gloria's doing. Tired and worn out, she headed to the back office. At least it was quiet here. Out of the way of the hurried plans being set into motion.

As soon as she closed the door behind her, she collapsed on one of the chairs and dropped her head onto her folded arms. She couldn't think straight any more. The drugs were still slowly making its way out of her system. She was tired and worried. She had not heard back from anyone in her family. Sian was talking to Taz and they were pulling more teams together. Medical teams as well this time. Everyone was heading to the mountain.

She hated that place. Hated what it represented and what it was trying to take from her. The irony that all those people hanging had been taken from someone else wasn't lost on her. But she wasn't going to let more people be lost.

It bothered her that Jared had stayed up there. He should be home where he'd be safe. Nothing up there was safe anymore – for human or vampire.

That mountain was sucking the life out of everyone.

Sian rushed in and then came to a skittering stop. "There you are. I've been looking all over for you. Taz says they have enough men to search the mountain and keep the two entrances covered. With backup all around the mountain in case there are other exits."

"Which there are as far as we know because Tessa was able to escape high above the snow line."

"Right. Well, I don't know that they thought about that potential exit, but there are going to be helicopters in the air as well doing an aerial search for anyone trying to escape the military net."

Rhia groaned but pulled herself upright. "I'm coming."

"Actually," Sian said, "I want to go, but I agreed to stay here and work with Gloria."

As much as Rhia would love to have Sian by her side, she understood. She nodded. "Yes, her hands are full, aren't they? Between picking up all the suppliers and shutting down those businesses and storage places, she needs all the help she can get."

Besides, Sian was pregnant. She should stay here. "I'm going though."

Sian looked at her, sorrow, regret, and determination on her face. "No. You're not."

Now that she hadn't expected. Sure, she'd thought Sian might argue, maybe try to talk her out of it. But not this 'the decision is made and I know you won't like it' tone of voice.

"Why is that?" Rhia stiffened, sure she wasn't going to like the next part.

Sian stayed silent for a long moment, and then said, "Because they left 10 minutes ago."

Rhia's breath froze in her chest. Pain and anguish filled her. "Why," she whispered. "Why couldn't I go?"

"Because Taz promised Serus he'd keep you safe. No matter what." And that was that her tone said. She'd do anything to make that happen too. "Serus would do anything to keep you safe. As I know Taz feels the same way about me."

Instead of the expected anger, tears sprung to Rhia's eyes. It was something she hadn't felt in a very long time. "I don't want to live if I lose my family," she whispered.

"And that's another reason you have to stay here. They are trying to get to *you*. If they succeed and you have returned to the blood farm, the whole lot of them will turn around and try to find you." Sian gazed at her solemnly. "This is best for everyone."

Rhia swallowed. "God, I hope you're right. Because if you're wrong..." she didn't finish the sentence. She couldn't. Sobs had clogged her throat. She turned and walked away.

As she left the room she barely heard Sian's sad whisper. "I do too."

CHAPTER 17

CODY STARED AT the closed door then down at his precious burden. Tessa appeared completely unconscious, her body soft and warm but harder to carry than if she were awake and holding on to him. "We need to find a way through that door, everyone."

"We're working on it," Serus snapped. He cast a quick glance over at Tessa then turned his efforts back to the closed and apparently impenetrable door.

"Or another exit," suggested Jewel.

Cody spun slowly, holding Tessa gently as he surveyed the large empty room. "I can't see any other exit."

Ian piped up, "And Tessa only saw the energy up at the top where you guys tangled with the two vamps."

Goran turned to look at him as if he'd said something surprising. Then he looked down at the remains of the vamps beside them. "That's actually a good point. The younger vamp didn't have any wings. How did he get up there?"

"Maybe he's a glider?" Serus suggested.

With a smirk, Goran turned to Serus. "I wouldn't tell you this under any other circumstance, but you are no ordinary glider. I doubt most could make it up to that office space like you did."

Cody had actually wondered about that because Serus was well known for his prowess whereas Wendy, another glider who'd been in on the initial search for Jared couldn't begin to do what Serus was capable of doing. He'd put it down to Wendy's age, but he didn't think so now. He looked up to where they'd found the dying vamp. There's no way another glider could jump that high. He vaguely remembered seeing Serus bounce off walls getting higher each time but still...

"You're thinking there is another way in or out from up there?" Jewel asked. "I don't think I can get up there."

"I'll go take a look." Goran took to the air while Serus resumed kicking the door in front of him.

"I should be able to knock this thing over, and yet it's still standing."

"As in vampire proof?" Ian walked over to search for the seams of the doorway. "That doesn't make any sense. This was a place *for* vamps. Why would they be trying to keep vamps out?"

"Probably only select vamps." Cody stared down at Tessa's pale skin. He wished she'd wake up. He hated seeing her like this. And although he was strong, he hoped he didn't have to carry for too long. Showing weakness wouldn't go down well. He did not want to have to ask someone else for help.

A shout sounded from above. Everyone glanced up to see Goran jumping over the edge of the half wall to land gently in front of them. "Tessa was right. There is another door up there. I haven't tried to open it. Thought maybe we should stick together."

Serus nodded. "It's going to take a few trips."

Goran grinned. "Sure will."

With a big laugh, he snatched Jewel up out of David's arms and jumped into the air.

Serus shook his head and took off after his friend, David

on his back.

Within minutes, Goran had returned, nodded at Ian to grab hold of him, then checked with Cody. "Son, are you going to be okay?"

Cody glared at him and lifted off, Tessa cradled in his arms. The distance was short, the space wide open so he could use his wings to land gently enough and not jar Tessa.

He folded his wings back and waited. While he watched, Serus walked to the new door and gave it a hard kick.

Silently, it swung inward.

❧ ❦

GORAN STEPPED THROUGH the doorway. No matter what they did, they were being forced to go deeper into the mountain. He came to a standstill.

Yeah, he might be old compared to these kids in the group, but he got it eventually. He turned, caught Serus's gaze over the heads of the others and said, "I'm starting to wonder if we aren't being herded in a certain direction. As if maybe they want us here in this place."

Serus's gazed hardened as he understood.

"That's not likely." David said. "Think about it. How would they know that we'd find this door?"

Everyone turned to look at the unconscious Tessa.

"Okay, so they might think we'd find our way here, but they couldn't *know* that we would."

"True." Goran turned back to the dark passage in front of him. It looked like another mine tunnel. Only there were no white tiles covering the walls or the floor. They really had no other option at this point. With the others following behind, he walked forward cautiously, having a hard time letting go of the idea that this was another trap.

A few more steps and he hit a corner. There was a new tunnel covered with white tiles. Maybe this was another way into the blood farm? Was that possible? Knowing that they were going to be more exposed against the bright tiles, he crept forward, a hand up behind in warning to the others.

A second corner loomed – and sounds filtered toward him.

∂≈ ∈∂

STUPID. HE SHOULD have left with Taz. He couldn't believe he was still sitting here all alone. No one had come out of the blood farm and no one else had arrived. His butt hurt and he was hungry. Hell, he was always hungry. How many meals had he missed when he was drugged in that damn place anyway? Technically none as they had fed him intravenously, but that didn't make up for hamburgers, fries, and milkshakes.

His stomach growled. He so shouldn't be thinking about food. He shifted his position and studied his cell phone. He'd been trying to track down the property owners and had found the name had been changed a dozen times in the last couple of centuries. Cool that all the registration records were online. So not cool that he only had a cell phone.

He could really use a laptop screen at this point. It would be easier.

Just as he switched websites again, he heard a noise coming up the road.

Please let it be Taz. He'd said he'd be back hours ago. At this point, Jared wasn't sure if he was pissed that the guy hadn't shown up or scared that something had happened to him.

Either way, Jared was tired of waiting around. The noise grew louder. And louder. It sounded heavy. He hopped to his feet and ran back to his hiding place behind the garage shed.

And waited.

❧ ❧

RHIA WALKED INTO the main room of the council hall to find Gloria and Sian working on laptops, phones at their ears.

She didn't want to be at this end of the action. She understood the logic of keeping her here, but she didn't agree with it. That's because she knew one thing – if her family died because this war, then she'd rather die with them.

The others wouldn't understand.

For a vampire, eternal life was the thing to preserve. She didn't have the same outlook. But she had something most of them didn't have – she had a family.

Sian would understand somewhat. She'd really understand when her baby was born. Until then, she only had a glimpse of that emotion that Rhia grappled with.

And Rhia knew the cost of this war. She'd seen it before. Had lived it before. She and Serus had survived back then, but the odds were against all her family surviving this time. And that scared her shitless.

Speaking of family, her sister just walked into the front hall.

Rhia stiffened. She had no proof her sister was involved. Either of her sisters. But it's something they'd certainly condone. Humans were food for them.

"There you are. I've been trying to catch up with you all day. You could have told me about the laptop, you know," she complained. "Instead I had to find out through Gloria."

Rhia spun around and stared at Sian, her mind racing. She could see the same questions mirrored in Sian's gaze.

"I didn't know you knew Gloria that well?" Rhia said, managing to keep her voice level and calm while inside, her heart raced. Had she trusted the wrong person? Her gaze switched to look at Gloria. Gloria lifted her head, her gaze going from one sister to the other, and then she rolled her eyes and dropped her gaze back to her laptop.

"Of course I do. So do you."

Gittoria walked closer. "Are you sure you should be out of hospital?"

Rhia stepped back instinctively. "I'm fine."

"I don't think you are, you know." Gittoria leaned a little closer. "You're not acting normal. I think you should let the doctors check you out again."

Rhia stared into the blackness of her sister's gaze and wondered at the extent of her involvement. She couldn't bring herself to trust in her siblings. Either of them. They were both catty bitches to the highest vampire order and they only did what was good for them.

"I'm fine." Rhia cast another glance over at Sian, then with a slight tilt of her head. "But I think I will go lie down."

"Good idea. Maybe I should watch over you."

Rhia snorted. "Like hell. You're just as likely to kill me." Her words found their target.

Gittoria stepped back, her head tilting to the side, a mocking look on her face. "Like I said, you aren't acting rationally."

"If anyone is going to watch over me, it will be Sian. But thanks for the offer."

She turned to walk away and found Sian already at her side, saying. "Let's go. It's actually not a bad idea to lie down, you know."

"I can't rest." Rhia kept her voice low so as to not be overheard. A quick glance around told her she needn't have worried. Gittoria had gone to speak with Gloria.

"What the hell is going on? Why is she here?"

"I don't know. If you go and lie down so I don't have to worry about you, I might be able to find out."

Rhia pushed her towards the other two. "Go now. I don't trust my sister. And if she's good friends with Gloria, I'm not sure I trust her either."

"I'll go see what they are up to."

Rhia walked to the door and waited for Sian to slip back into her spot and become engrossed in her laptop. She would get to the bottom of this. Of all the people in the hall, Sian was the one she trusted the most.

CHAPTER 18

"**C**AN WE MOVE a little faster?" Cody muttered. The tunnel stretched endlessly in front of him.

"I said I'd carry her." Serus's growl washed over him.

"I'm fine. But if there is some way out up ahead, I'd like to reach it." Cody walked forward slowly, knowing he should just shut up. Everyone wanted out, not just him. He looked down at Tessa in his arms. She's the one who really needed to get out.

He stopped suddenly. Was her color pinker? Or was that just the different light?

"What's the matter?" Serus crowded closer and peered down at Tessa. "Has something changed? Is she awake?"

"No, but I think her color is brighter."

Serus snorted. "Well that isn't much help. Now if she'd wake up…"

As if on cue, Tessa tried to move. Cody held her tighter, not wanting to drop her in case she was about to start struggling. Then she moaned.

"Tessa?" Cody said, "Take it easy. You're going to be just fine." At least he hoped she would.

"Tessa?" Serus said, "Can you hear me? Talk to me if you can."

Tessa groaned again, but she stayed motionless. Cody wondered if they should try to wake her or if she'd just go under again. It might be better if she slipped under until she was fully healed.

Then she opened her eyes and stared at him.

And frowned.

Cody?

Hey. There you are. How are you feeling?

Her eyes drifted closed and she slipped away without answering.

He raised his head to stare at Serus. "She said my name but now she's gone under again."

Serus frowned. He reached out and stroked her forehead. "Guess it's not a bad thing. She seems to be healing at least."

"I hope so." Cody shifted her weight gently in his arms and strode ahead. What he really wanted was out of this damn hellhole and get back home.

Me too.

There you are. Cody laughed. "She's talking again."

Only she was gone again. Damn. "She keeps drifting in and out of consciousness." That scared the crap out of him.

"Not good." Serus took one last look at Tessa then raced ahead, calling back, "Let's see if we have a way out. Goran could fly her home and she'd be getting the best care within twenty minutes."

Now that would be ideal.

Only somehow Cody didn't think it would happen. They weren't that lucky.

THERE WAS A warm sense of security wafting through Tessa's mind. She was moving. Being carried. By Cody. She recognized the feel of his arms. The caring touch. She barely remembered being carried by Goran and her father, but Cody's arms...she'd never forgotten that warm sensation. That loving touch.

She checked out the rest of her body.

Something was wrong. Ice and fire streamed through her body, muscles, and bones. She couldn't tell which was which as the pain shifted. As soon as she thought about the heat in her chest, ice joined it and put out the fire. But then when she wanted to shiver from the chill in her legs, fire blasted down her muscles, warming her legs.

Weird. Cool. And could be wonderful if there wasn't this horrible lassitude inside. She wanted to wake up but at the same time she knew she wasn't ready. It would be nice to roll over though, and shift around to ease the muscles that had become sensitive from being carried so long.

So long?

A part of her brain woke up at that thought. Just how long had she been out?

Was she injured? Cause otherwise, why she was being carried?

Carried. Cody. Blood farm. Shit.

As her mind made the connection, the images filled her mind. The old dying vampire. The young one she almost remembered. What had happened?

She combed through her memories, trying hard to piece together the sequence of events.

Then a flash of silver had her flinching.

Instinctively she pulled up her arms to avoid the thrust. And...

And what? She'd blanked out at that point. She shifted her arm. And cried out in pain.

Her hand.

And then she remembered.

Cody. My hand.

I know. Take it easy. We're lucky you're alive at all.

Did I lose my hand? She didn't dare open her eyes because the thought of a cripple or missing a limb terrified her.

Easy. You still have a hand. But the silver spike went through it. Your throwback genes saved you, but I don't know how much damage the silver did. Everyone has been so worried.

Yeah, me too, she joked. *Still don't feel great.*

No. And you're weak. It's like the silver stole your strength.

Hopefully not for too long. Where are we? She'd kept her eyes closed but now opened them. Colors bombarded her. She shut down her vampire vision, realizing that it was damaged in some way. At the very least, it seemed to be on overload. With her human vision, she struggled to orient herself.

"White tiles. God I hate them."

"You and me both."

"Can I try to stand?" She let her eyes drift closed. She felt safe this way but it wasn't fair to Cody. He had to be tiring.

"Like hell," he said good-naturedly in response to her thought. "I'm all vampire, remember?"

The arrogance made her smile. "So it's okay to play the injured female a little longer?"

"If you were playing, that would be a different story. But you're not. And you *are* injured, so please focus on healing. It would be so much easier to have you fighting at my side than me trying to protect you while you're down."

"Fighting? What fighting? The old vamp is dead, right?"

"Yeah but…"

Tessa listened in surprise as he caught her up on events. "So we're in a totally different part of the mine?"

"Looks like it, but there are white tiles here too."

"Gross. I wonder if this is where I was taken before."

"No way to know. There is something up ahead. The others have gone to take a look. We're last in line."

"Sorry about that. I know how you prefer to be out in the forefront."

"Forget about that. I'm exactly where I want to be – here with you."

She opened her eyes and watched his energy shimmer in the dark. *Beautiful. Just like him.*

He slanted a look of mock horror at her. *Hey, guys aren't beautiful.*

Yes they are. And you especially.

෨ ෬

SERUS COULDN'T BELIEVE how the knot in his chest loosened at the buzz in the air and the sound of Tessa's voice. He had no doubt Cody and his daughter were forming an alliance he'd yet to understand. Sure he could mindspeak with Rhia and Goran, but those relationships had been ongoing for centuries. He'd never seen anything like that happen in just days.

The problem was Tessa was unique in so many ways. And this appeared to be yet another way she was different. Cody was a fine young man. But Tessa was just a kid. She shouldn't be forming a relationship like this for a few more decades at least. He'd connected with Rhia much later and had wanted to wait. Rhia would have nothing to do with it and, he admitted, he hadn't tried too hard to change her mind. He knew women made up their minds so much faster than men, but Tessa was only sixteen.

And he wasn't ready to let her go. She was still in high

school, for Christ's sake. But she was also alive, and for that he'd learn to deal with the rest.

Are you done bitching yet?

Goran?

Who the hell were you expecting? Christ, that father stuff was getting on my nerves. My son is a good man.

I know that. But my daughter is so young.

It's just that they blindsided us.

Actually, Serus added thoughtfully, *I think this blindsided them.*

Goran chuckled. *I'm jealous in a way. Can't say I've found another relationship that's quite the same as my first wife. I'd like to but...*

Yeah, you're so not ready to settle down. If and when, then maybe.

I'm still a youngun. No need to settle down for a bit.

Huh, if you're a youngun, then your son is a damn pup.

Goran roared. *Yeah, well he's likely to be your son-in-law one day.*

Serus shuddered. *I got nothing against your boy...*

Hell, I know that. Up until this last week, I'd have taken him aside and asked him if he was sure about this, but now...

Yeah, he's changed. Grown into a man.

And your girl is growing up like I've never seen before. I say we step back and leave them to it.

Easy for you to say, Serus grumbled. *You're not the one with the daughter.*

And none of us will have anyone if we don't get out of this mess. So what do you say about getting your ancient ass up here and helping me open this door?

What door?

The one in front of me. Goran's tone of voice was both

affectionate and exasperated. *Earth to Serus. We might have another battle to fight once we get through this door.*

Good. Serus pushed his way past David and Jewel and then made his way in front of Ian. *I'm more than ready to take out some vampire ass.*

Wow. For a moment there I thought you were Tessa. That's something she'd say.

Ha. Like you haven't changed yourself these last few days. You're positively glowing. When you're not injured, that is. Serus finally caught up to Goran, reached out, and slugged him on the shoulder.

"Hey, what the hell was that for?" Goran grumbled, glaring at him.

"To get you in the mood." And Serus grinned up at him evilly. "Now in the words of those kids behind us – let's go kick some butt."

☙ ❧

JARED WATCHED AS several large army trucks pulled up and parked. The back of both trucks opened up and dozens of men in combat outfits poured out the back.

Instinctively, he retreated. That was a lot of firepower and a lot of men. At least they were human. Thankfully. He took a deep breath. And stepped around the shed wall to where they could see him.

En masse, the group of men raced to form a circle around him, and everyone had a hand on their gun – just in case.

He slowly put up his hands. He swallowed hard before taking a deep breath. "Hello. I'm Jared."

One of the bigger men stepped forward. "Hi Jared. Glad to find you safe and sound. We were hoping you'd be here. I understand you know a couple of ways in and out of this mountain."

"One for sure, and possibly the second one as well. It's a little hard to find, but I found it once so…"

"Good enough." He motioned to the men to split into two groups. "Show us how this garage floor works then you can tell my men how to get to the other entrance."

He hadn't actually opened the floor himself, but he'd seen how it was done. With a nod, he led the way to the shed and told everyone to step back. Then he hit the large button and watched, relieved as the floor obediently rose back up. As it rose, with the leader at his side, Jared crouched down and pointed in the general direction of the door. "The door leading into the blood farm is in that corner."

The floor clicked into place. The men moved onto it. Jared pushed the button again and stepped back into the floor. He strode across the platform to the steel door that they were in front of. "Nothing works in this place like you expect it to." He pulled his leg back then kicked the door. Nothing.

Crap.

He tried a second time. Nothing. Then a third. Still nothing. Then he remembered Tessa was shorter than him. And he aimed his next kick lower.

It popped open.

Thank God. He'd felt like an idiot when it wouldn't open. Now he stepped back out of the way and smiled.

"Good enough. We'll take it from here." More men jumped down as the leader led him back to the wall. He motioned to a ladder that had been dropped over the front edge. "You first."

Jared clambered up the ladder to find several of the other men waiting for him. The leader pointed to a group surrounding a map. "Now let's find the other entrance."

And Jared's heart sank. He didn't know if he'd be able to point it out on the map. It had been hard enough finding the entrance when he'd slid down the mountain to the road...but on a map? He wasn't even sure how to get to the road he'd found while escaping.

Taking a deep breath, he explained how he'd escaped and why he wasn't sure he could lead them back there. He thought he could from the inside, but he wasn't at all sure that he could from outside the mountain.

That wasn't quite what they'd expected. The leader stared at him for a long moment. "Then I guess you need to come with us. And we'll see if we can find the tunnel exit."

He smacked the hood of the truck and said, "Get in. We're rolling out now."

Shit.

Jared tossed one last look at the blood farm entrance and jumped into the front of the truck.

He pulled out his cell phone and texted Taz. *Searching for second entrance with army.*

Taz responded within minutes. *Guard your back. We still don't know which humans are involved in this mess.*

RHIA KNEW SHE should say something about her plans to someone. To Sian at least. But Sian was working to find out what her sister and Gloria were up to – if anything. She hoped not. She hated her sister sometimes like all siblings did, but that didn't mean she wanted her involved in this mess. But wishing it didn't make it so.

And she'd thought Gloria to be one of the stalwarts

against blood farms because of what she'd lost the last time. But that didn't make it so either. She also couldn't say that just because one might be involved that the other was.

But now she felt like she couldn't trust either of them.

She strode down the hallway to the far end. There were people milling about all over the place. That was good. She'd blend in and no one would remember her.

Just the way she wanted it. She opened the door and heard the sensor say the UV rays were too strong to go out. Damn, so it was still daylight out there. The council hall was just like home. She needed the sensors there too. She had been accidentally burned a few times already. She could use the motorcycle outfits that had been put away in the large cloakroom by the front entrance. But it meant facing the women again and she'd just as soon avoid them at this point. They'd ask questions she didn't want to answer.

She paced the office, wondering if there was anyone she could ask to retrieve a suit for her. Up ahead was Wendy, another of her son's friends. She'd been involved in the first trip to the blood farm and had stayed home after that. Good.

Wendy's face lit up when she spotted Rhia. "Hi. Have you heard anything from David and Ian? I keep trying their phones but no one is answering."

"I don't think the phones are working anymore." Rhia stroked her hair away from her face. "I haven't been able to contact them either."

Wendy's face crumpled. "I've been so worried. I stayed home after the last time and felt terrible when they all went back up there."

"It's not a good scenario at the mountain right now. Be happy you aren't part of it." Rhia meant that, but she understood what the girl was going through.

Wendy shook her head. "It doesn't feel like it's a good thing." She stared up at Rhia, tears glistening in her eyes. "I just wish there was more I could do. All the gossip makes this whole thing a nightmare. So many dead. So many more that are likely to end up that way. I hate this."

"I do too. I'm heading out, but I have a few things to collect before I go. I don't suppose I can ask you to go the cloakroom and grab me a full set of motorcycle leathers and a helmet, can I?"

Wendy's face brightened. "Sure. I'll be right back."

Rhia smiled. "Perfect." She waited by the back door for Wendy to return then groaned when her son's friend returned. Wendy had dressed herself in full leathers as well. She handed over the armload of protective clothing for Rhia to put on. She stared at Rhia, defiance mixing with fear and concern. "I'm going with you."

"Going where?" Rhia tried to think of an excuse to give Wendy, but she couldn't come up with a plausible reason. She quickly got dressed.

"To the blood farm." Wendy held out the helmet.

Rhia paused in the middle of closing her jacket zipper. She looked at Wendy curiously. "What makes you think that I'm going there?"

"That's where your family is."

Rhia's fingers stilled. "And why do you want to go?"

Wendy winced. Then took a deep breath. "Ian is my boyfriend. We've kept it a secret for months. But I can't stand not knowing what's happened to him."

Damn. How could Rhia argue with that logic when it was the same she was using for herself?

CHAPTER 19

TESSA TOOK A deep breath, feeling her chest expand and constrict normally...if somewhat painfully. "Well, that's a good sign," she said, her voice sounding weak, even to her own ears.

Cody gently lowered her feet to the ground but kept a supporting arm around her shoulders. "What is?"

"No pain." She opened her eyes and smiled up at him.

Her brother and Jewel crowded around her, big grins on their faces. Ian was there too. She grinned lopsidedly up at him. "Hey Ian."

He gave her a sheepish smile. "Hey Tessa. Nice to have you back in the land of the living."

She gave a small laugh. "Are you sure? I'm still a pain in the butt."

David hugged her gently. "Yes you are, but Cody is so much easier to get along with when you're not hurt."

"Really?" She turned to catch the discomfort on Cody's face. With a warm smile, she reached up and kissed his cheek. "Thanks for caring. And for being you."

"Hey, where's my kiss?" Ian protested with a big grin. "I'm being me too." He jerked back as Cody shoved him into a wall. "Ouch. Like that hurt." Then he sniggered. "Or maybe not."

David laughed, a sound filled with such joy that Tessa

reached out and hugged him again. "My hand still feels like someone shoved a spike through it but other than that... I feel pretty good." She wiggled her fingers experimentally, wincing as the fingers fully extended.

"About time. The ancients went through that door while we were engrossed in your being alive, and they didn't tell us." Cody stared at the still partially open door. "I also don't hear anything on the other side."

David stepped over. "We did earlier."

Tessa walked over, trying to study the ground around them. Her vision was different. Maybe stronger? Maybe not, but something odd had happened while she had been injured. The colors were brighter. The energy clearer. There was almost a buzz in the air.

"Can you see anything?" Cody murmured quietly.

She shook her head. "Not any more than the various energy signatures that should be here."

"Okay. Then at the count of three, let's find out why the elders haven't come back for us."

Just then the door opened and a very grim Goran stood in the open space. "You need to see this, but it's going to hit you hard. All of you."

He looked over at Jewel as if regretting she was there. Tessa's stomach churned. This was going to be bad. If they said it was bad, that meant it was really bad.

"Where's my father?"

"Oh, he's in there. And he's fine. Well, as fine as anyone can be after seeing this."

Goran shoved the door wide open and stepped aside. The small group surged forward.

Tessa's breath caught in the back of her throat but a small cry escaped. She barely heard the shocked gasps of those around her.

Her father stood in front of her, his head bowed.

She took a step forward, only to have Cody grab her and pull her back. "Careful."

Careful? Of what? The room in front of them was another blood farm. A horrible travesty of the one they'd already passed. These victims? Hanging so lost and alone?

Her own people. This blood farm was full of vampires.

☙ ❧

SERUS STARED BLINDLY at the room in front of him. He heard the others arrive and knew they were trying to assimilate what they were looking at.

He could barely even understand. And the little he did – hurt.

That his people could do this to their own kind was beyond comprehension. For what possible reason could they have for torturing vampires like this?

"Wait," David said, his voice shocked and not understanding. "This doesn't make sense."

"How and why would they need to hang vampires like this?" asked Ian.

Goran placed a hand on Serus's shoulder. In understanding and shared horror. The two had seen a lot over the centuries, but never anything like this. "Do you have any idea what they are up to, Serus?"

"No," he said, his voice cold and hard. "I don't. But we need to find out and we need to pull every one of these vamps down. They might recuperate if they are given a chance to. Our vampire DNA can heal them. If these poor creatures haven't been here for too long, they might survive."

Then Tessa spoke up and shocked them all. "They aren't real vampires."

"What the hell are you talking about?" Goran spun around to face her. "They are as real as you and me."

"Not according to their energy," she said firmly.

Serus turned slowly to stare at his daughter. That she was the only one to see this energy she was always talking about it made it difficult to confirm her suspicions. But damn it, she'd been right every time so far. "What are they then?"

Tessa grimaced, and then took a deep breath. "Something in between. I'm thinking they are 'created' vampires. Designed to the specs of whoever built this house of horrors."

Everyone stared at her face then turned to look down at the warehouse below them. Serus realized it was a much smaller room than the human blood farm. There were only ten vamps in a row and although he couldn't see how many rows there were, he could see the end of the room from where he was standing so he doubted that there were more than ten rows. So close to a hundred vamps hung here.

"So you're saying they aren't real?"

"They are real in that they are breathing living organisms. Animals, I guess." Tessa spoke carefully, choosing her words as if the wrong one could cause an explosion. "I'm thinking they might have been created in a lab and moved here to 'finish' up."

Ian whistled, a long low sound that was perfect for the shock running through Serus's system then said, "Wow. I hope you're wrong."

"So do I," she whispered. "What I can tell you is that they have a different look to their energy than anyone else I've seen to date, animals, human, or vamp."

Jewel asked, her tone so shocked it was almost silent, "A

new species."

"A hybrid," Tessa said, "A true hybrid." Serus listened to her voice. He watched her take another deep breath and announce, "I'm actually thinking that these things might be a hybrid of all three."

THE SUN BEAT down overhead as Jared studied the road, hoping to lead them to the tunnel exit. But everything looked so different. He wasn't even sure he'd seen this road ever before. How could that be?

"See anything familiar yet?" asked the driver.

"Not yet." Jared admitted, "I'm afraid that I won't recognize the entrance at all."

"We'll be turning onto the road where the barricade was put up to stop the masses from entering the blood farm. You should be able to find your way from there."

A wave of relief washed through Jared. That he could do. That would explain why he didn't recognize this area. They hadn't even gotten to the right road yet.

A few minutes later, the truck took a sharp left corner, the turnoff barely discernible. But the driver seemed to know where he was going. The driver continued in this direction for a few more minutes. Jared wondered about the change in terrain. It looked closer to the right area.

Then he saw it. He leaned over and pointed. "That's where I came out of the trees. The entrance is up a ways."

The driver nodded. "Good. Let's go."

SIAN TRIED TO keep her head down and her fingers working. She needed to be almost invisible and the only way to do that was to be studious and keep working away in the background. Only then would Gloria and Gittoria forget she was there.

Inside, she tried to sort through the information she had and the suspicions that they'd had about Gittoria. Not that they had anything there to go on. Hate didn't count.

That Gittoria couldn't be more different from Rhia was just part of it. If there was trouble brewing, Gittoria was usually at the edge of the disturbance, whether she made use of the final product herself or not. She loved to instigate trouble. She loved mind games and power plays. Sticking it to rest of them when they didn't know it would appeal to her nature.

For that matter, she might be 'sticking it' to Gloria in this instance, too.

The two women continued to talk as Sian tapped on the keys. She wished she had a better understanding of Gloria's involvement. Councilman Adamson appeared to trust her, but Sian was no longer so sure. She'd been all for sharing the intel with Gloria in the beginning under the assumption that they had to tell someone. And Goran apparently trusted her. Now, however…

A young man came over. "Ladies, I'm looking for Wendy. Have any of you seen her?"

Gloria looked up and frowned. "No, not recently. She was working in one of the other rooms earlier."

The man nodded. "She came in looking for two sets of motorcycle gear but we were missing one gauntlet. She grabbed a different one and said that would do, but it was a terrible fit." He held up a black leather one. "This is the right one."

Sian studied the black gauntlet. It might be the missing glove, but it was too big for Wendy. She was a tiny girl. "I haven't seen her. I presume she was picking out the suits for someone else?"

He shrugged. "One suit for her and the other one for Rhia."

Sian stared at him, a wave of ice slithering down her back. "Rhia?"

"Yeah, they were both heading out somewhere." He turned to leave. "I thought I could catch them before they left, but it looks like I just missed them."

Sian watched him leave, pain and loss setting in. She should have known Rhia wouldn't stay behind. No matter the logic, she'd gone after her family.

Sian, her hand to her belly, found it hard to blame her. As much as she wanted her friend to stay safe, she wouldn't have listened either. Not if her family was in danger.

☙ ❧

CODY WATCHED TESSA study the energy pattern floating around the floor level.

"Tessa?" Cody nudged her arm. "Can you see anyone here? Or signs of anyone being here recently?"

"That's what I was trying to see, but looking at the energy from this height, all the colors are blending into one big mess. I also can't see an easy way down. Surely these people know what stairs are?"

He nodded. "So down we go."

"Great," Ian said. He looked over the rail and gulped.

Serus let out a snort and picked Ian up before jumping over the railing.

Jewel and David jumped holding hands.

Cody studied Tessa. "I'll carry you down. I know you can jump, but if you misjudge the landing, it's liable to give you the mother of all headaches.

"Ugh. I don't need more of those, thanks." She stepped closer and wrapped her arms around Cody's neck. "Besides, this will never get old."

He dropped a kiss on her nose, wrapped an arm around her waist, snuggled her up close, and lifted off. "Good. I'm glad to hear it."

On the ground level, he floated down as gently as he could. The whole way they could hear Ian talking, "How come she's getting such royal treatment? Geez, Serus basically dropped me." But his grumbling tone was good-natured.

Tessa laughed at him. "You're lucky he didn't just toss you over in the first place."

The look on Ian's face made everyone break out in laughter.

Cody shook his head. "Uhm people, did anyone consider using stealth and not letting anyone know we're here?"

A vamp laughed. The sound came from behind them.

Tessa gasped. She closed her eyes.

Cody stared down at her, his muscles tense as anger surged through him. She didn't need another fight right now. She hadn't healed enough for that.

She opened her eyes to stare at him. Her thoughts were silent. Shocked.

When would things go their way?

Then the harsh cold voice said, "Like hell. We knew the minute you entered the tunnel up top." He gave a coarse laugh. "That's right – we've been waiting for you guys for quite a while."

A second vamp stepped forward from the large group that had suddenly surrounded them.

His sarcastic voice cut through the silence. "So, what do you think of your new home?"

7

CHAPTER 20

TESSA STARED AT the large group of vamps. They had a similar energy to the mess emanating from the hanging ones behind her. She thought they might be the same – only older. Because what she hadn't pointed out was the fact that all the vampires hanging behind them were young.

Young?

Yes. As in all the same age. At least the ones in the front are. There could be older or younger ones further back.

You really think these...things were made in a lab?

I'm not sure how else they'd get so many looking so similar and all the same age. Study them. Look at the similarities. Sure, there are a few differences. but not enough that they can't be related. They look like brothers. She thought about that. *And consider the fact that they are all male. As are all the hanging ones.*

I never noticed. So why no females?

Tessa had to wonder if they kept females as prisoners to service the men. And if that thought didn't make her want to puke, nothing in here would.

That's not likely. Don't even think about it.

She turned to study the space around them. There were about twenty vamps circling them. But no clear leader. She wondered where the boss was hiding.

I can't see one.

Neither can I, but there's been one every step of the way.

True. I suggest we take care of these assholes first then continue on our journey to freedom.

He said it so casually she almost laughed. *I wouldn't discount these guys so quickly. They could be a new generation. Look at their clothes.*

She felt Cody's sideways look.

"Hey. What's the matter, don't you guys work for a living? Your clothes are all brand new. All of you." She studied the confusion on their faces. "It's almost like you're brand new to the job…" she lowered her voice so only the rest of her group could hear her, "…or brand new to life."

Goran, standing by her shoulder, stiffened, a hiss escaping from his mouth. She knew he could talk with her father, but that left three of them out of the loop. She could only hope they heard her. Not that it made that much difference. These guys were going down.

But she didn't know yet if that was going to be hard or easy. If they were stupid turned vamps – no problem. But if they were state of the art designed and created vamps – that might be a whole different story.

Shit. Did you have to mention that? Cody's mental groan swept through her head. She giggled.

Goran gave her a sideways glance.

The vamps glared at her. "Think this is funny, do you?"

"Nah," she said. "I just can't imagine the size of the damn birthday cake you must have for all of you together."

They glanced at each other while she studied their reactions.

Goran whispered, "Seriously?"

She nodded. "As close as I can tell. Look at them. Similar features. All the same age, same brand new clothes."

His hiss turned to a growl.

She hastened to add, "Remember that they might be 'improved' versions."

"All the more reason to take them out."

The vamps shuffled uneasily in front of her. Tessa almost felt sorry for them. They had no idea. She didn't dare let herself side with them because that would mean she'd accord them the same rights as any animal.

Not going to happen, Cody whispered. *They are machines built to wage war.*

Only they may have a part of us.

Not even close.

As if Goran and Cody could mindspeak, they both lunged forward, grabbing and scooping up two vamps each. Goran flew straight up and dropped them – on top of some of the hanging not-quite-ready vamps. The one screamed as he fell all the way to the ground.

"Well, that answers one question – they can't glide or fly." Serus laughed.

David and Ian jumped up to meet the incoming group. Tessa turned to check on Jewel and found her father fighting at Jewel's side. Unfortunately, Tessa's strength wasn't back one hundred percent. She didn't dare try to kick ass. It would be her ass that took a kicking.

And before she could do anything, she was scooped up into the air and placed back up on the catwalk. *Stay here,* Cody ordered as he flew back into the battle.

Startled, Tessa didn't have time to react. She was still trying to grab the railing to stop herself from falling sideways. Damn, she hated not being able to help. She could only watch as her friends and family took out vamps and were beaten back as more joined them. The bad guys seemed endless. This was a war they couldn't win.

Shit.

She searched the room for something that would turn the tide in their favor. There were no weapons she could find. No other people to join in. What the hell could they do?

"Stop it. That's enough." A horrific whistle swept through the room.

The vamps all stopped, got back on their feet, and stepped back – like well-trained militia. Which they weren't.

She slipped out of sight as a huge vamp strode in from the right side. Where the hell had he come from?

"You can't win, in case you hadn't noticed. For every one of my people you kill, I have dozens more to take their place. You are going to wear down eventually."

The most horrible sound Tessa had ever heard came from Goran's throat. "Tyson?"

"Yes, of course. Who were you expecting?" The icy superior arrogance made Tessa mad. Asshole. Who was this guy anyway?

Trying to keep an eye on the proceedings, Tessa asked Cody, "*Who is Tyson?*"

His shocked grim voice answered, each word dropping like a heavy stone. *My brother.*

RHIA STUDIED WENDY once they were outside the building. She appeared completed dwarfed in the suit. "Let's snag a vehicle and drive up."

"Can we make it a vampire vehicle so that we can take off most of this gear?" Wendy asked hopefully.

Rhia shook her head. "Better to stay dressed in gear until

we get into the mountain."

"I wonder, after all the rumors flying around about experiments on vampires and potential gas and explosions, if we'll ever be safe."

"I hope so. This has to be over soon."

Not for the first time, Rhia found herself wondering if she'd look suspiciously at all her friends and family forever. Wondering if they were traitors and liars. She hoped not.

She pulled out the keys she'd snagged off Gloria's desk during their last conversation and pressed the button in the middle. A vehicle on the far side beeped. "Good. Let's go."

They both raced to the vehicle and got in. Rhia started up the engine and pulled out of the parking lot, hoping they would have at least a ten minute lead time before anyone noticed that they were missing.

She'd need at least twenty minutes to get up to the mountain. And who knew how long to find her family in that mausoleum? She could only hope the military had gone in and secured the place first. But even if they hadn't, nothing would stop her from going in to save her family.

⇜ ⇝

SIAN RAN TO where she'd last spoken to Rhia. She needed to know for sure. So she could warn the others. Rhia was a good vamp and there were a hell of a lot of angry well-armed humans heading up the mountain to take down any vamps that got in their way. Sian was afraid that they might accidentally harm the friendly ones as well.

She turned the corner into the room and found several other vamps, but not her best friend. They looked up at she skidded to a stop.

"What's the matter, Sian?"

"Has anyone seen Rhia or Wendy?"

"I saw Rhia about ten minutes ago. I'm not sure I know a Wendy," said the oldest of the three vamps in front of her.

Another said, "I saw Wendy carrying some gear a little while ago. I don't know where she was going though."

The third vamp just shrugged and went back to work.

Damn. Sian spun around and quickly texted Rhia. If she had her phone with her, she'd answer. At least Sian hoped she would.

Where are you? she asked.

Silence.

Sian waited a few minutes longer, then realizing that deep inside she already knew what Rhia had done, she texted, *You've gone up to the mountain, haven't you?*

It was a long time in coming, but the answer finally showed up. *Yes. I have to.*

❧ ❧

"TYSON?" CODY TRIED hard to keep his voice even, perplexed. Talking was already difficult, but to do so with a confused tone in his voice was damn near impossible. He'd shifted closer to his father, hating the way the ancient was reeling from the blow his brother had dealt him.

"Is this your operation?" He studied his brother's face. "Why?"

"Why not? It's who we are." His brother's cold face looked so familiar and yet so foreign. As if Cody hadn't ever really known him. Apparently he hadn't. Not if the man staring at him was the same one he'd grown up with. Then again, how often had they seen each other? Over a century separated them. He'd barely even seen his brother while he was growing up and there'd been no meeting of the minds at any time.

Tyson was a stranger.

But not to his father.

Cody risked a quick glance over at Goran, then forced himself to look away. Goran stared at his son as if his world was falling apart. His shoulders slumped and his face...Jesus...vamps were already pale to begin with, but his father's face looked like life had just become too much for him to handle.

Considering the depth of this betrayal – it probably had.

Cody?

He stiffened slightly. *Tessa, don't let him know you're there.*

I won't, but he might already know.

"How nice to have you all packaged into one tight group." Tyson said, his voice cold and amused. "Easy to take care of." He paused and smiled. Then he spoke again and confirmed their worst fears. "Only we need a few genetic samples from you first."

The large group of vamps, and surely more had joined them by now, surrounded her friends and family. Cody clenched his fists. *How the hell were they going to get out of this mess?*

"That's it?" His father spoke up. "You'll take our genetic markers and then kill us? We're your family. All you've got."

"Not quite." Tyson smiled, but the sight of it chilled Cody to the bone. "See all these vamps? Well, they are my kin. Your blood is still of interest to us. I don't have wings. Unfortunately, you managed to hand them down to Cody, but not me. Even though I'm an ancient as well, as was my mother. But you changed the brood mare in Cody's case and she cast true."

Brood mare? Cast true? What the hell? That was Cody's mother Tyson was talking about. She'd died before Cody was old enough to remember her. According to his father, Cody had been an unexpected surprise that he'd been delighted about. Particularly after his mother had died and Goran had devoted his time to raising Cody. They had an awesome relationship and as he stared at his forbidding-looking brother, this was likely to be part of the core problem.

Then Tyson spoke again. "Of course I took care of her."

Cody gasped. Shock slammed into him. Surely his brother hadn't said that, had he? Cody had never known his mother. But to think his brother may have been the reason for her death was too much to bear.

He couldn't imagine what that news would do to his father.

There was no time to question him as Cody's mind dwelled on all the other information.

Tyson didn't have wings. Cody hadn't really considered that as an issue. So many vamps didn't. But there were some that did. Like Ian and Jewel. Although their wings were smaller and weaker than those of the ancients, they were still functional. Cody didn't think he was any better than other vamps. He was different, as they were in their own way. They had other skills that he didn't have. But he was an ancient. The blood running through both his brother's and his veins was pure. As pure as they could get.

His father only had two offspring. And they'd taken opposite sides in this war. As he tried to sort through his brother's words, Cody realized it was worse than that. Tyson hadn't just chosen a side; he was actively involved in creating and developing it.

"Are you saying all these vamps are your family?" Jewel's incredulous voice rang out clear across the room. "Why would you want to do that?"

Tyson snorted. "It's not that they are family because that would make them close to being my equal and they aren't, but I used DNA to create them. Some of my DNA. Some from other people. I tinkered with it a little." He gave a smug shrug. "After all, we needed an army, but we didn't need them to be smarter than us. So I took care of that part."

Cody shuddered. Since when had his brother been into genetic tampering?

David spoke up, anger threading his words, "You're the young upstart taking over the place."

Tyson started. Then laughed and laughed. "That's funny. I *was* the young upstart. But now I'm one of the bosses. But thank you for reminding me that I need to keep an eye on my partner. Still, he's very young. I should be safe for awhile yet."

Truth piled in on top of truth as Cody tried to fit all the puzzle pieces together in his head.

Easy. Tessa's voice rolled through his mind. He was damn glad to hear it. He'd never felt so alone as he had a moment ago. Then she spoke and reminded him that he would never be alone again. And that she was their ace in the hole. Although he didn't see any way out of here.

Hey. I'm still here. Don't give up yet. She tried to inject some humor into her voice, but he could sense the fear building in her. *We don't know all of it yet. Don't jump to conclusions.*

Hard not to. And even harder to see a light at the end of this war. We're completely surrounded. I don't know if you can see them from up there, but there are several dozen goons down here.

I'm working on a plan. Give me a moment.

Tyson spoke up. "Hit them with the drugs and get them strapped down in the labs. I want them all dead within the half hour."

Cody stepped toward his father. "Dad? We have to do something."

His father raised his gaze to look at Cody. "Do what?" He stared lifelessly at the large group of vamps approaching them. "This is it. We did what we could. There's nothing left to do."

CHAPTER 21

S HIT. SHIT! TESSA couldn't move. She hadn't been noticed up above, but her presence wasn't going to be enough to tip the scales in their favor. And with Tyson walking away, she desperately wanted to take him out. She doubted the others would do it. At least not Cody or Goran.

Yes, I would.

Good. Hold on to that thought.

Tyson had almost reached the door when she took her chance, both fists clenched, silver spikes protruding between her knuckles. She glided as silently as she could and sailed toward him.

And misjudged the distance.

She'd blame that part on her injury.

Shit. She was coming in too high. If she couldn't drop down fast enough, he'd have the door locked and closed in time for her to slam into it straight on.

Instead she barely skimmed underneath it, ducking her head low to clear the top of the doorway. And in typical old Tessa style – she hit Tyson in the back as he stepped through the door to the other side.

"What the f…"

And she punched him with both spiked fists.

He blew up beneath her, her nose and mouth clogging with ash. Her eyes burned from the smoke.

She coughed several times as she staggered to her feet. *God, this guy was bad news.* Correction. *He'd been bad news. Now he was just another pile of ash.*

Are you okay?

Yeah, but your brother isn't. I'm sorry, but he's dead. I killed him.

Good, it saved me from doing a nasty job. And we could use your help back here.

Shit.

Turning around, she stared at the door that had closed behind her inelegant exit. *Please don't let it be locked.* Taking a quick look around, she realized she was in another stupid white tunnel. But this wasn't the time for sightseeing.

She refocused on the door and opened it, surprised when the knob turned under her hand. No kicks required.

As she went through the door, a rumble sounded somewhere in the distance.

The noise was long and slow and far away but was getting closer. Then she didn't give it another thought. The room was full of bloodshed.

She jumped into the fray. Jewel was struggling with two vamps trying to drag her down past the hanging vamps. Tessa jumped overhead and landed behind the vamps, arms outstretched and silver spikes driving into both vamps. They collapsed, screaming but not dead. Jewel stumbled free. "Oh thank God. I was so afraid," she cried out.

Tessa stabbed the men again, this time aiming for the heart. These men had been created with some kind of resistance to silver. Like what the hell? They were obviously a new generation. But they weren't completely immune. At her second stab, they seemed to smoke around the edges as something happened internally. She remembered the guy out in the sunshine. These models were a step ahead of him, and although an attempt had been made at silver immunity, they hadn't succeeded yet. She stabbed them a third time for good measure and watched as they started to burn.

"About damn time. But it took three tries." Only she was speaking to empty air. Jewel had gone to help David.

Tessa turned, her gaze catching sight of the hanging vamps. Vamps that could be the new version.

Cody, it took three stabs with the silver spikes to make them burn.

Got it.

Diving into the fight, Tessa slashed and cut her way through the crowd. She figured that the touch of silver was crippling enough to stop the force of their attack. She waded through the tumbling and burning bodies. Two men on Ian got a slice each, then she reversed her double-armed motion and took them both out permanently. Her father was doing some major damage, but she didn't understand what was going on behind him. It's as if Goran stood immobile in the center of the room. Cody was fighting protectively in front of him. And Serus was doing the same on his other side.

Goran wasn't fighting. He'd given up. Or had given in.

Cody, what's wrong with your father?

Finding out about Tyson.

Shit. Yeah, that might do it. But they needed him on their side. She sliced and diced and ducked behind the others to stand in front of Goran. His tortuous gaze locked on her. Damn. She hated to do this, but…

She transferred the silver spike from her right hand to her left, then spun around in a huge wind up and let her open hand fly.

And smacked Goran full on in the face.

He bellowed and stumbled back, shock filling his eyes. His face turned red. From her slap or his temper, she didn't know, but it looked better than the living dead imitation he was doing.

"What was that for?" he growled. His hand reached up to cover the bright red mark on his cheek.

"Getting you back in the game," she snarled back into his face. "We need you."

He blinked and looked around at the carnage going on. His face twisted, his gaze narrowed, and a hatred she couldn't have imagined took over his face. He roared at the top of his lungs and took off in a nasty whirlwind of wings and claws and roars. David and Ian ducked as vamp after vamp was tossed into a heap at their feet, compliments of Goran. After their initial shock, the two quickly stabbed and slashed until the vamps were nothing but a growing pile of ash in front of them.

And just like that...it was over.

Tessa stood shaking in place, her body barely recovering from the demands she placed on it when Cody wrapped his arms around her and pulled her into a tight embrace. "I thought we were done," he whispered into her hair. "Then you came along."

She could feel tremors making her legs quake. She needed to know that everyone had survived, but she was scared to look around.

Whispering back, she said, "I was afraid we all were. Please tell me everyone is okay."

He twisted to look around and cried out exultantly, "Yes, everyone is alive."

Tessa lifted her head to smile at those around her. She caught David's grin and smiled back, Jewel almost hidden in his arms. Checking out the other side, she found Serus standing in front of a glowering Goran. "Where's Ian?"

"Behind you."

She turned to find Ian leaning against the wall. He raised a hand in acknowledgement, an exhausted smile on his face. "I'm here, but I don't think I can keep doing this much longer."

David groaned. "Neither can I. Like what the hell? I never thought I'd be happy to go back to the routine I had before. Even university is sounding pretty damn fine at the moment."

Tessa giggled. Cody lifted her off her feet and twirled her around in a big circle while her brother scolded her, "School is hardly a laughing matter!" But his grin said he was teasing. "Besides, what do you care? You're still in high school. Talk about easy."

Held tight within Cody's embrace, she had to wonder. Cody was in university too. Would their ages matter? She still had a year to go. Although if she wanted to, she could finish it in half the time. She actually dumbed down her work because she always had top marks to begin with. She didn't know if her vampire genes gave her an edge over humans or if she were naturally smarter.

After what I've seen from you these last few days, I'm going to go with naturally smarter. And while at the moment our age difference might cause our peers to laugh at us, in a few years we'll actually look odd again because we'll be so close in age.

She laughed. *So true.* She hesitated a moment, hating to change the atmosphere, but it needed to be said. She whispered painfully, *I killed your brother.*

SHE DIDN'T APOLOGIZE. She just stated the facts. And she was right. It had to be faced. She couldn't even begin to understand the conflicting emotions he felt right now.

And your father, I'm so sorry for what he's going through. I hurt for what I did, she whispered painfully. *I don't know what to say to him.*

And that is what makes you so different. You have so much heart. He answered quietly, soberly. *My brother was not the man I thought I knew. I don't blame you. You didn't do this. In fact, once again, you saved us all. And as much as I thank you, it would be nice to save you for a change.* Try as he might, he couldn't keep the aggrieved tone out of his voice.

She wanted to giggle again. He could feel it. Almost as if he were the one feeling that way.

Then he could hear her thinking, *He had no reason to feel that way. He did his share and so much more.*

Thank you. She hadn't been speaking to him, but as he could hear her thoughts anyway...

She flushed. *Wow.*

True. And his warm caring laugher eased her embarrassment. *It will also keep us honest.*

So true. Still, I'm sorry. Not for killing Tyson as that was a man in dire need of dying. But that he was your brother and Goran's son.

Yes. I will deal with it later. Much later. Especially Tyson's comment about my mother.

I heard that. I'm hoping he didn't mean it.

I don't know. I'll have to talk to Dad.

And about your father...

Cody stared over at his father, who stood shoulders bent, head down, deep in conversation with Serus. *I'm hoping your father can make him understand.*

Yes, she murmured. *But I have to say something to him.*

And while Cody was still puzzling over what she meant by that, she pulled out of his embrace and strode toward the ancients.

He hurried after her. *Ah Tessa, that might not be such a good idea right now. Maybe pick a better time?*

There is no better time. In fact, there won't ever be a good time. I killed his son. How can there be a good time to face that?

❧ ❦

JARED POINTED UP the mountain. They were still driving in the big truck, but he could see the dark mouth of the mine opening up ahead. "We're almost there."

The truck slowed down and the man on his right leaned out the window and stared up the hillside. "I see something black up there."

"Yeah, that's it. It's an old mine entrance."

The truck slowed down. The driver shifted gears and the truck lurched hard before smoothing out and turning at that last corner. Jared couldn't help but feel excited and nervous at the same time. Was it a coincidence that he was here with a second rescue party? Or was it another trap? Nah. It couldn't be. These were the good guys. These were his people. They were here to help their people in the blood farm. And to take out the assholes who started this.

While he was busy worrying about that problem, the truck slowed down and came to a dead stop. The man beside him nudged him. "Does this look right?"

Startled, Jared looked at the black mouth of the cave and nodded. He swallowed. Damn, he was really going back in. "This is it."

The two men hopped out. One of them pounded on the side of the truck to notify the men in the back. At least that's what Jared thought was in the back. And as a dozen men hopped out and joined him, dwarfing Jared in their fatigues and sidearms, he realized they'd come for war.

That should make him feel better, but…

"You guys do know that not all the vampires in there are the bad guys, right?"

The leader snorted and said, "All vamps are dead vamps as far as I'm concerned."

"Dead right." One man behind him did something to his gun, making a hard clicking sound. "After what they've done to our people – all vamps should be dead vamps."

Jared stared at them in shock. "Whoa. That is so not true. My friends are inside. The family that came and saved me, they are here. Some of the techs that were helping Taz on the medical side, they are all good vamps."

The men gave a hard laugh. "There are no good vamps. They might pretend to be that way, but inside…no way. And any vamps we see will be dead vamps."

The men started to march forward.

"Wait!" Jared raced behind them. "You can't just go in there and kill everyone off. What about my friends?"

The leader stopped and turned to face Jared. "They aren't your friends, son," said the leader. "You need to understand that. Vampires are liars and cheaters and they will stab you in the back the first chance they get."

Another soldier cocked his gun and let out a harsh laugh. "So we'll get them first."

And the men strode forward. The leader stayed behind a moment longer. "Jared, I want you to go sit in the truck and stay there until we come back."

"No. No." Jared shook his head as his heart quaked. What had he done? He'd come to rescue his father but had somehow gotten involved in annihilating the vamps. And if Tessa or her family – like Seth – were still here, they'd be shot at first sight.

It would be carnage.

And he'd be partly responsible. Oh dear God. What had he done? And what could he do to stop it?

The leader shook his head. "You will stay here. That is an order. Do not go back inside that mountain. Do you hear me?"

Jared stared numbly at him. Then nodded. "I hear you."

"Good. Now get inside that truck and stay there. Do not come out under any circumstances."

The leader glared down at Jared until he nodded. Then he turned and strode after his men.

Jared watched them stride deeper into the mine. Good thing he'd never been any good at following orders.

RHIA STOOD OUTSIDE the garage entrance. She stared into the yawning mouth her family had descended into. Was she doing the right thing? Did she have a choice? There were trucks everywhere. Human trucks. And that should be a good thing, but it also gave her a chill to realize how many more humans there were in there than vamps. Not an easy thought. Still, there were no people milling outside. And she wondered about that.

Had they *all* gone down below? Was that wise?

At least it meant it was safe to go down.

She took a few steps back to stare up at the mountain. If

she were a flier, she'd choose to find out how her daughter had escaped up in the snow line. Get in that way and work her way down. But she couldn't get up there. Wendy was a glider, but she was not the same caliber as Serus and she couldn't go alone. And they'd have to wait for night to fall.

No. She turned her focus to the garage in front of her. It would have to be here and now.

"Rhia?"

"Yes. I'm just thinking that I'd feel better if we had more vamps with us." She tried to be reassuring, but it wasn't easy. "There is a heavy human population in there and they are angry at us. We had nothing to do with the mess, but they don't know that, and I doubt they care. They need someone to blame."

Wendy said in a small voice, "Someone like us?"

"Maybe." Rhia realized another truth. "I shouldn't have let you come up here. You need to go back. If you glide, you'll be able to make it home much faster."

"Maybe, but it's still daylight and I can't go anywhere until the darkness falls."

"Then hide in the trees out of sight until you can go home."

"And you, what are you going to do?"

Rhia stared down at the entrance. "I'm going in. I am a councilwoman. Some of them will know that. That should protect me." At least she hoped it would.

"Then I'm coming with you."

Rhia started to protest.

Wendy shook her head. "No. I'm not going to be safe alone. If they find me, I can hardly explain my presence, and nothing has changed about my reason for coming in the first place. Ian is here. And I know he's in big trouble."

At that, Rhia sharpened her gaze. "What makes you think that?"

Wendy shrugged and stared into the garage entrance. "I don't know. It's just that everything feels wrong."

Somewhere in the distance, a deep rumble sounded.

"Sounds like a storm is gathering." Rhia motioned. "Come on then. Let's get inside."

The two hopped down to the lowered garage floor before walking to the steel door.

"For better or worse," Rhia muttered. "I will have my family back." Then under her breath, she added, "Or die trying."

CHAPTER 22

TESSA STOPPED DIRECTLY in front of Goran.

Serus frowned at her. "Tessa, this might not be the best time."

Goran just stared at her, his jet black gaze shuttered and hard. Tessa took a deep breath and studied his eyes, seeing past the rage to the pain deep inside. There was so much hurt. But there was also anger. And she didn't know if any of it was directed at her. If it was, she needed to diffuse it.

She willed herself to get this right. For her sake. For Cody's sake. For Goran's sake. "I'm sorry."

Serus stepped up behind her.

Damn, her voice sounded terse. Cold. She winced. She hadn't meant it that way. She tried again. "I *am* sorry. I wish there'd been another way."

Clouds crossed his vision. He narrowed his gaze at her.

"But I had to." She added soberly, not able to hide her own pain. "He was trying to kill us all."

The room had gone deathly quiet.

She waited. They had to get past this as best as they could. She stared up at him, letting him see her own pain. Her own regret. Her own acceptance of his reaction.

The muscle in his jaw twitched as he continued to glare at her.

She waited.

His glare eased and a heavy sigh worked its way up from his chest. As he released it, some of the rigidity left his shoulders and eased the tight muscles of his face. He nodded.

"And he'd have succeeded if you'd been a moment longer," Goran announced, his voice gruff and thin with pain. "You don't need to apologize. You did what you had to do."

Tessa breathed loudly. She let her own strained shoulders ease. "I did," she said, "But I'm still sorry. He was your son and Cody's brother. I *wish* he'd been a stranger."

A ghost of a smile whispered across Groan's face. "In many ways, I guess he was."

"And in many ways, he wasn't." Serus pointed out. "We know there are going to be many more casualties before we're done."

Goran nodded, straightened his shoulders, and looked around. "And we need to stop this abomination. There's no way I'm leaving this nasty room and these...these things here to grow and come after us."

Cody stepped forward. "Is that what you want?" He waited until Goran turned to look at him. "I'm pretty sure they are all related to us."

A look of horror crossed Goran's face. "That doesn't make them family," he cried. "They are creations, test tube concoctions. Lab results. Not family."

Cody grinned. "Just checking."

Goran shuddered. "Do not joke about that.'"

Just then a louder rumble sounded. Tessa spun around. "Whoa. What was that?"

The others turned as the sound grew louder.

"I don't know," Serus said. "But it's not good."

Goran straightened and took several steps forward. "I want this place demolished. These...these things destroyed."

"We will. But it can't happen right now. We need to get out of here." Serus ran toward the door that Tyson had left through. "We have to go…and now."

David ran ahead, tugging Jewel's arm to keep her close to him. "What do you think that noise was?"

"I don't know. But it can't be anything good. We're inside an old mountain, remember? Inside an old mine riddled with unstable tunnels."

Cody rushed up and grabbed Tessa's hand. "Come on. Let's go."

She tugged back, her gaze off to the side. "Not without your father."

He turned to look at her. "What?"

"Your father. Look." She pointed to where Goran was busy trying to destroy some kind of panel on the wall. "I think he wants these things destroyed more than he wants to get out of here safely."

Cody groaned. "We don't have time. We have to go."

"I know, but look at him." Tessa studied Goran's face. "He looks possessed."

"He is. Tyson created all this," Cody swept his arm wide, "Using my father's blood. Tainting it in a way. He's not going to be able to live with himself if Tyson's creations survive."

"Can't we take care of it later?" she cried out. "The others are ahead again."

"Go. I'll stay here and help him."

"No. Not again." She shook her head. "He needs to come with us. We need to make him understand." A louder groan swept through the mountain, sending shivers down her spine. "And we need to get out of here, now!"

Cody rushed over to his father. "Dad, come on. We'll come back and take care of this later. But something is happening, and we have to leave."

Goran looked at Cody; Tessa could see the black tormented look in his features.

"Goran, please. There is something happening to the mountain. Either the vamps are blowing something up, or there is a quake or something. It doesn't matter. We have to get out of here. Please."

Goran shook his head. "No, you go. I have to make sure these things are destroyed."

"And do you have to kill Cody while you're at it?" Tessa cried. "You've lost one son. Do you want to lose another?"

His eyes widened in shock. "No. Go. Run to safety. I'll stay he—"

"No!" Both Cody and Tessa shouted. They each grabbed one of Goran's arms and dragged him out of the room. "We can come back later. We have to leave before we're all killed."

Just as Tessa finished speaking, a horrible groaning sound came from – everywhere. She cried out. "Hurry. The mountain is coming down."

Then she was swept up into Cody's arms and with Goran flying at his side, they raced down the corridor in the wake of the others.

Tessa clutched at Cody. Panic kept her breath locked into her throat. They weren't going to make it. She knew it inside her.

"Stop thinking like that. We've been through so much and survived that I have to believe we'll make it out of here."

She didn't bother answering him. They'd caught up to the others. She pointed to a black entrance up ahead. "There. It could be a way out."

Cody swooped into the big room, leaving the others slightly behind.

Frantic, she searched for a way through.

Dirt fell down on them, small stones bouncing as the mountain rippled all around them. More dirt fell, then more rocks. Cody darted and swerved, trying to get to the wall on the far side. She buried her face against his shoulder, fear clutching her heart.

She couldn't have imagined this. Not after all they'd been through.

A huge boulder hit Cody and he reeled from the blow. He cried out. They started to slip sideways.

She gasped as his left arm fell away useless She grabbed his shoulders. "Cody! Oh my God. Are you okay?"

He obviously wasn't. They were still falling.

"I can't hold us up," he gasped, "My wing." Small rocks showered down on top of them. Tessa struggled to help Cody correct their path, but he was too big to hold up. She was losing her grip on him.

Then something hit her on the shoulder and they both lurched to the side. Cody crashed into a wall and fell from her grasp. He tumbled to the floor below.

Tessa cried out. *Cody!*

She jumped toward him.

Cody, talk to me. But there was no answer.

Something smashed into her back and sent her tumbling in his direction. She cried out in agony. Dirt fell down around her as she twisted in a freefalling motion. Then the mountain gave an almighty shrug and sent a huge cascade of rocks down on top of her.

And she knew no more.

Vampire in Defiance

Book #5 of Family Blood

Dale Mayer

PROLOGUE

Please note – we left book 4 off with this chapter.

TESSA STOPPED DIRECTLY in front of Goran.

Serus frowned at her. "Tessa, this might not be the best time."

Goran stared at her, his jet black gaze shuttered and hard. Tessa took a deep breath and studied his eyes, seeing past the rage to the pain deep inside. There was so much hurt. But there was also anger. And she didn't know if any of it was directed at her. If it was, she needed to diffuse it.

She willed herself to get this right. For her sake. For Cody's sake. For Goran's sake. "I'm sorry."

Serus stepped up behind her.

Damn, her voice sounded terse. Cold. She winced. She hadn't meant it that way. She tried again. "I *am* sorry. I wish there'd been another way."

Clouds crossed his vision. He narrowed his gaze at her.

"But I had to." She added soberly, not able to hide her own pain. "He was trying to kill us all."

The room had gone deathly quiet.

She waited. They had to get past this as best as they could. She stared up at him, letting him see her own pain. Her own regret. Her own acceptance of his reaction.

The muscle in his jaw twitched as he continued to glare at

her.

She waited.

His glare eased and a heavy sigh worked its way up from his chest. As he released it, some of the rigidity left his shoulders and eased the tight muscles of his face. He nodded.

"And he'd have succeeded if you'd been a moment longer," Goran announced, his voice gruff and thin with pain. "You don't need to apologize. You did what you had to do."

Tessa breathed loudly. She let her own strained shoulders ease. "I did," she said, "But I'm still sorry. He was your son and Cody's brother. I *wish* he'd been a stranger."

A ghost of a smile whispered across Goran's face. "In many ways, I guess he was."

"And in many ways, he wasn't." Serus pointed out. "We know there are going to be many more casualties before we're done."

Goran nodded, straightened his shoulders, and looked around. "And we need to stop this abomination. There's no way I'm leaving this nasty room and these...these things here to grow and come after us."

Cody stepped forward. "Is that what you want?" He waited until Goran turned to look at him. "I'm pretty sure they are all related to us."

A look of horror crossed Goran's face. "That doesn't make them family," he cried. "They are creations, test tube concoctions. Lab results. Not family."

Cody grinned. "Just checking."

Goran shuddered. "Do not joke about that.'"

Just then a louder rumble sounded. Tessa spun around. "Whoa. What was that?"

The others turned as the sound grew louder.

"I don't know," Serus said. "But it's not good."

Goran straightened and took several steps forward. "I want this place demolished. These...these things destroyed."

"We will. But it can't happen right now. We need to get out of here." Serus ran toward the door that Tyson had tried to escape through. "We have to go...and now."

David ran ahead, tugging Jewel's arm to keep her close to him. "What do you think that noise was?"

"I don't know. But it can't be anything good. We're inside an old mountain, remember? Inside an old mine riddled with unstable tunnels."

Cody rushed up and grabbed Tessa's hand. "Come on. Let's go."

She tugged back, her gaze off to the side. "Not without your father."

He turned to look at her. "What?"

"Your father. Look." She pointed to where Goran was busy trying to destroy some kind of panel on the wall. "I think he wants these things destroyed more than he wants to get out of here safely."

Cody groaned. "We don't have time. We have to go."

"I know, but look at him." Tessa studied Goran's face. "He looks possessed."

"He is. Tyson created all this," Cody swept his arm wide, "Using my father's blood. Tainting it in a way. He's not going to be able to live with himself if Tyson's creations survive."

"Can't we take care of it later?" she cried out. "The others are ahead again."

"Go. I'll stay here and help him."

"No. Not again." She shook her head. "He needs to come with us. We need to make him understand." A louder groan swept through the mountain, sending shivers down her spine. "And we need to get out of here, now!"

Cody rushed over to his father. "Dad, come on. We'll come back and take care of this later. But something is happening, and we have to leave."

Goran looked at Cody; Tessa could see the black tormented look in his features.

"Goran, please. There is something happening to the mountain. Either the vamps are blowing something up, or there is a quake or something. It doesn't matter. We have to get out of here. Please."

Goran shook his head. "No, you go. I have to make sure these things are destroyed."

"And do you have to kill Cody while you're at it?" Tessa cried. "You've lost one son. Do you want to lose another?"

His eyes widened in shock. "No. Go. Run to safety. I'll stay he—"

"No!" Both Cody and Tessa shouted. They each grabbed one of Goran's arms and dragged him out of the room. "We can come back later. We have to leave before we're all killed."

Just as Tessa finished speaking, a horrible groaning sound came from – everywhere. She cried out. "Hurry. The mountain is coming down."

Then she was swept up into Cody's arms and with Goran flying at his side, they raced down the corridor in the wake of the others.

Tessa clutched at Cody. Panic kept her breath locked into her throat. They weren't going to make it. She knew it inside her.

"Stop thinking like that. We've been through so much and survived that I have to believe we'll make it out of here."

She didn't bother answering him. They'd caught up to the others. She pointed to a black entrance up ahead. "There. It could be a way out."

Cody swooped into the big room, leaving the others slightly behind.

Frantic, she searched for a way through.

Dirt fell down on them, small stones bouncing as the mountain rippled all around them. More dirt fell, then more rocks. Cody darted and swerved, trying to get to the wall on the far side. She buried her face against his shoulder, fear clutching her heart.

She couldn't have imagined this. Not after all they'd been through.

A huge boulder hit Cody and he reeled from the blow. He cried out. They started to slip sideways.

She gasped as his left arm fell away useless She grabbed his shoulders. "Cody! Oh my God. Are you okay?"

He obviously wasn't. They were still falling.

"I can't hold us up," he gasped, "My wing." Small rocks showered down on top of them. Tessa struggled to help Cody correct their path, but he was too big to hold up. She was losing her grip on him.

Then something hit her on the shoulder and they both lurched to the side. Cody crashed into a wall and fell from her grasp. He tumbled to the floor below.

Tessa cried out. *Cody!*

She jumped toward him.

Cody, talk to me. But there was no answer.

Something smashed into her back and sent her tumbling in his direction. She cried out in agony. Dirt fell down around her as she twisted in a freefalling motion. Then the mountain gave an almighty shrug and sent a huge cascade of rocks down on top of her.

And she knew no more.

CHAPTER 1

TESSA COULDN'T MOVE. Neither could she open her eyes. But she could sneeze...and cough...and sneeze some more. With every movement, pain radiated from her chest to her toes. Toes she felt all too well. Damaged toes. Damaged leg. Badly damaged knee.

Shit. Shit. *Shit.*

She tried to assess the damage. Obviously she was still alive, but given the little bit she remembered prior to this moment, she wasn't sure that was a good thing. Buried alive sounded like another living dead scenario – especially considering her long lived vampire heritage.

Then she remembered her friends and family...and Cody.

Cody? Can you hear me? Cody!

No answer.

Maybe he was like her, caught somewhere between awareness and unconsciousness. Or worse.

Panic set in and brought her screaming back to her physical reality. And the pain. It streaked throughout her body and ripped the foggy clouds away from her mind. She cried out as millions of sharp pinpricks covered her legs, her back, and damn...her head. She'd been fighting for days and now she felt like she'd been the loser of a mega battle. Oh wait, she was – Mother Nature had given her ass a major butt kicking.

Still, as she vaguely remembered the blood farm vamps'

earlier innuendos about something big about to happen, she realized Mother Nature might not have had anything to do with it.

Cody? She reached out mentally again, hoping to sense him. Sense anyone. But found nothing on that level. It was like she existed in deep space completely surrounded by...emptiness.

She coughed again to clear the dust from her lungs. She had to hang on tight to her emotions, or she'd break down and lose what little strength she had left. Now if she knew the others were alive...

Cody? Can you hear me? Please be okay.

Memories of him falling from her grasp caused a light film of cold sweat to pop up all over her skin. She hadn't been able to hold on to him. He'd been too big. Too heavy. She'd been injured and hadn't been able to hold on tight enough.

If he'd died because of her... Tears threatened. Impatiently, she brushed them away. She didn't have time to waste. He could be still alive. They all could be. The others had been just that much further behind them in the tunnel. If the tunnel had held.

She tried to take a deep breath. That brought on a major coughing spell. Damn, that hurt. Finally, she collapsed back against the rocks and opened her eyes.

And realized she wasn't even at ground level. She was lying on rocks, surrounded by rocks, and covered by rocks. In effect, she'd been buried alive, sealed inside a hollow in the middle of the rocks. She surveyed her prison. Cracks of light shone through in odd places so the rocks hadn't completely obliterated the cavern. That was the good news. With all the rocks flying around she was lucky she'd only been tossed around and bruised up. She didn't think she'd broken anything – except maybe her leg, only she didn't want to look too close. But…her hand had completely healed over as well.

How long had she been unconscious?

She could have broken and healed a dozen bones if she'd been out long enough.

Crap.

⤳ ⤺

CODY TRIED TO roll over and jolted awake as pain streaked across his wing. He cried out and collapsed back down, waves of agony rippled continuously down his body. Shit. The same damn wing he'd injured before.

When the pain finally eased, he slowly lifted his head and realized he had only inches of clearance before his head cracked into stone. His wing, stretched out beside him, was pinned under an even bigger boulder. At the sight of it, he remembered.

The cave-in. His brother. Tessa!

He groaned. He'd fallen with her. Instead of saving her, he may have killed her. Panic surged through him. *Tessa? Tessa!*

Cody? Is that you?

His heartbeat calmed. Thank God she was alive. *Tessa? Where are you?*

Not sure. Under a mess of rocks. And injured.

He gasped. *Badly?*

Don't think so. Just my leg. A huge rock is balanced on several rocks above me and I'm jammed in below.

He lay back down in relief. *Oh, thank God.*

After a long pause she asked in a timid voice. *Are you okay? I'm so sorry. I dropped you. I wasn't strong enough with my injured hand to hold us both up after a big rock slammed into us.*

That wasn't your fault!

But I couldn't save you, she cried.

He gave a short laugh. *And I've been thinking the same about you. I carried you into the middle of a cave-in where we were both injured.*

So you are injured! Her horrified gasp ripped through his mind loud and clear. He wanted to lie and say he was fin—

Don't bother. Now how bad is it? I'm searching for an exit out of my prison.

Be careful, he warned. *Any movement could bring those rocks down on top of you.*

I know, but lying here forever doesn't sound like a nice way to spend eternity. She almost smiled at the thought. Almost. *What about the others? Have you heard anyone call us? I wish we could talk with them.*

That would help, but no, I haven't heard anything.

Can you move? she asked.

No. My wing is pinned by a large rock.

Oh no, she cried out. *That's bad. Can you move the rock?*

He glanced up at the huge boulder and groaned. *I don't think so. It's huge.*

Then I'm coming to you.

No! But he was too late. Tessa, in her typical take charge and forge ahead regardless style, had left his mind.

And left him feeling lonelier than ever. Christ, he hurt.

He tilted his head and listened intently.

Someone was calling for him. And it wasn't Tessa.

"Cody!"

GORAN DID A slow wide sweep over the rock pile below him. Dust swirled, hiding much from his view. The cavern ceiling still held, but it's as if it had shed an inner skin and dropped it all to the floor below. He should have waited for the dust to settle, but he hadn't been able to. Serus watched from the tunnel entrance with the other kids while he did a flyover.

It looked bad. Not a sign of them anywhere.

He'd already lost his oldest boy. He couldn't stand to lose Cody, too.

Serus called out to him. "Any sign of them?"

"Not yet. But they might be anywhere," Goran yelled back. "The dust is making it hard to see."

"Cody fell off to the left," David yelled. Goran hovered in place and turned to look at David. He pointed in the direction David had said. David nodded. Goran swooped down and studied the fallen rocks, searching for anything that would indicate his boy and Tessa were alive.

There was nothing.

As he turned to do a wide sweep off to the left, he heard someone. Or something. He dove lower and landed on a huge boulder.

Serus's voice immediately jumped into his head. *Careful. They could be under any number of rocks.*

I know, but I needed to stop and rest for a moment. He hated to admit it, but he was feeling like crap.

I hear you. But we're going to feel a hell of a lot worse if we can't find our kids.

I thought I heard something here.

What?

Not sure. If you'd be quiet for a moment maybe I could find out, he answered, exasperated. Serus went silent...but stayed in the background. Goran didn't need to look over at the mouth of the tunnel to realize that Serus was staring at him something fierce. As if by will alone, he'd have Goran find his daughter.

They'd decided that it was too unstable for Serus to land his jumps on the rocks, but things appeared to be calming down. The dust was settling.

Then I'm coming.

No, wait. Goran spun around. He'd heard something. He was sure he had. He crouched down closer.

And heard it. Someone moaned close to him. He punched a fist in the air.

Who? Is it Cody? Tessa? Are they okay?

I don't know. I can't tell.

Well, move the hell over. I'm almost there.

☙ ❧

JARED WOKE UP with the mother of all headaches. What happened? The last thing he remembered was a horrible groaning as the mountain gave a huge shake. He'd wondered about it being an earthquake, but then had been afraid the assholes he'd led into the mountain had done something bad.

Except they hadn't had enough time. Had they?

He sat up and put a hand to his temple. The area around him showed a few fallen rocks, but nothing like he'd expected to see. The one beside him had drops of blood. So Mother Earth had taken a lucky shot and hit him in the temple, knocking him out. The rock on the ground appeared to be what he'd smacked on the way down. Damn, but that smarted.

What was he supposed to do now? Was the mountain done shaking and grumbling? Was it safe to go any further inside? Or should he head back to the mouth of the tunnel and wait it out?

Wait what out, Jared? You showed them how to get in. How can you sit here and do nothing while they go in and annihilate your friends?

Because by now he did consider them his friends.

And that was a hell of a lot better than his family.

At the thought, he jumped to his feet. What about his father? Could he have survived this? He searched his surroundings, realized he was still alone, and bolted deeper into the mountain.

RHIA WAITED, HER arms braced against the walls, for the waves to finally calm. Thankfully, the tunnel hadn't collapsed. Then they were in the deep rock section, and that *might* have afforded them a little protection. She glanced back at Wendy. A very wide-eyed and frightened Wendy.

"I think it's over."

"For the moment. What if it happens again? And was that an earthquake or a bomb?"

At the mention of a bomb, Rhia winced. She didn't want to think about that. Neither option was good. Earthquakes were bad news on their own. Add a blast that could have set off the earthquake and it was really bad. Mines were often established along fault lines as that's where the minerals collected. Still, the area had to be somewhat stable because humans used dynamite all the time. And as far as she could tell, this had once been a working mine.

"I disliked this place before. Now it just gives me the creeps."

The shiver in Wendy's voice made Rhia pause. Wendy shouldn't be here. Neither should Rhia, for that matter, but she wasn't going to go home.

Wendy was a different matter.

She turned back to her and opened her mouth.

Wendy beat her to it. "No. I'm not leaving. We're here. Let's find the others and get the hell out."

Rhia studied the younger girl's determined face, turned back to the tunnel and said, "Fine. Let's get this done."

CHAPTER 2

TESSA HATED THE shakiness wracking her soul. Never a huge fan of the great outdoors, this rock pile was bringing every old nightmare back to life while adding a slew of new ones. She might never sleep again. She shifted away from the hard rocky points jabbing her soft flesh. Dirt drifted, clogging the air. She shuddered, eying the boulder above her. That damn thing looked ready to crush her at any moment.

She heard voices and wanted them to be her family, but what if they were the assholes hunting her?

I think it's my father. Cody's whisper slipped through her mind on a warm wind.

Really? Do you think I should yell out? She perked up. Moments later she heard her father's frustrated voice calling out, "Damn it. They have to be here somewhere."

It is my father! She took a chance and cried out. "Dad?"

Silence.

The air filled with hollers. "Tessa? Is that you?"

"Are you okay?" Her father's voice moved closer. "Can you show us where you are?"

"Is Cody with you?" Goran's thready voice was thin with hope.

She sniffled back tears, unexplained laughter threatening to bubble up. "Cody is somewhere close by. But I don't know where. He says his wing is pinned."

Snaking a hand through the rocks, she poked her fingers upward as far as she could and wiggled them. "Can you see me?"

"There she is." She heard her father call out, followed by sounds of someone scrambling over rocks. She wiggled her fingers again. They were grabbed and squeezed.

"Gotcha."

"Oh, thank God." *Cody. My father found me. We'll find you as soon as I can get out of here. Your father is searching for you. Can you call out? Give him some indication of where you are at?*

Silence.

Cody? Damn it, Cody. Are you there? Can you hear me?

"Dad," she shouted. "Cody stopped answering me."

Fear propelled her to push up against the smaller rocks beside her. A small round circle of light appeared only to be instantly blocked by her father's face.

"Did you find Cody?"

Serus checked behind him. "Goran is searching for him. Let's get you out of here and we'll join in."

By the time the two of them had maneuvered enough rocks out of the way for her to slither though, she felt like she'd survived a session with a rock crusher. So not nice. And Cody still hadn't answered the calls.

Ignoring her own pain, she crawled over to the closest rock and sat where she could survey the cavern. Her damaged leg stretched out in front of her. As long as she didn't stare at it, the pain was tolerable, but if she let her gaze wander to the bloody mess, yeah, her stomach heaved and she almost passed out from the pain.

"Jesus, Tessa. Look at your leg," her father gasped.

She gave him a wry smile. "Actually Dad, I was trying

hard *not* to. Forget about my leg."

"Hard to do when it's right in front of me." Serus squatted in front of Tessa. "Can you make out Cody's energy at all?"

She shook her head. "Not from here. I need to stand up."

They both gazed down at her almost useless leg.

And then the pain started. Tears welled up and stabbing pains covered her left side. "Shit."

"Easy. You are doing fine. The leg will heal."

She glanced up at him. "Will it? How fast? Cody needs us now."

The rush of wings had her turning around to find Goran landing on rocks behind her.

"Tessa, glad you survived. Do you know where Cody is?"

She repeated what she'd told her father, adding, "If you carry me up high enough, I might be able to spot something."

With her father's help, Goran gently picked her up. She shuddered as her leg was jarred. She held it away from his body as he swooped upward until they hovered twenty feet above the rocks. She spotted David, Ian, and Jewel huddled against the tunnel entrance. She waved at them, relieved when they waved back. "Were they hurt at all?"

"No. We were just far enough behind you and Cody that by the time we reached the mouth of the cavern the rocks were already coming down."

She kept her gaze on the floor below as she listened to them. Horrible memories flooded her psyche, making it difficult to focus. Not being able to see much in the way of energy trails – just those made by the elders – made it that much harder. She swallowed hard and tried to concentrate. She watched her father's and her own energy trail from the rock prison rising into the air. But she couldn't find Cody's.

There should be his energy from the fall. If it hadn't dissipated.

Damn. She was looking at it wrong. "Can you turn around? So I can see his energy path from his fall?"

Slowly Goran flew in a wide circle as she pulled the story together. There's where she'd fallen, and Cody...his energy dove into that rock pile...thank God. He'd come down about thirty feet away from her. And closer to the wall. There was no visible sign that he'd moved after falling. She pointed out the spot. "I can't see him or his energy after he fell, so he hasn't moved."

She glanced behind her to find Serus already almost upon them. She wanted to help the men lift rocks out of the way, but she wasn't going to be able to stand on her own. And as long as Goran was supporting her, he couldn't help Cody. A flat rock sat off to the side. "Can you take me over to that spot, please?" He lowered her gently to the rock then flew off to help Serus.

Tessa stood on one leg and watched. Cody's energy lay low and quiet. Please let him be all right. *Please.* She watched her father toss rocks away fast and efficiently. Seconds later, he shouted, "He's here."

Oh, thank God.

Cody? Cody, can you hear me? Please talk to me.

There was only silence.

GORAN LANDED ON the biggest rock beside Serus. It was hard to pick the right place as he didn't dare land on a rock that might be holding his son down. He stepped over to where Serus stood and peered over the edge. Cody lay face down, half buried in rocks with only his shoulders and head free.

Working his way carefully downward, Goran cleared a path until he crouched beside Cody and placed a hand on his head. His boy was alive but unconscious with a huge boulder pinning his wing down, just as Tessa had said.

He winced. That had got to hurt. First things first. The rock had to go. After that, they'd need to find a place to hole up and let the two kids heal. Enough was enough – for all of them.

"Serus, give me a hand." With both of them on either side of the boulder, they might be able to lift it up.

Serus jumped down, careful to avoid Cody's legs, and crouched into position.

Goran looked at him. "We're going to have to lift it straight up and off to the side. So you'll have to jump at the same time I lift off – got it?"

Serus nodded.

Goran started the countdown. "Three. Two. One…"

With muscles bulging, backs straining, and their faces twisted with effort, both men finally managed to pick the boulder up off the ground. Below them, Cody groaned. Goran hoped that was in relief and not because they'd hurt him in the process of helping him.

Now that the rock was up, they needed to get it clear. At the count of three again, he unfurled his wings and slowly lifted. Serus jumped up and sideways. At the last moment, the boulder tipped to the side.

"Watch out!" Goran gave a hard shove, and the boulder rolled over to crash on the pile beside them. Rock shards flew in all directions.

Goran rushed back to Cody's side.

His son coughed, lifted his head and coughed again. A

plume of dust rose up into his face and set him off on another coughing fit.

Goran reached down and helped Cody into a sitting position. His damaged wing stretched limply on one side.

"Shit." Cody's face twisted in pain. "Now that is not good."

Goran braced Cody's shoulder, then, after a long look at the damage, popped it back into place.

Cody roared.

Goran winced. "Sorry, son. Your shoulder was dislocated. Now we can get your wing to fold back up." He reached over and used just enough force to get the job done. He firmly refolded the injured wing. Cody's shoulders hunched and he pulled free from Goran's grasp, gasping loudly.

"It should be able to heal now. The good news is that it's not broken."

When Cody didn't answer, he squatted in front of him. Sweat beads rolled off Cody's forehead and a pulsing twitch pounded along his jaw. Goran gave him a couple of minutes, then asked quietly. "Are you okay?"

Cody lifted his head and gave him a short nod. "I will be." *Cody?*

❧ ❧

HE GLANCED AROUND to find Tessa standing behind him. *Tessa. I'm fine. Or I will be. Are you okay?*

She nodded. *My leg is damaged, but I'm alive. That's what counts.*

Pride and joy surged through him as she stood, injured herself but worried about him. She was such a warrior. *You are so right. I'm going to be fine. Although I won't be taking you for a flight around town any time soon.*

She laughed, the sound bouncing through his mind and making him smile. Using his hands to push himself up, he slowly straightened. Once back on his feet, he took a deep breath and gazed around at the devastation. Rocks, dirt, and clouds of dust everywhere. Hearing a sound on his left, he turned to watch David, Ian, and Jewel approach.

"About time you woke up. All you're doing is sleeping on the job." Ian reached out to hit him, realized his fist was aimed at his injured shoulder, and swerved away at the last moment.

Cody glared at him. "Yeah. Thanks for missing me."

Jewel kissed him gently on the cheek. "I'm so happy to see you alive and well."

"Almost well." Cody straightened and shrugged gently, barely holding back the grimace of pain. "With any luck, I'll be fine in a few hours."

"And that brings us to the next item of business. We need food and rest. A place to stay in until you two heal and we can recharge. Doesn't have to be too long, but we have to make sure it's enough that we can fight our way out of here," David said with a pointed look at Cody's wing.

Cody nodded. "Damn good idea."

"Tessa can't move without help," Serus pointed out. "Goran, can you carry her back to the tunnel opening? We'll scout ahead and see what we can find."

Goran nodded. "Give me a minute to move the two of them over."

Cody snorted. "I can get over there on my own. Go get Tessa."

With an assessing glance at his son, Goran lifted up and headed toward Tessa.

Stubborn.

He grinned at Tessa's voice in his head as he made his way slowly back to the tunnel. *Maybe. But I can walk. You can't.*

True. Her disgruntled tone made him chuckle. He caught their friends looking at him strangely. He dropped his smile and shrugged at them sheepishly. "Sorry. Inside joke."

"You really can talk to her, can't you?" Jewel asked.

He nodded. "It's weird. And fun."

"Sounds like it," Jewel said.

Serus stepped up and said, "Talk when we're back at the tunnel."

Cody straightened, hating the damage his body had sustained. It had been a tough week. As long as he wasn't floating ash, he was good with it. But that tunnel appeared to be a long way away.

In a quiet voice, Jewel asked, "Are you okay? Do you want a hand?"

He hid his grin as he gazed down at the tiniest vampire he knew. "I'll be fine. But thanks."

David smirked at him. "I could toss you over there."

"You and whose army?" Cody scoffed. "You can barely drag your sorry ass around without trying to lift mine."

The gentle wrangling continued as they made their way to the tunnel entrance. The whole way, Cody had tried to talk to Tessa, but she'd closed a door between them. Up ahead he watched his father land and stand almost protectively in front of her.

Was she more badly injured than they'd thought?

Tessa?

I'm here.

His breath wooshed out. *You disappeared. I wasn't sure what happened.*

You were worried? Her smile rippled through his mind. *No need.*

Then why did you leave. It's like you shut me out.

I did.

Silence.

Why? He asked cautiously. But inside, frustration built. Why would she do that? And how did she do that? He had no idea how to leave her mind at all.

Because the pain was so bad I didn't want you to hear me screaming.

Oh shit. Are you that badly hurt?

My leg. It might be healing, but it sure doesn't feel like it.

Yeah, it must suck to be human. He couldn't imagine a leg taking six weeks to heal. A bad break could take a vampire six hours, but normally a couple of hours would put one back to good health. In Tessa's case, he had no idea. *And you didn't need to hide your feelings from me. I wouldn't have thought less of you if I heard you scream, you know.*

She smiled again, so faint it was like a whisper, something he felt more than saw. How weird was that?

I hated hearing your pain.

Oh shit. Yeah, that changed things. He thought she'd been worried about what he'd hear, and instead she'd been protecting him from being upset at her suffering. Somehow, he felt like he'd failed a test.

No! No tests here.

Maybe, but I didn't understand, and I feel like I should have.

She laughed. *We haven't had time enough to know how the other one thinks or reacts for that.*

I know. But you're right. I hadn't considered what hearing you scream would do to me. And you thought of it before I did.

So? It's not a contest. Quit your complaining and get over here.

But her words were warm and tinged with humor, making him once again aware of how mature she was.

Yeah, life is like that.

No, I mean it. You understand people like no one else. Except... He thought about it. *Your mother, maybe?*

Then that's easy, I learned it from her.

No. I think you learned because of the challenges you're faced. You might have gotten your big heart from her, but you use it differently. Look at Jewel and how you handled her. Look at Xana and how sorry you were that I'd been forced to kill her. She needed killing, but you were worried about the effect of doing so on me. See, that's all you. It comes from your heart.

Silence. He was almost close enough to see her face now. Her face was lowered. He wasn't sure, but it looked like she was hiding it.

Are you okay? He asked in alarm.

She lifted her face and he could see the shy smile and bright pink cheeks.

He'd embarrassed her. *I tell you the truth and you get shy and hide away.* He shook his head in bemusement. *You're going to have to get used to it. I'm not going to hold back when I see something fantastic. Honestly, you're something very different for me, and I'm learning a lot about myself through you.*

He could feel a hesitation in his mind. He rushed to add, *Different in a good way. You're warmer, more caring than other females I've known. You're almost...* and he held the words back.

But she said them herself. *Almost human?*

RHIA STRODE DOWN the long white tunnel with a confidence she didn't feel. She had no idea what they were up against, but she knew the balance of power had shifted some way. She'd had a hand in it, going to the humans for help.

Now that they were here in force, it was daunting to think she'd done something that could backfire on her people.

But whatever was going on down here had to stop. Even if they needed to change things up. She needed her family back safe and sound. With young Wendy here...she felt even more responsible.

"There isn't much damage here," Wendy said softly from behind. "I wonder why?"

"Good structure. We also don't know what caused this disaster, and that would determine where the worst of the damage happened. We need to consider that it could have been a blast sealing off one part of the mountain from the other."

"I don't like the sound of that."

"No. Neither do I." Rhia opened the last door and entered the section of the mine where there should have been an office full of computers on the left. Instead, fallen rocks and tiles covered the space. "Oh no!"

CHAPTER 3

TESSA HATED THAT her leg wouldn't heal at the same rate as a full blood vampire would. Hated that it would mark her as different yet again.

And she had to stop focusing on it. Especially when Cody could read her every thought – or almost every thought. So disconcerting.

Told you so.

She rolled her eyes. Cody stood in front of her, a good ten feet between them, a warm caring in his eyes that she'd never get used to. How could she not love the sense of acceptance? It made her realize how much she'd missed in her life.

But no longer.

She smiled as Cody's voice nudged the door open and slipped into her thoughts. He was right. She wasn't alone anymore. And didn't that thought curl her toes?

Then why don't you make those curling toes heal a little faster with that vampire heritage you're always calling on? Maybe it will help.

She gasped. "Why didn't I think of that?"

Her father squatted down beside her. "Why didn't you think of what?"

She groaned. Cody burst out laughing.

"I suggested she call on her vampire genes to help her heal faster." He stared down at her leg and winced. "How bad is it?"

"It's bad," said Goran. "She can't be moved much. We need to find a safe place to hide."

"And me," protested Ian. "Why does everyone forget about me? Geez." But his grin belied his words.

"Ha," Jewel said. "According to you, you're tough as rocks. According to the girls, you're dumb as rocks."

Cody laughed at Ian's mock gasp of outrage. His peals of joy ringing around inside the tunnel made the two stop to turn and look at him.

"What's his problem," David muttered.

It was Goran who answered. "He's happy. In fact, considering the scenario, he's damn happy. Are we sure there isn't happy gas or something floating in the air?"

Tessa grinned. She knew why Cody was happy and it had nothing to do with chemicals. It was her. And him. And all of them alive. Here and now. "He has a right to be happy. Just think of everything we've been through."

As she sat there, with the others all laughing and joking around her, she realized how much they'd survived. The emotional, physical, and mental trauma. They all belonged in a human shrink ward.

Speak for yourself. Cody said. *I am normal.*

And I am the new normal.

He chuckled, then laughed lightly only to start bellowing with joy... again.

Serus looked at her. "What did you say to him?"

She smirked. "I said I was the new normal."

Her father shot Goran a questioning look, then they both stared down at her, puzzled. "What does that mean?"

Jewel giggled. "It means she's the wave of the future and the rest of us had better adapt as she leads the way. She is normal – or what normal will be soon."

Goran reared back. He frowned. "Uh, Tessa...you've come a long ways...but..." he stopped helplessly.

Tessa giggled. He looked at her in total confusion.

"They are putting us on, Goran," growled Serus.

With a hoot, Cody said. "We know perfectly well that Tessa will never be considered 'normal', but she's never going to be a second class vamp again. She might very well lead *us* as she has some serious skills."

The admiration in his voice had Tessa straightening her back. Damn, that felt good.

And it's true.

"Sooo Tessa, any time you want to ditch this big guy," Ian said with a straight face, "you know I'd be happy to take you out to a movie, right?"

Silence.

Everyone turned to stare at Ian. He tried to keep a straight face but couldn't pull it off for more than a few seconds. He bent over howling and slapping his knees. "Oh my God. You should see your faces. Priceless."

Tessa watched Cody. There was no laughter on his face. A storm brewed. *Easy. He was only teasing.*

There will not be any teasing about that. Ever.

About me going out with anyone else? She couldn't stop herself from asking.

Yes. That was not funny.

No, but he's just trying to get a rise out of you.

Maybe I should get a rise out of him. If he thinks he's—

"Sorry Ian. I'm spoken for." She grinned up at the affable steadfast vamp that had fought by her side so much this past week and added, "Besides. So are you."

His eyes widened in horror. He spun around as if to

search for someone behind him, but it was the first thing out of his mouth that gave him away. He swallowed hard and asked, "How did you know?"

The others stared from Ian to Tessa and back to Ian. Cody's face twisted in thought as if trying to figure it out.

Jewel straightened, a look of shock on her face. "What? You are?"

David walked over to stand beside his friend, a huge grin on his face. "Well, well, well."

"Yeah, give over." Cody laughed, walking over to slap Ian on the shoulder. "We want all the details."

Ian hunched his shoulders and stared at Tessa suspiciously. "There aren't any." He narrowed his gaze at her. "Can you read my mind?"

She shook her head, helpless to wipe the wide grin off her face. "I don't have to." She motioned with her hand. "I can see energy, and that includes the bits and pieces of other people's energy we hold close."

Ian bent to look at his legs and arms.

She giggled. "It's mixed with your energy. So I know she's important to you." An impulse had her adding, "It *is* a female...isn't it?"

He gasped, and a visible shudder rippled down his tall lean frame. "Yes!"

That did it. The others cracked up.

Tessa knew the banter and humor was giving them all a chance to de-stress. It was also giving her a chance to heal. She'd called on her vampire heritage to fix her leg and although she wouldn't want to trust it just yet, it was starting to feel like it was improving.

Really?

I think so.

Cody crossed the last few feet and knelt in front of her.

Serus crowded around them. "What's wrong? Is your leg worse?"

Cody gently ripped the black material away and showed her father the pink flesh where there'd been damaged muscles before. There was still a ways to go, yet now she knew she would heal in decent time. "She's healing beautifully."

"No way." Goran leaned over and let out a long whistle. "Well, now if that doesn't beat all."

"Tessa, did you do something different?" her father asked, studying her leg.

"Only in that I made a direct request to heal my leg."

"A request" Jewel asked, her brows creasing in confusion. "To whom?"

Tessa chuckled. "I talk to my different genes when I need something from that side of my heritage. In this case, I asked my vamp genes to heal my leg."

She lifted her leg experimentally. It didn't send pain screaming through her. "It's much better."

Cody straightened. "But not all better. Let's see if you can put some weight on it."

She used his hand to pull herself upright. She slowly lowered her sore leg to the ground and put some weight on it experimentally. It hurt, yet it showed a hell of an improvement already. She let go of his hand and took a tentative step, then groaned and shifted to her other leg. "It's definitely not all better. My back still hurts too. I guess I was a little too specific with my instructions."

"Then sit back down and tell those genes to fix all of you," her father ordered. He glanced over at Cody. "And you, how is your wing?"

Cody stepped back slightly and worked on gently unfurling his wings. His right one opened with no problem. The left one barely moved outward and he winced. "No flying for me for awhile."

Ian snorted. "Join the club."

Jewel nodded. "I tried earlier, but they won't even open. More drugs haven't helped the ones that paralyzed our wings in the first place."

"Damn tired of it, too," Ian growled. "We could be so much further than we are now."

"Or you could be injured like Cody and Tessa are," David retorted.

Ian stopped, thought about it, then nodded. "True enough. But I have had it with being drugged by these assholes."

Tessa nodded. "We all need to be extra careful since each of us has been drugged at least once."

"Not me. No one has gotten close enough to drug me," Serus growled as he glared at her.

Goran snorted. "How about no more drugs for any of us?" He stood, hands on his hips, staring down the tunnel. "I think I'll go back to that damn cloning room and make sure they are all dead."

"Not alone, you aren't."

Tessa knew there'd be no stopping the two ancients now that she and Cody were on the mend and the truth was, she just wanted to get the hell out of here and go home. Only they weren't quite strong enough to make that happen.

"Dad, you need to find blood. Enough for everyone would be ideal. Just make sure it's drug free."

Ian groaned. "I really don't want anything from here."

"Neither do I," Jewel added in a small voice. "But I'm really hungry."

"I don't like it either," David muttered.

Tessa nodded. "I hear you, but I can see your energy levels and they are dangerously low. We are also in a blood farm. I don't know what will happen to any of you if you don't feed. I don't want you going off the wall and attacking anyone here." She made a face. "Especially me."

Silence.

"Shit. She's right, Serus. The kids haven't had anything in days. We grabbed some at the hospital."

"And that was still a long time ago." Cody straightened. "I think we should stay together. That means we'll all go to the cloning room. It's not far, and if there is any blood we can use, we'll all drink some in order to get out of this place."

"We're assuming that some blood survived the blast," Jewel pointed out.

"If so, then we have to assume some vamps could have survived as well," Tessa straightened up and moaned as her still-healing back shifted. "I vote we all go."

She took several steps back toward the other end of the tunnel.

And that's when she heard it.

JARED HATED THE darkness. And he really hated this mine. When he'd come this way earlier, there been light. Lots of it. A layer of fine dust filled his eyes and nose. He coughed, then coughed again. Something bad had happened here.

He could barely make his way over the rocks. The tunnel hadn't collapsed, but there was enough debris on the ground that he had to struggle through it in places. The weird smell added to the effect. Musty, dusty, and earthy.

Further along he saw a light still burning from behind a large boulder, giving the area a weird halo. He shivered and walked closer. There was no going back. Not now. With any luck, the soldiers would change their minds and he'd meet up with them as they retreated.

But he didn't hear a sound or see a soul. He entered the halfway station, which was how he called the wooden platform room connecting the two tunnels It was empty. Canisters sat on their side and shelves had tumbled to the floor, covering the contents that had fallen first. He made his way across the room and opened the door to the other half of the railway.

Empty. But not collapsed. It's as if one side took the hit but not the other. At least it made walking easier. Despite the low level headache bugging him, a sense of urgency was building inside. He didn't know what was wrong, but something was and that was good enough for him.

He might be tired, but he was alive and he wouldn't rest until he found his friends. With that thought uppermost on his mind, he picked up his pace until he was running down the tunnel.

☙ ❧

RHIA STRUGGLED TO keep her emotions in check, but she couldn't stop the small cry from coming forth. If this is what the early rooms in the mine looked like, what would they find below?

Wendy whispered. "Oh, this is not good. I'm sure those computers are important for something."

At that, Rhia took a second glance and realized there was no power in the room. There were no lights on the monitors, nothing showing on the screens. "If the people in the blood farm are connected to this power system, then…"

"—then they are dying right now, if not already gone."

What a mess. Rhia closed her eyes at the enormity of the cleanup they could be facing here. The decomposition of so many bodies, the condition of the blood flowing from the canisters, and the blood in the holding tanks going bad – all of it was a disaster. And a huge biohazard.

Turning resolutely to face the tunnel, Rhia said, "Let's hope the organizers of this nightmare have a good backup power system in place."

"I don't think anything could be good enough," Wendy muttered.

Rhia nodded. "I know. We'll find out soon." As they came around the last curve to where they'd ordinarily be able to see through the glass into the nightmarish hanging dead, Rhia realized all the glass was gone.

So were some of the support beams. The tunnel was still passable, and from what she could see the people were still hanging. That was good news. If they were still alive or not remained to be seen. The large double doors to the blood farm were damaged. She couldn't open it and was forced to knock out the remaining glass from one of the large screening windows. Then she climbed through.

"Watch yourself," she warned Wendy once she was on the other side, but she needn't have worried as Wendy hopped smoothly through. Together, the two walked down the left side of the warehouse, keeping a wary eye on the hanging population and the structural damage that showed in the lopsided supports from which they hung. The rooms on the left were damaged in an irregular fashion.

Some appeared to be fully sealed off behind fallen rock, while in others, the ceilings had come down. Rhia didn't see anyone alive – other than those hanging and their state of life was still in question. She so didn't want to walk any closer and find out. If she even could.

"There's nothing we can do for them right now, is there?" Wendy had stopped to stare at one man hanging at an odd angle due to the twisted structural beam he was strung up on.

"Not at the moment. Without power, they will die and even with power, we won't know if they will survive and for how long."

Wendy gave a slight shudder and turned to face Rhia. "Where do we go from here?"

"To the other computer room. Keep an eye out for the others. In fact, let me know if you see anyone."

"Human or vamp?"

"They are both down here." She glanced around, saw nothing moving, and strode toward the computer room. "We need to hurry. There could be more earth tremors at any moment."

"Do you really think this damage was caused by an earth-quake?"

Rhia hated to consider that it wasn't. "I hope so. If a blast did this, then we have to consider that there could be more set to go off at any moment."

Wendy's face scrunched up. "Let's go. I don't want to be here in either case."

"Too bad." A harsh angry voice snapped out behind them. "Cause you aren't going anywhere. Ever again."

SERUS STOPPED. "WHAT was that?"

Everyone froze, ears cocked to listen better.

But nothing was distinguishable. He shook his head and muttered, "I swore I heard something."

"Like what?" asked Goran.

He shrugged. "I don't know. A rumbling? Voices maybe?"

"I didn't hear anything," David said from his left. "Maybe it was just falling rock from the earthquake."

"Maybe," he answered, but didn't voice the worry in his head. It had sounded like voices.

Then we'll go with your gut. It's rarely wrong. Goran's voice whispered in his head.

You're right. My gut says the voices are trouble. Big trouble, but I can't tell you why.

I don't need to know why. Let's just be on guard and get the hell out of here.

Serus glanced around at the sad group behind him. Damn, how had they come to this? They were in tough shape before this last incident, but with both Tessa and Cody injured, holing up until they regained their strength and were fully healed was the only option.

"I'm going to scout ahead to check if that embryo room is safe. We can stay in there if it is."

Tessa looked at him, an oddly mature look in her eyes as she said, her voice whisper soft. "No, Dad. Nowhere is safe. We stay together. It's not far. I can make it."

Damn, she was stubborn. And prideful. And his. He was so crazy proud of his little girl. But he didn't want her hurt any more than she already was and she didn't seem to know when to quit. She needed to listen to him today. But even as he started to protest, he realized she was speaking out of concern for him. He stopped. He'd never considered that she might be worried about him for his sake, but more that she was still a child worried about losing her father for her sake.

She'd changed.

As evidenced by her actions once again.

He bent over. "So are you too old for a piggyback ride?"

She laughed in delight. "Never." With David helping, she was soon seated on his back. He led the way back to the room Goran hated.

And we can wait here now. Goran's growl filled his mind. *I want to make sure they are all dead.*

As long as you don't go off all crazy again.

Goran snorted at his side. He strode past Serus and led the way. Carrying his daughter had shifted Serus's view on getting things done. She came first.

CHAPTER 4

G ORAN HELD UP his hand for those behind him to stop. He placed his finger on his lip and motioned to both Ian and David to join him before slipping up to the door. Tessa struggled to slide off her father's back without jarring her leg. Tired, sore, and hungry, she wished a power nap was on the menu. Those had kept her energy levels up during her night and day lifestyle. She rarely got five hours in one stretch. Power naps were her answer.

Too bad her stomach couldn't do the same thing.

As if it had heard its name, her stomach started growling. Cody and her father spun to look at her.

"What was that?" Cody asked, confusion in his voice.

She winced. "My stomach."

They both looked at her. Then at each other.

Her father spoke up, "How serious?"

Cody pinned him in place with a glare. "What do you mean?"

Her father shrugged. "She eats human food instead of blood if she can."

Cody glanced at her, one eyebrow raised.

She winced. Nothing like springing one of her major quirks on him without warning. "Not really. I do drink synthetic blood if I have to, but I don't like it."

"But you need food for energy and there won't be human

food here. So therefore, you'll have blood," her father said, his tone of voice not allowing for an argument.

"If I have to, I will." And she would. But not unless she really had to. She kept her face carefully blank and her tone of voice carefully calm. But her father wasn't fooled.

He gave a loud snort. "Let's go. The sooner we get out of here the better. She can get downright mean when she's hungry."

She glared at him. "Do not."

"See what I mean?" Her father turned around to look for Goran. "Ah hell. Where'd they go?"

"They shouldn't have gone in without us." Tessa bit back a moan of pain as she slowly hobbled over to the open door. David and Ian stood just inside the room watching Goran check out the half-suspended vampires. On the ground were several piles of burning ash. Tessa closed her eyes as she realized Goran was finishing off the rest of the vampires. The rest of his family.

Don't call them family.

She scrunched up her shoulders at Cody's chastising voice. *Sorry.*

I know, but he's really having a hard time with that right now.

Understood. Still, she stood in the doorway and watched along with the rest of the group. *I suppose this is as good a way as any for him to work his rage off.*

Maybe.

Serus walked over beside Goran.

Happy to leave them to it, Tessa made her way over to the stairs she'd jumped off when she'd tackled Tyson earlier. This area looked to be untouched by the quake or Goran's actions. Good thing.

She didn't know what anyone else needed, but she needed food and sleep.

Stay there. I'm going to see if we can find something for us to eat.

She nodded and watched as Cody strode toward the back of the room. *Be careful.*

I will.

Jewel joined her a few minutes later, shaky and pale as she collapsed beside Tessa. "I don't think I can do this anymore."

"Cody is searching for blood." She motioned to the closed doors at far side of the room. More of the room was open to viewing as Goran cleaned up. She grimaced and turned back to Jewel, barely holding back the shudder of revulsion. She didn't like what Goran was doing, could barely stand the thought of it, but she knew her arguments against his actions weren't going to go over well either. But were all the hanging vamps bad?

"I hate what he's doing," Jewel slumped back against the hard stairs. "But I hate what those... things... represent more."

"I know." Tessa shifted so her back was to Goran's systematic actions. "The thing is, I have trouble believing that they are all bad."

Jewel opened her eyes to stare at her. "They are a messed up combination of all things and they aren't vampire or human or animal. They are just—"

Jewel stopped as words failed her.

"That's why I'm not out there fighting for them," Tessa admitted. "At the same time, I hate that we brought them to life at all."

"Not us."

"It was still one of us. Our people. Like what is wrong

with us?" Tessa cried out. "Look at this whole disaster. All caused by vampires."

Jewel rolled her head from side to side. "It's too big to take on the guilt. I'm not guilty and neither are you. Those madmen are the ones who did this, not us."

"I know that mentally, but inside, my heart is hurting. We are so vicious. Why couldn't we be a species of faeries or something?"

"Faeries?"

Tessa gave a half laugh. "Sorry, it's a human thing. A species of fictional people that are all things nice and sweet."

Jewel stared at her. "I think I'd like that. I've had enough nastiness to last me a lifetime."

"And considering how long we live…"

"While you two are busy talking, maybe you should multi-task and drink at the same time."

Tessa looked at Cody, caught sight of the two IV bags in his hand, and skittered backwards up the stairs. "Get those things away from me."

Jewel swiveled from Tessa to the bags in Cody's hands. She licked her lips.

Oh shit.

Jewel needed to feed. And bad. The smell of blood from her own injuries had stopped Tessa from noticing the heavy metallic smell that permeated the room. It had to affect her friends and family. Highlighting their need to feed.

But damn – from those IV bags?

She hoped not.

Why not?

Who knows what's in it? They could have all kinds of substances in there.

But we don't have a choice. Jewel is fading. You've never seen the type of damage a ravaged vampire in bloodlust mode can do. And if everyone drinks a little blood, then we can hold off that state.

Jewel reached out with a trembling hand. "Is it safe?"

Tessa watched, horrified as Cody held the bag toward her. Her own stomach was screaming...but no longer in hunger. In shock. In panic. In fear.

"How can it be safe? It's from here."

Jewel's hand fell away and she turned to look up at Tessa beseechingly. "I can't go on much more. I need to feed...eat." she corrected. "We all do." She took a deep breath and asked, "Don't you?"

Yes, she did. When she had to. But she mixed it with other stuff in order to get it down and make it stay down. Her body allowed for both foods, and she needed both but she didn't like the blood stuff.

She had no idea what would happen if she went past dizzy and fainting. If she was flat out unconscious, would she die? Did she *have* to drink some of the blood from this farm? Surely other blood was available? It would be too much to hope they had human food here. The vamps would have thrown out anything they'd found on the humans. She glanced down at her hand and held it out in front of her. It trembled slightly, but it was nothing compared to Jewel's hands.

Were the others the same? Were they going to go into a feeding frenzy if they didn't eat soon? And if they did, who would they turn on? Humans? Or if there weren't any humans around, would they turn on each other?

Or would they turn on her instead?

Don't ever think that. Cody's harsh voice slashed through her fear. *It won't happen.*

Are you sure? Even if you all become so lost in bloodlust, will you care?

Of course we'll care. Do not for one minute think you will become the victim of our hunger.

She closed her eyes and collapsed against the railing. *Sorry. I'm sorry. I must be more tired than I realized.*

You damn well better be.

The hurt and anger in his voice made her ashamed. She hadn't wanted to think along those lines, but once she started in that direction, the thoughts had just come.

Well, stop going in that damn direction. No one here is going to turn on you. That's your fear speaking. No one will ever again turn on you – and if they do, I'll be at your side keeping them off you – do you hear me?

The fierce anger in his voice had her sitting upright to study his face curiously. *You mean that, don't you?*

He gave her a clipped nod and said, "Yes."

She really wasn't alone any longer. Unbidden, tears came to her eyes. How long would it take before she felt that on the inside?

Now. You'll start feeling it now.

Then in front of whoever was watching as if he no longer gave a damn, Cody laid down both bags of blood in Jewel's lap and reached over to clasp Tessa's head firmly in both hands, leaned in, and kissed her. Hard.

He pulled back and said in a terse voice. "Believe it."

Still in a temper, he snagged up one of the blood bags and headed toward Ian.

Jewel giggled. "Wow."

Tessa slid her a sideways glance and grinned. "Actually I think that was more like…double wow!"

AFTER DROPPING OFF a bag of blood for Ian, Cody strode over to his father. He didn't understand the rage coursing through his body, but if anyone could spike his anger over nothing, it was Tessa. How dare she think they'd turn against her? So what if she had some throwback genes? No one knew if they were actually human genes. Everyone assumed that's what she had, but it's not like her family had done any tests to find out. Like how foolish could she be?

And how insulting?

Actually thinking they'd lose control. They weren't green vampires unable to control their urges. Hell, if that were the case, he'd have turned her over his knee a long time ago. Or thrown her over his shoulder and carried her off to his lair.

Just the thought of doing that made him feel primitive. And hungry. For her. Damn. What were the chances he'd be able to take this relationship where he wanted it to go anytime soon?

Zero to none.

Double damn.

He allowed his anger to re-ignite. It helped burn away the other fire in his system. One he was likely to be nursing for a very long time.

Damn female.

Not my fault.

He stilled.

Shit. He closed his eyes as he realized she'd heard the thoughts in his head. Yeah. This was not good.

I'm sorry. I should have left, but you were so angry I was try-ing to figure out how to explain, when you...

Shame washed through him. He wanted to run away and

hide.

Please don't. She sighed, a tiny breath that wafted through his mind. *I like that you feel that way about me.*

He opened his eyes. *What?*

A girl likes to know she's wanted.

He smiled wryly. *Yeah? You like knowing I'm suffering mightily for this?*

No. Not really. Her tone of voice changed and humor crept in as she added, *Well, maybe a little.*

He grinned. How the hell could she shift his emotions from one direction to the other so fast he felt like a hormonal teenager?

Her laughing voice filled his head, making him roll his eyes. *You mean like me? You aren't that much older, you know. Maybe it's your hormones that are going wild.*

Yeah, they sure are.

Is that…why?

He stopped and had to think about what she said. And still couldn't figure it out. *What are you talking about?*

Never mind, she said quickly.

No. Not never mind. I don't understand. And he wanted to.

I just wondered… and she stopped again.

Wondered what? Now he was getting impatient.

She rushed to answer. *You said it might be hormones so I wondered if that was the only reason you feel this way.*

He had to stop for a moment to figure out what the hell she meant. Then he got it. And he laughed and laughed.

It wasn't that funny, she muttered.

Oh yes, it is. Nothing, and I mean nothing is needed to make me feel this way. I don't need hormones to enhance anything.

Oh. She said in a small voice.

He grinned. *Tessa, I want you now and I'm gonna want you*

in a couple of centuries. No hormonal enhancements required.

She smiled, and damned if he didn't feel it as it spread through his mind. And how special was that?

"Cody?"

He spun around at the sound of his father's voice. "What's up, sir?

"Come here. I want you to see this."

RHIA TURNED AROUND slowly, her hands up in front of her. Wendy followed her lead. Together, the two women faced a large group of soldiers. Human soldiers. Pissed-off human soldiers.

Crap.

"Gentlemen. I am Rhia of the Vampire Council." She stood tall and straight. "I'm one of those who helped organize your presence here."

One of the soldiers grinned, but there was no humor in his face. Nor in his voice as he said, "Prove it."

She cocked her head to the side. "Call your commander. I worked with Councilman Adamson and Gloria of the Vampire Council. They are, as am I, part of the Human Council. They will vouch for me."

"If you are who you say you are, you wouldn't be here." A second man spoke, as cold and angry as the first one.

She understood the bitterness. This warehouse was full of their people. Humans who'd been badly treated by her people. She agreed with their mood, but she didn't dare have it directed at her and Wendy. She needed their help.

"She's telling the truth. I was at the Council chambers with her."

"And you... who are you?"

"Wendy. Daughter of Councilman Wilson." Wendy's voice was cool and composed.

Rhia was impressed. She couldn't imagine anyone else being this calm in this situation.

More men clustered around the first two soldiers. One in the back, asking, "How do we know you aren't responsible for this abomination?"

Rhia patiently reminded him. "That's why you should phone your superiors and confirm our identities. We need to get medical personnel down here to help these people. Taz was here, he needs to come back now that you are here to keep him safe."

"You know Dr. Taz?" The second man spoke up.

Rhia nodded. "He is a good friend."

"Not likely. Not with him being human and you being..." he broke off and waved his hand at her. "A vampire."

"Not true. We are good friends. His wife is my best friend," she added coolly. "Sian."

The men reared back slightly, looked at each other, but stayed silent. The first man, apparently the leader, pulled out his cell phone and walked a few steps away from the group.

"If you're telling the truth," the second man said, "Then we'll find out. But if you're lying... you'll be dead just like this guy." And he pointed to a vampire lying off to the side.

Rhia cried out. "But he's one of the techs who was here helping Taz."

The same guy snorted. "Like hell. He was trying to run away when we got here."

One of the men in the back laughed. "Like that was happening."

It was Wendy's shocked voice that put things in perspective and highlighted how dangerous this situation had become. "You shot him in the back?"

"He wouldn't stop. We ordered him to stop. But he wouldn't." The big man shrugged. "Then he wouldn't die."

Another man in the group called out, "Innocent men don't run."

"Maybe not," Rhia said in a hard pained voice, tearing her gaze away from the dead vamp. "Scared men do though."

"Scared? He's only going to be scared if he did something wrong and he's afraid we'll retaliate."

"Which we will."

"And did."

Rhia stared at the men so eager for payback, they'd killed an innocent vamp. As she stared down at her fallen peer, she had to question if he was innocent or not. If he was, then why was he still here? Taz had said all the vamp techs had been separated from the human techs. Once released, the entire group had left. She spun around to face the way they'd come in. He'd also said that Jared had stayed behind. If so, where was he now?

❧ ❦

JARED STUMBLED FOR what had to be the twentieth time as he followed his trail back to the staircase. He could only hope he'd recognize the entrance. With all the rock and debris, it was hard to recognize his surroundings. And in the piss poor light, he was lucky to see anything.

He clambered over another large group of rocks. He was starting to work up a hell of a sweat, too. He wiped his forehead on the shoulder of his t-shirt. Taking a deep breath, he jumped up and over the next boulder to the far side.

Was it getting hotter in here? Dustier? He wished he had water. He hadn't thought to ask the soldiers for a bottle before they left. Maybe they didn't have any. Or maybe they had cases of the damn stuff. Just the thought made him look back the way he'd come with longing. How long would it take? He coughed up more dust from his throat and cursed his stupidity. It would likely take another hour to just to reach the trucks. Too long.

He had to catch up to the soldiers and make sure they didn't shoot his friends.

If any of them were still alive. That he hadn't seen anyone dead or injured was a good sign. Maybe.

He dug deep and headed to the next pile of rubble.

Surely it couldn't be much further.

He came to a clear sector. He started to run. Just when he settled into a decent pace, he heard something up ahead.

Voices.

CHAPTER 5

TESSA GLARED DOWN at her leg. It still hurt like crazy. As much as she hated the pain, it gave her something to focus on. And it beat watching Jewel and David suck back blood from the bag. She hated to think of what might be mixed in the blood. Drugs? How could there not be?

Still, Goran had found it in a small cooler off to the side for the staff – or he assumed it was for the staff. From what she could see, her friends were tanking up. That should have made her feel better as they needed this. She was likely to be the one with the waning energy now. She knew Cody was healing nicely as he appeared to be using his injured shoulder just fine. She didn't know about his wing though.

Jewel groaned and leaned back against the stairs. "I'm drunk on blood," she murmured. "Now I just want to sleep."

Tessa bit back her warning about sedatives being in the blood. If there were any, it was too late for her friends. Besides, they did need to sleep so maybe... just maybe, this was a good thing.

She'd love to sleep herself, but her stomach was still growling at her. It wasn't bad enough yet for Tessa to grab a blood bag and suck it back like the others. She could and she would...if and when her situation became bad enough. She wasn't there yet.

And given the unlimited number of nasty things the bad

guys could have dissolved in the bags – she might never be.

She should try to power nap –boost her flagging energy and help her to heal.

With a quick glance around, she realized that whether as a result of overfeeding or the sedatives, most of her friends were already collapsed on the floor sleeping. At least they looked asleep. Her father was standing and talking to Goran at the far end. Neither appeared to be tired. And how the hell did that work? Still, if they were awake, then they'd stand guard and she could nod off. With a quick check on Jewel to make sure she was really just asleep, Tessa let her eyes close.

Ha. Thought you'd never stop worrying.

She smiled. *I thought you were asleep.*

Nope, just resting. We need this. So just sleep. Let your body relax.

His voice was hypnotic. Soothing. Comforting.

She felt the tension in her shoulders relax. The throbbing in her leg was distant, less of a pain and more of an ache.

Good. Now go deeper.

She sighed and felt her body drop off.

"Well, well, well. Look what we have here."

Tessa froze. *Shit. Cody. What's going on?*

She didn't move, although instinct had her wanting to run as far and as fast as she could. Which, given her leg, wasn't far at all.

Keep pretending to be asleep.

She heard footsteps as several people walked through the room. Where the hell had they come from? She thought there was no way out from this side. She assumed her father was still at the back of the room but she didn't know for sure. Cody was slumped against a wall and was pretending to be asleep. She peeked through her eyelids.

Humans. Armed humans.

Really? Like is this good news or bad news? Cody asked.

Not sure. She watched as one of the men dressed in an army green uniform prodded Ian with the end of his rifle.

"Hey, this lot is dead already," the guy said. He walked over to David and repeated his poking.

They think we're dead? Cody murmured.

She realized he was uncertain because they were humans. He'd had little to do with them compared to her.

"Good. Saves us the trouble of having to kill the assholes. What's with all the ash and crap floating in the air? What the hell were they doing in here anyway?"

"Who knows? Come on. There's nothing more here. The place has been destroyed. Let's head back to the tunnel and keep going."

A third man appeared in Tessa's line of vision. "Damn. I really wanted to kill something."

"Me too. But everything in here is dead already. Looks like the mountain did the work for us."

"Hell," muttered one male Tessa couldn't see. "I *really* want to kill something."

Tessa barely held back a shudder. She didn't dare let them see she was alive. They'd likely open fire on everyone to make sure they were dead.

"So fire into one of these corpses if you're so desperate to play with your gun. But remember, the mountain is already unstable. Start firing wildly in here and you might bring more rocks down."

"He's not going to start firing at anything," a clipped voice from behind her said. "We're here to take out the vampires who built this damn mountain. Not waste ammo riddling corpses with bullets. Now everyone head back to the tunnel before those rocks shift again and we can't squeeze our way back out again."

Tessa held her breath as she waited to hear the sounds of the men leaving. She heard so much noise then a slow drifting off as the men moved further away. She kept her ear tuned to their footsteps. As soon as they left, she was going to bolt over and check out the way they'd come in.

She wanted to peer around the railing and check if they'd all left, but what if one or two had stayed behind as a guard?

Wait. I can see the exit they used, but let's make sure they don't decide to come back and double check.

What a great thought.

It's what I'd do. What I've done, he admitted. *Why would you leave anything to chance? Just because a vampire is dead doesn't mean he stays dead.*

She'd done the same thing herself. *Stabbing seemingly dead vamps with silver to make sure they didn't get back up again was just common sense.*

Did they say they were killing vamps? he asked.

Sure, the ones involved in the blood farm.

Yeah, and how are they going to know who that is?

They aren't, she answered slowly, thinking about it. *And the one sounded like he couldn't wait to kill any and all vampires.*

A sudden movement from the side she couldn't see had her closing her eyes and holding her breath.

It's your father.

Oh. She straightened and peered over the railing. "Dad? Are they gone?"

He turned and nodded, a grim look on his face. "Yes. We couldn't take the chance of them mistaking us as the bastards who created this hellhole. Glad you stayed quiet."

"Cody is awake, too," she said, "But I think the other

three are out cold."

Serus glanced at the others stretched out in various positions. "Good thing too. If they thought we were alive, I believe they'd have shot us first and asked questions later."

"Me too." Tessa stretched her injured leg. "I gather there is an exit we didn't see before?"

"One opened up with the earthquake. I watched them leave," her father said, adding, "How is the healing going?"

"Getting there. I was just about to take a nap when they arrived."

"Do. I'll stand watch. We were at the far end when the humans surprised us. They didn't even walk down to the back of the room." He snorted as if disgusted with their lack of thoroughness.

She smiled. "The room is trashed, and with all the ash they probably thought nothing else could be alive."

She studied the large room and realized that it really did look terrible. All the frames that had held the 'growing' or maturing vampires were hanging drunkenly off the supports. Most of the tiles had collapsed and pipes and tubing hung everywhere, still spewing whatever nastiness they'd held. In fact, the back half of the room slanted slightly and all the horrible liquids had pooled at that end.

No wonder the men hadn't gone down there.

She wouldn't have either.

Just looking at the pool of glistening horror made her stomach churn in protest. She closed her eyes and dropped her head to her knees.

She so didn't want to pass out. But feeling faint appeared to be the dominant emotion right now. She needed food.

The hairs on the back of her neck rose, and she jerked upright to find Cody's hard gaze blazing down at her. He held a bag of blood up to her face.

"Drink."

❧ ❧

GORAN WAS WALKING toward Serus when he saw Cody jump up and thrust a bag of blood into Tessa's face. She did look weak, and they appeared to be arguing about something. But she was also standing up to his boy just fine.

Only her mouth wasn't moving and he couldn't hear anything.

As he walked closer, he understood. They were fighting mentally. How weird was that? It was as if he was watching a movie with no sound. His boy was glaring something fierce. Then Tessa leaned in and dropped her head against Cody's chest.

He reached for Serus mentally. *What's going on?*

I think Tessa is getting weak. But she's afraid of the blood. She doesn't drink much blood at the best of times. Hates the stuff.

How can a vampire hate blood?

Serus shrugged. *What can I say? She's had some flavored stuff she could get down, but that the blood comes from here and might be drugged is adding to her objections.*

Goran studied the three sleeping vampires. They were in a deep sleep. *Do you think the blood was doctored?*

I hope not. Serus added, *Jewel and Ian have been drugged enough already.*

Shit. Goran strode over to Ian and gave the boy's shoulder a good hard shake. No response. Ian's head lolled to one side, but there was no other movement. *That's not good.*

He spun around to see Serus shaking David awake. Goran tried to figure out how many times David had been drugged.

Once for sure, but was this the second or third time?

David groaned. Serus shook him harder. "David. Wake up."

"Why?" David asked, not opening his eyes. "I'm so damn tired."

"Yeah, as long as you're just sleeping and not drugged."

David's eyes popped open. "You think I've been drugged?"

"It's possible." Serus squatted beside him. "Ian appears to be affected by something."

Back on his feet, David stretched. "I feel decent."

"It might have been a sedative to keep the vamps calm. Happy," Goran suggested.

"Well, I definitely feel like smiling," David said with a big grin. He turned to look at the others. "How is everyone else?"

"Tessa won't drink blood. Jewel, like Ian, is in a deeper sleep than she should be. Both Goran and I fed, but we had just enough to take off the edge. Hopefully not enough to absorb too many drugs. We don't feel any different, which is good."

David made a mock face. "You might have told us that last part. Last I remember, you were handing out bags and telling us to drink."

"Yeah, but you missed the instructions – drink a little. Not the whole damn thing," Serus said in exasperation.

Cody walked over and joined them. "I had about a quarter. Kept the rest just in case."

David groaned. "I didn't. I had about half a bag."

Cody reached out and slugged him. "You always did eat too much."

"What about Jewel, is she okay?" He leaned around Cody.

But it was Tessa's voice that called back, "She's out. She's almost comatose. I can't get any response from her."

David stumbled to her side. Goran watched him, thinking that this was Jewel's third time. Maybe they were lucky and it was only a calming agent.

He caught Serus's eye. He motioned to Ian. "I think we should wake him up."

Everyone turned to look at Ian sprawled on the floor. "It's a good thing he was out like this when the humans walked through here," Serus said.

"Humans?" David called from the stairs. "What humans?"

Goran heard Tessa filling her brother in as he stepped to Ian's side. This boy kept getting knocked down. When was it one knock too many?

He tilted Ian's head toward him and lifted an eyelid. There was no flinch, no movement of any kind. With a heavy sigh, he reached out and whacked Ian hard across the face.

Ian didn't react.

Goran glanced over at Serus and Cody.

"He was hard to wake up last time. But he still made some response after I slapped him." Cody motioned to his friend. "He looks worse this time."

Serus reached over and hit Ian hard on the opposite cheek. "That means he's under the influence of some kind of drug."

"Possibly. I don't know how much he drank."

"How much is too much?" Cody asked, crouched beside Serus.

Goran glanced over at him. "One bag, two bags." He shrugged. "Your guess is as good as mine. Ian has been struggling since the first dose of drugs. His body might have just given up and needs to sleep for awhile."

"Only we don't have awhile." Serus straightened, his

mouth twisting. "We can't just stay here until he wakes up."

"Why not?" Goran countered. "The humans checked us out and left. The mountain has stopped rumbling and for right now, we have several people that need to do just that – rest."

Serus twisted to gaze at the three clustered by the stairs. "How is Jewel?"

"No change," Tessa answered.

"How are you?"

Goran followed Serus's gaze to study Tessa's face. She was holding up, but exhaustion showed in the very way she stood. In fact, he'd swear she swayed on her feet.

"I'm fine."

"Like hell." Cody bounded to his feet. "You're ready to drop. You need to drink a little blood. Not enough to be affected like Ian and Jewel, but enough so you can heal and regain your strength, like what I did and what our fathers did."

She ran a hand over her forehead. "I'm not sure I can," she whispered. "It's likely to come straight back up." Indeed, a greenish cast had washed over her face.

"I don't have any synthetic blood here, Tessa. This is what's here and you need to feed. Even a little bit." Serus walked over to his daughter.

Goran stayed behind and tried not to listen. He couldn't imagine what his old friend was going through right now. Having raised Tessa through many problems already, he was the best equipped to handle this one.

Who knew how long she'd hold out?

RHIA STOOD BESIDE Wendy and presented a calm, almost disinterested front. On the inside, she was a mess. She asked the leader, "Where's Jared?"

The second man glanced over at his leader, who was trying to make a phone call, before he answered. "Was that the kid waiting here for us? If so, he's gone with another group to some mine entrance with a mini railway." He shrugged. "We haven't seen anyone else alive."

That was good news about Jared. "Good. Jared escaped from that railway tunnel so he should be able to show the guys the way in."

The man nodded. "Apparently." He glanced over at the leader again.

Rhia could have told him that the phones would not work down here, but as she was the one who suggested he call…

The leader turned back, his face twisted in frustration. "I can't get any reception. I'm going to go up to the surface and try calling again." He stopped as if conflicted.

The second man nodded. "Go. We're fine here."

Undecided, then as if making a decision, the leader said, "I won't be long. We'd better sort this mess out now." He walked back toward the tunnel, calling back. "If I don't return, assume the worst."

He pivoted and glared at Rhia and Wendy. "Don't take any chances. Shoot them."

CHAPTER 6

TESSA WAS VAMPIRE in more ways than she had realized. This had been brought home to her resoundingly fast. In her cosy life, with all her needs met, she could ignore that part of her heritage. Now she came face to face with it. She had to feed. And now with the thin veneer stripped away, she felt naked.

Uncomfortable.

Vulnerable.

Again.

She could handle the synthetic blood if she had to. It wasn't even bad. The fresh stuff, even if it had been filtered and cooled, made her stomach heave. That it was likely drugged would make it impossible to keep down. Could she roll it around in her mouth and spit it out? Would that do any good?

There should be clean blood here. Not everyone would be drinking the drugged stuff. Surely?

With that thought uppermost on her mind, she stood up and turned her back on her glowering father and pissed off Cody. She slowly navigated around Jewel's sprawled legs and her brother hovering close beside her to head toward the back of the room.

"Where are you going, sis?" David called after her.

"To see if I can find anything better than drugged blood

to eat."

"Well, there won't be granola bars, that's for sure," he muttered.

"No, but maybe there is pure blood or synthetic blood." She limped forward until she came upon the remnants of Goran's actions to rid the world of his unplanned family. Piles of still smoldering ash covered the floor

She swallowed, lifted her gaze from the nasty floor, and searched the debris and hanging wires and pipes for another cooler. Some kind of cold storage where the workers would have kept lunch. Surely they had access to the good stuff here?

With so much downed bits and pieces, she struggled to make her way to the back of the room. When compared to the blood farm, this room was small. As in tiny. She reached the back wall in minutes – well, as close to the back wall as she could get and avoid the huge pile of liquid nastiness in front of her. She stood from her new position and turned to face the others. Everyone was resting or talking in small groups. Except for Cody. He stood and watched her. Glaring at her.

Tough.

She turned to study the funnels, pipes, filter system, and piping for the nutrients presumably being moved back and forth somehow. The growing pool of green brackish stuff still dripping from large pipes above her head told her no one had turned off the feeding system.

Or maybe they had, as the flow had slowed down to a trickle. Was that from the earthquake or maybe someone was watching them. Again.

She studied the corners of the ceilings and the monitors hanging above them. Snow showed on the one while the other was a black screen.

"See anything?" Cody asked curiously.

She hadn't heard him come up behind her. Or inside her mind. Such a curious thing. Maybe she'd blocked him out because she was mad at him.

Are you still mad at me? he asked shortly, temper simmering in his voice.

The last thing she wanted to do was set his anger off, but he didn't understand what it was like for her. She sighed. *No. It's just hard when the very act of swallowing this blood will make me puke.*

I doubt you will find anything different here. The people here lived on the home-grown stuff. They farmed it, remember?

I know. I just thought maybe there was someone else like me out there.

His hand landed on her shoulder and squeezed. *I doubt there is anyone else quite like you.*

She didn't know how to take that, so she ignored him. She pointed to the monitors. "Wonder if the monitors were to keep an eye on the hanging children or on the workers."

"Both."

She nodded and motioned to a door behind the rubble. "We should check out what's behind the door."

"Why? Maybe we should just go home and leave this behind."

She knew he was tired. So was she.

"I'm afraid the younger versions of your family will be in that next room." She sensed his surprise in her mind. She watched as he turned to consider the issue.

"They were all the same age," he said. "All relatively young, but not very young."

"Exactly. They were older than the ones we found hanging. Did we get them all? Or is another batch maturing and trying on clothes as we speak?"

Cody stared down at her, distaste twisting his edgy features. "What a horrible thought."

"But we have to consider it," she added. "They were grouped by age. The group that attacked us and then the group that was hanging. If we found two groups at those ages, why wouldn't there be younger upcoming ones? Not older as they would have already been sent into battle." She waved a hand at the mess of ashes. "Goran took care of the next batch, but it would be foolish to consider there aren't younger variations maturing even now."

That was enough to set Cody forward to clear a path to the door. "You look for more doors. Who knows how much more of this shit we're going to find?"

She turned to study the walls around them. How many rooms were here? It made sense to have an embryo room and something like a nursery for young vamps. If these guys were clones – the only observation she could make in this case – then the doctors would have to have a large clean lab big enough to include embryo storage until they were needed.

That would require exclusive equipment and specialists to keep this army production on track. Yet once established, it would be easy to maintain. A couple of doctors and several minions for all the labor work were all they needed.

So a layout to minimize movement from one stage handling area to the other made sense.

Cody shifted enough debris and pushed the door open enough to see in. She peered over his shoulder. "Is there anything in here?" she asked.

"I can't see far enough in." Pulling back, he cleared away more debris. She pressed the door wide open and stepped over the mess on the ground and into the room. A room virtually unaffected by the tremor. The room was an organized embryo system. Canisters full of greenish liquid filled the left side. On the other side were larger containers holding vamps not ready to be hung on their own but definitely past the embryo stage. Large silver canisters lined the far wall. Not big enough to hold a full size person, but maybe enough for embryos at half the age. She shuddered. She really didn't want to know what was in them.

They would need a fair bit of time to reach the stage like those that Goran had killed in the main room. Could that mean another room full of those in an in-between stage? Or several other rooms? Was it likely they had a succession of rooms like the tunnel ones they'd been in before, where each stage could be moved into the next room. Like a damn assembly line.

A shocked cry had her spinning around. Goran stood behind Cody at the open doorway.

There was so much pain and horror on his face she didn't know what to say. Thankfully Cody handled it.

"Easy, Dad. We don't know if any of these are viable. The power is off. Whatever was taking care of these things is offline now. The longer the power is off, the closer these things are to being dead all on their own."

She hadn't considered power. But he was right. The pumps were silent, the fluids were still inside the tubes.

Could anything still be alive?

She hoped not. She moved through the room, checking the contents and wondering with amazement at the highly scientific level of the process in place even as she winced in revulsion at the contents.

How could they do this? Were they actually playing with DNA to create the next batch? To create their next wave of designer army vampires?

"Where are the others?" cried Goran. "There must be more. Older ones than these." He waved his arm toward the canisters. The cold anger in his voice scared her. There was a detached ferocity that said he'd find every last one and kill them all.

She glanced over at Cody. He shrugged. "I don't know. Yet."

Tessa watched Goran's gaze search the room, searching for the next place. He stopped as his gaze landed on a glass window of some kind opposite Tessa. She hadn't made it to that side of the room. She raced over to the window. "They are in here."

And the window shattered in front of her.

∂∘ ∘ᕲ

"WHAT THE HELL?"

Harsh laughter followed the cry.

Jared ducked behind a large boulder, his breath caught in his chest. Well, he'd found the soldiers. But no vampires. What were the soldiers up to? He heard more laughter, but the voices and footsteps were moving away.

They were still moving down the tunnel.

He took a chance and ran behind them, hiding behind another boulder.

He tried to keep close enough to hear their conversation.

"At least they were all dead."

"What do you mean at least?" A low growl came from one of the heavier set army men said.

"I wanted to kill them myself. What good is it if they are already dead?"

More laughter.

"There will be plenty for all of us. Who knows, maybe we'll get lucky and the Human Council will decide to exterminate the Vamp Council. Hell, we could kill them all while they sleep during the daytime. One well-organized day and they'd be all gone."

"Not all of them, there are vamps everywhere."

"Yeah, but not here. Just think, we could have a vamp-free city. Once we put out the word, no other vamps will want to come here."

"Only until they realize what we've done and then we'll have a full scale war on our hands."

"Good. That's just what we need. Be a huge boost to the economy. Plus if we take over the vampire businesses, the humans will do much better, too."

The voices headed further down the tunnel.

Jared didn't follow. He was too stunned to think. A vampire extermination? He wanted no part of that. God help them all if that happened.

And what dead vampires had they found?

Please don't let it be his friends. As the tunnel resumed its tinny silence after the soldiers moved off, he heard something else. Glass breaking.

Shit.

Now what?

Stay and find out, follow the soldiers, or retreat?

At the murmur of voices and the sound of more glass breaking, he searched the wall for where the sounds were coming from. He spotted a hole in the wall high up behind him. He'd missed it earlier. Boulders and rocks had piled up around it. And it was back slightly from where he was crouched. That could be where the men came from. Except that didn't make any sense. They said everyone was dead.

Did that mean dead vamps and humans? Or both? If that was the case, then why the voices and breaking glass?

Had some of the army group stayed behind to wait for vamps to show up?

He groaned but darted to the hole in the wall. It was dark inside but there appeared to be some light in the space above. Creeping forward, he clambered over rocks and made his way through the hole. It connected to some kind of stairs, but they'd fallen into a twisted steel mess. As he searched for a way forward, the sound of the voices grew louder.

He popped his head through the hole and came face to face with Ian.

A very dead looking Ian.

AT GORAN'S BELLOW, Serus raced toward the back of the room. He hated leaving Ian and Jewel but knew he could count on David to keep an eye on them. In the state Goran was in, anything might happen and someone needed to keep a lid on him. Not that a lid was possible. He was the strongest bullish vamp Serus knew. And that was saying something.

He came to a skidding stop at the edge of a pool of black-ish liquid. "Shit. I almost forgot about this mess." Turning his attention to the narrow strip of floor close to the wall, he picked a way through to the open doorway. And came to a stop.

What the hell?

He bolted forward. "What's going on?" There was glass everywhere and Goran appeared to be rampaging through a second room killing…killing something. Serus couldn't actually see what that was, and that scared him more than anything.

"Dad? I'm over here." Tessa called to him. She was leaning against a wall, Cody by her side.

Serus rushed over. "What the hell is going on?"

Tessa pushed off the wall and pointed to the next room. "Goran lost it."

Serus could see that for himself. He took several cautious steps forward to see his best friend stomping tubes into the ground and stabbing life forms of all sizes. A nasty smell permeated the room. He lifted his nose experimentally then winced. "Gross."

"I think the embryos were affected by the blast." Tessa took two cautious steps forward to stand by his side. "Once Goran saw this other room, it's like he had a lifetime of rage to release."

"He probably does. Tyson's lifetime."

Tessa's small gasp resonated in the quiet space. "Finding out about him had to be devastating."

"It was." Serus could only imagine the mix of pain, guilt, and regret that his friend was dealing with right now.

"And I killed him. I wonder if he'll ever forgive me?"

Serus glanced down at her. "He blames himself not you. Feels he should have been there more for him. Taught him better. That he should have seen something in his son. Something he could have stopped before it was too late."

"Do you think that's possible?" she asked, curiosity in her voice.

He turned to look at her fully. She was so young. And yet so worldly. He struggled to answer. "There is no way to know. A parent's job is never easy. We do the best we can at the moment, but every child is different and every instance is unique. I really liked Tyson. But he's been a stranger these last few decades, and I didn't recognize the child I knew in the man that died."

Her gaze narrowed. As if she was looking inward or outward. As if she somehow had access to another way of thinking like she had another way of seeing. Or maybe that was the difference. Maybe her different way of physically viewing the world outside had given her a different way of viewing the world inside too. A different perspective.

This precious daughter of his was very special. She had much to teach them all. It was galling to admit that his way, the way of vampires for centuries, was being shown up as old, stale, inefficient, and dull. As if she was a breath of fresh air in an old system. A dying system. One that had long ago run its best race...and lost.

"What's with the depressed sigh, Dad?"

Depressed? He hated to think his own daughter could read him so well. Then again, Rhia could, so maybe she'd passed that ability on to his daughter. Or maybe she'd come by it naturally. Regardless, she was still waiting for an answer. Those striking green eyes stared up at him in warm loving concern. Her capacity for caring went beyond anyone he'd ever seen. Her mother was close, but years at the hands of the merciless vampire women she called her family had given Rhia a harder shell, a more protective stance when dealing with the world.

Tessa had been dealt some hard blows herself but she'd gone quiet and let the others do their thing. She'd hidden inside – coming out periodically to test the waters and see if her environment had warmed up enough that it was safe to come out. If Jared had never gone missing, he wasn't sure what she'd have done. She wouldn't have hooked up with Cody, that was for sure. His gaze flew to the young man who'd captured his daughter's heart.

Cody. The young man stared at his father. His fists clenching and unclenching helplessly. As hard as it was for Goran to deal with this mess, he wasn't doing Cody any favors here. Goran needed to stop and think about his other son. He needed to remember that Tyson had been Cody's brother, too. Cody had enough issues to deal with without Goran creating more.

Serus glanced down at Tessa. "Cody needs you. I'm going to calm Goran down. Give us a few minutes."

Her gaze widened in surprised understanding. She turned to look at Cody and her gentle features softened yet again. He waited until she approached Cody, slipping her hand into his clenched fist. Cody turned in surprise to gaze down into her upturned face.

As Serus watched, Cody enfolded her in a tight hug and buried his face in her hair.

Serus nodded. They really were well matched. For the moment.

He turned his attention to his fiercely angry and hurting friend.

Someone was going to have to go in there and stop him.

And that someone was going to have to be him.

᠗ ᠗

WENDY SHIFTED UNEASILY at Rhia's side. Rhia worried about her. It was one thing for Rhia to die trying to save her family, it was quite another for Wendy to face the same fate. Even if she'd volunteered. She hadn't fully understood what she was getting into.

Rhia had seen humans in action before. Sometimes they

were the worst of all the animal species.

The group of men watched their leader leave the immediate area to make his call. As soon as he moved up the tunnel and away from the wall of glass, the first one pushed his gun against Rhia. "Stupid vampire bitch. Do you really think any of us gives a damn that you are on the Vampire Council? You should be dead like all the other vampires who did this. As of now, the only good vampire is a dead vampire," he said, bitterness rolling through his voice. "These people didn't deserve this."

"No," she agreed. "They didn't. But then we didn't do it to them. And you know that."

Another of the men stepped forward, "Why do you say that?"

She turned her cool gaze on the new male. They needed to understand, or every vampire on the planet was in danger of finding their way of living going through yet another massive change. And although the vamps had always prevailed, the humans had a lot more technology available to them this time around. She knew the vamps could survive, but she didn't want to see them have to retreat and turn back into being hunters again. But they would if they had to. And that would mean the end of the life as humans knew it as well.

Humans would go from peace loving, believing they were the big predators on the planet, back to what they'd always been and had chosen to forget – prey.

"Because there is no way that this big an operation involving this many human victims could happen without humans helping," she added softly, just loud enough for them to hear, "A lot of human help."

Silence.

Then the room exploded with exclamations and shouts of

disgust.

"No way."

"Like hell."

"Fuck."

She watched the awareness, disgust, and disbelief settle on several of the men's face.

"Exactly. So just like there are nasty vampires who did this," she waved an arm toward the disaster around them, "there are also nasty humans who helped them. The very ones who should have been protecting your people not only turned their backs on them but helped the vamps hide their tracks and removed all the missing person's cases – before it was ever brought to anyone's awareness."

"That's a lot of accusation going on." said the second in command. "Without proof, I might add. It doesn't make the vampires any less culpable."

She shook her head and said sadly, "No. It doesn't. But it wasn't me. And you people could be just as guilty."

"Hey, I had nothing to do with this," said the same male.

"Or me," spoke up someone in the back. "And you're just trying to save your ass."

"If you want us to believe you are not one of the human traitors," Wendy said reasonably, "then you also have to believe us."

Indecision warred on their faces. Rhia watched the expressions carefully. These men were justifiably angry. They wanted targets to smash, enemies to kill, anything that would allow them to vent their anger and to feel like they've meted out justice. She couldn't blame them. If their positions were reversed, she knew she'd have killed them all instead of asking questions.

If they hurt her family, she still might.

Wendy gripped her arm and murmured, "Easy."

Rhia settled back. "I'm fine. Tired though and impatient to find the rest of my family."

Some of the aggression had disappeared from their faces. They stood more relaxed, their guns loose in their hands.

She appreciated that.

"We have to wait for Stan to return."

Rhia studied the area, trying to remember where the other exits were. She couldn't help but feel like time was running out.

Stan's face popped up in the window coming down the hallway. She wondered at the design that allowed the vamps working here to see an intruder long before they arrived inside the warehouse. They really should have a warning system when the door at the top was activated. And maybe they did.

She waited for Stan to arrive.

Hard footsteps warned her of his arrival. As he came into view, he hitched up his gun to point directly at her and said, "We've got a problem."

CHAPTER 7

TESSA WANDERED INTO the destroyed room, looking for anything that would give them an idea of what else was going on here. On the other side of the window, Serus was once again trying to talk Goran down off his mad. Cody wandered silently to her side. She understood his pain. There'd been so much death already, he had to be wondering when this would all end and who'd be left standing.

Hell, she certainly was.

As she bent over to check out a lab book on the ground, a wave of dizziness had her swaying in place.

Shit.

"You can't keep doing this," Cody growled behind her. "You have to eat."

She knew that. She'd come back here to look for clean blood and had found nothing clean about this place. Just more evidence of the nastiness of some vampires. In the background, she could hear Goran and Serus talking. Cody's name popped up several times. She looked over at him, but he seemed oblivious.

It wasn't her business, but it was impossible to avoid hearing parts of the conversation. Something about Cody needing Goran. Needed his father. Not this broken man. Goran had lost one son and he didn't need to lose them both to this nightmare.

She gasped. This had been hard on Cody, but she didn't think it was that bad.

I'm not. Your father is using that line to make my father calm down, see sense. I'm fine, he comforted her silently.

Thank God. She squeezed his hand. *He had me wondering there for a moment.*

No worries. I'm fine. No, I don't like what Tyson did, and I'm scared for my father. Cody pulled her closer into his embrace, dropping a kiss on the top of her head. *He didn't deserve this. He's really strong, but inside he's more puppy dog than you might believe.*

She spun around to stare at him in shock. *No one would ever call Goran a puppy dog. An injured wolf, maybe. But he never gets out of that predator status. He makes the council members cringe,* she muttered.

Cody laughed. *True. But it stopped you from worrying.*

She laughed, loving the lightness in his voice. Maybe he really was okay.

I said I was, didn't I?

She flushed. *I wonder if I'm ever going to get used to this.*

You and me both.

She cast another glance back at the men still talking, only this time her father had his arm around Goran's shoulders and was leading him back toward them.

"Looks like they are finished."

"And here I thought you were finished."

The shockingly familiar voice sounded behind her, startling her. She spun around to stare dumbfounded at David. And standing beside him was…Jared.

"Oh my God, Jared." She raced over to him and threw herself into his arms. She'd been so worried that he hadn't made it out of the blood farm.

He hugged her tight and laughed. "It's so good to see you. I was so afraid you'd died when that blast went off." He pulled back to stare down at her, a sloppy grin on his face.

She beamed up at him as she stepped back, his arms falling away. "We survived. And you did too, obviously. What are you doing back here. I sent you out with all the techs and Taz to keep you safe." She frowned and looked behind him. "And speaking of Taz, is he here?"

Jared shook his head. "No, he's not. He's supposed to be coming with another medical team to see if anyone can be saved from the warehouse." His face sagged. "I'm afraid they are all dead."

"Oh no," she cried.

"But we don't know that," cautioned David. "So let's not jump to conclusions."

Tessa studied Jared's face. Worry and fatigue had given him a worn haggard appearance. How horrible to have just found his father and now to lose him all over again. Although in truth, his father was barely a step up on the ladder of the life.

And that's something we also don't know. So no panicking yet please.

She snorted. *Who's panicking?*

At Jared's odd look and the flashes of amusement in David's gaze, she realized what she must look like talking to Cody in her head. She linked arms with him. "Sorry. Have you come with help?"

Jared winced. "I thought I did. But honestly, I'm not sure the term 'help' is correct." He started to explain, but David stopped him.

"Hang on. We need to get the elders over here to hear this."

David walked toward the busted window that separated the two rooms and called out. The elders were already on their way, but once they saw Jared they came running.

By the time Jared finished explaining, they were stone faced.

"We saw the group you're talking about." Serus said. "They came into the other room while everyone was passed out. They assumed the group was dead and left."

"But they left wishing they had come upon us earlier so they could kill us," growled Goran, his gaze hard and flat.

It was that look that bothered Tessa the most. He appeared to have crossed some sort of invisible line. She just didn't know if that was a good thing or a bad thing.

She desperately wanted to get out of this place but knew they had other people they had to be wary of. And how did that work?

Her stomach growled loudly. Aggressively. Cody glared at her. She sighed and looked away, catching sight of Jared's concerned face. She flushed. "Sorry. I haven't eaten since...well...forever."

"Tessa?" Jared scrounged in his pockets and drew out several granola bars. He held them out. "Do you want these?"

Her eyes lit up and she snatched them out of his hands. "Yes," she said gleefully. "I do." She ripped opened the first one and downed it in a few bites. She opened the second one and ate it more slowly.

"Lucky save," David said jokingly.

She laughed as she realized the others were staring at her. She held out the bar. "Anyone want a bite?"

"Can we leave now?" Cody spoke up for the first time, his voice tired...sad.

She spun around to look at him. "I hope so." She studied

his face intently. *What's wrong?* she asked silently.

He didn't answer and he wouldn't look her in the eyes.

Cody? Now what?

He stiffened and turned slightly away from her.

She studied him, puzzled. She popped the last of the bar into her mouth, feeling so much better with food in her stomach. Just as she was about to ask him what was wrong for a third time, David walked over and caught her attention. He leaned in and murmured, "I know you're new to this relationship stuff, but there's no way Cody is going to like or accept you greeting Jared with that much enthusiasm."

"What?" she whispered, shocked. "Are you kidding me?"

She turned slightly to stare at the stiff back facing her. And got angry. Like really angry. Red filled her mind and heat raced down her body. "He should know better than that!"

"Oh?" asked David, a hint of humor in his voice. "And how does that work? Last week he barely knew you and what he knew does not come close to the you of this week."

He took a deep breath and lowered his voice even more, forcing her to lean in so she could hear him. "Xana did the same thing."

Still pissed, she snapped in low tones, "Did what? Hug an old friend after almost dying? Wow, life's tough."

David sighed. "Look, she was always trying to make him jealous. She would flaunt herself in front of other guys, always touching them and flirting with them. It doesn't matter if that's not what you were doin—"

"It wasn't," she snapped.

He held up one hand in a placating manner. She glared at it, at him.

"But it's going to trigger the same old feelings he had about Xana's behavior. Whether he likes it or not."

She frowned as a fragment of understanding filtered through. She'd spent enough time dealing with her own emotions only to have the ones she thought she'd already dealt with sneak back in and bite her in the butt. She realized it was likely the same for everyone. Damn. She couldn't stay mad at him.

She looked around to find her father grilling Jared on who he'd spoken with and who he'd seen. Goran had slumped against the wall, as if the outburst of violence had left him drained and exhausted. David was watching her, that gaze of his seeing too much.

"Fine," she said, tired to the bone. "I'll fix it."

And she headed in Cody's direction.

IF THERE WAS such a thing as a reality check, watching Tessa throw herself into Jared's arms was it.

And as reality checks went, that had been a biggie. And yet, was he being unfair.? Tessa was not Xana, but most of his friends would say all female vamps were the same. They were all teases. But was that true in Tessa's case? Or was she just learning about that aspect of herself? Maybe as she was young and inexperienced it was a side of herself she was only just understanding. And how horrible was that? Not to mention tarring the whole vampire line with one stroke.

Serus had often said Rhia was not like the other females. His father had told him that and had often wished he could find a Rhia for himself. Cody thought Tessa, being her mother's daughter, would potentially be different too. While he stared moodily at the mess around him, he wondered just how different she really was.

Very, she snapped, suddenly standing in front of him, and she upped and smacked him across the face. *How could you even begin to think that? How could you think I'd do anything like that?*

Cody reared back, startled by the attack. Damn it. Had she read his mind?

I didn't need to, she said. And sniffled.

As he reeled from the shock of her words, he realized her eyes were starting to shine with moisture.

Oh shit. He'd take a smack over tears any day.

Too bad. You get both. But she tried to sniffle them back, wiping her damp eyes on her sleeve.

And he realized just how exhausted she was.

And how scared I was. And how hurt and worried about the others I was, she sobbed gently.

He couldn't help it. He tugged her into his arms and dropped his chin onto her head. He wasn't going to apologize, but he was willing to admit that their emotions were all over the place. So much had happened this last week that neither of them were feeling like themselves. Or thinking clearly.

She pulled back and stared up at him determinedly. *I was thinking and acting clearly when I hugged Jared.*

He stiffened, clenched his jaw, and glared down at her. Damn it. Just when he was getting over his mad, she had to start it up again.

But she wasn't finished. *But that's because I was delighted to see him alive and well. We almost died. He almost died. He's a friend and I like him. He's not my boyfriend and I don't feel the same way about him like I do about you.*

She pulled her arm free and smacked him on the shoulder. *And you should have known that.*

Even in his mind, her truculent tone sounded so clear and

so…hurt.

The words slipped out on their own. *I am sorry.* So much for not apologizing.

You should be, she snapped. *You'd never accuse Jewel of doing this. Would you?*

No. She's different. And stopped.

She narrowed her gaze at him, and dropping her tone menacingly, she added, *So am I.*

He grinned. She went from being a delightfully weeping woman to a snarling vamp. He loved it. And maybe, just maybe he was starting to fall in love with her. He just barely managed to keep that thought to himself.

He jumped into the silence. *I just might need a little time to remember that. To not see your actions as I've seen them in others so many times before.*

She snorted. *You have time. Five minutes exactly. Then get over it.*

With a shout of laughter, Cody picked her up and swung her around in joy.

❧ ❦

JARED DIDN'T KNOW what to think. Or where to look. But his gaze kept tracking back to Cody and Tessa. First they appeared to be fighting, then it looked like Tessa was crying, and now she was laughing her head off as Cody swung her around.

Like what was he to make of that?

Inside, he felt hollowed out. His fantasy burst like an air bubble. He didn't think Tessa'd had anything going on with this Cody character. From the looks of it though, he'd been wrong. But she'd gone to the movies with him. Not Cody.

And that had only been a week ago. So this, whatever this was, had happened recently. He tried to picture Tessa and Cody together before the movie and he couldn't. It didn't fit. Tessa had been so awkward, so innocent. So fresh. Cody would change her. Make her more worldly.

Take away her innocence.

A ball of fear twisted inside him.

Had he already?

Had he missed his chance with her? Had she become Cody's when Jared was busy looking elsewhere? And then came a sneaking sense that maybe this was right – as in meant to be right. Vampire to vampire.

And he should find a human to be with.

But Tessa was both.

As he watched, Tessa reached up and kissed Cody in a very non-brotherly way.

David spoke from his side. "Get used to it. They are bonded."

Bonded? What the hell did that mean? Was it some kind of vampire ritual or something? He wanted to ask, but David had already turned away. Frustrated, Jared kept an eye on Tessa and Cody and the other on David. But he was no closer to understanding what was going on, except that something had shifted in the relationships going on around him.

And he'd been left out.

SERUS WALKED GORAN back toward Ian and Jewel, both still passed out in the same room they'd left them in. Serus went to Jewel's side and checked her over. She was alive in that her chest was rising and falling with each breath, but nothing else moved. Her eyes never shifted under the lids. Her body never twitched, and neither did she make a sound.

"She's really out, isn't she?" Goran asked.

"Yeah." Serus rubbed his chin. "I'm not liking this one bit."

"Too deep and for too long."

"If we can't wake them up and we can't leave them, that means we stay." Serus took a good look around. "We're relatively safe here."

"Going home sounds like a better idea," Goran said. "We can get out the way Jared got in."

Serus straightened. "Except for Seth."

Goran frowned.

"And the trigger-happy soldiers." Serus ran his hand over the back of his head and sighed. "If my boy is here, I can't leave him. I can't leave because those assholes might find him and make a mistake I can't live with."

"Well if you ain't leaving, you know I ain't leaving." Goran snorted and stepped back, shaking his hands in front of him. "No way. I already lost one boy, we're not going to lose yours too."

"But these kids need to get home, and they need to get home in one piece."

Goran shook his head. "I'm not taking them. Send all the rest home. I'm coming with you."

With a hard laugh, Serus said, "Good luck with that. They won't go unless we're all going."

"Exactly right."

Serus turned around at the sound of Cody's voice. Tessa and Jared stood on either side of him. David snuck around everyone and took up his earlier position beside Jewel.

David laid a hand on her cheek. "She doesn't look good."

"But she doesn't look any worse," Tessa said with a small smile. "I might just be a bit jealous. She's getting a good sound sleep and I'm wasted."

Cody laughed. "Good point."

"You can carry them out, right?" Jared said, "Head out the way I came in? Specially with the fliers in the group." He grinned hopefully. "We'd be home in no time."

Tessa smiled.

Then her smile dimmed. Serus nodded. She'd starting thinking, started connecting the dots.

"Seth is here. His friends. My friends Catherine and Jill. What about Motre and his group? Even Bart doesn't deserve to be shot by those guys. We can't leave them unaware." She took a deep breath. "If they are even still alive."

"Whoa." Cody turned and slung an arm around her shoulders, tucking her up close. "Don't think like that. We survived. So did they."

But Goran was shaking his head. "It's not that simple. The mountain is a mess. They could be anywhere. And if they are injured, that's an even bigger problem."

"And all the more reason to find them. Fast."

Serus had always been good at making decisions. At knowing right from wrong. At seeing a path forward. At knowing what to do next. And now for the first time, he was stumped. He didn't want to break up the group.

His shoulders slumped. He didn't know what to do.

CHAPTER 8

TESSA STARED DOWN at her two comatose friends. They needed to wake up but she didn't think there was any way to make that happen. She could try to slap them awake but... that might not work so well. "You go. I'll stay here with them."

Immediately, noise filled the air as everyone expressed their opinion.

She shook her head and let them talk. Vampires were good at that part. She nudged Jewel with her boot. She thought she saw some eye movement but wasn't sure. She nudged her again and dropped to her knees in excitement. "Did you see that?"

David looked at her then at Jewel. "See what?"

"I saw her eyes move." She leaned over Jewel's shoulders for a closer look. "Jewel? Jewel, can you hear me? Jewel?"

No answer.

But her breathing had changed. Tessa pulled back slightly and David took her place.

"Jewel? Honey, can you hear me?" He tapped her on the cheeks. "Jewel?"

She moaned.

"Yes."

Serus and Goran both bent down and checked her over. She groaned.

"Looks like she's coming around."

"About time. Thought she was done for."

Jewel opened her eyes at that last comment. "Done for?" Confusion, drugs, and sleep clouded her vision, but clarity was slowly creeping in.

"Am I dead?"

Tessa grinned. Okay, so not quite enough clarity.

"Nope," she said cheerfully. "Just drugged. Again."

Jewel stared at her in shock, then in horror. She tried to sit up but could barely raise her head, never mind move her shoulders. David reached behind her and half lifted, half tugged her into his lap. Upright, she gained a little color back into her cheeks. Jewel raised a trembling hand to push her hair back off her face. "I don't feel so good," she admitted.

"You were sleeping very deeply. It's going to take a few minutes to get back to normal." David smirked. "Ian is still out cold."

She snickered. "He's going to be pissed when he wakes up."

"Especially when we're going to have to slap him awake now." Cody laughed. "In fact, I'm looking forward to doing that right now."

While Tessa watched, he smacked Ian several times on the face, hard. Ian finally rewarded him with a groan, understanding kicked in within minutes. He jumped to his feet with fire in his eyes and a punch in his fists. He was striking mad and lashing out at everyone and everything.

Cody, with David's help, managed to calm him enough to sit him back down until he was aware enough to understand what had happened and to whom.

Not that it helped much as Ian wouldn't calm down. His body vibrated with coiled tension. Tessa just didn't know if that was the drugs or anger. Knowing what he'd been through…likely both.

With wild eyes, Ian spun around looking for the exits. "I have to get out of here."

"We all do," Jewel groaned. "Please, can we go home now?"

Goran and Serus exchanged grim looks.

An awkward silence fell. Jewel groaned. "Now what?"

It was Tessa who answered. "While you were out, a group of human soldiers came in ready to kill us all, but as most of us were passed out…they thought we were already dead." Sadness crept into her voice. "They are hunting the vampires who did this, but…"

"But they aren't too fussy as to who they kill in the process," David filled in.

"And my brother and his friends are here," Tessa added gently.

"So wait, now you're saying that we have to worry about asshole vamps *and* asshole humans?" Ian snapped. "I wasn't kidding when I said I wanted to go home. If I get drugged again, I'm likely to turn on you all."

"I think this last time, you had sedatives, considering how deep you were sleeping. There didn't appear to be any mind control elements at all."

Tessa nodded in agreement. "Also, they'd have to be doing some kind of neural interference in some way for the mind control to work. The sound system here is broken, and you didn't have anything attached to your brain…" she grinned. "Except ears and that weird ear cuff thing you're wearing."

His hands slapped to his right ear and the metal piece that hung there haphazardly. Whatever it was came loose. He ripped it off and flung it across the room. The others laughed.

"I don't wear earrings," he said violently. Ian's gaze turned even more wild-eyed. His gaze went from one person to the other as he tried to focus.

David said, "Where the hell did you get it then?"

"And what is it?" Tessa walked over to where the metal piece had landed and picked it up gingerly. "Trackers? Then she remembered.

"One of the dying vamps said I had one." She slapped a hand over her right arm. The pain had long disappeared under the onslaught of new injuries and with the strain of what they'd been through, she'd completely forgotten. "I actually wondered if I'd had something injected under my skin."

"What?" roared Serus, striding over to her. "Why didn't you say so?"

She frowned. "Actually I thought I already did." She gave a headshake. "But who can remember if I did or who I told? I haven't exactly had a shortage of things to think about."

He jerked her arm around to look for himself. He ran his thumb over the upper flesh of her arm. "There's a mark here."

"Yes. It's been there since I woke up in the SUV."

He nodded, but there was no laughing answer on his face. "And I'm betting that there is something else inside of here as well." His thumb stopped moving to press deep.

"Hey, that hurts." She pulled her arm free and rubbed the spot gently.

"That's because either that's where you were shot with a needle and the area is still tender, or something was implanted and it's still bothering you. Like a tracking device."

David and Ian stomped over. The tech boys, as she thought of them.

"Get away." She shot them a warning glance. "Besides, if I was tagged like an animal, then you might have been as well."

Immediately, Ian started slapping at his arms as if looking for an implant.

David rolled his eyes. "Not likely, sis. You were left behind for a reason. Remember they wanted to see what you could do?"

She did remember, but she also wanted to forget. Glaring down at the red mark made by her father's thumb, she hated to think that something foreign was inside her. If there was something, she wanted it out. Staring at her skin, she realized there *was* something.

She could see a disturbance in the energy field. A blackness that didn't belong. And how was she going to get it out? She glanced down at her fingers and slowly extended the long nail of her right index finger. Taking a deep breath, she closed her eyes long enough to tell herself to get at it and then plunged the nail into her own arm.

"Shit."

"What the hell are you doing?" roared David, who jumped forward and grabbed her. "You don't have to do that."

"Yes, I do. I don't want any of their damn hardware learning anything about me. Do you hear me?" She jutted her chin in his direction for emphasis. Then she turned back to what she was doing.

It was deep.

Rather than digging her whole hand in, she ordered her nail to extend deeper into her flesh.

She barely held back a cry as a tremor of pain rippled throughout her system.

You don't have to do this now, you know. We could have found a doctor to take it out of you.

She almost smiled at Cody's comforting voice.

I had to do it fast. I'm such a baby when it comes to pain.

A tiny ripple of amusement slipped into her mind, followed by his voice. *So you stab yourself instead of waiting for drugs to stop the pain?*

No drugs, she said fiercely. *Ever.*

Silence.

Then a quiet understanding sigh. *Fine. Your way then. Just please don't do any more damage than necessary. Your body is already weak.*

Weak, yes, but not done yet. I do feel better because of the food. And who knows, maybe having this foreign thing in my system has been slowing my healing down. God only knows what kind of information it's been telling those assholes.

As we don't know for sure that there is anything there, I doubt we will ever be able to say.

It's there, she snapped. *I can see it.*

You can see what? he asked cautiously.

I can see the change in the energy. There's a thick black blob like a spot in the energy of my arm. I just need to… she gasped.

What? Are you all right? What did you do?

He was suddenly in front of her, peering down at her bloody arm.

She swallowed twice and pushed up under the black spot. Waves of greasy pain hit her stomach.

Please don't let me be sick, she prayed silently.

Take a deep breath. It will help. If you bend over, it will help too. He smiled. *But you'll have to take your finger out of your damn arm first.*

His attempt at humor fell flat and they both watched as a blood-covered silver dot rose slowly as she pushed it up through the skin, ripping and tearing as it went.

And then it was out.

She gasped with relief. "I don't know what it is or what it does... I'm just glad it's out."

David picked up the micro-sized unit from Cody's hand and lifted it into the faint light to see it better.

Jared walked forward.

And Tessa realized she'd forgotten about him.

His eyes were huge. And he was staring at her arm and her bloody finger.

She flushed and stared down at her feet. God, how she must look. So primitive. An animal ripping her own arm open.

Good thing he hadn't seen her when she had been ripping out the throats of the enemy.

It made her all the more aware of their differences. Before he'd arrived, she'd felt mostly normal within her vampire group. Accepted for who she was and could revel in it. Now she felt...odd. Different, as if something major had just shifted.

It made her feel uncomfortable in her skin. Again. And she didn't like it.

But it had changed something inside her. As if this had to happen for her to see her true self. Without all the doubts that had plagued her growing up. She might be different from the vamps around her, but she was as much one of them as David or Seth.

She'd tried to fit into the human world and she had...for a time. She could have made a home for herself there quite happily. But she'd have been hiding from her own true self.

Now there was no going back. No more hiding.

She could be friends with the humans. But she could no longer fool herself... she could no longer pretend to be one of them.

She was and always would be a vamp. Of mixed genetics. Of throwback genetics, or whatever they wanted to call it, but she was completely a vampire.

Finally.

❧ ❦

JARED STRUGGLED WITH what he'd just seen. The ease of what she'd done. Although it had hurt her, she'd done it anyway. He couldn't imagine the Tessa from school doing something so cold-blooded. As much as he understood the necessity, that she'd actually done it bothered him. He wasn't used to girls cutting things out of their bodies like that. It was an emergency scenario, but still...

"Do you think we have trackers?" Jewel asked fearfully. She'd regained her feet and stood with David's arm supporting her.

Tessa glanced over at her, one hand clasped over her wound. She shook her head. "Not that I can see."

"See?" Jared asked, giving a quick glance over Jewel. "How can you see something so small?"

There was an awkward silence. Tessa stared at him. Her green eyes were cool and assessing. Jared wondered what he'd missed. He remembered some joking about Tessa's abilities at odd times, but he hadn't realized there were actual skills involved. He'd heard her say she could see the black spot but he'd assumed she meant like a sliver. Although as Ian held the small metal dot in his hands, Jared realized it wasn't black at all. It was silver. So what had been the blackness she was talking about?

He turned and narrowed his gaze at her. "Tessa? What am I missing?"

She wrinkled her nose, then shrugged and relaxed. "I see energy. Peoples' energy. The energy they leave behind when they walk. The energy around their body. In this case, the energy of something foreign in my body." She gave a second self-conscious shrug. "It's no big deal."

Jared didn't know what to say. It *was* a big deal. He just wasn't sure what it all meant. Except that it was yet another difference between them. He glanced around at the other vamps. The elders were speaking off to one side, David and Jewel were watching him, and Cody and Ian were studying the weird metal device. "Can you all do that? Is that a vampire thing?"

David shook his head. "That is completely a Tessa thing. We're just normal boring old vampires."

"Who'd like to go back to living their boring old lives," muttered Jewel.

David tucked her up closer. "Soon."

Tessa spoke up. "As much as I want to leave, I don't like these soldiers running around here when we don't know where Seth is or why he's here."

Jared shrugged. "Neither Seth nor his friends said anything about why they were here when I was with them."

"Did you see where they went when you came inside?"

Jared hated that all gazes suddenly switched back to lock on him. "We came down the garage floor and walked down the hallway to the blood farm. Once we got inside, they headed to the back of the farm and I started looking for my dad."

"Wait, did you lower the garage door or did they?" David asked.

"Seth did." He frowned at them, shuffling his feet.

David exchanged worried glances with Tessa. "Did they

exclaim or comment in any way about the odd door, the hallway, or the blood farm? Or did they act as if it was all normal?"

He raised his eyebrows. "They definitely knew how to operate the floor. How to open the weird door at the top and to walk all the way down. They'd been here before. No doubt about that."

Serus's voice cracked across the room, "And you didn't see where they went or hear them say anything about where they were going?"

The fear in the elder's voice had Jared immediately shaking his head. Then he cleared his throat. "No sir, but they walked in, never made any comment, and strode right to the back of the warehouse. I never saw them again."

☙ ❧

GORAN COULDN'T GET his head wrapped around this information. The only way that Seth could have known about the garage mechanism and the weird doors was if he'd had prior knowledge. If he'd been here before, it followed that he'd had something to do with the blood farm. He wracked his brain to come up with something, anything, to explain Seth's knowledge.

And came up with only one explanation.

Seth had to have something to do with these assholes.

Just like Tyson. Seth was incredibly young to be involved though, a full century younger. Like Jacob. If these assholes were recruiting boys Seth and Jacob's age, were they recruiting through educational institutions? Tyson might have also been involved in the recruitment process.

That would be doubly hard. It was one thing to lose his

son in this mess, but another to have a son responsible for recruiting other people's sons.

His grief was not something he'd wish on anyone else.

Especially Serus's boy. He'd known Seth since he was little. And he'd never seen any behavior to indicate his involvement in something like this.

Then neither had he seen anything in Tyson's actions. Maybe he'd never wanted to.

But what could possibly cause these decent young men to willingly join this mess?

He watched the emotions ripple across Serus's face. The pain and shock, the awareness, and the grief as they ravaged his soul. His gaze, black pits of agony, had Goran's gut reeling from the crippling memories. *Tyson.* Goran had already lost so much…and Serus's pain was just bringing it all back to him. Again.

Damn.

He shuddered with the effort to keep it all contained when what he really wanted to do was to kill his son all over again.

CHAPTER 9

TESSA WALKED OVER to the hole in the wall where Jared had entered. She wanted to go home. But she wanted her brother to be alive even more.

When she found him, she planned to smack him good. And then she'd ask him what the hell was going on.

But she had to find him first. Before these soldiers killed him. She stepped over the heaped rocks, dirt layers, and crumbled supports to peer out into the tunnel. There was no sign of anyone.

Tessa?

She pulled back enough to face Cody. "We need to follow the soldiers and find out what and who is down there."

"I think Jewel and Ian should go home."

She nodded. "I agree. I just can't leave my brother. What if he's trapped somewhere? Or lying injured? Needing food?"

"I get it. I do. I just don't know what the answer is."

"The same as always." She shrugged, "Stay together. No one else can fly and Goran can't take all of you home and come back."

"I know but..." Cody studied her face for a long moment, then ran a quick glance down to her leg. "And then there is the issue of your leg."

Goran's voice called from behind them. "You kids are going to go home together. Serus and I are going to find Seth and his friends."

Tessa shook her head. "No—"

Goran cut her off. "Yes. You are injured. At this point you are more of a liability. We need to find the boys. And in order to do that, we need you home safe and sound."

David asked, "And how are you going to do that? Ian and Jewel can't fly yet. And Tessa can't jump, at least not very far."

"Not to mention that Cody's wing is still not fully healed." Tessa said coolly. "He won't speak up, but I will."

"Damn it, Tessa. My wing is healing. It's not that bad," Cody growled. "I'm fine, sir."

But Goran had stopped to stare at him thoughtfully. "It was a bad injury. And you haven't fed properly, so you are weak, too." He glanced over at Serus and shrugged. "I think that means we all have to stay together until these kids heal."

"And someone would have to carry me." Jared stepped forward. "I sure wouldn't want to be left behind."

"That wouldn't happen," Tessa said with a smile. "And it's good that you are here. You will be an asset if we meet the army."

A stone went flying as Jared let loose a bit of temper. "I don't know how much good I will be. They wouldn't listen to me before."

"But they aren't likely to slaughter us with you as a witness." Ian suggested with a grin. "So I'm happy to have you."

Cody snorted. "That just means they will shoot him too so as to leave no witnesses."

His face paling, Jared nodded slowly. "I'm afraid you just might be right. These guys are trigger-happy. I don't think they are bothered about who they take out."

Serus walked to the hole Tessa had looked out of. "If we have to stay together, then the best thing to do is get moving fast. So we can all go home."

"Home." Jewel sighed as if a dream had been dashed. "Like I'm ever going to see that place again."

David hugged her gently. "You will. We all will. This is almost done. We just need to make sure there aren't more of us that need help. I can't leave Seth behind."

"I'm still trying to figure out why he's here," she muttered.

"So am I," said David angrily. "There's no reason for him to be. For any of them to be here."

"You might want to consider things before jumping to conclusions," Cody said, "That if they were a part of this, they'd have known about the blast, if it was one, and wouldn't be here at this time."

Tessa perked up. "That's true. And the other consideration is those damn drugs. Seth is young and if he'd been given drugs over a period of indoctrination, he wouldn't know what he was doing. Just like mom."

Everyone there had seen the effects of the drugs on both willing and unwilling participants. Tessa knew that the reminder would at least keep back some of the fear and judgment the others were racing toward.

She didn't want to believe that Seth was involved. She refused to believe it until she knew for sure, and until then she'd treat this as yet another problem to solve.

It might not be that easy, you know, Cody's voice murmured gently in her mind. *Like Tyson, Seth could have signed up willingly, too.*

I know it's a possibility. But until we know for sure...

"So if everyone is in agreement? We follow this tunnel deeper into the mountain to find my brother. If we don't find him in the next bit, say a couple of hours, then we need to go home and come back with other vamps to help us look."

"Make it an hour." Goran added, "And I'll lead the way. One hour to search, then we go home and get help. We'll get a vamp army up here to combat the human army."

Tessa hated the thought of leaving if they hadn't found her friends by then. But at what point could she walk away? She felt responsible for Catherine and Jill's plight. Motre and the army had made the decision to go deeper into the mountain, but her friends were victims... they didn't deserve this. Still, she had an hour... with any luck it would be enough.

While Goran was still talking, Serus stepped around Tessa and slipped through the hole in the wall.

Tessa laughed. "Looks like you're not in the lead."

"Serus, wait up. Damn it, Serus."

And Goran scrambled after him.

The rest of them followed.

RHIA WATCHED AS the group stepped off to one side just out of her hearing range to discuss Stan's problem. She wanted to know what was going on, but they were just as determined to keep her from finding out. She understood. But she didn't like it. She and Wendy weren't prisoners exactly, but they weren't free to walk around either. Or were they?

She nudged Wendy. "Let's head to the back where the stairs are."

Wendy's gaze widened. She sent a nervous glance at the men.

Rhia shrugged. "Well, we can't be prisoners. That would be against the treaty." She arched an eyebrow at the one man standing watch over them.

He frowned and looked back at the others talking.

"No. Of course we're not prisoners." She turned to the long hallway. "We're going to go to the stairs that I know are here somewhere and look for my friends and family."

Walking backwards, she added with a determined look, "I came to find my friends and family. Join me or stay." She gave the soldier a bright smile. "I'll tell the others you're here if you plan on staying."

"And how can you tell them anything when we can't even make a phone call?"

Rhia laughed and turned to catch up to Wendy, who had marched ahead. She called back, "Because some of us are telepathic."

⤳ ⤶

CODY STOOD IN the tunnel and stared in the supposed direction of freedom. He'd walked down the tunnel days ago, but not far enough to find the exit. Now they had to turn their back on a way out to find Seth.

He just didn't think they'd like what they'd find.

Don't say that.

He winced as Tessa snapped in his head. *You're the one that reminded me to not jump to any conclusions.*

"Tessa, can you really talk to Cody in your head?"

Ooops. She turned to smile at Jared, who'd fallen into step beside her. "Hey, Jared. Sometimes I can."

He eyed her curiously. "And that's what you were just doing, right?"

Her lips twitched. "Yeah."

"And does that mean...something. You know some-thing..." he fumbled, "special?"

Uh oh.

Snort.

Let's see how you handle that question. Cody grinned.

She glared at Cody, slipped her arm through Jared's, and urged him to walk faster ahead of Cody.

"It does mean something special. Cody and I had never been able to do this before we went through this week of hell, though." She shrugged. "It started suddenly. We're still trying to adjust."

"Like a cold? Only one you won't ever get over."

Did he just say that? Did he? I ought to—

Tessa shut him off. *Stop. He doesn't understand. He's human, remember? Now let me talk to him.*

She tried to figure out how to explain the mindspeak stuff to Jared, but it wasn't something she understood herself. And decided to say so. "I don't know much about it. Neither does Cody. My parents can do it and the two ancients also can. So it's something that develops over time…but in our case it happened fast for some reason."

Jared pursed his lips. "So are you two like together now?"

"Together?" Damn. She was starting to sound like an idiot, but she didn't know what to say. She didn't want to hurt him. But Cody was her other half.

Damn right.

At least for the moment, she added with more than a little snark.

Ha.

Then her mind felt cold, empty as he left.

She tossed him a quick glance to see if she'd really upset him. He strode ahead without looking back.

"Is he upset?" Jared asked.

She'd never have thought anything of it except for the

tinge of hope in his tone. "Maybe, but he'll get over it quickly," she answered gently. "You do not want him angry."

His face twisted as he looked at Cody's stiff back speculatively. "So does this mean I shouldn't ask you to the movies again?" he half joked.

Cody twisted, shot him a look of fiery rage, then spun around and damn near raced to catch up to the elders.

Damn it, Cody, he's joking.

No, he's not. He's a guy. He's testing the waters to see what you'd say. To see what his chances are with you.

No, he's not, she gasped.

Like hell he isn't.

How do you know?

He gave a hard laugh. *'Cause it's what I'd do.*

No. You'd never have to. Cute Cody could have anyone he wants. You'd never have to even ask, she mocked.

You're wrong, you know.

The sheer starkness in his voice reminded her of his past relationships. *I'm sorry.*

Don't be. This is nothing compared to what we're going to face once we get the hell out of here. You especially. Let him down gently but firmly. And be prepared to be overrun by vamps once word gets out.

So not likely. She shook her head and winced as she caught Jared's curious look. "Sorry, Jared. I'm talking to Cody."

He winced. "Oh, I got that. It's just so weird to watch."

She wasn't sure she liked that concept either. He'd mentioned it a couple of times. She hoped she didn't look like a lovelorn dumbo or an open-mouthed fish as she did mindspeak. God, how embarrassing would that be?

Cody's laughter rippled through her head. *You look gorgeous – all the time.*

Says you, she muttered.

Ask Jared. He'll be happy to tell you.

Like hell.

"Hey!"

Up ahead, there were sounds of a scuffle. Tessa looked back at David and Jewel, who were bringing up the rear. "Come on. The elders are in trouble."

She raced forward, surprised to see that the elders had gotten that far ahead of her.

Then she wished she hadn't.

Loud metallic clicks were followed by rushing feet as a group of soldiers raced to surround them. Several vamps had been lined up in front of them. And they had guns to hold Tessa's group in place.

She studied the vamps. They weren't designer vamps. In fact, they looked normal. And young. These ones were kids like her. Or rather like David and Cody.

Do you know them? She asked Cody.

Hell yes. And so do you.

She didn't get a chance to ask anything else as more soldiers joined the first group – and pushed the vamps into the center.

"Seth."

JARED IMMEDIATELY PUT his hands up. He recognized the soldiers *and* the young vamps they were shepherding ahead of them.

"Hi again, guys."

The humans turned to look at him. He gave them a tentative smile. "Uh, remember me?"

He took a couple of steps forward. The guns were raised a little higher.

He cleared his throat, took a glance behind him at Tessa's group, then straightened his back. He faced the army with a boldness he didn't feel. "Remember I came to look for my friends?" He motioned to the group behind him. "Well," he smiled, "I found them."

The leader stepped forward, a hard laugh forming on his lips. "I told you to stay back at the truck."

One of the muscle-headed soldiers standing beside the leader grinned and said, "And I told you the only good vamp is a dead vamp."

Goran hissed.

Serus laid a warning hand on his arm. "Easy." He stepped up beside Jared. "Did you come down here to annihilate all vampires? Do you really think that is the answer to this travesty?" he growled. Even as Jared watched, Serus seemed to grow in size until he completely dwarfed the leader. He quickly switched his gaze to the soldiers, happy to see several of them scatter back a few steps.

The leader shook his head. "No. This is not annihilation. We're only after the ones that created this nightmare."

"And how are you making that determination?" Serus asked so coldly that Jared swore his own feet turned into blocks of ice. He couldn't imagine the effect on the other men. Jared knew he'd never want to be on the wrong side of the ancient. Damn, that man was scary.

Tessa had a hell of a family. And thinking about Tessa, he almost smiled as he imagined Cody having to face her father.

Then Goran strode forward to stand beside Serus. Between the two of them, they damn near filled the tunnel.

And effectively blocked the humans' exit.

The leader swallowed hard. "We just want justice. We figured that most of the vamps still here would be the ones to have a serious talk with."

Serus, his voice now dripping ice, pointed toward the young vamps. "And you assumed these kids had something to do with it? They are way too young to be involved."

The leader snorted. "There is no reason for anyone to be here unless they *are* involved."

"Unless they had other business here. Like we did." Serus walked over and lifted the chin of the first kid in the group. "Keegan. Councilman Mendes's son." He walked to the next one, but the young punk vamp glared at him.

"And Harding, Councilman Stengers's son. The other one is Warren, also a councilman's son"

Tessa gasped. Jared twisted slightly to look at her. She'd slipped forward so she could see the other men.

"Jared, are these the guys you came up with?"

He nodded. "Do you know them?"

"They are sons of several councilmen. Some of the bad councilmen," she whispered. In an even softer voice, she added, "We killed them."

"Oh shit."

CHAPTER 10

TESSA WALKED OVER to her brother. He straightened and glared down at her. She didn't know what to say. She knew what she wanted to ask him, but didn't know how to do that without making accusations. What she needed was to get him home where they could find out the truth. For that to happen, they had to get him and his buddies away from the soldiers.

"Seth," she asked cautiously, "Are you okay? Did they hurt you?"

"I'm fine." Seth snorted. "These guys haven't got the guts to hurt us."

Beside them, Tessa could hear the soldiers muttering angrily. He looked normal. He sounded normal. But the bravado of the words coming out of his mouth were anything but normal.

She studied him for a long moment. The stubborn tilt to his chin. The aggressive stance and the defiant gaze. She didn't know what had happened to him, but he was pissed. She just didn't know at what.

Or why he was even here.

"You know this guy?" asked the leader.

Tessa cast him a bright gaze. "Absolutely. Thank you so much for finding him. He's my brother. We've been looking all over for him."

The leader frowned. "Your brother? But he was in the offices with the rest of these kids."

"Kids is the right word too," Serus said harshly.

"Maybe..." the leader pointed to the group of young males. "But are they also involved in this mess?"

"Oh sure. Like they are going to answer truthfully." The leader's second-in-command stepped forward, his gun firmly gripped in his hand. "These punk ass kids were in the offices trashing paperwork. They were covering up for someone. That makes them involved."

"But we don't know how involved."

"And that doesn't matter. They were part of this human sacrifice bullshit. I say we punish them like we've punished all the rest." He stroked his gun barrel, leaving no doubts about his meaning.

"How many have you punished?" Tessa asked, hoping like hell it wasn't anyone she knew. "And you do know they have vampires hanging here too, right?" She didn't mention the cloning factory. She was thinking more along the lines of Darren and Moltere.

The leader frowned at her. "Why would they do that?"

Serus stepped in. "We don't know. It's one of the things we're trying to figure out."

Goran walked over, grabbed the two vampires closest to him, and damn near threw them in the direction of the exit. "Let's go. You will appear before the Council while we figure this out."

"Get your hands off me," snarled Harding. "My father will have you kicked off the damn Council for this."

Goran snorted and shoved the kid hard in the direction he wanted him to go. "Your father won't be doing anything."

"He'll kill you for this."

Goran shoved him again. The kid snapped back to his feet and turned on him with claws out ready to strike. He actually swiped at him, but Goran cuffed him like the cub in need of a tune-up he was and knocked him to the floor.

The kid bounced to his feet, fury loosening his tongue. "My dad and his friends will kill you for this. Do you hear me? You're finished."

"Shut up, Hardy."

Hardy spun on the second kid. "Easy for you to say. You're not getting slapped around."

Keegan laughed. "I didn't resist either. Keep your ego in check and it will all be fine."

"I'm not going into any cage or standing up in front of any Council. I don't recognize the Council as any authority. I won't be put in front of any kind of monkey tribunal." He straightened and spat.

Right on Goran's coat.

Tessa gasped.

Oh shit. Cody's voice slammed into her mind. *He's not going to tak—*

Without a sound, Goran pounced.

Harding was lifted off his feet and thrown a good forty feet down the tunnel where he slid another ten into a huge pile of crumbled debris.

Everyone watched as he lay still in place.

"Damn. Why can't we do that?" muttered the second in command. "That looked like fun."

"Hey, he didn't deserve that," Keegan snapped.

Goran, silent, his gaze black with rage, turned ever so slowly to face him. "You think spitting on me is appropriate behavior for a punk ass piece of shit like him?"

Keegan swallowed. "I...I didn't see him spit."

Goran pointed out the slime on his coat. "There. Now do you have something to say?"

The kid shook his head quickly. "No, I'm good."

~

SERUS HAD FROZEN at the sight of Seth silent and arrogant surrounded by his friends. What the hell was going on here? Did Seth have any idea about the kind of trouble he was in? Serus didn't dare speak. He'd kill the humans without a thought if it meant saving his boy, but...was his son involved in this mess? And if he was, what was Serus to do?

Goran's boy had been involved and he'd died for his actions. The thought of losing Seth was a pain he couldn't bear. What were his options? If Seth had been involved – none.

If he died here or if he was taken back to the Council, it wouldn't matter...death would be ordered as punishment.

Rhia would die of heartache. How could Seth do this? To his mother? To him? Where had they gone so wrong?

Easy there. Seth could be under the influence of the drugs, remember? These punks are assholes and need to be taken down a peg or two, Goran growled. *I doubt they know about their fathers yet, but something is definitely going on. We just don't know what. Until we do...don't jump to conclusions.*

Drugs. Right. Those damn drugs. Relief washed through him. His mind latched onto Goran's reminder. That had to be it. Like Rhia. His son had been recruited. Plied with drugs and brainwashed. It was the only reasonable explanation.

And for that, these assholes would pay.

Tessa had been silent through the whole exchange. He watched as she turned her attention to her brother. In front of Serus, Seth reached out and stabbed the group's second-in-command in the chest with a silver spike.

And chaos ensued.

❧ ❦

TESSA JUMPED BACK out of the fray, instinctively pulling Jared to safety with her.

"What the hell just happened?" Jared asked in shock.

Goran picked up Seth and tossed him into the air. She could imagine Goran would have given the old highlanders a run for it in days gone by. Her brother landed a good thirty feet away. And did not move again.

She wanted to run to her brother, but Goran was braced in front of the leader and his buddies. If he knocked them out, they'd never get any answers.

In front of him, the humans had surrounded the injured man.

Tessa kept her eyes on the injured soldier. She didn't know what she expected, but it was not this. The man was starting to smoke. To steam.

Like some of the prototype vampires she'd seen.

Not a quick death.

Not a good death.

But a death all the same.

She watched the look on his face as the emotions raced across his twisted features. Awareness, pain, shock...anger.

This wasn't a rescue party...this was a kill party. Or maybe only some of them were bad.

Shit. How could they tell?

Several of the men shifted around. Tessa jumped into the space that opened up and faced the humans and vamps down.

"What the hell are you doing?" asked the leader, rage

turning his face to a bright puce color.

"More to the point," she retorted, "Is what the hell is your injured man...and what the hell are you?"

The leader narrowed his eyes. "What did you say?"

"I asked what you are. Because he took a stab from a silver spike. Interesting that the vamps are using them, huh."

Two of his team stepped up on either side of the leader. She studied their build, the huge chests, massive forearms, the thick necks. She knew humans worked out to build muscles through specific activities. But did they get to this size? Or had they been 'enhanced' like so many of the vamps she'd met?

As she stared at the three men, her mind clicked and clicked and clicked, putting the pieces together. They locked in place.

These men, or some of them, might be helping the vamps. They were likely part of the human group that was helping to hide this blood farm.

She gasped. "You're bad guys?"

The leader laughed scornfully. "You don't know what you're talking about."

But silence was falling around them as her statement filtered through her group. Serus stepped up beside her. "What did you say?" His voice was harsh.

"I'm thinking that these guys, all or some, are benefiting from vampire enhancements." She pointed to the second-in-command, who was slowly losing what little color he had left. One hand was slapped over the slowly leaking wound.

"He sizzled, steamed when the stake went in. It's not like he screamed and then fell down bleeding. Instead, he's got like a slow poisoning going on."

"They are silver stakes," David murmured from behind her.

"Humans aren't poisoned by silver. It's toxic, but only slightly. Not like how it is for us vampires."

David turned to study the humans.

"They don't look like the others."

"They can't. Their basic foundation is human."

"What the hell are you talking about?" Another member of the team stepped forward. "Do we look like we're half-vampire for Christ's sake? What kind of idiot talk is this?"

"Maybe not yet," she snarled. "But how do you explain his physical reaction to the silver spike?"

"How do you know that it isn't a normal reaction?" He laughed. "Hell, we haven't ever seen a silver spike. How would we know what would happen?"

He motioned to the injured man. "And besides, the tip was likely poisoned. That would make more sense."

Tessa didn't have an answer to that. She continued to study the team. Could they all be humans but in the process of joining up? Or were already getting some of the enhancements? Maybe they were the human guinea pigs – and they didn't even know about it.

She caught the injured man's gaze with her own, peering into his eyes, willing him to give up something helpful. Then she saw it. A waver in his energy. A shimmer of something off.

Now she took a step back and shifted her vision as she sorted through the energy swirling around them. With everyone standing so close, it was almost impossible to separate the energy from person to person.

Or from vamp to vamp.

Jesus.

Cody, pull the elders back. I'm trying to look at the energy and it is damn near impossible with them standing so close to the humans.

If you think that will help. I think it's too late for that.

Yeah, it probably is, but let me try. It might help me understand what's going on.

Do you really think they are bad?

No. I'm not sure. There's just something...wrong about them.

Wrong?

She shrugged. *Yeah, but maybe not the way I'm thinking,* she added in frustration. *Damn it, why didn't I take a closer look before?*

Take it easy. You're tired and worn out. You can't do everything.

Maybe but talk about shitty timing.

She retreated several steps from Jared, trying to get the energy to separate. But it was all mixed up. Blending. She studied the humans. To see how different their energy was from the vampires. She'd seen Jared's and recognized it. She'd seen her friends' energies, Catherine and Jill, when she'd found them in their beds. But she hadn't been looking for differences between their energies and that of the vamps. The thought hadn't crossed her mind. Now she only had Jared as a comparison. And his should be normal, except he'd been drugged. And that would have affected him.

"What is she doing?"

Tessa ignored the human's question. It was hard enough to figure out the energy with all the distractions going on. To answer him would split her focus yet again. She squatted down, hoping to find some clarity in the mishmash of colors.

Nope. Not going to happen. The energy was everywhere and mixed to the point where she couldn't separate them. What was the chance she could separate the injured man's energy from the others?

She blinked as the energy in front of her pooled and then swirled in a dark vortex type of pattern.

What the hell?

Tessa? What can you see?

I don't know, she murmured. *It's really weird.*

Human energy is weird? Cody asked.

Well no, it's not just that, but there's also a blackness here.

A blackness like your tracking device? he asked cautiously.

She shook her head violently. *No, bigger, much bigger. Almost like a storm swirling here. I can't see why or where it's sourced from, but it's all over the humans.*

Cody walked over to stand beside her and stare at the humans glaring at them. Several shuffled restlessly.

The leader called out, "What's going on here?"

Goran smiled. "Our tracker has found something...odd with your energy."

"Energy?"

"Tracker?" Seth asked, confused, as he tried to stand up.

The leader stepped forward then turned to look back at his team. "What are you seeing? What's wrong with them?"

"I'm not sure," Tessa said frowning, "But something is."

She straightened and walked around the side of the small group. "Have you guys eaten or drank anything since you came into the mine?"

The leaders shook his head. "No."

"That's not true," said the second-in-command, on the floor with his hand still over his injury. "We had water."

"Sure, but we brought that ourselves."

Cody asked, "Sealed bottles? Ones you know couldn't have been tampered with?"

"Yeah." But the leader was starting to look worried. "You don't think we were slipped anything, do you?"

"I do, just not sure how." She turned to Jared. "Jared, you have an old film of this same blackness. It's not damaging your system at this point but it might have at the time."

Jared frowned at her. "What are you talking about?"

She shrugged. "There is a black mist to your energy. I'm presuming it came from when you were a prisoner here."

He stared down at his feet then held his arms out. "I don't see anything."

"That doesn't mean it's not there. Everything that happens to us is reflected in our energy. I'm only just seeing the impact on the energy waves." She brushed the loose hairs away from her forehead. "A week ago I'd have said I was crazy too. But time has changed many things."

"I'll say," muttered David. "Sis, can you tell where the blackness is coming from?" He motioned to the team standing on alert, a growing anger rumbling through the group. "They look like they need a little more convincing."

Tessa studied their human faces. "Did you get shots before coming up here? For protection against gases, diseases from these hanging bodies...anything?"

The leader's face darkened. "Everyone did because of the many medical issues and possible exposure to something we'd never seen before. It was a general issue immune booster."

"Was taking it a choice?" she asked curiously.

He shook his head. "I don't know, but we all wanted whatever protection was available." He shrugged. "Who knew what we'd find in here?"

"And who gave you the shots?"

He narrowed his gaze at her. "One of the medics."

She nodded casually, then took a deep breath and asked, "And did you know this medic – personally?"

"No, of course not. Besides, I rarely go to any medic." He

glared at her. "Most of us would rather do five hundred push ups than go to medical."

"Right." David groaned in humor. "So male humans and vamps have something else in common."

"How were you informed of this shot?"

One of the other men stepped forward, anger…or maybe fear, turning his face a blustery red. "What the hell kind of difference does it make? A human doctor gave us a shot to protect us." He motioned with his gun to the large group of vampires gathered around them. "Anything you say is just to turn us against our own kind." He growled to his leader. "Enough already, damn it."

"Easy, Tom. We don't know what she's talking about."

"So what? She's just twisting things around. She don't know nuttin."

A third man jumped in. "But what if she does? There is no doubt that something is wrong with Greg."

"He's been stabbed by a vampire stake, what the hell do you expect?"

"I expected blood and tissue damage, and a lot of pain," Tessa snapped, glaring at them, and smarting inside from having her opinion discounted. "I don't expect a slow hissing like a vampire would experience, or the blackening of the skin around the wound, or the slow poisoning that your friend is experiencing."

She walked closer to Greg, but the men jumped in front of her to stop her from getting too close. She motioned to their fallen teammate. "Surely this is not normal. This has vampire tampering all over it. Now I don't know if there was something in the shot you were given before you came into the mine or if you all willingly signed up for vampire en-hancements, but your friend isn't just injured. He's dying."

ॐ ॐ

CODY WATCHED AS Tessa glared the humans into stepping aside. She had guts, that girl. Just maybe no brains. Although her parents had bragged about her school marks, it was easy enough to achieve high scores when you were up against a mentally challenged race. And as he watched the army open their ranks to let her approach their fallen friend, he realized they really were not the brightest.

Then they did something that made his blood run cold. They closed ranks around her, completely engulfing her inside their group.

Goran growled.

Serus hissed.

Cody moved.

ॐ ॐ

SHOCK SLAMMED INTO Serus as he watched the humans completely enclose Tessa. He stepped forward and barely missed getting hit by Cody as he barrelled into the first human like a bowling ball.

Two stumbled out of the way, swearing. Several others raised their guns and pointed them at Cody.

Goran growled, "You don't want to do that."

The leader snorted. "He attacked us."

"You surrounded Tessa," Goran snapped. Serus only listened to the byplay with half an ear. He focused on Cody's attempt to reach Tessa. He was knocked back by one of the men, so he retaliated by grabbing that man's hand and squeezing it like putty. Screams rent the air and chaos resumed.

"Stop it. All of you." Tessa's frustrated voice screamed from the center of the body pileup. "We are not enemies. Now everyone stand back."

"Or else what?" mocked one of the men standing close to her. Serus turned on him, only to see him collapse soundlessly to the ground.

"What the hel—"

"I don't want to hurt anyone, but I will if you continue to attack or act in an aggressive manner," Tessa snarled, standing over the unconscious human. "Now stop pointing those damn guns at us."

"You just knocked one of my best guys out and you expect us to not fight back?" The leader's voice had gone past pissed off and straight into that fine line between panic and terror.

"I wouldn't have had to if you'd just listened." She sighed and stepped over to the prone man she'd flattened.

It was on the tip of Serus's tongue to ask his daughter what the hell she'd done – especially when she hadn't even touched the man. He'd been watching her at the time. So how had she taken out the man so quickly and so silently?

"Damn." Goran muttered at his best friend. "How did she do that?"

"I have no idea," he muttered back, "But you can bet I'm going to find out."

"Whoa, she's full of surprises. Talk about being our hidden weapon in this mess." Goran, laughter rumbling through him, grabbed his arm before he could take a step. "Look at Cody – he doesn't know what to think."

If the situation wasn't so serious, Serus would have grinned. Cody stood in the middle of the human group, staring at the downed man in shock before switching his gaze to Tessa, who was crouched at his side.

Even as they all watched, Tessa waved her hand in front of his face and the man woke up.

He took one look at her and scrambled backwards, his face twisted in fear. "Get away from me."

"Sure, no problem." Gracefully, she stood up and took several steps back. Serus watched Cody grab her around the waist and tuck her up against him while he glowered at the humans. He tried to tug her back toward Serus, but Tessa was having none of it.

She stepped forward toward the human she'd been trying to reach in the first place. After a moment, Cody followed.

Serus shook his head.

"What the hell is she up to?"

"I don't know. By now I wouldn't put anything past her. She's good, Serus. She's damn good."

CHAPTER 11

THAT HAD BEEN a crazy energy trick. How she'd managed to knock the guy out *and* bring him back to consciousness was wonderful. Without thinking, she'd reached a hand in his direction and temporarily halted the pulsing energy going to his heart. Now if only she could repeat it.

You did what? Cody's ominous voice pounded into her head.

Geez, knock the volume down, will you, she complained. *You're giving me a hell of a headache.*

Did you give the guy a heart attack?

She frowned and stared at the man now standing up, safely surrounded by the rest of his team.

I don't think so. She shrugged. *But I don't know. Maybe? I see things differently now. After being stabbed with the silver spike. Clearer. Brighter. And...well, I see the energy differently.*

Jesus. Silence. *You're scary sometimes, you know that?*

Me? She shot him a worried look. *Why? I just wanted to shift the power struggle.*

Yeah, but you do realize you weren't touching him you when you did that energy trick.

I was close though, she said, *Wasn't I?*

Obviously you were close enough. Maybe your energy went past your arm to do the job for you. He shook his head. *And that's just not possible.*

But wasn't it?

She might have let loose a bit more energy than usual. Every movement caused an energy trail so if she'd moved her arm, it would have left a trail. And in this case, it's as if she'd sent that trail to do what her arm couldn't. She shifted her position so she could view the man's chest. Sure enough, there were little bits and pieces of her energy in his heart chakra. She might not have understood what would happen, but it had happened the way she'd wanted it to.

And waking him up? How did you do that?

I scooped back some of my interfering energy, she admitted. *And I wasn't sure that would work either.*

You are full of surprises.

Maybe. But did it help or hurt?

She walked closer to Greg, the injured soldier, studying his energy. Could she scoop some of the blackness away? Would that even help?

It's worth a try. If you could help him, it might restore the atmosphere around here a bit. We're getting nowhere and I want to get the hell out of here.

So do I. She took several more steps. Two humans stood up in front of the injured man. She walked around them. He didn't look so good, like he was dying from a slow acting poison. She stretched out a hand and gently reached into the blackness and scooped way a cloud. Then another and another.

She did it several more times until the energy looked almost normal. The spike needed to come out. She could remove the blackness, but more was forming even as she understood it was coming from the spike.

As if responding to her thoughts, Cody reached forward and pulled the spike out.

The man gave a strangled scream and the others came running. Tessa continued to scoop away the heavy congestion of blackness, hoping it would soon stop.

"What is she doing?"

"She…is trying to help him."

"He'll bleed to death now most likely. Should have left the damn thing in to plug the hole."

Sure enough, a slow sluggish pool of blood welled out of the injury and ran slowly down his chest.

She frowned and scooped faster. Then stopped. On instinct, she reached out her index finger and plugged the hole. There was a slight hissing sound. She poured her own energy into the injury and forced the blackness out. Slowly, the darkness faded and her lighter energy blended with his.

He's still sick, but he should start to feel better now.

She stepped back and watched a more normal color came over the man's skin. "That's better."

"Hey, the bleeding has stopped."

Did you do that? Cody asked curiously.

I think so.

The others rushed to surround their injured man and she backed up several steps. She turned to face her own group, beaming with satisfaction. She'd actually helped someone. Like really helped.

And caught Seth's glare.

And the hatred in his eyes.

Her steps faltered. Her stomach dropped. Her heart squeezed tight. She whispered painfully, "Why, Seth? Why do you hate me so?"

JARED BACKED UP to the edge of an invisible line between the two groups. He wasn't sure what was going on or how Tessa was doing what she was doing, but a part of him wanted nothing to do with either group. They were both scary in their own way. As much as he liked Tessa, what she could do…

Jesus. He wondered if Jill and Catherine knew about her, about her skills? Did anyone know? They'd have a lot to talk about when they got out of this mess and life returned to normal – if the teens had been saved.

There were so many different groups wandering through this damn place, he had no idea. He doubted that Tessa had forgotten about them. But Seth certainly dominated her mind at the moment. Not having a brother himself, he couldn't pretend to understand what it meant. But he didn't understand Seth at the moment. He'd been controlled and detached in the car ride to the blood farm, but now he was positively glowing with hatred. For his part, Jared hoped none of it was directed at him. Humans were at a disadvantage against the vamps – especially a human with no skills training.

But then why would Seth have allowed Jared to return to the mine – had even given him a ride – if he'd hated him? Unless Seth *was* part of this nasty group and wanted Jared back in the blood farm. If that was the case though, why was Seth still here if blasts were set to go off?

Unless he hadn't known about the blasts.

Jared shook his head. This was beyond confusing.

And he just wanted to get the hell out of here. He hadn't been able to save his father. He doubted there was anything he could do to help any of the other prisoners.

"Jared?"

He turned to look at Tessa. Unshed tears shimmered in her beautiful green eyes. He couldn't ignore her pain. Her brother might be a twisted psycho, but Tessa was real and down to earth. He didn't know about all her abilities, but then he wasn't sure she did either.

He walked closer to her. "Are you all right?" he asked in low tones.

"I will be." She sniffled. "It's just hard to see him like this."

"Has he ever shown that side of his personality?"

She shook her head. "I have to believe that this is caused by drugs. It's too impossibly big if it isn't."

It was hard to work through her thinking, but he did understand. Her whole life as she'd known it would be called into question if her brother really did hate her as much as he appeared to. That had to be hard. Jared understood hate and relatives. Look at what his aunt and uncle had done to him.

"It is quite likely the drugs. But how can we tell?"

"Tyson could have told us if we'd asked." She shrugged. "But I doubt we would have believed him."

"Tyson?"

She winced and gave him a short account of Cody's older brother.

"Shit." That had to bite.

"Yeah, that's one way to explain it."

He couldn't imagine it, but if Cody's brother was a traitor, then it was quite possible that Seth was, too. And if that was the case, Jared didn't know what to think.

He had wanted to kill anyone involved in his father's incarceration. But it was one thing to imagine doing such a thing and quite another to actually act on those thoughts, particularly when he might actually know the man – and damn near impossible when he was related to those who had saved him.

"Pick up the pace, Wendy." Rhia never glanced behind to see if the soldiers were following her or not, but she wanted to get the hell away if that was a possibility. If they followed to see where the two women went, then fine. But she'd rather go alone.

They made it to the first of three doors. Rhia opened one to find a large room with beds. She closed it and walked to the next one. It was also a room with beds. The third door opened to a small hallway with cupboards, several of which were on the ground.

"The blast affected this area, too," Wendy commented.

"Maybe and maybe not. There was a lot of fighting here." She explored the small area and opened another door to find the stairway. "Yes. This is exactly what we're looking for." With a quick glance around to make sure they were alone, she motioned Wendy to go down ahead of her.

She closed the door behind her and followed.

"How far down does it go?" Wendy asked after they had gone down several flights of stairs.

"I don't know. But it's supposed to end at the mine, so we haven't missed it."

They went down several more flights of stairs and came to a sealed metal door.

Rhia turned the handle. It opened easily under her fingers. She pulled it open and stepped out into the destroyed tunnel, only to find the path blocked by large boulders.

Cody let Tessa and Jared have a few minutes alone. She

needed it. So did he. He couldn't school his thoughts the same way Tessa could. And she wasn't doing a great job of it right now. Pain and fear and shock all ate away at her. He'd gone closer to her, but she'd stumbled away from her brother and toward Jared. Cody wanted the direction to be accidental.

Her brother's hatred was not.

For that, Cody wanted to pound his face into the ground. Only Serus was there before him.

Before Cody could react, Serus had tossed his son into the back wall, anger vibrating through his face. "The only reason I'm not killing you right now is because I want to believe that drugs are responsible for this attitude. I've never seen it before, and I sure as hell don't want to see it again. You have no reason to treat your sister like this."

"She's a freak." Seth slowly managed to regain his feet, a wary eye on his father. "Look at her. She's not like us."

"And so you hate her?" Serus asked incredulously. "What does that make you? It makes you different. It makes you scared of the unusual. Well, guess what? That kind of thinking when you're five is a whole lot different when you're an adult. We're all different. Even you. Does that make you better than us? If so, then Tessa is better than you – because she's even more different," he growled.

Cody raised an eyebrow. *That had got to hurt.*

It does, Tessa whispered in his mind. *But Dad is right. We are all different. All unique in our own way. Seth is no better than us and him being similar to a large group of other people does not mean they are better because there are more of them—*

A terrifying rumble came from the base of the mountain. The ground shook beneath Tessa's feet. She gasped. Cody raced to her side, tugging her into his arms. He murmured against her hair, "It's okay. Just more aftershocks. Take it easy."

"I just want to get out of here." She shuddered. "But what about my friends – Catherine, Jill? And our friends – Motre and his group?"

"We've got teams searching now," said the leader. "Soldiers. We are going to go through this place and find everyone who is still alive. You need to go home."

Tessa turned to him. She wanted to trust him. She did.

Then do, urged Cody. *They came to help. Let them help.*

I really want to but…

But what?

"Tessa, are you all right?" David asked as he approached her from the far side. "You're just staring back the way we came. Are you ready to leave?"

Jewel cried out from his side, "Please, let's go."

Cody stared around at the sad looking group on both sides of the fence and realized it was the best thing for the group. But leaving Jill and Catherine behind was unacceptable to Tessa. And how could he leave Motre and his group? They'd fought on her side. Still, when did one step back and let others help?

"These humans came to search for survivors and to clean out the vamps." Jewel reached out with a shaky hand and pleaded, "They are professionals. Let's let them do their jobs."

David pulled her in for a hug. "Easy, Jewel. We're almost done. We're going to be fine."

"For the moment. What if there are more tremors? What if this whole damn thing comes down? Look, we said one hour and we said we came to find Seth. We found Seth and it's past one hour. Let's go home," she said forcefully.

"I second that motion," said Ian, limping back toward the entrance. "We've done what we said we'd do – let's go home."

Tessa's mind was spinning. Cody heard the wheels turning like a steady buzz. Worrying about her friends and the mountain coming down.

We can't do everything, Cody said quietly.

But we can do this.

Ask him.

She turned and studied her brother's sullen face. Determinedly, she took several steps toward him and shoved her face into his. "Where would the latest humans be kept?"

He sneered.

Without warning, her fist delivered a hard uppercut to his jaw. His head snapped to the side and he stumbled backwards. She got in his face again. "My school friends are here somewhere. I want them safe. Where are they?"

"How the hell would I know?" he snapped and glared at the wall behind her head.

His buddy Warren, Councilman Thompson's son, sniggered beside him. Cody picked him up and shook him hard.

Tessa spun around to face him.

"That means you know where they are," Cody snarled. "So give. Where the hell can we find them?"

"Why the hell should I tell you?" Warren snarled, trying to punch Cody in the face.

Goran growled and somehow grabbed Warren from Cody's grasp. Shielding him from the others, he bent his head and spoke into Warren's ear.

Cody tried to hear the conversation, but it was over before it had begun and all of a sudden the words exploded from the punk's mouth. "They're in the new section of the mountain."

"Hey, shut up," Keegan said. "You know what kind of trouble we're going to be in if they find out you told?"

"Who's they?" Cody spun around to face Keegan.

"None of your business." He turned his back on Cody.

Cody, in a move reminiscent of his father, picked him up and tossed him to the ground.

"You don't scare me," Keegan hissed as he bounced to his feet. "Let this be you and me. Just the two of us."

Cody opened his mouth, and a sound Tessa had never heard before came ripping from the back of his throat.

"No." Serus stepped between the two young vamps. He glared at Cody. "No, no, and no."

Cody could feel the insult and the anger sear through him. He glared at Serus, his fists clenching and unclenching.

Serus widened his stance and crossed his arms across his chest. "No," he said coolly. "This punk ass kid is not worth the time or effort. You have to save your energy for healing."

Oh, I'm sorry, Tessa cried. *I forgot about your wing.*

I don't give a damn. I can still take him, he snarled at her.

I know you can, but we need you whole and healthy and able to fly. And Dad is right. This miserable piece of shit is not worth fighting over.

His body had stiffened into a steel beam. He glanced around, trying to give his temper time to cool, and realized that the soldiers had surrounded them.

Shit. Take our eyes off them for one moment and they get the upper hand.

Cody glared at the circle of humans. He spread his fingers wide and opened his arms, then grinned at them. "Looking to watch a fight?"

"Or something."

The energy in the mine had changed, with anger and testosterone crackling in the air. Tessa shifted uneasily. Cody glanced at Jared. He was looking back toward the mine entrance as if going home was the thought uppermost on his mind. Not that he could blame him.

This situation has to be defused quickly.

What are you up to?

Just watch. She turned to Goran. Nodded at the punk he still had pinched in his hand and said, "Get directions."

Then she turned back to her father. "Knock Keegan and Harding out."

Cody spun. "No. Let me."

Serus snorted, eyed Tessa carefully, then shrugged and turned to face the young arrogant vamps. Cody couldn't see over her father's shoulder, but within seconds the young vamps were both unconscious on the ground. She turned back to the soldiers. She motioned to the vamps on the ground and said, "Pick a couple men to carry them and your injured man out of here."

The leader glared at her and growled, "Who died and gave you command?"

She grinned evilly. "Not you...yet."

That wiped the look off his face. She nodded in satisfaction. "Accompanying you will be my brother, Jewel, Jared, and Ian."

There was a chorus of protests around her.

Wow.

Cody, his arms crossed, the mad gone from his stance, a small smile at the corner of his mouth, waited.

She held up her hand for silence. "The ancients, the rest of the army, Cody, and myself will continue deeper into the mine to find the others."

Behind her, Goran growled, "And why the hell would I want to do that?"

Serus walked over to Tessa. "What are you up to?"

"We have other vampires to find. Ones that fought on our

side. I can't leave them any more than I can let the army find them and view them as the enemy."

"Motre," Cody explained quietly, supporting Tessa.

Tessa nodded. "Exactly. *And* I need to find Catherine and Jill. We will go to them. Hopefully somewhere along the way we will find Motre's group."

Goran harrumped and looked over at Serus. "Well, what do you think?"

"Maybe." He stared at the punk in Goran's grasp. "But do we trust the instructions?"

Tessa shook her head. "No. That's why Seth is coming with us."

"Like hell I am." Seth snarled from the side. "You can't fucking make me."

She turned to stare at him. "Of course we can. You might think you're a big part of this operation, but you're nothing. A groupie is all you are. A low level follower who thinks he's a big shot."

Seth roared and raced toward her. Serus tried to step in front of her, but she shoved him out of the way. "I got this."

Her brother had almost reached her side when she made a quick slicing motion and he stopped, a look of incomprehension coming over his face. He dropped to his knees then pitched forward to the ground.

Jesus. Cody couldn't believe what she'd done – even if he'd seen it before.

Everyone around her gasped in shock. She ignored them. Cody stepped forward and rolled Seth over onto his back.

Tessa bent over her fallen brother and made a second slicing motion in a slightly different movement, as if playing with something they couldn't see – which of course she was – and he opened his eyes. Comprehension dawned on him and he crab walked backwards as fast as he could to get away.

She straightened and glared at him. "Now that we understand each other, get up and lead the way."

She deliberately turned her back on him.

And gazed into her father's worried eyes.

With a quick glance at everyone else staring at her, she straightened her back and said defiantly, "I didn't hurt him, but maybe it will knock some of that druggie arrogance out of him."

Her father frowned, then snapped, "We're going to talk about this later."

She snorted. "Fine. Just remember the shots he took at me earlier. At least I didn't hurt him." She shot her brother a disgusted look and added, "Now if we don't get a move on, there may not be a later."

Cody turned to study the small group that collected on one side. "David, do you mind?"

Jewel reached out and clutched David's hand. He looked down at her exhausted face and shook his head. "No. We need to get them out of here."

"Thanks, David." Cody watched as two soldiers picked up their injured mate and worked their way over to David's group. Then two big men walked over to Keegan and Harding, picked them up, and threw them over their shoulders.

Serus growled, "Best to keep them out cold."

"And this one," Goran dropped the one he held. "Keep him out cold, too."

The leader smiled, motioning for another soldier to pick up the punk. "No problem. We'll enjoy that part."

The group slowly straggled back the way they'd come.

Cody nudged his father forward. Goran growled. "She could have ordered me home too, you know."

"No, I couldn't," she said quietly. "I need you and Dad as backup."

He stopped in his tracks. "What for?"

She pointed to the rest of the army men leading the way. "For them."

☙ ❧

SERUS MOTIONED TO his daughter to lead the way. *Goran, are you okay to stay with us?*

Hell yeah. Goran snapped, *But I'd like to know what's going on in her mind.*

Maybe Cody understands, Serus growled, *I sure don't.*

Hah. He's so in love, he can't see his way forward.

Ah, those were the days. Serus grinned. *In your case, you probably don't remember.*

I've been in love lots of times, Goran protested.

But never longer than a few months. With a snort, Serus picked up the pace and caught up with his daughter, leaving his friend spluttering in place.

"Tessa, what's going on?"

She picked up the pace.

"Running away isn't going to help."

Her steps slowed…slightly. She cast a glance over at him. Her face was a mixture of thoughts he couldn't read. She dropped her gaze. He raised an eyebrow. "What's going on?"

She sighed and jammed her fists into her pocket. She opened her mouth to speak. He leaned in to hear her. When she didn't say anything, he nudged her gently. "Tessa?"

"I'm having a hard time about this whole thing with Seth." She shrugged as if trying to shake off her problems.

Serus tried hard, but he couldn't hold back a heavy sigh.

"Please don't hold his behavior against him. He's under the influence of drugs. Like your mother was."

"Is he?" she whispered with a quick glance behind them at her brother.

"I have to believe it. Until then, I'm trying to be understanding."

"Understanding has nothing to do with the look of hate in his eyes. Even if he was drugged, all those feelings had to have been inside him already. He couldn't have been forced to feel that stuff. Not as strongly as he does. That means he's been harboring these emotions for a long time."

"No. He's been under the assholes' influence for a long time. He's had reprogramming and mind control."

Her steps slowed. She turned to study her brother.

Seth caught her gaze and spat on the ground. Goran cuffed him on the back of his head.

Tessa turned away, shivering. Serus put an arm around her shoulders and tugged her closer. Seth would pay for that. He'd make sure of it. But not right now. "You have to give him a chance. This is not the same brother you sat with a week ago."

"Yes, it is. They'd have been giving him drugs way before then. He knew what he was doing last week. We didn't know. And even now he's not sorry, he's only sorry he's been caught."

There was enough truth to her words that Serus held back any comments. "Besides, what does his guilt have to do with the reason we are going deeper into the mountain now?"

"Because this isn't over. Because there are more assholes here. More top level leaders to take out, and I want to make sure no one is left to restart such a nightmare ever again."

He could understand that. He didn't agree with it as their

group had become bedraggled and needed rest, especially her, but he wanted the same outcome.

"And…"

"And I want to find my friends. I thought it would be okay to have the army find them and get them help, but with this mountain rumbling like it is, I don't want to take the chance. They are here because of me and I can't leave them."

"They aren't here because of you, but I do understand your need to find them. But the army can do the job just as well."

"Maybe. But not these ones."

He gave her a sharp look. "Why?"

"There is something wrong with them. Not all of them, but the ones that stayed…oh yeah. That's when I realized I made the right choice. I think, outside of the injured man, that the ones who left were maybe okay. Their energy was more stable, but…" she motioned to the men ahead of them, "not these ones."

He let his breath gust out. "You think they are being enhanced?"

"No. I think…" she took a deep breath, "I think they are being turned."

CHAPTER 12

THE LOOK OF outraged horror on her father's face almost made Tessa laugh. Almost.

"You have to be wrong." He glared down the tunnel as the team moved swiftly ahead of him. "That process has been outlawed."

"And yet I mentioned it earlier, so this isn't exactly news." Only no one had listened to her at the beginning of this mess. No one ever did. That had only changed these last few days. "But," she conceded, "Since then I thought the differences I saw might have been the result of their enhancements or drugs." She raised her shoulders. "Now I am not so sure."

Goran and Cody crowded around them. Seth stood off to the side, a bored look on his face.

"Did I hear you correctly? You think the soldiers are being turned into vampires?" Goran hissed the words, but even then his voice was so loud she was worried the men ahead would hear them. Realizing that they were still moving forward, she switched her attention to her brother. He appeared completely disinterested in the going ons around him.

"Seth? Feel like answering that question?"

He shrugged but didn't volunteer anything. Serus turned on him. Seth snarled. "I don't know. I don't know anything."

She almost believed him, but it was too pat. Tyson was no fool. He'd know which buttons to push on these young men and being part of an inner circle would hold some kind of appeal. Hell, she'd seen that type of want in high school – young males on all sides were always looking to prove themselves. To gain respect. To be looked up to. To find their place.

Here they had young upcoming studs to replace the old useless men who'd hung on past their prime. Yeah, that would appeal to them.

But it didn't mean they'd have been let into the real inner circle. For now, she'd give him the benefit of the doubt.

And she wouldn't believe anything that came out of his mouth.

With a quick glance around at the small group, she picked up the pace to keep the army in sight. She didn't know what was up ahead, but she didn't trust anyone anymore.

Not even me? Cody's humorous voice rippled through her mind.

She couldn't help but laugh. *Now you I trust. These punks...not so much.*

They are all older than you, he added.

Years do not make a man. And I do realize how snotty and sexist that sounds, she added. *Besides, this last week has leapfrogged me forward in maturity.*

I'll say, he said with feeling.

She tossed him a quick grin. *Hey, you should be grateful. I'm not quite so young and innocent as I was.*

Ha. You are too.

Like hell, she said good-naturedly.

There was a weird silence.

Now what? she asked in exasperation.

You are still innocent, aren't you? he murmured.

Heat flooded her face as she realized what he meant. She

struggled with her answer and ended up not knowing how to respond. He should know she was innocent in sexual matters. Hell, no male had looked at her sideways until Jared.

Jared! he exclaimed, hearing that part of her thoughts.

No. No! She spun around and stepped sideways to face him. The others kept on walking. Thank God. *No! I was thinking that you should have known the answer to that question without asking me. No male has ever looked at me before Jared, and I only went to the movies with him.*

She watched him close his eyes and a visible shudder rippled down his frame. When he opened them again, it was to gaze deep into her eyes, sending a glowing ray of heat deep into her heart. He grinned and dropped a kiss on her lips. "Good."

He spun her around, still spluttering, and dragged her forward. "Come on. They are getting ahead of us."

Bemused and delighted, she quickly stepped into line. But she hadn't taken more than a couple of steps when Cody came to a stop. And, she realized, so had the others. "What's the matter?"

Her father turned to look at her. "The soldiers are gone."

RHIA STRUGGLED OVER the boulders. The path was treacherous. She could barely see up ahead. She jumped to another perch on the right, then scrambled upward to crouch unsteadily at the top. She couldn't stand up as the roof of the tunnel was too low. Checking back, she made sure that Wendy was doing fine, only to realize she'd taken a different route and had almost reached the small tracks ahead of Rhia.

With a couple of long strides, Rhia landed in between the

tracks. She straightened and looked around. This area appeared to have been hit the hardest. The tracks to the left had some debris, but it wasn't much and the path ahead appeared clear.

"Ready?" At Wendy's nod, Rhia strode down the tracks to the right. Her family was down here somewhere.

"Rhia?"

She stopped and turned. "What?"

Wendy pointed to the other direction. "Someone is coming."

Walking back toward Wendy, Rhia scanned the straggling group walking toward them.

"Oh my God. That's David."

❧ ❦

JARED HATED TO be sent on his way with the rest of the group. He'd come specifically to save his friends, hadn't he? Yet he felt like he'd been demoted by being sent back with the group. And by Tessa no less. Surely he deserved better. She'd taken Cody with her. That made a statement. Like how. As much as he wanted to get out of this place, he didn't want to be sent home like a child either. He wasn't exhausted like the others.

Or maybe he was just pissed that Cody hadn't been sent back with him. David and Ian had though, so that mollified his ego somewhat.

Jewel did appear to have hit the end of her rope.

Those damn drugs appeared to be more dangerous than anything he'd ever seen. That whole blood farm had been full of that shit. He watched the soldiers carrying the unconscious vamps. They moved so effortlessly, as if the extra weight was nothing to them.

Jared wished he had half their size and bulk. He'd require different genetics and hit the gym for the next decade to look like that.

The other two men were struggling to help their injured team member. Mostly because he was trying to do more than he should and was fighting their help. Jared shook his head. There was a time to be brave and stubborn, but if he was as injured as Tessa appeared to think he was, the guy was better off getting his sorry ass carried out of here. Fighting was only going to make the drugs work faster. Even as he watched, it seemed like there was a gray pallor to him And not just on his face.

Unable to help himself, Jared shifted so he walked on the side furthest away from the sick man. It felt like something bad was going to happen to...

And he didn't want to be in this damn mine when it did.

He caught David's questioning look and shrugged. If David couldn't see a train wreck about to happen, how could he explain it to him?

~ ~

"WHERE COULD THEY have gone?" Standing beside his father, hands on his hips, Cody stared down the dark tunnel. "And why?"

"I think the 'why' is the more important question here," Serus muttered. "I never trusted those assholes."

"Ha. You don't trust anyone. Human or vampire."

"Works for me. When you don't know who you can trust, then trust no one." He took several steps forward. "Let's go see where they went."

"Or not." Seth said.

Serus stopped and turned to look back at his son. Cody studied Seth's face. His features worked with some kind of internal struggle.

Tessa whispered in his head. *The energy of the team just stopped. I have to get closer to see where they went.*

He nodded. *Seth is looking to say something, but I have no idea what.*

I don't trust anything he does say, so why bother listening?

She walked in front of him to stand beside her father. Distracted by her movement, Cody spun his gaze back to her brother and caught anger twisting his features, followed by fear.

He's afraid.

Like I said, he knows so much more than he's telling. Of course if anyone sees him with us, they might wonder what he's told us.

We need to find out what he knows.

Good luck with that.

Serus said, "Why not, Seth? What's up there?"

Seth shrugged and turned to stare at the wall beside him. Serus crossed the distance so fast Cody didn't realize he'd moved until he'd lifted his son into the air and gave him a good shake. "You want all of us to die? Is that it? Are we so bad that you want to kill your whole family?"

"Not all of you."

Tessa gasped, a sound so full of pain and hurt. Cody rushed over to her and wrapped an arm around her.

"That's just sick. She's not one of us. Send her ahead. Let the animal see—"

A loud smack filled the air. Cody looked over to see Seth holding the side of his jaw, staring at his father with a hatred that made Cody's toes curl. He didn't know where this emotion was coming from but it was painful to see. As Tessa trembled in his arms, he realized how much worse it was for her. Could the mind control be responsible? If not, they were better off if Seth was dead. And how hard would that be to deal with?

Maybe there is something the vamps can do to switch his thinking. If mind control was responsible in the first place, maybe there is a reprogramming group as well for reverting this. She took a sobbing breath. And what if this is just the truth finally showing up? That he's hated me all this time. And just kept it a secret. Now that he's part of the chosen group...he doesn't have to hide it anymore.

Don't think that. You know him. You lived with him.

Did I? Or did I just live with the shell of my brother? A false front that he let the rest of us see?

He's not very old. How involved could he have gotten in the last couple of years? How high up the chain of command?

She took a deep breath and stepped back. I don't know, but if he can escape, he'll be a hell of a lot higher up the ladder now than he was before. We've taken out so many bosses he could be just a few rungs from the top.

Cody spun around to stare at the two men glaring at each other.

He couldn't imagine ever turning on his father like Seth had just done.

Which face was the real one? This naked angry poisonous personality, or the one he'd known for years growing up? A couple of years older than David, he'd been a replacement for Tyson who'd never been around. Could he too have so badly misjudged Seth? Or was this a careful process of infiltrating the ancient families and turn them inside out by poisoning the younger upcoming members from the inside? Seth was here with three other vamps, all from prominent families. All with dominant fathers who wouldn't give up control easily. But then, a couple of them had been on the bad side. So maybe some of the fathers had recruited the sons. Or the sons had been recruited as replacements for the fathers. And if that was the case, did the fathers know? Or were the sons to take out the fathers at some point and step into their place?

That's a horrible thought.

Cody started. He'd forgotten to guard his thinking. Maybe that was a good thing. Tessa was incredibly intuitive and intelligent. She'd proven to be a big help so far. He needed her to be clear thinking at this point. They all needed to be.

According to Seth, they'd hit some kind of danger point. But was going forward the dangerous move? Or was retreating?

They needed a lucky break.

We've never been that lucky.

Serus pushed Seth forward. "Move it. You want to be a leader, then lead."

Seth shot him a hooded look that left Cody guessing at what was going on in his mind. Then Seth took a long, careful look at each of them, shrugged, and strode forward.

Shit. I don't like the look in his eyes.

Neither do I, and I don't trust him one bit.

"Tessa?" Goran asked her, "Can you see anything?"

Serus spun around to stare at her, a question in his eyes.

"Nothing yet." She shook her head. "But I'm trying. I need to be closer."

Goran nodded. "Then closer we go. Just make sure you have an exit to fall back on. I don't like the smell of this one bit."

Serus nodded. "Yeah, I'm thinking trap."

Goran shook his head. "I'm thinking it is worse than that. I'm thinking annihilation."

Tessa swallowed. "And Cody and I are thinking the young males are in place to take out the old ancients. Seth for Dad. Tyson for Goran. Harding, Warren, and Keegan for their respective fathers. I don't know if they were indoctrinated to the cause by their fathers knowingly as their replacements."

ଚ୍ଚ ଚ୍ଚ

IT WAS HARD to hear about your own child being groomed to take your place after you were taken out. Brutal even. He'd never have suspected something like that from Seth. Even now, it was hard to get his mind wrapped around the idea. He had to believe this was all about the drugs. His son had served as an apprentice on the Council at his side for years. Who would think that they'd want to jump the natural order of things like this? Then again, it was only conjecture at this time.

Conjecture that had more than a ring of truth to it.

He turned to his daughter, as much of a surprise this last week as his son. "Can you come here and tell me what you see?"

She trotted to his side.

In a lower voice, he asked, "Can you see any black in your brother's energy? Anything off?"

"His energy is really dark. I can't tell if that's his anger or drugs or something else. But it's not like yours or mine."

"Does it still look like what it did a week ago? When we were sitting around the kitchen table?"

"I don't know. I saw his energy, but it wasn't the same. I

just can't tell you what's the difference." She shrugged. "Remember, I wasn't really looking then."

Silence.

He had to be happy with that. That he was even asking his teenage daughter for answers showed how shook up he was. He'd never have done this before. Still, she hadn't shown that she had these skills in the past.

It seems we were completely out of touch with our kids. Goran groaned. *How did it get to that?*

Not Cody, Serus pointed out. *He hasn't changed. Neither has David.*

True.

"Then again, the black of his energy is really condensed," Tessa added thoughtfully. "As if it's fresh."

Serus brightened. "Maybe he'd just received a new dose. It would help explain his recent behavior."

"Tessa," Goran asked, "Can you see where the army went?"

Serus watched her as she studied the tunnel. It was darker, more narrow than what they'd traveled so far. He knew that could be both good and bad. Were they walking into a trap.

I say we are, Goran snapped. *And better to assume that we are than to not.*

"The energy is all off to the left side," Tessa said and pointed up ahead. She lowered her voice, "I want to see what Seth does when we get closer. There is likely to be an exit somewhere. But how he'd have known about it…"

"He might have been here before," Cody suggested. "Or maybe the army was attacked."

"We'd have heard a fight." Goran closed the gap between the four of them. "Although they might have a weapon that could have taken them out silently." He added, "Like gas."

Everyone spun to stare at him. He shrugged, "I'm just thinking aloud."

Tessa shot him a dark look. "Maybe you can go back to thinking quietly?"

He grinned. "Better to consider all options and know what the enemy is up to rather than be caught unawares."

She gave a mock shudder before turning back to study the tunnel. "The trouble is, I don't know what the energy of a gas looks like. So I won't recognize it in time to give a warning."

"If it's gas, there won't be any warning. But they would be getting everyone down here, their own people and ours," Goran said.

Cody spoke up, "Which isn't likely to bother them as they appear to have lots of replacements. Or they *had* lots." Then he winced, as if realizing who was replacing who. "Sorry," he murmured.

"As long as you aren't in on this, I'm safe," growled Goran.

"Not me, sir."

Goran cuffed him affectionately on the shoulder. "Wouldn't have thought so."

Serus didn't want to upset the mood by bringing up the fact that Goran would never have suspected his older son either, any more than he'd have thought Seth could have been turned to the dark side.

Tessa held up her hand. And she came to an immediate standstill.

Everyone slammed to a complete stop beside her. Serus studied the way before them. There was only the deep dark never-ending tunnel ahead. He had no idea what Tessa saw. He wished he did.

"Tessa? What is it?"

Seth kept walking ahead, unconcerned by anything. Indeed, his walk was steady as a soldier. He neither looked left or right. He didn't care if they followed or not, nor did he check to see if they were there.

Odd.

Serus couldn't see anything wrong either, but he waited and watched. Whatever was bothering her, she'd tell them about it as soon as she understood.

Then he didn't have to hear it from her.

Right in front of them, Seth disappeared.

CHAPTER 13

"**U**H-OH," TESSA SAID.

"What the..." Goran exclaimed. "Where did he go?"

"I don't know, but I'm going to find out," Serus snapped, bolting forward until Tessa shouted. "Stop. Right there. He disappeared right ahead of you."

Frozen in place, Serus studied his surroundings, then put out a hand as if to touch something. He shrugged and turned to look back at them. "I can't see anything here."

Tessa led the others forward. At her father's side, she pointed out Seth's trail of energy. "He walked up to here." She kept her hand pointed on the trail.

She stopped. She looked back to see the shock on their faces. She took several steps back and watched relief wash over their faces. She walked forward.

"Hey, what are you doing?" Cody asked as the group raced toward her.

She stepped toward them again. And laughed at the shock on their faces. "Interesting. I gather I'm disappearing from view at that point?"

"Hell yes. What did you do?" Cody asked.

"It's a mirror trick." She pointed to the side wall.

Serus studied the angles of the mirrors. "Isn't this a little complex for a mine?"

Goran snorted. "But damn clever. If you were looking down this way, you'd think the tunnel ended with that pile of rock. If we hadn't seen Seth disappear..."

"And speaking of my brother..." Tessa turned to study the tunnel further down. "I'm assuming he knew about this trick and that he's now taken advantage of it to disappear?"

"Where?"

"As the army disappeared somewhere here as well... Let's spread out and look." Cody headed to the rock wall closest to him.

"Don't bother, Cody. I can see my brother's energy. He went up there." She pointed forward and to the right.

The group walked over carefully and stood in front of the wall. Cody reached out a hand and searched for a crack. "Are you sure? I can't see an entrance here."

"Well, there has to be something." She said equitably, "The energy wallows here. It doesn't go any further down the tunnel."

Serus snorted. "What sense does that make? They put up the mirror thing and then don't have anything down the tunnel?"

"Good point." Tessa looked down the long black tunnel and wondered. There was a black energy mixed with something else. She hadn't seen it before as everything had blended together in the distance. The army's energy – it was getting blacker. She spun to look at her brother's energy. It didn't look any different except the remnants were dissipating fast – faster than expected. "We've got a problem. Looks like the army continued down the mine, but my brother's energy doesn't move from this spot."

"It has to. He's not here."

She walked into the fading energy trail. She stared down

at her feet, then she tilted her head back and looked up into a narrow space in the ceiling. She studied the torn opening above her head. It could have been created from the blast, but it was the only possible explanation for her brother's disappearance.

The rocks were blanketed with his energy.

Taking a deep breath, she jumped straight up.

☙ ❧

CODY SHOUTED AS Tessa went through the ceiling. "Hey Tessa, what are you doing?"

"Seth came up here." Her voice sounded a long ways away. And he didn't like it one bit. But as he stared up the small opening, he wasn't sure he'd fit. Not with his wings. "Damn."

"I'll go after her. You two stay here. The army might come back this way, too." With that, he jumped up after Tessa.

Cody shook his head. "It's the first time I found something I couldn't do." He frowned. "Can't say I like it."

"Yeah," Goran studied the space below the opening and frowned. "Not sure I'd fit either. With the wings and all."

They exchanged frustrated glances then studied the empty tunnel.

"What are the chances that the tunnel leads to another blood farm? We heard there were four, didn't we?"

"Yes. Doesn't mean they are all here though."

"True. And we were told that the humans were in the mountain that Tessa escaped from. So that could presumably mean up top." Cody stared at the small hole above his head. "Possibly up that way if this is where Seth disappeared to."

"Could mean all kinds of things, but it doesn't change the fact that we can't get up that way." His father stared straight up beside him, their heads almost touching.

"Some of those assholes were bigger than us. They wouldn't fit either."

Goran stared at Cody, then spun around to study the walls. "There has to be another way up."

"Maybe." Cody studied the tunnel then glanced upward. "I think the blast created this opening. Maybe Seth thought it was a shortcut?"

"Or he saw it earlier." His father shook his head. "Still doesn't change anything."

Cody stared down the dark tunnel. "Unless the main entrance is just up ahead."

"Are you thinking to keep exploring?"

"Thinking…yeah."

"And what about Serus and Tessa?"

Cody glanced at his father and grinned. "Well, in this case, we can both talk to them so we can tell them what we're doing."

"Maybe we should ask first?" With a grin, Goran added, "Don't want Tessa to ream you out too bad."

Cody rolled his eyes. "She won't be mad."

Really? How do you figure?

He straightened as Tessa's voice rolled through his mind. *Did you find anything?*

Looks like another hallway up here. White tiles…everywhere. We're tapping into another part of the blood farm…or a different one.

We can't get up there, so we're going to carry on down the tunnel to find another entrance.

Okay. We'll keep going in the same direction from here.

Maybe we can find the entrance on our side.

And just as quickly, her voice left his mind. He turned to his father and shared her message, but Goran was already nodding his head. "I heard it from Serus. Let's go."

$\approx \ll$

RHIA'S HEART POUNDED with joy when she saw David. She ignored the military presence and the guns that were turned toward her as she raced toward him and wrapped him up in a hug. "I'm so glad to see you safe," she cried.

He stepped back, smiling at her. "I'm fine. We all are. Somewhat." He looked down at Jewel. "Jewel and Ian were both drugged again. They need medical care."

Ian said, "I'm fine."

Rhia laughed as she realized he had Wendy wrapped up tight in his arms, tears pouring down her cheeks.

David shook his head. "Well, well, well. So my sister was right again. You dark horse, you."

Ian rolled his eyes and dropped his cheek on Wendy's head.

Rhia glanced back at the humans. "Seems like a couple of these guys aren't in great shape either."

"It's just one of us that is hurt." The leader carrying the vamp said, fatigue evident in his voice.

"And the boys – what is wrong with them?"

"Yeah, Dad and Goran did that," David gave a short bitter laugh. "We found Seth."

"You did?" She cried out, her face lighting with joy. "Are they okay?"

David hesitated. Her stomach twisted in fear. She reached up with a hand to cup his cheek. "Tell me. Please."

"Dad and Tessa are fine."

"And Seth?" She tried so hard to stop the quaking in her voice as fear rocked her world. "What about your brother?"

David looked down at Jewel. She hugged him close and murmured, "Tell her."

He took a deep breath and nodded. He looked directly into Rhia's gaze and said, "Physically, Seth is fine."

Her breath whooshed out of her chest with relief. But it was the way he said it and what he didn't say that let her know there was so much worse to come. "And…" she pushed.

"We found him with his friends." David motioned to the unconscious vamps. "All of them are on the wrong side of this deal."

She blinked in confusion. "I don't understand."

David opened his mouth, then closed it. Jewel offered a gentle explanation. "From what we heard, it was clear that the four of them were in on the blood farm mess. They were an active part of it."

She stared at Jewel in shock. She shook her head, her long braid flipping with the movement. "No way. That's not Seth. Nor the other boys." She stopped. "They wouldn't have anything to do with this nightmare."

Both David and Jewel looked at her. Silently.

And she realized they actually believed what they were saying.

She spun around to look at Jared, who stared at her with compassion. "No. No. You have to be wrong."

"They might have been drugged as part of their indoctrination into the group behind this mess, but there is no doubt that Seth and the others were part of this blood farm."

Her thoughts whirled in panic, searching for an explanation. Any explanation. This was too preposterous. "There's no way."

She stared at the group blankly, her gaze going from one to the other. "You don't know what you are saying."

"Yes we do, Mom." David reached out and captured her hand in his. "Tyson tried to kill us all. He was one of the leaders. He'd arranged for one of the main organizers to die so he could take his place and move up. The organization is a mess as we've taken out so many of the people that the ladder upwards keeps shifting. Everyone is trying to climb up and they are stepping on each other's backs."

"Tyson?" She locked on that name. She'd looked after him as one of her own. "He's one of them?"

"He *was* one of them," Ian clarified. "Tessa killed him."

Tessa? Would the shocks never stop? "My little girl killed Goran's son?" She shook her head. "No. That can't be."

"It is. And in the process, she also saved us. We were fighting for our lives and he'd ordered the latest batch of vamps to kill us. Tessa got him before he could get far."

This couldn't be happening. She couldn't believe it. She wouldn't believe it.

As if reading her mind, David said, "Believe it, Mom."

Not possible. She whispered, "I can't. I won't. Not until there is no other option."

And she would get to the bottom of this – one way or the other.

❧ ❧

SERUS SLIPPED DOWN the hallway with his daughter at his side. Now if only he could find his son.

"Dad, over here," Tessa hissed at him. He spun around, realizing she'd slipped to one side of the narrow white-tiled hallway – ahead of the corner he was about to walk around. Damn, he hadn't been paying attention.

He slipped over to her. "What's up?"

"A different energy. Going in the same direction Seth went."

He leaned around her to stare at the corner. "Someone walked by?"

"Yeah, a little while ago."

"Well, that's to be expected. If your friends are in here, they'd need someone to be looking after them."

She nodded. "Seth turned left."

"So left is where we are going."

She shuffled closer, stopped and looked at him. "Could Seth really be one of the bad guys?"

He wanted to lie. He wanted to defend her brother. In fact, he wanted to blast her for not believing in Seth herself, but her gaze was so direct, so full of pain he had to face the truth. "I hope not, Tessa. But I don't know for sure. We have to remember what they were able to do to your mother in such a short time. And realize how much damage they could have done to your brother."

"And they had a lot more time to convert Seth." She stared down at the floor. "Maybe months or years."

"Exactly. Have a little more faith. And remember his energy – you said it was dark as if he'd had a recent dose of drugs. That could have been the final installment. The one that turned him this way. Or it could have given him a boost temporarily and will ease off after a little time."

She appeared to consider his words. And froze. "Would that also apply to Tyson? Did I kill a man who was no more responsible than any of the other vamps who'd been forced into this mess?"

The pain in her voice made him realize the loss of innocence…and the stickiness of guilt. She'd never be free from the killings of these last days but if she could understand the necessity, be free of the guilt of having made a mistake, it would help her to deal with the situation.

"I don't think there is any comparison between Tyson and Seth. Tyson had a hundred plus years on your brother. A full century to gain wisdom. A full century to learn values and to make decisions." Serus closed his eyes briefly. "Seth is young. He's not got the years under his belt to stand for his convictions. He hasn't had time to formulate ones that will go the distance. Neither has he had long enough to mature into a man strong enough to withstand the romance, the thrill of being one of the inner circle. In fact – he was an easy mark."

"And do you think Tyson marked him?"

"Either way, we need to find the truth and in order to do that, we have to find him." Serus studied the anger and the fatigue on her face. She wanted to be angry but was too tired to work up the energy. Anger without heat was a sick frustration. He should know.

"Then let's find Seth."

CHAPTER 14

A LLOWING HER FATHER to take the lead, Tessa, her head still baffled by the never ending questions with no answers, followed. "Can you see anything?" she whispered from behind his back.

He leaned his head further around the corner then pulled back quickly, flattening himself against the wall. "Someone is coming."

She held her breath.

Two people, their voices slightly raised, were discussing treatments. "I don't think we can. We don't have enough supplies. The damage in the main blood farm isn't the problem. They will close that on the next blast, but they need to do a better job directing the effects away from here this time. That blast took out several of our supply rooms and cut us off."

"How long can we function on what we have?"

"A couple of days...maybe." The man coughed, then coughed again. "I don't know. It wouldn't have been so bad, but they brought us all those new patients. That's what's stressing our supply line."

"What about knocking the patient list in half? Keep the prime subjects and remove the rest. We don't want to waste the drugs we do have."

"I don't know. The bosses aren't going to be happy.

We're short on donors and we're already short-staffed."

"Which is why we have to make the decisions. Who knows where the bosses are right now or who we can contact? I've been trying, but so far I haven't reached anyone."

"Damn…I hate the silence. The lack of order. We can only do what—"

The first male went down without a fight. Tessa had only made it around the corner when she saw her father go for the second man.

"Don't kill him. We need him," she shouted.

He glared at her. "No, we don't."

"Yes. You heard him. He knows where the new humans are." She turned to face him. "He knows where Jill and Catherine and the others are."

Serus shifted his position, lightening the pressure on the vamp's neck. He struggled, trying to twist free of Serus's hold. Serus clamped down tighter until he stopped moving. Serus lightened the pressure again. "If you behave, I'll keep you alive. If you don't, I'll take you out now."

The vamp gasped several times before nodding. "Okay. Okay."

Serus gave him a little more air. The vamp reached for his throat, massaging it as he rolled his shoulders gently. "What do you want?" He coughed again. "I don't know anything."

Tessa nudged the unconscious vamp. His body rolled slightly to the side. Maybe he was dead. She found it hard to care.

She turned her attention to the other vamp. Shoving her face into his, she asked, "I'm looking for two young human females." She gave quick descriptions of Catherine and Jill. "Where are they?"

He shrugged. "How the hell should I know?" He nodded

back down the hallway where he'd come from. "There are so many back there." He studied her features. "Why do you care? You are a vamp. They are human."

It was the curiosity in his voice that made her realize just how out of touch these people in the warehouse were. They didn't understand that the rest of the world was changing. At peace with the side by side society. And no longer living with the farm animal mentality – like the ones inside the blood farm.

"And vamps? Have you got rooms full of vamps hooked up to drugs, too?" Serus growled into the vamp's ear.

He stiffened, his nervous gaze going from Serus to Tessa. "They are volunteers. We don't force our own. They are not prisoners…they are men here for enhancements."

Tessa studied the sneer, the hint of disgust on his face. "You mean you don't know that many of the 'subjects' you work on have been forced…some drugged and delivered in that state, others under threat of death, to take part in your experiments?"

"You are wrong. I am a doctor working on volunteers. This is a legitimate organization. I would not be a part of anything like that."

Serus and Tessa exchanged long looks.

"You have got to be kidding me." Tessa rubbed her temple as she stared at the arrogant doctor. "I have spoken to dying vamps who told me how they were forced."

He shook his hair, his gray hair flying out in different directions. "That is wrong. So wrong. You have been badly misinformed."

"Wrong or not, it doesn't matter. It's true. And you are a part of it. I've seen several councilmen drugged, imprisoned." She glared at him. "And for that, you will go in front of the

Council and tell them exactly what you know. They will determine your punishment." Which she could only hope would be death.

He stared at her in shock. His voice dropped to just above a whisper, "It can't be."

"It is." Serus let him go. "And you are at the heart of this mess."

Tessa wasn't so quick to let him off the hook. "What about the blood farm? I'm sure you knew about that."

He gave a light dismissive shrug. "Animals. Not the same thing at all."

"And yet Darren, a friend of my brother's, is hanging along with Moltere."

At the ancient's name, the vamp's face twisted in distaste. "Moltere should have been turned to ash a long time ago. But Dr. Kroner wanted him alive." He straightened. "But that could change now that Dr. Kroner was killed in the blast. It took out much of the blood farm."

"Why was Moltere being kept alive?" Serus said.

"For his genetics. We were doing experiments and needed a regular supply of the original genetic material."

There was a shocked silence as Serus's face closed down. Tessa couldn't imagine a vampire being kept alive forever so they could use his genetic material whenever they wanted to.

She swallowed hard. "Does he know? Is he aware of what's going on?"

The vamp glanced down at her. As Serus's grip had loosened enough, he straightened his shoulders and readjusted his lab coat. "No, of course not. We might need some brain material, and who knows what a conscious awareness after decades of drugs would do to that. He's very valuable."

"Yes, of course," she whispered, hating the words that

came out of his mouth. "Of course he is."

"And the other vamps? The other ancients? Are they valuable too?"

"If we had any, they would be, yes." He cast a considering look at Serus. "Will you donate your DNA—"

Her father's face went hard and flat. "No way in hell."

The vamp sniffed, lifted his chin. "It's for a good cause."

Tessa doubted it, but she was more concerned with his earlier comment. "So you have no other ancients in your labs? Or none that you know of?"

"Young lady, if I don't know about them, how could I possibly answer that question?"

Right. It was a stupid question. They were also wasting time. "So first you are going to show us where the humans are being kept for your experiments, and then you will lead us to where the vamps are 'volunteering' for their experiments."

The sneer in her voice elicited an instant response from him. His nostrils flared and his lips pinched together. "They *are* volunteers. And it will have to be vamps first as they are closer."

"Good. You won't mind if we ask them ourselves." Serus grabbed him by the back of the neck and turned him around. "And don't try to sound any alarms or try to escape."

"Where would I go?" he said calmly. It was such a reasonable tone Tessa wanted to smack him out of his complacent world. He was part of this mess. The reason so many vamps had come to horrid ends.

She waited until her father and the doctor moved off in the direction he'd said to go then stared down at the vamp by her feet. Suspicious but not sure why, she pulled back and booted him hard.

A gasp escaped him.

"So you were playing possum."

She pulled out her stake and stabbed him in the shoulder. He exploded in front of her.

She straightened to find the doctor half turned, staring at her in horror. "Oh my God, what did you do? He was my colleague."

"*Was* is correct. What do you think all your experiments have been doing to us?"

He shook his head again in wild denial. "No. You must have attacked them. They are gentle. They are not killers."

That didn't deserve an answer.

Serus added, "They are killing every one of us they can."

"Only if you attacked them. They are programmed to survive."

Not strictly true, but Tessa thought it was close enough. "If this mine is the only life they've known, maybe the blast made them feel threatened. We found some growing – and before you have a hissy fit – we didn't kill them. The blast did that for you."

"Oh dear. Those were our maturing groups. They wouldn't have been ready for months yet. Some much longer. We'll have to start all over again." Distraught, he was almost running down the hallway.

Tessa kept to a safe distance behind him. She didn't know if he was as lost in his world to the extent that he appeared to be, but that still didn't make him a peaceful vamp. As far as she was concerned, they didn't exist.

❧ ❧

CODY WISHED HE understood the mess of thoughts flipping through Tessa's head right now, but her emotions were all

over the place and so were the thoughts. From the preoccupied look on his father's face, he wondered if he was talking to
Serus. Or if Serus was in the same state as Tessa. Doctors,
ashes, killers, and captives. It all rolled into a mess in his
mind. He ran steadily behind his father, Goran's big coat
flapping with every step. The only good thing about this trip
was his energy and strength seemed to be rolling in strong and
fast. It felt good.

Except he hadn't had a chance to test his wings. Somehow
he didn't think they were fully healed. Rolling his shoulders to
ease the stiffness, he said, "We have to get up a level."

His father's steps never slowed. He called back, "I agree.
Do you see any way to do that?"

"No. Damn it." He hated being separated from the others. Something always went wrong.

"Well, they've captured a doctor. He's leading them—"
Goran glanced over at Cody and read his face, "But then you
know that already."

"Yeah, but I don't want them walking into a room full of
volunteers. There's no guarantee they are drugged and
unconscious. For all we know, they have a small army up there
waiting for enhancements."

Goran shuddered to a stop. "Look."

A door.

Cody approached slowly. "It's almost too easy."

"Not if you think that they weren't expecting anyone else
to make it this far."

"I suppose." He walked over, turning to look at his father,
"Ready?"

At Goran's nod, Cody pulled the door open.

RHIA STUMBLED ON the uneven ground. She glanced back for the millionth time as the group urged her on.

"Mom, we have to leave. There is no way to let them know that you are coming. That just makes it a bad deal all around."

"I could tell your father if I could get closer."

"And what good would that do? They are trying to find the survivors from the blast. You need to help us get out safely."

"I need to help them," she stated baldly and balked at being dragged one more step.

David ran a hand over her shoulder. "Mom, I know you're worried. I'm worried. But this isn't about you or me. It's about all of us."

She studied his face. "How can I reconcile what you are saying about Seth if I can't see his behavior for myself?"

"You'll see it later. Or if you are lucky, he will have reverted back to being the man we know. They all will." He motioned toward the unconscious vamps being carried by the soldiers. "And they all need help right now."

She took a deep breath, her thoughts conflicted. There was no way she'd listen to them about her son. She knew him. Inside and out. Just like she knew David. He was worried. For her. For his brother. And his father and sister. But he also needed to get Jewel outside. She looked bad. Like really bad. And…Rhia narrowed her gaze to study the smaller woman's face. She appeared…different than when she'd just come upon them. Alert. Not as tired. Almost waiting in readiness…

She spun around to study Ian's face. Damn. He looked the same.

If these two flipped…

"Mom? What's going on?"

She swallowed and motioned to Jewel's face. Her alabaster skin was turning gray. Her mouth was almost colorless, but her eyes, it was the change in her eyes that worried Rhia. The sweet-exhausted-just-want-to-go-home-and-have-this-over-with attitude was gone. In its place...Rhia watched in fascination as Jewel's gaze hardened, darkened, and flattened.

"Shit." She didn't think, she just reacted to the threat. She jumped Jewel, knocking her back several steps while the others scattered.

"What the hell!" David rushed to Jewel's side, but Rhia beat him to her. She picked her son up and tossed him back several feet while her other arm reached out and clasped Jewel's neck. Into the one spot her husband had shown her a long time ago.

Jewel dropped to the ground.

"What did you do?" David yelled as he ran to Jewel's side. "Are you crazy?"

Rhia closed her eyes, hoping against hope she hadn't been wrong. But how was she supposed to explain it to her son?

Then she didn't have to.

Ian exploded.

He threw Wendy off to the side and jumped David.

Chaos exploded on all sides. The army moved in to restrain Ian.

Rhia caught a glint of silver as she tried to get close enough to grab Ian's neck and put him out, but the fists were pounding and bodies were being slammed down. One human went flying, then another.

She saw an opening and waded in. Grabbing Ian, she knocked him out in seconds.

Then she stepped back to survey the damage.

David was on his back, groaning. "What the hell happened?"

"I'm going to assume that it was a cumulative effect of the drugs. At least I hope that's why they just flipped and went batshit crazy on us," Wendy said, staggering over. "I don't want to believe Ian would hurt me otherwise."

"He wouldn't." David struggled to his feet. "I never saw it coming. They'd have taken us out before I understood that they'd turned on us." He shuddered, a visible ripple of emotional pain that started at his head and worked its way to his toes. "I'm sorry, Mom."

"No. I'm sorry. I didn't have time to explain. It just happened to fast."

"Well, maybe you could explain now. Because we have no idea what the hell just happened." Two of the soldiers stood up. One was still unconscious on the ground. The injured man they'd been trying to help out of the tunnel sat on the ground and stared. "I don't get it. It's like they were time bombs set to go off at some signal."

"That's possible, but more likely they were affected by the drugs in the blood we drank."

The men's faces twisted in revulsion. "You drank blood?"

David ignored them. He was a vampire. What did they expect?

He turned to face his mother. "We found a lab housing 'growing' younger vamps. We stayed there because Tessa and Cody were so badly injured." He held up a hand to stop her exclamation. "They needed a place to heal. There was a lot of blood around and none of us had fed in a long time. We were exhausted. Some of us were worse than the others. Ian and Jewel grabbed and drank complete bags of the damn stuff. I only had a half and even that was too much. I fell into a deep sleep."

"You're thinking the blood was drugged?"

He shrugged. "There was no way to know for sure. Tessa believed it was. She refused to have any." He stared around the room. "And maybe she was the smarter one after all."

"But why at the same time? Jewel is much smaller," Wendy asked.

"Yes, but Ian drank two bags." David ran his hand over his head, his features twisted with fear. "He was pretty wasted."

"And the one starting to turn could have accelerated the other's progress." Rhia reached out a hand. "What a mess. Is anyone else hurt? Like seriously hurt?"

"Tony over there is still out cold, but other than a few more bruises, we're fine." The human asked, "Did you kill them?"

"No. They are my children's friends. I couldn't do that. They are unconscious and if we are lucky, they will stay that way. At least for a while."

"Good thing you came with us. We can't handle all of these unconscious people without you." David stared down at Jewel, a terrible look in his eyes. "God. I feel so bad for her. I should have warned her about the blood."

"If she needed to feed, it wouldn't have mattered what you'd said to her, she wouldn't have listened."

She watched him crouch down to stroke Jewel's cheeks. "She'll be fine, David."

"I know she will be eventually. This has been incredibly difficult on her."

"Hell. It's been brutal on all of us."

Rhia studied Wendy crouched beside Ian. They were coupled up as well and she hadn't even seen it. They were all so young. She figured it would change and possibly break apart over time like so many young relationships, but it appeared that this last week may have cemented the relationships. Staring down at her son's bent head, she asked, "Jewel's really important to you, isn't she?"

David stiffened slightly then relaxed. He gave a broken laugh. "Very." He turned to face her. "We've kept it to ourselves for so long. Not on purpose, but because it was special."

Wendy piped up. "Same here. It's private. We hadn't wanted to share. And at the same time, we didn't want to have it change by letting others know. We'd get bugged, some might laugh, so we kept it quiet." She smiled at David. "But we thought you two were a couple."

He grinned. "It was hard at times. Cody knew, so I figured Ian did too."

She nodded. "Yeah. After Cody broke it off with Xana. I wondered who he'd be with next, but so far he's single."

There was a funny silence. Rhia looked at David's bent head and then over at Wendy's curious face. Jared spoke up for the first time. She'd almost forgotten about him being there.

"He's paired up with Tessa now. Bonded, I believe David said," he commented dryly.

Out of the corner of her eye, Rhia caught David hunching his shoulder.

Wendy laughed. "No way. That's so not possible." She shook her head. "Cody has dozens of women after him."

But Rhia watched her son. His bent head, his stiff back. "David," she said in an ominous voice. "What do you know that I don't?"

DAVID SLOWLY LIFTED his face to look into his mother's frowning face. "It's not for me to say."

She narrowed her gaze, temper lighting the depths. Yeah, that wasn't going to wash. He asked, "Have you spoken to Dad lately?"

Her gaze deepened, darkened. "No. I haven't been able to. What happened?"

David fell silent. What could he say? She'd have to find out sooner or later. His father and Goran had handled it relatively well. His mother... yeah, that was a whole different story. And he didn't want to be the one to bring on the storm. Damn Jared. Then in all fairness, he wouldn't know to keep off the subject. Plus as he might still be hoping to win Tessa back, it made sense he'd bring it up.

Rhia spun around to pin Jared in place. "What do you know?"

"Mom. It's not our place. You will find out eventually and there are a lot of explanations to come, but could we focus on the issue at hand and get these people to safety. Obviously Ian and Jewel need medical attention, as does the human. The ins and outs of our relationships are not the prime concern," David snapped. Then he closed his eyes. "I'm sorry, but you should not hear this from us."

An uneasy silence surrounded them as she contemplated his words. She glanced at Wendy then over at Jared, opened her mouth, and then snapped it shut. "Fine. But you, young man, have a lot of explaining to do."

She reached over, grabbed Ian, and tossed him over her shoulder. Then she snatched Jewel off the ground and threw her over her other shoulder.

Ignoring the jaw-dropping stares from the humans, she said, "Let's go. I don't have time for this."

With her spine stiff and straight, she strode ahead of the rest of them.

"Jesus, she's strong." Jared whispered in awe.

"Well, the temper is giving her extra strength right now, but yeah, she is." David strode after her. Wendy ran to catch up to him and asked, "Were you serious? Is there something going on between your sister and Cody?"

"You have no idea." He shook his head. "Honestly, so much has happened, I don't believe it all myself. It's going to be a hell of a shock to my mother, so please don't bring up the subject again."

"Fine, okay." She took a deep breath. "But first answer me this." She spun around to read his face. "You said they are bonded? For real? I thought that was a rumor."

"So did I, but it's not. It's for real. And for better or for worse – Cody and Tessa are bonded."

CHAPTER 15

TESSA DIDN'T LIKE the doctor or what he stood for. His morals and ethics made her sick to her stomach. To think that people like Jill and Catherine, Jared even, were just animals to him was disgusting. He was the animal. Obviously it was just a short step to culling their own people. How gross was that? She knew from her human history class that people had been doing it to their race since forever, but she'd never seen or heard of vamps doing it to their own people.

More fool her for being so blind.

Not blind. Young. All species cull their own. Whether to remove the ill or aged, all animals tend to get rid of dead weight, Cody said gently.

That's an awful way to look at the world.

Don't knock me for it, knock Mother Nature. It's her system, not mine.

Well, it sucks, she argued. *There's no way that someone who's old and has contributed to the society should get knocked on the head because they are slowing the pack down.*

But it's the law of the fittest, you know that. You don't have to like it, but...

And these assholes? she asked, *Why should they be the ones to say they are the rulers and everyone they deem unworthy should be killed off, hung up for lab tests, or enhanced?* she snapped.

Hey, I agree with you. Don't get angry with me. I'm on your side.

Sorry. She groaned gently as she rotated her shoulders. *They are starting to piss me off.*

Yeah, I noticed. Oh wait — yes — Dad found a door! Cody's voice rippled through her mind with waves of excitement. *Hopefully it will take us to your level.*

Be careful.

Always. And his voice dropped out of her head.

Damn. Why hadn't he told her what was behind the door? Dropping away like that was just creepy.

Cody? She asked cautiously. No answer.

Double damn.

She rushed up to her father. "Can you hear Goran? I was just talking to Cody. He said he found a door and then he disappeared."

Her father gave her a worried glance. "I was just talking to Goran, but he left too."

She pursed her lips, checking out the doctor's face to see if he knew anything, but he didn't appear to understand what they were talking about. Or wasn't letting on if he did. His nose jutted out at a snobbish angle.

"Maybe they went behind another stone wall and we just can't get through."

That made sense. Particularly if they were in another stone type of passageway.

She glanced over at the doctor again. "Do you know Seth?"

The doctor glanced from one to the other. "Who?"

"Seth. He was just here in this area a few moments before us. He was with us, but then we lost him."

The doctor shrugged. "That's easy to do. Unless you have GPS or blueprints, this place is a death trap." He spoke the way he walked, a sharp rhythmic staccato.

"So where can we get those items?" Serus asked easily.

The doctor reached into his pocket and pulled out a small tablet. "I never use this one. I keep it in case I get lost, but I haven't had to use it in months."

Serus turned it over in his hands several times, but he wasn't very techie. Tessa reached out a hand and her father passed it over without a word.

After turning it on, she checked out the icons on the main screen. There was a built in GPS and a communication system. "Has it got audio?"

"No. Well, yes, but that part doesn't work down here. You have to send messages like texts." The doctor took the unit from her hand and opened the instant messaging system. "See, like this."

"Yet you don't use it?"

"I don't use *that* one." He pulled out a shinier one from his other pocket. "This is a newer streamlined model, but the GPS on the old one is easier to use. Since when did technological updates make things worse?" He snorted in disgust. "Way too confusing and way too much trouble."

Tessa was in the address book of the messaging system, trying to read the names. Most she'd never heard of. She passed it back to her father, leaving the names on the screen. His gaze widened and his footsteps slowed as he scrolled through them. Several times she heard small gasps from him. "Can you read them to Goran?" she asked in a low whisper.

He was way ahead of her, scrolling down and almost lip reading as he went. She noticed the doctor was busy on his own unit. She picked up the pace so she could see what he was doing. They'd been stupid. For all she knew, he'd sent out a warning that they were coming. Shit. Stupid. Stupid.

"What are you doing?"

"Checking my emails." He waved the smaller unit around. "This one is so much faster."

"As long as you aren't letting everyone know we are coming."

He snorted. "Who would I tell? There's only a skeleton crew here at the best of times and now with that damn blast that the idiots overcharged, I have even less technicians. I've been complaining about needing more labor for months now. They want these damn experiments done but won't give me what I need to do it."

"Typical," she said conversationally. "Aren't bosses always like that?"

"These are shareholders more than bosses. In many ways, they are worse." He stuffed the unit back into his pocket. "Still, it's a necessary evil to keep the system functioning."

She could just imagine. Where the shareholders in that address book? Those that funded this monstrosity were just as guilty of all the despicable acts going on in here. That they could condone them, all from behind their facade of innocence. Not willing to live in the trenches and get their hands bloodied like the rest of the workers made her hate them all that much more.

She caught her father's hand motion out of the corner of her eye and shifted behind the doctor. He handed the unit back to her. A few clicks later and she found herself in the GPS unit. But without having any coordinates to input, it wasn't much help. Ian had the GPS coordinates for the big cavern room, but that area had likely gone down in the blast. Besides, she thought Ian might still have the phone. Bart's phone. In spite of the situation, she smiled at the reminder of the dumpy vamp she'd met several times in the oddest places.

There were several flashing lights on the next screen. She figured that the doctor had a couple of pre-set locations marked on the unit in case he got lost. Pretty smart actually. The flashing dots reminded her of something else. She glanced down at her arm and the fresh scab in place. It no longer hurt, but being as tired as she was, it hadn't healed as fast as she wanted it to.

"Were you the one experimenting with implanted tracking devices?" With some difficulty, she managed to keep her voice low and even, seemingly disinterested.

"No." He made a disagreeable sound. "That was the biotech department. I'm not in favor of metal implants at all. It stops our scanners from giving accurate results and could be throwing any number of our tests off."

"Tests?" she asked mildly.

"Blood tests, genetic tests, fitness tests. Everything is computer based." He picked up the pace as they approached another hallway. "Almost there. You'll see."

As they approached the hallway just slightly behind the doctor, Tessa kept her gaze on him.

His face lit up as they stepped around the corner. "See — these two rooms are full of volunteers."

"Vamps?"

"Of course," he said, his voice smug and condescending.

"And where do you keep the human subjects?" Serus asked, his voice hardening in exasperation.

"Down at the end of the hallway. That's the new testing wing. It wasn't supposed to be for them, but as someone blasted a hole in my old laboratory, I had no choice. The blood must flow."

Tessa hated that phrase. Hated what it stood for. If the doctor hadn't proven useful up to now, she'd have clocked him and knocked him out permanently.

"How does one get downstairs from here?" Serus asked, staring at the two white doors that resembled so many of the doors they'd come across in this place. "Are the stairs down close by?"

"What stairs? Downstairs? There is no downstairs here." He gave him a pitying look. "I told you this place is a maze, and that was before half the walls collapsed." He shrugged. "I just gave directions to someone who couldn't leave the way he'd expected to because of the damage. There's going to be a lot more of that going on now."

And he stepped forward and opened the door.

IT WAS HARD to hold back the boiling anger bubbling in her gut. Rhia was so tired, afraid, and angry that it drained much of her energy. But her own daughter? With Cody? Cody was a playboy. A guy's guy and every girl's dream guy. Rhia had seen many like him over the centuries. He was not what she'd have chosen for Tessa. And never while Tessa was as green and innocent as she was right now. Maybe after a century, when she was old enough to make up her own mind, she could date someone like him. Maybe. Right now...hell no.

Still, it wasn't like Cody had time to put the moves on her, what with running and fighting for their lives these past few days. Tessa probably looked to Cody as an older brother. Besides, both Serus and Goran were there. They'd make sure Tessa was fine. She wasn't like other vampire females. Tessa was a good girl. A nice girl. Not like the rest of her sex that would cut her up and serve her as an appetizer at the Council meetings.

She didn't have the thick skin and stiff spine to go up against those women. If anyone thought Tessa was hooking up with Cody – and didn't that phrase make her wince – they'd have laughed her out of the room.

No. David must have misunderstood.

Her daughter had more common sense than to fall for someone like that.

Besides, she had bigger things to worry about right now. She had five unconscious vamps. Two she was responsible for and others that she could hardly believe the stories she'd heard about them. David had updated her on much of what had happened this last week but had kept quiet about Seth.

Too bad her own mind wouldn't let go of the subject.

She'd sent him up here to help out his family. And something major had gone wrong. It had to be drugs and whatever mind control program the vamps had used on her firstborn. Like they'd used on her. She had flipped to the enemy's side within a few minutes. How scary was that?

Her glance landed on the human who strode slightly ahead of her. As if he couldn't allow a female to be stronger. She shrugged.

Humans were different critters. Still, these ones were helping out. She just didn't know which side. Gloria and Councilman Adamson had been coordinating the raids and working alongside the human army. They might have a better idea of what was going on. She'd ask them as soon as she had a chance. For that to happen, she had to get out of this hellhole. And if she did, it would only be to dump her charges before turning right around and diving back into the mine to find the rest of her family.

"Mom, are you okay?"

She blew a few strands of hair out of her face. She didn't

want to lie, but neither could she just blast David with the raw truth. She was pissed off. But she was a mother. "I'm fine. Or I will be when this is over. I want the rest of the family safe and sound and I want Seth and these others in medical hands where they can be helped."

"Do you think they can be?"

"I'm living proof that they can. But I do think time is an issue. The faster they get help, the better."

She tossed him a teasing glance. "And speaking of friends, how long have things been going on between you and Jewel?"

He flushed. "A few months." David turned to Wendy, who was walking on Rhia's other side. "What about you and Ian? How long have you two been together?"

She laughed. "Months and months. No one guessed."

"Except Tessa." David grinned at the surprised look Wendy shot him.

"How did she know?"

"Something about seeing energy that people hold close. She told Ian that she knew he had a girl and knew who it was. Flustered him pretty good."

Wendy laughed. "I can imagine. Tessa has some scary skills."

"Yeah, even more now. I don't know how she does it, but…" and he went into a long description of her cutting off the energy to the human guy's heart or something. Rhia tried to listen, but it didn't make any sense. And that it was his baby sister he was talking about – it really didn't make any sense.

"She did it so easily. When she did it to Seth, I couldn't believe it. When he woke up again, he was damn scared. She'd totally freaked him out." Jared hooted, admiration in his voice. "Hell, she freaked us all out."

The thought of Tessa having to hurt, or at least being in a situation where hurting Seth was the best option scared Rhia. How could this have happened?

"I wish I'd seen it." Wendy shook her head. "Seems like I missed so much."

Rhia negotiated around a mess of rocks on the ground, hating to admit the weight of the two vamps were making her less than nimble. Oh, when had she gotten so old?

"Yeah," Jared added with a snicker. "You missed getting drugged, beaten, knocked unconscious, and all kinds of bad things. Fun stuff."

The bitterness came from his own experience. Rhia knew that and she was sorry for it. He'd had a tough road this last week. But with any luck, he'd heal and move on and be a better man for it.

"But I also missed watching Tessa learn more about herself, watch you and Jewel grow closer, watch the ancients argue and fight like they always do." Wendy chuckled. "And I missed a chance to see Ian excel in tough situations."

And that was very mature of her. Rhia was proud of how well the younger generation was handling their experience. It had been dangerous and scary and tough for all of them. And they'd come through with flying colors.

She wasn't sure she'd done half as well.

GORAN STUDIED THE never-ending staircase rising in front of him. "Damn. This isn't going to stop anytime soon."

"How can that be?" Cody peered around his father's shoulder. "Tessa and Serus can't be more than ten feet above us. We've gone three times the distance. At least."

"And Serus said something about there being no downstairs to the section he's in. The communication is really spotty." He glanced at his son. "What about you? Can you talk to Tessa?"

Cody shook his head. "Not really. I know she's there, but it's all fuzzy like bad reception." He smacked the rock wall beside him. "I presume that this is responsible, although you are getting through to Serus."

"Just a little. I'm afraid this passage is leading us further away from them as well."

"Do you want to go back? We can." Cody shrugged. "We can even go to the hole they went up into and knock it open wider."

"It is lighter up ahead. Why don't we check it out quick? If it's a dead end, we'll go back."

Goran started up the next flight. This passage was very old. Maybe from the original mine. Likely a secondary exit cut into the rock in case of an accident and the men needed to find a way out. Something like what Tessa had escaped from originally. Maybe they were on the right track after all.

And if they were, where the hell were Serus and Tessa going?

❧ ❦

TALK ABOUT NOT fitting in. The trip was long and torturous with little talking. Jared hadn't meant to cause trouble – or maybe he had. He liked Tessa and if she wanted Cody instead of him, it would hurt but it almost seemed right. Still, he'd rather she chose him. Except that he didn't see how he could have a future with a vampire. But there was Taz, who'd managed just fine. Moodily, he kicked a rock out of the way and carried on down the tunnel in last place. Maybe Tessa and he would make better friends.

He shouldn't have said anything. But anything to do with Cody irked him. He had Tessa.

Jared was under no illusion which way that would go, but that was just another jab at him. And if him being around all the time irked Cody, all the better.

Feeling better for the first time in a long time, Jared caught up to the rest of the pack.

CHAPTER 16

S HE'D NEVER VIEW a closed door the same way again. Tessa knew that for the rest of her life, she'd worry about what was behind them. Worry that she'd see something close to what she'd seen today.

The room was jam packed.

Full of vampires.

Volunteer vampires, according to the doctor.

Everyone was connected to piping of some kind. Most were in beds. Some were standing and shuffling around, and many were collapsed criss-crossed on top of each other like casually tossed firewood on the floor.

Most appeared unconscious and the ones that weren't...didn't appear to be all there. The only sounds were disconcerting wooshes and beeps from the various machines.

"These are your volunteers?" she asked.

The doctor nodded. "And as you can see, we are in dire need of space. Techs are working to prep several more rooms so we can spread them around with one to a bed."

Tessa studied those closest to her but she didn't recognize anyone. "Is this the only room?"

He motioned to the second door. "The others are in there."

Instinctively, she moved over and opened the door.

And gasped.

Motre was in the first bed. His face was slack to the point where his skin looked too big on him. Surely that couldn't be? Beside him were more faces she recognized. Faces from the fights, faces of men that had fought on her side. Stiff with shock, she took several steps inside.

And the door shut and locked behind her. She spun around and froze.

She was alone. Her father hadn't followed her inside. And neither had the smug doctor. Scared, but needing to know, she reached out and tried the door. The knob turned a few inches but it didn't open.

Shit. She pounded on the door several times until a voice behind her shook her to the core.

"Don't bother. Once you're in, you don't get out."

She spun at the sound of a familiar voice and saw someone she least expected to see – Bart. Big old don't-want-to-get-involved dumpy Bart.

She turned to study him. Her instincts were on full alert. Was he a friend or foe? He had no tubing attached, which should have made him foe, but he was holding a mess of it in his hands. He held up the needle. "They misjudged the amount to give me and I woke up."

He looked around the small room, a hangdog look on his face. "I tried to stay hidden in the shadows, but that big guy at the end of the row found me. Him and the others. So many others. But some of them turned on him and things kinda blew up. I tried to run away and the next thing I know I'm in here with a killer of a headache. Like what's with that?" The plain face twisted into sheer ugliness as he touched his head gingerly.

"The drugs will do that to you." She studied his face but couldn't see any deceit in him or his energy.

"And you, you aren't a prisoner." He nodded at the door. "Other than that door?"

She shook her head. "I came to find Motre," she motioned at the big vamp in the first bed, "and his group. They were supposed to be finding and releasing captive vamps. Looks like he got taken instead."

"He should be coming around soon too. I doubt they'd have understood what someone his size would need for a dose."

She walked over and ripped the needle out of his arm. He never made a sound. Systematically, she walked from bed to bed and removed the needles from their arms. It didn't take long. This room wasn't as packed as the first one. And why was that?

She hadn't realized she'd spoken out loud until Bart answered.

"Because these ones are likely prisoners and the others...not so much."

"That would make sense. The good doctor said that both rooms were full of volunteers." She shook her head. "So I came to see if my friends were in this room."

"And you came alone?" Bart snorted and lay back down on his bed. "You are the damnedest one for walking straight into trouble."

He had her there. And she was tired, or there was no way she'd have come into here on her own. She'd pit her father against the doctor any day, but not if there were lots of techs with needles. She hadn't seen any earlier, but maybe those emails he sent had brought help.

Now she was starting to feel foolish.

She studied the room as she finished pulling the last of the needles out. "Is there any other way in or out, Bart?"

"Nah. One door only."

"Right. But two rooms side by side." She studied the simple white walls. "What's the chance they are just standard building walls? No rocks or steel in between them?"

"Why would they need that? These are sick rooms. No one has the strength to argue or fight their way out."

She laughed, hope bubbling up inside. "You are so right. But I'm here. And I'm healthy and strong and no, I am not drugged."

He stared at her, bolted upright, and came over to stand at her side, rubbing his hands gleefully. "Do you think we could break down a wall?"

With his help, she could. "Absolutely, but which side?" She turned to look at the far wall. She hadn't seen any more doors down the hallway, but there'd been a corner and that meant there could be another room on the other side here or at the back. But they *knew* there was a room on the other side. Only it was a room full of volunteers. Were they faking being unconscious? Because she didn't want to go from a bad situation to a worse one.

For a quick moment, she contemplated the door. It was reinforced with a decent locking mechanism. The builders expected the captives to try and fight their way out of here. And what about the ceiling? She tilted her head and looked up. Was it open space up there? She remembered the cavernous room where the vamps were hiding. And she couldn't help but wonder if this wasn't a similar thing. She walked back a few steps to try and understand the type of ceiling that was over their head. "Bart, have you seen a ceiling like this?"

"Like what? It's all over the place. So…?"

"It looks like tiles again." She couldn't reach up and touch it, but she could certainly jump up there and push against them. "What is with these guys, do they own a tile factory or something?"

"Wouldn't surprise me." He glanced over at her. "You aren't thinking to jump through that, are you?"

"It's either up or through," she motioned to the wall that connected to the other room full of vamps. "They have a similar door, I imagine."

"Or if they are volunteers, maybe not."

"And what if they are awake? They are the enemy." She walked over to the closest corner and pulled a bed under it so she could stand on the bed and push. The tile lifted slightly. She glanced at Bart, but he wasn't any taller than she was. She jumped slightly and pushed the tile out of its hanger. Darkness glowed above. Typical. She jumped and grabbed the cross beam holding the tiles up and hung there. Bart came over, grabbed her boot, and boosted her up. She disappeared through the space and found herself in a tunnel slightly bigger than the building, but not as big as the cave. She could also see signs of construction of a second floor going on down at the far end. Interesting. More expansion. If they had access to the outside from this part of the mine, they could shut the rest of it down, blast it closed, and keep the operations moving forward. She was very happy to know that.

She was going to shut them down.

All of them.

Permanently.

"Hey, what's up there?" Bart called to her from below. "There's no way I'm going to fit through the opening."

So true. She leaned over and said, "Not much. We're inside a large tunnel and this building is being extended. I'm on the surface of the tiles, not too much to stand on up here, just a few cross beams, but I expect I can get into the hallway and open the door from the other side."

"Hurry up. I don't want to be here any longer than I have

to be," he grumbled. He nudged his chin in a different direction. "Some of the guys appear to be waking up."

"Good. I'll be there in a minute." She turned to study the tiles in front of her, oriented herself to where she needed to be, and carefully lifted a tile that should be on the hallway side of the room Bart was in. She peered from side to side. There was no sign of her father. Considering that he was an ancient, chances were the creepy doctor wanted his DNA – donated or not.

And given that he'd likely have been taken out at the same time or soon after she'd been locked in, she'd bet he was in the next room.

Sliding the tile back to rest on the others was fairly easy. Taking the plunge to the hallway – not so much. But she landed softly, turned, and turned the door handle. Yes, it opened!

Bart raced out. "You did it!"

"Yeah, duh." She examined the knob in her hand. "There has to be some way to stop this from locking. I don't want to get caught in here again. And we need the vamps who are waking up to be able to get out."

The door was jerked out of her hand and in front of her stunned eyes, the knob was ripped off. "Is that acceptable?" Motre, swaying slightly, stood in front of her, his face hard and his gaze lethal.

"Yeah, that works." She grinned. "Glad to see you are still alive."

"Is that what you call it?" His fist slammed against the doorjamb then grabbed a hold. His fingers turned white as he tried to hold himself upright. "I feel like shit."

"Drugs will do that to you," she said cheerfully. "Got caught by surprise, didn't you?"

His glare deepened.

"Whatever," she smirked. "Did you find your boss?"

Motre's eyes widened. He spun around, stumbled, righted himself, then took a step back into the room. His shoulders sagged. He pointed to the back of the room on the left. "Councilman Bushman is there. Trondjent is beside him, and…" he stared off to the right, "and I think the other two councilmen are on the right." He nodded. "It looks like they are all here."

She stepped forward slightly and peered inside. "Good. Let's get them on their feet. We need to get moving."

"What about the others?" Bart asked. "In the volunteers' room?"

Tessa stared at the second door. "My father is likely in there. But there are dozens of hostile vamps in the room – in various conditions. Volunteers. And most likely ones that are going to be happy to kick our ass."

Motre straightened. "How many?"

Tessa studied the interior of the room Motre had been in. "Same size room, about the same number of beds, but stuffed with vamps."

"So we need the men back to full strength." He turned to the room of slowly waking vamps. "Everyone on your feet. We're heading into another major fight."

A few snapped awake, several groaned, and a couple that were ahead of the others stood up and walked closer.

"What's up?" asked the first one to reach them. He was rubbing his head as if he'd taken a major blow.

Quickly, Tessa explained.

"You think your father is in there?" Motre asked. "What about the others?"

That explanation took a little longer and by the time she was done, most of the men were on their feet.

"Goran? Councilman Goran and Councilman Serus?"

Several men asked, their voices climbing over each other.

She lifted her hands, palms up. "Yes. They are both here somewhere."

"That means a third of the council is here." Motre frowned. "And we've taken out several more. So half the council is accounted for."

He nodded. "We have to wonder about the ones not here, which side they are on."

"Probably both," she said, suddenly remembering the small computer GPS unit. She searched her pocket, smiling as her fingers closed over it. Pulling it out, she said, "This will give us a lead on some more members. The email list is big. The doctor has a smaller unit that's faster."

Motre took it from her and handed it to the vamp they'd been speaking with. "Chad, you go through this. See who we know and might be able to take down. We'll have to coordinate efforts with the outside world for that."

"As there is an army crawling all over the place already, that might be a bit hard," Bart suggested. "For the humans to be here, someone is coordinating something."

"Sure. But who with?" she asked. Realizing there were a dozen men standing and listening, she pointed to the door beside them. "Shall we?"

Motre motioned to several males. They stepped in front of Tessa and surrounded the door. Motre backed up several feet then ran several steps, jumped, pivoted, and kicked the door beside the lock. He landed lightly as wood splintered in all direction.

Popping the door open, the group he'd assembled rushed forward.

Expecting sounds of a fight, Tessa ventured forward when she didn't hear anything. She peered around to find piles of ash as Motre's men systematically cleaned up. The smell was almost as horrific as the sight.

"Is my dad in here?"

Motre shook his head. "No. Doesn't look like it."

"Shit. That means they took him somewhere else."

SERUS WAS BARELY conscious. He didn't know what the doctor hit him with, but feeling was slowly returning to his jaw. At least it hadn't been drugs. He welcomed the pain as it sliced through the fog clouding his mind. Hearing voices, he kept his eyes closed and tried to understand what was going on.

The same asshole doctor was speaking, "Hurry before he wakes up. We need his DNA."

Like hell they were going to get that.

Footsteps raced to the far side of the room. "Faster. He could come around any moment."

"If I had the right drugs, we could knock him out and keep him here." Drawers were opened and closed. "Shit. Where is everything?" More banging around gave Serus hope that they were all out drugs. The footsteps approached. "This is the last one. We need to go to the supply room and get more."

"I'm not sure there is more. With this place crawling with unfriendlies, it's a crapshoot as to who you're going to meet in the hallways." He coughed several times. "I want to take time up top. The air down here is getting bad."

"Unfriendlies?" the tech asked. "Do you mean humans?"

"Both. I got a message saying there's a human army down here somewhere and they are covering all the entrances. At least the ones they know about. And then I came upon this ancient. He had a girl with him. She's locked up but we need his DNA."

"Shit. What do we do now?"

"Nothing. They'll never find this place." More sounds of glass doors banging. "Besides, if they are in the main blood farm, they won't survive the next blast. It should close that part of the mine down for good."

"Can't say I like the idea of more blasts. Surely there is another way?"

"If there was, it's too late now." There was a heavy pause. Serus risked a look. The second male was prepping something on a nearby table and the first man was studying a bottle of something. Shit. It was now or never.

"Found the restraints. They won't hold him for long. Hopefully we can keep him out until we find the right drugs." Someone approached. "Give me a hand. We'll get the sample now – just in case."

"Like hell." And Serus lunged.

❧ ❧

DAVID HATED THE fatigue that ate away at him. He should be stronger than this. More capable. His mother strode ahead carrying Jewel and Ian effortlessly. It made him feel like an infant. A weakling.

"Keep up, David. Let's stay together."

Yeah, now he definitely felt like a kid again.

Until he heard Jared's snigger beside him. David glared at the human. "You're no faster."

Jared grinned. "Yeah, but I'm a weak human and you're supposed to be a strong kickass vamp." He motioned to the unconscious vamps being carried. "Apparently the rumors were blown out of proportion."

David's stomach twisted. He couldn't blame Jared for stating the obvious, but he wanted to.

No young male, human or vamp, wanted to be thought of as anything less than macho. And as he was the only male vamp still on his feet...he should be good. Then there was his mother. She looked invincible. And he admired her.

And envied her.

Right now he wanted to puke until his stomach emptied. Damn drugs.

"Anyone know what time it is? Are we heading into day-light or moonlight?" Having spent so much time underground, he'd lost track of the days.

"It should be night time when we exit the mine."

"Hopefully. It would be nice to have something go in our favor."

"I prefer daylight myself." Jared walked by his side, look-ing way too energized for David's flagging strength. He'd like to punch him out for that alone.

Which was small of him.

Tough. As he stared at Jewel's slack body hanging over his mother's shoulder, her dangling arms swaying with every step, he had to wonder how badly affected by the drugs she'd been to turn and attack like Ian had. Would she throw off the drugs, or did some kind of mind control kick in after a certain time?

He studied Ian's equally limp body. He'd had a bad time in this mine. Wendy walked beside Rhia on Ian's side. David shook his head. He hadn't realized the two were a couple. It had taken his sister to point it out. He had to wonder at how much difference a week had made for all of them.

Lost in his musings, he didn't notice anything around him.

Until Jared whispered, "Oh shit. We've got trouble."

☙ ❧

CODY PUSHED THROUGH the stairway to jump out behind his father. Into yet another empty room. Older, as this had stonework and not tiles. "What. This is much older than a lot of the mine."

"Yeah, I think it leads to the outside." Goran turned in a slow circle. "Like an escape hatch to the outside world in case of a collapse."

"Makes sense. Maybe we can find the others and leave this way." Cody crossed the empty room and pushed open another door. More stairs. "It must lead up and out."

He left his father at the base of the stairs and walked to the far wall. He tilted his head and studied the odd stonework. "Is this another door?"

"Not likely. I don't think this section of the mine is part of the vamp building."

Cody wanted to do a more thorough search, but he had to admit after a first and second glance that there didn't appear to be anything here and nowhere else to go but up. He glared at the small room. He hated to leave it. He couldn't help but feel like Tessa was likely on the other side of the wall. Somewhere.

He turned to follow his father. Goran started up the stairs.

A weird grating filled the room.

Cody turned to see a door open quietly beside him.

CHAPTER 17

TESSA FRETTED AS Motre insisted everyone be up and mobile before leaving as a group. Tessa agreed in principle. Only it was taking too long. She paced the hallway, swearing under her breath at the cloud of ash and smoke that seeped from under the door of the other room.

"We're ready, Tessa."

She spun around, relief making her giddy, to see Motre standing in the doorway, a large group of vamps assembled behind him. "Finally. Let's go."

"Which way?"

"This way." She raced down the hallway. It had been no problem to find the energy trail, but it was already dissipating. They were more than a half hour ahead. And these assholes could do a lot of damage in a half hour.

Footsteps pounded behind her as the vamps followed. Several corners and damn near a quarter mile later, she came to a screeching halt. She glanced over at Motre.

He stepped up and motioned to four other men to frame the two doors.

They looked to have it handled. She stepped back safely out of the way and watched as they broke the doors down. Screams erupted from both rooms. She stayed back out of the way as more men poured into the rooms. These vamps were all looking for payback. She was just looking for her father.

The sounds of fighting and chaos were equally noisy from both rooms. She looked from one room to the other as she leaned back against the wall and waited. Bart appeared to be of the same mind. Him and several of the less healthy looking vamps had slumped to the floor. Two she recognized as councilmen. Only Bart appeared to be asleep.

Then the left room went quiet.

Followed by the room on the right.

She took a deep breath and stepped forward to take a look.

From where she stood, she could see into both rooms and the devastation within. The beds were intact and so were the many patients tucked under sheets and attached to tubes. Ash filled the space between the beds. She walked into the right room first and saw the patients were human.

She slowly worked her way down the beds. She wasn't sure but some of their faces were familiar. Several she'd seen standing with Jared when he'd come back to show the humans the way into the blood farm. Had they all come to the rescue after her panicked call from the blood farm? After finding no sign of Catherine or Jill, she left everyone unplugging the humans from their drug source and walked into the second room.

Tears came to her eyes. Catherine was in the second bed on the left. Jill was another dozen beds past her. She'd finally found them. Now she needed to get them out of here safely and find someone who could help to rid their bodies of these drugs.

The mountain rumbled.

That made it an easy decision. She started with Catherine and unplugged the tubes in her arm, then moved on to the others. The vamps helped and by the time she'd made it about five beds down, the others had all been unplugged.

"Are they likely to wake up anytime soon?" she asked the group in general.

"They are humans, so who knows?" said Chad, one of Motre's group.

"Let's hope it's fast. We can't get them out in this condition. There are too many of them."

"We are many now," Chad said. "We could carry one each."

"And we may have to."

Just then the mountain rumbled again. A slow rumble rippled through the mine, causing several of the men to cry out.

"Why don't we just grab them and go?" one vamp in the back asked.

"The GPS unit shows an exit not far from here." Motre said, not looking up from the small machine.

The mountain rumbled again. This time, she swayed as the ground rippled underneath her. "I don't think they were expecting to have this area affected by the blasts."

"If they were setting charges in an old place riddled by these mine shafts, they are asking for trouble." Motre studied the dust filling the air. "The whole place is likely to come down."

"Yeah. But I can't leave without my father."

"What are you going to do?" Chad asked.

"I'm thinking of sending you and the men out with a human or two apiece – whatever number you guys can handle – and get them to the closest exit fast." She stared into the rooms full of beds. "How many humans are there? Maybe someone can do a head count."

"On it." A couple of men disappeared behind Chad. Motre stayed with her. He said, "I'm not leaving. You might need help finding your father."

"And Goran and Cody are still here. Not to mention a group of soldiers somewhere close."

"More humans?"

"Yes, they came to secure the area for the medical personnel to return, but…"

"They would be helpful to carry out their unconscious members." Motre motioned to the room full of humans.

"I wish we could find them."

Motre pushed some buttons on the GPS and asked, "How many were there?"

She twisted her lips as she tried to count the group in her head. "Eight or nine, I think."

"And they went down the tunnel when you came up?" he questioned her earlier stance on the tunnel.

"Yes. And Goran and Cody went down the same tunnel and found an old staircase on the opposite side to where my father and I jumped up."

"Okay, does this look right?" He held out the small unit and pointed to something on a map. The screen was small but clear enough to see the staircase and another cavern further down.

"Possible, yes." She tapped the screen excitedly. "So does this staircase meet up with us somewhere?"

"Let me look." He clicked away. The two men came back out from the rooms. "There are thirty-five humans."

"And vamps to carry them?"

"Twenty four."

"Are any of you strong enough, in good enough shape, to carry more than one human?"

Several of the men straightened in outrage. She rolled her

eyes. "I'm only considering that you were drugged. And may still be weak."

Several snorted in disgust at her. "Like that would be an issue."

"In that case, load up and let's get everyone safely out of here."

"I'm not going," Motre said, "and neither are Chad or Lenther. We're coming with you to rescue the others."

"And I'd appreciate the company, but I have to make sure that the humans are safe first."

"They'll be fine." She watched as the vampires helped load the unconscious humans onto each other's shoulders.

"Do you think they can carry them all?" she asked Motre quietly, needing to make sure they could do the job. She didn't dare leave any humans behind. They didn't deserve this.

"They are vamps. Strong and pissed off vamps. Carrying a few humans is no big deal." Motre answered her without lifting his attention from the GPS unit. "I have a route for them. That will be the fastest way out of here."

"And can they get the hell off the mountain from that point? No point in sending them up the mountain if it's going to collapse underneath them."

"True, it sounds ready to collapse at any time, but the exit looks good. They'll be fine." He looked up at her. "It's the best option at this point."

She nodded. The vamps came out in single file and none appeared winded by the burdens they carried. Motre spoke with them as a group and gave them instructions. Tessa listened with only half an ear. She was desperate to find her father, and this was once again taking too long. Both her father and Seth's energy appeared to go past these rooms, but she hadn't been able to leave her friends. Especially not now that they had a solution on how to get them all out. Finally, Motre finished and the men took off.

Bart brought up the rear – empty handed.

Naturally.

She nodded in the opposite direction to the three men that were left. "We have to go this way."

"Excellent. We should be able to meet up with Councilman Goran this way, too."

Finally good news for once.

Feeling better than she had in a long time, she raced after her father's energy trail. Maybe they'd actually get out of here safely after all.

☙ ❧

SERUS WIPED THE sweat off his forehead with his sleeve. Thank heavens Goran wasn't here to see that. He'd never live it down. Break a sweat over two humans, techs even. Yeah, that would keep Goran laughing for decades. It had to be the fatigue, lack of food…something. He was *not* getting old. To hell with that shit.

Now to find Tessa. Seemed like that was all he'd been doing this last week. He checked the two men's pockets, retrieving the doctor's computer unit and the matching one in the other man's pocket. This second male also had a key ring. He pocketed that too. He studied the room he was in and realized it was just one of many similar rooms he'd seen over the week. It had several beds and more equipment in a large wall cabinet. More of a lab room then. As they were looking to steal his DNA, it made sense. He strode over to the cabinet and wrenched the doors open. There didn't appear to be any cooler or other type of storage for other DNA, so maybe they were going to take the tissue samples here and move them elsewhere.

At least they hadn't gotten his. No one should have to worry about their DNA in the wrong hands.

There was only a single door in the place and nowhere else to go but out. With one last look around, he opened the door and stepped outside. Face to face with two more vamps, both in white coats.

He didn't think, he just reacted. Up went the fist and down went the vamp. At least the first one. The second one sliced at Serus's back, catching his coat. Serus pulled free by sliding out of the sleeves then turned and kicked the vamp in the nuts.

The vamp bent over, losing his hold on whatever weapon he had as he clutched his groin. A spike. Perfect. Serus moved. He kicked the tech in the face, then dropped, scooped up the spike, and stabbed the vamp in the chest. The second tech went up in flames.

He turned back to the first vamp.

Too late.

The kick caught him under the chin, snapping his head backwards. Serus shook the stars from his mind and roared. Then lunged. The other man had some training as he managed to get Serus in a head lock for all of two seconds before Serus flipped him down to the floor. He reached for the neck and latched on tight. The spike sat in the smoldering pile of vamp ash. He snatched it up and stabbed the second vamp in the thigh. No explosion or ash. Just a horrible slow escape of air and a nasty smell as the man's flesh sizzled. He was burning, slowly.

Serus backed away, coughing. "If that's what you guys call

enhanced...you are crazy to try it. If it does that to you when you're dead, what the hell do those enhancements do to your system when you're alive?"

He gave the slow burning corpse one last appalled look and took off in the direction they'd come from.

How many more of these assholes could there be?

And where the hell was his daughter?

ক্ষ শ্ব

THE HALFWAY STATION appeared up ahead. Jared raced forward and opened the door. It was empty inside.

Good thing, as he hadn't given a thought to the enemy possibly waiting for him.

Like last time.

"Wait. Jared, what's down this way?" David called out, pointing to the tracks running off into the distance.

Jared walked to the edge of the platform as the humans carried their burdens through to the other side. He stared into the blackness. "It must wind around to the other side of the mountain."

"Maybe to one of the other blood farms?" David stared, hands on his hips. "I wonder if we should check it out."

That was the last thing Jared wanted to do. But if more of his people were in trouble...

He glanced at the platform. All the people were through except for Wendy and Rhia, who stared down the tunnel.

"These people need to get out of here." Wendy said. "They come first."

David shook his head. "The exit is just on the other side. According to Jared, there are vehicles parked outside, you guys can drive away. Jared and I will take a quick look."

His mother snapped. "No. You stay right here. I'll deliver these two to the trucks, Wendy will stay with them, and the army can drive them off the mountain." She glared at the two men. "I'll be right back. I will go with you. Do. Not. Move."

She disappeared.

Jared turned to face David. "Are you sure this is a good idea?"

David snorted. "No, it probably isn't, but we're here."

There was no arguing that. Jared sighed, jumped off the platform, and started walking. "Then let's take a look."

"Except Mom said to wait."

"Yeah, but she's your mother, not mine."

❧ ❧

GORAN WATCHED AS Cody dashed around the back of the door and waited. The door swung back and forth but no one entered. "What the hell?" he whispered, "There is no one there."

"We activated the release somehow." Goran's gaze went from the open doorway to the stairwell. He'd only put his foot on the bottom step when this one had opened. That was the trigger. Still, why? Unless there was a different route and they wanted people to have that option. Or it was a trap. Something else that this place was famous for. He stepped through the doorway. It started to close and came up against Cody's foot, slowly forcing it out as it tried to close.

"There should be a trigger mechanism. Likely based on weight," Goran said. "The same as the stair I stood on when this door opened in the first place. Probably hinged on this first tile here."

"Tile?"

"Stone then. It's completely square so it's not a natural part of the mine."

"But what's down this way?"

Cody hated the two options. He really wanted to find the one that would lead to Tessa.

Then get a move on. Lord knows I could have used your help lots already.

"Tessa!" He laughed, "Dad, I can hear Tessa." But from the look on his father's face, he was in contact with Serus. Perfect. Maybe they could meet up with them after all.

Tessa, where are you?

Darned if I know. We have a couple of fancy GPS units that show us your staircase and we're moving in your general direction, but we need to find my father first.

What? What happened to your father?

He was taken. I did find Motre and his group, a room full of volunteer vamps that are no more, and even better, I found Catherine and Jill...and many other victims.

Wow. Cody didn't know what to think. He'd been climbing stairs while she'd been out saving everyone again.

She laughed, the sound a warm loving breeze in his mind. Man, did he love that.

And I love you, she giggled. *I didn't do anything. I've been wandering around here when I happened upon the two rooms. Oh, and guess what...I found Bart. He left with the group that hauled the humans back out to safety. Then again with Bart, who knows where he'll slip off to.*

How did you get them out? He couldn't imagine. Neither did he want to. His mind had locked onto her first words and wouldn't let go. She loved him? Had she meant it? Or was it a casual joking comment? Thankfully she'd carried on talking and hadn't heard his thoughts.

I rescued the vamp group first. Once they had their strength back, they were capable of splitting the unconscious humans up between them and carried them away.

And now...? They'd done so much already.

Now I have Motre and two of his men helping me to find my father. He can't be too far away.

Actually, it looks like my father is talking to your father the same way we are right now.

Oh perfect! she said. *Maybe he can tell us where he is. Then we can come to you. We need to get the hell away from here. The army can do the last sweep and find the others. If there are any others.*

There are still the other blood farms.

Yikes. I forgot about those.

The army can worry about them.

Speaking of the army, any sign of the soldiers?

Cody's stomach sank. *No. I forgot about them.*

Yeah, it's not like we are short on things to worry about.

As they waited for their fathers to stop talking, Tessa filled him in on the conversation with the doctor. The doctor who'd apparently turned on them.

He wasn't surprised. Most vamps couldn't be trusted. He hoped the humans were safe with the group that had carried them out.

I did consider that, but we were short on options. Also, the vamps were more than anxious to get the hell out themselves.

And you found a room full of volunteer vamps?

It was stuffed, she explained. *The men were standing room only. It was disgusting. Everyone was connected to something. The doctor said they were getting enhancements. I didn't recognize anyone. They were likely imports. Surely there couldn't be so many unknown local vamps that none of Motre's group recog-*

nized them either?

Makes sense. Not good, but understandable if they were afraid of tapping into those that might not be sympathetic to their cause.

Motre and his team were damn glad to have targets to take out.

Cody could just imagine. Motre and his team were deadly at any time – but in this situation, they were out for blood. So not a good scenario.

No, it wasn't. But he didn't go on a rampage or anything. He went really controlled. Really quiet. Damn, he was scary.

Did you check the room afterwards?

No, she whispered, *the smell told me everything I needed to know.*

He winced. Not a visual he cared to spend too much time on.

Goran turned. "Serus is looking for Tessa. Does she know where she is?"

Cody explained about her finding the others and having a GPS unit. Goran only nodded. "Serus has a few as well."

"Good, they should be able to find each other then. They haven't been separated that long – how far from each other could they be?"

CHAPTER 18

"**I**S THERE ANOTHER corner up ahead?" Tessa called out to Motre, who was studying the GPS unit again. While waiting for him to check, she sent another message out to Cody. Nothing. Damn this mountain.

"No. The hallway looks like it goes on a ways. Too bad these guys don't have some kind of subdermal implant showing us where they are all hiding."

At the term subdermal, she paled. "They injected me with a tracking device of some kind." She stroked her arm, still tender from her rough surgery. "I dug it out."

He started at her curiously. "How did you know it was there?"

Back to that again. She gave him a sheepish smile. "I could see a black spot in the energy of my arm. So I used my nail and pushed it out. Once removed, the black spot was gone too. Figured they had to be one and the same."

Lenther turned to stare at her. "I think I heard you say something about energy before."

"Yeah," she nodded. "I did."

"I wouldn't have believed any of it if I hadn't seen you actually do this stuff," Motre said, waving his hand at her arm. "So the next question has to be – if you saw that tracking device in *your* arm, can you see if *we* have any of the damned things?"

The other two men grouped around her. She opened her mouth to say it wasn't likely when she saw it. Motre's neck. Something black. Not very big. But deep and dark.

She stood on her tiptoes and leaned in.

"What is it?" he pulled back and glared at her. "What are you staring at?"

"There is something dark up here, but it's hard to see."

"Dark?" he asked suspiciously. "Like a tracking device?"

"I can't tell," she said in exasperation. "Crouch down a bit so I can see, please."

He dropped to his knees. "Now...what the hell is it?"

At eye level now, she pulled the collar of his shirt back a bit.

"Hmmm." She eyed the spot dubiously. "This is bigger and blacker than what I saw in my arm."

"You think it's a tracker? Something they shot into me while I was out cold?"

"I don't know." And she didn't. "But I suspect it's something like that. Maybe a little more complex. They were only trying to track my whereabouts – at least that's what the one vamp told me. I don't know if this is the same thing at all."

"Get it out," he snapped ominously. "I don't want anything inside me – especially not from them."

"And that's another issue. I'm thinking they took something from you and are using this to collect more data." She sighed. Or her imagination could be taking off again. She had no idea. "Or I could be completely wrong. We really don't have time for this."

"Take it out," he roared.

"It's going to hurt," she warned.

He spun around and gave her such an affronted glare, she lifted her shoulders then dropped them. "Okay. Don't move."

"How are you going to get it out?" Lenther asked. "You don't have any tools."

She snorted, held up her hand, and extended her sharp nails. The men stepped back.

"Jesus."

"How come you can do that?" Chad asked. They'd all crowded around her, watching and generally getting in her way. "And no one else can?"

"Yeah, I'm a little different." She studied the muscle running along the top of Motre's shoulder and pressed gently until she felt him stiffen. "Does that hurt? Like that might be the spot?"

"It doesn't *hurt*," he snarled, "But it doesn't *feel* normal."

"Right." Without warning, she held her index finger beside the place she hoped held the device and extended her nail. She felt the resistance from his flesh but her nails forged through the skin and tissue like it was nothing. He stiffened and gasped as she went deeper. She twisted slightly to get a better look and managed to scoop below the black spot and then force the black upward. It came out easier than she expected. Maybe it hadn't been in long enough for the pathway to have healed. It seemed to slide right up and…there. It sat in a tiny pool of blood on his shoulder.

"Got it."

He relaxed and pivoted to stare at her. "Let me see."

"Open your hand." When he complied, she dropped the tiny unit into his palm. "There."

He hissed as he stared at the metallic dot in his palm. "I don't know what they were tracking, but you said they took something from me. What did you mean?"

"Answer me something first," she motioned to his size now that he was standing again. "Is your size natural?"

He frowned.

"I mean, is this the way you are naturally? No genetic tampering, no enhancements."

"No. Nothing. This is the size all the males in my family are." The other two men nodded, confirming his words.

"Right. Then I suspect they stole tissue samples." At his confused look, she smiled. "They took your DNA so they could find out why you are so big naturally and gift it to their creations."

He stared, his gaze widening with horror as she explained what they found in the lab. "That is bad. Like so bad on so many levels."

"How do you think Councilman Goran felt when he found out about his extended family? And," she added, "I suspect that is also why they snatched my father. He is another ancient. They kept Moltere alive as a living tissue donor all these years for their experiments. They probably didn't need to, but there wasn't any point in losing his contributions by killing him either."

The other men paled as they realized what she was saying.

"I can't believe they are genetically modifying vamps," Chad said.

Lenther exclaimed, "And no matter what Moltere did, he didn't deserve his fate."

"Men have been looking to improve their species since time began," Motre said. "Human or vamp."

Tessa couldn't argue. "True. And now they have your tissue sample as well." She nodded at the device in his hand and added, "I don't know what that was doing, but I suspect it could track any number of things that would allow them to see what else your body could do."

"Thieves. Liars. Cheats," he spat. "If they weren't all dead,

I'd kill them all over again."

The group around him snarled their agreement.

Chad stepped forward. "Please see if I have any of those in my body."

"Then it's my turn," said Lenther. "I don't want them to have anything of mine."

Tessa realized they weren't going to go anywhere until she'd checked the men over. It didn't take long. She found one more black spot on Lenther's lower spine. She hesitated at the location then decided to be grateful that she didn't have to take the damn thing out of his butt.

It took a little longer with Motre asking questions every step of the way, but finally she had the device out of Lenther's body too.

And the look in his eye when he realized she'd been right was scary.

He was after blood now.

And not his own.

She hoped that they'd be able to find more vamps to kill. He had a serious need to punch someone or something. She hated being the bearer of the bad news. In the movies, the bad guys always shot the messenger.

That was not the end she wanted for herself.

❧ ❦

JARED HEARD DAVID racing behind him. He probably shouldn't have made that crack about his mother, but it was true. And he was feeling incredibly misplaced right now.

He didn't have a mother and hadn't had one in a long time. Or a father for that matter. He might have obeyed his uncle's rules in order to stay at his house until he finished school, but he'd be damned if he'd start this stage of his life by not following his instincts. Right now, his instincts said to get the hell out of the mine as soon as he could. If they had to check this tunnel, which he begrudgingly admitted they should, then he wanted to do it fast and be gone.

Footsteps pounded behind him. David, most likely. Whatever.

Until his shoulder was grabbed and he was spun around. By Rhia. A very pissed off Rhia.

"I did not search for you, nurse you back to health, and possibly lose family members for you to pull a stupid stunt like this. I want you alive and well and not collapsed in some damn tunnel under a ton of rocks."

He glared at her, trying to ignore the laughter on David's face. He opened his mouth to argue and stopped.

"You were worried about me?" he asked cautiously. How long had it been since anyone had made rules to keep him safe? To show they cared? To keep him from getting hurt? Damn. He couldn't be angry at her for that.

He wanted to be. But his anger drained as if she'd reached out and yanked the dregs from him.

She gave him a stony smile. "I don't know what your life is normally like, but in my family we care about each other. We take care of each other. And we don't let them pull crazy stunts that might get them killed. And regardless of your upbringing, you are no longer alone."

It was on the tip of his tongue to bring Seth's name into the conversation, but the look on David's face warned him that was a door better kept shut.

The darkness in the cave settled deeper as he marshaled his thoughts. Rhia still had a hard grasp to his shoulder, so she was waiting for something. His anger these last few days hadn't allowed much room for being chastised like a little boy again. Still...

He owed her something, and respect was a place to start. He took a deep breath and said, "I'm sorry. I should have waited."

The tension on her face eased. And her hand dropped away.

He added, "In my defense, I figured that the sooner we knew, the sooner we could get the hell out of here. I can't help but feel like the whole place can come down any moment."

She studied his face. He hoped the sincerity he felt was easily readable. He'd seen her strangle a man with one hand. She could break him in two without a thought. It was a hard reality.

"I know that," she said in a gentler voice, "However, it doesn't matter how fast we leave this place if we leave hauling out your carcass."

He winced. "Yeah, sorry again."

She led the way. "Now let's go. Fast in and fast out." She sprinted away into the darkness.

David fell into step behind her and Jared, who'd always considered himself a runner, lagged in third place. Damn. Was there anything these vamps couldn't do?

∽∽

SERUS STARED AT the computer unit in his hand. He was technologically challenged. He knew that. But this was the first time he wished he'd taken the time to learn all this stuff. And if he survived this nightmare, he swore he'd have David teach him. It would be worth the humiliation to know he'd not get caught in this position again.

This stupid little computer had the answers he needed and wouldn't let him have it without pushing all the right buttons. And damned if the buttons weren't on the small side. His thumbs were huge. And awkward. He clicked a few more times looking for a help button he thought he'd seen pass by.

Just when he was prepared to throw the damn thing, it buzzed in his hands.

"Holy crap!" He tossed it from one hand to the other. It kept making noise. He finally lifted it to his ear and yelled, "Hello."

Buzz.

His fingers danced over the buttons, looking for something that would shut the damn thing off. Shit. Shit. Finally it went quiet and left him feeling like he'd missed something important. He snarled out at the world in general. Damn place was full of tricks.

"What's the matter Dad, can't answer my call?"

At the sound of Tessa's voice, he stilled, then turned.

And caught her as she jumped into his arms. "Yay, I found you!" she cried.

She was alive. Thank God.

He buried his face in her hair and hugged her tight. She felt so solid, healthy. And he could barely hold his tears back. He'd thought for sure that this time she'd not get out of whatever jam she'd been caught up in. And once again, she'd proved him wrong. "Tessa." He wanted to say more but the words clogged the back of his throat. Finally, he dropped her to her feet and stepped back a bit to hold her by her shoulders. "Are you all right?"

She grinned, a beautiful smile that lit up her face and made his heart ache with joy. He snatched her back into his arms and squeezed her tight. Her laughter made him put her back down where she beamed up at him.

He lifted his gaze to the men surrounding her. Motre. Damn, that bastard was big. And pissed off. Serus grinned. "Glad to see you alive and well and not hooked up to an IV machine. Thanks for helping my daughter."

Motre snorted sheepishly. "It's actually thanks to Tessa that we are no longer hooked to the many machines that we were hooked up to," he corrected.

"And for taking out the tracking devices or whatever the hell they are that the assholes put into two of us," said the vamp standing beside him.

Serus raised his eyebrows and looked from the men's faces to Tessa's beaming face. "So you saved the day again?"

She shook her head. "So not. I got locked inside the room where they were. By the time Bart and I got out, you were gone. So I freed them and then they turned and killed all of the volunteer vamps that had been in the other room." She frowned. "And what happened to you? I wasn't in that room ten minutes before I managed to climb through the ceiling and saw you were gone."

"Yeah, I'm not exactly sure what happened. I saw you enter the room and the next thing I knew, I was waking up in a lab room where the damned doctor was talking about restraining me before taking samples of my DNA." He grinned, hard and flat, at his last few words. "They obviously didn't get anything from me."

"Good. They did from two of these guys and maybe from some of the others. There's no way to know how they are choosing who to get samples from. But if two of these three men had devices in them, we have to presume there are more in the others. We released dozens of vamps including two – no – four councilmen. I'm sure they have trackers. But we can't do anything about that right now. They've all left the mountain." She chewed on her bottom lip. "At least I hope they have, because they were carrying all the humans we found. Including my friends."

"They will be fine," Motre said. "They have a way out and they were all pretty anxious to leave."

"And Bart, did he leave too?" Serus had to wonder at that nuisance vamp. What was he up to?

She shrugged. "As far as I could tell. What that little weasel did after he was out of sight is anyone's guess. I wouldn't be surprised if he's hidden in another part of the mine."

"If he has, that's on him. We can't save those that won't let themselves be saved."

"Now that we've found everyone, can we get the hell out of here?" Chad asked.

"We need to find Goran and Cody, and I don't believe anyone has seen the soldiers that went ahead of us." She took a deep breath. "And I don't know about Seth."

Chad frowned. "We have no way of knowing where the soldiers went. And no way to communicate with them."

"As for your brother..." Motre lifted his unit. "Chances are he knows how to get out of here just fine."

She nodded slowly. She had no way to look for her brother and Motre was right. "He has insider knowledge of where to stay to be safe and how to escape this place."

She had to be satisfied with that. She glanced over at her father and saw the same fight warring on his face. Then he nodded. She added, "As for the soldiers, they came in prepared to do a job. So maybe they are fine, too."

"That's more like it." Motre said. "Now can we move on? I'd like to find the assholes that hooked me up."

"Hooked *us* up," Lenther pointed out.

Motre and his men were looking for a fight. Something they could release their frustrations on. But as Serus looked around, it looked like they were fresh out of bad guys.

For once.

RHIA TRIED TO rein in her temper but it defied control. She'd been chasing after these kids for days now and they were still taking off on her. They hadn't let her go after Serus but for some damn reason they figured they could come down this stupid tunnel.

"Mom, he didn't mean anything by it. I don't think he ever had much parenting."

Good point. In Jared's case. To David, she snapped, "And what is your excuse?"

David fell silent as he ran by her side. She snuck a glance at his face. He wasn't angry. He looked philosophical.

"I guess I couldn't let him go alone," he said quietly. "And it was my idea. He's been through a lot and still he's stepped up to help us out several times." He rolled his shoulders. "I figured I could do no less."

That she hadn't seen coming. She shook her head. When had her kids grown up?

Jared streaked past her as if they were racing to a finish line, but he was slowing down now. Then he stopped and pointed at something.

Now what?

CODY STARED INTO the black corridor. "I'm not liking this

part. Why all the tricks? If this was built for the miners, why have things like this to stop people from getting to safety?"

Goran laughed. "Traps to let those out that were allowed out and traps to stop those that weren't. Clever really. It is a great way to get rid of someone you didn't like."

"True, but what if they needed the exit themselves?"

Cody glanced from the dark corridor to the stairs. "You'd have to be crazy to go into that corridor when you could go up."

But as the words flowed out of his mouth, he felt the draft of fresh air.

"Or maybe this is the way out and not the stairs upwards."

Goran studied the corridor. "Or the fresh air is to make you believe this is the way out but is actually part of the trap."

"Damn." Cody hated his father's insistence that this was a trap. That could mean all kinds of nasty things were waiting in there. He did not want to go inside. "I wish we knew where Tessa was. There's no point in going in this direction if she's not on the other end."

"They said they had maps of this place and showed the stairs up here. That most likely means they can see this corridor as well. And will likely use it to find their way here."

Oh, now that wasn't good.

Goran looked from one door to the other. "I wish there was a way to stop this one from closing behind us as we enter."

"Can you rip it off?" Cody suggested. In his head he started calling for Tessa. *Can you hear me, Tessa? We think you might be walking into a trap.*

"Can you hear Serus at all?"

Goran wasn't paying any attention. He was studying the

way the door was hung. "I can't see any kind of hinge. How does this thing work?"

"I don't know. But if we can't prop it open, then we need to take it off."

Goran nodded. "Great. But how?"

Cody studied the door that appeared to be made completely out of one piece of stone and shrugged. "With brute strength, I suppose. Both of us together."

Goran raised an eyebrow. "Then get over here and let's see what kind of damage we can do."

Cody joined him and leaned his shoulder against the door. "One, two, and three…"

Slowly it creaked open.

Then Cody heard a cry from deep inside.

"Someone is inside." He went to go in but his father called out, "Stop! It could be a trap."

Frustrated, he turned to face his father, "We need to know who is making that noise."

Indecision warred on his father's face even as Cody backed up into the entrance of the hallway. The door started to swing shut.

"Wait." Goran tried to hold the door open, but it was beyond stopping.

Cody squeezed back to his father's side just in time.

"Damn," he said as he caught his breath in the small room. "We need to open it again. Help whoever is stuck inside."

Goran strode over to the stairs up and stomped on the bottom stair. The door slowly opened again.

"You stay here and keep this damn thing open. I'll go in and get him." He didn't give his father a chance to argue. He raced in, took a long jump past the first trick square, and ran inside. The tunnel was dark and narrow and the floor uneven. He walked as fast as he could. The faint cries were just up ahead.

He almost tripped over the man crumpled on the floor. After a quick inspection, it appeared the man's leg was damaged. There was no easy way to do this. Cody tugged him upward. As a flier, it was almost impossible to carry people on his back as it could damage his wings. But in tough situations...there wasn't much choice.

Cody called toward the open door where his father waiting. "Dad? I've got him. He's hurt though."

"Can you carry him out?"

"Working on it. The tunnel is too damn narrow." He grunted as he stepped over rocks.

"Can he walk?" Goran called out.

"It's his leg. Looks like a spike of some kind pierced it."

Goran frowned. "A silver spike?"

"No. Wood." The surprise in Cody's voice matched Goran's. Wooden stakes were old. It had to have been a trap that the guy triggered.

"Vamp or human?" Goran asked.

"Cody, is that you?" The vamp on his back struggled to get down. "Let me down. I can make it."

"Like hell you can. Stop moving. We'll be out of here in a minute." But inside Cody was stunned. "Uh, Dad... it's Seth."

❧ ❧

"SETH?" STARING INTO dark narrow tunnel, Goran wished he'd sent Cody to step on the stairs. Being left behind sucked – to use the kids' language.

"Yeah, we're almost out."

He could hear Cody's heavy breathing as he helped Seth into the room. Damn, that boy didn't look so good.

"How bad is it?"

"Need to get the wood out of his leg, but it might be better to let someone else do that. He's sweating really bad too. I wonder if the stake was poisoned."

"If it was a trap, then most likely."

Seth whispered, "It was. I was told to use this hallway. No one would find me and I'd be safe."

"Who told you?" Goran snapped. He'd kill the bastard himself.

"A doctor," Seth gasped out. "I don't feel so good."

And he didn't look good. Sweat poured off his face and his skin was clammy and gray. His hands shook as he stretched them out to show them.

"Dad, we need to get him out of here."

Goran stared down the tunnel. Then back at the suffering boy. "Was anyone else in that tunnel?"

Cody glanced over at him. "I didn't see anyone, but I didn't go all the way to the end."

"At the other end," Seth whispered, "More vamps."

Oh shit.

And Seth collapsed at their feet.

CHAPTER 19

FOR THE FIRST time, Tessa wondered if they all might actually get out of here. Find Goran, which hopefully wouldn't be hard as they had the GPS to guide them then they could find an exit. She squelched the concern over the soldiers. They'd come into the mine prepared. Surely they would be okay?

Except for that weird energy surrounding the men. Maybe enhancement and maybe drugs. Whether they were volunteers or not, she had to admit she felt safer away from them.

Motre stopped a few feet ahead of her. He'd been following some kind of map he'd found in the GPS unit.

"There should be door here." He turned to look around. "But I'm not seeing one,"

Tessa examined the walls on both sides of the hallway. They hadn't seen anyone since meeting up with her father. It was as if the place was completely empty. And she knew it wasn't. Creepy stuff.

She walked up one side and then crossed over to walk down the other. And saw a faint, like seriously faint whisper of Seth's energy.

Excitement rippled through her. "Dad, I think Seth went this way." She looked further down the hallway. But Seth's energy didn't carry on.

However his energy had blended to the wall. Everything

was energy. If she took that thought process one step further, the wall itself was energy and should show the space where the wall ended. And where Seth had entered.

Only she hadn't been able to see anything like that. Because she hadn't been looking for it.

Resolutely, she turned back, shifted her angle of viewing, and studied the wall. Her father and the others stood in the middle and watched her.

But no pressure.

She put them out of her mind and focused on what was in front of her. She could see the different energy of the floor material and the walls. They married together comfortably, but there was a slight change where they joined. So in theory, there should be something similar where the hinges were – and quite possibly where the latch was. If there was such a thing. As she'd found out, this mine was full of tricks. It was trying to figure out what a break in the material would look like when she saw layers.

In one place, it was eye level. She stopped and stared, puzzled.

"What do you see?"

"Layers of energy." That was another switch. Because of her injury. Instead of hurting her, her vision had improved. In so many ways.

Cool.

"Layers? What does that mean?"

The men arranged themselves to stand beside her to stare at the spot she pointed out.

She laughed even as she heard the whispers behind her.

"How can she see anything? It looks the same."

"No, it doesn't. There is something on top of the base layer. 'Ohh…' And she got it. Placing her hand on the spot, she searched for one at knee level and grinned. 'Here.' Keeping her left hand on the same spot, she stretched out her right hand as far as it would go then slowly slid her right hand toward her left hand. She'd only gone about a foot when her nails caught on something. She stepped sideways and realized the 'something' was actually a break in the wall. She reached out with her left leg and kicked.

Silently, a portion of the wall opened up in front of her.

"Hot damn, you found it," Chad crowed. He reached out and slapped her back.

She grinned. Damn, that felt good.

"Yeah," her father said, "But what did she find?" He nodded to the space in front of them. "Look."

"What the hell?" Motre's words washed over Tessa from behind.

She was speechless. "Are they alive?"

"How could they be?" Lenther asked. "They must have been here for years."

"But...vamps don't die." She hesitated. "At least not easily."

Serus brushed past all of them and stepped into the weird corridor. "Why don't we find out?"

He reached the first vamp slumped on the floor and checked to see if he was alive or dead. He frowned. "Hell, this one could still be alive."

"Oh no." Tessa gasped. "That's horrible. They'd prefer death to this."

"Wouldn't we all?" Chad said quietly.

"We have to make sure this door stays open. If those guys died in there – or almost died – it's because they couldn't get out."

Tessa left Motre and his men to figure out how to keep

the door open as she joined her father. She studied the dead looking vamp. "Are you sure he's alive?"

"Vamps can shut down into a state of hibernation. He's alive." Serus leaned forward to look at the female at his side. "And if he is, then chances are she is as well."

"How do you think they got in here?"

"Hard to say." He straightened. "But you can count on one thing, they couldn't get out."

"How horrible. What if they had families?" she cried out. "Waiting for them to come home."

"That's a sad truth in this case. These are Darren's parents. Remember we found him hanging in the main part of the blood farm when we first entered?"

She gasped. "That's right. So his parents disappeared – somehow getting locked up in this hallway – and Darren is left alone and becomes one of their victims." She sat back on her heels and stared at the two vamps. "Do you think they were part of the blood farm or trying to escape?"

"My gut says trying to escape."

She agreed. They'd never have left their son alone. "How can we help them?"

"They need more help than we can give them." Her father went to lift the male up onto his shoulder. "He doesn't weigh much. We'll be able to carry them out of here."

"Providing *we* actually get out," muttered Chad from behind her.

"Seth went this way and he's not here so it must lead somewhere," Tessa said. "Goran and Cody are close, too." She tilted her head, "I think I can hear Cody."

Serus's eyes defocused as if he was calling to Goran. Then he smiled. "Yeah, there they are."

She laughed. "Would have been fun if we'd rescued them from this hallway of horrors."

Hey, I heard that. Cody's voice burst through her thoughts, making her start with surprise.

Where are you? she asked excitedly. *You should see what we found.*

And you should see what we found. Damn we must be close if we can speak like this.

I know. I wonder if you are at the end of this horrible hallway. Looks like a dark stone corridor. But we found two vampires that look like they've been caught in here since forever. And they are still alive. Dad says they are Darren's parents.

That makes sense. We found Seth – injured at this end of a small squarish tunnel carved from solid stone. His voice grew stronger the more he spoke.

Damn. She bounced to her feet and searched the darkness. *I can hear you so clearly. We are at the same tunnel because Seth's energy came this way.*

Be careful. Cody said, excitement raising his voice. *He tripped some kind of trap and he's been staked in the leg.*

Motre is fixing the door to stay open so it doesn't close and lock us in. Like what happened to these hibernating vamps.

Hibernating?

They have been here so long, they look and feel dead, but Dad says they are alive. That our bodies can shut down and go into a hibernation state. They look really weird too.

Can you wake them up? Ask them what happened? Although if you do, someone will have to tell them about their son.

She winced. *Yeah, that would be tough. We don't even know if he's still alive. He was in the main warehouse.*

Cody's groan rolled through her mind. *That's not good.*

They won't be talking to anyone for a while. She watched her father pick up the two vamps and continue down the tunnel ahead of her. *We're on our way.*

ॐ ॐ

DAVID STOPPED BESIDE Jared. Damned if there wasn't a double set of doors leading to one side. They weren't well used, but neither were they sealed shut from disrepair. He studied them and wondered if they'd open. And if they did, what else they would find in this house of horrors.

What a place. He'd be happy to be out of it.

He looked down the dark tunnel, wondering how much else was there to find. And why couldn't the damn army find it all instead of them?

Right on cue, the damn mountain grumbled and rolled gently under his feet. He closed his eyes and shuddered.

Rhia gave the doors a hard wrench. "A quick look only. We need to get out."

The doors squealed as they shifted cantankerously.

"If this has been used in the last thirty years, I'd be surprised."

"Give me a hand." Rhia shifted to one side. David and Jared walked over to the far side and the three pulled. Hard. Finally, it gave a small groan and then popped open.

"What is it?"

Rhia shook her head. "I have no idea."

Jared coughed and cleared his throat. "I think I do."

They stood at the edge of a long wall of cabinets. There were handles evenly spaced over the wall. "I think it's like a morgue. A mausoleum of sorts."

David stared from the wall to Jared and back to the wall. "Why the hell would you think there are dead bodies in there?"

"I doubt there are bodies here," Rhia murmured. "It could be a memorial wall to the men and women who died building the mine. The mine is old. There would have been accidents."

"Still creepy."

"Okay, so can we go now?" Jared asked. "This just ups the weirdo meter. And I'm so done."

With one last look, Rhia turned to lead the way back to the halfway station.

"Uhm, don't you think we should close the doors? Out of respect for the dead...or something?" Jared said.

David watched Jared give a casual shrug like it didn't matter, but as he watched Jared glance toward the crypt, he realized that it did matter. David returned to the furthest door and motioned to the other door. "A little help?"

Rhia stared at him in confusion. "We're trying to leave it the way we found it when the mountain is likely to fall and obliterate everything anyway?"

"It's a respect for the dead thing." He motioned toward Jared.

She blinked and comprehension hit. Muttering under her breath, she started to push the door close and stopped.

"Now what?" David asked.

She reached forward and pulled a hanging disc from one of the knobs. Made of wood, old and dusty, it had been impossible to see. "Marie Moltere. At peace in Moltere's Mountain."

"What?" David crowded around to take a look.

"Is this a memorial to Moltere's family?"

She stepped back to eye the wall and found another hanging piece. She reached up and cleaned it off. Then read. "Monk Moltere."

"So it is his family?"

"Wow."

"Interesting." Rhia didn't know what to think. "It's not necessarily an odd thing. We are a long lived species, with so few of us dying." She reached to brush the dirt off a plaque at the top. "Moltere's Mountain."

"So not a mine after all – the mountain was their home." Slowly, Rhia finished closing the door, now a hint of reverence in her motions. "That explains why it's so old."

They closed it with a hefty slap. Then turned to walk back to the platform. David fell into step behind her. And stopped.

"Did you hear something?"

He turned to look behind him.

And saw the two soldiers almost on top of them.

❧ ❦

SERUS? CODY IS telling me about Claude and Mara. It's so hard to believe. They've been missing for years.

I know. They are in bad shape. If they survive, they may not be the same.

That bad?

Yeah. We're on the way to you. How bad is Seth?

He'll live – if we can get him some help. I think the stake was poisoned. Goran's voice rose. *We need to get off this damn mountain.*

We're coming as fast as we can.

We'll stay at this end to keep the door open. These damn things are tricky.

Motre propped our end open.

Unless someone comes along and unprops it.

Thanks for that. Serus winced and shifted the load over his shoulders. He'd worked harder this last week than he had in years.

Make that decades. You're getting soft, old man.

Ha. Like you're one to talk. You're older than I am.

Silence. Serus grinned. Goran never did like to be reminded of his age. *Aren't you, old man?*

He frowned. Why wasn't he answering? He strained to sense his friend's presence. There was a buzz as if to say he was there, but...

Serus. Go back. Go back, Goran yelled.

Serus froze. Shit. *What's wrong?*

No answer. And then the mountain started rumbling.

Instead of heeding his friend's warning, Serus raced toward him.

⌒ ⌒

JARED WATCHED THE two remaining soldiers struggle to stay on their feet. From the beaten and exhausted look on their faces, they'd either barely made it out of harsh battle intact or they were fighting some major disease.

Considering Tessa's observation before they'd left, it could be either.

The problem was there were no vampires with the group.

"Where are Tessa and the others?" Jared cried out.

Rhia spun around to look at him. He quickly explained who the men were.

"We went ahead and somehow got separated from them," said the closest one. "We followed the tracks and found one room off to the side, but we were attacked. We're the only two that survived. We were weak. Something's wrong with us. We fought hard and lost most of our group. We made it back to the tracks and just kept going." He wiped his forehead. "Figured this tunnel would never end." He looked around.

"Even now I don't know where we are."

"You've come full circle," David replied. "And I'm glad you did. At least now we know that we don't have to go all the way down the same tracks."

"But where is my family?" Rhia cried. "I knew I should have gone after them."

"And done what? We needed your help and as long as they are all together, you know how resourceful they are. I'm sure they are fine," David said.

Jared wasn't so sure, but figured they'd have a better chance of getting out better than if anyone went back in to look for them. "Let's return to the platform and get out."

Rhia looked torn, but David tugged on her arm. "Let's go. We have to trust in them."

She closed her eyes briefly and swayed as if it was all too much. Jared realized how much she stood to lose if this turned out bad. Husband, son, daughter, and best friend.

Then as if underlying her fear, the mountain started to rumble…and rumble…

"Shit. Let's go." David ran past Jared with his mother bringing up the rear. Jared turned to make sure the two newcomers were following and found the thought of being buried alive had kickstarted them. In fact, as Jared turned back to see Rhia and David getting further ahead of him, the army men raced past him.

Jared was in last place. Again.

So much for his track and field medals from school.

The platform loomed ahead. With a last surge of adrenaline, he jumped up onto the platform and through the doorway to the other side. The others were waiting. At the sight of him, they turned and ran to the entrance.

Just as a huge blast tore though the mountain.

CHAPTER 20

TESSA HAD ONLY taken her gaze off her father for a second. She swore she had. But he'd raced so fast she'd lost him in the tunnel ahead. With the mountain crashing around her, she couldn't hear her own screams. She checked back once to make sure the others were following. They were in fact on her heels and pushing her forward. Crap.

The mountain had finally given in.

The stone walls went on forever. She couldn't imagine the work involved to build such a place. She'd have expected it to be yards long and not the miles it felt like. Her heart pumped and her lungs screamed as she ran down the narrow passage. Motre wanted to pass her but it wasn't wide enough. Calling on her vampire genes, she begged for more energy to get out of this hellhole in time.

Cody, can you hear me? she cried. There was no answer. *Cody!*

Without warning, the tunnel ended and she'd barrelled into a tiny circular room – a tower-like room – with a mess of rocks. But where were the two men?

"Tessa, over here. Goran and Cody have come up here." Motre passed her to race up the stairs behind her father.

The floor under her feet rippled, tossing her sideways. She struggled to her feet, found her arm grabbed, and was shoved forward into the stairwell.

She stumbled, regained her balance, and bolted upward. When her feet hit the floor at the top, she spun around to see where they were. In a room. A tiny room.

With a large opening on the side.

Only there was nothing out there but black sky. They'd climbed so high within the mine that there was no place left to go but over the cliff.

And none of her group could fly.

❧ ❦

RHIA RACED INTO the darkness of the night. The two soldiers jumped into separate vehicles and started up the engines. Dirt swirled and rocks kicked up as they turned the trucks around. The rest of the group hopped into the canvas-topped back of the second truck. Jared ran for the cab and piled in as the truck jumped forward.

"Drive, drive, drive!" he yelled, his head out the window, watching clouds of dirt and dust billow from the mine entrance.

"I am." The driver punched the gas and the truck flew around the corner. Rocks pounded on the hood as the mountain careened on the edge of self-destruction.

The truck swerved. "Shit. Hang on. This is going to be rough," his driver screamed.

Up ahead, Jared watched the first truck rip around the corner, raising a plume of dust. They were pulling ahead of his truck. Damn. He wished he could drive. Hell, he wished he could fly.

"Faster," he yelled. "Look at the others. They are way ahead of us."

"Not in a moment they won't be." The road opened up to

a long straight stretch and they jumped forward.

Jared twisted out the window to watch the devastation going on behind him. They might just make it.

The roar was building to the point that he couldn't hear anything but the pounding of his own heart. The mountain looked ready to explode.

Taking everything and everyone out with it.

Including Cody, the ancients and...Tessa.

☙ ❧

CODY SOARED, SO grateful his wing had healed enough for his wild jump off the tower. He circled and swooped, loving that sense of being whole.

Except it was short lived. He wasn't whole and if he lost his friends...and Tessa... he'd never be whole again.

"Dad, did you warn Serus?" He looked over at his father, carrying Seth effortlessly over his shoulder.

"I tried to, but knowing him..."

"You think he kept on coming?"

"I'm afraid they didn't have a choice," he shouted. "The mountain made that decision for them."

"Shit. That means they are likely to be crushed inside."

Goran hovered in place where he watch the exit they'd flown from. "There's no sign of them. They might have gone back. Found a different way. Don't lose hope."

The growl from the mountain had become deafening. He had to shout to be heard. "We have to stay here and make sure."

"There is any number of other possible exits they might escape from."

"No. Look!" Cody pointed to the ledge they'd flown off

491

of.

"Someone is up there."

A blast rent the air, sending both Cody and Goran tumbling backward with the force.

RHIA COULDN'T BREATHE. She didn't dare. She was afraid she'd lose something precious if she did. She couldn't help but want to turn back. And knew it was no longer possible.

Not anymore. Her beloved Serus would survive. He had to. And he'd do anything to keep Tessa and Seth alive. Even if it cost him his life. As she would in his place.

She called out in her mind again. *Serus, please, my love – answer me.*

No answer.

Rhia shuddered, rejecting the promise of the pain to come. They'd survived this the last time, were they lucky enough to survive it again?

"Mom. They will be fine," David murmured quietly at her side.

She turned her black gaze on her son. "Will they?" she shook her head and stared silently out the window. "I wish I could be sure of that."

The truck slowed. The gears grinding, the box bucking with the force, before it came to a rolling stop.

Rhia strode to the back of canvas covering and threw back the canvas. And found herself surrounded by gunmen – vamp and human.

All pointing their guns at her and David.

"HEY, WHAT'S GOING on?" Jared asked. He'd been escorted out of the cab in time to see Rhia and David being held under guard.

As his gaze swept the area, he realized there were dozens, maybe hundreds of people here. Vamp and humans. Most of the humans were unconscious on the ground. His gaze landed on a group of teens. Human teens. Sarah. Aaron. Jessica. Even Stephen. Damn, it was good to see them safe. He'd been afraid they'd never made it back to town.

He rushed over to them – and came up against several gunmen as they stepped in his path. Jared glared. Then switched his gaze to the large group of pale vamps standing beside the humans.

And the anger and confusion in their gazes.

He looked around. The soldiers had been separated from the vamps. Ian and Jewel appeared dead. Wendy was crouched beside them, anger and yeah, that was fear on her face.

So she didn't know or like what was going on either. Damn. Would this never end?

Seth's three friends that the soldiers had carried out had been laid on stretchers. Carefully. Unlike Ian and Jewel. So they were bad vamps and this was a group of equally bad vamps retrieving their fallen comrades. Nice. *Not.*

He was getting damn tired of this shit.

WENDY KEPT HER eyes on the proceedings while pinching Ian to wake up. She could only hope he'd be himself when he did. They needed him. What should have been a welcoming party had turned into what she suspected was a clean-up-the-stragglers party. And she was one of the stragglers.

They'd been surrounded and basically ignored in the beginning, but now that the others had arrived, things had changed. She figured they'd been waiting to see who else had survived.

Gloria walked over to where Rhia was standing.

"Nice to see you again, Gloria." Rhia's voice was cool, wary. "I don't know how well all the raids did, but this mountain appears to be finished."

Wendy agreed silently. They'd seen too much stuff right now to believe anything anyone said.

In her hand, Gloria held a small computer type unit. "True enough. We've been tracking you. Well, some of you. You did quite well. That you will lose the two ancients is sad, of course, and you've lost your daughter. And for that," she took a deep breath and smiled. "I am grateful. I'd have preferred to have killed her myself to make sure that nastiness was stamped out permanently. However, as the creator of that obscenity, I'll be happy to kill you instead."

Wendy gasped.

Rhia stiffened. Her gaze went cold. "I wondered who was the organizer behind such a large operation. Especially when you started coordinating the raids. It seemed like you were so anxious to help, the first one to compile the computers, the ledgers. To box the information to look at later. As if you were going to be the one going over the material. At the time I didn't think anything of it, but now..." she frowned. "Are my sisters in on this?"

"No." Gloria gave a mocking laugh. "We couldn't trust any of them to keep quiet." Then she smiled again and Wendy's blood chilled. "We should have taken you out at the beginning, but we were too busy trying to salvage the situation. Besides, if any one of you had been taken out early, the others would have torn the mountain apart looking for answers."

"And the rest of my family?" Rhia answered coolly. "What have you done to them?"

"Oh, me nothing." Gloria smiled, a dead iciness to her eyes. "The mountain will take care of them. Or *will* take care of them." She held up the device in her hand. "It's a remote detonator. I have one more charge to go. And that should finish it. My husband was part of the Moltere clan, you know. I hate to see the place go, but it's not the only location I have at my disposal. If you'd stayed up there, you'd have been buried like all the rest. We were hoping a few other members would make it out of there, but... now it's too late."

She lifted the device.

"Wait," Rhia shouted. "Why not wait and see who else survives?"

"Because I'll probably just have to kill them. I was hoping to see some we'd been working on for years. I had a lot invested in those kids. We've got three and will take care of them, but they aren't as far along as the others in their programming. One of the missing you know very well."

Wendy knew. She didn't know if Rhia had connected the dots, but it wouldn't take long.

David gasped.

Rhia whispered, "Seth?"

"Yes, Seth." Gloria laughed. "I'd planned his transformation personally. To target your mutant daughter. Too bad I never had a chance to see how that turned out. Looks like he didn't survive the mountain either. He still needed several more sessions to make the programming permanent." She shrugged, mocked, "Oh well, what's done is done."

Her smile turned sly. "You remember Goran's boy, Tyson, don't you? See, we couldn't get to your men so we decided the best bet was the next generation. They were born to replace you, after all. And replacements were exactly what we needed. Tyson, already being a son of one of the higher council members himself, came up with the idea of going after others like him. It was a great idea."

Wendy reeled as she realized how many vamps had been involved and how many she knew personally. And how many Rhia must know. Talk about betrayal.

Ian groaned softly. She gasped and leaned over him. "Quiet. We're surrounded."

He stilled, then his eyes opened a slit. She stared down into them. Damn, was he with them or with Gloria? And how was Wendy supposed to find out?

❧ ❧

DAVID LUNGED TOWARD Gloria and came up short as guns butted against his chest. "You used my brother as a tool? A weapon to destroy my family?" he asked in outrage.

Gloria stared at him, her gaze flat, dead. "We gave him a gift. He would have a chance to live. To carry on his family's genes – the right way. He had been trained to assist Tyson."

David shook his head. "You have no idea what you've done."

She laughed. "Of course I do. And thanks to Goran's emails to Markus, Tatia, and Cleary – we knew right from the beginning. Of course he also asked me about the Enforcers. I'd already taken care of them a long time ago. Join or die. It was that simple."

"How could you?" Rhia shook her head slowly, as if coming out of a deep sleep and couldn't believe what she was hearing. "You lost your own son and husband in the last war!"

"Yes." Gloria's gaze hardened. "Because of the humans. The humans killed my family before I even understood we were in trouble. But I made them pay. Back then and every day since."

David stared at the vengeful woman he'd known all his life. He'd always been wary of her. Had heard bits and pieces about her over the years but never questioned any of it. There had been no reason to. Until now. And realized how a simple misconception of what had originally happened to her husband and son had let them be so blind to someone who was a really obvious suspect. Now that he understood, hindsight was a bitch.

"I should have known," Rhia said painfully.

"Why? I went out of my way to keep you from even considering me."

David stared at the car Gloria had exited. Was it rocking? He studied it carefully. Yes. Someone was trapped in the trunk. He glanced around at the group holding the guns. Boredom was starting to wash over their faces. They might be henchmen, but they were nothing like Motre's men.

He walked over to Jewel's side. Guns were raised as he moved, but no one stopped him. He crouched down beside Jewel, wishing she'd wake up. He gazed into Wendy's worried gaze. She motioned downward. He glanced at Ian and found his friend staring at him. Anger like he'd never seen before burned deep inside. The car jerked beside him. David looked up at Wendy and tilted his head toward the car. She shrugged. Damn, she didn't know who was in there either.

Behind him, Gloria barked, "Let him out."

Soldiers immediately raced over and opened the trunk. They lifted out an ancient male vamp and helped him to his feet. The men cut the bindings on his hands and legs. They stepped back.

"Oh no," whispered Rhia.

David twisted to see who it was. Councilman Adamson.

"I'm so sorry, Rhia," he said painfully. "I had no idea."

"Now that we all know where we stand, let's take care of this problem first." She lifted the device in her hand.

David straightened and started moving, his fingers already clenched around a spike hidden in his pockets. He just needed a chance… any chance…

"No!" cried Rhia. "Don't."

Gloria laughed. "Too late." And she pushed the button.

CHAPTER 21

"SHIT, DAD, NOW what?" Tessa huddled back against the mountain ledge as cold wind blasted them. The dark of night was their only saving grace.

Where were Cody and Goran, the fliers in their group? Some of the others here might be jumpers, but there was no place to jump to. The valley glowed with rivers and fields and was a hell of a long ways down. The ledge they were standing on was takeoff spot for fliers. And the worst for any others of their kind.

"I might be able to glide down." Except her father's voice didn't have that strong confident tone she wanted to hear. They were standing in the middle of nowhere with no place to go. She needed hope.

"Anyone else here a jumper? A glider?"

The others all shook their heads. "None of us," Chad said. "We went into the security side of things because we are big and strong. We don't have those advantages so we needed training to make up for it."

"Yeah, little good all that training will do now." Fear threaded through Lenther's voice. She felt for him. She *might* survive the fall as a glider. She did not know about them. She'd never made an attempt from so high up, and the landing might be a bitch, but she'd likely live. She could possibly carry *one* of them. But there were *five* to split between her father and her.

It was too many.

And they were all huge. And she...well, she was a hell of a lot smaller and weaker.

Then the choice was taken from them.

The mountain exploded. She grabbed two men and jumped.

GORAN REGAINED HIS balance, shifted his weight, and spun around to look at the spot where he'd seen Serus and the others just moments before. That section of the mountain was gone. Not just damaged but completely missing.

"Cody, can you see them?" he screamed over the wind.

Cody hovered in place, his gaze frantically tracking boulders as they fell. "No, I can't!"

"They're falling." Goran dipped down. "They have to be, there's no other place for them to go."

And he dove into the mess of falling rock.

Cody tore after him. *Tessa! Can you hear me?*

Cody! Help!

Where are you? I'm looking everywhere but I can't find you.

We're falling. The mountain blew up. I jumped. But it's too far.

Her panicked cry tore into his heart. *I'm coming. Hold on.*

He tucked his arms tight against his body, folded his wings back, and bulleted downwards.

DAVID GRABBED THE closest vamp and stabbed him, then

spun around and slashed at two more. A shout rose up around him.

Councilman Adamson joined in the fray. David ducked and kicked and cut and burned to ash every vamp he could touch. He heard Ian roar behind him. David turned and realized Ian was slaughtering Gloria's henchmen, Wendy at his side. He laughed. "Glad to have you back, Ian." He ducked and barely missed a spike in the shoulder. "Oops." He landed an uppercut and took out the guard.

"These assholes are going to die for what they did," Ian cried out.

Then David didn't have a chance to hear anything as he was punched, kicked, and knocked to the ground. He rose with blood in his mouth and started to spin, spikes in both hands as he tore through the enemy, hoping that the others would finish off the ones that he wounded. He came to a staggering stop, exhausted and out of breath. He crouched, both hands out waiting for the next attack.

And found there were no more attackers.

His chest heaved as he searched the group. His mother. Jewel, still unconscious. Ian and Wendy. Even Jared – holding two spikes of his own. Wow. That guy had hidden depths.

He struggled upright, realizing his mother held Gloria to her knees on the ground.

Councilman Adamson walked over. "Gloria, how could you do this? You killed so many of our people."

"Your people," she snapped. "Not mine. I am not one of you."

He stared at her, pain and hatred mixing in his features. "Then I have no trouble doing this." He stabbed her in the chest with a silver spike.

She exploded and covered them all in ash.

$\approx$ $\ll$

SERUS HAD TWO vamps over his shoulders and Motre wrapped around his chest. They were freefalling. He'd pulled off some major stunts in his lifetime, but he didn't have much hope of a happy ending this time.

Goran, save my daughter! Please. She's doesn't have my experience. You need to help her.

Cody is on that. I see you. Almost there. Shit. How many are you carrying? Goran laughed. *Show off. What am I going to do with you?*

Well, you could help us to land for a start. And taking half the weight would be good too, Serus said humorously. The ground was rising rapidly. He couldn't land gently with the weight he carried and he didn't have a free hand. *Actually, how about you just slow us down enough that we don't slam into the valley floor?*

Goran swooped down and grabbed the back of Serus's pants, adjusted his grip on Seth, and said, "Hang on everyone. This could be a little rough."

I can't lift you all, but... And he heaved backwards, using the power of his wings to slow their descent and angle them away from the falling rocks.

$\approx$ $\ll$

TESSA CRIED OUT as another rock smashed into her shoulder. One of the men clinging to her lost his grip on her arm and wrapped his big arms around her waist instead. She could hardly see where they were going because he was so big.

Tessa, hang on, I'm almost there.

Hurry!

A cold wind whistled past so fast, bringing tears to her eyes. Moonlight shone overhead but she could barely see. She blinked her eyes to clear them but they filled instantly.

She couldn't hear. She could barely see, but she was feeling way too much. Everything hurt.

And then she was grabbed under the arms.

Got you!

Tessa was jerked up hard than pulled sideways as Cody tried to control their downward plunge. The ground swerved sideways as he pulled them away from the peak they were ready to slam into. They were going way too fast even now.

Up ahead the valley opened up.

Look.

Vehicles clustered in one spot with a large group of people standing in a circle. They were too far away to identity anyone but Tessa could see a mix of vamps and humans. Tessa said, *Looks like the others made it out safely.*

Good. And our fathers are slightly ahead of us.

If you could slow me down enough, I could get down on my own.

I'm not sure about that. We are still going too fast. You're carrying too much weight.

But the truth was, with the two men hanging onto her, Cody was carrying too much weight, and it was showing. His wing might have healed, but this would tax any flier.

She could hear Cody's wings as he struggled, his breathing labored.

I'm fine, he gasped. *We can do this.*

They were coming in low and fast.

And she understood what she needed to do. She said, *We can. But not quite this way.*

She called out to Chad and Lenther. "Hey you two. Can

you grasp on to Cody? It will ease the weight for him."

Instantly, the two vamps reached out and grabbed Cody's legs. They swung wildly in the air while the weight was redistributed. *Okay Cody. Let go. I'm fine.*

You say that, but...

She wiggled her shoulders. *Let go, Cody.*

Hang on, I'll slow it back a little more then drop you.

She felt the force as he pulled back on his wings to slow their descent, then he let her go.

∂ ∽

SHIT. HE SHOULDN'T have released her. Even as he whispered that under his breath, his shoulders eased and the pain in his arms disappeared.

She laughed. *Yes, you should have. I'm fine. Look.*

You are traveling way too fast.

Unless he could get back to help her before she hit the ground.

Stronger with carrying just the two vamps, he swooped down to the crowd, relieved when he saw his friends all standing and watching them, and lowered himself enough that the men could drop to the ground. His father came in behind him with Motre and Seth. But no Serus. And Cody realized they'd done what he'd done. Split up the weight.

Goran and Cody rose immediately to fly off in tandem to help Tessa and Serus.

Tessa had almost reached them. He raced to her side, meeting her as she was about to attempt her landing. Her face was twisted with concentration.

I'm here, Tessa. I can grab you.

I think ...I'm... and she hit the ground. Hard.

He cried out. And heard the cries of the others as they watched her go down. Hard.

And then she came up.

And down.

And up and down.

He stared. *What the hell?*

She laughed, her voice free and joyous. *I can do this – remember?*

She landed again and took off into a long smooth glide that allayed the force into something manageable.

You look...

Ridiculous. Right?

No. Not at all. I can't say I expected a graceful ballet dance of a landing but you are...beautiful.

TESSA BEAMED. SHE could see her father standing, exhausted but alive, with her mother in his arms and Seth crumpled at their feet. David hovered over Jewel, who appeared to be sitting up. Ian stood with Wendy wrapped in his arms. Tessa grinned as she realized she'd been correct about the two of them.

Even Jared was there, talking to a very exhausted looking Goran.

And they were all watching her come in.

Great.

Talk about arriving in style.

No pressure...again.

Sweetheart, you have a style all your own. Don't even try to be anyone else.

Cody's comforting voice wrapped around her. *How could*

she not love this guy?

I hope you mean that.

I guess we now have a chance to find out. She laughed again, feeling a freedom she had yet to experience. *And I for one can't wait.*

Moments later, she landed cleanly in front of her family and friends. She was instantly engulfed by their cheers.

Life was good.

No. As Cody landed and snatched her up and twirled her around in a big hug, she realized life was better than that – life was great!

Vampire in Conflict

Book #6 of Family Blood

Dale Mayer

CHAPTER 1

*A*ND SHE THOUGHT *she'd come home to a hero's welcome – why?* Tessa stared at the clear pathway in front of her. She'd just entered the high school to find students lined up on either side watching, silent, solemn, as she walked down the long hallway to her school locker.

No one said a word. There wasn't a smile for her... oddly enough, neither was there a frown.

Tension permeated the air.

A sense of watchfulness. A sense of waiting.

Already, she wished today was over. Instead, she'd just walked inside the double doors ahead of the morning bell.

She hadn't *really* expected a warm welcome. After all, she'd been more or less ignored when she'd been in class before – except for her circle of friends. She knew most of the kids in her grade, but there were many grades attending the school. She was a stranger to most of them.

Unfortunately, they appeared to know who she was now.

Putting steel into her backbone, she tossed her hair back and walked to her locker. As she opened the lock, the silence was filled in with whispers. She'd walked the gauntlet and survived. Now they could talk about her in their little cliques.

She shrugged. After what she'd been through, what was a little gossip? Many had talked about her before this last week, so this wasn't new.

Just then a soft voice entered her mind. *You don't need to be there. You have a choice.*

Cody.

Miss me? The warmth of his voice had her dropping her head against the locker, a silly smile on her face. *So much,* she answered. *I'd almost rather be fighting in the blood farm than struggling through this day.*

And yet you are there by choice. His tone was puzzled, confused. None of her family and friends would understand her need to come back to her human school.

Maybe that was because she couldn't really explain it herself.

I know. She struggled to come up with an answer that would help. In the end, all she could say helplessly was, *I had to come back – even if only to say goodbye.*

Then do what you need to do. I'll talk to you later. His voice took on a humorous tone as he added, *And if you need me, just call.*

Thanks, she whispered, feeling her world righting itself yet again. So what if these people didn't want anything to do with her? She had Cody.

Damn right, he said, then he was gone. Like a warm wind blowing through her heart, he'd popped in when her discomfort reached him and now that she was fine, he was gone again. And she was fine. Now.

She pulled her books out and relocked her locker and headed to her first class. She wished she'd had more sleep. But she'd had horrible nightmares about that crazy jump off the mountain. Every time she woke up as she stepped into the abyss.

Sighing, she pulled out her new phone and checked for calls. Still none. Her phone had been suspiciously quiet since she'd returned home from Moltere's Mountain – or what was left of it.

She'd tried calling her friends several times since, but there'd been no answer. She hadn't seen Catherine or Jill at the end because once the rescue vehicles had arrived, everyone had disappeared into dozens of different directions. Her friends should be recuperating. Some, like Ian and Jewel, had been taken to the hospital. Of Jared, she had no idea. His testimony was going to be huge against the rogue vampires. Even her parents and brothers were all involved in treatments or heavy meetings. The Councils on both sides were gearing up for talks and if that didn't work, war.

The Vampire Council had a mess on their hands.

And she was caught in the middle and yet left out. That last part stung.

She was a mere teenager and needed to let the grownups deal with this. At least, that had been her aunt Gittoria's comment.

As if Tessa hadn't been through hell this last week and come out a different person. Yet it was like everyone was trying to slot her back into the old insecure meek teenager role. A role that no longer fit.

Once again she felt caught in-between the old Tessa and the new Tessa. It was weird – as if she didn't fit into her new skin. She needed to adjust to a new normal – whatever that was. Or rather she needed her life to adjust to the new 'normal' Tessa. She'd been on a roller coaster of danger and action for so long. A crazy ride where she'd acted and others had followed. Where she'd spoken and others had listened.

She had loved that.

She wanted that back.

Instead, in the aftermath, her parents, friends, and all the new people she'd come to know, like Motre, had specific jobs to do. They'd all headed off, leaving Tessa more or less alone. Even Cody had to deal with the fallout of his brother's involvement and his subsequent death. Sometime later today, he was supposed to see a specialist about his wing.

She'd have been better off alone actually, but Aunt Gittoria had arrived to look after her. Talk about insulting. Then to make matters worse, that witch of an aunt had been very free in her opinion of Tessa being nothing but a mutant teenager. That had been fun. *Not.* Gittoria had kept up the jabbering until she'd walked back out the front door leaving Tessa alone.

Taz had arrived soon after and put her through a mess of tests. Then he'd left, too.

She'd been lost. Her family had so much to deal with, they'd been gone all weekend. Leaving her to heal – to recuperate.

How could she do that? She'd been exhausted, true. And sore. And at odds. She'd tried to sleep, had the longest bath possible, and had eaten several times. Then she'd woken up early and realized her family had come and gone while she'd slept and she was once again alone.

That had sent her bad mood to an all-new low.

She'd immediately had a shower, shampooed her hair then with a pair of scissors cut her hair. She'd given herself bangs and lost the tiny streak that was left of her old dye job. Personally she thought it did a lot to shake off the old Tessa look. Dressed in new black jeans, new short boots and a deep blood red t-shirt she felt almost normal.

Seconds later, she'd also realized it was a school day after having missed a full week. Catching up on her homework was going to be nasty. Still, there was no easy way to rejoin the normal world but to show up.

She'd dressed, feeling odd to do such a simple task, and walked the few blocks to the human school. With every step she took, she felt like she was doing the wrong thing. By the time she'd passed the mall, she was wondering about the brilliance of this incredibly stupid idea. But it was late in the school year. How could she switch now without failing her classes and losing the entire term? Besides, she was desperate to reconnect with Catherine and Jill.

She *could* have gone to the vampire school. At least she thought she could have, but until she tried to change she didn't know how that would work. Besides, would switching have been better or worse? And that brought her back to her human friends. She knew the girls weren't likely to be here today as they were still recovering from the drugs. And neither were answering their cell phones. She didn't know if they no longer had their phones, weren't conscious, or were ignoring her.

That the last was a definite possibility hurt. Big time.

And Jared? She had no idea. She had no cell number for him and he didn't have hers. She could only hope he'd be here at school.

Tessa hitched up her jeans for the umpteenth time that morning, realizing she'd dropped so much weight last week that her clothes barely fit. She needed to go shopping.

Or she could just eat more. She patted her pockets, which held several granola bars, and entered the lively classroom. Conversations bustled on around her until slowly people noticed her presence. Conversations died.

Leaving an awkward silence.

Great.

Looks like it was going to be a long day.

Just as she resigned herself to being on the outside and

shunned – again – there was a commotion at the door.

She turned to see Jared at the doorway, surrounded by friends slapping him on the shoulder and high-fiving him. She chuckled as he was sent from side to side by his friends' good-natured jostling. He looked good. Damned good.

I heard that.

And that made her brighten that much more.

Cody, she said, *What are you doing here again? I thought you'd be busy doing important Council stuff all day? Not checking in on me all the time.*

I should be. He laughed. *And I definitely shouldn't be talking to you during class.*

Class hasn't started, and I'm already wondering what I'm doing here.

Admiring Jared apparently. His voice took on a disgruntled tone, making him sound like an upset two year old. She sighed with happiness.

At that, her world righted itself for the second time that morning. She was here to see if she should continue to go to this school. To find out if this place matched the Tessa who'd returned from Moltere's Mountain. She would give herself some time to make that determination. She had friends here but if she went to a vampire school, she knew that she would lose them eventually. Maybe not at the beginning, but over time…she would. That made her sad to think about.

Yeah well, I'm pretty sure that Wendy and Jewel are missing you badly, too.

Tessa sat up straighter, then slumped. *Nah, they might like me…now, but they have a whole mess of vampire friends. Besides, they are David's friends, not mine.*

Why can't they be both? Cody questioned. *Ian would be insulted to not be considered your friend. Honey, we went through hell this last week. We're all different. Our values have been shaken, our ideals and ethics questioned. Our sense of right and wrong, what we thought of as our history and what we want for our future…everything has been torn apart. I'm different, you're different, and so are they. David can be your friend and your brother. Jewel and Wendy can be your friends and introduce you to more. You don't have to feel as if you don't belong in the vampire world anymore.*

It might be different for me in that world, she said, *but I don't know how different.*

Time to find out. We're all doing a get together in a couple of days. I want you to come.

Now she grinned. *Really?*

Hell yeah. So book it in – no excuses. And he disappeared.

She turned to glance behind her to see that Jared was finally making his way further into the classroom. Now *he'd* gotten a hero's welcome. He deserved it. She was happy for him.

He was one of the good guys. And there were few left of them in this world.

She watched as Jared's gaze swept the classroom, whipped past her, hit the brakes, and ripped back toward her. His face lit up. "Tessa!"

She jumped to her feet and ran toward him.

Instantly she was engulfed in his arms.

JARED HUGGED TESSA tight. He couldn't stop laughing as he rocked her from side to side. "I can't believe we made it out alive. All of us. Like freaking all of us. And the way you got off the mountain…after we thought you'd been blown up inside it." He shook his head in wonder.

There had been cries of horror as rock flew in all directions and part of the mountain toppled sideways. Worse had been the realization that there'd been people standing at the top. He'd died a half dozen times, petrified that Tessa had been one of those people. When he realized she had been – everything had been so much worse. He, like all the rest, had watched in horror as the mountain had blown up after Gloria pushed that damn detonator.

Time had passed in slow motion as everyone waited for news.

When she'd come crashing down at that speed, they'd all figured she was gone. Then she'd done that weird ballet-jumping thing and somehow pulled off the landing of the century. Jared remembered how her parents had cried out in horror then shock and then roared with laughter as she'd made her way toward them in classic Tessa style. But that damn grin of hers had beamed so bright…he knew he hadn't been the only one affected by her presence.

God, he'd been so proud of her.

He squeezed her again before backing off slightly so he could look her in the eye. "I never got a chance to see you afterwards." He gave her a lopsided grin. "At least not for long."

In truth, there'd been a hell of a party of all of about ten minutes before all the ambulances had arrived to pick up the injured and the drugged. He'd been neither, and he and a few other humans had been carted away in separate vehicles. The Councilmen had banded together – drugged and injured vamp and human members alike – and had taken off in a different convoy.

And he hadn't had a chance to tell her how much he'd

admired what she'd done. Or anyone. Well, he could fix that now. He looked around to see everyone who'd cheered his arrival at school today standing and staring at them. Some had doubt on their faces, others cringed at the thought of him touching her, and even more were intrigued that he had her in his arms.

Speaking of which, it was a damn good thing Cody wasn't here. He'd break Jared's arms for touching her. And damn if the hairs on the back of his neck didn't rise. He had to cast a quick glance around to make sure he wasn't about to get his face punched in.

Well, they were as alone as they could be in a roomful of teenage humans. Just to be sure, he whispered, "Cody isn't here, is he?"

She shook her head, her eyes sparkling with laughter.

He grinned and turned to the students surrounding them at a distance. "Everyone, I want you to know that Tessa has been going to our school for years. I've been lucky enough to be her friend this last year, and I have to tell you, she has saved my life…more than once this week."

He paused, his voice serious, and added. "I owe her everything. *We* owe her so much. She rescued the humans that were recently kidnapped. She brought in a large group of vamps to help rescue the others, and she fought so many of her own kind, and…" he winced, "Some of our kind, to bring an end to that blood farm."

He grinned. "Tessa is gorgeous inside and out. And if you get any ideas about her, Cody, one of the most vicious vamps I've ever met, will rip your arms off."

The guys all stepped back. He laughed. "Just kidding!"

Tessa upped and slugged him gently in the stomach. She smiled at everyone, still that shy lilt of her lips that had caught his attention in the first place. She'd been quiet, studious, and slightly on the outside of everything at school. He'd barely noticed her at the beginning, but once he'd noticed, he'd been unable to stop staring. He'd lost that battle to Cody but he counted himself blessed to call her a friend.

He smiled at everyone. "Seriously, she's the best friend any one could have, and she stepped forward to save our way of life." He stepped back slightly and started clapping. There were a few seconds of hesitation, then several others joined in and within minutes the room exploded with applause.

Jared smiled at Tessa as color washed over her face. Good. She deserved this...and so much more.

But this was a start. She could find acceptance here – now. And that meant he could see her on a regular basis. He'd been worried that she'd no longer go to his school and he'd never see her again. That would have been difficult. He knew of no other friend or family that would have done what she'd done for him.

༺ ༻

CODY SAT BACK and glared at the doctor. "The wing is just fine."

The doctor, an old friend of his father's, said, "It isn't fine. It will be, but it's not there yet. You did too much too fast."

Cody rolled his eyes as he turned away. And damn if Goran didn't cuff him. Cody sighed and settled back. "I didn't have much choice. People, good people would have died if I hadn't gone back to help."

"I heard about that ruckus." He turned back with a large needle in his hand.

Cody was off that bench and backed against the door before the doctor had a chance to say a word.

"No needles," Cody said tersely.

"Oh stop. You're too old to be acting like a kid anymore," the doctor snapped. "I have to adjust that bone inside the wing."

"No needles." Cody didn't give a damn what he had to do to his wing, he'd never let anyone come close with another needle in his life.

"It's going to hurt like hell," the doctor snapped.

Goran stepped in. "I'm on Cody's side. No needles."

"Fools, the pair of you." The doctor shook his head. "I thought you had more sense."

"I do," Cody said coldly, his eye on the needle. Damn, was he going to be suspicious of everyone now? Even the doctor he'd seen since birth? He wished he could see energy like Tessa could. Maybe she'd be able to see if the doctor was good or bad – that he couldn't pissed him off. Since they'd made it back from the mountain, Cody was constantly looking behind him, searching for the location the next attack would come from. He wondered how long it would take for that feeling to pass.

Sleep had been hard to come by. He'd woken up a dozen times in a panic. Usually searching for Tessa.

Wakefulness wasn't all that great, either.

In the mine, he'd been with Tessa most of the time – unless one or the other had been kidnapped. After the first few days, they'd been together telepathically as well. That had been what had gotten him through the first day home. Knowing that Tessa had been there on the other side. They'd spoken sporadically – enough to stay in touch as their lives split in different directions. That she'd chosen to return to the human school blew him away. And kept their schedules out of sync. Finding time to be together was going to be next to impossible. He should be in classes himself, but his wing had been screaming at him and he figured there was something his body was trying to heal but couldn't. His own father had suggested he come here.

Thankfully, just then the doctor was called out into the hallway, giving Cody a chance to reassess. Now as he eyed the good doctor leaving, Cody had to wonder – just how good was the doctor?

❧ ❦

SERUS GRABBED THE hair on the side of his head and pulled. "All right," he cried. "How was I to do anything? I'm telling you, you had to be there. Then maybe you'd understand."

Rhia glared at him. "You let that...bad boy hook up with our daughter." She poked him in the chest. "I like Cody just fine. He's a good man – or he will be when he grows up – but she's..." Rhia poked his chest again. "Too...young."

He threw up his hands. "And I'm saying she's not as young as she used to be. And Cody didn't do anything wrong."

He glared down at the wife of his heart and had no idea how to make her understand. "What I saw happen over those few days between Tessa and Cody was...magical." He ran his hands over his face. God, he was tired. But this had been brewing since they'd met up safe and sound again after the mountain blew up and Cody had gathered Tessa up into his arms and hugged her close.

Rhia had been brooding ever since. And although he was a warrior and braver than most men he knew, this wasn't a battle he wanted, and neither was it one he could win. Goran had slapped him on the shoulder and had wished him luck then taken Cody off to herd the injured vamps home.

And had left Serus to deal with Rhia.

Right about now he wanted to run away himself.

"Damn it, Rhia." He glared at her, and then brightened when he realized what he had to do. "You need to talk to Tessa." He backed up, his face beaming with relief. "That's who you need to be talking to."

"Serus, are you running away from me?" Rhia stalked closer, gearing up for a fight.

"Honey, I love you. But I'm not the one you need to talk to." And he escaped to another Council chamber.

The surviving members of the Council had been deep in talks since they'd returned home. Their numbers decimated, they were trying to sort out if other Councilmen had been involved or if they'd purged all the assholes.

Councilman Adamson was leading that charge. He had what little was left of the evidence his longtime lover and traitorous bitch Gloria had left behind. Of course she hadn't intended for anyone to find the stuff, as she'd been planning on setting up shop somewhere else after killing Adamson and everyone else on her list.

But that hadn't turned out so well for her. A savage grin swept over his face. Although sore and tired and feeling every year of his age, Serus went off in search of Goran.

Serus, where are you? His old friend called.

Coming your way. Where are you? Serus frowned. Suspicious now of everyone and everything, he hated the tone he thought he heard in Goran's voice. His own voice hardened as he said, *What's up?*

We got trouble and could use your help.

CHAPTER 2

TESSA SETTLED INTO her class routine by mid-afternoon. She'd been overwhelmed by some of the kids' overtures and then made decidedly uncomfortable by some kids who obviously wanted to be anywhere but in the same room with her. She realized that for all she'd been through, many of *these* people had only heard about the blood farm aspect and the vampires who'd done this. They'd associated her as part of the whole vampire group. And she was...but she wasn't one of *those* vampires.

Her homework was done in five minutes flat. The rest of the class was struggling with the in-class assignment. She wondered if it was fair to be here. She couldn't stop the heavy sigh as she considered the problem. The kids needed to know that they were safe from her, and if her being here made them feel unsafe...then that wasn't good either. And it's not as if the schooling was hard. Maybe she would get a better education in a vamp school. She'd be more challenged at least. She didn't know what to do. At least in vamp school she wouldn't make the others feel bad. She was one of them.

And if that didn't beat all. She was finally realizing she was a vamp and belonged in a vamp school. Revelations flooded through her. In her old life, she'd been hiding away with the humans. She'd felt safe here. The humans didn't pose a threat to her. Not the same as her own kind did. But she wasn't that same person.

Look at the difference a week made.

She'd waged war on her own kind only to feel a greater kinship with them at the end of it.

She hadn't seen that coming.

She checked her cell phone and smiled. The day was almost over. Good. It had been a very odd day today, and she couldn't wait for it to be over. She hadn't seen Jared since this morning's class. He'd been surrounded at lunch, regaling the others with his adventures. Not wanting to rehash any of it, she'd left him to it. She'd killed many people this last week. That was nothing to gloat about.

Then again, she was female. It was men who loved war stories. She wished Catherine and Jill had been here today. But so far she hadn't seen them. She had texted them – still no answer. She had to consider they were still in the hospital or at home recovering.

Maybe after school she'd walk by Catherine's house and see if she was there. She needed to know they were okay.

The afternoon bell rang, and grateful this day was over, she went to her locker, put away her books, and walked out.

No one spoke to her as she left.

It saddened her. Jared had done a wonderful thing this morning, and she appreciated his efforts. People had been friendlier after but that had waned as the day went on. Or maybe as the excitement died down. She didn't know. School just felt different now.

Tessa changed her direction and headed to Catherine's house. She lived with both parents and a younger sister. Surely someone would be home to fill Tessa in on her condition. The house was cold and empty looking as she approached. Curtains were closed as if the owners had been gone for several days. Her blood quickened slightly with nerves. Would Catherine's family know what role she'd played this last week? Would they care? Would they remember her as Catherine's school friend? Or would they see her as a vampire and hide inside?

When no one answered the doorbell, she had to wonder if the latter wasn't true. Damn. She walked around to the back of the house. How could she find out if they were home and hiding or if they were gone – and gone a long time if the overgrown yard was any indication? She frowned. Catherine's family was a closely-knit one. They did a lot of things together. Her father...she paused trying to remember what Catherine's father did. It had something to do in the medical field. She brightened. He should be able to help his daughter.

Maybe they were all at the hospital – visiting Catherine. She spun around, wondering where the human hospital was. Jared would know. She pulled out her phone and texted him, glad to have his number back on her contact list. It was the first thing he had given her this morning after that little introduction in class.

New phones had been the first order of the day for everyone, as promised by her father. Serus had been happy to hand them all over. Apparently these had nifty GPS trackers, navigational tools, and tracking systems. All kinds of things that she had yet to play with. Jared's response was immediate. He gave her the address. When she clicked on it, it gave her a map to get there from where she stood. Too cool.

Then she received another text from Jared asking her why. She texted back, *Catherine and Jill.*

No answer on that one. She turned around slowly, watching the map shift and change to accommodate her new position, and realized she was only a few blocks away.

As she was in human territory, she didn't want to jump her way to the hospital. She'd likely raise alarms about another vampire invasion. It was a sunny day, and after the prolonged time in the mine, the warmth and brightness was welcome. For a long moment she tilted her face skyward and smiled up at the sky. Then she started walking.

The hospital parking lot was stuffed with vehicles, and there appeared to be people rushing all over the place. Then again, there were a lot of victims from that last raid. Thankfully, Motre's group had managed to get them off the mountain before it blew up. She had no idea if anyone had gone back to the mansion or if that area even still stood. She'd like to think the army was dealing with that. And hopefully searching for human survivors from the blood farm.

From what her mother had said earlier, Tessa had understood that the people were better off hanging until they could be helped properly. Not just unhooked from the machines and hope for the best. The mountain blast had taken the decision away from them.

And there'd been hundreds of humans in need – if not thousands. The humans didn't have the infrastructure or the medical personnel in place to help that many people at once.

She realized as she stood in the parking lot that she was avoiding going inside. Was she obviously a vampire? Her hair might give her away. She pulled it to one side and quickly put in a side braid. Maybe that would help. She was tall, but dressed in a t-shirt and jeans, she should look like she used to at school – and no one had known her as a vampire before.

She straightened her shoulders and walked inside. There were people everywhere. She winced. So many hurt and hurting. Families sobbed in groups. Others stood silent and broken off to one side. In the middle of the melee, she found a familiar face. Taz.

She made a beeline for him. "Taz?"

Harried, he looked up, spotted her, and his face lit up. "Tessa!"

The noise around them dropped away until she stood in a sea of silence.

Ah hell.

Was she famous here, too? Or maybe infamous was a better word.

CODY WALKED OFF the pain. It had been hours...and still it damn near crippled him. Serus had come to help hold him down after he'd refused to be given a needle for the pain. He'd tried hard to take it in stoic silence, but damn...

Shudders wracked his tall frame as another stabbing pain hit him. His shoulder also screamed in agony. He thought the doctor said a bone in his wing was damaged. If that was the case, then why was his shoulder hurting so bad? He'd never have sat down again to get that wing fixed if his father hadn't stood guard.

The good doctor thought he'd stood by ready to hold Cody down, but it was more to protect Cody in case the doctor was one of the assholes.

Now the two men stood to one side deep in discussion. He heard snippets. Something about Rhia. Tessa. Then he heard the word pissed.

Cody massaged his shoulder, mentally telling his vampire genes to kick in and heal his system – like now. Another of Tessa's habits he'd picked up. After a few more moments of walking and waiting, the pain had eased noticeably. Maybe there was something to Tessa's techniques.

Instinctively he went to speak with her and had to stop himself. She was at school. And that had to be tough. He admired her for returning. For refusing to let that fear of how she'd be treated get to her. She could defend herself from any physical attack as she'd proven many times this last week, but he knew verbal attacks would be a different case. She wasn't used to that and had a tendency to hide inside. It was her instinctive response, honed after years of rejection.

He wanted the Tessa he'd found this last week to be the one the rest of the world saw.

That might be difficult.

Hopefully she'd look around at the humans and the school system and realize she didn't belong there anymore. That worked for him. He wanted her on a vampire schedule. He was selfish, wanting her to spend time with him, and that was going to be damn hard to do if she slept all night and went to human school in the daytime.

For the first time, he found his inability to walk in daylight restrictive. When he lived with others who moved in moonlight, it wasn't a bother. However, with Tessa, he wondered if she'd be happy living in a dark world. She, of course, could live in light and dark, but she also got to go outside in the sunlight. He wouldn't be able to go with her.

He turned to face his father. Goran had changed this last week. He was older, stronger, more appreciative of what he had, and more aware of what he'd lost.

Cody hadn't processed his loss yet. Or the ramifications of his brother's actions on Cody's own future. That Tyson, his older brother, had been one of the main forces behind the blood farm made Cody cringe inside and yet he hadn't had anything to do with it. Tyson had besmirched their good name. And damned if that didn't feel wrong. He hadn't realized how traditional his views were or how well tradition sat on his shoulders. He'd have laughed it off before. Now having experienced firsthand some sidelong looks and whispers behind him, he had the barest understanding of how bad the situation could get.

He straightened his back. He refused to let others opinions impact him from doing what was right. He had real friends. The others could go to hell.

There was still so much he didn't know about what had happened to the others when they had been separated. There'd been no time to fill in the gaps. He had few details of what had happened on the ground at the end. Even Jared knew more having been with David when Gloria had been killed. Such a horrible time. He was grateful everyone had made it out, but the cost had been high. Too high.

He still couldn't forget the sight of Tessa boldly jumping off that cliff, two vamps gripped in her hands. She hadn't had a hope in hell of landing that jump, and she knew it. But she'd done it anyway. She might have made it if she'd been alone – might have – but being Tessa, she wasn't going to leave anyone behind. He broke out in a cold sweat just thinking about it. Damn that girl.

He already missed her. He hadn't seen her all day. How were they going to do this? Serus might accept them having a relationship, but he wasn't at all sure Rhia would. It was different having a son over a daughter. Plus Serus and Goran had seen their relationship develop. Too fast to be comfortable for any of them, but not one person that had been there could doubt the sincerity or the strength of their bond.

Somehow Rhia was going to have to deal with it. He had no plans to stay away. Or even wait until tomorrow to get his

Tessa fix.

As they walked down the hallway, he heard more rumbling behind him. The ancients. He sighed and turned to face them. "Okay, what's the matter now?"

Instantly, they both straightened and gave him a superior look. His father said, "We weren't speaking to you, Cody."

"No, you might not have been, but you were speaking *about* me."

Goran drew himself up to his full height and looked down his patriarch nose. "Were you listening in on our conversation?"

"I didn't have to." Cody laughed. "You just answered the question yourself. So like I asked earlier, what's the matter now?"

His father slid a look at his old friend Serus, then shrugged. "You might as well tell him. He's going to need to be prepared."

Cody took several steps toward his father, his stomach sinking. Now what? Hadn't he had enough trouble for a lifetime?

He glanced over at Serus. He respected both men. He'd given it to them all his growing years, but this last week they'd earned it and so much more. At the moment though, something big was bugging Serus. And that couldn't be good. He asked quietly, "Serus?"

Serus flinched then sighed. "It's Rhia. She's not real happy about you and Tessa."

"Ah hell." Cody stared at him then asked cautiously, "Not happy? As in how not happy?"

"As in she'd likely rip your throat out if you come near Tessa again."

૨૦ ૦૬

RHIA PACED THE private room. Her best friend sat complacently by her side and let her rant.

"My God, Sian. She's only sixteen."

She spun around to glare at Sian when she remained quiet. "Did you hear me? She's only sixteen."

"Almost seventeen if I recall correctly," Sian said quietly.

Rhia threw up her hands. "We live to be thousands of years old. What's a few weeks?"

"If you put it that way, what's a few years? It's just a blip on the screen of life."

That did it. Rhia could feel her temper building to the point that she didn't know how to contain it. She stopped at the black curtain covering up the massive windows in front of her.

She should be asleep. Sian should be asleep. Instead they'd been working hard to get to the bottom of this nightmare before anyone else complicit in this atrocity had time to hide their tracks and burrow underground. Or worse, start up the whole operation again.

But she couldn't concentrate. She'd seen Tessa in Cody's arms. That had been such a shock. Even though she'd had a little warning from David, she hadn't been prepared. She understood the two kids hadn't been prepared for this either. But it had happened and like two parts of puzzle, they'd slipped into their relationship very smoothly. Maybe too smoothly.

And everyone around her just seemed to accept it. That blew her away. That Serus would let his little girl hook up with someone like that. Goran's boy. Jesus. Cody was a good kid. She'd had him over at her house for years. He'd make a good man – eventually. But young bucks lived a wild life, and she'd heard about Cody's relationships. She wanted something better for her baby girl. She wanted someone steady – like Serus. Someone who'd stand by her girl and protect her if she needed it, encourage her to be the best she could be, and be there for her when times got tough. Vamp women were the most vicious creatures on the planet, but not her Tessa.

She was unique, and her partner needed to understand that. Rhia also didn't want anyone permanent in Tessa's life for a long time. Decades. Maybe even centuries.

"Rhia, how old were you when you hooked up with Serus?"

Rhia stiffened. "That's a low blow."

"Why? You were the same age. Did you listen to your parents? Was Serus any less of a bad boy?" Sian chuckled. "Like hell he was. Both him and Goran were hell raisers. But once he found you, Serus went straight and solid."

"He was solid to begin with," Rhia murmured.

In a gentle voice, Sian added, "And so is Cody. He's not his brother. He'd been dealt just as big a blow as Goran, but he's standing strong. He's been there for Tessa all week."

"Week," Rhia spat. "That's the problem. They'd only really been together over this last week. Relationships don't start off like that."

"Sure they do. Add in the danger and stress, and of course that flare of attraction grew into something much bigger."

Rhia bowed her head, shaking inside. "How much stronger is the question. She's too young."

"They haven't taken their relationship to the intimate level yet. There's been no opportunity. You don't know that Cody will push for that or if Tessa will even want to."

"Cody will push, he's male. And Tessa doesn't know what

she's doing in that area." She closed her eyes and tilted her head back, letting her long hair flow down her back. "I can't even believe she might be close to that stage."

"Vampires enter puberty long before humans. They form sexual relationships young. Tessa is actually late to be entering the ring. You know that."

"I know, but she's not like the others." Rhia held out her hands, pleading for Sian's understanding.

Sian gave her a warm caring smile and asked the one question guaranteed to make Rhia stop and think. "Do you trust her?"

Rhia's shoulders sagged. That of course was the real issue. She had to think about her daughter, her growth this last week. The solid decisions she'd made and the way she'd taken charge. For all her youthfulness, Tessa had done what was right.

She sighed. "Yes, I trust her."

"Then let her be. Have a talk with her, sure. But don't be arrogant, aggressive, or overly protective. She's grown a lot this last week. Allow her to keep growing. Don't try to stuff her back into the old form. She won't fit anymore, and it will damage your relationship if you try."

Such words of wisdom. Rhia slumped down on the couch beside Sian. She clasped her oldest friend's hand and smiled gratefully at her. "You're going to make a great mom, you know."

A twinkle entered Sian's gaze, and with her free hand she rubbed her slight tummy bump. "I hope so. You've been a great teacher."

CHAPTER 3

TAZ MOTIONED TESSA into a small empty room, a supply closet from the looks of it. Taz came in behind her. He closed the door and the overwhelming noise that had risen sharply behind them dropped to something reasonable. Instantly, the frayed edges of her temper eased back. She smiled with relief. "Thanks. That noise out there is brutal. I don't know how you stand it."

"It's a mad house today." Taz ran his fingers through his hair.

Tessa took a closer look at him and winced. She'd had a good night's rest, a long bath, and all the food she could get down. Taz on the other hand looked like he'd worked through the whole weekend. "You haven't been able to leave here, have you?"

He shook his head. "There are too many patients from the blood farm. The large group that was brought out before the collapse, and even now a few are being brought in by helicopter from the army's rescue efforts."

That was news to her. She hadn't known there was anything left to rescue. "Wow, I'm so happy to hear some people survived."

"Yes, but we're overrun, and everyone who is missing anyone has shown up looking for their kin."

"I'd be doing the same." She gave a small laugh. "Actually, that *is* why I am here. Catherine and Jill, found in one of the blood farm rooms, were sent out with the injured vamps. I saw the girls at the end being loaded into ambulances – enough to know they'd survived. However, they aren't at their homes, at school, or answering their phones, so I'm here," she took a deep breath, "hoping for news."

He nodded, brought out his tablet, and started clicking through lists. "The two are in the same room on the second floor. They are both doing fine."

She brightened. "Can I see them?"

He checked the notes on his tablet. "I don't see why not. There were some family members there when I saw the girls earlier, but don't ask me when that was."

"That's fine. I want to speak to Catherine's parents anyway." She opened the door to leave. Immediately, the noise swelled around her. Desperate to ease all the noise back down – for his sake and hers – she slammed the mental door between her and Cody shut, after whispering, *Sorry, it's too noisy.*

Wincing at Taz, she said, "I'm going to end up with a hell of a headache if I stay here much longer. I don't know how you do it."

"It's been a crappy couple of days," he admitted, "But hopefully the worst is over now."

"I hope so. But somehow I doubt it." Taking a breath against the crowd and noise to come, she walked out and made a beeline for the stairwell. Inside the smaller space, the noise once again receded. She didn't envy Taz's job one bit.

At the second floor, she checked the room numbers until she came to the right room and stuck her head inside. Catherine slept on the first bed. Tessa's heart lightened at the sight of her friend. "Oh, thank heavens you are all right," she whispered as she walked to the foot of the bed. She glanced over to see white curtains around the other beds. Only Catherine's bed was open to view. She frowned. How could she find out if Jill was in here and if she was okay? She didn't want to poke her head inside the curtains. The curtains had to be closed for a reason.

"Jill?" she called out in a soft voice. No answer. She pulled up a chair beside Catherine's bed and wondered if her parents were still around. She hoped so, but Taz had no idea when he'd seen them. They might have left by the elevator while she'd climbed the stairs, or they could have left hours ago. As far as she could tell, she was alone.

She reached over and covered Catherine's still hand with her own. "I'm so sorry, Catherine. I wish you'd never gotten caught up in this mess."

Catherine never moved. Her pale face never shifted and her hand never twitched. Unnerved, Tessa studied her friend closer. There was a light pink bloom across her face, and her chest rose and fell as she breathed. She was just in a deep sleep. Like a drugged sleep. Tessa flinched. Damn drugs. She'd hoped the girls would have thrown off the medication by now. Instead, Catherine looked seriously out of it.

How could that be? She'd been away from Moltere's mountain for at least one, if not two days – hadn't she? Regardless of how many hours exactly, the drugs should have left her system after all this time. They couldn't stay in her bloodstream for so long without a booster, surely. Tessa stopped and straightened as she worried about this problem. Were the girls still drugged? As in had someone in the hospital given them more drugs to keep them comatose? And if so, why?

She knew she was overly suspicious of everything and everyone after what she'd been through. Some of the assholes had escaped, and many human assholes were likely trying to cover their tracks. What a great place to find more victims for the blood farm. At the hospital. All the records were here about next of kin, addresses, health conditions, etc.

She flinched at the thoughts that wouldn't stop running through her mind. She needed to talk to Taz again. Find out what was going on with Catherine – her sleep looked anything but natural.

She stood up and turned.

The side of her head exploded, and she collapsed.

CODY RETURNED TO the main Council chamber with his father. Silent and brooding, he'd kept his mouth shut after Serus's announcement over Rhia's attitude regarding a relationship between him and Tessa. Rhia had to get over it. He and Tessa belonged together. It might take them a while to be able to live together given their ages, but it was not like he had a choice. They were bonded. He had no idea how or why, but it was not something that he could stop. Walking several feet in front of the ancients, Cody headed for the main chambers. He entered and came to a dead stop. Rhia and Sian were sitting on one of the couches off to the side. He sighed. "Hello Sian, how are you feeling?"

She gave him a warm sigh, reminding him that some of the vampire women were stunningly beautiful inside and out. She'd chosen a hard road with a human partner. Choosing Tessa as his partner wouldn't be the easiest, yet it was easier than Sian's choice. At his own wording, he paused. Earlier he'd said he'd had no choice. Now he was saying he'd chosen her.

Which was it?

Both.

He hadn't known he'd had a choice in the beginning, but now that he knew, he'd made the choice voluntarily. Tessa was his. She might not have made the decision that he was hers...she hadn't had a chance to choose or even sample the others in the universe – but for him there was no longer a choice.

"What's with the long face, Cody?" Sian said.

He brought himself back to the room. "Tired," he said shortly.

He turned and faced Rhia. "Where is Tessa?"

She raised her eyebrows and said, "Can't you tell me?"

He stared at her and called out to Tessa. *Where are you?*

And got no answer. He hated that. He'd been trying for the last few minutes, but she'd said something about closing a door. As if she couldn't hear something on her end and needed to close him off to hear better. Like how did that even make sense?

"No. She closed the door between us."

It was the first he'd spoken of the telepathic communication between Tessa and him with Rhia. Serus had known for a while, but Rhia apparently didn't like this development.

He stared at her, calmly waiting for her to make the next move.

She frowned. "Sounds like a smart idea on her side."

"No," he said. "It's a dangerous move. We might have survived Moltere's Mountain, but there are more bad guys out there and many of them are humans. She's gone to a human school."

Rhia's frown deepened. "Besides the fact that she should

still be home resting, she went to that same school all year. She should be safe there."

"Saying that about Tessa doesn't work." Cody's lips quirked. "She can get into trouble like no one else."

A black stabbing jolt suddenly slammed into his head. He gasped and fell to his knees, his hand on his head.

Goran jumped forward. "What's the matter?"

"Pain, horrific pounding in my head." Cody tried to regain his feet, but waves of greasy pain continued. Then stopped completely. As in nothing. He stood back up and knew the elders surrounding him were as confused as he was.

And then he knew. "Damn. That wasn't from me, that was Tessa's pain. She's hurt." He spun around, as if hoping she'd materialize behind him but knew there was no way she could. She wasn't here. She was at her damn human school. Or was she? He checked the time. She should have been out and home again at least a half hour ago. "Where is she?"

Serus looked at Rhia. Rhia looked at Serus.

"School is over, so she should be home." Rhia was already dialing as she spoke. Her phone rang endlessly. Serus grabbed his phone and called as well. Cody shook his head. Tessa was in trouble after one day back at school. Already. Like that girl was a trouble magnet.

"Where could she have gone?" Sian asked quietly.

"Maybe to look for her friends. She's been worried about Catherine and Jill. If they weren't at school, she might have gone looking for them." Cody frowned, thinking about the short blasting noise he'd heard just before she'd closed the door. "Either to their homes or to the hospital."

Rhia clicked through the numbers on her phone. "I have Catherine's number here." She dialed it and trained her anxious gaze on Serus and Cody. "No answer."

"She could have gone to the hospital," Sian said. "Taz said they are overrun with people from the blood farm. And her friends might not have been released yet. Particularly if they were still feeling the effects of the drugs."

Goran frowned. "Would Tessa go to the hospital alone?

Sian held up her phone. "I'm calling Taz. Maybe he's seen her."

With everyone watching, she connected to Taz. And found within seconds that Tessa had been there and was now in Catherine's room as far as he knew.

Sian explained what had happened to Cody. Even Cody could hear Taz's exclamation. Sian held the phone slightly away. "He's gone to look. Said she'd been there about twenty minutes ago."

The noise from the hospital clearly came through the phone only to fade slightly as Taz raced upstairs. Everyone waited, staring at the phone in Sian's hand.

Taz spoke again, his voice filtering into the air. Sian pulled the phone in closer. "Yes, I'm here. We are all here." She gasped. "What do you mean she's not there?"

Rhia stepped forward and cried, "Where could she be?"

Cody was already on his feet heading for the door. "Ah hell. That girl…"

❧ ❦

DAVID WALKED INTO the main Council rooms looking for Cody. And found him stalking toward the underground garage. His jaw was clenched, and damn if his face wasn't twisted in anger. David stopped to watch his best friend. He'd only ever seen him so frustrated when a girl was involved. "What's up, Cody?"

"Your damn sister." Cody spun around to glare at him. "She's not answering her phone. She's not answering telepathically." Then he explained about the sudden head pain.

"You think she's in trouble?" David's own alarm bells sounded. What the hell? "Only Tessa would go to a hospital and disappear." Still in denial, he shook his head. "She's likely just walking home. She's used to doing that, you know."

"And the head pain?" Cody demanded.

David shrugged. "I don't know what to say about that. You guys haven't had anything like that happen between you before – good thing as neither of you would be able to fight if you were crippled by each other's wounds – so I don't know why you'd think it was from her now."

Cody just stared at him helplessly.

"I know she's got a nose for trouble," David added, "but surely it's safe now."

"Ha. This is Tessa we're talking about, remember?" Cody massaged the back of his neck. "I don't know what to think. She should have reported in to someone. Both your parents have been trying to call her, but she's not answering."

David lifted out his new phone. "It's the latest and greatest, but it's hard to learn. I found I missed several calls myself today, but the ringer had turned off in my pocket. Did you send her a text?"

Cody stared at him then groaned. "No. I never thought of it."

"See, that's too much telepathic communication. Sometimes old tech is the better answer." David sent off a quick text to Tessa. *Where are you?*

And waited.

Cody did the same. He asked David in an absentminded voice, "How's Jewel doing?"

"Tired. The drugs are still clogging her system and she's got no energy. She just wants to sleep the night and day away."

"That's to be expected. We had a hard week."

"Yeah, Ian's a little worse. The drugs are still causing him trouble. He won't let the doctors do much. They want to run tests and he keeps fighting them."

Cody snorted. "I don't blame him. My damn wing was a bitch to get fixed. I wouldn't let the doctor come near me with any needles, so he set the bone without it."

David snickered.

"How about I'll stand by and watch these strange doctors give *you* a needle," Cody threatened.

"They are hardly strangers. You've been going to the same doctor since you were born."

"Uhuh, and that was what – twice?"

David considered that. "True enough. I wouldn't let anyone poke me either."

Cody looked at him. "Did you ever wonder what happened to Bart?"

At that name, David started to laugh. "I think Tessa said something about him leaving with the group of humans she and the others rescued…but…" he frowned. "Come to think of it, I don't remember seeing him afterwards in all that chaos with Gloria."

"Or later when the ambulances and the army arrived." Cody turned to look out at the darkening sky that wasn't dark enough for him to travel in yet. "What do you want to bet he snuck away before then?"

"If he snuck away too early, then he's not likely to have survived the blast."

Cody stepped out onto the covered front deck of the

Council building, staring out in the early evening. "I wouldn't count on anything with that sneaky bastard."

"I wouldn't either."

"But Tessa had a soft spot for him."

"Maybe, but she's no fool. There's no way she'd trust him. Hell, at this point, I doubt she trusts anyone." David didn't know what to do. He'd planned on visiting Jewel. But if his sister was in trouble…

"Yeah?" Cody said, looking down at his cell phone as he waited to hear back from Tessa. "So where the hell is she then?"

∽ ∾

TAZ RACED FROM room to room on the second floor of the hospital. There was no sign of Tessa. She couldn't have been missing for long. He'd seen her barely thirty minutes ago downstairs. He hoped she was walking home.

He walked back to her friend's room. Catherine still slept. And the room was empty of visitors. He checked the other patients, surprised to see no visitors. When he'd been here an hour ago, there'd been a good half dozen family members. And…he paused, casting his mind back. They'd been angry, restless. And very volatile about what had happened to their kin.

Could they have seen Tessa and recognized her as the vampire she was? Vigilante justice wasn't good for anyone, but when a person was angry and saw a likely target…someone who could as easily have been one of the assholes who'd hurt their family, emotions were easily overloaded.

Could one of them have attacked her? Just taken their rage out on her and run? They might have been scared of their own actions. He'd seen people pull some pretty crazy stunts and then been horrified afterwards. Rage and grief often showed up as anger. And anger made people do all kinds of things.

He searched the whole second floor. There was no sign of Tessa.

He called Sian back. "She's not here." He ran a tired hand over his rumpled hair, wishing this last week had never happened. And very much afraid things were going to get much worse before they got any better. "I can't find her anywhere."

CHAPTER 4

TESSA MOANED SOFTLY. Damn, her head hurt. What had happened? She'd been injured somehow, that much was obvious, but her mind drew a blank over the actual events. And that wasn't good. She'd barely recovered from the week from hell and now this. She opened her eyes to find herself lying on a cement floor. Stairs going up appeared on her left. She lifted her head slightly. And damn if stairs didn't go down to the right. Had she fallen down a flight of stairs? That wouldn't be unheard of, but she'd hoped that she'd moved past that awkward stage.

She slowly stood up, gasping as the inside of her head pounded from the movement. If someone had attacked her, they hadn't done a good job. Or they might have believed her to be dead and had run. Neither scenario made any sense right now. She lifted her hand to her head and winced more from the stickiness than actual pain. She checked her fingers.

Blood. Of course.

She'd been injured enough, damn it. Moving carefully, she struggled up the flight of stairs and opened the fireproof door in front of her. Where the hell was she?

There was a long white hallway in front of her.

She froze...and swallowed hard. It couldn't be. Don't panic. More than one building had white walls. And as her gaze roamed the area, she realized these weren't tiled walls.

She wasn't in the blood farm.

Of course she knew that. The blood farm was gone. She closed her eyes and swayed in place. Her mind instantly argued that there were supposedly four blood farms. And she had no idea if all had been destroyed when the mountain collapsed.

From the looks of the hallway, she was likely still in the hospital. She remembered sitting at Catherine's bedside and getting up. That was where her memories stopped. She gave herself a mental shake. Had someone knocked her out and thrown her over the stairs thinking that it would look like the fall had killed her? Of course it wouldn't have, but would her attacker have known?

She tried to contact Cody, but her mind was too fuzzy. She couldn't focus.

She needed to find Taz and have him check her head. She hated stitches, but it was better than waiting for a gap in her scalp to close. She paused. Or maybe not. She closed her eyes briefly and instructed her vampire genes to kick in and heal her head injury. Then started down the hallway. All she wanted at this point was to get home safely. At the first corner, she turned to look back the way she'd come. The stairwell said fire exit. So an exit, but likely not the most commonly used one.

As in out of the way and with minimal traffic. She could have lain there for a long time before anyone found her. If she'd been human, that fall could have killed her.

Had her attacker not known she was a vamp? Or hadn't realized how hard vamps were to kill? Or had he been interrupted before he finished the job?

After having been chased by too many people looking to kill her already this month, she'd figured she'd run through her quota of good luck. She needed to be very damn careful. She had no idea who to trust.

Up ahead was a wall of elevators. Her heart stalled yet again. This all looked so much like the blood farm that her stomach was twisting into knots. Please not...

But anything was possible.

She needed to go home. Her family had to be worried about her. Oh wait, they were busy at the Council instead. She'd been deemed to need rest at home. They'd come and check on her eventually. And possibly already had. How would she know? She hadn't even made it home today. She had gone to school this morning and had yet to return. She had left a note though. Just to make sure, she pulled out her phone and checked. Missed calls and texts. Great. Now she was going to have to explain what she was doing that she didn't answer.

Sighing, she stepped into the elevator after noting she was still on the second floor she let it take her to the ground floor.

With the blood oozing down her temple, she should fit right in.

When the elevator doors opened, the noise almost brought her to her knees.

~⁚ ⁝~

SERUS WALKED INTO hospital and almost threw up. The smell. Rot. Antiseptic. Pain. Anger. Grief. Dominating all the rest was that insidious aroma of fear. He hated even being in the vicinity of it no matter what the reason. It was only when he saw the features on the first human that he realized with Rhia at his side and Goran and Cody behind him, they must have looked a fierce sight.

The mass of humans took one look, cried out, and the sea of people parted. Actually, they pretty near ran in the opposite direction screaming. He rolled his eyes. "We're not going to get much help from anyone here."

"We need to find Taz," Rhia said as she slowly turned around, trying to find someone recognizable in the shifting wall of humans.

"Taz," Goran bellowed. "You here?"

Serus shook his head at his friend's bullish but effective methods.

"Yes. Hello." Taz rushed through the crowd toward them. "Goran, you're looking better." Taz grinned at Cody. "I bet you're not flying yet, are you?"

Cody shook his head. "Need to heal a little longer. To-morrow I should be good to go."

"Taz," Rhia said anxiously. "Any sign of Tessa?"

His worried gaze shifted back to Rhia. "No, not yet."

He motioned toward a wall of elevators behind him. "I can take you to where she said she'd be going, but I checked the area over and she wasn't there."

Serus said, "We'll be checking for ourselves."

Taz nodded. "And I'll be going with you. Some of those people have been traumatized. I don't want your presence to set them off even more." He waved a hand at the crowd standing in clusters, watching from what they hoped was a safe distance.

"Good. Let's go. The sooner we find her, the sooner we'll be gone."

Taz pushed a button and they waited for the elevator to reach them. The one on the left opened first. Serus was stepping toward it when Tessa, blood dripping down the side of her face, stumbled out.

Rhia cried.

Serus growled.

Goran howled.

Cody moved. And caught her before she hit the floor.

❦

CODY CRADLED TESSA in his arms. "Easy Tessa, take it easy. I'm here."

She opened her eyes to stare up at him. "Sorry. Got taken unawares." She moaned. "I don't feel so good."

Taz spoke, "Cody, let me take a look at her head."

Cody clutched her closer to his chest. His father placed a heavy hand on his shoulder. "Let Taz take a look."

Cody shifted her slightly so that the doctor could check out her injury. From what he could see, it wasn't that bad. Still, she'd had more than her fair share of them lately. Too many. She needed time to recuperate. She should never have gone to school today. And she should be living on a vampire schedule so he could be with her and protect her when she wasn't in school. "How is it?" he said abruptly, glaring at Taz.

Taz glanced up at him, smiled slightly, and patted him on the shoulder. "She's starting to heal already."

Cody gave an abrupt nod. "Good."

Taz looked around. "We're causing quite a disturbance. Do you want to take her home or for me to find a room for her here to finish her healing?"

Rhia started to speak, but Cody cut her off. "Home. She's safer at home."

"You may be correct." Taz grimaced. "I wish I knew what happened here, but we're going to have to wait until she wakes up and tells us."

"Do you have security cameras?" Rhia asked.

"Of course." Taz looked at Rhia. "Ah, you want to check the camera feed?" He thought about that. "I should be able to arrange something." He glanced at his watch. "Give me a moment." And he disappeared into the sea of curious faces.

Cody turned to Serus. "Let me take her home. You two can stay behind and figure out what happened."

"I'm coming home with her," Rhia snapped. "You're not going to be alone with her in my house."

Silence.

Cody turned slowly to face her. He drew himself up tall and straight. It was on the tip of his tongue to blast her for that unfair accusation.

But both Goran and Serus stepped in. Goran said, "Cody, easy."

Serus stepped in front of Rhia. In a quiet but determined voice, he said, "That's not fair. You have no reason to speak to Cody in that manner or imply he'd be anything other than proper with our daughter. I will not let you speak to him this way."

The silence shimmered with tension, then Rhia gave an abrupt nod. "I'm sorry, Cody. The news of your relationship to my very young daughter has come as a surprise. I'm not happy about it."

Cody hated that he didn't get a chance to snap at her, but how could he when Rhia had stepped right up and apologized? He could do no less. "The issue at the moment is Tessa," he said. "I have never wanted anything less than to keep her safe." He glanced at his father. "I'd fly her home, but with my wing…"

"No way. And that means I am flying her home." Goran turned to Rhia and Serus. "You two see what you can find out. We'll keep her safe. Like Taz said, she's healing on her own. And in this last week, we've seen her do some amazing things. She just needs a bit of time."

Appearing torn but as if grudgingly realizing the sense of his words, Rhia nodded. Serus said, "Thanks, Goran. We'll be there as soon as we can."

Just then, Taz called them over. Rhia and Serus raced to join him.

Goran and Cody walked out of the hospital. The evening darkness had fallen. Thankfully.

Cody carefully transferred his precious burden to his father. They both took to the air and headed home. Goran strong and sure, Cody weaker and lagging behind with a bum wing but keeping up as best as he could. He'd be damned if he was going to be separated from Tessa again.

☙ ❧

IAN WOKE UP with a slammer of a headache. He glared around his tiny ass room — a room he didn't recognize. Somehow while asleep they'd moved him, and he didn't know why or where. He'd never been in a hospital his entire life, and now every time he woke up, here he was. Who knew a vampire hospital even existed? Seemed pointless to him. He'd have healed on his own just fine.

If they'd left him alone.

The longer he was here, the grumpier he was getting. Damn doctors and their needles. He wasn't signing up for any more of those in this lifetime. As soon as Wendy returned with some clothes for him, he was getting the hell out of here. He could finish healing at home where he should have been the whole time. At least he was no longer hungry all the time, but the blood tasted medicinal here. Nasty stuff.

He sat up, hating the grogginess. So what if he'd been drugged a time or two? His body should have thrown those off in no time. He lifted a hand to brush his hair back. And froze.

From his arm dangled a long skinny tube.

His heart seized. He swallowed several times. And followed the tube to the back of his hand. And the needle in his arm.

"Holy shit." What happened next was normal, he told himself. Anyone who'd been through what he'd been through would have done the same.

He ripped the needle out of his arm. And growled as it took a bite out of his arm at the same time. He flung the nasty mess onto the ground then added the tape that had been holding it onto his skin.

"Where the hell am I, and where the hell is Wendy with my damn clothes?"

Realizing he'd seen both David and Wendy here made him feel better. He had to be safe. She wouldn't have been here as a guest if he was still in the blood farm. That was foolish thinking. The blood farm was gone. Blown up. Collapsed in on top of itself. Everyone inside was all dead.

He had escaped with his friends.

He was in this place because of all the drugs he'd received. Relieved, he tried to lie back down, but the needles and tubes on the floor made him want to run as far away as he could. Wondering why he had to have needles at all, he kicked the mess out of sight under the bed.

Then he heard footsteps. Not the soft gentle ones of a woman, but the hard clip of someone in a hurry. A large someone in a big hurry.

Hating the fatalistic attitude swarming through him, Ian sat and waited.

Friend? Or foe?

CHAPTER 5

T ESSA WOKE WITH the hard jolt of a landing. The shaky movement caused her stomach to revolt. She struggled, only to realize she was being carried.

Her heart surged, hoping it was Cody. But the man was too big. Too strong. Yet familiar. Goran.

"How is she?" she heard Cody ask beside her. She fought back the nausea, feeling her throat wanting to seize up before upchucking. She struggled to be put down.

"She's awake and fighting to get on her own feet, so I'll take that as a good sign." Goran put her on her feet, keeping a steady hand on her shoulder. She took several stumbling steps, stopped for a few deep breaths as she fought the nausea, and realized where they were. She took two steps to the bushes at the side of her house and vomited.

And then again.

"Jesus." Cody laid a hand on her shoulder, "Tessa?"

"I'm all right," she whispered, "Give me a moment."

"Ha, she's obviously not all right. Probably should have left her at the hospital with Taz."

Another shudder rippled through her at his words, but she managed to keep the nausea back. Slowly, with Cody's arm under hers, she straightened. Taking a long deep breath, she let it out in relief when the queasiness seemed to have faded. "I think that's it."

"Time to go lie down." Cody said firmly. "I'll bring you a glass of water."

She really wanted to brush her teeth, but the thought of doing so brought her queasy stomach to life again. "Thanks. Lying down sounds good at the moment."

Goran hovered behind her and Cody as they made their way inside. "Didn't you see anything when you were at the hospital?"

"No," she whispered. "I found Catherine but I couldn't see the other occupants as their curtains were drawn for privacy." She stopped at the top of the stairs, feeling sweat roll down her back. She paused, gathering up her energy, and added, "I remember being beside Catherine then my head exploded in pain." She thought for a moment. "I think someone threw me down the stairs."

Cody's grip on her arm tightened, and she gasped. He loosened it immediately. "God, I'm sorry. It's just the thought that someone threw you away like that..."

He guided her down the hall to her bedroom.

From behind her, Goran said, "They'd have to be strong to carry you that distance."

"Or there was more than one person," she said. "I honestly don't know."

Cody pulled the covers back on her bed. "Lie down. Dad and I will keep watch."

"Thanks," she whispered. "If Mom catches you in here, there's going to be hell to pay."

"Yeah, I got that."

The sour tone in his voice made her lips twitch. "Are you going to open the door between us or keep it closed?" She knew Goran was still in the room, but damn it, having that door closed all the time was irritating.

"It's open on my side, sweetie. I figured you'd closed it and just kept it that way."

She frowned, trying to remember. "I closed it at the hospital because of the horrific noise." She could barely remember anymore. "Obviously I forgot to open it again."

"Don't worry about it. Just rest."

With a heartfelt sigh, she lay down on her bed and closed her eyes, smiling when she felt the covers being gently placed over her shoulders. "Thank you," she whispered.

Cody placed his lips against hers in the sweetest of kisses. He always made her world right.

And she slept.

❧ ❦

"WHAT AM I going to do with her?" Cody asked his father. Both stood quietly in the darkened room as she slept. There was something off about the way she slept. Her breathing was too deep. The sound a little too raspy. Her body lying too heavy and still. Cody hated that she'd been injured again. "I thought she'd be safe now."

"I'm not sure any of us are yet. Her in particular. She brought this blood farm mess to light, so you could say she caused all this. And those assholes trying to save their butts are going to blame her."

"And yet she insisted on going back to school today – human school, no less."

"What else was she supposed to do? She was trying to step back into a normal life." Goran stared down at the sleeping girl. "Chances are good she didn't realize how much her normal had changed. She won't think she fits in with the vampire world yet either as she hasn't fully made that transition."

"Will she ever?" Cody wanted her to fit in, for his sake and hers. He couldn't imagine anyone not liking her.

"She will, but she has to let go of that human lifestyle first. Otherwise, she'll always be torn."

"She has many human friends and few vampire ones. Not sure she can make that switch."

"As the vampire bonds strengthen, she will see where she stands much better."

"And me, where does any of this leave me?" That was the real issue he'd wanted to bring up. Cody didn't know what to do about Rhia. About Tessa being so young. About the heat that flared between them. A heat he couldn't do anything about.

"Patience. Tolerance. Look after her and if you are serious, stand by her side and love her as she walks through this maze." Goran's steady voice helped stabilize the shakiness inside. If there was one thing his father had experience in, it was relationships. Maybe not long term ones...but definitely longer than most humans had.

"And Rhia?

"Give her time. Don't forget, to her, Tessa is still young – *her* little girl – the same young girl that went to the movies with her human friends." Goran reminded him. "Rhia missed seeing much of Tessa's transformation."

"I understand that. Tessa *is* young."

Goran looked at him. "Second thoughts?

"Hell no. But waiting for her to be ready is going to be a bitch," he said forcefully.

Goran started to laugh.

Cody rolled his eyes and pushed his father out of the Tessa's room so as to not wake her. Tessa might not need blood to keep going, but he and father did and he could use some sustenance right now.

RHIA SAT IN the small security office and watched the cameras roll. They'd been switching camera views to find Tessa and track her back to the stairwell where she'd woken up. They'd picked her up at she'd entered the hallway from the fire exit. Rhia had gasped at the sight of Tessa barely managing to stay on her feet. Obviously disoriented, she probably had no idea her nails were extended. A defensive motion that made Rhia see just a little of what her daughter had been through this last week.

Serus wrapped an arm around her shoulders. She leaned in closer.

The security guard backtracked the cameras to that same exit but it was just out of sight. Many people had walked the halls, but there was no one suspicious and no one carrying her daughter. Then again, that stairwell wasn't covered by any cameras. Of course it wouldn't be that simple.

"How could this happen with no record of anyone around?"

The security guard shrugged. "I can't say. We don't have security cameras in the stairwells."

A longer shuddering gasp escaped Rhia's chest as her lungs squeezed in tight on themselves. "What could have happened?"

"I'll go through all the security feed we have for the entire hospital over that hour she was here, but it's going to take time."

Serus tugged Rhia back a bit. "Please do so, and call us if

you find something. We'll go home and keep watch over our daughter."

Rhia let Serus tug her out of the security room. She was angry and tired and hurting...and she wanted answers.

"How could they not know what happened to her?"

"They don't know *yet*. Maybe he will find something and maybe he won't. Let's leave quietly so as to not cause any more disruptions."

"Like I care about that," she scoffed in a low voice. "Not now that one of them has hurt my daughter."

"And we don't know that," he replied, trying to keep his voice low enough so the security guard couldn't hear. "We are vampires inside the human hospital, so how can we know for sure that there aren't others like us here?"

She frowned, hating his logic. She wanted to lash out at something. Anyone.

Back at home, she realized she had a target.

Cody.

∂∞ ∞6

IAN HELD HIS breath. The footsteps had stopped. He could hardly breathe, his chest had squeezed so tight. Now he waited, not knowing what to do.

What he wanted was to get the hell away.

He studied the room and realized that even if he was in good vampire hands, he still wanted out.

He reached for his cell phone for the millionth time, once again realizing it wasn't here. That wasn't good. Then again, he didn't have his clothes on either. He looked down and realized he had on a scary variation of the dreaded hospital gown. It was bare from the back, judging from the fresh air he felt. He figured his folded wings covered part of him but they weren't long enough to cover everything. How could he escape with his butt hanging out?

The room was damn small and had no cupboards. So where were his old clothes? Like his boxers?

He knew he'd been sleeping for days, but surely the hospital staff wouldn't have tossed his clothes. At the back of his mind, he heard Wendy mention washing them for him. Had she taken them away? Cause that wouldn't be good. He wanted to get the hell out of here.

Like now. It seemed like he'd been waiting since forever for Wendy. How much longer would he have to wait?

And damn, those scary ass footsteps started up again.

Coming his way.

JARED COULDN'T BELIEVE he was back in the same damn group home. Okay, it was better than his uncle's place, and whatever happened to that old geezer, anyway? He'd told the cops about him and his sister, but Jared had no confidence that anything had been done. There had been no time for one thing. Just time enough for his father to have died when the mountain came down. Although there were rumors that the military were still bringing out survivors. But he didn't know if they meant survivors as in people that had been hanging at the blood farm or survivors as in those that had been part of the rescue crew. He'd seen dozens of soldiers around when he'd shown them the tunnel entrance. He doubted they'd made it out.

But how could he find out? He knew Dr. Taz's name but felt bad calling him. The man had been run off his feet before.

He couldn't imagine what his life was like now. Jared also wanted to contact the Human Council and find out what was going on. Only they wouldn't share any information with him.

He felt cut off and cut out.

And hated it.

Surely there was something he could do to help.

He wandered in the direction of the kitchen for a glass of milk and maybe a piece of fruit. The other kids here appeared happy to see him, but they didn't know or seem to care much about where he'd been or what he'd been through. Then again, they wouldn't likely believe it. Hell, he damn near didn't believe it.

And what about Tessa? He'd tried to help her out in the morning at school, then he'd lost track of her during the day. He'd been a celebrity at school, and that had felt decent. Better that than a pariah.

Still, this issue obviously wasn't mopped up. And he wanted to be part of the cleanup crew.

At least to help him gain closure. And if he was really lucky, his aunt and uncle would get locked up for the rest of their lives and he wouldn't have to deal with them any longer.

The back office doors were closed. Just a sliver of light shone through. He realized he hadn't seen any of the staff in a while. Normally there were a half dozen staff on duty at any given time. Right now, as best he could tell, they were in the office having a meeting. He tiptoed closer.

"I tell you. Half the Vamp Council is already gone. We could just finish the job and wouldn't have to worry about them anymore. Wouldn't have to wonder about our missing relatives and or if our kids are going missing in the near future."

"You're talking crazy talk. The Council might rule the vampire clan, but the entire species isn't living here. They are all over the planet. We'd have to take them *all* out before we could be safe, and you'd never know if you ever got them all or not." There was a pause then the same voice spoke again. "We'd never be safe – ever."

"But they do sleep at night. It would be easy to go from house to house with a special gas and kill them all while they slept."

Ah shit.

Jared hated to hear this kind of talk, but knew this wouldn't be an isolated incident. If these men were talking like this, then many others were, too. He had to warn his friends. After everything they'd done for him, he couldn't stand by and let them be murdered.

He'd been texting with Tessa earlier. He quickly sent out another one. "We've got trouble. Need to talk."

⸎ ⸎

DAVID SAT AT Jewel's bedside. She looked terrible. He was glad he'd decided to come here while the rest of his family went looking for Tessa. It had felt disloyal at the time, but now seeing the shape Jewel was in…

"David…"

He leaned forward. "I'm here, Jewel. You're supposed to be sleeping."

She gave him a sleepy smile. "I've done nothing but sleep." She stared over his shoulder, worry sliding into her gaze. "I heard the doctors talking earlier."

"And," he reached over to clasp her hand in his. "What did you hear?"

She couldn't meet his gaze, "Something about the paralysis possibly being permanent."

He started. "What?"

"Both Ian and I. Neither of our wings are responding to their treatments." She lifted her gaze to his, and he could see the fear deep inside. "I need to be able to fly, David."

David winced and immediately shifted over to the bedside. "Remember, the doctors don't know what we're dealing with here. And therefore, they don't *know* what will happen."

"But they said our vampire genes should have fixed the problem by now. As they haven't..." and she let her voice trail off. But the worry in her beautiful eyes damn near broke his heart. Maybe sleep was the best thing for her.

He said as much to Jewel.

"I've been trying," she whispered, "But it's hard to not worry."

"And yet the worry itself is going to hinder your healing." He smiled down at the most beautiful woman in his world. He reached up and stroked back the hair lying on her cheek. "Remember what Tessa did? She told her vampire genes to kick in. Maybe yours have been suppressed by the drugs, but I bet if you told yours to knock it off and to get into the game, they'd be happy to help."

She laughed in delight. "I'll try."

David's new phone went off. "Hopefully that's Cody."

He frowned. "Interesting."

"What?

"It's from Jared. He wants to talk. Says he's heard something. Something bad."

CHAPTER 6

TESSA WOKE UP to hard voices, and a tension so thick in her room she couldn't imagine the state of affairs downstairs. She sat up carefully, feeling a sense of déjà vu. Delighted to find that her headache was gone, she stood up – and was forced to wait for the room to stop swaying. She'd have chosen a shower, except it sounded like she was needed more downstairs.

She tested the door between her and Cody to find it solidly closed.

Not good. As fast as she could, she raced down the stairs to the living room.

Her mother stood in the middle of the room ripping a strip off Cody. Yep. Déjà vu.

"You will not date my daughter. She is too young."

Oh shit.

Cody never said a word. He stood tall and straight, his hands behind his back. Neither did he do anything but stare over Rhia's head.

He wasn't going to defend himself. And from the looks of it, both Serus and Goran were out of their element.

But Tessa wasn't.

She strode between Cody and Rhia and stood tall, her feet planted apart, her hands on her hips.

"Stop it," she snapped. "Leave him alone."

Rhia, now in a full rage, turned her gaze on Tessa. "What are you doing out of bed?"

Tessa snorted. "I was woken up by your screaming."

"Do not push it, young lady."

"Me?" Now Tessa could feel anger of her own rising to the forefront. "You want to do this now? Then you damn well better pick on someone who can fight back. Cody respects you too much. He won't fight back. But I'll be damned if I let you kick him like this." Tessa lifted her nose in the air. "You've got a problem with his relationship with me, then you come to me. Not him."

Rhia was livid. "You think you're so grown up that you can argue with me like this?"

"When you are in the wrong, I will. I have to. There is no one else here willing to go against you when you get like this. And that." Tessa glared at her mother. "Is wrong."

"Are you saying I'm wrong?" Rhia gasped. The shock and pain poured from her features.

"And overreacting." Tessa nodded her head. "Yes."

And just like that, in a rush of emotion stealing the ire from her spine, Rhia collapsed on the closest chair. "You are too young," she wailed.

"For what?" Tessa said, aware of Cody relaxing slightly behind her. The door between them eased open a crack.

Stay quiet for a bit longer, she whispered mentally.

He snorted. *I'm staying silent until I get the hell out of here.*

No. It will be fine. She just has to accept us.

I don't think that she's willing to do that.

"What are you doing?" Rhia asked suddenly, a new worry in her voice.

"Talking to Cody telepathically. Telling him that you will calm down in a minute or two." Tessa tilted her head to one side. "He doesn't believe me."

"Don't put words in my mouth," Cody protested.

Tessa and Rhia ignored him.

"So it's true?" And damned if her mother didn't look crushed.

"Why does our mindspeak upset you?" Tessa studied her mother, trying to understand.

Then Cody piped up. *I don't think there is any understanding this. She can mindspeak with your father, so why is she upset with us being able to as well?*

"Mom," she said gently. "Why does that upset you?"

Rhia sighed heavily. "I wanted you to wait. To live a little first. You have your whole life ahead of you." She flung her hand toward Cody. "It's one thing to date or have a fling," she quickly interjected, "But to bond like this? It takes away your choices."

Say what? Tessa shook her head. "Wait. Are you saying I should go and date anyone other than Cody? In fact, I should go and date a lot of guys and not Cody?"

I wouldn't try that if I were you. Cody's heated voice growled through her mind.

I won't, but I'm trying to get my mother to see how silly she's being.

"No, I don't want you to date anyone," Rhia cried.

Serus stepped forward. "Rhia, honey, you're not making sense."

And then Tessa got it. All the anger slipped away. *It will be okay, Cody.*

She walked over to her mother and crouched down in front of her. "Mom, I know what the real issue is here."

Rhia reached out to gently tug on Tessa's new bangs, a wry smile on her face at the new look. Then, exhausted and frustrated, she said, "Good, because I don't."

"Neither do I," snapped Serus.

"You're not ready," Tessa said simply. "For me to grow up. For me to be an adult. For me to not be your little girl anymore."

Tears filled her mother's eyes. "No," she whispered. "I'm not."

CODY STARED AT Tessa's mother. She'd always been the most welcoming and warm-hearted woman he'd known until this weekend when she'd found out about Tessa and him. After being at the hospital tonight, she'd really blown her top. He hadn't known what to do. His father and Serus had been frozen at his side. Both of them wanting to defend Cody's position but not knowing how to without making things worse.

Then Tessa had shown up to defend him. Again. God, he loved that girl.

She spun around and stared at him.

Damn.

He hadn't meant to say that. She narrowed her gaze and let him dig his ass in a little deeper. *At least, I didn't mean for you to take it the wrong way.*

Tessa sniffed and spun back to her mother. "I'm not going to jump into anything. This mindspeak thing came on quickly for us. There was no preparation or choosing. It just happened, but with it came a bond that's hard to describe. It's new; we're still learning how it works. We're forever treading into each other's thoughts." Tessa flinched. "In a big way."

"You can read each other's thoughts?" Rhia sat forward.

"So you can both talk to each other, hear each other, and you can hear the other person's thoughts, even when they aren't talking to you?"

"Sometimes." Tessa nodded. "And feel his pain when something happens to him, and sometimes other emotions." She shrugged. "We have a door between us that we can close or open at will. Earlier, I had shut the door because the noise level at the hospital had been horrific. I closed the door to help save him and give myself one more layer of silence to help combat the pain." She smiled wryly. "And that meant he didn't hear me when I got hurt."

"I felt it though. Like a blinding pain on the side of my head." Cody lifted a hand to his head. "That's how we knew you were in trouble."

"Even though the door was closed?" Tessa thought about that. "That's new."

"I think that if one of us is in trouble, it won't matter if that door is closed or not. The urgency of the situation will still come through. I just wish you'd seen your attacker. If you'd thought about it then, chances are good I'd have gotten a name and we'd be on the hunt for him now."

The frustration in Cody's voice finally caught Rhia's attention. She stared up at him for a long time. "You really care about Tessa, don't you?"

Silence.

Tessa smiled. *It's okay to answer. I won't hold it against you.*

Ha. Cody's warm smile whispered through her mind. *If she had any idea how much I care, she'd kick me the hell away from you.*

Maybe not. Maybe she'd realize that I'm not just the next notch on your belt.

Cody nodded to Rhia. "Very much."

She ran a gentle hand over Tessa's hair. "I can fight a war, organize a massive sweep over a big blood farm operation, and any number of other things I'd had to do lately, but I'm completely undone at the concept of my baby growing up." She shook her head, the gentlest of smiles forming on her beautiful features. "You make sure you only do what you're comfortable doing, do you hear me?"

"I will," Tessa said promptly, knowing that could mean anything or nothing.

Make it anything.

"And Cody?" Rhia's voice sharpened to razor edges.

"Yes?" He straightened.

"If you ever treat my daughter like a Sunday special to throw off on a Monday morning…if you ever whisper your exploits with my daughter to your buddies or…" Her voice grew ominous, "If you ever hurt her, you know I'm going to gut you and hang you on the remains of Moltere's Mountain…right?"

Dead silence.

Cody swallowed hard and said, "Yes. I understand."

"And you're still willing to have a relationship with Tessa knowing this?" Her sharp eyes assessed his every moment.

"Yes." He said calmly. "What you don't understand is that I have no choice. Neither of us do. This relationship is here in front of us. It doesn't understand if we're ready or not. It's either take this walk or forever wonder what we missed out on. And I'm not prepared to do that."

Goran's hand came up on his shoulder. "He's a good boy, Rhia. Serus grilled him earlier, and now you. I say we leave them alone and see how it goes. For all we know, they'll break up in a few months."

Rhia brightened. Cody shook his head, but Tessa…Tessa

spun around and glared at Goran. Cody almost laughed as his father backed up several steps.

Goran took a deep breath. "Easy, Tessa. I was just joking."

She stood up. "Not a joking matter."

Studying him to make sure he understood, she switched her gaze to Cody, caught his grin, and glared at him as well.

"Now do you think I could have a shower and maybe a bit more sleep? I have school tomorrow and need to know that roasting Cody is no longer on the menu," she asked in a plaintive voice. "Or…" She lowered her voice in a threatening tone, "Do I need to keep him in my room so I can be assured that he will be safe?"

Cody and Goran grinned.

Rhia glared at her daughter. "Not funny."

"Yeah well, there hasn't been much funny about any of this."

Just then David came racing inside. "Oh, thank God. You're all here." He gasped for breath. "I just got a text from Jared. He thinks there's a human uprising going on. To take out the vampires. The blood farm news has tilted the balance and now the humans are out for revenge."

Cody watched as everyone but Tessa surrounded David. "You aren't concerned?" he asked her quietly, stepping closer.

She nodded. "Yes, I am, but I'm also ready to have a normal life again. I'm supposed to go to school in a few hours." She yawned. "And before then I need food and a shower."

He wrapped an arm around her shoulders and tugged her closer. She ignored the fact that everyone else might see and cuddled in closer. "My head is really sore, too."

"Not healing?"

"Yes, it is, but the dried blood is tugging on my hair. I need a shower."

"Why don't you slip out now and grab one. I'll catch up with David and get the news and pass it on as I find out."

She grinned. "One of the advantages of telepathic communication." She cast a quick glance around, saw everyone was paying attention to David, and turned back to Cody. She reached up and kissed him gently. "Keep me updated."

And she left.

Cody couldn't help himself. He lifted several fingers to his mouth as if he could hold it there. After a moment, he rejoined the group and listened in as David showed him Jared's texts.

"That could explain what happened to Tessa. Maybe someone recognized her at the hospital. It might be as simple as someone wanting to get payback for a missing loved one," Cody said.

"We can only guess at what happened to her," Serus said, frowning.

Rhia's gaze flew to Serus, "Speaking of which, we haven't heard anything back from the hospital security department."

"I'll call Sian. We need to contact the Human Council and let them know."

Goran spoke up. "And that's where our input ends. The Human Council needs to handle this. But..." he added, "We need to talk to our Council so they are prepared."

"Do you have any security here, Serus?" Goran looked around. "Just in case the humans do know where to find us?"

"Which they do, because Jared came here and spoke with Seth. That's when Seth and his friends took Jared back up the mountain. So if he found us, others will."

There was a long thoughtful silence as everyone considered their predicament. Cody didn't want to add anything. He was surprised that Jared could even find his pants in the morning, but the thought of anyone coming here to throw poison gas at Tessa's family filled him with dread. Had they fought one war only to end up in the middle of another?

☙ ❧

SERUS SHOOK HIS head. "Not enough security for this." He knew he looked bad, aggressive. Bullish. He didn't give a damn. "This is wrong. I understand that they want revenge, but this is anger looking for a target, any target."

"I agree, old friend," Goran said, studying him closely. "What do you want to do about this?"

"Do? Nothing. I want to tell the right people and I want to leave this well enough alone. Look at us; we're a ragtag group of tired, worn out people."

"Warriors. We're tired and worn out, but we're refueling and can be ready to go now if necessary," David said, excitement in his voice. "I know we lost a lot of people, but we've regained a lot as well. There are many vamps who'd want to step up and fight."

"Fight humans?" Serus drew himself up to his full height. "Like Taz. Like Jared? Is that what you want?"

"No, of course not, but if they come at us and try to kill us, I'm not going to lose any sleep over taking them out," David said hotly. "If they want a war, they can have it."

"Easy, David. You don't mean that." Cody hoped he didn't mean it. David was the gentle one in the group.

"Maybe I don't, but I don't feel like this is over. Sure, the blood farm is gone, but what about all the humans that were in collusion with the vamps? What if those same asshole humans are the ones that are driving this uprising to hide their involvement?"

Cody had to admit that was a hell of an idea. "But we can't just blame everyone that is charging at vamps right now. They aren't going to be the ones that were involved in the blood farm. They are going to be people that lost someone or whose loved ones have gone missing. The ones fanning the flames, pushing life into the cool embers, are the ones we need to find."

"But it wouldn't take much sniffing around in the background to figure out who is pushing these people forward. Maybe they have an agenda, maybe not, but some humans were feeding their friends and family to the blood farm. Getting paid to get rid of unwanted people. Those same people don't dare get caught, and they are the ones we need." David said. "Assholes like Jared's uncle. That man needs to be picked up. Someone should sit him down and give him a serious talking to. I doubt anyone else has had a chance to yet."

David looked around expectantly at the group. The silent group. "Oh, come on. Are you serious? Are you really happy to be able to just walk away at this point? Don't you want answers?"

"We've got answers. And all I want is right here at home," Rhia said firmly. "You should be fine with that, too."

Serus realized that Rhia wanted to be done with this issue after the hell they'd been through. As if they dealt with the vampire side of the problem and now the humans needed to deal with their side.

Goran whispered in Serus's head. *She's right, but it won't be that easy. We have to make sure we warn our people.*

And that's likely to set off another war.

Then war it is. We did what was right, Serus, but we can't lie down to be slaughtered in our sleep.

No, we can't. We're going to have to stop this before it goes any further.

Damn.

☙ ❧

IAN WAITED BEHIND the door for the person to enter. The door was pushed open. He sucked back his breath and froze.

No one came in.

Shit.

The door slowly swung closed, and damned if he didn't hear it snick shut then click as the person locked the door. He'd been locked in? Why?

He stepped in front of the door and studied the room. There was no way to have seen him behind the door. Then again, if he hadn't been in the bed, he was either behind the door or gone.

And he'd locked the door just in case.

Except there were no sounds of his footsteps leaving. So the asshole was waiting on the other side of the door. But waiting for what? Ian reached out a hand to turn the knob and stopped.

If he turned it, then the other guy would know Ian was locked inside. But if he didn't, then the other guy would have no idea if Ian was here or snuck out.

He slowly dropped his hand.

And waited.

And waited.

Just when he figured the guy must have left already, Ian heard someone call out. "There you are, Dr. Horander. I've been looking for you."

And the footsteps started up again and faded soon out.

Ian sagged against the wall.

The guy had been waiting for him to make a move. All this time.

Ian studied the room, trying to find anything to make sense of what was going on. There wasn't even a big enough window to deserve that name. It looked more like a hastily converted cupboard.

He knew he'd been moved from one room to another. But why the downgrade?

Even more importantly – why had he been locked in?

∽ ∾

JARED GLARED AT the clock on his cell phone. If he were a vampire, this would be his time of day. He didn't like the hot sun or early mornings. He was a nighttime kind of guy. Talk about living the wrong lifestyle. Then again, he wouldn't want to live on blood. His phone had stopped ringing as his friends had dropped off to sleep and his vampire friends were apparently heading out to contact more vampires for a meeting.

He lay there staring at his phone and realized something. For all he'd hated the last week, there were so many things he'd enjoyed. The action. The adventure. The sheer joy of feeling alive and doing something good. That whole hero thing. And now he felt left out. Alone. And damn it, he didn't want to be cut out of the action.

He wanted to be fighting for what was right. He wanted to do…something.

Throwing off his covers, he paced his tiny room. What

could he do?

Sleep was necessary, but every time he closed his eyes, the whole saga kept running through his head.

Tessa wouldn't be sleeping with this going on. She'd be telling everyone what to do. Hell, she'd likely be leading the next charge.

As always.

And damn it, he wanted to be there, too.

CHAPTER 7

TESSA LOVED THE hot shower, except for the stinging of her scalp from the heavy spray. The warmth also did wonders for improving her mood. Washing her hair, however, was a pain. She was tired from the injury and the requirements of healing her body yet again. It wasn't supposed to wear her out like this but today...it was.

The wound had closed on her head, but the area was super sensitized. Just trying to work shampoo into the long strands made her wince. It took several tries, but eventually she got the blood off. Turning off the shower, she took a moment to listen. No yelling. No arguments. No fighting downstairs. Good. Maybe they'd get through this after all.

She was glad she'd thought to pass over the phone numbers to Jared at school. They'd all made connections this last week. They'd been through so much, she knew David had come to respect Jared – a lot.

So did she. But he wasn't Cody.

This last week had taught her so much about vamps, humans, Cody and especially herself. They were lessons she could have taken a decade to learn any other way. She was glad she'd had the short intense course. Self-confidence flowed through her body now, and that made her look at the world different, too.

It wasn't any rosier, but it was more manageable this way.

One of the biggest differences was she was no longer alone. Cody, for better or for worse, was always there.

She hoped this was a lifelong thing. She'd always expected to have a relationship like her parents had. And hadn't ever really thought, deep inside, that she'd get it.

Relationships had looked to be for other people. Not Tessa. That she'd started down that path with Jared and made a sudden detour bothered her a little, yet she could see how important that detour was to her life. And considering how Jared was handling it, he was better off, too.

She hadn't really thought of it as a human to human relationship or vamp to vamp relationship, but more that as much as the thought of going to the movies with Jared had made her happy, the thought of going anywhere with Cody made her toes curl and her heart sigh with a sense of rightness.

She half expected Cody to pop in with a snide comment as he so often did when she thought about Jared, but he'd gotten better. Maybe also because she was choosing Cody over Jared, he didn't feel the need to step in and let her know how things stood.

As if she'd let him make that decision.

She snickered. That was something else that had changed. Tessa had grown a backbone.

In her room, she checked her own phone and realized Jared had sent her a message as well. She read it quickly. Shit. As she hadn't responded, there'd been no follow up message. She dressed quickly.

Are you done? Cody asked.

Hey. Yeah, just trying to braid my hair then I'll be down.

Come here and I'll braid it for you.

She paused, hairbrush in midair. *You know how to braid a woman's hair?*

Yes. His tone was more of a smirk than anything. She thought about that, the door between them open, so he could read her thoughts as she worked her way through what that meant. His presence was there, but in the background. If he knew how to braid hair, that meant he'd done it before. And if he'd done it before, he'd have braided his old girlfriend's hair. Cody did not have a mother or sisters to practice on. How did she feel about that? Odd, but it was before her time. And besides, she was going to reap the benefit.

Decision made.

Sure. I'll bring a brush and hair tie.

Good. Laughter rumbled through her mind. *Glad you worked your way through that.*

*Me too. You have a past. I wasn't part of it. I can't change that. So…*she gave a mental shrug. *Here we are.*

And within seconds she was walking down the stairs and heading to the living room. There appeared to be some major discussion going on. She walked over to Cody and handed him the brush, then turned so he could access her hair.

"You cut your hair," he said in surprise.

She flung him a saucy look. "I did, thanks for noticing."

He grinned. "Oh there's not much about you I don't notice." He stroked the brush through her hair. "I like the look. Makes you look older too."

"That's a good thing right now." She stared at the others. "David, I got a text from Jared as well. Did he send you more?"

David looked up, saw her, and walked over. He quickly explained.

Her heart sank and she groaned. "Ah crap. I guess they want revenge." She winced as her head was tugged gently on the tender side. Cody was being very efficient and kind, but there was a certain amount of brushing required to braid her hair. She said to David, "We did too, if you remember?"

"I do remember," David said, "I still want revenge for what those assholes did to our own people."

David studied Cody behind Tessa's shoulder. "I wonder what we can do to stave this off."

"If the Human Council would step up and say they are doing a full investigation..." Cody said, "Maybe that won't stop everyone, but it would stop the bulk of them.

Tessa said, "There are always going to be some that don't think the government does enough."

She thought about it. "I should talk to the principal at my school and ask him to make an announcement about this issue."

"He'll probably kick you out of the school when he realizes that you're a vamp. Or if he already knows, he'll likely tell you to leave voluntarily to stay safe."

"Still, the school kids need to understand." And maybe he'd make the decision she didn't want to make or wasn't ready to make. He might kick her out of the human school, giving her no option but to go to school with her vampire people.

"What are you thinking?" Cody's warm voice drifted down the nape of her neck, sending chills down to her toes. Damn, he was good. And special.

She smiled, knowing he could hear that last thought.

There was a weird smooch in her head. She shook her head slightly, then turned to cast him a sideways look. "Did you just blow a kiss in my mind?

He grinned. "I did."

She shook her head. "That was the most bizarre sound."

"Yoohoo? Are you two there?" David glared at them

mockingly. "It would be good to have some input here."

The ancients walked over. "We're heading to the Council offices," her father said. "Your mother, Sian, and I are going to the Human Council," he glanced down at his watch, "In a few hours. We'll call them in early." He glanced over at Goran. "Goran and you three should go to Councilman Adamson and discuss options with him."

Tessa straightened. Inside, she beamed. She was being included. Then he took away her sense of satisfaction.

"I'd prefer to leave you home, Tessa, but if the threat is real, I can't leave you alone in bed unprotected."

Damn. She glared at him. "Thanks for nothing, Dad. Here I was happy thinking I was being included in Council business, instead you're wanting me to tag along because you don't have a babysitter to look after me."

Cody's whispered in her mind, *Easy, Tessa.*

Why? She said in disgust. *Has nothing changed?*

But as she watched her father's expression, she realized something had changed. He knew it too, but didn't know how to adapt – what to do differently.

"Let me rephrase what you just said. The three of you go with Goran and speak with Councilman Adamson. We'll meet up before Tessa heads off to school." And she waited, her gaze steady as she watched her father fumble through this shift.

He smiled and nodded. "Okay. That works."

As he tugged Rhia toward the kitchen, he said to her, "We need to contact Sian and get Taz involved. He's overworked now, but there's no help for it. He doesn't need hundreds more humans landing in his morgue either."

"Oh no, Serus," Rhia cried. "That would be terrible."

"And that's why we can't leave this to the Councils. We

have to make sure they do what's right."

She sighed and said something, but she was too far away for Tessa to hear. She turned to Goran and said, "Where's Councilman Adamson?"

"At the Council Hall," Goran said. "The fastest way to get there would be to fly."

David shook his head. "Cody shouldn't, I can't, and Tessa's head injury means no jumping for her. You can meet us there if you want, but I'll drive."

Goran nodded. "Make sure the three of you stay together."

"And you stay safe," Tessa said. "Not all humans sleep at night, and if you're visible in the air, you're also a target for shooters."

He paused, considered the options, nodded once, and said, "They won't get a second shot."

And she had to be satisfied with that.

She turned to her brother. "Shall we?"

"Are you sure you want to come, Tessa?" David asked. "It's going to be hard to go to school in a few hours without any sleep."

She winced. "I know. Still I *should* go to school, only there's not much choice. I'll have to find a quiet place at the hall where I can crash for an hour or two."

"You could skip the day at school," Cody said. "You're a top student. You'll catch up fast enough."

"I'm considering it except I should speak to the principal. See if he understands what's brewing." She followed them outside. "I'll see when the time comes."

David led the way to the car. She got into the middle of the front seat, Cody beside her. She leaned her head on Cody's shoulder and said, "Wake me when we get there."

And closed her eyes.

        ॐ ॐ

CODY TUCKED TESSA in closer and stared out into the murky night. He'd done so much lately he'd been losing track of day and night. He was also in school and had no idea where his own college classes were at. For all he knew, the school had closed for a few days because of this problem.

"Are you okay?" David asked.

"Yeah, I think so."

"Mom got her claws into you, I hear."

Cody snorted. "Yeah, she tried to. Woke Tessa up when she was supposed to be in a healing sleep."

"I was actually outside for a bit. Too scared to get involved." He chuckled. "Mom is quite the force when she gets going. But you survived."

Cody smiled, glanced down at the sleeping woman in his arms, and said, "I survived because of your sister. She came down and stood up to your mother."

"Really? Damn, I wish I'd seen that."

"Took the stuffing right out of Rhia." Cody leaned his head back. "It's not like I could say much to defend myself."

"I'm actually surprised that Dad didn't go after you, too."

"We settled our differences in the mine. Your mom missed that."

"And that was too bad."

"Hopefully she's good now."

"Yeah." David was quiet for a few more minutes. "You know that she's not ready, right?"

Cody groaned silently. "I'm glad everyone is concerned about my sex life. However, I never had any problem before, and I don't expect to have any now." He snorted. "I won't push Tessa into doing anything she's not comfortable doing."

Giggles rippled in his mind. He glanced down at Tessa.

I thought you were asleep?

Not quite.

Enjoying my being grilled by yet another family member, huh, he said in disgust.

No. But happy to hear you are doing just fine defending yourself. Families are tough, but they are all we've got.

He thought about that. *You're lucky you have everyone.*

Yes, she whispered. *And I'm so sorry about Tyson.*

Don't be. He shifted slightly to settle her more comfortably against his chest. He had one burning question in his mind. The same question everyone else had cared about. *Damn it.*

What?

Nothing. He winced, knowing she'd know that he was lying.

No. I'm not ready. But that doesn't mean I won't be ready tomorrow. Or later today. Or if we were alone and had time, in an hour.

Don't do that to me. He groaned. *That is sheer torture.*

Honestly, I'm not sure I'll be ready for months yet. This is all so new.

And it should be new. Just because I have some experience with relationships doesn't mean I have experience with anything like what we have. He took a deep breath and knew that what he was going to say was going to cost him, but he had to be honest. *I don't want you to be intimate with me because you think that's what I want. Oh, I want to be alone with you. In a big way. There is so much to introduce you to...*he paused then continued painfully. *I don't want making love to be a tool, a* *power trip, or a bargain between us. I want you to want me as much as I want you.*

The warm breath of air brushed the gentlest of kisses through his soul. A shiver slipped down his spine.

Not a problem. She smiled. *I'm almost there.*

Ah Jesus, Tessa. You need to get ready damn fast.

"Hey, are you two talking or sleeping." David's irritated voice interrupted them.

"We're both here."

"Yeah, that's what I thought." David said. "Damn irritating."

Tessa laughed, the sound rippling through the car. "Sorry, David. It's taking a bit to figure this out."

"Ha. The only thing to figure out is that you shouldn't do it around others."

"Not going to happen," Tessa said cheerfully as she sat up. "So get used to it."

Cody shifted around to look out the window. "Where are we?"

"Almost at Adamson's place."

"I thought he was at the Council offices?" Cody said.

"This is on the way. Thought we'd stop by and check here first."

As he stopped talking, he turned the powerful car to the left, took another left, and pulled into a huge driveway.

"I wonder how he's doing after Gloria," Tessa said. "That had to have been horrible."

"He finished her off," David said, "So I imagine that part helped."

Cody agreed. Betrayal was one thing, but a chance at revenge – priceless.

❧ ❦

Rhia strode into the Council building. Sian was waiting for her.

"I just spoke to Taz. The medical community is worried. Fights are breaking out all over the place. Small groups are stirring up trouble."

"That is so not good. Did you contact the Human Council yet?"

"They aren't answering. It's early for them."

"And yet this needs to happen," Serus interjected, "So we have to get them up."

Sian nodded. "I've been trying. So far no one is answering."

Rhia frowned. "We have their home numbers. Why wouldn't they answer?"

Sian shrugged. "I have no idea."

"Unless they know who is calling and are trying to avoid talking to us," Serus suggested.

"That would not be good," Sian said. "But given the hour of the morning, I think it's more likely that most of them are asleep. We just have to be the first people they hear from in the morning.

"Do we have the address of the members we met with earlier? If so, why don't we go to their houses and wake them up? If there's an uprising brewing, it's going to be early intervention that shifts the power struggle here."

Sian tilted her head slightly, considering the idea. "I'm not sure that's a good idea. They are intimidated by us already. It will seem overwhelming to them if three of us arrive at their homes."

Rhia could understand that, but given that they had to

stay up late, it seemed only fair that the humans could get up early to meet them halfway. "What do you suggest?"

"How about we send humans to their houses?" Sian suggested. "Although I'd have to contact Taz and find out who he'd suggest."

"Is that a good idea? Bringing in strangers when we can't be sure whose side they are on? The only humans I trust are Taz and Jared. Taz is needed at the hospital, and Jared is still a kid," Serus said, frowning at her.

"And Jared's been involved enough. We need to keep him out of trouble."

"And yet he's been our warning signal already," Sian reminded Rhia. "He would make a great liaison."

❧ ❦

WENDY WALKED INTO the hospital, a hospital she hadn't known existed until this blood farm mess, and walked up to the front desk. She smiled at the receptionist. "When I was leaving last time, Ian was being moved to another room. What room is that? I've brought a change of clothes for him."

The receptionist held out her hand. "I'll take the stuff to him. Thanks."

"No. I want to give it to him. I also want to see him." Wendy couldn't have explained why her fingers locked on the bag she was carrying or why her back went up at the idea of this woman giving Ian his stuff. Ian was hers, damn it, and she'd done a lot to make sure that guy survived the damn mountain. She wasn't going to dump him here.

"I need to see him myself," she said firmly.

And waited.

The receptionist gave her a razor thin smile. "Sorry, Ian's

condition has been downgraded. He's no longer allowed visitors."

Wendy felt something wobble inside. She steadied herself. "Then you must be thinking about someone else. Ian was fine when I left him a few hours ago. They were moving him to another room, and they said I could see him when I returned." She hardened her voice, fear giving her an edge. "Guess what? I've returned and I want to see Ian."

The receptionist smiled, a slow chilling movement that sent shards of ice down Wendy's back. "Ian isn't allowed any visitors."

Wendy studied her, then dropped her gaze to the name tag. Misha.

"Well, Misha. I suggest you tell me his room number before I decide to take this way above your pay—"

"What appears to be the problem here?"

Wendy turned and sighed with relief. "I told you I'd only be gone an hour." She held up the bag for Ian. "Now where is Ian so I can give him his clothes?"

The doctor gave her a somber look. "I'm sorry. After you left, he took a sudden downward turn. We had to isolate him. He's in a special ward with round-the-clock care. You can be sure we're doing everything we can for him." As the doctor spoke, he urged Wendy back out the front door. "If you want to leave the bag, I'll be sure to get it to him when he wakes up."

Wendy shook off his arm. She hadn't gone through what she had without learning something, and her instinct said this doctor was trouble. And that she was in trouble. Worse, so was Ian. "You're lying. And I will see you in hell before I believe a word that is coming out of your damn mouth."

His face went granite hard. "I was afraid you'd be trouble." He shifted and Wendy caught a glimpse of a needle in his hand. Uh oh. She twisted, ducked, and bolted for the front door.

"Stop her. Call security. She can't leave the grounds. Stop her!"

❧ ❦

JARED DRESSED FOR school. He'd rather leave super early than lie here for another hour. He didn't think he'd closed his eyes for longer than a couple of hours, and those hadn't been restful. He walked downstairs to find the kitchen empty again. He shook his head. What the hell was everyone doing? He headed to the office and looked inside. Empty. He wandered through the other rooms. Everything was empty. He spun around, suddenly worried. It was early – but surely there was someone here.

He wandered throughout the place, more disturbed with every passing moment.

Where were the night staff? Some of the kids here needed serious assistance. Then he realized the night staff were likely attending to the other kids upstairs.

He hated that deserted feeling. Walking back, he stepped into the office for a second glance. Instinct had him walking around the big overloaded desk.

And found one of the missing staff.

Crumpled on the floor.

He raced to the man's side. With two fingers, he checked for a pulse but knew instantly there was nothing to be done. The man's flesh, thick and pudgy, was already cool.

Jared straightened. He had to call the cops, but he hated to. They'd look at him as a suspect again. And he'd had enough of that. He should go back to his room and wait. If he left early like he'd planned, the cops would get suspicious yet again.

He stared down at the dead man and realized his fingerprints might be detectable. Might not be, but he wasn't willing to take the chance.

Feeling foolish, he took a tissue and wiped the spot he'd touched. Then retraced his steps back to the kitchen. The last thing on his mind was food.

Another sick thought caught him. What if the other staff members were dead as well? Surely they'd have called the cops about their friend. He turned back in the direction of the office. Why had he assumed the death was foul play? Maybe the guy had a heart attack. He hadn't seen any blood. Or visible trauma. Now he felt a bigger fool. If it was a natural death, the cops wouldn't give a damn who found him.

Jared retraced his steps to his room. He checked every open door on his way – and found nothing or anyone.

Crap. Now what should he do?

CHAPTER 8

TESSA EXITED THE car outside Councilman Adamson's place and stretched under the gray-just-before-dawn sky. They didn't have much time before the sun rose. Hopefully they could get to the Vampire Council by then. "Do you think he's home? The house looks pretty deserted. And dark," she added as an afterthought. "Then again, he could be already in bed."

"Or not." Cody pointed to the sky and the large shadow circling overhead. "Wonder what the chances are of that being him?"

David looked up. "If it is, why won't he come down here?"

"Because he doesn't know us. Or trust us. Because some-one close to him tried to kill him." Tessa waved skyward. The circle swooped lower and lower and lower.

Finally Councilman Adamson landed in front of them, his cold gaze going from one to the other. "Visitors again. I could go months to years without a visitor and yet in the last few days I've had several."

"Getting popular, sir," David said with a grin.

"This kind of popularity I could do without." He glared at them. "I presume you kids have a specific reason for coming?"

"We need to talk to you. As your place was on the way to

the Council Hall, we thought we'd stop here and see if you were home."

"And now that you know?" His demeanor eased slightly. "What can I do for you?"

Tessa studied the man she knew only by sight and realized he looked weary. As if in the aftermath of the bitter betrayal, life wasn't worth living anymore.

"I'm sorry," she said in a quiet voice. "For your loss. And for the damage she caused."

Adamson pinned her with a sharp piercing gaze. She felt a tingle, as if he could see into the heart of her. "Tessa, Councilman Serus and Rhia's daughter, I presume."

He spoke in such a quiet tone of voice, she didn't know how to take it. She didn't hear anything condescending. Going on instinct, she nodded and said, "Yes, I'm Tessa. The one Gloria worked hard to kill – quite possibly by the hand of my brother Seth."

His eyes glittered. "That woman has a lot to answer for."

Adamson switched his gaze to David and then Cody. He nodded to both of them. "The three musketeers. Although there is normally a couple others in your group. Haven't you stirred up enough trouble?"

"We didn't stir up anything," Tessa said coolly, "The situation was waiting to explode."

"True indeed." He studied the males. "Why are you here now?"

David explained about the texts from Jared and the calls from Taz. The Councilman listened quietly, shaking his head every once in a while. "That's not surprising. We'll have to stomp the resistance out of course, and fast. That I'd like this to go away doesn't mean it will."

"I wish it would though," Tessa said. "I've had enough

war to last a while."

"Me too," said Cody.

The Councilman smiled a real smile this time, maybe with a tinge of respect. "You've grown up through this mess. War will do that." He walked up the stairs, the front door opening automatically in front of him.

It was that door, so reminiscent of Moltere's Mountain, that made her pause, her breath catching in the back of her throat.

Instinctively, she shifted her gaze to using both her vampire and human vision. And took another look at the Councilman before he disappeared inside.

And damn if his energy didn't swirl with black.

"Crap," she whispered.

Cody stopped mid-stride. He spun around. "Crap what?" he said in a hoarse whisper.

"His energy," she hissed. "It's nearly all black."

David was at the front door already. He turned around, but kept walking backwards. "Hey you two, what's going on?"

Cody motioned to him to step back down. Only David continued walking backwards into the house. Tessa glanced at Cody and then at David. "I don't know what the black is, so let's stick with David."

Cody, as if realizing that David was about to be separated from them if that trick door shut, ran up the stairs after him.

"What's the matter?" Councilman Adamson said from deep inside the house. "You're all acting like this is a trap."

"And maybe it is," Tessa said. "Nothing personal, but we haven't found many vampires lately that we can trust."

"Your parents trust me," he said in an affronted voice.

"They trusted many vampires, Councilmen even, that they shouldn't have." Cody snorted. "And that didn't turn out so well for us as several tried to kill us."

"Good point. I knew they were involved but wasn't aware that they'd personally attacked you." He opened his mouth, hesitated then asked, "How did you get away? They were ancients with serious skills."

David laughed. "They were. But we had a secret weapon and some friends that were on our side."

Tessa didn't think Bart counted, but finding vamps like Motre had been a godsend. But she stayed quiet and studied the corner where the Councilman's voice came from. She understood Gloria had lived here with him. She racked her brain trying to think of reasons why his energy would be cloudy and dark. Was he ill? Had Gloria poisoned him? Or was he taking enhancements? Yet supposedly Gloria had tried to kill him, only when she failed, he'd killed her. But could he have been a part of this mess and Gloria had planned to get rid of him anyway? Once again, nothing was clear and straightforward.

Tessa hated the confusion, but until this was sorted out, she had no plans to trust this or any other Councilman.

The Councilman spoke up. "What secret weapon?"

David opened his mouth to answer, but Cody jumped ahead of him and said, "He's joking, sir. He just means we were lucky. Fate or whatever you might want to call it was on our side."

Tessa whispered to Cody in her mind. *Thank you.*

No problem. I gather you think he can't be trusted.

Until I know more, I'll reserve judgment. And that means I don't trust him. Yet.

RHIA WALKED TOWARD the Human Council offices, her coat over her head. It was piss poor timing with the morning sun breaking through. This was the last place she wanted to be. She should be home resting and enjoying time with her family. She hadn't heard from Goran or her kids. And that made her mad, too. She knew David would be levelheaded enough to keep on track, but with Cody and Tessa doing the courtship tango, she wasn't so sure. She remembered mooning over Serus to the point of losing interest in everything but that man. He'd been the only one for her even back then. Now centuries later, she couldn't imagine being with anyone else. Ever.

She hoped for the same for them – down the road. As much as she wished it wasn't happening for another couple of decades, she also hadn't been looking forward to Tessa having multiple relationships and hurting over each and every one, either. Tessa wouldn't date just anyone. She'd have to care. And that meant she'd hurt when the relationship hit the rocks. And most would. It was ingrained into the vampire nature. But Tessa was different. And she'd hurt for everyone that came and went in her life.

Yet she was starting with Cody.

Rhia shook her head and tried to toss the worries over her daughter from her mind. Humans were cagey. They hadn't kept their spot on the food chain by being stupid. She needed her wits about her for the upcoming meeting.

Like last time, Rhia wasn't coming with good news. That the two Councils had worked together well last time gave her hope. But then she'd been admitting failures amongst the vampire clan. This time, she was broaching failures in the human side of this war.

She didn't think her reception would be quite the same.

She turned to make sure Sian and Serus were behind her and watched dozens of vehicles pulling into the parking lot. Her nerves kicked in. She motioned to the others behind her.

There were way more humans here than last time.

Sian studied the new arrivals. "I don't know many of them."

"I don't know any of them," Serus growled. "And I don't like being outnumbered."

From behind them came a deep and familiar voice. Rhia was happy to recognize the same man they'd worked with last time. "I'm sure you couldn't be nervous physically, so I'm presuming you don't like crowds."

Rhia turned and put a smile on her face. "Councilman Smithson, this is my husband, Councilman Serus."

The Councilman's eyebrows shot up to his hairline. He held out a hand. "A pleasure."

Serus shook his hand and nodded in return. Great time for Serus to turn reticent. She motioned to the crowd of humans walking up the stairs. "Why are so many here this time?"

He sighed. "Because everyone has heard about the blood farm, so everyone wanted to be involved."

Sian spoke up for the first time. "Let's hope they still want that when they find out why we're here."

Within ten minutes, Rhia knew the answer to Sian's comment.

They weren't.

❧ ❦

JARED DID SOMETHING he hadn't expected to do when in trouble. However as he'd texted David earlier, it seemed like the natural next move. He texted Tessa and her family for help.

He couldn't decide why that was the right thing to do when the police were the obvious choice. Dead human should have meant human cops. But he'd met the human cops... and he hadn't been impressed. While he waited for someone to get back to him, he crept through the house searching for the other staff. It was possible there'd been a falling out amongst thieves and one had killed the other. In which case, the killer should have taken off – unless he wanted to appear innocent and went about his daily work as if nothing had happened. Jared closed his eyes against the headache from hell. He thought for sure this would be all over and life could return to normal. Instead, it appeared to be anything but.

Yet neither could he connect this dead male with the blood farm mess. But could he disregard the possibility given the crazy talk he'd heard about a human uprising?

He searched all of the nooks and crannies downstairs, even forcing himself to open closets and the pantry to make sure no one was hiding and that a second dead body wasn't hidden from view. He had yet to go outside and check the grounds. He figured he'd do that after he'd determined who and what was left in the house.

There should be a good dozen guys like him here, so why was he the only one up? It was early, but not as early as it had been. He checked the clock and realized it was past 6:30 am. The place should be buzzing with people by now. He shook his head at the wrongness of the atmosphere.

And wondered...nah, no one would kill everyone in this group home. Surely. Cause if that were the case, Jared would be dead, too.

Still, he couldn't let the idea go as he crept upstairs to the first bedroom. He opened the door and found it empty.

Relieved, he crept to the second one. Someone slept in their bed. Good. He went on to the next and the next. Half the bedrooms were empty and half were occupied. That might be normal. He didn't know. The first time he'd been here, the place had been pretty full, but he knew several were heading home. Some were being transferred to a different group home, and two were going to the hospital for more surgery. So it was possible that there were only a few people here again. With as many staff as they had, the house had appeared full. He just couldn't remember if that meant full with kids.

His phone beeped. He checked his messages. Tessa. He grinned. Gotta love having a gorgeous girl talking to you whenever you called. Her response. *Oh hell no. Get out.*

And he realized that she was right. If there was hell going on here, he'd not only be caught in the crossfire but he'd also likely become a victim.

And he echoed Tessa's words. *Hell no.* He grabbed his pitiful bag of stuff including all his schoolwork and crept down the back door. The security alarm wasn't on. He frowned, quickly texted that to Tessa, and slipped out into the back yard. And promptly tripped over a second body.

Ah shit.

WENDY DASHED INTO her vehicle and struggled to fit the key inside the ignition. She thought she'd lost the two men following her, but she didn't know for sure. She'd crept through the parking lot, which was full, thank God, and snuck up to her car. Now she lay sideways across the seat until she could get it started. But she couldn't see. She dropped the keys. Shit. She scrambled to find them, taking several tries before snatching them up. Her fingers shook so hard she couldn't fit the key into the ignition. Closing her eyes briefly, she struggled to take a deep breath. She needed to get herself under control. Ian needed her help.

And damn it. She needed help. If she didn't make it out of here, it would be over for both of them.

And no one would know what had happened.

Finally the key slid in. She turned it and cried when the engine fired up. "Oh thank you. Thank you, thank you," she whispered.

Sitting up cautiously, she took a quick look around then reversed the car out of the parking spot. She wanted to race out of there as fast as she could, but she didn't dare take the chance that she'd bring unwanted attention to her vehicle. If they found out what car she was driving, they could track her down.

At a sedate pace, she drove the car to the exit. The sweat dripped from her palms, making the steering wheel hard to hold. She also couldn't control the small gasping cries that escaped her mouth. As she pulled out onto the main road, she heard shouts behind her.

She sucked in her breath and gunned it. Gravel spit out behind her as she ripped down the road as fast as she could push the engine. She figured she had a couple of minutes, but that was all and that was only if there were no fliers outside. It was overcast, but the sun was cresting the horizon. Some vamps could navigate at this hour. Enhanced ones definitely could. She'd heard about those experiments from David. If there were enhanced fliers out there, they'd be able to track her to her home. Just the thought sent chills down her back.

Where could she go? Where could she get help? Where

could she hide and stay safe?

Nowhere. If they'd gotten her name, there was nowhere safe for her anymore.

And she burst into tears.

CHAPTER 9

TESSA STARED AT her cell phone. She couldn't believe what she was reading. "Jared has found a second body! He tripped over it while slipping out the back of the building."

"Really?" David shook his head. "What are the odds?"

"Not good ones." Cody read the texts over Tessa's shoulder. "What the hell is going on?"

"Why are you concerned with a human finding human bodies?" Councilman Adamson's voice came from the darkness at the other side of the room. He walked toward them, an odd look on his face. Tessa studied his features and realized he was really curious. Like her father, he was old. Like seriously old. He'd lived through centuries where humans were prey, as if they were ants scurrying about their day. He really didn't understand.

She waved her cell phone around in her hand and said, "He's a friend. A human friend. And he's in trouble. He warned us that several of the people in the house he lives in are gathering to discuss annihilating vampires. After news of the blood farm got out, many became afraid and angry. Some consider us the enemy and those that lost friends or family – they want revenge."

"And what the devil does that blood farm business have to do with this body?" Adamson asked. "Or even you?"

"Maybe nothing and maybe everything, because this nightmare is not over. You want it to be over so you can move on. But for many of the humans, they can't until they get closure."

"Well, they need to," he snapped. "We all lost loved ones. The only thing left to do is let this die down so we can forget about it."

Tessa studied him. Old and tired, he looked like he was done with the world. As if his longevity was a burden now and death a welcome release. And she understood. He'd loved Gloria. Maybe as her parents loved each other. If one of her parents had died, they'd have done everything they could to make the killer pay. They'd have wrought a terrible price for messing with their loved ones.

In Councilman Adamson's case, he'd killed Gloria himself. He'd already gotten his revenge. There was no one else to blame. Nowhere to direct his all-consuming anger. That there'd been no other choice didn't help. Gloria had been trying to kill him. And that betrayal was eating at him. He had no recourse for the pain in his soul. He'd already meted out the only punishment he could. And it wasn't enough. He wanted Gloria back, but he wanted the woman she had been or the one he thought she'd been.

And that was never going to happen.

Taking a chance, she said, "You can't take back what Gloria did or what you had to do, but you can help stop her poison from continuing."

He hissed and drew himself up tall and deadly, his eyes glowing with hate. "You dare talk to me about that? About something you know nothing about?"

Cody and David stepped up beside her. David said, "Yes, she does. So do I. And Cody. We were all her victims. I was there at the end when you killed her but if you hadn't, I would have."

"Just like we killed the other Councilmen involved in this mess. But it's not over," Tessa said coolly. "If you aren't going to step up and deal with this mess and clean out the dregs of those responsible, then we have to."

"How dare you call me out on this?"

Tessa glanced behind her. The front door was closed and although there were three of them, she didn't think they were going to get out without a fight. She resisted the urge to back up. Retreat wasn't an option here. Where the heck was Goran? They should have told him where they were going. "We didn't come here for a fight. We came to you for help."

"You are nothing and know nothing." His voice trembled rage. "You haven't even lived. How could you possibly understand?"

The front door burst open behind them. As one, they spun around as Goran charged, anger rippling across his face. His gaze swept across the three of their faces, as if counting to make sure they were all fine before settling on Adamson.

"And me, Adamson?" Goran snapped. "Do you think you are so special that no one else knows your pain?" He strode forward. "Including me?"

Surprised by Goran's unexpected arrival, Tessa wasn't watching Councilman Adamson's face when Goran spoke, and she was sorry she missed seeing that initial reaction. It might have helped her to understand the man more. As it were, it was as if seeing Goran's pain had drained the stuffing right out of him.

"You can't hide away from this one," Goran said. "I went to the Council looking for you. They told me they hadn't seen you since the mountain collapsed. Or shall I make it plainer –

since you killed Gloria."

Councilman Adamson turned away, his shoulders slumped and his head bowed.

His grief was palpable. Tessa hated to see him in pain like this.

Really? Why? Cody said derisively. *I got the distinct impression he was about to do some serious damage to us.*

We were pushing into his hideaway. Backed him into a corner. He was just lashing out like any animal in pain. She kept an eye on both Goran and Adamson. The differences just underlined what was wrong with Adamson. "His energy is definitely black. I just don't know if it's something other than those nasty drugs. Or if he was given them unknowingly over time."

David caught her low whispered words, shooting her a surprised look.

So did Goran. He spun. "What did you say?" he bellowed.

"Really Goran, we're all in the same space, I'm sure yelling isn't required," Councilman Adamson's voice sounded irritated and weary. Tessa figured that was better than not caring about anything.

"Tessa?" Goran waited impatiently.

She wasn't sure how to bring it up, but somehow he had the same black energy she'd been seeing at the mountain. "I know that this will sound insulting and I don't mean it that way, but your energy has the same blackness in it that the men on the vampire drugs had."

There, she'd done it. And damn if she didn't back up several steps as she waited for him to blow. After all, she'd accused him of possibly being one of them.

He stared at her. In a conversational tone, almost as if he

were talking to a dimwitted child, he said, "My energy? What are you talking about?" He glanced over at Goran. "I understand this is Serus's daughter and that's she's...troubled, but surely you don't let her go around talking like this?"

David snarled. "She's not troubled. And if she says your energy is full of blackness, then it is. I can't see it, but that doesn't mean it's not there."

"So what if it is? I'm depressed. Black sounds like a great color to me."

"And drugs?" she asked determinedly. "Are you taking enhancement drugs from the blood farm?"

Insulted, he curled his lip, prepared to blast her, when Goran stepped in. "She means it, Adamson. She's never been wrong yet."

He frowned, his gaze going from one to the other. "Seriously?"

As everyone nodded, he threw up his hands. "No, I haven't been taking any of those damn drugs. Why would I? Like Goran, I am one of the oldest ancients alive today. One of the originals. I don't need enhancements," he spat out.

Goran looked down at Tessa. "Then what is it?"

Tessa sighed. She figured she knew, but saying so was going to deliver another blow to a man that looked like he'd received too many already. "Is there any chance that Gloria might have been giving them to you somehow without you knowing?"

He glared at her.

She rushed in to add, "Any special blood she's been treating you to? Any medications she could have tampered with? Any creams, lotions you might use on a regular basis?" She winced at all the males looking at her in shock. She rolled her eyes, "Yes, I know that isn't likely, but Gloria was female and she might have given you all kinds of things that I don't know about. Are you sure there wasn't anything she made for you on a regular basis that you used or consumed?"

Silence.

He tilted his head then shook it. "I can't think of anything. I'm not on medications, and that whole concept disgusts me. I'd never have taken anything willingly. No." He shook his head. "You are wrong."

But she wasn't. She knew that. She tried once more. "No special drinks that you shared together?"

He frowned and glanced at the kitchen. "We often had blood coffees together."

Tessa winced. It was popular drink amongst the older set, but she couldn't imagine it for herself. "And who would make it?

"Normally she would. It's not hard. We kept the coffee in a special jar. I often make myself one when I'm alone."

"May I see it, please?"

"The jar?" He shrugged, then as if humoring a child, he said, "Whatever. It's over here."

He led the way to the kitchen. Tessa walked forward slowly, searching for energy that seemed odd or displaced. And found nothing. If Gloria was using the same drugs, she hadn't left any sign in this room. She might have been getting enhancements herself, but was more likely waiting until they were improved upon. But that didn't mean she wouldn't use her love as a lab rat. As Tessa remember all too well, the group had a particular fondness for vampire lab rats.

He opened a cupboard, removed something, and turned around with the jar in his hand. He held it up. "This is it."

Tessa stared at the jar and backed up one step then another step. "That," she said faintly, "is so poisonous I can feel it from here."

Cody placed a reassuring hand on her shoulder. "And you say you've been drinking that?"

Adamson frowned. "Every day for years. Since she's been gone, I've had several in her memory."

"So even now," Tessa said, "That she's dead and never to return, she's still killing you – a little bit every day."

THE COUNCIL CHAMBER filled with the humans to the point that more chairs had to be brought in. Rhia, more concerned than ever, watched as more than three dozen people showed up for today's meeting. Serus stood alert at her side. Sian smiled genially at everyone as they walked past, but the three of them hadn't made a move to sit down.

Talk about being overwhelmed by numbers. Councilman Smithson called to her. "Councilwoman Rhia and Serus, Sian, if you'd take your seats, please."

As one, the three moved to sit at the massive table. All three sat together.

"Now, Sian, if you could explain the purpose of this meeting."

Sian took a deep breath and explained about the rumblings and news that Taz had shared. There were a few gasps of surprise from a couple of the members but as a group, there was very little surprise.

Councilman Smithson said, "We've heard rumors. It is to be expected that some of our people are upset. Of course we don't condone vigilante justice."

"Or hiding those guilty of selling your own people."

The councilman frowned. "We are conducting an investigation into those claims. As we haven't had much time, I can't say how deep this goes or how many people may have been involved in that despicable act."

"If any," snapped a different member at the table. "We only have your word that humans have been involved."

"So of course you can produce the missing person files for the more than 1,000 victims we found hanging in the blood farm?" Rhia said smoothly.

The man's face turned a mottled red. "There could be any number of reasons why we can't find all of those. It's ridiculous to think any human would do such a thing to one of their own."

"Only we have proof that many have indeed done that to their own. Keep your blinders on if you wish." Rhia said in a scathing voice, "Or keep protesting so that I'm tempted to have your own family line and financials examined to see who's gone missing in your world."

A growing anger surrounded her at the table.

"This is at the highest level, people. I can guarantee you that at least five if not two dozen of you are involved in this hypocrisy," Rhia cried. "We didn't come her asking for your help to save us. We don't need it. But if you refuse to calm your people, we will defend ourselves."

The rumble spiked as several members jumped to their feet in protest.

She slammed her hand down on the table. "Are you all so young with short term memories that you've forgotten what life was like for you before? Sure you can burn us out, kill as many of us as you can. And you will never be free to live a normal life again," she said, fury building inside. "I want nothing more than to live a peaceful life." She glared at the angry faces staring back at her. "You don't have to calm your people. You don't have to look for the poison in your own midst. You can let this develop into a full-blown war. Maybe I will survive. Maybe I won't. But not one of you." And she stopped to look into everyone's eyes. "Not one of *you*...will."

   🍀

JARED DIDN'T KNOW what to do next. He'd bolted away from the group home as fast as he could. He had what little he owned in his backpack. The rest of his clothing was at his uncle's house.

As he walked down the sidewalk on the quiet street, he had to consider that. He could really use some more clothing. His big backpack would be helpful, his camera. There were a few mementos he'd like to have of his father. There wasn't much option but to go and ask for his possessions back or sneak inside and take back what was his. He'd hoped that both his aunt and uncle would have been placed under arrest by now, but he had the feeling that wasn't going to be the case.

Still, his uncle worked the morning shift and shouldn't be at the house. As school wouldn't start for a long time yet, Jared wondered at the sensibility of going and retrieving his stuff. He didn't want to face his uncle again. So now might be his only option. If his uncle had been arrested, for all Jared knew the house and its contents would be confiscated by the Council and sold to go to their coffers. His uncle certainly didn't deserve any of it. Or his aunt.

He also had his own future to think about. He doubted he had a job any longer after not being able to show up for the last couple of shifts. Although his boss was a good man, it was hard to ignore an absentee employee. And that meant the little bit of money Jared had saved wasn't going to go far. He needed clothes. As far as a place to live, maybe he could make a deal with one of his buddies' families. Work in exchange for room and board. At least until he finished school. Something that was looking to be further away than ever.

Shit. Determined to regain what was his after a quick assessment of his meager worldly goods, he turned in the direction of his uncle's house. It was only a couple blocks away. In the early morning light, the sleepy town looked right and cheerful as if nothing bad could ever happen here.

He snorted. Talk about deceptive. This place was full of intrigue. And once again, he was in the middle of it.

❧ ❦

IAN BOUNDED OFF the bed at the sound of yelling and cars racing. At the window, he watched men running all over the place. On the road, he watched a small maroon car peeling down the road. It was going way too fast to be healthy. If that driver had done something – anything to piss these assholes off – Ian would cheer the driver on.

It turned a corner, wrapping around the hill below the hospital, and he caught a better glimpse of the vehicle and just an impression of the driver.

Christ. That was Wendy.

Trying to escape these assholes.

Ian started cursing as his blood was alternately frozen with fear and heated with rage. They were after his girl. That meant she'd been here and hadn't been allowed to see him. At least, that was the best reason he wanted to contemplate for what was going on here. If she'd been taken hostage earlier and had just now escaped, he'd go crazy thinking about what they'd done to her while he'd slept.

Stupid. That's what he was. He'd had an opportunity to escape earlier and had been worried about not having pants.

He slapped himself up the side of his head. Idiot. He could have gotten pants from somewhere. Hell, the damn techs here wore scrub-like uniforms. He could have knocked anyone out and taken them.

His gaze never left the car as it burnt through the pavement to escape.

Then he saw a flier soaring in the sky. In the early morning light? *A daylight flier.*

Wendy was no longer safe. A flier would track her home.

Ian slammed his fist against the window frame and felt something give in his back...and with his paralyzed wings.

Hope flared inside. Maybe the paralysis that doctors were talking about wasn't permanent. There was only one way to find out. He went to work testing the theory.

CHAPTER 10

T ESSA WAITED OUTSIDE on the small porch. The front door stood open behind her. The Council had sent someone to retrieve the coffee and search the rest of Councilman Adamson's house. She hadn't gone looking for anything else suspicious. Now that they knew what to look for, the lab techs could find anything else.

She glanced at her watch. "Crap." She called behind her, "David, can you give me a lift to school?"

"Sure. Is it time?" He walked over to the front door. "We're going to make a dash for the car."

Tessa walked to the car. "David, throw me the keys and I'll turn on the SunGard." With the keys in hand, she walked over to the car, unlocked the doors, and switched on the UV protection so any vamp could drive. Then she slid over the middle and waited. Goran stepped out on the front porch beside the guys, hollering and waving his arms.

She peered through the windows trying to figure out what was going on. Before she had a chance to get out and find out, they were all racing to the car, coats over their heads.

"Change of plans," David said as he hopped into the front driver's seat and slammed the door closed. The other two scrambled inside. David turned the car on and pulled out fast, gravel spitting behind them as David drove at top speed. "Mom is in trouble."

She gasped. "What?"

"Serus contacted Dad," Cody said. "Your mother kinda lost it and basically threatened the Human Council to smarten up. If not, she said she'll make sure they don't survive the next round of this war."

Tessa gasped. "She wouldn't have done that without a good reason."

"Except she's not exactly been herself lately." Cody's comment had both David and Tessa turning to stare at him.

He shrugged. "Just saying."

"Serus said they need reinforcements. So we're all going. I don't know how many they are up against, but with Sian pregnant and Serus worn out and your mother still recovering from the heavy drugs, they are not in the best position to fight. Humans are easy, but if there are any there with the same weapons of war that those vamps in the mountain had, they are in trouble."

Tessa brooded. She knew her mom was really struggling right now. On many levels. She could easily see her losing it if the humans on the Human Council didn't appear to believe her or seem willing to help.

Tessa had nothing against the humans, but with the crap that Jared was going through and the stuff that anyone associated with the victims of the blood farm had been through, she wouldn't be surprised if there was trouble at every corner for the next several months.

The people needed to see that the two councils were going to step up and make sure the perpetrators were caught and punished. The Vampire Council was working on their side of the issues, but was the Human Council?

"School or home?" David asked.

"Mom, always. If it turns out to be nothing, I'll still make it to school." She added, "What about Council Adamson? Is he going to help?"

Goran spoke from the back seat. "He's gathering up some more men. There are more than three dozen humans attending that meeting. If something blows, we don't want any of them getting free."

"Shit," Tessa said half under her breath.

David shot her a worried look, then hit the gas and sent the car careening around the corner. She smiled. If he had anything to do with this, they'd have been at the Council Hall already.

Goran spoke from the back seat. "Serus says it's bad. He's about to take a step that will forever finish the treaty. He's giving them a small chance but if they attack Rhia, he says it's over and he'll take out as many as he can."

Tessa froze. Her mind jumped from horrible option to horrible option.

"This was supposed to be a meeting," Cody said in alarm. "What went wrong?"

Tessa spun around to see Goran's faraway look. "He's talking to Dad now. How far away are we, David?"

"Five minutes. Maybe less."

"Is there anyone else out there we can call for reinforcements?" Tessa wondered out loud. "We need to make sure the Human Council knows that they can't hurt Mom and Dad without reprisals."

"I think Rhia actually threatened to make sure no one in the Human Council survived." Goran grinned.

Yes, someone had said something to set her mom off in a big way. Tessa shuddered. "Anyone who sees her gentle features might make the mistake of thinking she's just another pretty face once, but never twice," she said. "She doesn't threaten. She makes promises. And she'll be damned if she's going to go out of this life without making sure she keeps that promise."

Inside, her gut had locked down, and thoughts of school and everything else had fled her mind. Both her parents were in trouble. Enough was enough. She didn't want to hurt any humans, but if they killed anyone in her family…

Not one person in the Council Hall would escape her wrath.

❧ ❧

JARED APPROACHED HIS old home warily. The last time he was here, he'd gotten a hell of a shock. He didn't want to meet his family. Ever again. Unless they were in prison and he was on the visitor's side. Even then, he couldn't imagine any reason to see them. The house was dark and quiet. He frowned at the vehicle in the parking spot. His uncle should have been at work. Why wasn't he?

Or had the car broken down and he'd gotten a ride to work? He could also have been fired. That put a smile on his face. He slipped to the back door and peered inside. No sign of life anywhere. Should he go in? He really wanted to grab his stuff.

He studied the old clapboard exterior of the house. It was in desperate need of paint. And new windows. Likely new doors. His uncle may have gotten a chunk of money for selling his brother and Jared, but Jared had no idea what he could have done with it. As long as he'd known him, there'd never been obvious cash. Maybe his uncle was hoarding his money in the bank, or knowing the old bastard, under the damn mattress he slept on.

Still, if his uncle was home and he caught Jared inside, then what? He was entitled to get his clothes, wasn't he? Sure he was. His uncle had done him wrong. Not the other way around. As he thought about it, he could feel the stirrings of justified anger. Maybe he should step inside and actually accuse his uncle. Let all that hurt and anger find a target – the right target. He'd just have to make sure that he didn't let that anger get out of control. It would be just Jared's luck that he'd be the one to end up behind bars.

As the drive to take his uncle's neck in his bare hands and squeeze the life out of him became too strong to control, he realized he didn't dare confront the asshole.

Not yet. Maybe never. If that was the case, then he wanted his shit back. He might not be able to get the revenge he was due, but he'd be damned if he left behind what was rightfully his.

He tested the doorknob. It opened easily in his hand. His uncle never did give a damn about security. Maybe because he was already sleeping with the devil.

In the kitchen, Jared stopped by the first counter. The coffee maker sat on the corner. He reached out a hand and touched the pot. It was off and cold to the touch.

His uncle wasn't even up yet. How could that be?

Then Jared relaxed. The bastard had run. It was the only explanation. Happily, Jared realized he wasn't going to see his uncle at all. His nerves slid down to a normal level and he walked quietly to his room. He pushed the door open to find it completely trashed.

His mattress was half off the bed, the bedding in a heap on the floor. The drawers had been pulled from his dresser and dumped on the floor. The closet door was open, and it appeared that everything he'd ever stuffed into the back and forgotten about had been hauled out and tossed in the center.

Why?

What could he have that anyone could possibly want? He didn't have any money. Neither did he have anything worth any decent money. He was a kid. What could he possibly own of value?

Or was this about the damn blood farm? Were the people involved afraid that he'd kept some incriminating evidence? Something that would get them in trouble?

He hadn't.

But he wished he did.

He stared around at the remnants of the last decade and swore softly. Not wanting to be there any longer than necessary, he switched from shock to gathering up what he needed. His backpack, although turned inside out, was whole. He stuffed it with his clothes, quickly sorting as he went through the mess, collecting everything useable in just a few minutes.

His heart slammed against his chest and a film of sweat formed on his skin. He couldn't get rid of the feeling that he needed to get the hell out of here and fast.

He peered around the bedroom door and stepped into the hallway. There wasn't a sound in the house. It wasn't normal. His uncle always had the radio on, or the computer was always playing something. The silence sounded wrong.

Felt wrong.

He stared at his uncle's bedroom door. He should not open it.

Yeah, he should, said his conscience.

He really didn't want to. So what if there was something wrong with the bastard? After what he'd done, he deserved to be ill.

But he wasn't his uncle.

And the state he'd found his bedroom meant someone had come in here that wasn't friendly.

Christ, his headache was getting worse the more he tried to sort this out.

He groaned. Given that his uncle had a connection to the blood farm and given the mess in his room and the fact that there was no sign of his uncle...

He walked silently to his uncle's doorway and put an ear to the wood. Not a sound.

Shit.

He turned the knob and opened it just enough that he could look around the edge to survey the room. The curtains were closed. The room was dark and gloomy.

And the aroma...

His gaze zeroed in on the bed... and his uncle lying fully dressed on top of the covers. Jared's heart slammed against his ribs. He closed his eyes briefly. *Please don't let this be another one.* He hated his uncle but...

He pushed the door open wider and stepped to the bed-side to make sure. "Uncle?"

No answer. He gulped hard, his gut churning, and turned his head away from the sight of his asshole uncle lying with his head twisted the wrong way.

Oh, his uncle was dead all right. But he didn't die from natural causes.

This was his third dead body today. And the only one to make him squeamish.

Bile rolled through him and crawled up his throat. He spun and ran as fast as he could down the stairs, blasting out the back of the kitchen door and over to the bushes lining the property to the neighbor's side.

And his stomach emptied.

ॐ ॐ

SERUS STARED AT the humans who dared to piss Rhia off. Chances were good they were heading into a bloodbath that would mark another massive change in the life of the humans.

Were they really ready for the chaos they were about to wreak? He'd gladly die at Rhia's side fighting these bastards, but what really pissed him off was that he'd asked these same men to help them. To preserve their way of life.

He glanced over at his beloved wife and realized she was as close to losing control as he'd ever seen her. Since the last war. And she'd been a warrior like none other then.

She had the softness and compassion to save those that were in need, but the killer in her would destroy any and all that threatened her or her family. And he'd include the pregnant Sian in that group right now as well.

The humans might think that they had the upper hand in numbers, but they had no idea about the danger they were in. Not one of these humans would walk free if anyone laid a hand on the three of them.

He heard car doors slam and sounds of running feet.

Human or Vamp? He could use a few more vamps, but he didn't want his kids involved. If he was going down, he wanted to know that his kids were safe.

For once.

The door rattled. He growled. The damn thing was locked.

Even as he judged the distance he had to cross so he could open it himself, the doors exploded.

And Goran and Cody rushed in.

Serus grinned. Perfect.

Then he saw David. Shit. As the males spread out, damn

if his errant daughter didn't stroll in as if she was the queen of the place. Her eyes assessing, she scanned the place, her gaze coming to rest on Sian, her mother, and finally him. Relief filled her face and she beamed a smile his way.

"Nice to see it was a false alarm, Dad."

He groaned. Only his daughter could take the knife edge of tension and interject some humor.

He sighed. "Tessa, why aren't you in school?"

❧ ❧

WENDY DROVE FAST until she hit the main road to town. The tears had stopped finally and now her mind worked furiously. She was still alone, and as far as she could tell, she was not being followed. She figured she was safe – for the moment. If she could get somewhere in a heavily crowded place and ditch the car, she might stay safe.

There was only one place to do that right now. The mall. She parked close to the front, and jacket over her head, she bolted for the front door. Inside the entrance, she stood, shaking so hard she wasn't sure she could take another step. She stared around, realizing she'd come to the vamp mall. Was this the right place to be? If she'd gone to the human mall, she'd surely have been safe. Except she stood out as a vamp. And that might have been worse. She envied Tessa for being able to travel wherever she wanted and at whatever time she wanted.

She was really the future of vamps. Most looked at her as a throwback, but in essence, she was what every vamp wanted to be. No wonder the nasty doctors had wanted her blood.

And that just brought her to Ian. Why would they want to keep him? He'd been drugged so many times, he was barely able to recover.

Her eyes closed briefly as the answer hit her. He had had so many drugs and had turned, albeit briefly, before Rhia had knocked him out. What if they were trying to bring that asshole Ian back? He was already on the edge of being there.

She strolled to a corner of the mall where they had large comfortable seats. With her back to a wall where she could keep an eye on everyone, she pulled out her cell phone and called David.

His family had to help.

There was no one else she could trust.

⤝ ⤞

IAN MANAGED TO get the window open enough to lean out and see what was going on. Thankfully, he was in the shade, but the sunlight was coming out strongly across the courtyard. There was no way fliers should be out now. Not unless they could withstand light like Tessa. Like the ones involved in these nasty experiments.

Was that what this place was all about? He'd never been here before, but he presumed that Rhia and everyone else had been brought here to the same hospital, too. If not here, then where?

The sun broke through the clouds and hit the building beside him. He had maybe another half hour before the rays came inside. His old room had black curtains to keep the sun out. This one didn't.

He couldn't go after Wendy until darkness fell.

He had no way to get out of this room, either. He stopped at that train of thought. He hadn't actually tried the door handle. Maybe it wasn't locked or maybe it wasn't a crazy secure lock. He'd heard about Tessa opening the locked door in Moltere's mansion with a credit card. He didn't have one of those, but even though he was tired, he still had incredible strength. He frowned, staring down at his bare feet and hairy legs. At least he used to. He had no idea what the drugs had taken from him. He still couldn't move his wings. He closed his eyes and tried to ruffle them. He strained as hard as he could, felt his wings begin to unfurl, then it stopped. He shuddered. Sweat beaded his skin and his stupid gown was soaked – from just that little bit of effort.

Yet he'd managed to move his wings. Sure, it was just a little and nowhere near enough to fly away from here. But they were responding. And that was a first.

He just needed to keep pushing it and gain a little more motion each time. He could do this.

Then once the darkness fell, he'd squeeze out that damn window and get the hell away from here.

CHAPTER 11

T ESSA KEPT HER voice light and calm as she spoke to her father, her gaze lightning fast and assessing. The atmosphere was twisted with tension. No doubt they'd arrived just in time. She cast a slow glance at the group of humans glaring at the new arrivals. The balance of power had shifted, and no one knew what to do.

A huge crash had her spinning around. Shards of glass filled the air and sunlight beamed into the center of the room.

Her gaze landed on a large male as he smiled at her and tossed a rock from one hand to the other.

Tessa snorted. As if. And stepped right into the middle of the pool of the sunlight. "Thanks, this really brightens up the place."

Shock and anger wiped the jubilant looks off the humans' faces.

"You don't burn," cried out one of the leaders.

She turned to face him. And realized something else – there was a black shadow around him. She stalked toward him. He quivered in place but held his ground. She smiled.

"No, I don't. But maybe you do." She grabbed him by the shoulders and tossed him into the light. And winced as he screamed in terror and his skin started to sizzle and burn.

He jumped out of the light and stared down at his skin in horror. "What did you do to me?" he shrieked.

She said, contempt oozing from her voice. "*I* did nothing. It's the deal you made with the blood farm assholes."

The man stared at her in horror. He stared around at the others watching and shook his head. "I didn't do anything," he cried out. "Honest."

"Then why did the light singe your skin?" asked one of the men standing closest to him. "How could that possibly happen? And..." He turned to glare at Tessa, "How did you know?"

Tessa stared at him. How did she know? *It was the darkness in his energy.* She stepped back to study the rest of the Human Council.

So much black oozed around all of them. Surely not? She turned to check on the rest of the humans milling around in fear and confusion.

She pointed at the guy nursing his burns. "You stand over there." She waved her arm to indicate where he should go. Then pointed to the two men behind him. "And you and you."

Taking her time, she wandered around the rest of the group, studying their blended energies. The one guy standing off to one side appeared normal. She motioned him to a different corner of the room. By the time she finished the first group, she had an almost even split of humans in the two groups.

Then she approached the largest group.

"I am not moving," snapped the first man.

Tessa shrugged. "Cody, this guy needs to go into that group." And she pointed to the group of humans with dark energy. Then she turned her back on him.

He screamed. "Get the hell away from m—" only he was flying across the room before he'd finished speaking.

Goran protested. "Hey, how come Cody gets to have all the fun?"

Tessa laughed and pointed to the two men beside her. "You can assist these two over to the same group."

"What do you think you are doi—"

They sailed through the air to land behind the others.

Tessa smiled at one man, and he damn near raced to the group. She caught him by the arm and said gently, "You belong over there." She pointed to the smaller group of humans without the black poison in their systems.

He took off in the right direction. With Cody and Goran's assistance, she finished separating the last group until she came to the last three men standing close together. She stopped. "Oh, this is interesting."

"What's interesting?" Goran asked, bending in place as if trying to see what she was seeing.

"They all have a similarity to each other, but they're different from either of the other groups."

She walked around them. Her curiosity was piqued. She hadn't seen anything like this before. Each had a black hole in their energy, but it was like a cylinder at the base of their spine all the way through to their lower belly. As if they had a hollowed-out spot.

"Very interesting."

"What? What are you doing?" The man's voice quavered. "Why are you separating us into these groups? What do the groups mean?" And damn it he didn't sound liked he'd crap his pants if she said boo.

She pulled back. She didn't want to scare them like this. She hadn't thought what her actions would look like from their perspective. The other group without the black energy was the calmest. Angry, but in an affronted way. Then again, they were innocent.

The group with black energy was a problem. They were either receiving enhancements willingly or unwillingly, possibly being poisoned like Councilman Adamson.

And then there was the group in front of her. There was something odd about the three men. She stepped back a few more steps so she could see their full energy. The blackness was more a murky gray black. As if they had just started a treatment perhaps.

One of the Councilmen from the normal group spoke up. "Now we're in the groups you wanted. Tell us what they mean."

She shrugged. "I can tell you that your group has had no vampire enhancements. And aren't being poisoned – at least not by vampire poison."

Shocked cries filled the air. When it calmed slightly, she continued, "That makes you the more objective of the humans here."

The Councilman stared at her. "Of course I'm innocent. Wait…" he stared at the other two groups. "You mean they aren't?"

"Tessa, what are you doing?" Rhia asked, her tone disbelieving and shocked.

Tessa spun around in time to see her father grab her mother's arms and tug her closer to him. He bent and whispered into her ear.

Rhia turned a hard assessing glance at Tessa but stayed quiet.

Good.

"This group," Tessa walked toward the men whose energy had filled with blackness. She studied their faces and realized many were going to be like the army soldier. It was possible they had taken something innocently and not known about the enhancements. It was also possibly a scenario like Gloria and Councilman Adamson. Speaking of which...

She frowned. "How many of you are married?"

All but two lifted their hands. "Let me clarify a little further, how many of you are happily married?"

Two more men put their hands down, and the remaining four stood slightly apart. She asked, "Do any of you four have any business dealings with the vampire community?"

Everyone shook their heads. "Do any of you belong to the military?"

More head shakes.

She frowned.

"Tessa?"

She looked at Cody. "They are as chock full of poison as the army sergeant was. I'm trying to find out why."

"Poison? What are you talking about?" The man standing in the front of her asked. "I've been feeling like shit for weeks, but no one has mentioned poison."

He tugged at his shirt collar. "I've even been to see the doctor, but he couldn't find anything wrong."

"Me too," said one of the men behind him.

"And I spoke to one," cried a third.

Tessa looked at the fourth man. "Did you go, too?"

He shook his head. "No. Don't like them. But my brother-in-law is one, so I spoke to him." She nodded and asked gently, "And who is your brother-in-law?"

"Jensen. Dr. Jensen."

"Hey, that's my doctor."

"And mine," shouted the other two in unison.

Tessa turned to the Councilman in the clear energy group. "I highly suggest you pick up Dr. Jensen and question him about running experiments on humans on behalf of the rogue vampire group."

Cries broke out. And suddenly, everyone wanted Tessa to tell them what was happening to them.

She bared her fangs and hissed as they surrounded her until a warm hand squeezed her shoulder and Cody stepped up to her side. "Back off. She'll answer questions, but one at a time."

Thanks, Cody.

As always. He paused then added, *Are you serious, all these men have been poisoned?*

I'm not sure about all. But those four, yes. She turned to look at the four men with black energy who were not related to Dr. Jensen. "Do any of you have anything to do with Dr. Jensen?"

All four shook their heads. She pointed her question at the two men who weren't happily married. "Have your wives gone to the doctor for you? Said she'd drop by at the drugstore or pharmacy any time recently?"

One shrugged and one nodded. She smiled sadly at the one who nodded. "I'm sorry, but in your case I'm afraid your wife will need to be looked at closely."

His jaw twitched. Then he gave a curt nod and stepped off to the side. She looked at the next man. "And you?"

"I don't know. I'm not happily married, but she wouldn't kill me. I'm the breadwinner. She has no money at all."

"And your girlfriend?" Tessa hated to bring up his private issues in a group like this, but the man's energy was covered with more than one female energy. "Does she need you, too?"

He winced. "No. She's more likely to try and kill me. I broke it off with her a couple of months ago. It went on far too long and wasn't a good scene."

Tessa frowned as she tried to sort through the old and newer layers of black and gray energy. "The poisoning may have started months ago, but it's still fresh in your system, so if it was her, you're continuing to take the poison since you two split."

He frowned at her, and then a dawning awareness and a look of horror took over his face. "She's a nurse. I have a skin condition and she refilled the prescription for me. I use it daily."

"Then that's where your investigation should start. With that cream." And then that bitch, only Tessa didn't add that part. He already knew what to do next.

There were still two men in the group, but Tessa couldn't pinpoint the exact cause with them even though she'd tried. Deciding that the humans could figure that out, she turned to the oddball men with the cone of blackness. And realized how deeply ingrained that blackness was. This wasn't superficial in any way.

She snorted. "This other group was all being poisoned, and yet you three are poisoning yourselves. Every one of you is taking – willingly – vampire enhancements."

And all three launched themselves at her.

❧ ❧

RHIA SURGED FORWARD, only to be tugged back to Serus's side. "Damn it, let me go. Tessa is in trouble."

Serus laughed. "And this is why you don't see Tessa as she really is now." He grabbed her stubborn chin and turned her around so she could see Tessa. The first man was on the floor, out cold. As she watched in shock, Tessa waved her arms and the two remaining men dropped beside them.

"What on earth," Rhia whispered. "What is she doing?"

She knew she sounded dazed and slow, but she didn't understand what her daughter had just done. "And how?

"See, we've been watching her this week as she grew and figured out what she could do and what she couldn't." He pointed at Tessa. "This stuff, she just learned on the last day. It's got something to do with her slicing through their energy and creating a disruption to their pattern or some stupid thing." He leaned closer as Tessa knelt beside the men and did a reverse kind of motion. "Now watch."

The first man woke up and bolted backwards. Fear tightened his features even as his Adam's apple bobbed in panic. "Whaaa...t did you do to me?" he cried, his panicked gaze shifting from her to the other men on the ground and back to Tessa.

"Maybe the better question is what your association with the vampire clan is." She took a threatening step toward him. "And the truth. We've had enough damage from your greediness."

"They promised we'd be bigger. Stronger. Better," he cried out.

"Bigger, better than who? Other humans? Do you think you'll ever be bigger or better than vamps? Look what I just did. Do you think getting an enhancement is going to change that?"

"They said the vampire clans were shifting. Becoming weaker. That we had to be on their side or else we'd become one of the farm animals."

She paused at that and turned to look at the other two men. She walked closer, bent over, and waved her hand so their energies blended again. Both men groaned, waking slowly. She gave them a moment, then asked, "Were you also in on the procuring process to replenish the blood farms?"

One man shook his head. "No. I was just trying to stay alive after the vampire war was over. They said we'd be harvested if we didn't join them. We weren't good enough to join right now if we didn't have the enhancements." His voice faded away. He stared up at the ceiling. "I don't feel so good."

"That's because the enhancements are unstable. They were also built on vampire DNA, not intended for humans specifically. But *adapted* for humans. Not that they care if you survive or not."

A wave of depression settled on his face. He sighed. "I didn't see a choice."

She pursed her lips and stared at him. "Besides being a traitor of your species, what else do you know that can help the humans find the other traitors?"

"Names and places. I'm one of the accountants." A whisper of hope lit up his eyes.

"Shut up, Lew," said one of the men. "She doesn't know anything. Fucking bit—" and he went flying.

Thanks, Cody.

Any time.

She glanced down at Lew, who seemed to be waiting for some pronouncement. "And you'll help them capture the others? Be fully cooperative and help us clean out the poison in both our societies?"

"God, yes," he exclaimed. "I only went this way because it seemed like there was no other option."

Tessa nodded. "I'd wondered."

"Tessa?" David asked. He'd stepped up to her side. "What are you doing?"

"I'm thinking we could use this one." She shifted her hand to Lew and then to a second man. "And maybe him."

"Hey, what about me. I can help," protested the third man who Cody had flung to the side.

"You're not my problem. That's up to the Human Council. As far as I'm concerned, you're a dead man walking."

"What? Why? What are you talking about?"

"Well, the vamps will know that you were cornered, and very soon they'll come looking. Did I mention there was talk of other blood farms? Ones we didn't find?"

He collapsed to his knees. "No! You have to help me."

"No, I don't." As she went to turn away, she stopped at the accountant and did something strange. She reached out a hand and tugged at a cloud of blackness from the man's belly. "There's some kind of implant here."

He gasped. The others gathered around. Rhia couldn't believe what she was seeing. Not only was Tessa in complete command of the situation, she was the only one who was. Cody and David both deferred to her, and damn if Goran didn't as well. He stood at the back, the silent, surly watch guard, just hoping someone would make a wrong move.

She missed what Tessa did, but suddenly she held up a small metal pill-sized object. She handed it off to David casually.

He held it up. "This looks like the implant you had, Tessa."

Rhia stiffened. "What?" she said furiously.

Serus called to David. "Likely the same lab."

Tessa stood in front of Lew, and damn if he didn't open his eyes and smile gratefully at her. "Thank you. There's been pain there for weeks."

Cody reached down and hauled the man to his feet. "Remember, your agreement. If you don't, I'll be sure to bring Tessa back for a visit."

Instead of cringing, the man said, "I'd like that." He smiled at Tessa and reached out a hand. "Thank you."

Rhia stared in shock as her daughter shook hands with one of the men who'd attacked her.

She said in a furious whisper to her husband. "What the hell has happened here? Where is my daughter? What have all of you done to her?"

~ⅎ ⅋~

NOW THAT THINGS were calming down, David pulled out his phone and checked for messages. He'd had it on mute since before arriving at Councilman Adamson's. They'd left so fast he hadn't had a chance to change the settings. Crap. Four messages. All from Wendy.

He listened to the first one, spun, and grabbed Cody by the shoulder. "Listen," he ordered and held the phone up for both of them to hear.

Cody's face turned from surprise, to shock, and finally fear.

"Oh no. Not Ian."

"What about Ian?" Goran said, nodding at the phone. "Is that boy in trouble again?

David nodded and set his cell phone to replay the messages then called his parents over. Tessa stood behind him. When everyone was within hearing distance, he replayed all the messages. Wendy's teary voice filled the air as she tried to explain what happened and where she was. She ended the last line with, "Please hurry."

David immediately called her back. When she answered the phone, he ran a tired hand down over his face. "Wendy, I'm on the way. Stay exactly where you are and make sure you can be seen in public. If anyone tries anything, scream like hell. We'll be there in ten minutes. Got it?"

"Yes," she said, her voice trembling. "Thank heavens you called. Please hurry."

"We're on the way."

David closed the phone. "Okay, this is bad. In a big way. We have to get Wendy, and now I'm terrified about Jewel. She's in the same place as Ian."

∂ ৎ

WENDY SLUMPED INTO the big scoop chair. Her heart was slamming against her chest when two men sat down not far from her. She'd been prepared to ignore them. They were young, after all. Then they'd started pointing and making snide comments.

As a single lone female, that was always a problem, but the mall should have afforded her some protection. Instead, she was wondering if she hadn't played into the assholes' hands. The place was almost deserted. Then again, most vamps would be sleeping or safe in their houses right now. However, like many human teens, the young vamps hung around to look cool. Or to look for trouble.

She didn't want any trouble. In fact, she'd be happy to never have any more trouble ever again.

She checked her phone. Nothing new. Once again, she searched the area. No one she knew. A few people came and went. No females. And that made her leery. There should be female vamps here. Shouldn't there?

She sank lower into her chair. And closed her eyes.

Hurry, David.

She didn't dare think about Ian. Or what those assholes

could be doing to him. It was the endless unanswered questions swirling in her head about what and why that was killing her. And the thought that Ian might already be dead.

Another young male joined the two that had been sitting and watching her.

This was getting scary. She sent another text to David. The last thing she wanted was to have her friends walk into a trap.

CHAPTER 12

TESSA BOWED HER head against the oncoming headache. She knew the blood farm cleanup would be a bitch, but she hadn't really thought to be involved at this level. She'd been devastated to be left behind at home while her family had taken off to mop up. She'd hoped to be included in a minor way. That was it. And yet it seemed like it was once again on their shoulders to sort this mess out.

Well, she'd done what she could here.

Good thing. Ian was next. No – Wendy. She didn't know how many people were at the mall for Wendy to hide amongst, and that was a problem. The vampire mall wouldn't be busy right now given that it was daylight outside, yet for that reason it had an underground entrance like so many of their social and business venues.

Tessa glanced around and caught the eye of the Councilman she'd deemed to be free of the black energy earlier. She walked over. "We have to go. Can you handle these guys?" She motioned to the various humans around them.

He nodded. "We've got this. Your parents came to ask for our help to stop the rioting. We see now that it's partly our fault too and will do what we can to help."

He held out his hand. She shook it. Her parents stepped forward and shook his hand as well. Sian said, "We can coordinate our methods to make this as clean and least damaging for both our people."

Tessa left them talking and headed over to David, who was already walking out the front door. "David, wait up."

"You stay here. I'm going to pick up Wendy. I need to take her home. We can plan our next move from there."

Tessa waffled. She didn't know if she should go with him. Or go to the school and talk to the principal.

Cody made the decision for her. He said, "We all stay together, David. If the humans are rampaging, we shouldn't be separated."

"And our parents?" David asked.

Tessa stopped and turned back to see her parents in heavy discussion with Sian and the Councilman.

"They don't look ready to leave. Maybe they can get down to business now," Goran said, standing at the edge of the commotion. "Serus won't leave your mother, and I'm not leaving you kids. So that's how this gets divided."

Tessa shrugged. "Works for me.

David stood impatiently at the door. "Come on. We have to hurry." His phone rang at that moment. "It's Wendy." After answering it, he held it up for the others to hear her speak.

"David, where are you? There's a group of vamps hanging around here. I'm getting scared."

"We're on the way. Hold tight." He raced out to the car, yelling back. "Let's go."

Tessa followed him. They were in the car and racing down the street in seconds.

She hated to think of anything happening to Wendy. Thankfully the mall was close. They ripped into the underground parking lot and came to a screeching halt. She had the door open and was running toward the stairs when she heard the others call her.

"The elevators will be faster, Tessa." David called.

She shook her head. "Maybe, but they are more dangerous."

She was through the door and halfway up the first flight before she heard the others behind her. Once at the mall level, she walked quickly toward the spot Wendy said she'd be.

"Wait up, Tessa."

She turned and tossed Cody a big grin. "Why are you so slow?"

He grabbed her arms and said in a low voice, "Wendy texted again. She thinks the group is after her. Either waiting for someone else to arrive or waiting for more people to leave so they won't be noticed."

Tessa stopped and checked their position. Wendy should be just around the corner. Ahead, a group of three young males loitered. And damn if their energy wasn't completely black.

Tessa studied their faces. She didn't recognize any of them. *Cody, do you know these guys? They have to be your age. Have you seen them before? Their energy is black.*

Cody walked slowly forward to her side and studied them.

No. One maybe I've seen with Jacob, but not the other two.

Strolling along quietly as if looking at the store windows, Tessa wondered when the men would notice their presence.

They aren't very aware, are they? she asked mentally.

No. Maybe they are too young for this. Or just tired. Or... he sighed. *Maybe they have nothing to do with this mess and they are totally unconcerned. Not everyone is a bad guy.*

Do you think Wendy was imagining these guys?

Not necessarily. But remember in the blood farm after being chased? It seemed like every vamp we met after seemed to be against us. As if our perspective at the time was slanted.

Tessa did remember. She'd thought, *hoped,* that stage of looking at every vamp sideways was over.

David passed and walked around the corner, purpose in his step. The men sat up and watched.

Here we go, she said. *Asshole alert.*

The men stood up and followed David.

Tessa and Cody tracked them. She didn't know where Goran was, but he'd be around.

And likely show up when least expected.

❧ ❦

DAVID SPED PAST Tessa and Cody doing their mind thing. He couldn't stop the thread of tension running down his lean body. If Ian was in trouble, then Jewel was in trouble. And that he couldn't handle.

Tessa and Cody were safe together, so where the hell was Jewel? He'd texted her several times since hearing from Wendy and so far nothing. He'd tried calling, but it went straight to voice mail. He'd also tried to contact Ian.

Next he planned to contact Motre. Many of his friends had been in that same damn hospital. Although none of the others that David knew about had been drugged the same number of times that Ian and Jewel had. If he wasn't so suspicious, he'd think they'd kept the two of them in longer for more testing. Now he figured they wanted to see the results of their earlier work.

David noticed the three punks lounging in the chairs. There were young males always hanging out here. With a game shop and an all-night blood club around the corner, Wendy couldn't possibly have picked a more dangerous area to be alone. She wasn't as striking as Jewel or as unusual looking at his sister, but Wendy was one of those curvaceous females that always had men sniffing around her.

That Ian had won that particular contest still surprised David. Then again, maybe not. Ian had gone quiet with more excuses to not go out these last few months. David had been grateful as it had given him time with Jewel, so he hadn't paid much attention to what the others in the group were doing. Of course, Tessa had noticed.

Up ahead, he saw a small collection of scoop chairs. But no sign of Wendy. Shit.

Wendy stood up from where she'd been hiding on the far side of the last chair. "Oh thank God, David. I thought you'd never get here."

She threw herself into his arms. "Please tell me you didn't come alone?" she said nervously, her gaze locking on something behind his shoulder.

David turned to see the three punks standing behind them. He curled a lip. He hoped they tried something. He was in the mood to tear them apart.

Behind them, his sister and Cody moved into position. David grinned and called out. "There's enough to share. Don't you be getting greedy."

Cody called back. "Nah, they are all mine."

The three men stopped and looked from one group to the other. One man swallowed convulsively, his huge Adam's apple bobbing with his words. He tried to back away from the other two, his hands out in front.

"Hey, no need for talk like that." He motioned to the door in front of Wendy. It was one of the exits that led outside. "We were just leaving."

David snarled. "Then go. We'll watch to make sure you

make it."

The one man furrowed his brow, then took several steps forward.

"Hardy, don't be an idiot."

The third man never said a word. He spun around and grabbed Tessa.

Then put a knife at her throat.

$$\approx \ll$$

CODY HATED SURPRISES. And not seeing the third man make his move was one of those unpleasant ones.

He growled and stepped toward Tessa. *Don't move, Tessa.*

She closed her eyes. *I wasn't planning on it, but now that you mention it…*she lifted her hand to grab the arm around her throat.

Cody watched, wondering if she could do that energy trick.

No, I can't get to his energy from this position.

Take it easy, Cody said. *We'll get out of this.*

Yes, we will, but I'm still pissed at getting caught. She glared at him when his lips twitched.

I didn't even see him make his move, Cody admitted.

Yeah, he was fast. Too fast. Tessa said somberly. *He's on enhancements. In his case, I'd have to say they are working.*

Great. Cody shifted his mind to the possibilities when the asshole spoke.

"This is how we're going to play this. We want the other girl. And you want this one. So we'll swap. Straight across."

Do it, Tessa whispered into his mind. *As soon as I have a better position, I can take this one out.*

Cody hated to do so, but regardless of what agreement he

made, he'd never let these assholes leave with Tessa. "Fine," he said, his voice cold and edgy. These guys had no idea how close they'd come to death. But they'd find out. In about three seconds.

"Move over to the other male. And send the female over to me."

"Ha. You three back up," Cody snapped. "Both women can step into the middle and then move to each side."

The man seemed to consider it.

He stepped back as if to follow instructions.

And Cody watched his forearm tighten. The bastard was going to slice Tessa.

I know. I just need...

And damn if her nails didn't elongate and stab into the man's arm.

The man screamed, the knife falling from his arm as she spun and did her weird hand thingy. Cody jumped the guy with the big Adam's apple. He went down without a fight. *Damn it.* He hadn't meant to knock him out. He spun around to find David holding his male in a headlock on the floor. *Yes.* Now they had someone to answer questions.

Tessa, on the other hand, hadn't bothered with the niceties. It looked like her guy was dead.

"Damn it, Tessa. I wanted to kill that guy," he complained.

She crouched beside the downed man. "Do I let him live?" She turned to look at the other two. "It's different now that we're not in the mine."

"He's big in the organization."

"But not everyone had a choice, so we'll give him one chance." Tessa nodded, reached down, and waved her hand quickly. The guy gasped for breath.

"Of course, I might have left it too long," she said. "There could be some permanent damage."

The injured man continued to gasp for air, and then he shuddered and opened his eyes. He focused on her. And groaned. "You must be Tessa."

She curled her lips. "And you must have a death wish."

He shuddered. "I think I just stared death in the face."

"You did, and I brought you back. Don't make me regret it."

"Then you should have killed me," he said quietly. "Now my father will just have to do the job."

Cody walked over to stand behind Tessa. "Who is your father?"

"Councilman Baker. I'm Vince."

Tessa shook her head. "He was one of the Councilmen we weren't sure about, Adamson brought him in to help early on. Him and Councilman Wilson."

"They are running the hospital together."

Cody reached down and hauled the kid to his feet. "And speaking of that hospital, what the hell are they doing to our friends?"

The kid coughed several times. "Checking the results of all the drugs they'd administered. And giving them more."

Wendy cried out at the news. David hauled the conscious male over, Hardy, and dropped him by Vince's side.

"You do realize these are vamps like us," David said, dragging the Adam's apple guy over.

Hardy shouted. "You don't get it. We weren't part of that whole gross blood farm thing, but the team is out of men. You killed off their up and coming vamps so we've all been pressed into this. It's your fault we're in this mess in the first place."

David shook him hard. "Do you think we care? We've

been attacked and damn near killed a dozen times, and still this isn't over. We want it to be over. We want out. But instead our friends are captive again – when they should have been safe."

"There is no out. Don't you see," Vince said. "There is no safe. This is it. They have the power and they aren't going to let go. There's no school anymore, there's no business future. It's with them or against them." He leaned back and closed his eyes. "And now that we've failed, there is nothing left for us."

"Maybe there is." Tessa stood up. She studied the energy of the three men. "What drugs are you taking?"

"Who knows," Hardy spat. "We don't have a choice with that either. They took samples of our blood, cross-referenced it with something else and bam...." He collapsed onto the floor beside his friend. "We're given something based on the results."

"Oh, you have been given something. No doubt about it. And they are killing you with it." She looked at Vince. "You aren't suffering as much as your friends. Either you have different drugs or are on different doses."

"That's because of who he is." Hardy groaned. "I'm a nobody. I'm expendable."

"I thought you said they were short on manpower. If that's the case, you are more valuable alive then dead."

"No. They are growing new batches of vamps. They only need us until the first crop matures."

And damn if the kid didn't have tears in his eyes when he added, "Our way of life is over. Only a special few will survive, and it will be at the discretion of these powerful men."

"Like hell," David said. "I'll make sure these assholes don't survive this war for what they've done to Ian and Jewel."

"And the others," Tessa said. "We're going to beat them

like we beat those at the blood farm. Now the real question is – are you with them – or us?"

GORAN SLID AROUND the corner of the stairwell where he could keep an eye on the elevators as well. He didn't like these underground parking lots. He understood the necessity but not the value. Then again, he wasn't in the business of bringing more vamps into the place. At least this way they could run all-night gaming halls here. Good for business. Bad for the vampire community. Most gaming halls had a tendency to lean toward the darker side of life, and what went on here catered to the darkest of appetites.

He doubted the kids knew about that. Especially Wendy. She'd never have come here to hide if she did. The criminal element was darker than Goran cared to see – and he'd seen much of that side of life.

Time to have a talk with Cody. Make sure he understood just what went on here.

The kids had gone upstairs to find Wendy. Goran was torn between wanting to follow to protect them and wanting to stay down here and see if their arrival had been noticed by anyone.

He blended into the shadows and waited. There was nothing for the longest time. With a patience he'd learned over the centuries, Goran figured the kids should be back down soon. That they weren't was a bit concerning. Just as he decided his overactive imagination had been making up scenarios instead of real concerns, several vamps detached from the shadows on the far side. Goran slipped deeper into the darkness. Had they seen him?

If so, his cover was blown and the kids were likely in danger.

Cursing himself, he sent out a warning to Serus. *Not sure what's happening. I'm in the underground parking area of the mall. The kids have gone up to get Wendy outside the gaming hall. They haven't come back and now I've got a few vamps that appear to be up to no good.*

In that area? Serus responded. *You know most of them are up to no good. Why the devil would Wendy go there to hide?*

She likely thought there'd be safety in numbers.

Except most of those numbers would kill her for the high. And they'd do it for money in a heartbeat. If it moved them up in the power chain or because someone would owe them for doing this, well, they'll be fighting off a dozen others trying to kill her for the same reasons. Serus's voice sharpened in Goran's head. *Why didn't you stay with them?*

Because I was afraid that we were being followed. A weird sensation when we came into the parking lot. As if someone came or left on the sly. And I wanted to know who.

It's most likely some of the drug dealers, Serus said impatiently. *They're likely doing a lot of deals in that place.*

Goran thought Serus would have made the connection, but obviously the mess going on at the Human Council was occupying his thoughts more than Goran's issues. *Exactly,* he said quietly.

It took Serus a moment to pull his thoughts together. Then he exploded. *You think the drug dealing at the mall is connected to the drugs from the blood farm?*

What's in common? Goran asked. *Drugs.*

Serus's low hiss slithered through Goran's mind. Yeah, now Serus was listening.

And I ask again, why did you leave the kids alone?

Now fear and anger mixed in his best friend's voice. Goran, humor rippling through his words, said, *Tessa was with them. I figured there wasn't much she couldn't handle. I was likely better off down here to grab as much intel as I could. Instead, the place has been as silent as your grandmother's grave until now...*

❧ ❦

JARED RAN DOWN the block toward the school. He didn't know why there versus anywhere, except he thought there might be safety in numbers.

He'd been texting David steadily. David had only been able to tell him his parents were dealing with the problems. He'd also asked if Jared had a place to go to stay safe. Jared had wanted to go to Tessa's house but understood that might not be the best option at the moment.

So school it was. At least until he figured out where to go after that. He wondered if the teachers or administrators there knew anything about this mess. The problem was so secretive and pervasive. And that blood farm had operated under everyone's nose for so long...

Talk about a slow burning poison eating at humanity.

He'd seen the results and didn't like them. Any of them.

The dead men at the home and his uncle were just more. He shuddered. The school grounds were up ahead. He could sit in the playground until the doors opened.

He checked his cell phone for a news update. The early morning news hadn't reported any deaths at the group home, either. Would it even make it to the news, or would it be squished down before that happened? Could the people behind this mess keep something this big hush hush? And his uncle? Was he going to be listed as a suicide or an unsolved murder in the years to come? He doubted anyone would make that mistake in reality, but those people appeared to be able to twist the news the way they wanted to.

When had he become so cynical? Oh yeah, after he'd been kidnapped at a movie theater.

He walked onto the school grounds, surprised to see a lot of vehicles parked. An early morning meeting?

Not that it was that early anymore. Other kids were here. The playground was occupied as well. He checked his watch. Classes wouldn't start for fifteen minutes. If anything, the place should have been busier. He shrugged and walked inside and down the hallway to his locker. There, he unloaded his heavy bag stuffed with his stuff from his uncle's house. He had no idea what else to do. And he was grateful that he had a big locker. He stepped back and stared at the full interior.

This was everything he owned in the world. He was essentially homeless. And an orphan.

"Hello, Jared." The principal spoke from down the hall. Jared quickly pulled out his school books and closed his locker before turning to face him. "Good morning, sir."

"I hear you're quite the hero." The principle smiled. And damn if Jared didn't wonder if that smile was for real. He would be forever wondering about the people around him now. Wonder if they were involved in his attempted murder and the murder of both his parents. After all, that's what the blood farm was. A murder machine.

"I'm no hero," he said. "But I won't be a victim anymore either."

CHAPTER 13

T ESSA GLARED DOWN at the punk kid in Cody's arms. No one had said a word since she'd asked whose side they were on. "Answer me."

When the kid opened his mouth, she studied the energy flowing from him. She heard his words but looked at what was going on around them. Fear. Betrayal. Pain. And the need to survive.

She could understand all of it. She nodded at Cody. "I think these guys need to be taken to the Council. Let someone like Motre get what they need from them and set up a sting of some kind."

"Not sure what Motre is doing. Many of his friends were injured or are recovering, so I'm sure that's what he's focused on right now," David said, a tremor to his voice.

Tessa hated to hear the fear in everyone's voices. She understood it, but fear crippled people. Instead of action, they fell into inaction. And this was not the time for that. "We need to get these guys to the Council. Let Adamson deal with them." She waved her arms toward the three punks. "If Motre is around, even better. I'm sure Chad and Lenther would like to be in on this, too. They were at the top of the mountain with me when Gloria blew it up."

Cody grinned. "Not sure they want to be anywhere close to you at this point. As I recall, you grabbed them and jumped off the top of the mountain. How you were going to land, carrying not one but two full-sized vamps from that high up, I don't know."

Wendy gasped. "Is that what happened?" She stared at Tessa. "I saw you arrive on the ground, but I never did hear about how you got out."

"Yeah, that wasn't much fun." She shook her head. "But there are a few guys that are likely to be grateful to me for saving their lives."

Cody lifted the kid to his feet. He glared at him. "You get one chance and one chance only."

The kid nodded rapidly. "Understood." He glanced at his friends. "What about them?"

Cody glanced over at the one still out cold and the other one sitting quietly in front of him. "Tessa, any reason these other two don't get the same chance?"

"No. They each get one chance. Blow it and we'll kill you," she said calmly.

Cody watched the look exchanged by the two men in front of him.

There was no doubt they believed her.

❧ ❦

CODY COULD ALMOST read their minds. These men were staring at this sixteen, almost seventeen-year-old female vamp who was talking about killing them so casually – completely at odds with her dynamite looks.

He grinned. God, he loved her.

And heard her gasp in his head.

Did you mean that? This time?

He was quiet, not knowing quite what to say. He'd surprised himself.

She giggled. *Right. Guess that answers that question.*

No, it doesn't. See, I don't know, he said quietly, *I don't know what that emotion is. I've never been able to recognize it and I've never said it to anyone.*

No one? Not even Xana?

No. Definitely not her. But…I thought I was in love with her. And I know now that I wasn't.

How do you know you weren't?

Because I didn't feel for her what I feel for you.

He couldn't see her smile…but he felt it.

You like that, huh?

Of course, she murmured. *Every woman wants to know that she's special. Even to a man with tons of experience. No female wants to be the same as another, and especially not the same as the last one.*

You will never slide into that category, Tessa. I have never known any woman like you. I can't imagine anyone even coming close. He grinned. *Honestly, I don't think the world is ready for another Tessa.*

Her laughter tinkled through his mind.

After what I've been through, I wouldn't wish being me on anyone.

True, but look where you are now. Isn't that worth it?

He could hear her think it over, her mind operating on one level even as her body operated on another level. She'd picked up the second kid at her feet and shoved him over to where the third one was out cold. Cody watched her, wondering if she'd answer.

Then she turned and said *Yes.* And turned back to the business at hand. "Wendy, are you okay?"

Wendy nodded. "Now that I'm not alone. I didn't know

what to do or where to go once they started chasing me." Her voice quavered at the memory. She wrapped her arms around her chest. "What's going on? I don't understand. This nightmare was supposed to be over. I got to relax for what... one day, two days maybe. Now it's chaos again?"

David wrapped his arm around her. "Take it easy, Wendy. We'll get to the bottom of this."

"But will we get there in time to save Ian?" She lifted swollen eyes to David then over to Cody before locking on Tessa's face. "Please help me save Ian."

"It's not just Ian," David said. "All our friends that were at the mine are potentially in danger. And so is," his voice thickened. "Jewel."

Cody slung the unconscious vamp over his shoulder and led the way back to the underground parking lot. He kept a hawk's gaze on the other two vamps. He didn't dare let any of them escape. David was helping Wendy, and Tessa walked beside him, quiet yet stoic.

Are you okay?

Yes, she murmured. *Just had hoped...*

I know. Sorry. I'd like nothing better than to have this over with myself.

The elevator was dark, empty, and creepy. Cody almost laughed. Since when were elevators or even large underground spaces creepy? Since the damn mine. He wished he could spend more time up above ground in the light. Tessa had no idea how lucky she was.

I'm starting to, she answered in response. *Makes me wonder if there would be a way for others to enjoy it.*

And that's what got these experiments started, Cody said. *And no good can come from that.*

I know. We all want what we can't have. Vampire nature.

And human nature. It seems like they are willing to do anything to have what they can't have. The elevator descended to the underground parking level.

Just before they reached their destination, David glanced over at him, a grim look on his face. "We need to call in someone to help transport these guys. The car won't fit four of us in front, and I'm not comfortable with all three behind me while I drive."

"That's not going to work."

"No, it's not." David pulled his phone out. "I'll make the call." He called Councilman Adamson.

"Sorry to bother you, sir, but we have three vampires who have been working for Councilmen Baker and Wilson." He winced at Adamson's indrawn breath. More betrayal. Barreling ahead, he added, "We have Vince, Councilman Baker's son. Both councilmen are apparently behind the mess at the hospital."

David hung up the phone. "A truck is on its way."

"Good. Now where's your father, Cody?" Tessa asked. She looked around. "I've been expecting him to pop out the whole time. I lost track of him when I ran up the stairwell."

"He stayed behind," Cody said. He looked around, concern shifting through his thoughts. "He wanted to keep an eye out just in case our arrival brought some unwanted attention."

"Good plan – where is he then?"

❧ ❦

IAN WAITED FOR someone to come to his room. Anyone at this point. He had what passed as a port-a-potty, and damn if that wasn't humiliating, but peeing out the window didn't exactly appeal to him, either. Besides, he was trying to lie low until he could escape out the window. It was a bitch of a first step, but he figured it was better than being dosed with more drugs. Besides, he had worked his wings to the point of straining them, but they'd started to move.

Paralyzed my ass, he thought. *I can do this.* Sure, he'd rather get the hell out sooner than later, and preferably not by jumping out of the eighth floor window. But he'd do what he had to do, then he'd go find Wendy.

Snick.

He spun around.

He'd checked the door earlier and it had been locked.

Did that mean it was now unlocked?

He waited. Then crept to the door. Was someone waiting on the other side? He turned the handle, and the door made a tiny sliding noise as it opened.

He held his breath.

And pulled the door toward him. Shit.

ʠ ‎ʠ

TESSA SLID TO the left as soon as the elevator opened on the parking lot level. On one side, energy flashed and danced in the murky darkness.

Two people were fighting. Goran appeared to be one.

She held her arm back, stopping the others from leaving the elevator. She pointed in the direction of the fight. Behind her, the light went out.

The men stirred. One of the punks hissed. "If we're caught in here, they're going to know we failed to grab the girl. We won't have a chance to get away safely."

Wendy turned to glare at him. "Good. Maybe I should tell them myself so they know. And I'm Wendy, by the way. It might be harder to kill me if I have a name."

He glared. "We weren't supposed to kill you. Just hold you until they came to take you back to the hospital. What would you care if you had a mind wipe? It's not exactly going to make a difference – you wouldn't remember this anyway."

"A mind wipe?" she gasped. "That's what they were going to do?"

"I doubt it," David said, "You've already proven to be too much trouble. That might be what these punks thought, but they'd have killed you in a heartbeat if you'd showed any resistance. They can't afford that anymore."

Smack.

Tessa spun around to see Hardy holding a hand to his cheek as he glared at Wendy. "What was that for? I didn't do anything, remember."

"Yeah, but you were going to," Wendy hissed. "And you still might if you got a chance."

Tessa grinned. "You go girl. Next time, use a fist and maybe you'll knock him out. That way we don't have to listen to his convoluted logic."

Hardy sneered. "I heard about you. Big mouth and sneaky tricks."

Thunk.

This time, the guy crumpled against the back wall, barely staying upright. The blow had come out of the left field.

Cody glared at him. "Open that mouth against Tessa again and I'll close it permanently."

Noises off to the side stopped. Cody stepped forward and calling out, "Goran, sir?"

"Yeah, I'm here. Call for a Council transport truck, will you. I've got two that we need to take in for questioning."

"Already done. We've got three here for transport as well."

A loud snort sounded out of the darkness. "Just so you don't think you did better than me. There are four of you against three of them," he grunted and suddenly appeared in front of them, tossing two unconscious vamps on the floor beside them. "Whereas I'm all alone."

Tessa grinned. "Ha. I figured you could handle these guys alone, otherwise I'd have offered to help."

Goran's grin flashed. "Thanks for not insulting me. I told your dad the same thing about you."

Pride swelled through Tessa, making her stand up taller. She liked the sound of that. "Maybe you should say something similar to my mom."

"Like hell. I'm not getting within an arm's reach of her. She bites."

Tessa laughed.

She motioned to the unconscious males on the ground. "Do you know these two?"

"Nope." Goran bent down and rolled the men over so both faces were visible in the light of the elevator. "Do you?"

Tessa shook her head. Cody said, "No."

David echoed the same response. Wendy stepped forward. And swayed in place. "He was at the hospital. He's one of the men who chased me."

"Yeah?" Goran looked down at the man slowly regaining consciousness and kicked him. "Asshole."

Sounds of a heavy truck approaching drew Tessa's gaze. The lights shone bright in the heavy darkness. The glare landed on the waiting group. Tessa instinctively stepped back out of the light. She couldn't explain the need but if she'd learned anything this last week, it was to listen to her instincts. David stepped behind her.

"What's up, sis?"

"Not sure. I just didn't want all of us to be sitting ducks in case they decided to sacrifice the truck if that meant running over all of us."

Tessa heard Wendy's shocked gasp, and she skittered further into the shadows on the other side of Tessa.

Goran growled as he studied the truck and the occupants barely discernible behind the special windshield. "Anyone know them?"

"We're hoping it's a Council truck. Now who's actually driving it remains to be seen," Cody murmured quietly as he studied the surrounding area.

Tessa watched as the light pinned the group in the glare. The rest of the underground parking lot was basically open. They couldn't see with the light in their eyes. There could be a dozen people about to jump their group. Tessa slipped further off to one side. David raised an eyebrow in question. She smiled. "Just making sure we're not all at one place. A little backup so to speak."

He nodded and stayed where he was.

The truck came to a screeching stop.

Tessa shifted so she could see the faces of the three punks they'd caught upstairs. If they knew something, it would show on their faces. Sullen and fearful, the three huddled together, but there was no recognition on their faces.

She took yet another step back and prepared for anything.

❧ ❦

SERUS HAD HAD enough. They'd done nothing but talk, set up plans, and talk some more. The biggest issue was who they could bring in to help out. Who could they trust? Who was available to help? And who would keep their mouth shut?

Serus didn't understand all the distinctions. Why not just ask who they could trust? Sian understood his point, but she said humans were different. As if they operated on a points system and certain values were worth a certain amount of points. Other characteristics were worth a different amount of points. When added up together, each person had some kind of dependability level.

It was bullshit as far as he was concerned. People were people. They could only be trusted to do whatever suited their needs at the time. There was nothing else to it. He rolled his eyes.

Goran, where are you at?

In the underground parking lot. I caught two bogeys and the kids brought three down from the mall level. So five of us and five bad guys. A Council truck has just arrived. Should be on our way back to the Council Hall soon.

Just be careful.

Maybe a little more than careful. Your daughter just slipped into the shadows. Cagey girl, that one.

Yeah. And good instincts. She obviously doesn't like who's driving the truck.

Not sure if that's it or not. With the truck driving toward us, we can't see the rest of the darkness. A perfect blind for an attack. I'm moving back, too but don't want to get too far away from the others. Several are out and I want to keep them that way. Uh oh, Gotta go.

Damn. Goran was getting all the action. Serus almost grinned at how different that saying meant now versus life before Rhia. His grin wiped off at the idea of Cody using that in relation to his own daughter. Not so funny now.

He growled.

"Serus? What's up?" He glanced over at Rhia. No way was

he sharing. "Just fed up. Goran's having fun beating up bad guys and I'm stuck here."

"Leave then. We'll be fine. Sian and I are going to be a couple of hours yet."

"Hell no. I'm not leaving you. Just give me something to do."

"Wait – did you say Goran is fighting?" she asked, her voice incredulous.

"No. Not at all. The fighting is over," he groused. "He caught them both. Even the kids captured three." His glare deepened and his lip curled. "While I'm in meetings."

"Go," she said. "Our kids shouldn't be fighting. This is supposed to be over. They are supposed to be safe."

"Well, it didn't happen. Wendy is safe, though. But now the Council is there to collect all the bad guys so they can interrogate them."

"You have to go. Get whatever information is available," she said immediately. "We need this over."

"I'm not leaving you," he said, letting just enough anger leak from his voice to let her know he was serious.

"You have to. We'll be fine."

He just gave her a look. He wasn't going to move one step without her. "I'm not leaving you."

She glared at him. "Serus, don't be difficult. You are needed at the Council Hall."

He smiled. "I'm not leaving you."

She growled and threw up her hands. "You have to."

"Not without you." He was implacable. He wasn't leaving Rhia's side. Sian either. That woman was pregnant. Neither of them were going to be alone again. Not until all talk of human-style vigilante justice stopped. And so what if he was missing out on the action? He'd lost out before and survived.

This was no different.

"Go, please."

"No."

Sian started to laugh. "Rhia, we can do our stuff from the Council Hall. It's just mostly phone calls from here on out."

Rhia stopped, uncertain.

She studied Serus's face then turned to look at Sian. He turned to study Sian's worn face himself. If Rhia couldn't see that Sian needed to go back, she wasn't looking very closely.

"Fine." Rhia threw up her hands. "We'll all go back."

Serus couldn't help it. His grin shone. "Now we're talking."

"You better not have manipulated me into this." Rhia peered into his gaze closely.

He gave her an injured look of innocence. "Me? How could I do that? I want what's best for you."

She glared at him, then gave in gracefully. "Fine."

Serus waited while they gathered their stuff. With any luck, he could still get in on the ground floor of the interrogation.

Finally he'd get to have some fun, too. If they got back before Goran hogged it all.

CHAPTER 14

TESSA WATCHED FROM the shadows as several men hopped out of the truck and walked toward Goran. "Are you the one that called for assistance?"

Goran nodded toward David. "He did. But these are the men that need to be taken back to Council headquarters."

One of the men kicked the man closest to them. "What did they do?"

"Attacked me," Goran growled.

The two men looked up at Goran, frowned, then looked down at the two unconscious males in their prime. "You beat them both up?"

Tessa wanted to giggle. They'd be making a big mistake if they judged Goran as old and nothing to worry about. Others had made the same mistake about her in the past. They wouldn't a second time. She hadn't eased up her guard. These two could be from the Council, but she wasn't so sure.

"Let's load them up." The driver walked to the back of the big truck and opened the big double doors. He lifted up the first unconscious vamp and tossed him into the back. The second vamp tried to lift the other unconscious vamp, but he didn't have the strength. "Give me a hand with this one, Reilly," he said. "I can't lift him."

Goran snorted, scooped up the prone man, and threw him up and into the back of the truck like he was a bag of garbage. Goran stepped back and glared at the weak vamp. Muttering to himself, he motioned to the three other vamps. "Have you got room in there for these three?"

Tessa watched as the driver nodded. "Yeah, I presume they are going to the same place?"

Goran nodded. While Tessa watched, the men hopped up one at a time to sit on the benches. The back of the truck had no windows so once they were in, the men were going to stay in. Tessa watched as the driver locked the back and walked around to the front of the truck. She'd been looking for an opportunity to study their energy, but in the parking lot with dim lights, the place was dark. Too dark. She couldn't tell if he had black in his system or not. Even the energy of her group, which was lighter in color, was hard to see down here. She didn't understand why.

And because she didn't understand, it made her suspicious.

Then again, everything did that lately.

"Goran, are you going to travel in the front of the truck?"

He turned to look at her then checked his watch and realized he couldn't fly yet. He nodded. "Good idea. I'll meet you at the Hall."

Goran walked up to the front of the truck where the driver and the second man were waiting. They looked a little nervous. He grinned. "I'll be riding with you. I want to make sure these guys get there safely."

The driver laughed. "Old man, you're welcome to come along for the ride. It won't make any difference. These guys are going straight to the Council."

"Good. Call me old man again, and you're going to be riding in the back of the truck with the others."

That wiped the smirk off the driver's face. He rolled his

eyes and said, "Whatever."

He hopped up to the driver's side and turned on the truck. Goran waited for the second man to hop up, then with a wave to Tessa and the others, he got in.

"We'll be right behind you," David called out leading the way to the car. They hopped in, and waited until the truck drove away.

Inside the car, Tessa sat in the back with Cody. Wendy sat in front with David.

"Tessa," David said, "Did you see anything odd?"

She sighed. "What was odd is that I couldn't see anything. It was so black and murky I had a hard time seeing your bright healthy energy. Maybe I'll be able to see something more at the Hall."

The truck rumbled forward. The car followed behind.

They pulled out onto traffic and bright daylight. Tessa watched as the truck turned left onto the busy highway and picked up speed. Just as David completed the same corner, a big semi slammed into the Council truck.

Tessa cried out, her gaze locked on the truck carrying Goran and seven others as it flipped completely in the air before landing on its roof and sliding across the highway. Other vehicles crashed into it, and even more slammed into them.

It was chaos.

David slammed on the brakes. The car spun wildly out of control. Wendy cried out while Tessa clutched Cody. He wrapped his arms around her as the world spiraled out of control. And suddenly the car came to a rocking stop. Wendy sobbed in the front seat, her hand holding her head.

"Jesus," David whispered. He turned to look around. "Is everyone all right?"

Tessa cried out when she saw David's face. He must have

hit the windshield. A cut split his forehead, and blood dripped down his cheeks.

"I'm okay, Tessa." He turned back to check on Wendy.

Beside her, Tessa watched as the semi backed up awkwardly from where it had landed on the shoulder and eased past the mess it had created on the road before driving away.

Tessa twisted as it drove past them, trying to see the license place. She couldn't catch a clear glimpse.

Then it was gone.

David started the car engine and pulled the big car off to one side and out of the way. For a long moment no one moved. It was daytime outside. The car sat under the bright hot sun.

As soon as her mind cleared as to what had happened, Tessa bolted out of the car and ran to the cab of the Council truck. She had to climb over debris to get to the passenger side. The door had been ripped open and hung in a crumpled mess of steel. Goran had tumbled out but was hidden in the shade of the vehicle. But not for long. He looked bad. Unconscious, he was bleeding from the side of his head, with one arm bent at a weird angle. She reached in to grab his hand and felt for his pulse. Vamps were notoriously difficult to kill, but as it had been proven many times, they could die.

Tessa, grateful he was unconscious, threw her jacket over him, picked him up, and struggled to get him to the car. Humans were racing over to help until they realized the vehicle was full of vampires. Then they stopped and milled around helplessly, not knowing what to do.

Or what they wanted to do.

By the time she'd reached the car, Cody was outside, his coat over his head to protect him from the sun. With his help, they got Goran into the car.

She raced back to the others.

Where she smelled smoke. *Cody, the vehicle is going to explode.*

Ah shit.

She grabbed the closest vamp. She had a bit of shade on the one side, but she couldn't get all the vamps out. The sun would burn them to a crisp.

"Help," she cried out to the crowd. "I need blankets, coats, something to cover these guys from the sun."

"Why bother," cried one man. "Let the bastards die."

She shot him a bitter look. "Is that how we should help your son if I find him in an accident?"

The man glanced at the ground. One man raced toward her. He had several blankets in his arms. "Here, use these."

With a grateful smile, she ran back to the van. While wrapping the first man, she realized the blanket was big enough for two. With some difficulty, and hating that the second man had regained consciousness and was crying out for help, she dragged him out, too. She gasped for breath as the smoke filled the interior. Her muscles screamed with her efforts.

Her instincts screamed at her to run.

She straightened. And there was Cody. He'd found a human truck with a canopy cover and was carrying both men to the pickup box where they'd be out of the sun. Thank heavens for that. Tessa worked her way around to the back of the truck. And saw the first sign of flames.

Crap. This day was just getting better and better.

"Are there people in the back of the van," called out one woman.

"Yes, five." She looked up. "I need more blankets. Covers. Something for them."

The door had been locked. She looked at it, realizing that it was stronger than it looked and was going to give her nothing but hell. And once again Cody was there.

Wearing a motorcycle helmet and gloves.

She grinned.

Love the outfit.

Ha. Move over. We're losing precious time.

He ripped the door off the hinges, raising a cry of surprise from the humans watching. Sunlight shone into the back of the van.

Tessa jumped inside with a blanket. The top three in the pile were the young punks from the mall. The top man was conscious but groggy. She covered him with a blanket and passed him up to Cody.

She turned to the next one and repeated the same movements.

"Tessa, hurry up," Cody called. "The flames are getting higher."

"I'm trying. Here's Vince." She passed the unconscious male over and turned to the third man. She didn't have anything to cover this one with, so she lifted him up to Cody, who wrapped the man up in another blanket. He disappeared from sight with his burden. Tessa turned to the remaining men. And she could see the two males Goran had knocked out. Damn. The first one was smoking. The smell inside the vehicle was putrid. Smoke filled the small space. But was it smoke from the gasoline around the van or from the vampire? The second vamp looked to be still alive. And he was huge. And she was tired.

"Tessa, you have to get out now. We can't wait any longer. I can fly, but not in the sunlight. We have to get away now. This thing is going to blow."

"This is the last one." She groaned as she tried to lift him. "The other one is smoking."

"Smoking?" Cody scrambled in beside her and cast a horrified look at the dying vamp before grabbing the big male and crawling back out the van. Tessa struggled to get out behind him. Just as she reached the top, she heard a weird sizzling sound.

Panicky, she jumped from the back of the van, as far and as high as she could.

The van exploded below her, sending her tumbling into the rocks on the nearby hillside.

❧ ❧

CODY WANTED TO scream from the scorching sensation in his lungs. The heat as he jumped free, one big-assed vamp in his arms, was intolerable. He gasped for air, terrified Tessa wasn't behind him. "Tessa," he roared. "Get your ass out here."

He didn't know if she heard him. He raced over to dump the injured vamp with the others in the back of the truck then turned to look for Tessa. There she was. Her head was just popping outside the back of the truck. Oh thank God. He ran toward her as she took one of the biggest jumps he'd ever seen her do.

And the vehicle exploded. A ball of flame rippled in widening waves, lifting him off his feet and slamming him back against several vehicles. He bounced several times then lay still. He groaned, waiting for his head to stop ringing.

"Hey, dude. Are you okay? That was a wild landing, man."

Cody rolled onto his side before trying to stand. He made

it upright, but he was weaving on his feet. He could barely see, and the blurred vision and the ringing in his ears made everything more difficult. He tried to focus on the people surrounding him, their hands out to help if he fell over. He took one unsteady step, then another.

"Tessa," he croaked.

"Well, if your landing was crazy, hers was epic. She can like jump!" The admiration in the young human's voice had Cody straightening, barely holding a cry back as pain lanced through his back. Crap. Not his wings again. He didn't dare check. He had an oversized jacket on, which protected his wings from the sun. He didn't remember where he got the motorcycle gear from, but he was wearing it. And that's what had allowed him to go help Tessa. He looked toward David and found him guarding Goran and Wendy.

What a bloody mess.

His gaze turned to search for Tessa. "Where is she?"

"Halfway up the hillside. Man, I wish I could jump like her."

Cody's gaze searched as his mind called out to her. But he wasn't getting any answer. And that scared the hell out of him.

His gaze flicked past the scenery, then hit the brakes and slid backwards, landing on Tessa. She was standing, holding onto a big rock. She appeared to be dazed, but more or less fine.

"She really got blasted."

Cody glanced at the huge kid in front of him. And damn if he wasn't the one wearing the rest of the motorcycle gear.

In the distance, he heard sirens approaching. Hopefully more Council vehicles were coming to help move the injured. And a fire truck would be good. The damn truck looked to be ready to burn for quite awhile.

Tessa, honey, are you okay?

She straightened as if she was getting some message, but she wasn't responding. At least, given the ringing in his ears, he wasn't hearing her.

Tessa, can you jump down?

He closed his eyes and concentrated. *Tessa? Tessa, please talk to me.*

No answer.

He took a deep breath and shouted, "Tessa! Can you hear me?"

The crowd turned to watch Tessa on the hill. She seemed to hear something. She turned. Took an unsteady step. Tried for another one. And staggered.

The crowd cried out.

"Oh no." As Cody watched, he realized the hillside was steep. As in too steep. "Tessa, wait. I'm coming. Don't move."

And she straightened, lifted a foot, obviously dazed, and tried to take another step.

"Man, she won't quit, will she?"

Cody groaned. "She doesn't know how."

Tessa tried for one more step, and fell down...and down... and down the rest of the hill.

ॐ ॐ

SERUS WALKED INTO the Council Hall. He'd been trying to reach Goran for the last ten minutes to get an update. So far, Goran hadn't answered.

And Serus hated that.

It was rare for there to be silence between them. That door had been open for centuries. Always available to contact each other in case of an emergency.

Goran hadn't called for his help, so in theory, he should be fine.

Or he was out cold.

"Where are they?" he bellowed. The two hapless vamps within his earshot slapped their hands over their ears. Serus grinned. That felt much better.

Rhia smiled gently at the two men. "He means where are the vamps coming in by transport to be interrogated? Serus is looking forward to that part," she added wryly.

The two vamps looked at each other, then over at Serus.

"We've just had word that the truck carrying vamps has been involved in a bad accident with a transport truck." The other male vamp added, in a low voice, "There is one fatality."

Blood rushed to his head. Serus wanted to pound someone into the ground. And the two vamps in front of him were the only ones available.

Rhia placed a calming hand on his arm, "Do you know who?" Her voice was sharp but not trembling.

The odds were good that Goran wasn't the deceased vamp, but neither could Serus forget that he'd been with the kids. And one of them might have been in the big van with the men. He shook his head and tried to shove that thought deep down. "Where?"

The street was named. Serus turned without a word and headed back to his car.

"Wait, Serus," Rhia said, "Maybe they have more information."

Serus turned to face the men, but they were both shaking their heads. "Nope, they don't."

And he walked away. He called out to Goran. *You there?*

Still no answer.

Damn it.

❧ ❧

SCHOOL WAS ALMOST over. He hadn't seen Tessa all day. He checked his phone. Nothing from anyone.

"Hey Jared." He turned to face Greg, one of the nicer guys at the school. He planned to be a doctor if he could get into med school. His marks were solid but not spectacular, and Greg had to work for those.

Unlike some people. And damn if that didn't remind him of Tessa again. He checked his phone yet again. "Yeah, what's up?"

"Did you hear about the big accident on the highway?" Greg asked. "Some vampire truck was involved in a big accident. Along with another car full of vamps. They were talking about a couple of people that were involved in saving them. There are tons of pictures on the Internet. Like crazy pics of when the van blew up. I wondered if it was Tessa."

Something inside Jared froze. "I haven't heard anything. I wonder if that's why she wasn't at school today."

"That's what I'm asking you." Greg held his hands out. "I thought you two were tight."

"We are." He spun around, looking to see if there was anyone else he could ask. "I have no idea where she is, but that would make a terrible kind of sense. She hasn't been answering my emails or texts all afternoon."

But he'd find out for sure.

As he looked down at his phone, he realized that was also likely why David wasn't answering, too.

They couldn't.

CHAPTER 15

TESSA SLAMMED UP against a big boulder and hung suspended for a long moment before rolling back to lie face up. She groaned and stared up at the blue sky. It would be pretty if the clouds didn't dance up and down.

She hurt – everywhere. Who'd have thought a landing like that could rattle her brains so much?

Tessa!

Cody. She smiled and said, "I'm over here."

Tessa, talk to me.

"I'm over here," she called again in a louder voice, but it still came out as a squeak. She tried again. "Here." She lifted a hand and tried to wave it.

And cried out in pain. Crap, her arm was injured. She turned her head slightly and saw how far down she'd rolled and wanted to laugh – but groaned instead. She assessed the rest of her body and realized she'd gotten off lightly. Outside of some aches and pains – and depending on her arm – everything appeared functional.

Good thing.

She looked around for Cody but couldn't see him. But then her vision was still wonky.

Damn it, Tessa, I'm inside your head, can't you hear me?

Oh. I can, she cried. *But for some reason I thought you were talking to me out loud.*

How badly are you hurt? he asked worriedly. *You don't sound very good.*

I'm fine. Just bruised. Then again, I haven't stood up. Memories of the blast filled her head. *Are you okay? Did you get hurt?* She struggled to sit up, biting back the cry of pain when she accidentally put her weight on her arm.

Struggling and swearing, she made it to her feet. And heard a cheer. She turned to find a large group of people gathered around parked vehicles and a still-smoldering truck cheering for her. She mustered up a smile and waved.

The cheers rose into a deafening noise.

Well, I'm up, she said. *Can't say much more than that. Did we all survive?*

Except for the one. Cody reminded her in a grim voice.

I remember now. I don't know exactly what was going on there with him. I'd seen that before, but only after being hit with silver or sunlight. I wish I knew what killed him.

Chances of finding out now aren't good.

Moving slowly, Tessa limped over toward the crowd who still cheered. What was their problem? She groaned as she landed heavily on the uneven ground, jarring her head. *Cody, how's Goran?*

I'm heading over there now. I'll let you know.

By the time you find out, I should be at the car.

Take it easy, he said. *Apparently you literally flew. They are calling it an epic jump.*

Really? Feeling better already, Tessa said, *Go check on your father. I'm fine, just a little shaky.*

She watched as Cody raced to the car. She was surprised that David and Wendy hadn't gotten out. Then the car was parked in the bright sunlight, pinning them inside. Hopefully, they were recovering from their slam into the windshield.

Cody had been the only one wearing a coat.

She took a deep breath and slid around the rock. She could do this. After what she'd already done today, this wasn't a problem. So what if the ground was wavering as if she were drunk? And the heat seemed too hot and her arm too sore. This was nothing.

It could have been so much worse.

Tessa, Cody called. *Dad is in a bad way. We need to get him some help.*

Won't he heal on his own?

Normally, but it looks like his leg is broken and needs to be set.

I'm coming. And she was. Just slowly. Sirens echoed in the distance, gaining in volume the closer she got. The air stank, too. Horrible black smoke plumed upward into the sky. She kept her focus on placing one foot in front of the other. As she approached, the crowd stepped back slightly.

She grimaced. "I look that bad, do I?"

One massive guy in front grinned. "You look like you took a beating. But that jump flip thing you did was seriously awesome."

She didn't want to ask what he was talking about. She remembered the jump – not the flip. But that might explain why so much of her hurt – particularly if that flip was how she landed.

She smiled at the good-looking male, his face still filled with awe. "Don't suppose you caught on film, huh? Be nice to have a copy to see what I survived."

Tessa, Cody growled. *We need to go.*

She waved at the crowd to let them know she was okay and walked as fast as she could the rest of the way to the car.

Sirens were cut off as rescue vehicles arrived.

As far as she was concerned, this was a great time to leave.

DAVID DROVE CAREFULLY. His headache boomed through his skull. Wendy looked the way he felt. Both had smashed into the windshield, neither of them having thought to wear seatbelts. So not a vampire invention. For the first time, he considered the merits of such things. Still, he'd heal without much effort. He understood humans wearing them all the time. They were so delicate, their bodies fragile. He wondered how the species survived. Even as he settled into the slow pace of driving past the piled up vehicles, he realized his head was feeling better. In the rearview mirror, he studied Tessa's features. She looked like she'd been blasted to hell and back. Her skin, always pale, now looked white. At least the little bit he could see of it. The rest was covered in soot and grime. She needed a shower in the worst way. And likely a long rest in bed.

Wendy held her own head as if she had a massive headache. Then again, she'd been banged up pretty damn good, too.

They were a sad looking lot. This accident had been the last thing they'd needed. Had it been as simple as that or had the Council truck been hit on purpose? Outside of the semi that had caused the accident driving away, he had nothing suspicious to prove it either way.

Cody had survived the worst of the blast, but now that his father lay in his arms, he looked almost as bad as Tessa. Cody leaned his head back and closed his eyes, his lips in a grim line.

David returned his gaze to the road. They'd survived so

much. He knew the odds had been against them from the beginning. That everyone had survived was wonderful – and tested fate. He wanted to quit while they were ahead. Quit while they were safe. They were supposed to be safe.

And they weren't. He'd been trying to call Jewel and Ian and hadn't gotten an answer from either of them.

"Cody, what about those other vamps, is someone driving the truck for us? I never even thought about them. You could have driven that truck."

"The owner is bringing them in." Cody twisted to look out the back window. "He's coming up behind us."

"Where do we go?" David asked. "The hospital is no longer an option, and the human hospital is completely overwhelmed – not that they'd be much help in any case."

Tessa's phone rang. She opened it and spoke to the caller. From what David could hear, it was their father.

She explained where they were and that there was a truck full of injured vamps following them.

By the time she hung up the phone, he thought he understood. "We're to take them to the Council Hall?"

"Yes," Tessa said tiredly. "Dad is going to track down medics. Supposedly there are enough rooms for them to stay there until they heal."

David nodded. "Good thing. We all need rest."

"Not me," Wendy said. "I need Ian. Alive and whole."

"Let's get everyone to the Council Hall, then we'll organize a group and go take the damn hospital back under our control. Just think, at least they are all in one place."

Tessa spoke up. "The mine was just one place. That didn't make it any easier."

"I suggest we surround the hospital so no one can get out, then go in with a vamp army and clean the assholes out."

Cody's tone was vicious.

David glanced in the mirror. Cody's jaw twitched with temper.

"How's he doing, Cody?"

"Not good. Get us to the Council Hall. Then I'm heading to that goddamned hospital. If anyone there can help him, I'll find him and bring him back with me."

"How can you know who to trust?" David asked curiously.

Cody grinned, but it was a movement that hardened the planes of his face and highlighted the anger in his eyes. "Tessa."

❧ ❧

CODY SAT BACK, anger churning a hole in his gut. He'd half expected Tessa's tinkling laugh to slide through his mind after his comment. He meant what he said. If she could determine who was infected in some way by this disease, then he was going to line them all up and have her separate them into groups. The guilty group he'd dispatch immediately.

With the others, he might have to listen to the how and why to determine the extent of their guilt.

But maybe not. As far as he was concerned – anyone involved was guilty.

Tessa, are you all right? You're awfully quiet.

No answer. He studied her up in the front seat. She'd leaned her head against the car door and her eyes were closed. Maybe she was sleeping.

"Wendy," he whispered. "Is Tessa sleeping?"

Cody listened inside her head. He hadn't heard anything when she'd gotten knocked out. Was she okay?

Tessa? Please answer me, sweetheart.

Again, no answer.

Damn it. She was hurt worse than he thought. Cody couldn't move with his father stretched across his lap.

"She looks asleep." Wendy leaned over and frowned. "Tessa, are you okay?"

She nudged Tessa's shoulder.

Tessa's head rolled to the side and hit the door – hard.

And she never made a sound.

David hit the gas and the car lurched forward.

SERUS PACED BACK and forth in the underground secure parking lot at the Council Hall waiting for David and the rest to arrive. Rhia leaned against the closest wall, eyes closed. She'd insisted everyone eat then had sent Sian upstairs to lie down. Good thing. All of this couldn't be good for the baby. Not that Serus knew much about babies, but Rhia had alternated from being the sweetest woman in the world to a woman on a rampage to a zombie barely functioning at times. He'd only been able to watch and be there for her. And sympathized. Most of the time, she hadn't wanted anything to do with that, either.

He wished Taz and Sian well.

This wasn't the easiest of journeys. Look at him. He was waiting for two of his kids to arrive, and he barely knew about their condition as it were. On top of that, his other son was in the hospital and if Goran was correct, Seth was either a prisoner of some asshole or he'd been recovered so his evil training would resume.

Serus would do anything to stop that. He hadn't had a

chance to even speak to Seth since the mountain blew up. His son had been unconscious the whole time. At least the doctors had said he was. Now he had to wonder. What if they'd kept Seth separated? Knowing who he was and what he'd been singled out to become. And were even now regaining lost ground.

If that happened, he swore he'd kill every last bastard. They had nerve to be involved at the hospital. It's not as if they could hide up there for long.

He frowned, thinking about that. So far this group had been wily and resourceful. They'd operated under everyone's noses for decades. No one had any inkling of what was going on and that took some serious smarts to pull off. They had to have a game plan. Other locations. A way to escape. Something.

A vehicle came screaming into the parking lot. Damn it. That had to be David. He'd been telling that kid to ease his lead foot up since he'd started driving.

Then he caught sight of his son's face.

Behind David came a pickup. Serus didn't know the driver but from the looks of him, the driver was human. Probably bringing the injured vamps. He alerted the medics he had waiting.

David parked and hopped out. "Tessa is unconscious."

Rhia raced over to Tessa's side of the vehicle, opened the door, and caught her daughter as she slumped sideways.

Serus turned around to find the first of the medical team running toward them. Rhia wouldn't surrender her burden, choosing instead to carry her directly upstairs. Serus wanted to do the same. He directed the men to the second vehicle while he, with Cody's help, tugged Goran out of the car. Serus studied the face of his old friend. He was alive, but barely.

David raced beside him. Serus glanced back to see Wendy and Cody going to help the vamps in the back of the truck. While David held open the door, he took one last look into the parking lot and watched as vamp after vamp was tugged out of the back of the truck. He walked toward the stairwell and started to climb. "Jesus, David. What the hell happened?"

As David gave him a short version of the events, Serus realized that the semi truck had to have targeted the vamp vehicle. Surely there'd have been no other reason to run off. Still, humans were charged for accidents, especially if they were at fault. Vamp road rules were different. Still, he'd love to talk to the driver of the semi in order to find out for sure.

"Did you catch the number on the license plate? Did Tessa?" he asked David.

David shook his head. "Sorry, Dad. We were hit at the same time, and it was all I could do to keep us on the road." He reached up a hand and touched the side of his face. That was the first time Serus realized that likely everyone in that damn car had been injured in some way. They were all very lucky to be alive.

ॐ ॐ

IAN STARED AT Motre standing in the hallway outside his room. The grin on the other man's face was something. But was he friend or foe? Ian really wanted him to be a friend.

"Well, are you coming, or are you going to sit in here until they come back with more drugs?"

Ian's gaze widened and he bolted to the other side of the door, his loose hospital gown flapping around his legs. "That's what I thought." Motre shut and locked the door behind him. Then motioned to the far end of the hallway. "Let's go. They are having a big meeting right now. We need to get clear before they come to check on you."

"What about the others?

"I've got some men releasing prisoners on the lower floors. I came up here because I overheard Wendy earlier. Figured you must be in one of the rooms they'd hastily pulled together to accommodate new patients."

Ian barely heard the rest after Wendy's name was mentioned. "Wendy, is she all right?"

Motre shook his head. "I have no idea. I just heard on the radio that a Council truck was involved in a big vehicle accident. There is a fatality." Motre snorted. "However, according to the human news, some female managed to drag almost everyone out of the vehicle before it blew up."

He shot a sideways look at Ian. "Can't imagine what female that was, can you?"

"Tessa." Ian crowed. "Oh my God. That's so awesome."

"Yeah, now it would be really good if we find out she didn't cause the accident in the first place. Cause damn, that woman can get herself into trouble."

Ian laughed and laughed. He felt like a huge weight had been lifted off his shoulders. He might not be completely free, and Wendy might not be completely safe, but the status quo had changed and things were finally swinging in his favor.

He'd get out of this yet.

CHAPTER 16

TESSA WOKE UP to a splitting headache, partly from the yelling somewhere close by. She groaned softly, wishing they would all just shut up.

Shh. Easy. Don't move. That blast apparently did more damage than you first thought.

Cody? She smiled and nestled deeper into the pillows. She was glad he was here with her.

I'm there in spirit. But I'm actually sitting beside my father. He's not pulling out of this spell very well. We've got good medics here, including Taz, but Dad is still unconscious. He smiled, a ripple of a movement in her head that was almost palpable. How cool was that? *I'm really glad you've woken up.* A wave of love washed through her. She didn't know if it was her love for him or his love for her – regardless of what they were willing to admit – but it filled her to the brim and brought tears to her eyes.

She sniffled them back.

Are you hurting? he said in alarm.

No, she whispered. *Just glad to be alive and hearing your voice.*

You say the nicest things, he said. *Then again, you are also the nicest vampire I've ever met.*

Ha, that's not necessarily a good thing. Certainly not in the vamp world.

It's a good thing, he said firmly. *Besides, it's who you are. Don't ever change. You are you and personally, I can't imagine you being any different.*

As long as you like me, then...

Oh, I do. This time she could see his smile in her mind's eye. How weird was that? It was also special. She knew she couldn't be actually seeing his smile because he wasn't there with her, but to know that she knew his face so well that she could picture every twist of his lips...yeah, that was special.

I wish they'd stop arguing, she whispered. *It's killing my head.*

Can't you tell them to stop? To take it elsewhere?

She gave a mental shrug. *I don't know who they are.*

It's not your mom?

I don't think so. It's a woman and a man, but I don't recognize either voice.

Hmmm. Your mother is supposed to be standing guard.

She probably just stepped out for a moment.

We've been talking longer than that. I wonder where she is.

I don't know. She groaned. *Now they are really going at it.*

She tried to sit up, but everything hurt. It was as if her body wouldn't listen to her commands. She didn't get it. She tried to roll over.

And froze.

Cody?

Yeah, I'm here. What's wrong?

I'm chained to the bed. Her heart jackhammered against her ribs. She tried to stay calm... tried but didn't succeed. *Cody! I'm like seriously chained to the bed!*

Chained? As in you can't move chained? he asked cautiously, as if not wanting to jump to any conclusions, *As in you're a prisoner?*

Yes, she cried. *As in there are links around my wrist and a small chain around the metal bed post.*

What the hell?

His shocked voice made her feel somewhat calmer. But not by much. *I gather you didn't know?*

Obviously!

She studied the shackles. Some sanity returned. There had to be a reason. Not a good one obviously, but still a reason. She was at the Council Hall after all. As she half listened to the argument going on, she realized the chains were a hot topic. Good. Someone was on her side.

Your mom grabbed you and ran. Your dad carried my father and I stayed behind to help unload all the injured vamps we'd placed into the back of the truck. Once that was all taken care of, I came to find my father and Serus went to you and your mother.

Hmmm. She tried not to let her panic overwhelm her. Just the thought of being a captive again was enough to make her want to kill the two people screaming beside her. She opened her eyes a tiny bit. It was Gittoria and a stranger. Why hadn't she recognized her aunt's voice? Then again, screaming like she was, no one would have recognized her.

Tessa tried to study the man's features, but she couldn't see him clearly. Neither could she see her aunt very well. She wished they'd come closer. Maybe she'd be able to see their energy. Figure out if they were good guys or bad guys.

Cody, it's my aunt Gittoria and a strange male.

A new voice jumped into the fray. "Stop that. You're going to wake her up. If you have to argue, do it in the hallway," Rhia snapped, her voice cutting and frustrated. "She needs to heal."

"Ha. Wait until she wakes up and finds out that you're the one who chained her up."

"If that's what I have to do to keep my daughter safe, then that's what I have to do," Rhia snapped. "I love her and she is not going to continue gallivanting around the world getting injured all the time. She needs peace and quiet and rest."

Tessa lay on the bed, reeling from her mother's words. She quickly told Cody.

What? Surely not.

Yes. What I don't know is if she's under the influence of those damn drugs. His shocked voice helped. She didn't feel quite so alone. *She sounds like my mother, she's acting like a concerned mother, but damn, who chains their daughter up to a bed to stop her from hurting herself?*

There was a long dark silence before Cody said, *I wonder if she's really Rhia.*

You mean like an imposter? That scared her. *The vamps aren't doing that kind of stuff, are they? Cloning specific people. To replace the real ones in all ways. No, can't be. Cloning doesn't work that way. You can't guarantee that a clone will look exactly the same as the original one you've taken the cells from.*

Maybe they couldn't before, but what if they can now? he said.

No. She rejected that idea immediately. *No way. This is my mom. I just don't get why she'd go to these lengths to keep me safe.*

Ah, that's easy. She loves you and she's lost enough people in this world that she doesn't feel she can lose you, too.

I wonder if my father knows. Or David?

I don't know. But I think I'll go and see. Don't struggle. Don't try to escape. As long as you are there, we should be able to find you. But don't let them know that you are conscious.

Got it.

And he left her mind.

They were getting better at that part. Being there but not

being there. Together but still apart. It was smoother now. They were closer too – if that was possible. It was such a weird feeling but at the same time, she couldn't imagine life without it.

She snuggled down into the bed.

There was an abrupt halt to the conversation. Footsteps walked over to the bed. "Tessa honey?" her mother asked. "Are you awake?"

Tessa lay quietly. She wasn't going to give the game away. But damn, she wished she could open her eyes enough to see her mother's energy. And the energy of the other two.

It was the only way she knew to understand the influences here. Even then, it didn't tell her who willfully signed up for the drug program, but at least she'd have an inkling as to why their behavior seemed so odd.

All she could do was wait.

❧ ❦

CODY TOOK ONE last look at his father. Pale and still, it was the closest he'd seen his father to death's door. And he didn't understand why. Neither did the doctors apparently. What happened in that truck?

He mulled it over as he searched out Serus. He found doctors moving amongst the other patients. Wendy had crashed and was sleeping on the couch in one of the Council rooms, reminding him that they had no word about Ian or Jewel yet. Speaking of which, where the hell was David? They were supposed to plan their next move to rescue Jewel and Ian from the hospital.

He continued to search until he found Serus. Relieved, he walked over to where Tessa's father was deep in conversation with several Councilmen.

He coughed lightly. Serus turned, saw Cody, and worry immediately filled his face.

Cody immediately said, "No change in Goran's condition."

The frown deepened. "Damn," he said softly. With the other two men listening in, he didn't feel comfortable mentioning Tessa's condition. He took a deep breath. "Can I speak with you privately, sir?"

Serus nodded and walked Cody over to the far side of the room. "What's up?"

He winced. "It's Tessa. She's awake." Serus's face lit up. Cody held out a restraining hand. "Wait. She hasn't told anyone she's awake, and now she's really scared."

"Why the devil would she be scared? Her mother is with her. Even her dratted bitchy aunt is there."

Well, that answered some of Tessa's questions. "Yes, sir. That's true. She's also been chained to the bed."

Serus's gaze widened. He shook his head.

Cody nodded.

Serus started to growl deep in the back of his throat. He spun and raced down the hallway.

Cody was right on his heels.

A fleeting thought crossed his mind as he raced behind Serus. *Where the hell was David?*

❧ ❦

DAVID THOUGHT HE had at least an hour before anyone noticed he wasn't upstairs in the main Council hall with the injured vamps. He'd fed quickly, then returned to the parking lot where he thanked the truck driver for bringing the vamps in, gotten the guy's name and number, and waited until he'd driven away.

Then he'd gotten inside his own car and followed the man out of the underground parking lot. It was getting late, but not late enough for him to be outside yet. He'd grabbed several of the blankets used to wrap the injured vamps up in and had thrown them into the back of the car. Who knew how many vamps he could free up at the hospital? Given the time of day, they'd need to wrap up. He hoped night would have fallen by the time he managed to get there and figure out a plan, but he was going to be prepared if his luck held. He'd tried to call Jewel again – several times. And he'd tried to call the main hospital. No answer at either number.

He drove steadily, his mind racing. He knew there was an underground parking lot. Had to be. Most visitors used the outside lot as there were many long covered walkways that gave the necessary protection in daytime as well. But he wanted the privacy of an underground lot. He also wanted the service entrance. Not the public one.

He'd thought long and hard about going alone. He wished he could've told someone, but with Tessa and Goran out, it meant that Cody needed to stay behind. Serus and Rhia were organizing some kind of task force to retake the hospital. And Wendy, well, she was still feeling the effect of the car accident.

He was too, but he'd never live with himself if anything happened to Jewel. He was terrified that Ian was already lost to them, but if he could save Jewel, he'd do anything he could to make that happen.

She had to be terrified. If she was even conscious. When they'd come out of the mountain, they'd been exhausted. Healing, but slowly. Too slowly. Ian was a little worse. The powers that be deemed it best for both of them to rest in the hospital where tests could be done to determine just what drugs they'd been given.

David hadn't questioned that wisdom. It had made sense to him at the time.

But Jewel had been sleeping almost every damn time he'd gone to see her. Was that normal? Now that he thought about it, he figured that should have been the first sign of trouble.

Ian had been moved. Even though he'd been walking and talking and doing fine, he'd been moved. According to what the doctors had said to Wendy, he'd had a major setback and was now in intensive care.

That David didn't believe.

Ian was a loveable oaf, but he was not stupid. And he was very careful to make sure no one got close enough to him to do any more harm. So they'd done something to him to stop him from leaving. Last thing David remembered while sitting between Jewel and Ian was him telling Wendy to grab his clothes and be back in an hour so he could get out of the place. David had left just after that.

That certainly didn't sound like a man on a downward slide. In fact, it was probably because of what he'd said that got him into trouble. If they hadn't realized he was planning on leaving so fast, they wouldn't have taken measures to have him stuffed away where he couldn't be found and likely where he couldn't escape.

The hospital appeared up ahead. Nice and creepy. On a hill like that, he wondered idly if they had more underground than anyone suspected.

Like what if they had a way out of the hospital into some underground tunnel?

Nah, he was just remembering the crazy blood farm mess.

That didn't make any sense in this situation.

But he couldn't help that little voice at the back of his mind asking him if he was sure. After all, they never did find all the other blood farms. This was a perfect place for one. Right under all their noses.

෨ ෯

IAN FOLLOWED MOTRE down the hallway. Questions rolled through his head, but Motre had made it clear to stay silent. Besides, Ian was free again and that's all he cared about. Questions could wait. Although he could really use some damn clothes. Up ahead was a laundry cart. It only contained bedding from what he could see. He gave it a quick search, then turned to follow Motre. And saw his grin. He glared at the big man, who was lucky enough to be fully dressed and not running down the hallway with his bare cheeks hanging out. He was grateful the front of him was covered, but sheesh.

"It's not funny," he growled in a low undertone.

Motre's grin widened. "Actually, it's damn funny. You've got huge knobby knees. Who knew?" With that, he picked up the pace, damn near flying down the hallway.

Knobby knees? Ian glanced down at his legs below the hospital gown. He was tall and lanky. He could use an extra twenty pounds. He'd always been that way. What the hell? Now he had to be worried about things like feet and knees? He snorted. Hell no. Wendy loved him just as he was. And when he saw her again and got her into a private corner with just the two of them, he'd asked her about those body parts. Maybe. Because he didn't want to hear her laugh, too.

Did girls notice feet and knees? Hell, maybe he should ask Tessa. She'd give him the straight goods. She'd grin, but she wouldn't mock him.

Motre came to a dead stop just short of the next corner. He put a hand out to stop Ian's headlong rush.

"Orderlies up ahead," he whispered.

"Let me at him," Ian snapped.

"I know you want to kill these guys, but remember, we don't know whose side anyone is on."

"Screw killing them. I'm going to knock them out and steal their pants."

☙ ❧

JARED DIDN'T KNOW where to go. He'd checked out the news on his phone, and there were sketchy details of the accident. He wanted to know for sure, but how? He could only think to go the vamp hospital or the human hospital. And honestly, the vamp hospital gave him the willies. Vamps. Blood. Needles. Hospital. Hell no.

He turned his feet toward the human hospital. Maybe he could find Taz and find out what was going on. How hard could it be to stay in touch with everyone? He should have gotten Cody's number. It would have hurt to call him, but right now, he'd do it. Ian was part of the whole group, too. Why hadn't he gotten everyone's number? Then again, Ian and Jewel had been hauled off for medical treatment, so who knew what condition they were in?

As he walked the few blocks to the hospital, he wondered at the several items missing from the news.

The two deaths in the group home and his uncle's death.

But who'd report his uncle's death? The man had no friends. It would likely be his sister. Jared frowned. Unless his aunt had been given the same treatment as his uncle –

meaning she'd likely been murdered, too.

His steps slowed down. Damn. Should he go check?

He didn't have her number, but he knew where she lived. He didn't want to break into the house but wasn't sure how else he'd find out. Given the amount of trouble that could possibly be laid at his feet, it might not matter if he broke in or not.

Shit.

She was still family.

He turned toward his aunt's house. What he should have done was grabbed his uncle's car keys and borrowed his damn car.

All this walking was getting seriously old.

CHAPTER 17

T ESSA LAY QUIETLY in bed. Everyone had long since left. Her mother appeared to be pacing the hallway. Tessa's patience had gone the same way. Cody had told her he was following her dad and they were both on their way here. Except that was at least twenty minutes ago. She'd tried to contact Cody since, but the door between them was closed. Not from her side. He wasn't as good at opening and closing that door and often closed it when he needed to concentrate. Or when he was getting ripped by someone. Although she usually could sense the emotion in him at times like this.

The spotty communication could also be from her head injury.

At the reminder, her head started pounding. She moaned lightly and shifted yet again to try and get comfortable. Before she'd realized her hand was chained to the bed, she'd been fine, but now that she knew, she felt so uncomfortable that all she could think about was changing positions.

Arggg. Where were they? She wanted out of here.

Shh. There's something going on. Your dad and I are trying to find out what. Rest up. It's likely to get hairy soon.

Rest? she shrieked. *I'm chained up. Switch places with me and you can be the one to lie here and rest,* she snarled.

She felt his smile. And sighed. *Just hurry up then.*

He left her mind and she opened her eyes to study her

room. She was in the Council hall supposedly. When did they have all these rooms? It looked like a bedroom that had been converted into a hospital room. It made sense to have space for their own people, but she didn't think anyone lived here full time. But she could be wrong.

Vampire Council operated in a very different way. She'd always been on the outside, but she'd kept her ears open over the years. She'd wanted to be part of the Council since forever. Follow in her parents' and her siblings' footsteps. Yet that wasn't likely to happen. Although she'd changed the vampire landscape, she doubted it had changed enough to be of any value to her.

It could be centuries before she'd find acceptance with the older members. Especially if they understood how many of their own she'd helped kill. There was probably some archaic law that stopped her from being part of the Council forever because of that. Her brothers were already apprentices of the Council, so chances were good they were operating on the Council's behalf by taking out the poison. She was on the outside and wouldn't be given the same consideration.

She had to wonder if the Council was sexist. Her mother was on there, but there were only a couple of other women that held similar positions. Most didn't show up to meetings anymore. One of them was seriously old.

Tessa had never met her but had heard her mother talk about her. She'd been a powerhouse in her time. She was over a dozen centuries old and still in good health, but she'd apparently made some comment a while back about how time had given her new meaning to life and she'd return when they were over their foolishness.

As that comment had been long made before Tessa had been born, she wasn't sure what foolishness she'd been talking about. What would she think of this blood farm mess? As an old vampire, she had sustained herself on human blood all her life. Or maybe animal blood. Tessa didn't know. Many of the older vampires were similar.

This old lady, Deanna, was also a glider like Tessa's father. They'd been friends since forever. Her father said she'd done her time and if she wanted to retire in peace and quiet and avoid the young punk vampires, which to her meant anyone under three centuries, who could blame her?

Besides, as an ancient, her bloodline was one of the purest. And that said a lot. Tessa wondered how she'd feel about this damn genetic testing on vampires. She was sure the blood farm scientist would love to get their hands on her.

And how horrible would that be?

The old lady would be devastated to be hunted by her own.

Tessa hated the thought. She understood greed and the need for power, lust and the need for revenge. She didn't understand using her friends and enemies as lab rats. But they were. They also looked at the vampire population as a whole sample pack. They could open it at any time and grab what they wanted and when they wanted it.

There was something very wrong with that way of thinking.

A noise outside in the hallway alerted her to the fact that she was about to have some company. About time. She wanted to get the hell away from here.

The door opened.

"Are you awake, honey?" Her mother whispered from the door.

Tessa tensed. She'd tried hard not to, but it was impossible. Horrible thoughts about her mother being involved with the damn vamps again made her skin crawl. She desperately wanted to jump up and run away – and she'd drag the damn bed with her if she had to.

She lay quiet and waited. Then the door was pushed wider open. Damn it. It sounded as if her mother was coming inside. Sure enough, soft footsteps crept closer to the bed.

Her arm was lifted up. The sleeve pulled back.

Ah shit. Please let her not have a needle in her hand. *Cody. I need help, Cody.*

And damn if she didn't feel the prick of a needle against her skin.

Her scream ripped out. *Cody!*

❧ ❧

CODY HEARD THE scream rip through his mind. Damn it. *Tessa. I'm coming.*

"Serus, Tessa is screaming for help. Rhia is trying to give her a needle."

"It can't be Rhia," Serus said, running in the direction of Tessa's room. "She knows how terrified Tessa is of needles now."

"Would she do that to try and protect her?"

Serus shot him a look as if to say Cody was stupid.

"I just mean she's so upset, how far would she go to keep Tessa safe?" *And away from me*, but he didn't add that part. Serus already thought he was crazy.

"Another option – albeit a crazy one – is cloning. We know they have our DNA – at least DNA from some of us – what if they are making reproductions of us? Not cloning in terms of building an army with the best of many vamps, but what if they had Rhia in a different room and this Rhia was a copy?"

"What?" Serus ran faster, as if he could outrun Cody's words. "I don't want to hear crazy talk like that."

They whipped around a corner and came to a single door on the right. Serus pushed it open and stepped inside. Cody was on his heels.

It was the first time he'd seen Tessa since the accident. She'd been unconscious then.

She wasn't now.

She was standing against the wall, holding her hands in front of her as a shield. And damn if there wasn't a rusted chain attached to her arm, dragging the bed with every hand movement Tessa made. Rhia stood, a needle in one hand, a metal sheet of some kind in the other, and was trying to reach Tessa. The bed, dumped on its side, was between them.

He couldn't believe it. He'd heard Tessa tell him what was going on, but the reality was so much scarier.

Serus appeared too shocked to know what to do.

Rhia turned to face them, but the look in her eyes was a terrible thing to see. "Serus, I will not have her killed over this mess. I've arranged for her to leave. She'll go to my relatives until we've solved this."

He stared at her.

Rhia tried to convince him. "I can't lose her."

"Oh, but you are willing to sacrifice David and Seth."

She snorted. "Seth is already gone. The doctors in Europe have said they can help him. If I send Tessa too, we'll know they are safe. We can protect David, and if things get crazier, then we'll ship him out as well."

Serus took one step closer. "You would do this to her. Knowing she's terrified of needles. Knowing that she would be lost if she woke up alone. Knowing that she'd think she was a prisoner again."

"But…" Rhia snapped. "She'd wake up."

Serus shook his head slowly. "I can't believe you would do that to her."

Rhia straightened up, and even Cody could see the effort it took her.

She was hurting. And badly.

Cody walked around Serus. Rhia's leg looked odd. As if it was broken. "When did you get hurt, Rhia?"

"What?" She glanced down at her leg and she flinched. "Oh, I don't remember."

"Honey, give me the needle. Let me take a look at your leg."

She looked from the needle in her hand to her daughter and then glanced down at her leg. Her eyes rolled up into the back of her head and she collapsed.

☙ ❧

IAN WAITED FOR Motre to give the word, then he stepped around the corner. Two orderlies rushed up to him. "Sir, you shouldn't be out of bed. Let's get you back to your ro—" and the first man went down.

Motre had his hand clamped around the second man's neck before he'd had a chance to make a sound. He caught him in his arms and carried him around the corner.

"Grab the other one. We need to find a place to stash these two so they can't raise the alarm," Motre called back to Ian.

That was the last thing on Ian's mind. He'd already judged this guy to be closest in size. And while Motre had grabbed the one man, Ian was already busy stripping the clothes off the man in front of him. He'd be damned if he was heading into another major fight with his crown jewels hanging out. Why the hell had they stripped him to the skin? They should have left his boxers on. He didn't want to wear another man's underwear so he made do with his pants, shirt, socks, and eureka – the shoes were a fit, too. A bad fit, but anything was better than running through this place barefoot.

He'd almost gotten the shoes tied up when Motre came barreling around the corner. Ian hopped to his feet, feeling like a vamp once again. He grinned evilly at Motre. "Now I'm ready to kick ass."

"You mean now that yours is covered up, right?"

And Ian's grin widened. "I was feeling a little too cool for my liking."

Motre shook his head, grabbed the guy's lab coat off the floor, and threw it at him. "You might as well put this on to complete the costume."

He threw the unconscious vamp over his shoulder and disappeared. Ian struggled to get into the lab coat just as he heard voices behind him. He took a deep breath, walked a few steps forward so he stood where Motre would be able to see him, and stopped as if he were searching for something he'd lost in his pocket. Motre approached from the side. Ian held his hand up in front of his body in warning, but in such a way that the people coming up behind him wouldn't be able to see.

"Are you lost, or what?" said someone from behind him.

"Sorry. Just looking for the notes I had on me this morning. Can't find them now." He rustled around, searching an inside pocket in an absentminded way.

The two men passed him. "Look at what kind of help we have now."

As they walked past, Ian jumped one and Motre took down the other. Quickly, they delivered the two men to the same room as the other two.

"I wonder how many more we'll have stashed in here before we're done," Ian growled.

"No idea. Let's move it."

"Who are we trying to rescue?"

"All the ones we rescued from the mine were brought here for observation," Motre said. "So far, no one has been released."

Ian shook his head. "So we managed to accomplish nothing by bringing down the blood farm?"

"I didn't say that. I'm sure many of the hospital staff are honest vamps. Once they started moving people to new rooms for all kinds of different reasons, I knew we had something odd going on."

"They moved me just after Wendy left. She was going to pick up some clothes for me and my cell phone. And she never came back, until..." and he quickly explained what he'd heard and seen from his window. "So I don't even know if she's alive or dead. If she's dead, I'll be razing this damn place to the ground."

He could feel the same panic welling up inside that he had before watching her run for her life away from these bastards.

Motre had his cell phone in his pocket. He nudged Ian close to a fire exit door and started pushing him up the stairs. "I'll call Goran and see if he has any news."

He tried once and got no answer. "Not sure what's going on, but we need to move. I'll try later."

He tried once again. Still nothing.

CHAPTER 18

TESSA DROPPED THE bed frame and stared shakily over to her mother. If that creature was her mother. "Dad, what's going on?"

"I'm not sure, Tessa. She's definitely not acting normal. But I don't know if what happened to everyone in the mine is the reason why she's being so afraid now. Or if this is something else. Maybe she's been drugged again." He brushed her hair back from her forehead. "I really don't know." He glanced over at Tessa. "Can't you tell?"

"There is a little darkness there. But I don't know if it's residual blackness from before."

She looked down at her wrist still chained to the bed. "She did this to me. She came at me with a needle and that metal sheet so I couldn't just knock her out. That's when I fought back." She shook her head. "I didn't want to hurt her, but she left me no choice."

"Did you break her leg?" Serus asked incredulously. "Your own mother?"

Tessa's eyes filled with tears. She studied her mother's energy, her heart singing at the slight blackness in her system. Less than before, but there was still some. Maybe she'd been given a different dose or a different type of drug.

"Yes," she said quietly. "I did. I kicked out once while I was on the bed, and that was all it took. And if you came at me with a needle after having chained me to something, you can be damn sure I'd do my damnedest to hurt you, too."

She stared at him, proud and defiant. Bitterness clogged her throat. "Do you really think I wanted to hurt her?" She glared at him, her own temper working up to a blinding rage. "Do you know what it's like after everything I've been through to wake up and find out my own mother had done this?" She lifted her arm, the bed rattling with the movement. "What was I supposed to do? Let her drug me, too?"

He shook his head. "No. No, of course not. I'm sorry. This is so messed up. Everything is backwards and people aren't acting rational."

The last he muttered so low, she barely caught it. "Like who else?"

He heard her but didn't acknowledge her question. Just then, Cody returned. A medic raced to Rhia's side. Cody came to Tessa's side. He had a long-handled tool in his hand.

She glanced at it, one eyebrow raised. He smirked. "For your chains. Although you'd make a great slave girl."

Relieved, she held out her arm while threatening in a mocking voice, "You really don't want to go there."

Cody positioned it at the one link wrapped around her wrist and closed the long handles. It snapped instantly.

She rubbed her arm. "Thank you. I hated that feeling. I never want to be anyone's prisoner again." She stepped further back as more people crowded into the room. Overwhelmed with what had just happened, she could only think about escaping. She inched around behind the crowd and ran out the door.

Cody called out, "Hey, wait for me."

But she'd already booked it.

She didn't know where to go, but she had to get out.

Somewhere where she would have a chance to deal with the confusion and pain, the sense of betrayal in her head. God, she'd actually hurt her mother. Even though she'd chained and drugged her, Tessa couldn't help feeling terrible. Surely there'd been something else she could have done instead. She'd tried to interrupt her energy like normal but when that hadn't worked, she'd panicked. She'd just reacted.

Just like she'd run from the room now. Running from the horror of what her mother had done. From what she'd tried to do and the words that had poured out of her mouth.

It made Tessa wonder now what she meant by that. What did she know? Tessa found an empty room and went in and closed it behind her. She didn't mean to shut Cody out. Hadn't thought about it. She'd just wanted to be alone.

A gentle knock on the door had her spinning around. She eased open the door in her mind. And smiled.

Cody. Sorry, I just needed to be alone for a bit.

Are you sure? I'm okay for you to be in there on your own to deal with this, but I need to know that you're okay. That you aren't going to do anything stupid.

I'll be fine. Just give me few moments. I need... I don't know what I need.

She heard the confusion in his voice, the pain in his own emotion. *It's not you, Cody. I just feel like my foundation is gone.*

And yet you won't let me help? Be there for you? Now he was getting pissed. And she realized she'd turned her back on him the same way she felt her parents had turned their backs on her.

She walked back to the door and opened it. Cody stood in front of her. She stared at him, wondering how he'd become such a huge part of her life, when the tears started to fall.

He opened his arms and she walked into them.

❧ ❦

CODY HELD HER close, loving the chance to be here for her. She was so special. He wasn't sure exactly what had happened between her mother and her but knew it had hit her hard. He cuddled her close as he moved her inside and closed the door. He wasn't sure what this room was, but there were easy chairs and a big couch as if it were a lounge for visitors or something similar. The best thing about it was it was private, and he hadn't had her alone to himself in a long time. And never like this. He urged her toward the couch, making sure the door was locked behind him first. There were too many people in this place. She needed some downtime and so did he. He wanted to give that much to her.

Even if it was only for a few moments.

She moved like an automaton to the couch and collapsed. He sat down beside her and tugged her into his arms. She curled up against his chest.

It was the silence that bothered him. The quiet inside and out. He didn't know what to say. If anything…maybe just holding her was the best thing to do. He dropped a kiss on her forehead while gently stroking up and down her back. Her body was long and lean yet so fragile. He knew how strong she was, how much she'd coped with. She'd deal with this, too. And he'd be there to help her.

He was so grateful she'd opened the door for him. When she'd run, he'd been afraid she'd run from him, too. Thank heavens she hadn't. They had so much going for them; he wanted them to make it. So few did. And they had nothing like what he already had with her.

She was his and he'd do everything he could to help her through this.

"She hasn't been quite normal since the blood farm," Tessa murmured.

Cody didn't have to ask who 'she' was. "No, she hasn't. Maybe someone slipped her another dose. We thought we were safe so we let down our guards. Instead, it's like those around us were placed where we hadn't expected them to be and pulled off a secret attack while we relaxed our guard."

"When could that have happened?" she asked.

"Anyone in the Council could have given her something. Anyone at the Human Council could have. Think about Councilman Adamson – he'd been taking Gloria's poison even though she's no longer alive."

"True. And Mom had returned to the hospital to see the doctor again. She's also been there with Seth. If she's been dosed again, then likely Seth has been, too. According to her, he's been shipped to Europe. I got the impression he was in a coma or something." Tessa sat up, her face troubled. "How can we find out where he is? If he's not here where we can keep an eye on him, it's going to be so much harder to get him free of the drugs."

He couldn't argue with that. "The only way is to contact the hospital and see if anyone there knows."

"And that we can't do because the hospital appears to be under a rogue vampire's control."

"Maybe some of the vampires we brought in for questioning will know." Cody's phone jangled. He shifted slightly so he could pull it out. He swore softly. "It's from David. I wondered where he'd disappeared to."

"He's missing?" she asked, shifting back slightly so she could look up into his face. "Where is he?"

He tilted the cell phone so she could look.

"Oh no!" After reading the short message, she cried out,

"He's sneaking into the hospital."

David PULLED INTO the underground parking lot and parked. He turned off the lights and sunk low in his seat. He wanted a moment to get the lay of the land. Something was wrong in this place, and he didn't need his nerves to tell him that. This place felt wrong. Like a menacing energy lived down here. It was palpable. He shuddered and wished that he'd at least let someone know the details of his plan. Maybe he still should. He was still going inside after Jewel. He'd find her, but he couldn't go in as a crazy man. He'd learned enough last week to realize that he didn't have to do something stupid. Hopefully he'd find allies in the hospital. He knew many vamps had been brought here after being rescued.

What he didn't know was how many might have been drugged again while they were here. He'd come back with help once he understood what they were up against. He didn't think he'd ever been here before and didn't know his way around. That put him at a definite disadvantage.

He stepped out of the car and closed his door quietly.

Feeling exposed, he crouched behind the vehicle and turned slowly to check out his surroundings. Seeing nothing wrong, he slipped between the vehicles and flattened himself against the closest wall. He hated that his nerves had woken in a big way. Even his stupid hands felt clammy, cold.

Why had he decided to do this alone?

Right now, it looked like a supremely bad idea.

He'd sent a text to Cody, but it hadn't been explicit. Now he realized he needed to send another one. He opened his cell phone and took a moment to tell Cody to get his ass over here.

He needed backup.

SERUS DIDN'T KNOW what to do. Rhia wasn't the Rhia he knew. Had she been given more drugs? And how could he possibly tell? Was her behavior really a reaction to almost losing everyone? He carried her into a single small room he often used at the Council hall when he needed space from everyone. He was a loner. He hated crowds and wanted nothing better than to spend time with his family.

He went to pull out his phone and realized he didn't have it on him. He grabbed Rhia's and called Sian. After arranging for her to come and sit with Rhia, he called Taz and explained what happened.

"It could be the drugs she'd been given initially. Some drugs take longer to take effect," Taz said. "If she'd received a booster, it would be even more likely that it's the same drugs. I can't say for sure. At this point, I'm not sure I know a vamp doctor to recommend. You guys never needed one, so it's not like you have many to call on."

Serus winced. He understood but damn it, his wife needed help.

Taz said slowly, as if he'd been thinking long and slow, "You know, it could also be the brainwashing. If they'd given her some triggers, they could easily put her back under their influence. That way they would be able to get her to do whatever they needed her to do. Including moving Seth and potentially many other vamps out of the country."

Brainwashing.

Serus stared down at Rhia, remembering what Cody and

David had said about her behavior before. How she'd appeared completely normal except for the things she had said and the things she appeared to be completely happy to do – like administer drugs to her son. "Is that what's happened to you, Rhia?" he whispered, hating to think she'd been triggered, as Taz had called it. But it actually might be better than the thought of her receiving more drugs. The drugs were insidious. Then again, so was the brainwashing. Who knew what they had already done or continued to program her to do?

The door opened behind him and Sian rushed in. "I can't believe she chained Tessa to the bed."

"And tried to inject her with something." Serus fished the needle out of his pocket. He wanted it analyzed, but he had to find someone he could trust to do it.

"I can analyze it." She took it from him. "Actually, if you can wait here, I'll get this started then come back and watch over her." She headed back out the door.

"Wait, have you heard anything about Goran? Is he going to be okay?"

She shook her head. "No one seems to know. He's unconscious and not showing any signs of waking up."

She walked out, leaving Serus alone.

Worse than that, he realized for the first time, he was seriously alone – possibly forever. Goran wasn't there, and his beloved Rhia wasn't there in his mind where she'd been for centuries.

He felt bereft.

And lost.

JARED COULDN'T HELP that his pace slowed the closer he got to his aunt's house. He didn't want to see her. And he wanted to see her dead body even less. After realizing his uncle had been murdered, the reality was that he didn't want revenge any more. He hadn't heard if there had been any survivors like his father from the blood farm, but he knew inside that his dad had died a long time ago. That was brutal. It was sad, but it was also a fact.

He couldn't do anything about it. It broke him apart to think of his dad hanging there all these years, but at the same time, there was a sigh of relief after the mountain collapsed. His father was now buried. Not the way Jared would like to see him. Not the way Jared would have wanted to have it, but it was the way it was, and it brought him closure. Just a tiny bit. His uncle's death brought another tiny piece. And now maybe he'd see his aunt and realize that this was really over. If she was alive, he wanted her to pay, but he couldn't honestly say he'd be happy if she was dead.

He'd seen enough death to last him a long time.

The house was around the corner and a block away. He walked steadily, wishing he could have driven. The town was small, but that was both good and bad. It wasn't big enough to support any type of public transport, so that meant he had to walk everywhere. It was also why everyone owned a vehicle – who wanted to walk?

There were neighbors out beside his aunt's place. One was mowing his lawn. Two women were talking over their fences, enjoying a break in their day. He didn't know if he should just walk up and knock on the front door. It would make sense, but at the same time, he didn't know what to say to her if she did answer.

He decided to be bold. After all, the neighbors were

watching him. He needed to make it look like he belonged here. He couldn't remember the last time he'd been here, but he was pretty sure he'd been forced to do her chores every damn time. She'd had someone living here at the time, but that person had either left or wasn't around at the moment. He frowned, trying to dredge up the man's face. And damn if something at the back of his mind kicked in. He could see the guy's face superimposed with plastic. He stopped and bowed his head. Damn. Had his aunt sold her live-in lover to the blood farm? What had she done after that? Gotten another one for as long as it worked out then sold him, too?

That old anger burned his belly. What a bitch. Had his uncle known?

Had she split the money with him? Although why she would do that, he didn't know. Except that they'd both known each other's secrets. They had to keep their twisted bond strong. He lifted his head to knock on the door, but it opened as soon as his hand hit the wood. The smell that slid out the crack in the door had him backing up and coughing like mad.

"Oh dear. Are you all right?" one of the neighboring ladies called out.

He shook his head and pointed to the open door. He didn't want to see, but the aroma was unmistakable. While he coughed again, the women came running. They bounded up the stairs and into the house.

Then the screams started.

CHAPTER 19

T ESSA RACED OUT of the room, all thoughts of a time out forgotten once she realized what was going on with David.

"We have to tell Dad."

"And I need to check on my father." Cody frowned. "I really hate to think of us going into something like this without backup."

"Like David did?" Tessa hated that her brother had taken such a chance. She needed him after almost losing Seth. Seth might live, but he might never recover and even if he did, he might not be the same as he was before. She hadn't determined if that was a good thing or not.

Sian was walking past when they reached one of the main chambers. She had a needle in her hand. Tessa's breath caught in the back of her throat. She stared at the needle like it was a serpent going to strike her.

Sian smiled gently. "Yes. It's the one your mother was holding. I'm testing the contents for your father."

The breath gusted out. "Thanks. I'm glad to hear that. Where is Dad?"

She pointed down the hallway. "He's inside the last door on the left, watching over your mother."

Tessa winced.

Sian laid a gentle hand on her arm. "Don't hold this

against her. She's either been drugged again or some of the brainwashing has been triggered. Either way, she's not herself. She's not the woman you knew. But that woman will return. You know that, right?"

Tessa nodded immediately. Not because she agreed – she didn't know what she believed – but because Sian was looking for reassurance.

"We'll go and talk to Dad now."

"Good idea. When I'm done testing, I'm going to watch over Rhia so he can go to Goran."

"How is my father?" Cody asked, his voice husky.

"I won't lie, Cody, we've never seen anything like this. If he were exhausted, then maybe he'd take this long to heal. If he were injured with silver or something that was holding him back from healing, then maybe that would make sense. But in normal circumstances, he'd have woken up already."

Tessa studied Sian, her words finally clicking in her head. "Hang on. You're saying he's not healing – as if something is stopping him?"

Sian shrugged. "In theory. I can't explain it clearly."

"No problem," Tessa said. "We'll go see Mom and Dad for a few moments then stop by Goran's bed to say hi."

"Good idea," Sian said. "I'll be back in a few moments."

Tessa led the way to her father. She opened the door, saw her mother in bed, and walked in. She didn't know what to think at this point. She wasn't angry anymore, just shocked and scared. What was it going to take to get her mother back? She realized that if her mother had received another dose of drugs or if she'd been triggered with that dumb mind control stuff, it had likely happened at the hospital.

As soon as the thought crossed her mind, she realized everything was going back to the damn hospital. And that was the final bit that helped wash her mother's actions away into its proper place. She walked forward and sat down at her mother's side. Her father stepped back slightly, giving her room. Tessa reached down and stroked her cheek.

"Poor Mom."

"Exactly."

She sighed. "I don't hold it against her, Dad. I just wish this hadn't happened. There are so many things wrong now."

Cody stood beside her father and showed him David's text.

Serus roared.

Tessa shrieked and clapped her hands over her head.

Rhia moaned.

"Now look at what you've done, Dad."

Serus rushed over and gently stroked Rhia's head until she went back under. Then he turned to Tessa. "Did you know what your brother was up to?"

"No. I would have gone with him in that case," she retorted. "We need to help him now. I had hoped you'd sent a team up there while I was out cold. I only woke up a short while ago, remember?" she said bitterly. "Instead, look what I woke up to."

"We haven't had a chance to organize a group to deal with the hospital." Serus said with a groan. "That's probably why David took off on his own."

"Of course. Jewel and Ian are both in danger." She frowned. "Where's Wendy?"

"She's sleeping somewhere. She smashed her head pretty bad in the accident. She has not fully recovered either."

Tessa grew grim. "Not a good showing. One car accident and most of us are out of the running. The accident has to be connected. They slipped in behind our guard when we weren't expecting to see them. With that step, they've already gained the high ground."

"But we're not down and we're not out."

"Do we have a way to contact Motre or his men?" She looked at her father. "I'd like to have them with us. They are good men."

Serus opened the phone and realized he still was using Rhia's. He checked the contact list but she didn't have Motre on there. He stood up and slapped his other pockets and swore. "I've lost my phone. I've been using your mother's."

"Did you have it when you found Mom?"

He stared at her. "Yes, I think so."

Sian returned just then. "I'll watch her now. You go and do what you need to do. We won't get the results for a while."

Serus nodded. He led the way. "First thing is to find my phone."

They retraced their steps to where Tessa had been. It wasn't far – just down the hallway and past a few rooms. She entered and winced.

The damn bed was still in the far corner, and her mother's blood still dotted the floor.

Kicked to the side in all the excitement was her father's cell phone.

She handed it over to him.

He turned it on and checked it. And crowed. "Motre texted me. He freed Ian and they are on the way to releasing more prisoners."

"Good." Cody said. "Tell him that David is coming up from the underground parking lot and that we're on our way."

The three looked at each other, then turned as one and headed to the main area.

"What about Goran? Maybe we should stop by there

first," Tessa said.

Serus shook his head. "No. He's unconscious and will heal at his own rate. He should be improved by the time we get back."

Tessa hesitated, torn. "I might be able to help him."

Serus already heading out the door stopped, turned. "Do you think so?"

She shrugged. "I don't know."

Serus stared at her then said, "He was in an accident not drugged or implanted with anything weird." He started back out to the hallway. "We'll go help David and if Goran isn't improving when we get back, then you can take a look. Agreed?"

"Agreed." She smiled, loving the change in her father's attitude toward her. "Let's go."

෮ ෩

DAVID WATCHED AS one man left the hospital underground parking lot, driving away in a Council van. He barely had time to note the license plate and time of departure. Maybe they could track the driver and figure out whose side he was on. Thinking about that, he sent another text, this time to Sian. Maybe she could track it down and get the name of the driver. He hoped his sister, father, and best friend were on their way here. He also hoped they had pulled together a damn army.

Not that the last part was likely.

Another vehicle arrived. He watched from the shadows. The man, who David didn't recognize, walked straight to the double doors and entered. No alarm lights shone. No beeps or buzzers. And no key or card required.

Good to know.

After he gave the man a good ten-minute head start, David strode over and opened the door. It opened easily. He took a deep breath and walked inside.

He hoped this wasn't the stupidest thing he'd ever done.

His phone buzzed. He slipped off to one side and checked the incoming text. And grinned. Motre and Ian were free and knew he was coming. Now if only he had some way to know where they were.

He texted back asking for details and said he'd gained entrance from the underground lot. He explained the plan to go straight to the top and come down checking every floor one at a time.

Then he put his phone away and started to run up the stairs. There was something close to ten floors here. He stopped halfway up the first flight and looked over the railing. The stairs went down. Like way down. He stopped to think about that. He'd come in one level down from the ground level, through the underground parking lot. But the stairs showed that the hospital went a lot further down than he expected. From where he was standing, he could see a dozen flights or so burrowing down into the bowels of the hill. He hated what his mind was thinking.

But he couldn't stop his feet from retracing their steps and starting down the other set of stairs. He really didn't want to see what was going on down this deep, but he knew if they were going to hide anything or anyone, it would likely be there.

Damn.

He really hated this part.

But if Jewel was stashed somewhere here, he was damned if he'd leave without her.

❧ ❦

IAN FOLLOWED MOTRE as they worked their way from room to room. They found many vamps, but most were in bad shape. And they didn't recognize anyone.

That in itself was odd. "How did you know which room I was in?" he asked.

Motre tapped his ear.

Ian wasn't sure if that meant they needed to be quiet so they could hear anyone coming or if he meant he'd heard someone say something about where Ian was being moved to.

Motre held out his hand to stop Ian.

And he tilted his head. With a sharp warning look at Ian, he slid closer to the next door and held up his finger in warning.

Ian sidled up to the opposite side. On the count of three, they opened the door and jumped in.

❧ ❦

JARED SPOKE WITH the police when they arrived. Said he hadn't seen her for a few days and although he'd called his uncle, he hadn't managed to reach him. No, he didn't know if the death of his aunt was related to his uncle's silence, but he gave them his uncle's address.

At least this way his uncle's body would be found and dealt with.

He told them he'd been in the blood farm mess and had spoken to the two officers about that already. There was no point in lying. They'd be able to find out easily enough. When they'd finished, they asked him if he wanted a ride back. He shook his head and made up an excuse that the walk back might help him clear his head of the shock. Knowing they might be watching, he took the route back to the group home. If he felt the penetrating stares as he walked, he put it down to common sense on his part. He'd found one body and was steering them to find another. That they hadn't mentioned anything about the bodies at the group home scared him shitless. Like what could have happened here? The last thing he wanted to do was go there and find out personally. He'd rather find Tessa and her family and stay with them. It was infinitely safer that way.

Sure, the humans were talking about rioting, but were they going to or was it all talk? All he'd seen so far was dead humans. That didn't say much for their planning.

Not sure if the police were going to follow or check up on him, he walked all the way to the group home and approached it casually. He saw people through the windows. A couple were in the yard tossing a ball. Really? What happened to the dead guy he'd tripped over on the back step?

He'd just decided to keep walking when a cop car turned the corner and drove down the block.

Crap. He'd been afraid they'd check up on him.

He opened the gate and walked into the yard, as if he belonged. He walked around the side of the house to the back yard. He stopped where he could see the cop car. It pulled up to the side of the road and parked.

Double crap.

He'd hoped they'd drive on. He walked around to the back kitchen door and stared at the spot where he'd seen a body that morning.

The spot was empty. Clear. Clean.

He pulled his shirt away from his chest and swallowed. Had he imagined it? Surely not.

The wooden door was open, but the screen door was closed. Inside, he could hear the cooks working in the kitchen. His stomach growled. Should he go in or run like hell?

He walked back to the corner to see if the cops were still there. Not seeing the car, he walked around to the front and saw the cop car pulling away up ahead. Good. That was one problem gone.

"Jared? Hey, you left early this morning. What happened?"

The manager of the home was standing on the front porch.

"I couldn't sleep, so I left early."

The man's eyes sharpened. "What time did you leave? I thought you were sleeping late until I went and checked on you and saw you were gone."

Jared nodded. "I lost so much school that I wanted to get in early and speak to the teachers. Get the backlog of work done." He shifted his pack, having left his big one at school. "I went to my aunt's place on the way home." He let his voice fill with emotion and walked to the bottom step. "I pushed the door open and saw something I hope to never see again. She was dead – might have been for awhile." He gave a shudder, one that came easy considering the day he'd had.

"I had to stay to talk to the police." He motioned to the car that was now out of sight. "I walked home and they just checked to make sure I made it home safe."

The manager, who'd always seemed like a nice guy, said, "Christ, you've had a day of it. Come on then, there is leftover roast beef and potatoes." The manager turned around and held the door open. "Let's get you a solid meal and an early night. Things will look different in the morning."

The roast beef sounded damn good. But going back into

that house…he didn't know.

Was it safe?

❧ ❦

DAVID DESCENDED THE stairs. He wondered when they would end. Surely there was no need for this many floors for a vamp hospital. Few vamps got sick, and even fewer needed more than a bone set right or a busted wing pinned up until it healed. Vampires healed on their own ninety-nine percent of the time. This massive complex made no sense. He knew the structural building was old. He had to wonder if it had always been a hospital.

The building looked modern enough on both the outside and the inside, but he didn't remember it being built in his day, and if it had been built in his father's day, that would mean it was still hundreds of years old. Why would they need something this size? He struggled to make sense of it. At every flight of stairs, there were doors going into another floor. He'd peered into the glass window at every floor hoping to see something – anything – on the inside. Yet saw nothing. He didn't get it. It's as if this lower half of the hospital had been built and never used.

He frowned as he descended yet another floor. The place was clean. Very clean. So someone was looking after the place.

Why? Actually, the why made sense – it was a hospital after all, and that meant cleanliness was important. Being empty, it had to be an easy enough job. Mop a few floors, do a few repairs.

He knew the vampire community had loads of space. Most houses were mansions, and many had multiple houses. They lived a long time and they liked their privacy and space.

But honestly, these floors could house everyone in town and still have enough space to not trip over each other.

And he couldn't fathom it. While he descended, he texted his sister and Motre.

This place was unbelievably huge and if they were looking for bad guys, they were out of luck, because they could be anywhere.

CHAPTER 20

TESSA SAT BESIDE her father as he drove toward the hospital. Cody was in the back seat. She'd been sending texts back and forth between David and Motre and getting them to connect. And to let everyone like Sian know what they were doing and why.

By the time she was done, they were at the hospital. Her father pulled into the underground parking space and stopped the car. The place appeared deserted, but she didn't know or care anymore. As far as she was concerned, this place could burn to the ground.

She'd had enough. Sian hadn't had any luck tracking down Seth, either. And that just sent fear racing down Tessa's spine. She just knew that once he left the country, the chances were very slim that she'd get her brother back. She didn't know if getting him back now would be any different, but to have him go so far away would be terrible. Who knew what these guys would do to him...no. She swore it wasn't going to happen.

That David had taken off on his own was something else she planned to rip him a new one for. He hadn't contacted their father or even Cody to go with him. Like crazy. And stupid. And freaking nuts. She loved both her brothers, but she didn't love what either of them were doing.

Or her mother. In fact, she was pretty disenchanted with

all of her family right about now. Except her father, and wasn't that a switch?

They aren't all bad. It's just a tough time. Cody said in a gentle tone. *Give them some space and understanding. Seth isn't responsible, and neither is Rhia. It's a tough time. Hang in there, Tessa. You're tired and hurting emotionally.*

She closed her eyes, loving the way his voice wormed through her heart. It felt so good. It filled the cold empty places inside and made her feel not so alone.

Thanks.

I'm angry, she whispered shamefully. *That this nightmare isn't over. I want it to be over. I want to go out on Friday night with you and your friends and be normal teenagers for a change.*

You might want to be a normal teenager. I'm past that stage, thank you. But his voice was both humorous and wry.

True. She smiled and teased, *You're like really old. Almost your father's age.*

He laughed at that, and she felt infinitely better as his joy lifted her own spirits.

I'm worried about Seth and Mom, she said. *I can't believe Jewel and Ian are once again in trouble. It's always been those two.*

Yes, and I wonder if that is why they've been singled out now, Cody said. *Maybe the scientists want to see the end results. Or maybe they want to move onto the next stage of their testing — whatever that is.*

God help us all if that's the case. She shuddered. *Also, I don't understand what's happening in the human world with Jared finding four bodies today. He has no one left now.*

And that made her sad. She had so much in comparison.

He didn't go back to the home, did he? Cody said. *Surely he's too smart for that?*

He has nowhere else to go. She frowned. *Maybe a friend's house? But how can he? He's expected to be at the home. If he doesn't show up there, they will put out an alarm about him missing. I imagine there is a curfew and possibly some kind of bed check at night.*

I always imagine it to be one step away from prison.

She laughed. *I don't think it's that bad.* Her laughter died and she started texting again. *I'm going to ask him where he is. If nothing else, he can bunk at our house. The thing is empty and there is lots of room. I should have made the offer earlier.*

There was silence. She turned to stare at him. Then got it. She gasped. *Surely you're not jealous?*

He grinned. *Honey, when it comes to other men, I'm never going to be happy to have them sleep under the same roof as you.*

Ha, she motioned outside the car. *See where we are? The only one getting sleep this night will be Jared.*

The gloominess in the underground lot surrounded them as Tessa walked to the entrance with Cody and her father. "Are we going downstairs after David or upstairs to help Motre and Ian?"

"Downstairs after David," her father said immediately. "Then the four of us will go and get Ian and Jewel. Then home. We're not here to fight a battle. Just retrieve a few friends that haven't been able to leave on their own."

Tessa hoped it would be that easy.

It won't be, Cody said with a groan. *It never is.*

He walked over to the big door and pulled it open. "Are you ready?"

Serus walked through first. Tessa next. Cody slipped in behind them. The three of them stared at the staircase that seemed to go on forever. And damn if Serus didn't look up, then down over the railing, then with a wicked grin at Tessa and Cody, he said, "See you at the bottom."

And he dropped over the side.

"What the..." Cody said as he raced to look down. Tessa was already there. She grinned. "He's taken the fastest way."

"Oh no, you don't," Cody said. "I'm not jumping over that edge."

She laughed. "Okay." She jumped to the center of the landing and then down a flight of stairs to the center of the next landing. And repeated it. Again and again.

Cody raced behind her, swearing and crying foul. She laughed and for the first time all day she felt good – in fact, she felt great.

She dropped down several more flights of stairs and realized her father hadn't called up to them. He was long gone. She leaned over the railing and waited for Cody to catch up. There was no visible end to the stairwell. Just blackness.

And her stomach sank. There was no bottom. Her dad had jumped.

But he was a glider. Not a flier.

"Dad?"

No answer.

Her father was gone.

"Dad!"

The cry echoed around and around.

Nothing.

Author's Note

Thank you for reading Family Blood Ties Books 4–6! I hope you enjoyed reading it as much as I loved writing it. If you enjoyed the book, please leave a review.

Dear reader,

I love to hear from readers, and you can contact me at my website: www.dalemayer.com or at my Facebook author page. To be informed of new releases and special offers, sign up for my newsletter. And if you are interested in joining Dale Mayer's Fan Club, here is the Facebook sign up page.

If you'd like to read about other books I've written, please turn the page.

Cheers,
Dale Mayer

Thank you for reading *Family Blood Ties Books 4–6*. If you enjoyed reading about Tessa's story the series continues with Vampire in Chaos.

COMPLIMENTARY DOWNLOAD

DOWNLOAD a ***complimentary*** copy of TUESDAY'S CHILD? Just tell me where to send it!

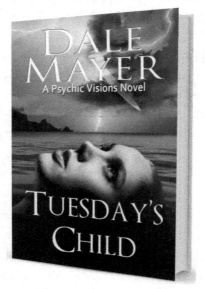

http://dalemayer.com/starterlibrarytc/

Vampire in Chaos

Buy this book at your favorite vendor.

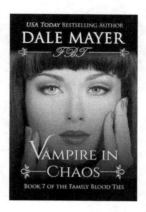

Family Blood Ties Series

Dangerous Designs

Drawing is her world…but when her new pencil comes alive, it's his world too.

Her…Storey Dalton is seventeen and now boyfriendless after being dumped via Facebook. Drawing is her escape. It's like as soon as she gets down one image, a dozen more are pressing in on her. Then she realizes her pictures are almost drawing themselves…or is it that her new pencil is alive?

Him…Eric Jordan is a new Ranger and the only son of the Councilman to his world. He's crossed the veil between dimensions to retrieve a lost stylus. But Storey is already experimenting with her new pencil and what her drawings can do – like open portals.

It …The stylus is a soul-bound intelligence from Eric's dimension on Earth and uses Storey's unsuspecting mind to seek its way home, giving her an unbelievable power. She unwittingly opens a third dimension, one that held a dangerous predatory species banished from Eric's world centuries ago, releasing these animals into both dimensions.

Them…Once in Eric's homeland, Storey is blamed for the calamity and sentenced to death. When she escapes, Eric is ordered to bring her back or face that same death penalty. With nothing to lose, can they work together across dimensions to save both their worlds?

Design series

Gem Stone (a Gemma Stone Mystery)

A juvie kid trying to stay on the right path stumbles into trouble...

Gemma takes her camera everywhere. From juvie hall to a halfway home, the new hobby gives her a focus she'd never had before and... hope in a future. Until she takes pictures of something that could get her killed.

And not just her...after she and another juvie girl are chased by a stranger to the halfway home that same night, the other girl goes missing and Gemma knows she needs help. But who can she trust?

Not the authorities that's for sure. Trusting them is impossible for a girl with her damaged history, and besides, who cares about a troubled kid...especially when trouble just naturally seems to find her.

In Cassie's Corner

Faith and loyalty are tested as a young girl learns what it is to believe – in herself, in her friends, and in life after death.

Cassie's best friend, bad boy Todd, is gone. Gone as in dead. Gone as in he's now a ghost.

But she doesn't realize that when he wakes her in her bedroom and begs her not to believe what they say about him. It's not until the next day when her parents tell her about the accident that she learns the truth...

The police believe Todd was living up to the family name, drinking and driving and coming to a predictable end. It's up to her to find out the truth and clear his name.

Todd is shocked at his sudden change in circumstances...and angry. He struggles with his new ghostly reality, realizing all he's lost as he watches his brother build a relationship with Cassie as the two pair up to find out what really happened to him.

The truth isn't always pretty, and Cassie has to be stronger than ever before. Especially when the whole world seems to be against her.

About the Author

Dale Mayer is a USA Today bestselling author best known for her Psychic Visions and Family Blood Ties series. Her contemporary romances are raw and full of passion and emotion (Second Chances, SKIN), her thrillers will keep you guessing (By Death series), and her romantic comedies will keep you giggling (It's a Dog's Life and Charmin Marvin Romantic Comedy series).

She honors the stories that come to her – and some of them are crazy and break all the rules and cross multiple genres!

To go with her fiction, she also writes nonfiction in many different fields with books available on resume writing, companion gardening and the US mortgage system. She has recently published her Career Essentials Series. All her books are available in print and ebook format.

Connect with Dale Mayer Online

Dale's Website – www.dalemayer.com
Twitter – @DaleMayer
Facebook – facebook.com/DaleMayer.author

Also by Dale Mayer

Published Adult Books:

Psychic Vision Series

Tuesday's Child

Hide'n Go Seek

Maddy's Floor

Garden of Sorrow

Knock, Knock...

Rare Find

Eyes to the Soul

Now You See Her

Shattered

Into the Night...

Psychic Visions Books 1–3

Psychic Visions Books 4–6

Psychic Visions Books 7–9

By Death Series

Touched by Death – Part 1

Touched by Death – Part 2

Touched by Death – Parts 1&2

Haunted by Death

Chilled by Death

By Death Books 1–3

Second Chances...at Love Series

Second Chances – Part 1

Second Chances – Part 2

Second Chances – complete book (Parts 1 & 2)

Charmin Marvin Romantic Comedy Series

Broken Protocols

Broken Protocols 2

Broken Protocols 3

Broken Protocols 3.5

Broken Protocols 1-3

Broken and... Mending

Skin

Scars

Scales (of Justice)

Broken but... Mending 1-3

Glory

Genesis

Tori

Celeste

Glory Trilogy

Biker Blues

Biker Blues: Morgan, Part 1

Biker Blues: Morgan, Part 2

Biker Blues: Morgan, Part 3

Biker Baby Blues: Morgan, Part 4

Biker Blues: Morgan, Full Set

Biker Blues: Salvation, Part 1

Biker Blues: Salvation, Part 2
Biker Blues: Salvation, Part 3
Biker Blues: Salvation, Full Set

SEALs of Honor

Mason: SEALs of Honor, Book 1
Hawk: SEALs of Honor, Book 2
Dane: SEALs of Honor, Book 3
Swede: SEALs of Honor, Book 4
Shadow: SEALs of Honor, Book 5
Cooper: SEALs of Honor, Book 6
Markus: SEALs of Honor, Book 7
Evan: SEALs of Honor, Book 8
Chase: SEALs of Honor, Book 9
Brett: SEALs of Honor, Book 10
SEALs of Honor, Books 1–3

Collections

Dare to Be You...
Dare to Love...
Dare to be Strong...
RomanceX3

Standalone Novellas

It's a Dog's Life
Riana's Revenge

Published Young Adult Books:

Family Blood Ties Series

Vampire in Denial
Vampire in Distress

Vampire in Design
Vampire in Deceit
Vampire in Defiance
Vampire in Conflict
Vampire in Chaos
Vampire in Crisis
Vampire in Control
Vampire in Charge
Family Blood Ties Set 1–3
Family Blood Ties Set 1–5
Family Blood Ties Set 4–6
Family Blood Ties Set 7–9
Sian's Solution – A Family Blood Ties Short Story

Design series
Dangerous Designs
Deadly Designs
Darkest Designs
Design Series Trilogy

Standalone
In Cassie's Corner
Gem Stone (a Gemma Stone Mystery)
Time Thieves

Published Non-Fiction Books:

Career Essentials
Career Essentials: The Résumé
Career Essentials: The Cover Letter
Career Essentials: The Interview
Career Essentials: 3 in 1

CPSIA information can be obtained
at www.ICGtesting.com
Printed in the USA
LVHW082159161120
671890LV00018B/285